THE STORMS OF LIFE

Diane Ashley-Roberts

Published by

**MELROSE
BOOKS**

An Imprint of Melrose Press Limited
St Thomas Place, Ely
Cambridgeshire
CB7 4GG, UK
www.melrosebooks.co.uk

FIRST EDITION

Copyright © Diane Ashley-Roberts 2014

The Author asserts her moral right to
be identified as the author of this work

Cover designed by Jeremy Kay

ISBN   978-1-908645-59-3

Printed and bound in Great Britain by:
Martins the Printers, Spittal, Berwick upon Tweed

THE STORMS OF LIFE Characters
TREM-Y-MÔR

Sir William Rowlands married (1) Letitia
    (sons): William (died), Twins (died), Richard (died), Edward
    (daughters): Letitia (died), Jane (died), Margaret, Katherine, Penelope
Sir William Rowlands married (2) Mariana
    (daughter): Mariana
Cook/housekeeper: Mrs Jones (daughter of George Reece)
                    (sisters: Jemima and Keren)
Butler: Wilson
Head Groom: Owen Lewis
Groom: Thomas and Evan Lewis
Maids: Bridget and Biddy Lewis
       Elin, Kate and Peggy
          (sisters: Anne and Mary)
          (brothers: John & two others)
       Owen Lewis married Bridget
          (sons) Thomas, Evan, Morgan, Owen, Adam,
       Peter and Francis
          (daughters) Biddy, Martha, Margaret, Hanna & Mary

SIR WILLIAM'S LONDON HOUSE

Governess: Miss Buckley
Footman: Barker
Servant: Cowley
Nanny: Caruthers

SILK WEAVER'S HOUSE

Sir William's brother, Richard married Anne
    (daughter): Sarah

STRULEY CASTLE

Sir William's daughter, Margaret married (1) Humphrey Struley
Margaret married (2) Walter
    (sons): Walter and Henry
Coachman: Gradeson
Maid: Perrin

LITTLE OAKS
Sir William's daughter Katherine married Alexandre Barnsley
Coachman: Wade
Butler: Cooke
Housekeeper: Hoddy

PEN-Y-BRYN FARM
Sir William's youngest daughter Penelope married Robert Roberts
 (sons): Llewelin, Robert (Robbie) and David
 (daughter): Sarah
Servants: Thomas Weller and wife Mary

PLAS HYFRYD
Lord Wynne
 (son): Henry Wynne married Hanna
 (children): Henry, Isabella and Sarah

CARREGFAN
Sir Meyrick Parry married Elizabeth
 (daughters): Esther, Francisca, Jane, and Ellenor
Butler: Pocock
Governess: Jane Fotherwell
Sewing woman: Anne

TY CRAIG
Matthew Cutland (Cutlass)

THE VICARAGE
Rev'd Griffith Owen married Barbara
Housekeeper: Mrs Beacon
Maid: Jennett
Cook: Cook

WINTER

HENRY

Henry braced his legs against the swell of the wooden deck as a wave rocked the ship. He pulled the collar of his cloak up to keep the sea spray from his face, but the taste of salt remained upon his lips.

He peered across to where he thought the land should be, but it had disappeared behind a curtain of clouds. A storm was brewing. Were they going to make it? he asked himself. Were they going to make it in time for the party? Oh, if only his business in Chester had been concluded yesterday then he could have caught an earlier boat, the *Summer Sunset*, rather than the *Abundance*, and even now he would be sitting in his carriage heading towards Holyhead or arrived at *Carregfan* with the other guests or even on the dance floor with his wonderful Mariana in his arms.

Suddenly, before his eyes, was his love, his betrothed – well, nearly betrothed – because tonight, at the party, the entire world would know that he and she were going to be married!

He had first met Mariana ten, or was it eleven, years ago? He and his sister, Isabella, were coming around the edge of the house during their afternoon walk on a very ordinary day in June. They had decided that today, with nothing better to do, they were going to walk along the beach to the path that led across the fields to the village. However, both he and Isabella came to an abrupt halt when they saw a small girl slip out through the drawing room windows, march across the newly mown lawn, and straight into the sea.

Isabella gasped but he just stared. Who was she? Where was her nursemaid – she didn't look more than five? Why had she come from their drawing room? And, why had she walked into the water, without removing her shoes? What was wrong with her? Was she simple? All these questions jostled in his brain in the few seconds it took for Isabella to dash across the grass. It was now his turn to gasp when he saw his burly sister push the girl, who landed facedown in the water. Henry ran after his sister:

"Izzie! Don't do that!"

As he reached the water's edge, the child came up, spitting out water and sand, and shouting abuse in Welsh, but he noticed there were no tears in her eyes. Before he could say anything, this wild cat flung herself at him, fists flailing. He caught her wrists in a powerful grip.

"It wasn't me!" he shouted.

Whether it was her imprisoned hands or his English voice, he didn't know, but it was as though all the hostility had gone out of her. Her arms went limp within his grasp but a splash of water sprayed up to above his knee-length breeches as she quietened. Had she done that deliberately or had it been a wave?

"Who are you?" growled Isabella, sensibly retreating across the pebbles towards the grass.

"I am Mariana."

Henry, at nine, reckoned that many a child would have claimed a relationship with a revered adult, who could have defended her, but later he discovered that Mariana always fought her own battles.

"If I release you, will you stay still?" he questioned.

"Yes," came the meek reply. But immediately she was let loose, the raven-haired girl fell on the unsuspecting Isabella, biting and kicking with as much vigour as any child from the gutter.

It had taken both Henry and a lately arrived nursemaid to separate this tousled animal from his bawling sister and it was several weeks before he saw Mariana again. He found out that Mariana's father had forbidden any more visits to *Plas Hyfryd* until she promised to behave.

Looking, back, despite the inauspicious beginning, Henry was surprised that his sister and Mariana didn't grow to be friends, for they were a similar age and the same sex, but it was his company that the younger girl seemed to seek. He noticed that Isabella soon withdrew from the close relationship, which sprang up between himself and Mariana, and hid behind a sustained, ladylike dignity, refusing to clamber along logs in case she fell, and running home rather than setting forth in rowing boats to the mainland and regularly reporting all manner of other pranks to a distraught nursemaid. However, nothing could separate his adoring companion from him and no threat of punishment, nor its administration, stopped the pair of them from thinking of new escapades… until he went to Eton.

What had he missed most on his arrival at that famous school? Was it his grandfather – a perceptive gentleman who seemed to understand him better than his own parents? Was it the handsome estate on Anglesey overlooking the Menai Straits where he had been allowed so much freedom? Or was it his little friend, Mariana, who followed him everywhere?

The day after he had returned for his first holiday, she had sought him out, bursting into the parlour.

"Henry?" She frowned, jerking to a halt when he turned from looking out the window. "Henry, is it you?"

"Ah, Miss Rowlands," he had found himself saying in that deeper voice that had come in the last year and he still hardly recognised as his own. "I wondered if you would be calling."

"Henry! You've never called me 'Miss Rowlands' before. What's wrong with you? What have they done to you? Why have you changed?"

And he had stared. Stared at this slight girl, her face achingly familiar and identical to the face of his dreams. How often, in those hellish days of the past year, had he thought of her? How he had longed for an ally amidst the terror of arriving in a strange environment and the subsequent degradation of being a 'new boy'! And, he knew, although only a girl and younger than he, she would have been an ally. How many times had he contemplated running away, back to *Plas Hyfryd* or even *Trem-y-Môr* (Mariana's home) to see just one friendly face! For, first the unaccustomed routine, and then the awful impact of the bullying had changed him from an outgoing boy into a shy and solemn adult. He had hidden his homesick tears, saving them for his silent pillow at night and he had learned quickly to be mute, retiring and obedient to all commands, whether from his masters or from older boys. He had discovered, in this way, that those who played cruel tricks on the callow lads did not notice him. After several weeks of unremitting torture at the hands of Edwin Marshall and his cronies, he also learnt the wisdom of jumping to the orders of Marshall for whom he 'fagged'. And only once in the whole year had a master whipped him. Yes, once had been enough for him to swear to himself that he would never allow himself to be in that position again.

On the first morning of the holidays, he had overheard his father commenting to his mother, "Henry has changed. He used to be so... exuberant and now he's very quiet. Almost moody. What would you say?" And his mother had replied, "He's growing up, dearest. He's beginning to take his responsibilities seriously."

Oh, if only they knew the truth! Why didn't they? Especially his father should have guessed what was wrong because he had been to Eton in his youth. Had his father not experienced some of what he himself had been through? Henry walked away from his parents' bedroom door and determined not to blab. He would hide his misery and, if anyone asked, he would say:

"I'm very happy at school, though the food is abominable!"

However, he had found it impossible to slip back into that easy relationship with Mariana. For some reason, they only managed to meet up for a few days during that long summer, and on several of those occasions she had been very cross with him. She had even stamped her slim foot when he had refused to follow her on some mischievous adventure.

Why had he not wanted to go? It just all seemed rather childish now. What was the point of catching one of his father's horses and riding bareback when he could call a groom to saddle a mount for him any day? Why tiptoe into the kitchen garden to steal strawberries when the very same fruit would be served up with cream in the dining room that evening? Yet, he didn't want to hurt his childhood friend. He couldn't share any of what had happened to him, but on the last day, unexpectedly she was kind and sympathetic – maybe because of his imminent departure. He didn't know why she seemed to accept him, but it gave him assurance that maybe they would be able to recapture some of their closeness, during the next holidays.

Of course, the second year was much, much better, because he was accustomed to his routine and he was no longer the newest boy; some other poor hapless lad was enduring the torment and torture. By the following summer, he felt he was his old self again, although he always remained much more conforming in his behaviour and often chided Mariana gently for some of her more hare-brained schemes.

With the passing of the years, his increasing awareness of sexual matters led him to visit an inn near his home to discover for himself the joys of female company. An older woman there knew how to deal with his embarrassment at his virginal state and taught him a number of ways to please both himself and any woman he chose to partner.

With some experience of women to his credit, he was delighted at the stirring in his loins when he saw the changing figure of his faithful friend. Mariana was blooming from a pretty child to an attractive young maid and he realised suddenly that he wanted this girl to be his and his alone. He knew many of his sisters' friends and many of his friends' sisters but no one compared with Mariana, even though, he speculated, her full beauty was still in bud.

Having decided on a course of action, he could be stubborn. However, he did not speak to his parents about it until he was catapulted into revealing his plans when his father broached the subject of him going to Cambridge.

He saw the hue of his father's face darken to crimson when he announced:

"I don't want to go to university, Father. I want to marry Mariana."

"Now, listen, my boy. I know the girl is devoted to you. I know that you've lived in each other's pockets for many years, but your mother and I have only allowed this because Mariana's father is your grandfather's best friend. However, we had hoped, your mother and I, that now you've mixed in society a bit... It's why you spent your holidays with your Uncle John. All those parties you went to. We wanted you to meet other girls. Yes, yes, I know. Don't look like that! Mariana is a beauty, but she's never been anywhere and certainly not to London. Parochial, my boy. Very parochial! We wanted you to broaden your horizons.

"Your mother and I... We have found someone who we think would make you a wonderful wife. You remember George Stuart. You met him last April at that party gathering in Sloane Square. Big chap with slightly bulging eyes. No, I don't suppose you remember. Well, your mother and I have known him for many years. Good friend of mine and he's got a very sweet daughter. Only daughter too. Well, only child actually, and she'll bring a good dowry with her, for George doesn't have anyone else to leave his fortune to. She's a little young for you at the moment, but when you've finished at Cambridge, she'll have matured..."

"Father, you're not listening to me. I'm not going to Cambridge. I'm going to marry Mariana. We've known each other for so long."

Henry watched his father pull out a decorative snuffbox from his waistcoat pocket and pinch a minute amount of snuff between his fat fingers. He knew his father did this when he was thinking and he could almost hear his father's brain clicking over. What argument would he use? He knew his best bet was to let his father finish what he was saying and then do what he wanted to do anyway. He could be as implacable as his parent! But the silence lengthened. Finally he ventured:

"Father, Mariana and I have already spoken about getting married..."

That jolted the other man out of his reverie.

"You insolent puppy!" His father leapt from his chair. "I ought to forbid you to meet her again, but I know that wouldn't work. That wilful minx would find a way to…"

"Father, she's not a minx!"

"Well, maybe not a minx but you can't deny she's wilful. Very wilful. William needs to discipline her more. But, that's by the way. She's not right for you, son. She's a nobody. She's not just the daughter of a country squire but she's his youngest daughter. Let your mother and I guide you in this matter. My father chose your mother for me… and look how well we have done. Your mother comes from the Pennants of Wiltshire and they can trace their ancestry back to William the Conqueror. Your mother has served me well." His voice softened. "I know we've buried four sons, God rest their souls, but your sisters…. We have you and all your sisters. Yes, we've done all right and we do know what's best for you. Now you must apologise to me, for you did wrong. You shouldn't have spoken to her when you hadn't even consulted me!"

Henry sighed to himself whilst his father crossed the room towards him. He had cultivated a deferential, pleasing demeanour during the last few years. He was, after all, his parents' only son and he understood, in spite of what his father said, his sisters came second to him. He had heard his grandfather describe the family as a quiver full of daughters with one sharp arrow of a son. However, on this particular matter his mind was made up.

"I am sorry, Papa, if I've upset you, but you must understand. Mariana and I talk about most subjects and especially if they are dear to our hearts…"

"No, Henry!" his father bellowed, apparently uncaring that his voice was carrying to the furthermost parts of the house. "I'm sorry. If you marry that chit I will… I will disinherit you."

Henry turned away and left the room. There was no point in trying to convince his father now. He knew that the threats would go unfulfilled. Probably he had chosen the wrong day to broach the subject, but when his pater had started droning on about studying at Cambridge, he had felt it was wise to apprise him of his own plans. He knew that his best strategy was to keep out of his father's way, preferably until his mother had had time to calm and soothe him. She would make him see sense. She would probably quietly tell him that he had handled the interview with his son badly and she might even be able to make him regret his outburst. Therefore, he would leave the house and ride across to confide in his friend, Jenkin. Let

8

the old boy calm down!

And so it had been. Two days later his father had talked to him again. His parents had decided to agree with his proposals, with the proviso that no formal engagement be announced until his twenty-first birthday. Henry had to fall in with their plans and after a discussion with Jenkin he had made some concessions too: he decided to go to Cambridge before learning how to run the estates at *Plas Hyfryd*, as long as he and Mariana were allowed to see each other often and pledge to spend the rest of their lives together.

Thus it was that he had faithfully promised to his beloved that he would arrive in time for this special occasion when their betrothal would be officially announced. He snapped out of his reverie when a shower of rain struck his face, and made his way to find the Captain. He needed to know what time they were expected to arrive.

Mariana and Elin

Carregfan was the only house on the whole island that had a room large enough for a grand Twelfth Night party, and so, each year, if its owners were in occupancy, people flocked to it. Set high above the village of Holyhead, with magnificent views over the sea and towards the Snowdonia Mountains, its presence dominated the smaller houses scattered around it.

However, as the first guest to the party walked the short distance from the harbour up to *Carregfan*, her eyes were not on the house but scanning the horizon. She was willing herself to see the faraway sails of the *'Abundance'* speeding towards the haven and herself, because it was carrying Henry and it was eight weeks since she had seen him.

What she saw, in the distance, but coming perceptibly nearer whilst she stopped to stare, was an enormous bank of purple clouds rolling across the sky like huge barrels careering along a grey stone quay. The girl screwed up her eyes and unconsciously pulled her crimson cloak closer around her slender body. A storm was coming. Not tonight… not tonight when her Henry was on the sea!

"Sweet Jesus," she whispered, "make him arrive before the storm."

Having been born practically in the water and having lived by the sea all her life on the tiny island off the coast of Anglesey, Holy Island, she knew about the suddenness of storms and the terrible havoc wrought by them. Shipwrecks were common, but this winter had been incredibly mild, with winds softly caressing the land, that not a single ship had been lost this season. Yet, even as she watched, the wind blew stronger and the clouds bumped and jostled one another to be the first to arrive overhead. The girl shivered and clutched her cloak with anxious hands.

"Are you all right, Miss Mariana?"

She turned to see her maid, Elin, panting up the slope in her wake.

"Look!" Mariana spoke in Welsh to her servant without thinking. Brought up by a Welsh nursemaid, freely allowed to mix with all the servants from babyhood, she spoke fluently both Welsh and the English that her father used. Without faltering, she flitted between the two languages as the occasion demanded. She continued, "There's a storm coming. Oh, where is Henry's ship? Why hasn't it arrived already?"

Mariana let her eyes dwell on the harbour, barely more than a creek, below her. The tide was in, the sand covered and the packets and fishing boats were floating upright, pointing their masts to the sky. At low tide the port was dry and ships and boats alike floundered in the sand. Now there was only one ship of the size of the *Abundance* and Mariana could clearly read its name – *'Mair'* – the Welsh name for Mary.

* * *

"Come now, Miss Mariana." Elin's voice was as though speaking to a child, but in fact, she was the younger. "Don't fret. The Lord Almighty will look after him. Come now, up to the house. Thomas will be bringing your clothes and Mistress Parry will have seen you already and be wondering what is keeping you."

Elin led the way up the grass verge. There was a track, wide enough for a carriage, but at this time of year the mud made it impossible to get any wheeled vehicle along it. She had heard that there was talk of making a path from the house down the less steep slope on the other side of the hill and around in an arc to the harbour, but for the time being, travellers had to use the squelching morass that served as a driveway.

Elin's boots, a sign of her good fortune in working at the Manor House, *Trem-y-Môr,* sank into the grass edge, already churned by other feet that had passed before. She placed her steps carefully, keeping her gaze on the ground, but she was aware that her companion was watching those fast-moving clouds while she trod the border of the track.

Elin turned to make sure that Mariana did not fall and, seeing a frown of worry crease her mistress' smooth brow, she was reminded of the first time she had seen Mariana.

It was the same day that her father had brought home his new wife, a bare seven weeks after her dear mother had died.

Widow Davies was a fierce, barren woman, who came to her third marriage armed with her own dark oak chest, initialled AG, bequeathed to her by her mother from her mother before her, who had received it for good services, which, it was rumoured, ended with the birth of a child.

She brought a sizeable broomstick also and she began to brush the cottage clean, literally brushing her reluctant stepchildren out the door before immersing them in a nearby stream. Then, she lined them up in front of her in order of height, badgering them to tell her their names – the youngest girl, not out of napkins, sat on the grass at the end of the troupe! Elin was the second daughter of the family but she was taller than her elder sister, Anne, and ended up at the head of the row. Widow Davies (Elin was never going to call her *'Mam'*) scrutinised them, her mouth grim. She glared at Elin before beginning her tirade:

"Now, you! Yes, you the eldest! Eleanor, isn't it? You must take these snivelling children away. I've only got one day to tidy up this hovel. Tomorrow, I must be back at the farm. So, go! Take them! I can't work with them under my feet all day. And, whilst you're at it, you can find yourself a job. A girl your age with no job! It's disgraceful! My, when I was your age I was slaving dawn to dusk – and sometimes longer – as a scullery maid. Find yourself something that'll bring us in good money. None of this picking up stones for the ploughmen so they can till the soil. No! Get yourself a decent job, preferably with board and lodgings too. Get along now and stop standing there with your mouth open!"

Elin was only too glad to hasten away from this sharp woman, with her raucous voice, who was turning their lives upside down. How dare she call their home a hovel – it was far superior to a cow shed! Who did she think she was? And what had her father been doing marrying such an interfering old hag? Was she a witch? Certainly she had a broomstick. Did she fly around on it? Life might be better for her father in the future, but it looked as though her life would be miserable under the tyranny of her stepmother. Suddenly Elin longed for her own mother's loving presence.

Hitching her youngest brother, John, onto her hip, she marched away, followed by her two smallest sisters, Peggy and Kate (Baby Mary she had left with the others). She knew that it would be impossible for her to "find a job", for she had lived here all her life and she knew everyone in the district. However, she saw the wisdom of staying out of Widow Davies' way and the child in her decided to go to the beach. At least the little ones could play in the sand and the sun was shining.

Across the fields, past quietly nibbling sheep, they went. Peggy had just begun to grizzle noisily when a tall young man, dressed in liver-coloured breeches and a green mud-bespattered smock, appeared along the path. He had lost his hat in his hurry and his bare feet struggled to grip the stubbly grass. Elin recognised him as Thomas Lewis, a stable boy at the Manor House, *Trem-y-Môr*.

"Help!" he gasped. The word was barely audible for he had bent over to catch his breath. "She… She needs… help. Up at… the… house."

"Who?"

"The young mistress. Mrs Jones… has… has fallen badly. She's cut her… her head and isn't breathing."

Elin knew who Mrs Jones was: the housekeeper and cook at *Trem-y-Môr*.

"Where are you going?" Elin asked, lifting John from her side into her arms, to stop his legs against her stomach.

"For the Master. He's ridden over…"

"Hurry then," interrupted Elin. "I'll go and do what I can."

Thomas, with his ragged breath more even, started off again at a run and soon disappeared. For a moment, Elin wondered if she had imagined him. All was quiet except for a skylark twittering high above her head. Then a gurgle from John, as he tugged her hair sharply, reminded her of the crisis and she hurried to the Manor House, dragging the reluctant toddlers with her.

Elin had never been near *Trem-y-Môr* before and, at first, she was overwhelmed by the size of it close-up, and by the complete and deep silence that hung over the yard and outbuildings. Cautiously she followed the rutted path around to the front of the house. There she saw, basking in the May sunshine and staring unblinking at the azure sea, a thick-set, stone house, whitewashed with lime a few years ago but now peeling, after the effects of salt and wind. Four windows on the upper floor, nestling beneath the hardy roof, faced the sea and there was a fifth window blocked in. Beneath this was a solid front door with two windows either side of it. The coarse grass grew from the edge of the path straight to the end of the land, where a three foot drop fell to the sandy cove. In places, the sea had eroded away the cinnamon earth and the broken brim had sunk on to the sand. Away to the right of the house, rough-hewn steps, paved with huge, irregular, slate slabs allowed an easier descent to the private beach.

One look at the front door showed it was seldom used, and Elin hurried to survey the back of the house. Here, also, there were four symmetrically placed windows on the upper floor but above these, just peeping from beneath the very eaves and looking as if they were supporting the roof themselves, were a row of windows. Elin decided these must be the windows of the garrets, where the servants slept. The ground floor of the house had been extended to include, she guessed, such rooms as laundry, stillroom, hot bake house and possibly a brewery.

Elin allowed her eyes to wander along all the windows and even towards the half-door of the stables in the hope of seeing some sign of human life. Nothing except a scraggy dog. Where was she supposed to go? She gripped Peggy's hand all the while to prevent the inquisitive child from investigating the mucky yard and urine steaming in the sun. Suddenly she noticed a backdoor, swinging in the breeze. This must be where she ought to go! Spurred into action, she jumped the two steps up into the cool, unfamiliar interior of the house with her train of sisters behind her.

Once inside the flagstoned scullery, she turned left into the Manor House kitchen. Again, she stopped. Forgetting her reason for being there she gaped, awestruck at its immense size, for the room was large enough to engulf the entire cottage where she and her family lived. Dominating the high-ceilinged room was an enormous fireplace with its chimney disappearing amongst the blackened rafters. To one side of it, at about shoulder height, was a wooden wheel, but its occupant – presumably the skinny crooked-legged mongrel she had noticed lying on the dirty cobbles – must have taken advantage of the crisis to run off. Thus the spit was still, with the meat burning, its juices hissing when they fell into the flames. A wooden rack over the chimney-piece held the spits, but all of a sudden, Elin's eyes were drawn away from the great iron pot that swung over the fire; away from the vast, scrubbed table covered with wood and pewter bowls, a butter pat, a jug with muslin draped over its rim, three jelly moulds and a ladle; away from the rows of copper pans arranged on a shelf above a door in decreasing size, reminiscent of the Widow's inspection parade; away from the inevitable oak *cwpwrdd deuddarn* displaying the blue-flowered china and pewter plates neatly marshalled on its shelves and interspersed with glass and china ornaments from earlier generations; away from all the furniture and utensils that she had never seen in her life before, to the two people who were in the kitchen.

There was Mariana, tiny, with her long ebony hair, un-styled, the way she always loved to wear it (as Elin would later discover). It was pulled back loosely from her forehead to reveal that W-shaped furrow that Elin was to see again and again and learn to both love and dread. The child, for child she was, jumped when Elin entered and barked in English:

"What do you want? Go away! We don't have beggars here."

Elin, unable to understand the words but understanding the message, had just caught sight of the other person in the room, or rather their legs, clothed in thick, woollen stockings wrinkled down to their ankles. Mrs Jones was lying like the stranded whale Elin had seen on the beach once, on the numbing, stone floor of her own domain – the Manor House kitchen. She lay completely still and lifeless.

"I've come to help," Elin bravely stated in Welsh. She was glad to see a look of comprehension come to the other child's face.

Elin noticed that this diminutive girl (for to Elin she appeared younger than herself), had blotches of dried blood on her skirt and there was bright scarlet on her hands and the crumpled piece of towelling she was twisting between her fingers.

For one horror-filled moment Elin thought that Mariana was injured also, until she saw the puddle of sticky fluid seeping along the floor. She dropped John to the hem of her own skirt and, with a command to Kate to hold him, she moved forward to look more closely at the prostrated housekeeper. Kate dispassionately gripped a handful of her brother's curly hair and watched, with interest on her face, her elder sister, unmindful of the blood, bend to inspect the bleeding woman.

"She's going to die, isn't she?" Mariana's voice cracked.

"Give me the cloth," demanded Elin in reply. She snatched the rag from Mariana's fine hands. She knew, from dealing with the wounds of her brothers and sisters, that the head bled freely and she realised that there was so much blood everywhere because it had been allowed to flow unstemmed. Once the pad was placed on the ugly cut, Elin bowed low over the woman's lips to feel her breath. Even though Mrs Jones was lying still, her chest unmoving, Elin felt the whisper of life from between her ashen lips.

"She's alive, but we... you... must get me more cloths and some cold water and... and maybe... yes, fetch me needle and thread." Elin spoke with authority for, although she was in awe of the Squire, she was unable to connect this trembling slip of a girl with him. "Kate, take the little ones outside. Don't touch anything – go down to the sand. Quickly! More cloths! A needle and thread!"

Mariana stood unheeding, although Kate trailed away. Elin realised the

Squire's daughter was deep in shock. Had it been too much for her to be left to cope all on her own? She rose and gently took the other girl's hand.

"Where is the housekeeper's room? Go and bring her sewing box or whatever she keeps her sewing things in. Please, Miss."

Mariana turned slowly, as if she was in a dream, her brow puckered, but she did return a few minutes later with a wicker basket. By this time Elin had reduced the flow from the wound by pressing hard on the pad, and had mopped up the pool of blood with her own skirt. Knowing that this young girl needed her help too, she risked leaving the housekeeper and, taking Mariana's arm, led her firmly to a rocking chair standing by the fire.

"Sit here now. Close your eyes. All will be well. She'll live. Just let me deal with everything." She kept her sentences short, for Mariana appeared to have gone into a kind of trance now that someone else had arrived to take charge.

The meek girl obeyed and Elin deftly sewed the wound and then, finding a huck-a-back tablecloth, she carefully lifted the woman's head to push the cushion beneath it. Seeing a shawl hanging on a hook, she covered the inert figure, after checking once more that Mrs Jones was not dead. Then she gave her full attention to the shaking girl.

"Now, Miss, come with me. Take me to your room. You should lie down."

"Blood," shuddered Mariana. "There's blood everywhere."

"Don't you worry. Come with me. I'm sure there's a basin in your room and some water. You can wash before you lie down."

Elin's fast thinking and neat stitching saved Mrs Jones' life. This was to be the first and only time that Elin saw the housekeeper with her tongue stilled. Much to her surprise, Elin was asked to stay. Mrs Jones was patently incapacitated and Owen Lewis' wife, Bridget, was swollen up with some dropsical condition pending the birth of her ninth child. Then there was Maggie, who had been doing the work of pantry maid, dairymaid and under maid. Elin was told that she had recently gone to Bodedern with her new husband. Thus there was no one left to do even the meanest tasks. In the next two days, Elin learnt as many jobs as she possibly could, by running between the beds of Bridget and Mrs Jones. She repeated instructions, asked questions and listened diligently. The Squire and his daughter were so grateful for her timely help that Elin never left their employ again.

Now, five years later, Elin had been elevated to Mariana's personal maid and her two sisters did her jobs in the kitchen. Elin knew better these days than to offer a hand to assist her mistress up the slippery hill to the party at *Carregfan*, for the quivering, shocked kitten she had met that day had given no clue of the stubborn wild-cat that Mariana would grow to be. Elin had discovered that Mariana had been reared by an inexperienced nursemaid who was too timid to oppose her unruly charge's wishes. She had been spoilt by an ageing father, who after ignoring his daughter for the first year of her life had then lavishly loved her in an attempt to assuage his guilt – at least this last was according to Mrs Jones. The housekeeper had informed Elin that the Squire saw his favourite wife in his grown-up daughter, and therefore allowed Mariana to behave in ways that would have made her mother turn in her grave.

"Oh, Elin, do you think Henry will be all right?" Mariana's hushed voice reached her maid's ears above the ever-increasing wind.

"Yes, Miss Mariana…"

"Oh, don't speak too loudly! God might hear and make the storm come quicker."

"Miss Mariana, don't talk such nonsense! Here we are at the house. Come now, and let's get you ready for this evening. Mr Wynne will be here very soon, marching up this path and asking where his bride-to-be is."

At last Elin had said the right thing. By alluding to Mariana's forthcoming marriage she set that young woman's eyes shining with excitement and her stride, in spite of her long skirts, lengthened.

* * *

Mariana passed by the maid. Her cheeks began to glow as her thoughts turned in anticipation of this evening. Tonight, she and Henry would make known their betrothal. The services of the *gwahoddwr* or bidder would then be needed. He would put on his flower-crowned hat, snatch up his long, carved staff, also decorated with flowers, and send the 'bidding' letters, inviting guests to the wedding. He would go from house to house, not merely to request their presence at the ceremony but reminding the people of any *pwyth* or obligation. She could almost hear his musical voice now in her head exhorting them to bring money or gifts.

Mariana smiled to herself. She knew that when the *pwyth* was dutifully returned on the wedding day, she and Henry would be given all manner of useful gifts. Of course, they would hardly need the homespun cloth or wooden spoons or handmade baskets from the local people, since Henry's family were well endowed and Henry was the heir. However, Mariana would appreciate the thought behind the contributions and she would know that they were given with a cheerful heart in repayment for all the times when her family had bestowed presents on others. But the most important point about needing the services of the *gwahoddwr* was that her love for Henry and his love for her would be made public at last!

Mariana had hugged her love for Henry inside for such a long time. She had known him for… it felt like forever. Of course, his family were important locally – his grandfather, Lord Wynne, had been a Member of Parliament until quite recently. With her own father, Sir William Rowlands, often being asked to be a Justice of the Peace, it was obvious that he and Lord Wynne should meet regularly to discuss county matters and to ride together. What was more natural than for the Squire to take along his only daughter? Thus, from an early age, Mariana had accompanied her father on his visits. Sometimes she travelled by carriage and on other occasions she rode on her father's horse behind him. Leaving the restrictions of the nursery, Mariana had journeyed to *Plas Hyfryd*, where the Wynne family lived, chattering in her high-pitched child's voice for all to hear.

Soon Mariana grew to love the well-kept estate, from its sweeping gardens (originally landscaped by Nathan Lister of London), to the immense house with its maze of rooms. The present house had been built only thirty years ago, although the new stone building replaced a wood and plaster mansion. The house had three storeys with towers at each end. The east wing overlooked the Menai Straits and had a spectacular view of the ancient castle of Caernarfon on the other bank.

As a child and even now as a woman, Mariana had not only been overawed by the size and number of rooms compared with her own home, but also by the wealth and magnificence of some of the chambers.

She had stood open-mouthed in the Staterooms with their intricately carved gilt mirrors, which showed what seemed like a thousand images of her. One day she had been wearing a lilac over-skirt revealing a white petticoat. Clinging to her narrow shoulders was a close-fitting, long-waisted, boned bodice of the palest lilac whose robings, the same colour as the skirt, dipped in a deep V to show a simple under-bodice barely rucked by her newly-formed bosom. She had twirled in front of the mirror, for once taking notice of her image reflected again and again and again. Blackberries and cream swirled together.

Then there were the side-tables gracing the long corridors sent from Cumley and Moore. She had marvelled at the smooth, polished finish attained by some menial servant. She had been dumbstruck by the fantastic half-tester, State bed, which was hung with dazzling Indian embroidery, also from London. In childhood, she had stroked the decorative, resplendent Gobelin tapestry adorning the wall in the dining room.

Quite recently, she had realised that one day she would be mistress of *Plas Hyfryd*. Would she ever dare to change any of the furnishings or furniture, possibly replacing some of the old-fashioned oak furniture with the latest walnut pieces with their finer grain? She had heard that one could even purchase dining chairs with legs ending in lions' paws!

However, although she loved to wander through the house, she usually, even to this very day, felt restrained in them, as if she remained an infant and had been warned not to touch anything. She had always been happiest when she was outside the richly furnished rooms and strolling in the gardens. On every occasion her memories showed the immaculately attended lawns bathed in sunshine, the expanse of grass stretching from the gravel path right down to the water's edge with their unimpeded views of the mainland and of Snowdon and her handmaidens. Tucked away behind a soaring stone wall was a kitchen garden that supplied the whole household with a variety of vegetables and herbs all year round. Further from the house were several orchards and beyond these were the fields of the home farm; altogether a big enough kingdom for any child! Since no one bothered to watch what Mariana was doing when she was outside, she had preferred to be out of the house and in the grounds of *Plas Hyfryd*.

Added to this, it had been in the garden that she had first encountered Henry, and this added richness in her memories. That day, as usual, she was bored by the old men's conversation and had slipped away, down to where the tranquil waves were licking the pebbles on the beach. It was completely different from the untamed coast where she came from, where the wind furiously kicked the waves onto the shore. She had decided to test the water by wading in, never guessing that she would end up soaked by the sea. And thus she had met Henry!

What pleasure there was to be found in friendship! How she loved her older companion, for, although she had many ideas on how to have adventures, some were beyond her capabilities, but with Henry, four years her senior, the world was at her feet. His greater height, wider knowledge, braver attitude and, most importantly, his willingness to spend time with her, cemented their relationship from the start.

It nearly broke her heart when he went away to school. Then, for a whole year, Mariana had pined for her partner and for weeks before his arrival home for the summer she talked of no one else. She waited but a single day after his return to *Plas Hyfryd* before begging her father to take her to see him. Laughingly Sir William had told her that he could not refuse her eager face and, actually, he did have something to discuss with Lord Wynne. They were soon on their way.

When they rode side by side along the driveway lined with immature trees leading up to the house, Mariana could hardly contain her excitement. Riding into the stable-yard, they were greeted by one of the many grooms who knew them both well and who informed them that his Lordship was sitting on the front lawn.

The young girl wasted no time, but impatiently leapt from her pony. She thrust the reins into the hands of the surprised groom, and raced around the corner of the house, skirts bunched up in her fingers to increase her speed. But Henry was not with his grandfather, nor was he on the beach, nor in their favourite hideaway near the orchards. Finally Mariana returned, breathless and hot, from her fruitless search to enquire of the old man, who had settled into conversation with her father, where the elusive Henry was.

"Henry is in the parlour, m'dear," Lord Wynne offered. "But I wouldn't disturb hi…" His words were wasted on Mariana's back. "Ah, the energy of youth, William, eh?" Barely did she hear his last words.

Henry was in the parlour and Henry was not in the parlour.

There stood a tall, young man, dressed in a close-fitting, bottle green coat with a fully-flared skirt which he had left unbuttoned to reveal a collarless waistcoat of the same expensive cloth with identical, but smaller, silver buttons. Tied loosely beneath his chin was a cream cravat. His stockings were gathered over the end of his knee breeches, which were buckled at the sides and on his feet were deep, square-toed shoes with high, square heels. On his head, and making him look almost unrecognisable, was a pigtailed wig. Mariana had never seen him in a wig before.

"Henry? Henry, is it you?"

Fear washed over her. This quiet, solemn stranger was very different from last summer – what had happened to him? Had she lost her friend? She needed him so much, for she had no other friends.

His sister, Isabella, wasn't her friend. That unfortunate first meeting had led to a barely concealed hatred.

There was another family who lived nearer to her than Henry. Sir Meyrick Parry of *Carregfan* (where the party was being held) had four daughters who were her contemporaries. However, *Carregfan* was not their main residence and repeated absence made it hard for Mariana to relate to the two elder girls. Also their daily lives were rather different from hers: lessons each morning with a governess, sewing samplers in the afternoon, accompanied walks. Mariana didn't like any of these activities and she found herself behaving badly whenever she visited. This seemed to deepen the rift between the girls. No, Esther and Francisca couldn't be her friends. And the twins, the younger daughters of Sir Meyrick. Well, they were just babies!

Of course, there was Elin. Over the years her father had travelled away from *Trem-y-Môr* often, leaving her in the company of servants. She spoke their language but there was an unseen barrier between them, which she understood was because she was the Squire's daughter. Once Elin was promoted to be her personal maid… was Elin her friend? No, for Elin never allowed Mariana to forget that she was the mistress. Surely, it was loyalty rather than true sharing that bound them together.

If truth was told, Mariana was happier with boys than girls. Isabella, Esther and Francisca were usually fearful of reprisals from their nannies or governesses. That was one of the reasons that she spent time with Henry… used to spend time with Henry. Not only was he stronger and bigger and taller than she was *and* prepared to join in her mischief, but he was a boy! Yes, she had always preferred male company, not least because she often wished she had been born a boy!

What about her father? He had taught her much of life but, he, of course, was not the same age and generation as her.

No, she had no friend apart from Henry. Her riding filled many hours of the day and she used to lose track of time when she was galloping across the beaches or ascending the steep cliffs, but she rode with no companion.

She needed Henry. He was the same generation, same class and had the same interests as she did. And for as long as she could remember he had been there for her. What had happened?

She pondered long and hard, but it wasn't until the day before he left for Eton that she came to any conclusion. With sudden maturity she knew that this metamorphosis was no natural growing-up but that her childhood friend had suffered. This was the reason for the change! She knew, in a limited way, what it was like to be different from others and instantly she forgave him and the sympathy increased their closeness.

When she and Henry entered a more mature phase, she began to think of marriage. In fact, it never entered her lively head that she would marry anyone else. After all, her father and Lord Wynne were lifelong intimates and would surely approve of the match, and she and Henry were very happy in each other's company. (She took little account of Henry's father in whose hands her future actually lay.) Blissfully she was unaware of any obstacles that might beset her way, and she hurried through the years like a hurricane, wishing her childhood away, anticipating sharing each and every day with Henry for the rest of her life.

And, at last, the day had come – from today everyone would know that she was to marry her dearest Henry.

Now, the impressive wooden door of *Carregfan* swung open, as a whole new world would open to her when she married Henry, and there stood a black-clad individual with a sober face. It was Pocock, the butler, who, Mariana knew, travelled with the Parrys to each of their homes. Silently he ushered Mariana and Elin into a spacious entrance hall. Mariana glanced over her shoulder once more at the threatening weather before Pocock closed out the first spots of rain.

The entrance hall was a room in itself and its wide fireplace was ablaze with what looked like an entire tree chopped into logs. Either side of the welcoming flames, but set back from the intense heat, were two oak chairs and a matching chest, thick with carving too. At the far end of the hall, the main stairs ascended and disappeared up into the darkness. Although there were plenty of wall sconces, each bearing four branches of candlesticks, the majority of the light came from the burning wood and Mariana's eyes were drawn to the apricot and gold flames.

ELIZABETH

Elizabeth Parry, the hostess of the Twelfth Night party, walked down the stairs to greet Mariana. She stood on the bottom step and regarded her guest. She had leant against her chamber window whilst the approaching storm had robbed the sky of its last vestige of daylight (even though the clock had not yet struck two) and she had noticed Mariana pause and stare at the sea. She had seen the chariots of clouds bolt across the darkening heavens and she had ordered all the fires to be banked up and the candles lit.

Now, when Mariana stepped towards the glowing logs, her maid just behind her, Elizabeth observed the two girls. They were of similar age, but here the similarity ended. Mariana, raised on wholesome food, with never a day of hunger, was diminutive: slim, with dainty hands and feet. Her luxurious black hair, parted in the centre, hung down her cloak in heavy waves. Elizabeth knew she had dark, expressive eyes fringed with charcoal lashes that curled downwards to rest on her creamy cheeks and her lips often gleamed red. Altogether, she presented a picture of beauty, which, so it was said, made strangers turn their heads wherever she went.

The maid, born in a cottage not many miles from here, would have known days and even weeks of near-starvation in her early life. However, in latter years, she had blossomed with the plentiful kitchen food at the Manor House and her short, stout figure belied a childhood of want and hardship. Friendly brown eyes contemplated her mistress. She was wearing the local *pais a betgwn* – petticoat and bed-gown, both made of Welsh flannel, dyed in the home to brown with a dye from rock lichens. The striped material made her look thinner, but her breasts were pushing the bodice to strain at its front fastenings. Her three-quarter-length sleeves were covered with a generous shawl, for, although probably she had been offered one of her mistress' old cloaks, she would have felt more comfortable in what she was used to wearing. Her straight brown hair was hidden beneath a red headkerchief, tied to keep out the wind. Her straw hat had slipped back, making her serious, concerned face look younger.

Elizabeth returned her gaze to her youthful guest, wondering what was to become of her. Oh, how her beauty caught the eye! It must rouse the blood of all manner of men, from nurslings to patriarchs, and few women would deny that special, secret quality Mariana possessed that made her popular with men. But Elizabeth knew she continued to be a headstrong, untamed child, and she speculated about how her forthcoming marriage to Henry Wynne's only son would turn out.

Elizabeth had known about the betrothal for a long time but had agreed not to tell. In the beginning, like his parents, she had hoped that their infatuation would die and more recently she had held her tongue to save the surprise until tonight's ball. She sympathised with Henry and Hanna Wynne who would have to cope with all the difficulties, which were sure to come. She knew the girl well enough to see the unsuitability of the arrangement. Young Henry was a conformer; Mariana was a rebel. Henry was quiet; Mariana was a chatterer. Henry had been well brought up in normal surroundings, which befitted his future as Lord Wynne, whereas Mariana had been reared by an assortment of servants and an old man. Elizabeth sighed when she noticed how close the maid was standing to Mariana. What was the wench doing here? Why had she not gone around the back and through the servants' hall?

Elizabeth shook her head. She had tried! Dear God, she had tried! When she had first met the scrawny little girl, pity had stirred in her breast at the plight of this motherless child. With four daughters of her own and three sons, instinctively she had wanted to draw this pathetic babe under her motherly wing, but Mariana would have none of it. Prickly to the touch, the child had shunned all approaches and Elizabeth had found not only her sedate, well-behaved daughters, but also their governess, petrified of Mariana and her unpredictable behaviour. None of them had ever come into contact with anyone like the tempestuous imp who exploded into their snug world, whenever they were at *Carregfan*.

"Never still for a moment," was the way Jane Fotherwell, the governess, had described Mariana. A changeling. Of course, if she had been fair-haired, many would have said she was a fairy child. She was certainly beautiful enough to be from the other world. There were many tales in these parts of men marrying fairy maidens. Was this where Mariana's mother had come from? No, Elizabeth did not believe in fairies and she did not listen to the idle chatter of servants.

Fortunately, the Parry family seldom stayed long at *Carregfan* or they might have had to find a new governess. Sir Meyrick had interests in South Wales in the shipping business and he could rarely leave their town house. Elizabeth remembered how appalled she had been when her husband had first showed her *Carregfan*.

The original house was medieval, and after her sumptuous home in Cardiff, Elizabeth had found its primitiveness offensive. However, her husband had become so interested in architecture that he had delegated some of his work in the city in order to design a more modern house up here in the north for his family.

His plans left the splendid medieval hall, complete with balcony, unchanged. Instead of building a low timber ceiling across from the balustrade (which could have provided a set of upstairs bedchambers), he had extended outwards along the hilltop using local stone and craftsmen from the village. Thus, the original size and grandeur of the hall was retained. He had kept a perfect symmetry either side of the hall by erecting two identical wings, each three storeys high. Now the house boasted several distinctive rooms downstairs including a drawing-room, formal dining-room, family dining-room, study and back parlour. Upstairs there were a host of spacious rooms. Hidden from the front of the house were the kitchens, sculleries, laundry room and buttery and all manner of rooms where the servants worked.

Elizabeth had to admit that once the improvements were complete she enjoyed coming, for she saw more of both her husband and her children here. No wonder she had not wanted a cuckoo-child interrupting their family life together!

As she had grown older, Elizabeth mellowed. Between the two wings of the house, behind the hall, was an enclosed garden. Sheltered from the harsh winds and warmed by the sun, Elizabeth found peace and security in planning and caring for her secluded garden and now her greatest wish was to settle her daughters in marriages to good men and enjoy a well-deserved rest.

Marriage. What an all-important part of life it was! She was preparing all her daughters for motherhood – for marriage and domesticity. She had, at one time, dreamed of young Henry Wynne for one of her own daughters – the Parrys and the Wynnes of *Plas Hyfryd*! – but she had known that the

Wynnes would have had higher hopes for their only son. Good lineage! Good family connections – that was what people wanted. Yes, Mariana was a beauty, a water nymph, but what about her family? Her father came from excellent stock. William Rowlands' grandfather had been a wealthy landowner in Caernarfonshire and it was only in recent years that their estate had been sold to pay the gambling debts of William's father, so she had been told. Sir William's present house came from his first wife's side of the family. But what about Mariana's mother? Where had Sir William picked up his second wife and what was her background? No one knew. She had been brought from London – and from before that was anyone's guess – and was dead within the year in childbed. Mariana's mother had remained a mystery. Where had all this fiery loveliness come from? Not from William, that was certain! No, Elizabeth had always been glad that she had no unmarried sons left whose heads might be turned by this gorgeous butterfly.

"Mariana, my love, how are you?" Elizabeth spoke loudly above the rattle of rain. The sky was hurling down the raindrops to strike the windowpanes in a heavy squall.

The younger woman moved to greet her hostess.

"Good day, Aunt Elizabeth."

"Come upstairs, my child. I have given you the blue room and I've had a fire alight in there all day."

Mariana, along with several other guests, had been invited to stay the night. Although Mariana had only three miles to travel, Elizabeth offered hospitality to this lonely girl every time. Much to her surprise, Elizabeth's youngest twin daughters had grown up admiring Mariana. They had put this dazzling girl on a pedestal, never seeing her faults, even now, though they were fourteen. Elizabeth suspected they would give Mariana a warm welcome this afternoon, even if Esther, her nineteen-year-old, and Francisca, who was the same age as Mariana, would probably be withdrawn, both for their different reasons.

When the two women were climbing the stairs, with the maid following, Elizabeth heard a whisper, "Henry!" She realised that Mariana was imagining Henry's ship, storm-tossed and battling against the tempest.

"Now, Mariana, you mustn't worry about your Henry. He might be a little late for the party, but I just know he'll be here in the end. I was surprised to hear that he was leaving his return until the actual day of the party, but I understand his business commitments haven't allowed him to come any sooner. Why isn't he enjoying a holiday after Christmas, like everyone else? I've had a room prepared…"

"That won't be necessary, Aunt. He wrote to say that he would change in the inn, just in case he was late. He said he wouldn't want to arrive here in his travel clothes amidst the other guests."

"Oh, he is such a well-mannered boy! There really was no need to worry. I hope he'll stay the night here – especially with this storm blowing. I am expecting his parents very soon, and, of course, Isabella and Sarah; but I'm glad you've come early. Now you will have time to see my girls and there'll still be plenty of time for you to prepare. Here we are." She escorted Mariana to the bedchamber. "Your gown arrived yesterday morning and Anne, my sewing woman, can make any last minute adjustments."

Elizabeth halted just inside the threshold of the room. The bedchamber faced west and was usually aglow with the setting sun, but today there were no gleaming rays to shine on the blue stuff-bed in the centre of the room, nor to pick out the painstaking stitch work of the lined tapestry hangings on two of the walls. In the corner stood a great chair and near the fender was a stool. The flickering flames bowed to their reflected partners in a large dressing glass, giving the impression of hundreds of candles alight in the room.

Hovering beyond the bed, and straightening the non-existent creases out of Mariana's gown, was a scrawny girl: Anne. She looked up when her mistress entered and stood proudly next to the bed as if she had fashioned this creation of elegance herself. In truth, the gown had been commissioned and made in London following the strict orders of Sir William, who had sent Mariana's measurements to the seamstress, and this was the first time Mariana had seen it.

White silk, richly embroidered and decorated with tiny pearls, cascaded over the quilt on the bed like a mighty, rushing waterfall and the never-still candle flames accentuated each pearl in turn to heighten the image of moving water. Yards of expensive silk covered nearly half of the four-poster bed and its long train was draped over the chest set against the end of the bed. Lying at the pillow end of the bed was the glossy, plain, white silk petticoat, which would show beneath the plush overskirt. The un-boned bodice, of similar material and glamour as the skirt, was edged with ermine on its long sleeves; it could be seen floating on this foam of silk. Mariana would wear a padded stomacher beneath her bodice, whose low, square neckline was bordered with the same sleek fur and boasted a latticed pattern contrived with more seed pearls.

Such an outfit was virtually unseen in this area and, Elizabeth guessed, that if Mariana had not been in such a state over the wellbeing of her young man, she would have been thrilled. As it was, the girl barely glanced at her clothes; instead she marched to the window to draw aside the curtains and peer out over the dark horizon. Elizabeth followed her to look over her shoulder. All was ash-grey, both clouds and sea, merging together in rounded pillows, but she couldn't really see anything because of the ceaseless rain buffeting the panes.

Elizabeth turned away and moved across to touch the rich material of the dress. She knew that Mariana would not only be the most beautiful girl at the party but also the best dressed. She sighed again at the waste, for even if Mariana had been less agitated, she might well have passed by her glorious gown: she was never one to care for clothes and had even been seen in male apparel astride a horse! Elizabeth knew how terribly excited her own daughters would have been at such an expensive costume and she saw in both the servants' eyes the sort of anticipation and thrill one would have expected to see in the true recipient of the gown.

"Mariana, come away from the window," chided Elizabeth. "It's like night out there. Come and see your clothes. Your father had them sent all the way from London. We really need to try them on you so that Anne can see if they fit you."

"Oh, Aunt, must I? I can't be bothered to put them all on, just to take them all off again, just to put them all on again."

"Now, Mariana, my child, you must have a final fitting – or rather a first fitting. You must look your best for the party and for Henry. It's a very special occasion and you are to be the most important person. All eyes will be on you once everyone knows… knows your news… so you must be patient. Your maid is here to help you, and Anne, of course. I shall leave you in her capable hands whilst I order you a small repast. We shan't be eating until nine o'clock tonight, so we're all having a light meal now to prevent us from feeling faint.

THE WOMEN

Mariana pressed her head against the cold pane of glass when she heard her hostess leave the room. She noticed the gown. Who could have missed it? And a wave of pure delight had run through her. She was aware that she was attractive to men and had learnt to cope with shunning their coarser advances, partly because she only wanted Henry and partly because she wanted to be accepted for her own self and not just because they wanted a tumble in bed. Also she knew that white suited her dark skin and she and Elin had tried out several innovative styles for her hair ready for tonight but... but she just could not concentrate now. Those ominous clouds, so quickly bringing the storm, had doused the fire of excitement in her heart as surely as if she had been out into the rain herself.

Oh, where are you, Henry? her heart cried silently. She was not normally pessimistic. What was wrong with her? She had a feeling. Yes, that was it. A premonition? No! She shook her head. She must think good, strong, positive thoughts and no harm would come to her love.

She felt someone approach.

"Shall I take your cloak, Miss Mariana?" Elin asked and Mariana spun. Anne remained near the dress, suspended, as though she would lose her identity if she left its side.

"Yes, thank you, Elin," Mariana returned. She must be stout-hearted. Yes, no weakness, no tears, no hint of inner turmoil. That was what she had learnt when she was a child – better be mischievous than weeping – and now she must try on that splendid gown and stand still whilst others' hands pinned and tucked and sewed. But it would all be worth it, for very soon it would be Henry's hands that held her! He would be more pleased if she were happy and bubbling with joy, not broody and anxious. Any minute he might arrive, flinging off his sodden cloak, striding into the room, his long legs quickly covering the ground between them and she would feel his familiar arms around her and hear his hearty voice telling her that he had been sailing on the savage sea but here he was, ready to dance with her and her alone. She smiled as Elin began helping her out of her everyday clothes.

* * *

Mariana was astounded at the image of herself in the dressing glass. Who was this woman? Yes, woman, not girl or child. The expensive gown kissed the floor when she turned this way and that before the mirror. The hairstyle Elin had created made her look older. The maid had caught her hair high up at the back, allowing just one or two stray tendrils to frame her face. Her heavy tresses stayed piled up with the aid of silver pins studded with pearls, which matched the pearl necklace around her neck. The pins were a surprise from her father, given before she set out that morning. Her father had told her that he was glad that she was going early to the party to mix with the womenfolk of *Carregfan*. Hugging her farewell, he had said, "Make sure you're the most beautiful girl at the party". But, as she stared, she decided that this was no girl reflected here, but a woman, mature enough for any man.

* * *

Elizabeth tried to suppress the feeling of regret that had arisen in her heart when she beheld Mariana in all her finery. It was a shame that Mariana was not her daughter, after all! Wearing the stylish gown, the girl had left behind her restlessness and rebelliousness and become still and poised. Minutes before Elizabeth had been with her two eldest daughters, who were both attired in new outfits for the party, but nonetheless who would look like young girls compared with this ethereal creature. Yes, Mariana's small stature, softly curving bosom and unbelievably narrow waist made her look like a princess.

* * *

Elin was brimming over with pride, as well she might be, for had not she helped to dress this woman and in particular used her skilful fingers to arrange Mariana's hair? But, more than that, since the beginning, Elin had felt that she had been involved with the very upbringing of her mistress and friend, ever since the drama in the kitchen five years ago. She had watched over her and guarded her, giving advice and even scolding her occasionally. Tonight was the culmination of all her hard work. Usually she felt older than Mariana but it seemed as if, during the last few hours, her mistress had overtaken her and she was now again in reality the younger.

* * *

Anne was satisfied. Her last minute stitching was invisible – an extra tuck in at the waist and a slight widening of the shoulders did not show, but Anne's experienced eyes could see that the bodice hung properly now, where before there had been a looseness. Thus the whole gown hugged Mariana's body. The woman was truly magnificent!

* * *

Elizabeth's twins, Jane and Ellenor, were speechless at the change wrought in their friend. Only babies when Mariana had first visited them, they were neither piqued by the beginnings of her beauty beneath her pale face, nor old enough to realise how exceedingly trying was her intractable behaviour.

Years later they had found out that their eldest sister, Esther, had resented the arrival at her lessons of a child who could not only get answers right when she tried, but also when she did not... and most of the time, she did not! They guessed that Esther, two years older than Francisca, had, until Mariana's appearance, always managed to be the best at everything. But suddenly, along came a child who could turn from sullenly rebellious to charmingly docile in a trice. Esther must have felt threatened. The twins suspected that the governess would never have succumbed to Mariana's winsomeness, but they knew that Esther considered the Squire's daughter a nuisance. In truth, Esther ruled her sisters and still thought of Mariana as an interloper.

Jane and Ellenor understood that Francisca was much too shy to interact with strangers. Apparently she had lived in perpetual fear of Mariana's pranks bringing punishment on the entire nursery. The reticent child had grown into an almost monosyllabic adult and the twins knew she kept away from Mariana whenever she could.

Of the four sisters, only they themselves liked Mariana. They were captivated by her loveliness, delighted by her inventiveness at mischief, thrilled if the lessons disintegrated. Impervious to the shouting that ensued, they used to encourage Mariana to disrupt the lessons as much as possible. They both admired her in every way, envying her freedom at home and wishing that they could live with her.

Now, all of a sudden, when they crowded into the blue bedchamber to see the party gown that their mother had told them about, they discovered that here was not the Mariana they knew, whose skirt was often muddied and torn and who would run barefoot on the beach – here was a woman, and they turned to each other and clasped hands for reassurance that even if Mariana was lost to them in adulthood, they had each other forever.

* * *

A knock at the door broke the silence and Mariana twirled around eagerly. Surely this was Henry at last!

"Come in," she called gaily, but it was only a maid, who bobbed a curtsey and said:

"Please, Madam?" She turned from Elizabeth to Mariana in apparent confusion. "Mr Pocock has asked me to tell you that the guests are beginning to arrive."

"Thank you, Owen." Elizabeth spoke with authority. "Would you inform Goodwin so that he can tell my husband?" Immediately she ignored the maid.

Mariana watched the girl hasten out of the room. Obviously Elizabeth Parry expected her orders to be obeyed, because already she was clucking around her daughters.

"Right. Away with you, Jane, Ellenor. You've seen Mariana and you can watch the other guests from the top of the stairs later. Go back to your room for a moment whilst I get organised. Come, Mariana, let's go down. My husband will be waiting."

On leaving the bedchamber, they were joined by Esther and Francisca and Elizabeth continued:

"Ah, there you are girls. My, how pretty you all look tonight. Esther, Esther, darling, do take that scowl off your face. Young men won't ask you to dance if you're sulking. Francisca, lift your eyes from the floor. Esther, you must go first, being the eldest. Then, Mariana next and then Francisca."

"No," disagreed Mariana. "I'll go last. This is your home and your party. Your daughters must go first."

Mariana ignored the look of surprise on her hostess' face. She knew she wasn't one to sit in the background usually but suddenly she wanted to bring up the rear. She allowed Elizabeth to escort her chicks downstairs.

"Well, that is very considerate of you, Mariana, my love. Now, Francisca, hold your head up and shoulders back. Don't keep staring at the ground as though you're frightened of everyone. Be careful, Esther, that you don't trip."

* * *

Elin stared around at the untidy room and sighed. Articles of clothing, towels, brushes, powder and even jewellery had been thrown to stay where they had landed. The quilt on the bed was crumpled and Elin watched whilst Anne scuttled to rescue her needles, threads and scissors from the chaos before she left with a quick farewell.

Elin sighed again. Very soon she would have to change into her 'uniform' and report below stairs to help with the serving of supper. Of mustard-coloured linen sent from Wrexham and skilfully made into petticoat and bodice, it was her most treasured gown and she felt like a lady when she wore it, but tonight she was tired. Momentarily, she wondered if her assistance would not be needed after all, if there were going to be fewer guests. She could hear that the tempest had not abated at all; it swirled around the house, hungry to enter the meanest crack. Could she afford to sit down for a few minutes before she started to put the room in order? She had been up and on her feet since well before four this morning and her neck ached from bending over to arrange Mariana's hair. She flung a back-laced corset and frilled tucker off the nearest chair on to the floor and sank gratefully on to its hard seat. She glanced at the bed – the feather mattress looked extremely welcoming. Maybe…

Her mind turned to the past. How long it seemed since she had slept in a bed with five of her brothers and sisters! And that had been no feather bed!

Elin had been born in a *Tŷ â siambr* – a house with a chamber – more a rude cottage made of stone with one room, which boasted a partition between the living quarters and the straw upon which the family slept. The floor was mud and the roof thatched with rushes. Two inadequate, unglazed windows gave light to the murky interior but the wide, open fire burned peat, producing a curling smoke that added to the gloom. The room was dark even in the daytime.

Elin's father was an agricultural labourer who was paid daily for his work, which meant his wages were irregular. Their cottage squatted near the farm of Joachim Thomas, one of Mariana's father's tenants.

Elin's mother. Ah, how she loved her mother, and the picture that repeatedly came into her head, even now, years later, was of her mother working. She was never still, never resting; always busy, always spinning or knitting to produce wares to sell to supplement their meagre lifestyle. After sheep shearing, Elin's father would procure a fleece (or sometimes two), for his wife. And the children would beg for scraps of wool at the end of the day when the shearers were clearing up the field. Then the complicated process of turning sheep's wool into garments would begin.

All the girls of the family were taught how to card the wool and spin it, and Elin's favourite moments during childhood were sitting close to her mother's knee, leaning against her mother's secure, familiar body, learning what to do; listening to her mother's quiet voice explaining and instructing her daughters. By five, Elin could spin adroitly, although even before a child could spin, he or she was involved in this home industry, for Elin, like her brothers and sisters after her, were sent to increase the supply of wool by gathering any strands caught in the gorse and briars around the fields. None were ever too young to be included in the family business!

Sometimes her mother had simply spun the rough flax ready to be sold to others who could make it into their own sheets or towelling. If she spent all the hours of light sitting at her wheel she managed to produce nearly two pounds of flax a day. If she ever made her own plain sheets she took all winter to complete one pair. However, more often, she had used the wool not only to provide her family with warm clothes, but also to make stockings, wigs and caps (put on the head when wigs were removed) to sell. Elin could hear the ceaseless clatter of needles across the years. But, with girls in the family, her mother had ready helpers since, from an early age, each daughter was able to make, from raw wool through to finished garment, four pairs of full-sized stockings every week.

Towards the end of the week, Elin and her elder sister, Anne, with their ever-faithful brood of younger siblings, were sent to wait near the crossroads to sell their handiwork. For this, they needed loud voices to catch the attention of travellers and an ability to persuade the customer that no finer garment than this very one (and so reasonably priced!) could be found anywhere on the island.

"You'll need thick stockings if you're crossing by boat to Dublin, Mistress."

"A cap for those winter nights indoors and this one could have been made for you, Sir. It looks like your size, Sir."

Elin remembered the patter well. Yes, the joy of returning to her mother with coins jangling in her neckerchief had made Elin work hard even when she had stood for hours in a brisk wind, glad of her own adequate clothes, waiting for a passing customer. When she thought of all the time her mother had spent bent over the wheel in an ill-lit room, it seemed as nothing that she should have to linger by the side of the road with superb views of the windswept island and the company of her chattering brothers and sisters. Yes, Elin remembered the work and the rewards.

Yet it had not only been the women of the family who had worked so industriously; Elin's father, although leaving the cottage each day at dawn and not returning until dusk, had been able, by the light of a single, rush light, to teach his sons how to make wooden utensils. These too were sold and the money added to their father's wages of six pence a day in summer and five pence a day in winter. Sometimes small amounts of food from the farm came their way as gifts and they had eked out a happy life together… until Elin's mother had died.

The other strong memory that Elin had of her mother was that she was always with child. Eleven children in almost the same number of years. As the second eldest daughter, Elin became accustomed to living her whole life with one baby astride her hip and a dirty toddler clutching her gown. When year succeeded year, each baby was demoted to the ground to struggle as best it could on its bare, unsteady feet and the latest demanding babe gripped her waist with its spindly legs. More than the bashful Anne, Elin had cared for each child whilst her mother shrunk and shrunk; her skin pulled tighter across her face after each weary year her bones protruded, her only girth an unborn child.

Three of Elin's siblings were lost by the time Elin was ten, the last taking her mother with him to the grave an hour after his arrival. Elin had not wept; her dead mother's face proclaimed the rest that she had never found on this earth, and innocently the young girl had believed that her life would continue as before, except that no new, crying babies would come to replace the year-old infants. How wrong she had been, for within two months Widow Davies had come into their lives and she had met Mariana!

* * *

Mariana held back slightly from following her hostess. She did not want to go and meet the other guests. With the preparations over, her mind had returned to Henry and his plight. If he had arrived already, surely he would have presented himself because it was all of eight weeks since she had seen him. He had not come to her; this must mean that he was not here yet. Anxiety made her stomach churn painfully and her head ache. She longed to remain in her room with her fears, but she remembered what her Aunt Elizabeth had said to Esther and she forced a smile to her lips. He would come. He would come soon and until then she must pretend.

Mariana was halfway down the stairs when the great door resounded with someone beating on its timbers. She had been told that Pocock and his footmen had opened the door earlier, but the wind had driven the rain inside and howled around the hall. Now only one unfortunate footman was stationed outside in the downpour. Surely this was not him, rude enough to announce a guest in this unseemly manner? She saw Pocock frown and glide forward to open the door.

There stood no familiar footman but a soaked stranger whom Mariana didn't recognise at first as one Evan Gloff from the village. He removed his hat, presumably in respect at entering the home of Sir Meyrick Parry, but then harshly shouted:

"Hello! We need help! She's asinking fast. The *Abundance* – out beyond Ynys Cybi. Oh, please help."

Such an unceremonious speech would have resulted in an instant rebuff and possibly the messenger being thrown out in places like London or Chester. However, in a close-knit community where shipwreck was common, every man was needed to assist and the request was accepted. Usually the women and children went too, as often to garner the duty-free flotsam and jetsam (if they could pick it up unobserved by the custom men), as to help the injured and dead. However, there was a moment of startled silence whilst the information was digested. Then Mariana moaned:

"No! No! Henry! Oh, Henry!"

She picked up her skirts and turned back up the stairs, rapidly ascending where she had just recently come down. She tripped at the top but righted herself and sped along the corridor to her room.

She saw Elin leap up with a start when she hurled open the door, pulling at the fastenings of her clothes as she moved.

"Miss Mariana! What is it? What's happened? Why have you come back?"

"It's Henry. His ship has sunk. Get me… get me out of these clothes. I'm going to find him."

"No!" barked Elin, clutching at her mistress' hands. "Leave that, Miss Mariana! Don't ruin your gown. You can't possibly go out in this weather and…"

"God's bones! If you won't assist me, I'll go as I am." She tore away from Elin, anger blazing on her face. "You can't stop me. Henry needs me. Evan Gloff came. He asked us to come… come and help. Henry needs me."

*　*　*

Elin heard the frenzy in Mariana's voice. Instantly she calculated that it would be impossible to prevent her mistress from going – she was never one to listen to reason, even when she was calm. Where was Mistress Parry? She might be able to steady Mariana.

"Now, Miss," started Elin in an authoritive tone. Maybe she could delay Mariana. "If you must go, then I think it's best for you to change. I will get you out of them…"

"No! No, there's no time. I'll go as I am. Hurry up! You must show me the way down the backstairs. There's no time to lose."

"The backstairs?"

"Yes, I can hardly go down the main ones, can I? They'll stop me, won't they? Quickly! Hurry! Which way do I go?"

"Oh, please stop," wailed Elin. "Don't go in that expensive gown. Oh, Miss, it'll be ruined in the rain."

"My life will be ruined if anything happens to Henry. He may already be…" Mariana's voice caught on a sob.

"No, Miss Mariana, you must not go. Not only would Mistress Parry and her husband disapprove but your father would too. Even Mr Wynne…" This last was a guess for she knew that Mr Henry Wynne did not always chide Mariana for her wilder schemes.

"Be quiet! There's not time to listen to you. I am going, with or without you." The resolve in her voice and eyes was unmistakable. She opened the door. Elin snatched up a cloak and followed her out.

"Turn right," Elin instructed. She was no match for Mariana at her most determined. It would be best if she went with her. She guided Mariana to the narrow door which all the servants used. In fact, until today she had never used the main stairs but she had been so worried that Mariana would never enter *Carregfan* (but would turn down the hill and sit by the creek until Mr Wynne arrived), that she had accompanied her mistress through the front-door in spite of the blatant disapproval in Mr Pocock's eyes. Come to think of it, there was always disapproval in his eyes – and even in the way he stood. If the truth were known, she was terrified of the stiff butler, but her concern for Mariana had made her brave today.

"Here, Miss Mariana, put your cloak on. You'll be less noticeable with it on."

She laughed silently inside. Less noticeable! Less noticeable! Her mistress would never be less noticeable even if she was wearing an old sack!

* * *

The cloak hung from neck to floor, with two slits for her arms and buttons all down the front, but Mariana simply threw it over her brilliant gown and hurried to descend the narrow, dimly lit, stairs. She had to turn half side-ways to allow the width of her skirts to pass along the cramped passage. Fortunately, before she had left her room to accompany her hostess she had told Elin to pin up the generous train.

They met no one until they reached the lower floor of the house and emerged on to the corridor leading from the kitchens to the main entrance hall. The light from the corridor illuminated the lower steps. Mariana stopped on the fourth step up, just out of view of anyone passing by.

"Which way is it?" she whispered to Elin. She knew that undoubtedly what her maid had said was true: both her father, if he had arrived by now, and the Parrys, would not only forbid her to go to the beach, but would probably lock her in her room to prevent her from doing so. Part of her haste in not changing her gown came from the dread of someone coming into her room to check on her or even to try to comfort her. Having escaped, she had no intention of being caught by some senior self-important servant who would recognise her and report her. "Could you go back, Elin, and fasten my bedchamber door and pretend I'm asleep or something?"

"Certainly not," came the tart reply.

"Ssh!"

"I'm coming with you," Elin continued, lowering her voice.

"No, you're not..."

"Yes, I am." Mariana heard that Elin's whisper was as resolved as her own. "If you go, I go. So turn left at the bottom of the stairs."

Mariana could not see her maid's face but she knew from experience that Elin could be stubborn like herself. Therefore, she wasted no more time on fruitless arguments, and lifting up her skirts once more, she descended the last few steps. When she reached the corridor she whirled away to the left with her head bowed.

* * *

Nelly held the stack of plates against her apron. They were heavy and she understood that, whatever else she did tonight, she mustn't drop them. She didn't usually work at *Carregfan* but she had been hired to help out at the party. She halted when the resplendent woman appeared before her. Nelly had lived in Holyhead all her life and reckoned she knew everyone, but she didn't recognise the woman who pushed past her rudely. She decided that she must have come from Cardiff. What one of the guests was doing in the servants' hall, she couldn't guess – probably up to some ridiculous caper. But why anyone would want to disappear out of the door on a wild night like this and in such an extravagant gown she didn't know nor care. She was just glad that her precious cargo had not smashed. She returned to the kitchen, shaking her head at the ways of the rich.

* * *

Mariana stopped to gape at the confused scene before her. She had slithered rather than walked down the hill, surprised that there was no one going up to *Carregfan*, nor anyone leaving it. Over the windy bridge, with her skirts weighed down with water, she and Elin had made remarkable time,

39

considering the darkness and the rain. They had struggled around the curve of the creek and with the village houses left behind them, they had paused for breath.

Before them were the mountainous seas, swirling and tumbling under the influence of the storm. Of the *'Abundance'* herself there was no sign. Had she been swallowed by the tumultuous waves or was the driving rain hiding her from their anxious eyes? Mariana scraped her drenched hair away from her face. She had not fastened all the buttons on her cloak and it billowed out in the full force of the wind, allowing the costly silk robe to be saturated. She had not even tried to lift the hood of the cloak, and the tempest had torn at its elaborate style so that it hung down her back. Belatedly she searched with her fingers for the pearl pins, thrusting them into Elin's hands for safe-keeping.

Now that she had halted, she realised that her heart was thumping and her ribs were heaving; her legs were aching from striving to keep upright on the muddy path; her feet were raw, for she had lost one of her shoes near the top of the hill when they set out, and the other one near the creek, and her stockings had disintegrated from their rough usage. However, overriding all these physical discomforts was the despair inside her heart as she squinted at the disordered beach.

Hundreds of figures, it seemed, were scurrying back and forth, dragging people from the crashing waves. Mariana frowned. Maybe those limp burdens were not bodies but packages and boxes. It was difficult to see from this distance. Other knots of villagers hung together – were they the women? – swaying in the hurricane, all apparently facing the sea, observing the work of the others. Why didn't they go and help? Mariana felt panic rising in her throat. How was she ever to find Henry in all this? If truth were told she had not considered how she was going to help when she had left the house; she had just known that she could not stay quietly at home whilst Henry was in danger.

The noise of the wind and relentless waves filled her ears and hindered clear thinking, but, as she began to cross the grass down to the sand, another sound came to her: a deep, haunting wail of grief from the crowd on the beach.

Mariana seized Elin's hand and cried despondently:

"Oh, where shall we start? Where is he? How can we find him?"

* * *

"We must look and we must ask," Elin soothed, gripping her mistress' frozen fingers. Although she had been unable to fetch a shawl for herself in the hurry of departure and therefore was soaked to the skin, she was hot from the heavy exertion of trying to follow Mariana. She was used to hard work but fast walking was an exercise her stout body hated. She was surprised at how cold Mariana felt. She looked at her slight friend. Suddenly she realised that, after leading all the way down here, now Mariana was turning to her for guidance. She herself had no foolproof plan, but she decided that they had better start at one end of the beach and inspect the half-drowned and drowned alike.

Elin learnt afterwards that those who saw her mistress that night thought she was an angel. Her cloak surged out behind her, flapping like wings, and her pearl-studded gown seemed almost to glimmer in the dark. Elin noticed that several men and women crossed themselves when they saw her hurry from one inert figure to another, searching and checking. Was she the angel of death, like at the first Passover, hovering over the bodies, taking the breath from these distressed people, or was she the angel of life, touching and healing the injured and the dead?

Elin sensed Mariana was sinking into discouragement as they moved along near the wintery waves which pounded ceaselessly, carrying in more and more debris and the waterlogged bodies. One time, she watched a tiny baby being spewed up on to the sand, but a single look told her that it was beyond saving and she pulled Mariana away so the downcast girl did not see it. All the time, grit blew in their eyes and up their nostrils and stuck to their own soaked clothing, making them more cumbersome.

Elin noticed that most of the bodies were men. Anyone in skirt or froth of petticoats Mariana ignored but all in breeches she approached, bending over to stare at their faces and touch their clothes. They had to check each and every one because in their bedraggled state it was impossible to distinguish squire from peasant, homespun cloth from fine. The majority were already dead but some stirred at her mistress' touch. None was Mr Wynne.

* * *

Mariana raised her hand to wipe her hair from her brow for the thousandth time. She acknowledged that the chances of finding her beloved Henry alive were very low, but she had to go on. She had to keep looking. She felt so tired, hope gradually fading as she saw more and more dead.

Suddenly she was grasped by strong hands from behind and a voice said:

"Mariana, what are you doing here?"

She turned to see her father, hatless, wig askew, coat sagging and his face streaming with water.

"Oh, Father, I'm looking for Henry." She couldn't keep the weariness out of her voice. And disappointment. For a brief moment, she had believed those hands had belonged to Henry.

"You must go home. This is no place for you…" Her father sounded unfamiliar; he was hoarse from shouting above the gale.

"No!" shrieked Mariana, wrenching herself free from his grasp. She sprang away from him and stumbled over a figure lying in the sand. Whilst she pulled herself up from the clogging ground, the body fell from its side to its back and Mariana stared into sightless, glassy eyes.

Her scream soared above the groaning of the injured; the wailing of the grief-stricken; the roaring of the waves and the bellowing of the wind. It seared the sky and reached the heavens. It was a scream of pure despair, catching at the very core of the soul and turning it to ice.

Henry!

SUMMER

WILLIAM AND GRIFFITH

Sir William gazed out of the window at the familiar scene before him. He was seated, facing the restive sea, in his library in *Trem-y-Môr*, his home. He had settled in this house, after a lifetime of travelling between his various estates, nearly eighteen years ago. He had sat in this very chair at exactly the same angle on so many occasions that he had lost count of how many times he had looked out of the window. However, the scene continued to hold his attention and was different each time he saw it. The land directly in front of him was clothed in green grass, which remained the same whatever the season; but beyond this, the ground dropped precipitously down to a half moon of shifting sand, which was washed regularly by the turbulent Irish Sea. It was here that he saw the changes.

He had seen the beach, his own private beach, smooth and cool on a calm, moonlit night, and hot and shimmering, with slowly lapping waves, under a fierce, full sun. He had seen it, as it was today, with the sand reduced to a narrow ribbon and the sky and sea dominating his vision; black and plum, bruised clouds, brimful of rain, apparently resting on the inky sea, which, chameleon-like, mirrored the menacing sky. Like the sea, Sir William's thoughts reflected the foreboding heavens, as the problems of the future hung over him.

What was he to do? His daughter's future lay in his hands. Of course, all his daughters' futures – Margaret's, Katherine's and Penelope's – had lain in his hands in the past, but Mariana was so special to him, so important to him and her happiness was what he desired. But there were other, unknown factors: for example, how long did he have to live?

How many scores of others down the ages had asked this same question? People facing illness or old age, most of them: and he was both of these. In his sixty-fifth year he felt that he had taken from life all it had to offer to him and, with the terrible pains in his chest recurring at shorter and shorter intervals, he knew that his life would soon be over, and then what would become of his unmarried, unprotected, youngest daughter?

If only Henry Wynne had not perished six months ago. What a tragedy that had been, and how badly his Mariana had been affected by his death!

If only Edward would return. Why had he never written to his son, begging him to come back?

If only he knew that the Lord God would grant him a few more years on this earth.

If only…

Sir William closed his eyes and rested his weary head on the back of the chair. The air was sultry and he had removed his heavy wig nearly an hour ago. He particularly favoured the full-bottomed wig with its mass of curls framing his face and falling to shoulder-length, but it was far too hot to wear in this oppressive weather. He wished the storm would hurry up and break. Now June in London could be a time of close, languorous weather but, at least there, refreshingly violent thunderstorms would clear the air and wash the grimy streets. But here in North Wales, thunderstorms were quite rare. Rainstorms abounded but they were hardly ever accompanied by the drums of thunder. He sighed. He hoped that the threatening rain would lighten the stifling air.

He fingered his cap, reopening his eyes. It was round-crowned with a flat, turned-up brim. Maybe he could afford to remove that too. Surely no one but Wilson, his manservant, would disturb him, and that reserved man had been with him for years and had seen him in his… well, in his altogether. So, yes, he would remove it. Ah, that was cooler. How delightful to be able to divest oneself of one's hair – not like women! Take, Mariana, for instance. She had wondrous hair, just like her mother, but she could not cast it off in weather like this. Mariana. Mariana.

He closed his eyes and imagined her mother. She had been slightly taller than Mariana, but with the same slender build. People had been heard to say that she had not been such a beauty as her daughter but, in his opinion, there could be no one to surpass his wife, Mariana – his Mari. Initially he had resented the fact the child was named after her mother. But he had been so distracted after his wife's death that he had given no guidance as to what to call the babe, and by the time he had come to his senses, the child was known as 'Mariana'. He used a pet name for his wife – Mari – which he had kept only between the two of them, and he had found over the years that he had thought more and more of his dead wife as 'Mari'. Because of this he had never shortened his daughter's name.

He could remember as clearly as if it was yesterday the day he had met his darling Mari. He allowed his thoughts to wander back in time.

It had been this time of year, June, and he was returning from the Westminster Coffee House after drinking a dish of coffee with his friend, Lord James Clarkson. He felt relaxed enough to hum a tune because the atmosphere in those newly-founded coffee houses was restful. Many customers went in simply for a peaceful read or to get away from their nagging wives, but he liked to visit them to meet old acquaintances and to catch up on the latest snippets of news. Since the seats were all separated by wooden wainscoting it was possible to have a completely private conversation with one's friends without fear of interruption. Whenever he was in London, he used to make sure that he had time to visit the Westminster Coffee House.

On this occasion, as usual, he was staying in his townhouse. He had left his friend at the coffee house and, when he turned the corner ready to cross the River Thames, he saw her.

Looking totally lost and somehow abandoned, Mari was standing at the entrance to London Bridge, which was the only way to cross the river. She looked completely out of place in her lemon gown, for the bridge was a bustling street supporting many different kinds of workshops. Tanners, brewers, soap boilers, lime burners and dyers filled the air with pungent smells and the noise they made competed with the sound of the rushing water of the river flowing between the starlings (the boat-like buttresses) of each archway. Wrinkling her nose against the fumes (a movement that would soon be familiar and very dear to him), and with her mouth in an attractive pout, she caused his heart to thump loudly.

Hastily he stepped forward to aid this alluring stranger. Ever the gentleman, he offered his services to help the lady in any way he could. Her problem on that particular morning was that she was lost. He was able to escort her to her destination, by a circuitous route, enabling him to begin to forge a relationship with her.

Theirs had been a whirlwind romance: it was only six weeks before he proposed to her and married her. How he had adored her!

Mari had not been his first wife. Being the eldest son, his first wife, Letitia, was chosen for him at an early age, for the land which she would bring with her to the marriage. He remembered that this very house. *Trem-y-Môr*, had come to him through his marriage to Letitia. She had been very different from Mari. His parents had described Letitia as a sober, worthy young woman and he himself had found her to be so. He had no complaints about her. She had run his several households efficiently and had borne him his children and, if there was no love between them, there was at least respect and familiarity. Twenty years of marriage and for it all to end with that terrible illness! They had shared a bed even up to a month before she died, where Letitia had always been compliant. She had given birth to twelve children in all. She was a good breeder, responding well to pregnancy and child-bed; she lost no child at birth. It had been during their early years that so many of his offspring had been taken: William, his namesake, at nine months; the twins at only three weeks, little Jane at two years old. There were others too but hardly could he recall them now, nearly forty years later. All that was left from his union with his first wife were three grown-up daughters and one son.

One son. One son. Dear Edward. Oh, why had he argued with him? What foolishness had filled his head, causing him to alienate his only son and lose his friendship forever? How the years had passed! It was such a long time since he had seen him that now his son was a man himself.

Of course, Mari had been the cause of the row. What a heavenly creature she had been! So young, so marvellously ingenuous, so loving, so unaware of her own charms. She had transformed his life with love and it was not until she had appeared that he had realised what his relationship with Letitia had lacked.

Come from nowhere, some said. In fact, Mari had never told him her past, but for his second marriage it had not mattered. Maybe money and a good lineage had been considered the first time he had married but, for the second time, he could afford to marry for love. Where she came from and what her life had held before he saw her standing alongside the river on that sunny London morning had not worried him at all. She never even told him her age, although he would have placed her at about eighteen or maybe twenty. One thing was certain, no other man had had her. Thus he had ignored the vicious gossips and not lowered himself to defend his new wife or the reason for their short betrothal. All that had mattered then was the present, the now: Sir William had found himself young again at forty-six, with his new love.

However, his past had been important to Mari and she had been avid to hear everything. She had wanted to know every minute detail of his life and she had taken his routines, his possessions, his houses, even his family, into her heart as though she owned nothing of her own. Still he wondered sometimes if that had been the case, but he had never probed her for information.

Naturally, such a youthful stepmother could have caused trouble. Certainly, Margaret, his eldest surviving daughter, had resented Mari, and had behaved ungraciously towards her, since she was of a similar age to Mari. Fortuitously, Margaret was married herself by that time and was not living at home. Katherine had interacted well with Mari, although she was on the verge of marriage herself, and spent much of her time with her betrothed's family. Penelope, his youngest daughter, had been a firm favourite with Mari and really his main problems had been with his son.

Edward had been fourteen then and Sir William imagined that he had been feeling the budding stirrings of manhood. The lad had become besotted with his stepmother. Mari had thought it was a tremendous joke and had teased her husband about it, in the privacy of their bedchamber, but he was intensely jealous. Increasingly he was delighted that such a captivating young woman could be in love with him, but he feared that she would turn from him. To have his own son ogling her had played on that fear and driven him to anger. He had felt that he could not bear to lose her now that he had found her – and especially to his son!

Within a few weeks of his marriage, Sir William had been plunged into a financial nightmare. The year before he met Mari his own father had died. Although he had been informed that his father's finances were tangled, it was not until after he had married Mari that the full extent of his father's debts became known. After the Civil War a large proportion of the family's riches had gone in fines, but all would have been well if his father had not loved gambling.

Nearly four months of mad rushing from house to house, inquiring of the stewards and sifting through the books, had revealed that Sir William's only hope of escaping imprisonment for his father's debts was to sell some of his property.

Although his heart had wept at the loss of this heritage, his new-found love had suggested that he keep his land on Anglesey and the house, *Trem-y-Môr*, together with his London house and a small parcel of land in Cardiganshire. In fact, he knew that Mari's favourite domain was the solid comforting house near Holyhead and, after Katherine's marriage, he and his wife had repaired there to await the arrival of their first child and to enjoy some time together alone. Later in the year, before the snows made travel across the mountains impossible, Penelope and Edward had arrived from London.

Sir William could picture their entrance now. He and his wife had been in the library, he recalled. She had been standing in front of a glowing fire, whilst he was searching for a book for her to read in bed. Since her pregnancy had begun, she had suffered from insomnia and she had asked him for something to read in the night in order to rock her active mind back to sleep.

He could even remember what his Mari had been wearing. She was dressed in mellow peach velvet and, with the tight lacing of her corset, the roundness of her breasts was accentuated. The gathered, open skirt was attached to her bodice, revealing a satin cream petticoat making her slender hips look wider. There was no sign of the baby – he could only see that when she was undressed – and he had felt desire rise within him.

He had gone forward to hold her, ready to whisper that he could think of a much better way of spending the next hour than reading, but before he reached her, the door burst open. There stood his daughter and son, both giggling helplessly. Their lack of manners, coupled with their untimely arrival, had vexed him but, when Mari herself within a short time was giggling too (and over something that he did not think was remotely funny), he had felt pushed out, an outsider, and ever after he viewed his children's presence as an intrusion.

During their stay, Edward and Penelope seemed to have endless vigour and their high spirits lasted through the Christmastide and into the New Year. Seeing his wife beginning to tire under the constant commotion created by the lively youngsters, Sir William's festering anger began to boil and he decided to arrange for his children to depart as soon as possible.

The very day he had come to this decision, he had returned from visiting one of his tenants to find his wife in the arms of his son. Unheeding to their protestations of innocence, not caring where the truth lay, five miserable weeks of pent-up emotion exploded and he had sent his son to a school in Winchester.

Although he had felt better after the departure of Edward, he had found Mari strangely distant and she had spent most of her time with Penelope, leaving him to feel the awkward interloper still. However, much to his delight, not two weeks later, a letter had come from his eldest daughter, Margaret, begging Penelope to set off immediately to aid her in the nursing of her son who had contracted smallpox. Since Penelope had survived that illness already, suddenly Sir William found himself alone again with his wife.

Even so, he and his youthful bride never recaptured the bliss they had experienced in the autumn. Nevertheless, over the years he had allowed his memories to blur, so that now he half believed that they had picked up again their close, loving relationship.

Sir William stretched his legs out in front of him. The clouds were continuously massing but as yet there was no rain. By God, he was hot! Should he ring for Wilson to bring him a drink? He closed his eyes. He remained lost in reminiscences. No, Wilson would intrude on his thoughts.

He let the years roll back. He and Mari had never discussed his dismissal of Edward because he had refused to talk about it. Yet that Christmas had only been the beginning of his estrangement with his son.

The following May (and a hard, frosty May it had been, he recalled), with the time of the birth of the child drawing nearer and nearer, a letter came from the headmaster of Edward's school. Therein lay a complicated tale about Edward and the local judge's daughter, ending in a plea for Sir William to come and see both his son and the headmaster. Assured by Mari that there was a full three weeks before the baby's arrival, impatiently he had left his wife's side.

For years the very thought of that ill-fated journey had caused a leaden knot in his breast, but now he just sighed and gazed sightlessly out of the window. It all seemed so long ago!

He remembered that he had barely reached Llandrindod Wells when a speedy horseman caught up with him, bearing the news that Mari had been brought to childbed and been delivered of a child, though the messenger knew not whether the child was a boy or girl. Now Mari was dying.

Riding his horse and himself to exhaustion, Sir William had reached Mari a mere two hours after she had died, and, refusing to see the baby, he had locked himself in his library to drink himself into oblivion. As the alcohol had filled his body, hatred for Edward had filled his heart, because he blamed the boy's misdemeanour in making him leave Mari. Believing (wrongly, he found out later), that his presence by her side would have prevented her death, he had written, that very night, a letter full of bitter, raging thoughts and while grief still tore at his heart he sent it to his fifteen year old son.

What a mistake! Sir William shook his head in sorrow and placed his cap back on his head absentmindedly. What a terrible year that had been, after Mari's death! He had alternated between his library and bedchamber, refusing to venture out and refusing to see anyone: a recluse. An eccentric recluse. His thoughts had dwelt on his lost love and he had forgotten Mari's last gift to him: the baby.

It was past the first anniversary of his wife's death before he glimpsed his daughter for the first time. Nonetheless, he smiled to himself, he had not sought her out of his own volition; it had been a case of mistaken identity.

Some sensible servant, not having been given any instructions on how to clothe the child, nor on what to do with the late mistress' gowns, had used the very same peach velvet of his memories to make his daughter an identical outfit. Sir William had seen the tiny figure at the other end of the beach from his library window. With a padded bonnet covering the short profusion of black curls, for a moment, he had let himself think that it was his Mari returning to him and that she would grow bigger and bigger as she approached him. Running from the house, reality dawned on him when he heard Mariana's childish shrieks. Immediately he had felt his dead wife's admonition: he had neglected the fruit of their union. And he had gone to meet the child, sweeping her up into his arms.

Mariana had peered at him, as if he was a stranger, which, of course, he was. She had sobbed so passionately that she had to be returned to her nursemaid, whom Sir William vaguely recognised as the woman Mari had engaged just before her demise. Once safe in familiar arms, the child had turned off the tears and stared boldly at him. His heart was captured! Thus father and daughter had met and, for him, his love for her had come as strongly and as quickly as he had loved her mother before her.

The pretty child had grown into a striking young woman, resembling her mother in face and figure.

Sir William returned his thoughts to the present and the difficult problem that lay ahead of him. If his daughter was a beauty, and she certainly was that, she was also a handful and she would need a firm man, who could curb some of her wilder ideas…

Yet, why was he thinking like this? For, since the tragic night of the Twelfth Night party, Mariana had changed. Yes, she still rode her horse, and mostly without a groom, he knew that. But, apart from this daily, early morning excursion, she remained in the house, usually confined to her bedchamber. She did not look ill: her face was still as comely as ever, but she no longer chattered and she hardly ever smiled and he had not heard her laugh for over six months. He had not received any complaints from his neighbours or tenants coming to him with stories of Mariana's pranks and wanting compensation for the damage she had done to their fields or livestock. Actually, it was very rare to see anyone coming up their path these days. He appreciated that he had neglected to visit both his friends and the people under his care. It was months since he had been to anyone's house and he had not attended the Quarter Sessions or the Great Sessions in April. He was truly guilty of introspection.

All this would have been bad enough; he could have coped with, and understood, Mariana's behaviour (for had not he himself been cast into gloom after her mother died – and he had had the bottle for comfort too!), but what really disturbed him was the talking into thin air. At least, from his point of view, it was talking into thin air, although, according to her maid, Mariana believed that she was conversing with Henry. Sir William had never heard her. If truth were told, when she deigned to come to the meal table, it was very hard to get a word out of her. However, in the privacy of her own room, evidently, she talked quite openly to Henry and often asked her maid questions on his behalf.

Sir William frowned and scratched his head. Mayhap he should take her to see someone; but he did not want her diagnosed insane and removed from him and locked up in one of those dreadful asylums where people flocked to stare. No, she was not hurting anyone. No, he would leave her; hopefully she would get over her grief eventually. Which brought him back to where he had started from: what should he do about her future?

A knock came on the door and before he had time to whip off his cap and settle his wig on his head, Wilson, his manservant, appeared. He had employed a butler in each of his larger establishments many years ago, but when he had come to settle here, he had found that his tranquil, country life hardly warranted paying a butler, and Wilson was well able to act as butler and his own personal servant. Growing older, he decided that a small staff suited him and Wilson was very competent in every job he undertook.

"Wilson?" The wig was on and already making him perspire.

"I beg your pardon, Sir, but the Parson has just called and is anxious to see you. If you are unable to receive him, he is willing to call another…"

"I may have said that to you, my man, but I really would be most grateful to see the Squire."

It was the Vicar pushing his way past Wilson. He was a squat man dressed all in black with an ostentatious grey wig, parted down the centre, with a long curl hanging tied in a knot on his right shoulder. Sir William noticed that he carried no hat; he must have left it in the hallway. Sir William knew that the Vicar was a fastidious man, who always looked very well-groomed, but the Squire was surprised to see him in such a curly wig for he was very religious: usually his attire was plain. Was this some special occasion?

Sir William was irritated by the man forcing his way in, but he rose to welcome him. He could hardly deny he was in now!

"It's all right, Wilson, thank you. Maybe the Parson requires some refreshment. Port or ale?"

The Vicar patted his rotund stomach. Sir William knew he was partial to both food and drink and he watched the other man fingering the buttons of his waistcoat as if checking that they were still fastened.

"A glass of port would be much appreciated," he returned.

"Fetch us some glasses, Wilson."

"Very good, Sir."

"Won't you sit down, Parson?"

* * *

The Vicar looked around the library. He would have preferred to be received in the parlour. This was a singularly scruffy room with its tiers of dusty books. He did not believe in reading. Well, only the Bible. Yes, the best book to read was the Bible. If you read that you couldn't go far wrong. He looked for a chair. There were only two in the room and the most comfortable was impossible for him to take because the Squire was standing in front of it. He did not really want to sit down at all, for his coat was stiffened with buckram and it made movement difficult. Furtively he undid a few of its buttons in order to push back the heavy cloth and perch on the edge of the chair.

Hidden in the very recesses of his mind was the picture of himself as seen in his looking glass before he set out. He had been extremely pleased with the image for, today, for the first time in years, he was wearing a new suit, in honour of this auspicious occasion. He had given precise instructions to his tailor and the man had obeyed him to the last stitch.

The suit consisted of black breeches to the knee that had a very wide angle at the crotch and a capacious, loose seat. He had reasoned that since no one ever saw the top of your breeches he might as well order them baggy. He hated close-fitting clothing because it made him itch, especially in this weather. Likewise, he had asked for the waist of his breeches to be loose since his corpulent figure often grew during the summer months. He had stipulated that there should be only a small buckle on the knee band so he could pull his black stockings or 'roll-ups' over the knees easily. He had purchased brand new black garters.

Over the breeches, hiding the fact that they were not too tight (for he did not let his coats curve away to reveal his breeches, which was the fashion nowadays), was a marvellous waistcoat, whose front was made of exactly the same material as his coat, but whose back had been made from cheaper cloth according to his own wise instructions: for again, who saw the back of this garment? And he was a thrifty man! Since his early youth, he had kept a strict eye on how his money was spent. The Bible says: **"Honour the Lord with thy substance and with the first-fruits of thine increase"**. Yes, God was looking over his shoulder to check that he did not waste money. His waistcoat was clinging snugly to his upper chest, but he did not mind that. It made him feel manly if he had to squeeze himself into a waistcoat and coat. Like the coat, his waistcoat was stiffened, making it flare out at the back – hence his difficulty with sitting. The buttons, made of the same cloth as the suit, were always kept done up as low as he could, although he noticed that the Squire's were not fastened below the waist.

His coat was a masterpiece, reaching down below his knees and gripping his shoulders at the top. It had side vents so that he could put his hands into the pockets of his waistcoat, if need be, and its collarless neck revealed a glimpse of a plain linen shirt, peeping from beneath a starched, simple white, crossed, lawn cravat.

Black, with just a dash of white! That suited his position as the Vicar of Holyhead!

Of course, he was not vain. **"And they rejected His statutes and His covenant that He made with their fathers and they followed vanity and became vain."** No, vanity was an abomination to the Lord, but today was such an important day. After all, he was here under the Lord's guidance. This was why he had dressed in his new suit and new wig, so that the Squire would be impressed; for the Squire had something he desperately, desperately needed: Mariana.

Reverend Griffith Owen had initially seen Mariana nine years ago when she was a mere child, and he was a married man. The chit had not stirred any passion in him then. However, when she had developed from thin child to sensuous woman, he had found himself more and more attracted to her. Five years ago, the Lord had seen fit to take his wife from him, and during the last two years, he had found his thoughts turning repeatedly to Mariana. He had battled in prayer and Bible-reading to remove his lust for her from his heart. How he had begged the Lord to release him from it and yet the more he had tried to be free, the more he had been bound by it! **"Dearly beloved, abstain from fleshly lusts, which war against the soul."** What a war he had been involved in!

Last year, he had heard that Mariana was going to marry Henry Wynne. Even today, a shudder went through his body. If that had happened… **"Thou shalt not covet thy neighbour's wife."** That was one of the Ten Commandments! He had been saved from this worse sin only by the shipwreck at the turn of the year!

Then, just a few weeks ago, he had read in Paul's letter to the Corinthians: **"I say therefore to the unmarried and widows, it is good for them if they abide even as I. But if they cannot contain, let them marry: for it is better to marry than to burn."**

Suddenly, as if the Lord Himself had spoken to him with a human voice, he had realised that Mariana was of marriageable age and that he could ask for her hand immediately. Thus here he was, this afternoon, sitting in the library at *Trem-y-Môr*, feeling sweat rippling down his back, ready to ask permission of her father. And yet, so far, the conversation was about everyday matters. He must speak soon!

"Well, what can I do for you?" Sir William queried with an impatient tone. He lifted his glass to his lips as the Reverend Owen took courage and admitted:

"I would like to marry your daughter."

Sir William choked on his drink and coughed and spluttered until his face went dark red to match the port that ran down his chin.

The Vicar was delighted to see the Squire in such a state. It gave him an advantage. An elderly man with spit dribbling down his face! And his wig was crooked. He had always found the Squire a difficult man to get to know. Yes, he was steadfast in his attendance at church, but when he met him around the Parish, his attitude often had an air of condescension. This embarrassing incident could give him the upper hand right at the start of the conversation, although he must tread warily and watch his tongue and his manners. If he made a mistake during this interview, the girl could be lost to him.

"My dear Sir Rowlands, may I be of assistance?" He half rose from his seat but the Squire waved a flustered hand at him. He resumed his position and waited until the other man had returned to a normal colour before continuing, "I see this has come as a great surprise to you, Sir, but may I assure you that this is no sudden decision on my part. No, indeed, Sir. As you may well recall, Mrs Owen departed this life five years ago. She was a woman adorned with a meek and quiet spirit. Although we asked the good Lord, on many occasions, to send us a child, He did not see fit to do so. **'But the Lord had shut up her womb.'"**

He paused out of reverence to the Holy Word but since the Squire made no reply, he went on:

"Within the last year or so, I have asked the Lord to find me a new helpmeet. I hoped then that God would bless us with children but… but, more importantly, I would have someone beside me in my work in the Parish. I have been watching your daughter and it has lifted my spirits to see her very regular and proper attendance at our services every Sunday. However, more than this, reports have reached my ears about how kind she is towards others. Jones the Fish – do you know him, Sir? He works… well, never mind. He was saying just this week how your daughter had visited his sick wife last year when he was away at sea. Yes, your daughter is a real credit to you, Sir. Honesty and charity are the most lovely things I know. And God Himself commends us in His Word: **'And now abideth faith, hope, charity, these three; but the greatest of these is charity.'"** He cleared his throat. Was the Squire even listening? He ploughed on; he couldn't stop now! "Hmmrph… I hope you don't consider me too old for your daughter. I am in fact only in my forty-third year."

* * *

Sir William crossed his legs. So this was why this jackanapes had come! He had noticed the other man's smart clothes and presumed that the Vicar had wanted to give a good impression in order to squeeze some money out of him. He had suspected that the cunning clergyman wanted him to agree to pay for the Parson's tithe for a certain section of the Parish. This meant he would pay the Vicar a set sum of money in advance, and then he himself would collect the tithe in kind from the different parishioners. After all, it was easier for him to deal with the rye, wheat hay and so on, than for a clergyman. Also it meant that the Vicar was assured of money. But it wasn't money he was after at all!

He sat up with surprise when the Vicar announced his age. He had assumed visitor was nearer his own age, from his appearance and demeanour. Fortunately the Vicar was gazing at his interlaced fingers and missed his own incredulous look, and carefully he was not drinking anymore after revealing his shock with that untimely coughing fit. Certainly for a man of three and forty the Vicar droned on more like a seventy year old!

"I married... married at twenty the first time and have had several parishes before coming here, namely Llanfair and Llanbedr and... well, I..."

The man glanced up as if expecting some sort of answer. Sir William nodded for him to continue. "I won't bore you with a list of my previous incumbencies. I have been vicar here for eleven years and feel well settled. However, in recent times, I have found my task more arduous without a wife and companion by my side. Not... not that your daughter's tasks would be tiresome or difficult for, naturally, I have a very capable housekeeper who manages the house for me. Nevertheless, the people of the Parish do so like a woman's presence and face... face in the Vicarage. And a young face and person would be welcomed by many, myself included. Well, and... and... I miss the comforts of a woman and..."

"We all do, my dear Parson." Sir William could listen no more. "Aye, we all do. I can, of course, say nothing about the disparity of age since my second wife was also quite young when I married her and there's no doubt that a pretty, young wife brings a new light into one!"

He watched the other man's face redden. Good! He had hoped to make a dent in the Vicar's pomposity. He had a shrewd idea why this man wanted his daughter and it wasn't for her attendance at church! In fact, church attendance didn't have much to do with duty or even belief in God nowadays. Many people went just to avoid getting a presentment from the Churchwardens to say that someone had not attended church for over four weeks. This was the very reason why he himself had insisted Mariana accompany him during the last few months even though she was sunk in grief. Each Sunday, obediently she had sat next to him in his carriage all the way to Saint Cybi's church and silently followed him into the dark, mystical interior. If only he had left her at home; maybe he wouldn't now be trapped in this unpleasant interview. He must dissuade this man from saying anything else. He went on:

"Yes, a pretty, young wife is an asset. However, in spite of the praise you give Mariana, especially in the realm of her interest and care for others, I'm not sure whether she is suited to be a parson's wife. Yes, she does visit and she helps in the village if she can, but sometimes... how can I put this? I certainly have no desire to criticise my own daughter but she can be quite... quite selfish. No, selfish is not the right word. She often has her head in the clouds. Not flighty as such, but just unaware of others' needs. And she can be very, very stubborn. She has a very strong character. She has led an unconventional life up until now, without a mother to guide her, and I'm not sure that she would settle into the role of a vicar's docile wife..."

"May I be so bold as to interrupt you, Sir? I do know that your daughter is a trifle headstrong, but surely that is just youthfulness and the responsibility of a husband and a house to run might well calm her down. Although..." The Vicar paused as if afraid to say more before continuing: "Although, from all accounts, she has already sobered... well, matured, in the last few months... since the death of her... her betrothed. Unofficially, that is! I don't mean to cause offence, Sir. I know there was no official announcement. I believe that it is the sorrow she has suffered which has made her... her grow up. It is the good Lord who knows best what to do with us all. Soon your daughter will realise that God has favoured her with many blessings – a young life and health for herself, and countless more opportunities to serve Him on this passing earth."

Sir William ceased to listen; his thoughts straying away. So others had noticed Mariana's behaviour. However verbose this stout little man was, he was accurate about the remarkable change in Mariana. She *was* introspective. One might almost say she was as silent as the grave, except in her strange conversations with the dead Henry. God forbid that anyone else had discovered this and definitely not this man who went from house to house visiting as part of his parish duties! Perhaps what Mariana needed was a fresh environment, away from this house and its memories. Also there was his own fear of being called to meet his Maker. If he died and word spread about her bizarre behaviour… she would be condemned to an asylum – or worse. With her jet hair and her imprudent behaviour, old escapades would be recalled, fingers would start to point, and tongues might begin to chant, "Witch! Witch!" This kind of accusation was still common amongst ignorant folk!

No, Mariana might well be safer under the care of a husband – and a clergyman at that – if anything happened to him. Again, he silently argued with himself, although it was distasteful to think of this round, fussy man in bed with his beloved daughter, children might well snap her out of her obsession with the past. His mother had always believed that what every woman needed was a babe suckling at her breast.

Besides, who else was there? He didn't know of any eligible men in this area now Henry was gone and Mariana never went out socially anymore, anyway. It was no good contemplating taking her to London; he felt too drained and ill. Furthermore, his town house had been sold and that would mean he would have to impose on his brother, Richard, which would be awkward for him, since he and Richard had never had a close relationship since Edward…

Edward.

Oh, where was Edward? If only he would return, then he could take care of his sister in the event of his own death. Edward could protect her from carnal men like this one. Yes, he had seen the glint in this man's eyes. He knew all about desire, begod he did, although his own had been dampened somewhat since the loss of his love. He had a woman he visited sometimes in…

He came back from his musings to hear the Vicar say:

"My father was a clergyman too but I come from a good family. My great-grandfather was Sir Edmund Owen of Maentwrog and though I haven't much money, the living here…"

Sir William hated the Vicar's sanctimonious tone. He had managed hardly ever, to actually listen to sermons preached in Saint Cybi's church. He had found it exceedingly easy to switch his mind to other matters (as he was doing now) and, more recently, to doze during the long, dull monologues. Only once had he seen this man animated in the pulpit and that was when he had preached about... Oh, what had it been about? Yes, it was about lust... Lust. Yes, not a subject for the delicate ears of some of those who sat on the benches or even stood at the back of the church, and not a subject that should be brought up from the pulpit. At least, not in his opinion. Nonetheless, if he remembered aright, the Parson had the attention of the whole congregation for that particular sermon!

Suddenly, Sir William's mind was made up. Whatever merits this boring man had, he did not like the Parson. There was something not quite... not quite... It was hard to define. He knew the Reverend Owen was very religious, and fond of quoting the Bible, but then he himself was always wary of fanatics. No, it was more than fanaticism. What was it? It was more than desire. It was lust. The man had a ravenous look in his eyes whenever women were mentioned. No, his darling Mariana would not go to a man like this! She was too precious by far!

Yet... yet, what was he to do? Mariana had had eyes for no one but Henry Wynne for so long that there were no suitors left. Possibly the best way ahead was not to dismiss the idea completely. This might be Mariana's only offer. He would speak to her about the proposal. Yes, that was what he would do. She would soon tell him what she thought of the Vicar, for she was not one to hide her feelings and often she took instant likes and dislikes to people. She might even find the Vicar attractive. Who knew what went on in the minds of women?

"Now, Parson," he ruthlessly interrupted. "I think our best recourse is for you to go away and let me think about what you've told me. I won't hide from you that this has come as a surprise to me. However, as I have already said, Mariana and I are both rather unconventional and I would like to speak to her before we discuss marriage settlements and so forth. If she is willing, and this is my only stipulation, if she is willing, I will send word to you and we can talk again."

* * *

Unconsciously the Reverend Owen checked the buttons of his waistcoat were fastened, smoothing out the cloth over his stomach. These last words were a dismissal. He could hardly disguise his disappointment. His host had not even been listening to all his attributes, including the adequate legacy from his Uncle John, which would supplement his living and enable them to live comfortably. The Squire had not seemed concerned with his ancestry: his Aunt Sarah had married a lord. There were other points in his favour! The chit would be mistress of a sizable house and yes, indeed, of a busy and important Parish. He knew Holyhead was a busy and important Parish. She might not be Lady Wynne but that opportunity had passed. It was no good giving yourself airs. Above all this, there was himself to consider. He believed that he was a good catch: young enough to stoop to her level, yet mature enough to provide wisdom and advice for some of her more frivolous plans – if she still had any!

As he bade his farewells, he realised that he had failed. If he could have persuaded the Squire to agree, then he might have succeeded but to ask, to actually ask, a young girl what she wanted – that would be the seal of death to his chances! He knew, deep-down, that he had been no match for Henry Wynne when that dashing fellow was alive, but now he was competing with the memory of a dead man, tinted with grief. So be it. He would just have to return to his praying and maybe some more days of fasting. Sometimes fasting helped too…

* * *

Sir William would have been surprised at the despondency in the Vicar's heart, for the more he pondered, the more he wondered whether his recent visitor might not be the right husband for his daughter. Given his own short life-expectancy (and he could not rid himself of the idea that the end was near), what other man would Mariana meet and marry in the next few months? Even assuming that she did meet someone, who would take her, with her private talks with a dead man? One thing was sure: this suitor wanted Mariana!

Sir William glanced out the window. He screwed up his eyes. What was that hovering out there? It looked like a white light dancing above the grass. He shook his head. Oh, he was so hot and tired! He must be seeing things. He felt weary with life with all its attendant duties and problems.

Suddenly, with no warning, a stab of pain shot through his chest. His mind began to blur as his body broke out in sweat. He tried to call out but could not. He must remain conscious, for with unconsciousness came death: he felt sure of that. Death! Had the white light been an omen? No, he could not die yet; he must see Mariana married to… to Henry. No, not Henry. It was someone else. Who? His distraught mind could not remember. He must see Edward, his only son again before… before…

MARIANA

Mariana sat up in bed with a jolt. Someone was calling:

"Help me! Save me!"

She listened for the voice, but all she could hear was a hurricane of wind howling outside and the frenzied waves pounding on the beach. It was a storm, a terrible storm, like the one at…

Henry! It was Henry. It must have been Henry who had called her. She had to go immediately to help him.

Leaping out of bed, she ran to the window. Although the room was enfolded in darkness, she knew exactly where all her furniture stood and she reached the dense brown curtains without knocking into anything.

Initially, she could see nothing, for the clouds were hiding the moon. However, she could feel the fierce wind rattling the window-frame and there was a draught against her fingers when she leant on the sill. She could hear the deafening roar of the sea. It sounded so loud that she wondered if it was crashing on the grass, or even threatening to come under the front door, as it did sometimes during the high spring tides.

Unexpectedly, a jagged flash of lightning illuminated the scene and Mariana saw, out beyond the point of land, a ship. She was battling to reach the safety of the port. Even as the light disappeared the ship sank below the crest of the waves and Mariana realised how high the waves must be, for them to hide an entire ship from view. Despite the cool sky, Mariana could see, etched in her memory, a picture of the battered ship, her sails ripped and hanging useless in long tatters. Mariana knew the name of the ship. It was the 'Abundance' and Henry was aboard and she must save him.

A caterwaul of thunder resounded above her head and spurred her into action. She raced to the door. Her bare toes chanced upon some clothing. It was an over-skirt which she had thrown on the floor, before going to bed. She bent to pick it up, not wanting to waste any time searching for a cloak, and flung it, shawl-wise, over her upper body. Nimbly she ran along the highly-polished landing and hurried down the stairs, moaning: "I'm

64

coming, Henry. I'm coming."

She reached the front door in no time, but precious minutes were wasted whilst she struggled to pull back the seldom-used bolts before she was out. She disappeared into the night as the tempest caught at the door and banged it shut.

Leaving the shelter of the building she gasped at the strength of the wind: it tore her makeshift cloak from her and swept her hair into a madly flapping banner of black. She could barely open her eyes against the force of it but she could feel the spray of the sea on her face and neck. The water was high, tearing at the land in a frenzy. Shielding her eyes with one hand, she staggered down the slippery steps with her body bent against the fury. Still echoing around her head, but now silent on her lips, she cried:

"I'm coming, Henry. I'm coming. Don't die."

She fell at the bottom of the steps onto the beach, landing partly in the wet sand and partly in the foaming lace of the water's edge. Remarkably, the water felt warm. She pulled herself to her feet and stared at the sea, her hands cupped around her eyes. There was no sign of the ship.

"Henry, where are you?" she shouted, but the words were snatched away. She licked salt off her lips.

Fortuitously, another blaze of lightning filled the air and she saw him! He was lying at the perimeter of the sea, and, whilst she watched, he was sucked back into the water where a huge wave broke over him.

"No!" she shrieked. Lifting her shift above her knees, she struggled towards him resisting the force of nature.

She gripped him under the armpits and dragged him against the downward pull of the sloping sand and the sucking of the retreating tide. Then she tugged him further up the beach until the water only swirled around his feet.

She paused for breath before heaving Henry's body on to its back. Using the edge of her lawn shift, she wiped the sand from his mouth and eyes.

"I'm here, Henry. I'm here," she soothed. "Don't worry. I'll get you to the house."

Somehow, in fits and starts, she hauled her beloved Henry up the beach, across the rough grass, around the corner of the house and in through the kitchen door.

She was surprised at the darkness of his hair. She remembered it had been fairer as a boy, before he had started wearing a wig; it must be because of the sea-water. His nose seemed larger and his chin was covered with the beginning of a beard; it must be an oversight on his part, because he was travelling aboard ship. He was very thin, too thin she thought, with his muscles and fine figure gone to almost skeletal proportions. However, it had been a long time since she had seen him. She must bake and cook her most tempting dishes for him. She noticed that his breeches were almost all torn away, and blood was trickling both from his leg and a nasty-looking gash on his head. But it was hard for her to estimate exactly how much blood there was, even when the lightning straddled the sky. It never entered her head to go and summon help to lift him instead of dragging him, like a killed deer. All she knew was that now she had found him she was never going to leave him again.

By the time she reached the end of the sand she was panting from half carrying her cumbersome load and her arms ached, but pure determination gave her the strength she needed. It was not until she arrived at the back door that she allowed herself. Up the two steps she bumped him, crooning softly that his ordeal was nearly over: and then they were in the deserted kitchen.

Here, the embers of last evening's fire lay hidden beneath a coat of ash. After pulling him close to the warmth, she found a poker and stoked up the fire, throwing on some of the twigs that Mrs Jones used for kindling. They sparked into life and she stood upright, pushing the aching small of her back with gritty, wet hands. Then she bent again to light three candles which she lined up on the kitchen table.

She looked around; everywhere was spotless. She knew that Mrs Jones never retired without returning all crockery and pots and pans to their rightful places. The housekeeper even set Peggy, Elin's sister, to scrub the floor as her last task at night. Mariana screwed up her face. Into the midst of the neat kitchen, she had brought disorder and mess, with all the sand, seaweed and sodden clothes. However, she did not care really, for hadn't she rescued Henry?

A mature Mariana knew how to cope with bleeding cuts and it was not very many minutes before she had placed a cloth on his head and, without any sign of embarrassment, ripped the final shreds of his breeches from him, searching for the source of the seeping blood on his leg. As she touched the cut, high up on his thigh, the man groaned and, for the first time, she dared believe he was alive.

WILSON

Wilson heard the front door bang and went out of the library to see what had happened. He had not gone to bed yet. His final duties of the day were to lock all the doors and then check that his master required nothing further. He would then climb the stairs to make sure that everything was ready in the bedchamber. It was his custom to lay out Sir William's night clothes and turn down the covers, and, in the winter, he would put new fresh wood on the fire and sometimes light some candles. After all these tasks, he himself was permitted to retire, for Sir William had never wanted his help to undress, unless he was ill. In fact, his master had always resented servants hovering around him at any time of the day, and didn't mind telling them so! He called them 'over-anxious nannies' and shouted at them to leave. Wilson had soon learnt to be unobtrusive, but, nevertheless, on call if needed.

Thus it was that during the early evening, not long after the Parson had gone home, Wilson had left Sir William undisturbed with idle chatter. He had returned to the library to clear away the glasses, but his master had been sitting staring out of the window with the back of his chair towards the room. Since Sir William had not uttered a word to him, Wilson had assumed that he wanted to be alone and had scooped up the dirty glasses quietly and left. Several times over the hours, Wilson had knocked and put his head around the door but his master had not moved. Therefore Wilson was forced to spend most of his evening listening to a lecture given by Mrs Jones on the best way to pluck a bird.

Returning a little after midnight, Wilson had asked Sir William:

"Do you require the candles lit, Sir?"

When there was no reply, suddenly Wilson had wondered if there was not something unnatural in his master's continual stillness. He had crept towards Sir William, ever ready at the last moment, if a bark of anger had come, to pretend that he had simply been about to draw the curtains. For a terrible moment, when he reached Sir William's side, he had thought his master dead, but a tentative touch to the other man's hand had found it warm. As relief flooded his senses, Wilson's mind had flown back across the years, for he had known Sir William since he was a child.

Dick Wilson had been born in London nearly fifty-four years ago in a scummy hole of a house near the River Thames. Even now he could remember the permanent, all-pervading smells from the drains in the street outside and from the river at low tide. His father had been unknown to him, but he remembered his mother. Mostly she was slightly inebriated and, when she was not, she was full-blown, roaring drunk. At these times she was very handy with a stick and soon young Dick learnt to stay out of her way when she started on her third bottle. However, after one of her serious drinking bouts she slept for two or three days and woke listless, which Dick preferred, for she never touched him then.

Sent out to beg the money for her drink, naively Dick thought that his life would be better when he was sold to a tall, portly man, a Mr Lysons, who paid his mother a few bottles of gin for him. Much was his terror then when he discovered that his buyer ran a gang of chimney sweeps, of whom he was the skinniest and smallest.

Each day, he had spent numerous hours crawling along scorching, black chimneys. When he had finished, exhausted at the end of the day, ready to fall on to his thin mattress to rest, he never managed to rid himself of the smell of soot in his nostrils, nor of the dirt ingrained in his skin. His whole world was bound up with darkness and he resolved to escape as soon as possible. It took him a year to pluck up the courage to run away. Then he had to learn to live by his wits, with a constant eye over his shoulder, in case the evil Mr Lysons found him. He didn't bother to return to his mother – the sense of betrayal continued to rankle – and he found that he could survive better without her.

With begging as his principal means of income, he realised the advantages of being maimed and cold-bloodedly broke his own leg and developed a limp to gain sympathy. With his big, green eyes and undernourished body, he made a meagre living. When winter drew closer and persistent rain kept people indoors, he began to steal and soon became extremely adept at taking food from the meat-pie vendors and market stalls.

One December day, his desperate hunger and cold made him careless. He saw the crusty, hot loaves lined up on the baker's tray ready to be lifted on to the head of the delivery boy and carried through the streets.

Dick abandoned caution and snatched the loaf, scampering away with the bread clutched to his famished breast, its warmth spreading over his frozen fingers and chest, its smell making saliva run from his mouth.

He heard the cry, "Thief! Thief!" but reckoned if he dodged down the labyrinth of alleys, he would soon be lost in the maze of passages and twisting back streets which made up the city. Surely he knew every route in the area!

How was he to know that this particular baker had tired of having his livelihood stolen, and only just above the poverty line himself, had recently employed a stalwart lad who could run faster and further than the undernourished thieves (and who could carry twice as many trays of bread as any previous boy probably, when he was not chasing after the culprits)?

It didn't take Dick very long to work out what had happened for, almost immediately he could feel his pursuer coming nearer and nearer. He ran on, although his chest was bursting for breath and his damaged leg cried out for rest. The bread was squashed into a misshapen lump; its heat dissipated now, its tasty aroma overpowered by other more pungent smells. Likewise, Dick's appetite had disappeared, for he knew that if he was caught he would not necessarily simply be whipped or put into the stocks; he might possibly be hanged! One of his friends, Molly, had been hanged, for stealing a handkerchief, only a month ago. He had forced himself to go to witness the event. He had wanted to shout out at the loss of such a young life, for Molly had been only ten; but instead, he had slunk to the back of the crowd, hoping his thoughts of sympathy would fly above the jeers and cries of excitement at this well-attended spectacle and reach his condemned friend. He had slipped away when the noose tightened on her cry of despair, sickened by the crowd's amusement and obvious delight at someone else's suffering.

Suddenly, desperately, he did not want to die himself; he cursed his stupidity and greed in not being more discreet in his theft. The baker's lad stamped through the grime, the sound of his hobnailed boots echoed along the alley. Dick was sure he could actually feel his pursuer's breath on his neck. Abandoning the bread, his bare toes frantically seeking a grip in the slime, Dick skidded left and across a broad thoroughfare. Such was his haste and panic that he neither saw nor heard the four monstrous horses galloping along the street pulling a handsome town carriage. Immediately the small boy was caught in a tangle of thrashing hooves; briefly he heard the horses' snorts of terror and then he was lying motionless in the mud.

He was told later by one of the grooms that the carriage came to a precarious standstill but the frightened horses continued to paw the ground against the tight pull on their reins by the shocked driver. The groom never mentioned his pursuer. With the passing years, Dick reasoned that his would-be-captor would have come to a slippery stop after him and watched the affluent gentleman descending from the carriage. The baker's lad would have seen him lying inert with his plastering of mud and excrement and thought he was dead. He would have turned tail and disappeared, deciding that it was better not to get involved: after all, he might be blamed for the child's death.

Why had a youthful Sir William bent over the bedraggled heap of humanity to check if he was alive, which was what the groom reported the master did? And, maybe more of a mystery, why had Sir William lifted Dick into the carriage whilst the groom concentrated on trying to calm the horses? Had it just been a rich man's whim? Or an impulse of the moment?

Even now as a man, Dick had no answers but he had never forgotten that his master had saved his life literally, as well as saving him from years of poverty and grief. To one brought up to live on the edge in the back-streets ghetto, homeless for such a large part of his boyhood, Sir William's town house had seemed like paradise. Although for several months he had suffered from nightmares of being chased, it was not long before Dick had settled in to a new life as boot boy to the household of the Rowlands.

This was why fear had clutched his heart when he had thought his master dead. He had fetched a candle near to his master. Noticing Sir William's pallor he had entreated:

"Sir! Wake up, Sir!" Cautiously he had shaken his master's sleeve. There was no response. Foreboding returned. Sir William was ill. What should he do? Was Sir William dying? He knew all about the pains that his master endured. Was this the end? Should he move the sick man? He didn't look comfortable in his chair. Wilson undid Sir William's silk cravat and several of his waistcoat buttons.

It was as he straightened up, wondering if he could manage to carry his master upstairs, that he had heard the noise. He went to investigate.

ELIN

Elin heard the front door close and came from the corridor leading to the kitchen. She had been woken by the thunder. She had tiptoed downstairs in the hope that maybe Mrs Jones might be awake also and the two of them could find comfort in each other's company. Elin had not admitted to anyone her disquietude of thunderstorms. Fortunately, they occurred so infrequently that she was able to hide her fear, but the housekeeper openly told everyone that she hated thunder. Elin prayed that she would find Mrs Jones ensconced in the kitchen, her feet on the fender, waiting for the storm to pass. However, the kitchen was empty and she had just decided to return upstairs when she heard the boom.

Elin and Wilson stared at each other. They were carrying a candle apiece which threw a halo of light around their faces.

"Oh, Wilson, it's you." The maid breathed a sigh of relief.

"Elin? Is that you? What are you doing up and out of bed?"

"I heard a noise."

"So did I. We must have heard each other! I'm sure no intruder would be mad enough to be abroad on a night such as this! Come, my dear. I need your help. Sir William is indisposed. I thought at first he was sleeping but he doesn't respond to me when I speak to him. He's in some kind of a stupor. Maybe I should send for a physician. I certainly think he would be more comfortable in bed. Could you come and assist me?"

With another person to talk to, and a task in hand, Elin forgot her trepidation of the thunder. She was not surprised to see that Wilson was still dressed, for she was aware that both he and the master retired late; but she was acutely conscious of her own thin shift. However, she reckoned that this was no time for modesty.

"Is he in the library?" she questioned shyly in English. When Sir William had first brought his valet to *Trem-y-Môr*, Wilson had been very much the outsider, but when the staff had come to know his gentle ways they had tried to include him in their conversations. Much of his time was spent in the company of his English-speaking master, but Elin knew that Wilson had learnt a few phrases of Welsh and used them to welcome guests. However, he never contributed any comments when the kitchen staff were gossiping, or there was a quick interchange in the corridors. Since many of the servants were as unfamiliar with English as Wilson was with Welsh, Elin had tried to interpret as best she could between the two parties with the limited knowledge of the foreign language she had picked up from Miss Mariana. Usually she stood a little in awe of the solemn butler, although tonight he looked so tired and sad that she resolved to forget her reservations of him and concentrate on the important issue of their sick master.

Together the butler and maid went through into the library but again there was no response from Sir William.

'What do you think is wrong with him?" Elin asked.

"I don't know. We had better send for Mr Lloyd."

Elin nodded. Mr Lloyd was the coastguard, waiter and searcher, as well as the acting surgeon for the whole island since there was no qualified doctor nearby.

"I think he would be better lying down," she suggested in a low voice. She couldn't bring herself to talk loudly, although she understood that the master was not sleeping. She observed Wilson matched her tone:

"It's too far to his room."

"I know! What we need is a truckle-bed! There's one under Miss Mariana's bed, but we won't disturb her. I'm sure there's one in the Back Chamber. I assume Sir William doesn't have one."

She saw Wilson smile briefly and felt his approval. These truckle-beds were low servants' beds which slid beneath the four-poster beds. They were used by all kinds of people from nannies with fretful charges, to visitors who required their servants to sleep in the same room as themselves. Although rather narrow (and not meant for the master!) one was just what they needed here because of its portability.

Working in companionable silence, Wilson and Elin carried down the bed, after lighting candles in the halls and on the stairs. Then Elin returned upstairs to bring down two blankets and a pillow. Again she took these from the spare room; not daring to enter the master's own bedchamber, in spite of the fact that it was unoccupied.

"Should you undress him?" Elin whispered nervously. She hoped desperately that the answer would be 'No'; it would be too embarrassing to see the master disrobed.

"I think we should only remove his coat and waistcoat. He wouldn't fit on the bed in his coat and besides, he would be more comfortable without it. If only I knew what ailed him! I'll remove his shoes, of course."

When Wilson had done this, he motioned Elin to lift Sir William's feet and they shifted the unwieldy man on to the low bed. Elin realised it was rather fanciful but she thought her master looked more peaceful lying down.

"There, that's better," Wilson intoned softly. Elin wasn't sure if he was speaking to her or the prone man. "Thank you for your help. I couldn't have lifted him by myself. Maybe we shouldn't bother rousing Mr Lloyd. He won't be pleased to be called out on a bad night like this one and Sir William does look more at ease now. I'll sit and watch him."

Elin glanced at the older servant, hearing the love in his voice. She had always pitied him. He didn't appear to have ever married and she felt he led a solitary life, far from London where presumably he had family and friends. He seldom took time off, or if he did, he spent it in his own cramped near to Sir William's bedchamber. Elin wondered what he did when he was alone. He never went to a tavern; in fact, she had never seen him drink alcohol at all. He did not visit women, not to her knowledge. He accompanied his master to church, standing near the back with the other servants, but since the service was conducted entirely in Welsh, Elin could not see how he could get any pleasure or understanding from it. Sir William was acquainted with Welsh. Did he ever speak Welsh to his manservant? Did the two men ever talk together apart from discussing what Sir William wanted to wear? She frowned. She didn't know hardly anything about this man. Yet he had been here when she had arrived five years ago. He looked very lonely tonight. She enjoyed the company of others and she hated to think of people as friendless.

"Can I fetch you something to drink? Some hot milk perhaps?" she offered, unable to keep the pity out of her voice. Why had she ever felt in awe of him? He was just a solitary old man, after all. He gave no reply; he seemed lost in contemplations. She repeated the question and saw him raise his head in surprise. Had he thought she'd gone away? Then a look of kindness came to his face. Surely he didn't pity her.

"Yes, that's very good of you. But I will only drink it if you will join me."

"I will and then, if there's nothing further you need me for, I'd better be returning to my bed. It's nearly time to leave it again!" She hoped the small quip would relieve his haggardness. "Shall I go and blow out the candles on the stairs? I've already done the ones upstairs."

"Yes."

Elin extinguished the lights and then, with her original candle in her hand, she pushed open the door of the kitchen. She jumped in fright.

"Miss Mariana! What have you been doing? Where have you been?" She went forward and stopped at the sight of the half-drowned man on the floor. "Who is this?" The final question was a mere whisper.

"It's Henry, of course. I've saved him."

"Henry?" Elin repeated. "Mr Wynne?" One glance told the truth.

"Yes. He called me to save him and I found him on the beach. The *'Abundance'* has sunk but there aren't any other survivors as far as I can tell."

"But where... where?"

"I've told you," snapped Mariana. "I found him on the beach. Our beach. Now, let's not waste any more time. He needs bandages – possibly a surgeon, unless you're prepared to get a needle and thread again like..."

"What's going on here?" It was the sharp voice of Mrs Jones. She stopped abruptly on the threshold of the kitchen and stared at the tableau. Elin could imagine what it looked like, because she herself had been shocked when she'd come into the kitchen. Elin was sure her own face was the colour of finely ground flour, as was Mariana's, but her mistress was also standing in nothing more than a sodden shift, clinging to her body, revealing her breasts and moulding to her slim hips. And then there was the body, obviously male, without Miss Mariana's fantastic claims, naked, except for a few makeshift bandages.

"Miss Mariana!" Mrs Jones barked. "What have you been up to?"

Elin knew she had read the housekeeper's mind accurately as she watched the bulky woman bustling forward and throw her own voluminous shawl over the man. Scandal was now written not just across Mrs Jones' face but in her posture too. Elin could imagine the comments later: "I've never seen anything like it and I'm used to Miss Mariana's pranks. The girl is always up to some mischief, bringing trouble into our lives, upsetting the peace." Elin sighed. Mrs Jones wasn't one to keep her opinions to herself!

"It's Henry!" wailed Mariana, looking from one person to another.

"He's bleeding and he needs a doctor. We must send for Matthew Cutlass. He's not far and he'll come out and tend to him. Go, Elin, go and wake Thomas and send him to fetch Matthew."

"Now, Miss Mariana…" began Mrs Jones with dogged determination.

"No!" Mariana's shout filled the kitchen above the weather, which threw a heavy spatter of rain against the window panes. "He's not going to die…"

"It will be all right," promised Elin. "I'll take care of him but you must change out of your clothes. You're soaked to the skin, Miss…"

"I'm not leaving him." Mariana knelt by the man's side and pressed the bandage on his head. "Elin, you must go for Thomas to fetch Matthew or you'll be held responsible for Henry's death and I shall never, never forgive you." Mariana's statement was suddenly calm and cold.

Elin met Mrs Jones' eyes over the top of their mistress' head. She saw reflected there her own thoughts: a silent message which plainly said that Miss Mariana had finally lost all sense of reality. Whoever this man was, he was not Henry Wynne! And, anyway, how could a slip of a girl have brought this man all the way from the beach? No, probably he had been involved in a drunken fight and had dragged himself to the back porch and Mariana had opened the door to him. Or, peradventure she *had* been right out in the storm, for she was certainly extremely wet. Perhaps she had met this stranger on the sand but he could not have been shipwrecked. There was no evidence of a ship in distress and where were the other survivors? All this flashed between them in an instant, but Elin's reasoning raced on.

She knew that there would be no convincing Miss Mariana that this person was not Mr Wynne. Mrs Jones, although sympathetic with her mistress' fantasies, had believed that the best way to cure her was to talk to her normally. Probably her aim now was to make Miss Mariana change out of her filthy clothing and snuggle into a warm bed. Once that was done, Elin guessed, the housekeeper would have no compunction in sending this embarrassing stranger on his way. At that moment the injured man gave a loud groan.

"May I be of assistance?" This came from Wilson who had just arrived. Elin realised that she had forgotten all about taking him some hot milk. He must have come to see what was keeping her. The butler glanced around the room.

"Oh, please, Wilson, will you go for Cutlass?" pleaded Mariana, "He must look at Henry. There's so much blood."

"Miss Mariana, you mustn't stay here in those dripping clothes," complained Mrs Jones. Her mistress was a child. "Come along and get changed."

"No," argued Mariana grimly. "I'm not leaving Henry. I'm not. I'm quite all right. I'm drying by the fire anyway. Henry needs me."

Elin caught Wilson's eye before he bent down to inspect the stranger. Elin understood that he, like all the indoor staff (and probably all the outdoor staff too) had heard about Miss Mariana and her belief that Mr Wynne was still alive. Wilson had always treated Miss Mariana with great respect. Did he realise that the kind of grief the mistress had suffered could temporarily unbalance her perception? Had he come to understand what had happened to Miss Mariana? His words seemed to confirm that he had because he observed quietly:

"Miss Mariana, I think your father would want us to carry your young gentleman up to the Back Chamber and fetch Mr Lloyd to him."

"Not the Back Chamber!" stated Mrs Jones as Miss Mariana protested at the same time:

"Not Mr Lloyd! Please not Mr Lloyd. He's rough and he's got coarse, hard hands. Please send for Matthew Cutlass. He knows so much about wounds after being in the Fleet. He'd be much kinder to Henry."

"Mr Wilson," put in Mrs Jones firmly. Elin was in no doubt that the housekeeper hated to see her kitchen in chaos and her authority taken from her. "I really do think this man would be better in the stable." She folded her arms purposefully across her ample bosom.

"No!" cried Mariana for a second time, flinging herself on to the wounded man's chest and gripping his shoulders with her hands as if to prevent anyone else getting near him.

"Mrs Jones," enunciated Wilson. His inflexion suggested that he was surprised that any God-fearing woman would be prepared to turn away a man this badly injured, whatever his class or standing. Elin believed that he understood what the housekeeper did not: Miss Mariana was beyond listening to reason. He continued in a tone that brooked no argument, "Mrs Jones, I shall carry this poor fellow upstairs. Please come with me; I shall need your help in staunching the bleeding until the surgeon arrives."

He turned to the distressed woman crouched on the floor.

"Miss Mariana, I absolutely promise you that I personally will not allow this man of yours to di… to come to any harm whilst he is under my care."

Elin watched as manservant and mistress fixed their gaze on each other. Was Wilson remembering her as a small child looking trustingly at her father? Certainly she resembled a child at the moment, with her hair in a tangle and eyes widely staring, fear at their edge. Would there soon be trust for this man, who was her father's closest servant, in those dark eyes?

"So, Miss Mariana, if you would like to retire to your room and change out of your wet clothes, then I will allow you to see Mr Wynne when he is in bed and bandaged. Of course, it wouldn't be seemly for a young woman to attend her young man before their wedding day. Once he is settled and you are dry, you can… you can stay by his side all night."

Elin drew in her breath at Wilson's apparently rash promise. With one sweep, he lifted the frail man up and led the way out, without a backward glance. The butler had never overridden the housekeeper's decisions before. Her astonishment melted to meekness and she followed in his wake.

Elin, urged again to seek out Thomas for him to fetch Matthew Cutlass, waited only long enough to usher her mistress back to her bedchamber before she snatched up her shawl and braved the weather. It was streaking from the darkened sky in long ribbons at a slanting angle that struck her bare face. Pausing fleetingly to listen for the thunder, she hurried across the drenched cobbles, glad that the noisy thunder-clouds appeared to be retreating, although it had left this stinging rain. She was relieved that the house sheltered her from the wind.

She headed for the stables. Scurrying across the slippery yard, she thanked the good Lord that she was being sent only to the nearby outbuildings and not half a mile away to Thomas' parents' cottage; just recently Thomas had moved out from the family home.

When she neared the stable doors, she raised her head and was surprised to discern a dim light flickering through the window: Thomas must already be awake. Pulling the half stable door firmly, she bent low to pass through just the lower half and entered the warm stable with a sigh of relief. She pulled the door shut behind. Then she shivered. A new fear assaulted her. She looked anxiously round for Thomas.

The stables were a single storey building, with three doors opening on to the outside: one at the back that enabled the horses to be released straight into the meadow, and two at the front that led on to the yard. Elin had just used the narrower of the two latter doors, for the wider door allowed both carriage and farm cart to pass through it. These vehicles were stored at the far end of the stables, where the wooden partitions of the stalls had been pulled up to accommodate them. Originally, there had been twenty stalls altogether; but only eight remained and of those, only four were occupied.

In the first stall, Elin could see Sir William's elderly hunter, and next to him stood the two carriages. These were glossy chestnuts whose coats glowed in the hushed light. In the last stall, with his eyes rolling nervously, was Mariana's stallion: a strong-boned, black creature, as hard to handle as his mistress. It was he, in particular, who made Elin nervous. Always she was wary of horses and the animals seemed to sense her panic and become agitated themselves.

"Thomas," she called. Where was he? Was he asleep, after all?

A tousled head appeared from behind one of the partitions.

"Why, Elin, is everything all right?"

"I was about to ask you the same question."

"Oh, everything is sorted out now. The horses always get upset during thunderstorms."

THOMAS

Thomas came out from the stall as he spoke, a broom in his hand. His reply deliberately gave no hint of the difficulty he had experienced in soothing the animals and, particularly, the great stallion, Mars. Miss Mariana had told him that she had named him after a Roman god, but he could think of some other names tonight! He had been tempted to summon his mistress to come and pacify the great beast, but his own pride had prevented him. He asked, "Can I help you?"

He stepped towards Elin. Surely the girl had not come just to enquire after the horses? Had she come to see him? She had never before approached him at this time of night and in her shift by the looks of it!

Thomas had brought a woman or two to the stable since he had left home. Purportedly, he slept in one of the empty stalls in order to attend his charges during the night and to give more room to his growing brothers and sisters in the family bed in the cottage. He had been delighted to move, for his new accommodation was easily as comfortable as the old one and much more spacious, since he had it all to himself. However, on occasion, he chose not to sleep alone and had passed a few wonderful nights with only the horses for spectators to what went on between him and Lily or him and Nancy. He knew this was not a pleasure he could have indulged in at home! He understood he had to be discreet, but, thus far, no one seemed to have noticed, so why had Elin come? Surely not for this! He would describe her as comely, but they had known each other for such a long time that he regarded her more as a sister than a bed-mate! She looked pale and was standing nervously with her back pressed against the door; but that might be because of the horses. He knew she was ill-at-ease with them. Why had she ventured out on such a wet night?

It did not take the young woman long to explain some of the events that had happened in the nearby house, but it took the information that Sir William was indisposed to bring Thomas to life. If his master was ill, he had best get on with his errand. Immediately he started to. Like guns of war, silent after victory, the thunder had stopped; but he could not leave the horses until they were completely unperturbed again. He felt Mars nudge him as if in agreement. It would be no good asking Elin to stay.

"There's a problem…" he began.

"Shall I send Kate to stay with the horses?"

Thomas smiled broadly with relief. Although young, Kate was a real natural with animals.

"Yes. Yes, I'll wait here whilst you send her over. They're calm enough now to be left with her. Then I'll go as fast as I can for Cutlass."

Soon, Thomas was striding across the drenched fields, with a sack thrown over his head. Although the night was starless and the wind constantly tried to rip the makeshift coat from him, he was familiar with the path and the elements impeded his progress hardly at all. He was not aware of the hazardous conditions, for he was lost in the past; he had forgotten Sir William's plight temporarily and his mind was fixed on Mariana and her stranger from the sea.

For many years, the vision of Mariana had filled his waking thoughts. Even as a child, he had perceived that he was fortunate. He had never wanted for food, or love, since his parents were a devoted couple, and secure in his father's job as groom at *Trem-y-Môr*, they had provided a sheltered home life for their large family.

Forever it seemed, Thomas had had an insatiable interest in horses and if he had been asked at an early age what he wanted to do with his life (an unrealised luxury for anyone he knew; they would have laughed if asked), he would have breathed, "I'd like to work with horses". When his greatest desire was fulfilled, he settled into contentment. His relaxed outlook on life made him popular with both lads and lasses.

For as long as he could remember, Mariana had been his standard and, finding none to match her beauty, he had shunned a close relationship with any of the village girls, although he could have had a good choice of willing partners.

Once both he and Mariana were old enough, he had been appointed Mariana's personal groom and it had become almost a game, at least for her, to see if she could lose him on her mad gallops across the countryside. Competent at jumping, clever at hiding, Mariana had succeeded in her aim on more occasions than he cared to recollect. Even now they were both adults, Mariana still lost him when she chose to, he mused dryly.

Initially, Thomas had feared that he would get into trouble because of his lack of attendance, but he soon found out that Mariana never reported her escapes. With the passing years, without actually speaking, they had agreed that they would meet near the dip, just out of sight of *Trem-y-Môr*, and walk the horses to the stables together. He assumed that, in this way, Mariana avoided being scolded and he, although he hated the lies, was glad not to draw attention to his inability to keep up with a girl! Also, he admitted to himself, he quite enjoyed his own solitary rides, for he could go where he pleased. Recently he had discovered that many of Sir William's friends from all over the island had reported Mariana's unattended riding, but for ages, he and she had become comrades in deceit.

Strange it had been then, three summers ago, when the sun had blazed from a perfect blue sky, unmarred by any clouds, that Mariana had not even tried to outrun him, but had led him away from her home to a deserted beach. He could recall that day as if it were yesterday.

Mariana was cantering down the path towards the burning sand when suddenly she fell from her horse and lay on the ground. Thomas' concern was tinged with incredulity. He decided that there must be some hidden pitfall, for Mariana was far too experienced a rider to fall on an easy slope like this one. In his opinion, Mariana was the most superb horsewoman he had ever seen! Digging his heels into his horse's flanks, he sped to her side and flung himself down to bend over his mistress.

Mariana's arms flew about his neck and pulled his face close to hers. She planted a delicately-scented kiss on his unsuspecting lips. He sprang back but her arms imprisoned him.

"Don't go, Thomas," she murmured. "Don't you like kissing me?"

He felt his cheeks suffuse with red and he blinked twice and swallowed an enormous lump in his throat, his Adam's apple bobbing painfully. Then he stared into the dark, compelling depths of her eyes.

"I thought you were hurt, Miss. Please let me go."

"Oh, no!" she remarked with a saucy smile. "Now I've caught you, you must pay a forfeit."

He could have pulled away from her with no difficulty, but the heat of the day and the hot smell of her were arousing him. How many times had he dreamt of holding her in his arms, of kissing her pouting lips? He closed his eyes, his good resolves melting.

"Come now, Thomas. A kiss. One kiss and then... then... Well, maybe

I'll let you go." She brushed his lips with hers again.

He jerked away. What was he doing – allowing himself to be so close to her? She was the master's precious daughter and only fourteen! He stood up, leaving her lying in the sand with her arms outstretched above her body, empty of where he had been. He turned away from her gently rising breasts which were pushing up with round firmness from her low-cut bodice, revealed because her neckerchief had fallen sideways on to the sand.

"Miss… Miss Mariana. We… we ought to be going back. It's nearly time for your meal and your father will be wondering where you are!" He kept his tone level and directed his gaze out to sea, squinting at the water shimmering hazily in the sinking sun.

"You'll have to lift me up. I've hurt myself."

He glanced at her. Was she really injured? He saw the hint of a smile.

"Come on, Miss. Stop playing games."

"Have you ever lain with a woman?"

Thomas stepped away from his mistress. Languidly she put her hands behind her head. He gathered up the reins of the horses in an attempt to cover his embarrassment. He was not going to admit to her that he had never been with a woman and it was all her fault! He had used her as his yardstick and every other woman had fallen short. She might only be a month or two short of her fifteenth birthday, but her body was ready… He rubbed his eyes with his knuckles. Was this all a nightmare?

"I'm here, Thomas." Mariana's voice was a caress as balmy as the heat of the afternoon.

Was she really offering herself to him, here, right now? Could he have her… the girl – woman – of his dreams? Should he taste her…?

He turned abruptly. Best put all these sorts of thoughts from his head. She was a child, after all, in mind if not in body. She was trying to seduce him, albeit rather inexpertly. He shut his eyes again, wishing he could block his ears as well.

"Thomas, why don't you come and sit down? I like you, Thomas. I've always liked you. Anyone who loves horses the way you do would have found a place in my heart, but you… there's something… something special about you. I don't love you, though. No, but I do like you more than most people. Thomas, I'd like to try… try it with you. I might as well admit it, Thomas, I've never had… had a man before…"

His blush reached his ears and down his neck. He must stop her!

"Please come home, Miss," he whispered hoarsely. "Otherwise I'll have to go without you."

"Thomas, I want you to…. I've seen you working in the yard, pumping the water, mucking out the stables with your shirt off and… and it makes my heart beat quickly. I've seen horses… horses and dogs doing… doing it and… and, well, even once a man and woman… Not that I actually saw anything, you know, but I have spied on courting couples, years ago… in the graveyard. It's not that I enjoy watching others. It was just that I was interested to see… to know how it's done. I was only eleven then and it all seemed so fascinating and grown-up, but I'm all grown-up myself now and I want to try… try it for my… with you, Thomas."

He heard her sit up and, out of the corner of his eye saw her undo the lacing across her yellow stomacher. The neckerchief, which usually crossed over the stomacher and was secured by ribbon bands to the robings, she discarded. Her bodice she allowed to slip from her shoulders and she pushed her breasts so that they fell, ripe and ready… oh, so ready, passion cried out to him, over the top of her disarranged clothes.

"Look at me, Thomas," she purred. "Would you say I was grown-up?"

In an instant he was angry. How dare this child – girl – woman behave so! Purposefully, he turned from the sight of pink revealed flesh and snapped:

"Get dressed again, Miss! I'm sorry if you thought that I would… would oblige you. I can't and you know that your father would kill me if he found out. My father would too, for that matter…"

"Who'll tell them?" argued Mariana. "I won't. You won't. There's no one else here. Who has told them you don't accompany me everywhere on my rides? No one. Please Thomas."

He said nothing and, all of a sudden, she leapt up, pushed past him, sliding her arms fully out of her chemise. Of the stomacher and neckerchief there was no sign. He looked resolutely over her head but he was very conscious of her nakedness.

"Thomas, I need you," she persisted. "Please take me. Please show me how! Henry won't tell me anything. He said I was too young, but I'm not, am I? I so want to know how it's done, what it feels like. Please… please, I beg you…"

Thomas moved away again.

"I'm going home now, Miss," he insisted. "I shall await your return there."

"Don't you dare! Don't you dare leave me! I'm your mistress. You must obey my orders. You will lie with me. You will. You will."

Thomas disentangled Mars' reins from his own horse's reins and, reversing the animal away from the other, he started to plod up the hill, determined not to look back.

"If you don't, I'll tell them you did!" Mariana shouted after him. "I'll tell them that you lured me to a quiet beach and that you… you used me. I'll make sure you lose your job and your home. You'll regret this, Thomas Lewis! You'll regret walking away from me!"

Thomas hesitated. She was quite capable of carrying out her threats. Should he take her maidenhead? How often had he longed to do so! But not like this! He had heard her stammered words: that he had not been picked for himself but because he was the only suitable man she could find whom she thought she could command to lie with her! No, he wouldn't degrade himself. Maybe if she had kept her forthright tongue at bay, he would have weakened, but no, dear, honest Mariana Rowlands had decided to tell him that she wanted to experiment and, really, any available man would have done!

Thomas resumed his walking. He hoped she would not cost him his job, but after all, she was the master's daughter and even if he did enter her, he had no guarantee that she would not tell anyway. Yes, she hadn't told anyone about his inability to remain by her side when she went riding; but he believed she held her tongue on her own account – because she enjoyed the freedom of riding alone – not to save him from being upbraided. However, in this instance, once… if he was foolish enough to show her what happened between a man and a woman and, hell's teeth, he had been tempted to do so in order to teach her a lesson… No, if he had been angry enough or foolish enough to take her, she would have had what she wanted and might decide to ruin him, just to spite him, for his slow response. To think of the master's daughter begging him and him resisting! No, he had done the right thing! He would have to chance it and pray to God to protect him from this voluptuous girl!

Thomas mounted his horse at the top of the path and, still without looking back, rode into the nearby village of Rhoscolyn. Here, he bought himself a tankard of ale and presently found himself joined by four other men. Within minutes their talk turned to coarse jokes, and, feeling rather sensitive on the subject of the fairer sex, Thomas rose from his seat, resolving to find a woman who could satisfy him. Mariana had disturbed him.

Having discovered the pleasures of bedding a woman he returned to the secluded beach, half to make sure that his mistress was safe and half with the intention of complying with her wishes and teaching her that long overdue lesson. However, she had gone and now worry replaced anger. What tale had she told? He made his way home slowly, fretting and fuming alternately, and all to no avail! There was no dismissal, no row, nothing! Mariana had not mentioned the incident. He did ponder about her reasons: did she feel humiliated that he had rejected her, or had the threats seemed pointless once she had calmed down? He never found out.

Nevertheless, *he* had been changed by the incident; he was wary of her from that day. He knew it would break his parents' hearts if he left the area completely, especially if he was unable to give an explanation for his departure. Therefore he reasoned that leaving was not a way out. If he was truthful, he did not want to start a new life elsewhere. Thus, unable to request not to be her groom and yet still remain at *Trem-y-Môr*, he had decided to keep his distance from his tempting mistress.

Thomas stopped at the boundary of Matthew Cutlass' land. He was nervous. He had never been nearer than this to the house, *Tŷ Craig*, before. There were stories of ghosts. The man who had designed and built the house was said to walk around his estate to this day. Thomas knew the present owner, Cutlass, had two black dogs that were trained to keep out intruders, but it was the ghost that made him halt. He cursed his own stupidity in agreeing to fetch the retired ship's surgeon. It was all very well for Miss Mariana to come here, which he knew she did, but to demand that he carry her message… He swore again at having to serve such an unpredictable mistress and then strode through the gap where a wooden gate had once hung, calling loudly:

"Cutlass!"

THE GIRLS

Mariana stood in her bedchamber, the Parlour Chamber, watching the primrose streaks of dawn illuminate the pale sky, listening to the dull murmur of voices coming from the room next to hers. She had been banned again from the Back Chamber, whilst Matthew Cutlass examined the patient. It must be him talking to Mrs Jones and Wilson. Elin, as far as she knew, was boiling more water in the kitchen. It had been an interminable night.

Mariana twirled a curl of her hair around her finger and wished she could return to her post by the side of the bed. She had been told that her father was ill but she had not seen him, since he was sleeping and could not be disturbed. However, all her thoughts were for Henry and how he was faring and hardly had she considered her father's condition. She turned, when a knock came at the door, and Elin entered.

"They've finished with the… Mr Wynne, Miss, and they say you can return now."

"Thank you, Elin." Mariana touched her servant's cheek. "You're looking very tired. Why don't you go to bed? I'm happy to sit with Henry."

"No, Miss, it's time I was up. There's… there's so much to do…" Her voice caught on a sob.

"Why, Elin, what is it? What's wrong?"

Her maid shook her head.

"It's nothing, Miss. Nothing is wrong. I'm just…"

"Why don't you have a little rest? Surely you could lie down for a few minutes."

"No, miss, I wouldn't… I couldn't… Not with the mast…" She fled the room.

Fear pierced Mariana's heart. What was the matter with Elin? Why was she so upset? Was it to do with her father or Henry? Not Henry, for they had told her that she could go back to see him. He couldn't have had any sort of relapse. It must be her father and hadn't Elin started to say 'The master'? Mariana bit her lip. Please God, don't let him die! Leave him here on earth a few years more, sweet Jesus, she prayed, hurrying from her room.

When she entered the Back Chamber, Mrs Jones was just tucking the covers over the patient, smoothing down the bed linen as she spoke.

"There, that's better," she was murmuring. "Now that kind Mr Cutlass – you'll soon find out that isn't his real name, but everyone calls him that. He used to wear an enormous cutlass at his waist when he first moved into the community and, of course, his real name is 'Cutland'. So you can see how the nickname stuck. Yes, Mr Cutlass has bandaged your cuts and bruises and we've given you a wash – got rid of all that seawater and sand. You were half-drowned, no doubt about that! But you can start to mend now. I'm sure Sir William won't miss this old nightshirt. And what is your story? Those old scars on your back – looks like you've had a good whipping in the past. Maybe you're a pirate. But then, what about your raw wrists? Who tied you up? Are you an escaped prisoner?" Here the housekeeper gave a little shudder.

"Mr Cutlass says it's more likely a pirate tied you up! He told me that you had been bound too tightly and for too long. So who are you? A gentleman kidnapped for a ransom? I'm sorry... I'm sorry that I suggested putting you in the stable earlier. It was just I was so worried about my little chick, Mariana. She was as pasty faced as you are. I think she's all right now – no ill effects from helping you. But we can't be too careful for there's no saying who you are or what your background is. Mr Cutlass says you'll mend, though you'll have a mighty headache when you wake. I'll say this for that Mr Cutlass, he seems to know what he's doing all right. He explained he wouldn't bleed you because you'd lost enough blood already..." She lifted her head and caught sight of her mistress.

"Miss Mariana! How are...?"

"Is he all right?"

"Yes, *Cariad*, your Mr Cutlass has seen to him. He hasn't woken up yet but it's because of all the blood he's lost. Mr Cutlass..."

"Not... not Henry. Father."

"Father?"

"Yes, my father." Mariana moved into the room, her skirts swishing against the floor. She had dressed herself after her drenching rather than changing into dry night attire. She had been far too wide awake to go to bed! "Oh, Jonesey, Elin was upset by something and..."

"There, there, my little one. You've enough cares on your shoulders without adding more. Sit down. Elin has brought some tea. It'll be cold now, for sure."

Mariana felt cold herself – not cold from being wet and out in the wind, but cold inside. She knew without being told that her father was dead. Whirling from the room she ran downstairs and knocked into Matthew Cutlass, who was leaving the library.

"He's dead, isn't he?" she shrieked. "My father's dead. Let me see him. Don't try to hide it from me."

Cutlass gripped her arms.

"Hush, Mariana. Calm down." He paused. "I'm afraid to tell you that your father passed away whilst…"

"You should have saved him," she accused him. "You could…"

"No, Mariana. He died much earlier in the night. Wilson left him in a kind of… trance and he just quietly slipped from this life into the next. When I arrived, I asked Wilson if I could see the Squire and he told me then… that he had gone. So I went to see the other patient."

"I must go to him," she shuddered.

Mariana sagged. Cutlass released his hold on her.

Wilson had left his master on the truckle-bed, with his hands crossed at his breast. Above his head, on the table, two candles were lit.

Mariana reverently knelt beside her father and took his fingers in hers. His flesh was chilly. She bent her head. Her lips began to tremble and then her hands too. Slowly, her shoulders started to shake. Tears fell as the truth hit her.

She was all alone.

Her father was dead.

Henry was dead.

Faced with her father's demise, she understood at last that Henry was dead too. In fact, Henry had been dead for six months. Like gradually waking from a deep sleep, reality seeped into her mind and the burden of sorrow filled her very being and she cried and cried, soundlessly, as though she was never going to stop.

* * *

Elin saw Matthew Cutlass standing in the open doorway of the library. She came up behind him and touched his arm. He hushed her, and motioned for her to look inside. There was her mistress kneeling by her father. Although her loose hair hid her face she could see the torrent of tears splashing on her hands and the lifeless body of the master. Matthew Cutlass pulled the door shut quietly.

"Leave her for a while," he suggested.

"Oh, Mr Cutlass, I can't believe she's crying. Praise be to God! All these months and never a tear dropped for Mr Wynne. I could see her sealing up her grief like sealing up a bottle of fruit preserves and…"

"Now it's broken, my dear. It was bound to be. Perhaps she will mourn them both together now."

"I've prepared some food for you, Mr Cutlass. Mrs Jones baked *bara brith* yesterday and…"

"How thoughtful of you! There was really no need. I won't stay long. I'll leave you some powders for your mistress. She must sleep later. She has had to cope with too much tonight… as you all have. Please will you call me if the stranger upstairs awakes before I return? He too may need something to ease his pain and make him sleep. However, I'll come back tomorrow… Nay, today! Then I can see how his wounds are."

When Elin returned to the library with the medicine for her mistress, she found that Mariana had disappeared. Elin stood without moving. Her mistress must have run away; probably she had ridden off on that horse of hers. Usually that was what she did when she was discomposed. A loner, was Miss Mariana. Not one who sought out the company of others when she was perturbed. Not like herself; Elin preferred a real live shoulder to cry on.

Elin slowly retraced her steps to the kitchen.

* * *

Mariana wept until she was sure she had no tears left. Then, kissing her father farewell, she ventured upstairs to view the stranger who had arrived from the depths of the ocean. With the understanding that Henry was dead, she knew the man in the bed was not her beloved, and, on inspecting his face, she marvelled that she had ever thought that he was Henry.

This man had dark, shoulder-length hair, which proclaimed that he did not normally wear a wig. His face was much older than Henry's and was much narrower too, with the skin stretched across his cheekbones. Even his nose was narrow and his lips were just a thin streak of colour, hardly noticeable, amidst the paleness of his face. Henry used to have full, rich lips, which drew the eyes when he talked. Mariana put out a finger and touched the stranger's lips.

"Why couldn't you have been Henry?" she cursed softly. "If only you had been, then I would have loved you… but you're not. That's obvious. Henry has gone and so has my father. Dear Father, how I shall miss you! I miss you already. Dear Henry, how I… Oh, Henry, Henry what am I going to do without you? Who shall I talk to you? Who shall I marry now? There's no one else I love; no one else I know even! I shall never marry now." The tears welled up; bravely she tried to brush them away and prevent them from falling. She must not start crying again, she admonished herself.

She left the bedside and leant against the window sill, looking but not really seeing. Her mind was filled with memories. She recalled all the laughter and fun she had had with Henry. She remembered how full of hope she had been with their forthcoming marriage. They had been in love and were going to stay in love all the days of their lives. They would have shared as much of every day that they could. Of course, Henry would have had duties and responsibilities around the estate but he would return to her each evening and then at night… She blushed, her thoughts recalling the time she had tricked Thomas. How could she have been so naïve and… and brazen! She would never have acted out such a scene with Henry. Instinctively she had known that Henry wouldn't take her to his bed before they were married. He would have been shocked even to hear her talk of such things. She had always believed that she and Henry could converse about any subject, but he did not ever speak about what went on between a man and a woman in private. Mayhap it was discussed with other men in a back room of an inn on a winter's evening but not, she supposed, with a frankly curious fourteen-year-old he intended for his wife!

However Thomas… Thomas had been different. At least, she had presumed he would be. She had been surprised, at first, when he had refused her request. She had conjectured that her groom would willingly have sported with her. When he stood up, momentarily she had thought that perchance he was as ignorant as she, but surely not? All men knew about that sort of thing! Finding those velvet kisses had not worked, she had convinced herself that presenting her half-naked body to him would bring him round. When that hadn't changed anything, she had become confused, not knowing how to continue. Her own feelings had perplexed her. It was all so mysterious. No one would explain it to her and, unlike the sons of her father's friends, she could not go to the nearest village to find a partner, as she heard some did! She had almost re-dressed and slunk away, but she tried once more. If he could only be made to look at her! Her cheeks stained red, even after all these years. Brazen was the word indeed! After the pleading, when he had rejected her, had come anger and then those ridiculous threats! It had taken only the time to ride home for her to become ashamed of her childish plot to ensnare her groom. She would never tell anyone and never try anything like that again, with Thomas, or any other man. Over the months, following the incident with Thomas, she had come to understand that the intimate caresses of a man should only be shared with the one you loved, and more and more she had longed for Henry to seduce her. Henry was a real man, not a callow youth like the groom. Then, with the passing years, finally she had realised that Henry held back not because he did not desire her but out of respect for her. And today even this dream was gone!

She pulled a chair near the window and covered her eyes with her hands. No more crying, she chided herself. She was so tired and despondent; there didn't seem anything left to live for! The two loves of her life were gone. How she had loved her father! She had perceived that he spoilt her but it was very comforting to feel cherished. She knew that whatever she did he would always forgive her and love her. As a small child, she had never hidden from him if she did something wrong. No, she would run straight to his outstretched arms. He had not scolded her – at least, it seemed like this to her in her recollections. Dear, dear Father. She had assumed that he would always be there, loving her, supporting her, behind her in everything – and yet he was gone, just like Henry.

Mariana stared ahead of her, tears blurring her vision. She could see Henry, in her mind's eye, the last time she had seen him alive.

"Don't forget to write," she had begged whilst his carriage had drawn away.

"As if I would!" he had called back. "I love you."

"Love you," she had echoed.

Love you. Love you. Love you.

There was no one left who loved her now. She slumped in the chair and gave herself up to grief.

"Are you all right? Are you an angel?"

The voice made her jump. Mariana glanced at the man. She was surprised at his cultured voice after all that talk from Mrs Jones about pirates and prisoners! She walked towards the bed and stared into the most brilliant blue eyes she had ever seen. They made her heart jolt.

"Yes… No. Yes, I am all right and no, I'm not an angel," she stammered. She reached for a handkerchief through the slit in her skirt to her petticoat pocket and wiped away the last traces of her tears, looking, immediately, as if she had never been crying. Others had told her how lucky she was not to have one of those complexions that turned blotchy with weeping or leave your eyelids red, but she just accepted that the tears simply rolled over her pearly skin and fell away. "You must forgive me, but I've just had bad news."

"I'm sorry."

The man paused and she wondered if he was expecting her to expand on her statement, but she remained silent. Somehow she found that she could not talk about her loss with a complete stranger.

"How are *you* feeling?" she proffered eventually.

"Not too good." He gave a short laugh, which was cut off in the middle of the sound. "Ouch! That hurt! I feel as if I've been in a boxing match."

"Well, you have in a way, except your partner was the sea."

"The sea?"

"Yes. We found you on our beach."

"Where am I?"

"On Holy Island."

"Where's that?"

"It's off the coast of Anglesey, which sits off the coast of North Wales."

"North Wales!" That made the man half sit up and then he groaned. Mariana saw the few tinges of pink on his face pale to chalk. His lips formed a line of pain and he closed his eyes. Instinctively she reached out to him.

"Steady now. Don't sit up! You've had a nasty knock on the head."

He gripped her as if she was a lifeline. Almost she could feel the pain surging through his body.

"Dizzy," he muttered.

She said nothing but looked at his strong hand, claw-like with thinness, clutching her slim fingers. She was shocked to see the red bands of marked skin which criss-crossed his wrist, raw, and in some places, oozing clear liquid. When the creases of discomfort left his face, she mumbled:

"How did you get these marks on your wrists?"

"I don't remember."

"Someone's tied you up," she pointed out. "They look like rope burns to me. Are they painful?"

"Not as bad as some other parts of me!"

"Were you a prisoner?"

"I don't remember."

"What do you mean, you don't remember?"

"Just as I say: I don't remember."

"What? *Nothing*?"

"Nothing."

"Can't you remember what ship you were on? Or where you were bound for?"

"No, nor where I came from." He stopped, before finishing in a whisper, "I don't even remember who I am."

Mariana frowned.

"Not even who you are!" Her voice, a mirrored whisper, as though their conversation was private and confidential, was incredulous. "You *must* remember who you are!"

Mariana sat down on the edge of the bed and then stood up again when she saw him grimace.

"Oh, I am sorry," she apologised. "I didn't mean to hurt you. I'll get the chair. I'm very tired. We've been up all night and you were quite a weight to carry."

"You didn't carry me, did you?"

"Hmm, not exactly carry. No, I suppose I dragged you, really. I'm not sure it did your cuts and bruises any good."

"How far did you drag me?" he asked whilst Mariana fetched the chair to his bedside.

"Oh, from the beach to the house. Not far, but in the middle of a storm, with the wind blowing and the sand in your eyes, it feels like a hundred miles. Can you really not remember who you are?"

"No, I have no idea."

"That must be awful."

"Well, now I come to think of it, I suppose it is. But maybe when my head stops aching, I'll remember."

"I wonder if I can guess your name. Is it Mark or James or Samuel? I'm not thinking of Welsh names because you're not Welsh."

"How do you know?"

"Your accent. It's definitely English with a hint of... I don't know, but it's not Welsh. Matthew will know. He's been all around the world."

"Why don't you tell me your name instead?"

"It's Mariana."

"Ah, that's a pretty name and it goes with a pretty face," he complimented her.

"Don't say that!"

"Why not? I thought you were an angel, albeit a sad and sorrowing angel, but with your hair and your face..."

"Don't!" Mariana turned away, her fingers once more over her eyes.

"Hey, don't cry! I'm sorry. I didn't mean to upset you. I'll say you've got horrible hair and an ugly face..."

That made her begin to cry in earnest: tears at first and then, within seconds, wracking sobs which shook her entire body.

"Mariana?" He touched her hand lightly. "Mariana, what is it? What have I said? I'm truly sorry. Hush!"

Gently he pulled her hand and slowly, almost without thinking, she allowed herself to lean towards him until he could reach her and then she laid her head on his bruised ribs and ranted out loud:

"It's not fair! It's not fair! Why me? What have I ever done wrong that God has taken everything from me? First Henry and now Father. Everyone. Everyone has gone. There's no one left. I'm all alone. Why? Why?"

He stroked her hair.

"Ssh, Mariana, ssh. You can't be completely alone. You must have other friends and surely there are other members of your family around."

She sat up and glared at him.

"You don't understand. I've no one else. My mother is dead and I have no real brothers and sisters – only half ones. And they don't love me anyway and there's nobody... nobody like Henry."

"You may say that you have no one but think, Mariana, you have yourself, your identity. You know who you are. *I* don't even know who I am."

Mariana's anger dissipated as fast as it had arisen. What magic charm did this mysterious stranger have which could comfort her? It had to be those startling eyes. They engendered trust. Mariana suddenly yawned widely, caught off guard.

"Oh, excuse me." A dry sob heaved her breast. "Would you mind…? Would you mind if I laid down my head again? I feel very sleepy."

"Not at all." She caught a glimmer of a grin on his face. Was he laughing at her? Now, what had she said wrong? She yawned again. It didn't matter. She put her head on his chest and was asleep.

* * *

Peggy woke with the light as usual. She sat up and looked for her two sisters. Both beds were empty. Elin must have started on her chores for the day, but where was Kate? Her middle sister loved the warmth of her bed and made sure she was the very last to get up and use the basin. Peggy slipped from the room. Finding the door to the main part of the house ajar, she tiptoed out into the upper hallway. Were Elin or Kate through here? The hall was empty. Why was there no one around? Where was everyone? In all her eight years she had never experienced anything like this before. She pressed on, her bare feet noiseless on the carpet. Passing through the back lobby she noticed another door, half open. She knew it led to the Back Chamber, but nobody ever went in there except to dust, occasionally. Yet it was used, if visitors came; maybe someone had arrived late last night. Her curiosity was aroused.

She pushed the door open cautiously, although there was no sound coming from inside the room. She started in surprise. There was a man lying with a bandage swathing his head and with his arm around Miss Mariana, who was fast asleep on a chair pulled up to the bed! Miss Mariana's head was laid on the man's chest and her glorious hair was spread over them both like a silken mantle.

Peggy ran from the room, down the backstairs, bursting to find out what had been happening during the night. Who was this visitor? She halted outside the kitchen, hearing voices at last.

"She's gone." It was her elder sister, Elin, sounding exhausted and sad.

"Gone!" exclaimed Mrs Jones. Peggy was glad not to have rushed in a few minutes ago. If the housekeeper was angry, she preferred to keep out of her way. "Where's she gone?"

"I don't know. She didn't come this way or you or I would have seen

her. I'd better go and see Thomas and find out if she's taken her horse."
Peggy understood: they must be talking about Miss Mariana. She leant
against the kitchen door.

"Oh, dear Jesus!" Mrs Jones voice was full of panic. "She shouldn't be
riding in her state. She might fall off. Quickly, Elin, run…"

"I know where Miss Mariana is. Why is she sleeping with a man?"

Peggy stood by the door as both women turned to her, open-mouthed.

"Where is Miss Mariana?" asked Mrs Jones whilst Elin scolded her for
wandering round in her night clothes.

The child led the two women upstairs to see for themselves this picture
of serenity.

"Let's leave them. They both need the sleep," instructed Mrs Jones.
"Now, Elin, you are to go and have a rest for at least an hour; you've been
up all night. Peggy can help me and then I'll call you later, after I've laid
out Sir William. I'm not sending for Mrs Parry. I… I want to do it myself."

She wiped a solitary tear from the corner of her eye. Peggy thought
she looked as if she had already been crying and she guessed that the old
woman would cry again whilst she performed this last task for her master.

EDWARD

The tall gentleman leaned wearily into the wind. He was sore from being in the saddle for twenty hours almost continually and his amputated leg ached atrociously. The wooden peg-leg, attached where his knee should have been, poked out at a strange angle causing folks to look twice at this traveller on his roan horse.

Here, at last, was the town of Conwy and, with it, a hazy, lazuli sky. The wind had chased away the few remaining clouds overhead, with their threat of rain, and to the west a slowly retreating sun shone, already changing from buttercup to orange in its descent.

Edward Rowlands sighed. He had left London yesterday and rode until midnight. Then, after snatching two hours' sleep, he had arisen very early that morning, whilst the stars remained, mounting up in the frosty yard of the 'Carpenters' Arms'. He had heard the twittering chorus of birds welcoming day after many miles were behind him. Some inner urge had made him want to reach Holyhead as soon as possible, and whilst he journeyed he had kept altering his goal. Firstly, he had thought that if he could reach the ancient city of Chester by nightfall he would be pleased and he could sleep there before pressing on the following morning. Then, he had set Conwy as his finish for the day; but pausing briefly above the walled town, which was dominated by the circular towers of the castle, he saw that the tide was out, leaving a silvery trail of water down the centre of the river estuary. Suddenly his spirits lifted. If he galloped, he would be able to use the post-boys' route around the coast and across the Lavan Sands to the edge of the Menai Straits rather than travel along the road to Bangor. The latter entailed following the tortuous bridle path, which made progress slow; any stumble by the horse, and the rider was faced with a sheer drop down to the sea, many feet below.

"Come on, girl," he crooned to his horse. "Shall we try to make home tonight? Now that would be an achievement for a cripple like me! London to Holyhead in a day and a night! And you've served me well today from

Chester."

When he reached the margin of the river, he noticed 'The Ferry Inn'. What he could do with at the moment was a generous tankard of ale and a slice of steaming pie! Dare he risk stopping?

"Hey, you!" he called to a lad sitting by the water's edge. "Is the tide going out or coming in?"

The boy squinted up. Edward appreciated that, with the extra height of the horse, he was towering over the lad, like the imposing walls of the nearby castle.

"It's a-coming in," he prophesied and then added, "Sir."

Edward tossed him a small coin with a word of thanks.

There was no time to waste then. The thought of a challenge had chased away his tiredness. He quickly dismounted, still very awkwardly, for he was not used to the saddle after years away from it, and his leg hampered him. If he positioned the wooden tip straight towards the ground and slid from the horse's back, he could usually manage but he always kept a tight grip on the pommel with his hands, so as not to let his whole weight land sharply on his tender sore. This time he accomplished it without falling, although on many occasions he had toppled over, especially when first he had started to relearn how to ride with his disablement. Mounting a horse was almost as hazardous, but if he stood on a raised platform or mounting post (or even a large stone), he could put his good foot in the stirrup and swing his unbending leg right across the horse's back. Sometimes he caught the horse's rump and over-balanced, and sometimes the animal moved with panic at this peculiar way of mounting. Altogether, getting on and off this horse was a problem, and he did it as infrequently as possible.

He waited impatiently for the ferry to return to his side of the river and then, having boarded, he stood holding his horse's reins whilst the boat set off again.

With all the difficulties that riding gave him, Edward had found that it was impractical for him to wear a long cloak, even if it had a deep vent at the back which supposedly made it suitable for riding. The long cloak tended to become entangled during his laborious ascents and descents; thus instead he wore a Roquelaure cloak, which was shorter. It had two collars: a capacious one which lay across his shoulders, and a smaller one which he pulled up and buttoned in bad weather. At present, both collars were lying flat. Beneath his cloak was a costume of dark blue, consisting of breeches and waistcoat. Again, he had dispensed with the coat of the suit as too unwieldy for riding; the cloak had to suffice as protection against the weather and cold.

Quite apart from his wooden leg, often Edward found people looking at him. He would have said that his light brown eyes were unremarkable. Yes, his skin was tanned from his years at sea and he had a crescent scar on his left cheek, but, when he viewed himself in a glass, he felt that his face wasn't particularly arresting. Usually he wore simple wigs with the masses of hair tied back into a 'queue' to keep them out of the way. Today, atop the wig was a forest-green, three-cornered hat to match his cloak, with one point facing the front, as if showing the way. He saw that several women on the ferry were openly staring at him. Did they wish him to notice them? He kept his eyes in the far distance because he was calculating his chances of reaching the Menai Straits in front of the returning sea. Was he taking unnecessary risks? he asked himself. Yet it had to be said that he thrived on risks. Wasn't that how he'd become captain of his own ship at such an early age? Again and again he had won against the odds, except that once with his father! But hadn't even that argument turned out for the best? For through it he had joined the Navy and made his money during the War!

Disembarking, Edward glanced at the sun, which hung in the western sky over the regular road out of Conwy. He was surprised to see how fast it had sunk in the time it had taken him to cross the river. Nonetheless, even if he could reach Beaumaris tonight… He readjusted his sights anew.

He rode his horse at an easy trot, allowing his body to match the rhythm of the horse's stride, renouncing the hunger-pangs that growled inside him. Nothing would deter him now. He had been hungrier than this many days at sea! Anyway, he had stopped for a hasty meal at the 'Four Cross Inn' in the middle of the morning, although that had been hours ago!

His journey led him past Penmaenbach, the smaller of the two mountains, and soon he reached the sand. Following the track, he skirted the base of Penmaenmawr, which soared towards the heavens on his left. It was covered with heather on its lower slopes, as yet not in flower, and he noticed many dots of white high up: sheep grazing on the top pastures.

Once he had passed the mountain, he searched along the width of the beach to find the place where the sand was firmest, so as not to slow their progress or chance an injury to his mount.

During his ride, Edward saw the sea advancing, moving visibly nearer each minute, it seemed. Here, at last, was the wide expanse of gold sand separating Anglesey from the mainland, with only the fast-flowing channel of the Menai Straits, never dry, to cross.

For a moment, Edward halted, allowing joy to fill him as he saw the misty edges of Anglesey rising above the sea, with its hump backed islet away to his right. He may have been to faraway lands, and there was no denying that some of the beaches west and east of here were far more glorious than this, but this was home – this was where his family lived and he had played here many times as a child. Familiarity lent warmth to an already beautiful land. The sand near the sea, wet from its recent soaking, was about to be covered again. It glistened in the sun, whose rays had broken through the cloudy horizon bathing the scene with shafts of amber light. Neither a foot-mark, nor a hoof-print, marred the miles of copper expanse. Up near the land, where the earth was drier, children had been playing, tousling the grains with their bare feet and fishermen had laid out their nets to dry; but this evening the shore was deserted, except for one old crone digging for worms.

Edward shielded his eyes against the sun's dazzling light, feeling the wind blowing in his face. Soon, very soon, he would see his father and all would be well between them. For years, Edward had harboured hatred for his parent; but when he had lain ill – dying, by all accounts – in the hospital in Plymouth, he had realised that nothing was too bad to forgive – nothing was that important – and he had resolved to mend the broken relationship. He had decided not to write, for then he would have been waiting for a reply; and what if it never came or its contents were still angry? No, he had made up his mind to go himself immediately he was better and, spurred on with a reason for living, he had recovered much more quickly. Now, with his convalescence behind him, here he was with maybe only thirty miles between him and his home and his father's embrace, for somehow he could not believe his sire would refuse a welcome to him.

Crouching over the horse's neck, allowing his wooden leg to lie forward rather than down, and giving encouragement to the plucky animal, he raced across the sand, a song of happiness in his heart, enjoying the pleasure of a horse beneath him again. He had missed riding during his years in the Navy, and whenever on land had sought every opportunity to borrow or hire a mount for a canter over the fields.

Once he neared his destination, the beach tapered with the sea flowing back, gaining momentum in the deep channel that ran between Anglesey and the mainland. Although there remained a spacious area of shore behind him, ahead he could see only a narrow strip of dry land left for him to cross; then he caught a glimpse of the ferry ready to leave to take its passengers across to the port of Beaumaris.

Edward felt his mount slow. Although both he and the horse were dripping with sweat, he called for one more ounce of strength to get them through the shallow sea. Giving a shout of triumph at this success, he caused the two passengers in the boat to look up in consternation.

"Hey, wait for me, please," he entreated. Skidding to a halt in a flurry of dirty water and sand, he saw the upturned, frightened faces and the stoutest man put a hand to the pocket of his coat. Through Edward's mind flashed a picture of himself: his cloak ballooning out behind him; his hat askew; his muddy appearance; his heathen cry. Perhaps they thought he was a highwayman or some kind of robber bent on taking their valuables. Neither the boy nor the boatman seemed well enough dressed to have any money but that unconscious movement of the older man… Was he a farmer who had driven his herd of cows across the Straits to market earlier? Had he got a good price and hidden from view a leather bag of clinking, gold coins? Edward flushed red. "I hope I didn't startle you. I was simply having a race! With the sea!" He laughed and the men appeared to relax.

"Ah, it's good to win a challenge!" he commented, looking over his shoulder. Already his pathway had disappeared under the relentless, incoming tide; no one would get through that way until later when the tide retreated again.

"Have you room for me to travel?" he murmured politely, although there was plenty of space on the ferry. He hoped the last of the tension on the men's faces would evaporate if he reaffirmed that he was simply another passenger.

"You're not a post-boy," accused the boatman, implying that only post-boys were allowed to use the shore route.

"No, indeed, but I'm in a hurry to be home and I knew I'd never get this far tonight if I came over the mountains; so I chanced the sand. Pity Septimus wasn't here. We could have gambled on the odds and I would have won!" He laughed again.

"You'd better be getting in unless you want to swim," growled the boatman.

"Thank you. If maybe one of you could give me a hand… I lost my leg in the War and I have no desire to fall into this sea up to my neck."

Edward looked from man to man. He reckoned that the lad was probably the farmer's son and it was he who stepped out from the boat to help him descend.

Once they reached the other shore, Edward left behind the grumbling boatman who had told him that he was very lucky not to have been trapped on the sands; that he should have been accompanied by an experienced guide otherwise he might have become disorientated; that he had been fortunate to have caught the ferry and on and on.

He stopped for a short interlude at the 'Fair Winds' inn – a rest which revived both horse and rider. Although he could have set forth on a fresh horse from the inn – there were several in the stables there – he chose to continue on the roan. He felt a comradeship with this animal which had safely brought him through the sea. It had been as exciting as Moses crossing the Red Sea, he chuckled to himself whilst remounting. There was no longer any need for haste. He would never be able to cross the strand at Holy Island (since the tide was full in), and he could pass over at Four Mile Bridge at any hour.

He trotted along the track past Tincolet and, as the sun waved its last farewell, he rode past a gibbet. No criminal's gruesome remains hung there but it caught Edward's attention and took his mind whirling back into the past. Over the years, he had seen many men, both mutineers and deserters, hung from the foreyard arm aboard ship, but the first time he had seen someone dead from hanging was at his school at Winchester.

His mind sped back to the time when he had arrived from North Wales, miserable and fatigued, feeling a strong sense of injustice and hatred against his father smouldering inside him. He was shown to a spotless dormitory containing twelve beds, one of which he was allotted. A plate of congealed stew followed by a lesson in Latin (and he was not excused, even though he had been travelling all day), left him silent and resentful.

Soon after supper, the lad in the next bed introduced himself: he was John Lucas and he told Edward not to look so glum. He promised that the best way to survive was to escape each evening after lights-out, down to the tavern; and sometimes, even, into the arms of a friendly woman! Since the only woman whom Edward could think about was his youthful stepmother, he had turned down the offer to accompany Lucas, using tiredness as his excuse and he had lain down to sleep.

Staring at the wooden rafters above his head, he cursed the day God had given him a father who would not listen to reason. Yes, he was prepared to admit to himself, that he had desired his stepmother, Mariana, but she had eyes solely for his father, if only the short-sighted old goat could have seen it! Oh, she enjoyed a giggle and she was great fun to be with; but there were times when she refused to join him and his sister, Pen, in some of their high-jinks and she would laugh:

"I'm a married woman now. I mustn't behave like this."

"Worse than that," Pen had rejoined on one occasion, "you've got two nearly grown-up children."

Mariana had wrinkled her nose.

"Don't say that! You make me feel old."

"You *are* old," Edward had put in. "In fact, two of your children are married."

"No, no. Not my children. My stepchildren. I think of you as my brothers and sisters."

"Not Baggy Maggy!" chanted Pen. "Not her! No one wants her for a sister."

"Hush, Penelope, dear." Mariana rebuked gently. "You mustn't say such things. Your eldest sister has troubles on her mind."

"What troubles?"

"I'm afraid that they are troubles that you wouldn't understand at your tender age."

"In other words, mind my own business. Well, I don't care! I wish Margaret wasn't my sister!"

"Penelope, don't let your father hear you say that," Mariana had warned.

Yes, Edward recalled, turning over once more on the uncomfortable bed, Father was never far from Mariana's conversation. She positively worshipped him. He could not understand what she saw in his father, for his nose was bulbous and often red, his stomach stuck out and he snored so loudly he could be heard from outside his bedroom! Indeed, however hard Edward had tried, he was unable to get his stepmother to notice him, *really* notice him! Now he cursed the day she had offered to teach him a few steps for the party at *Plas Hyfryd*. Of course, he, who could never be near enough to her, had not refused. He had been thrilled to grasp her hand in reality and indeed, even encircle her slim body in a loose embrace. Oh, he had stood on her toes several times and she had laughingly complained, but she had been close enough for him to be able to smell the rose-water that she splashed on her skin, and see right into the black, mysterious depths of her eyes. He was exactly on a level with her, shooting up last year from a puny child to a strapping man. Well, at least in his opinion, he had attained manhood. Why had she not wanted him? How could she prefer that old man, his father, who had spawned a woman older than herself? How could she stand to have *him* hold her in his arms, breathe his boozy breath, see him with no clothes on, allow him to put inside her his…?

Edward sat up in bed. He was here – a boarder at this strict school – banished from *Trem-y-Môr*. He must stop thinking of her or he would go mad. What evil mischance had brought his parent home at the precise moment that Mariana had been telling him how to hold a woman when dancing: close enough for comfort, but not so close "that your great, clod hopping feet trample on her satin slippers, Edward!"? He could hear her voice across the miles and his father castigating him. God damn the man to hell!

Now he was in this awful place where he was being treated like a child. He would probably never see her again; or, at least, so infrequently that it would not be worthwhile.

Gradually he became aware of sobbing. Well, he felt like crying too, but *he* was not doing so!

"Shut up, you snivelling bastard!" he swore. "Some of us are trying to sleep!" He punched his pillow and lay down as a muffled whimper came from the other end of the room and then no more.

Later he had been awakened by half-stifled laughs and whispers and several loud bangs and he assumed that his fellow-pupils were returning from their escapade into town. Much, much later, when a watery moon shone through the window, he heard scraping as though someone was moving furniture. He groaned. Oh, to be back in his own room at home instead of sharing his bedchamber with a roomful of restless boys!

He woke early the next day, but then he usually did. There was not much light, although a faint grey morning was creeping across the dormitory. He could hear rain and some other noise, a sort of creaking. A slow, rhythmic creaking. He opened one eye. Something was hanging from the ceiling; it looked like a bag. Perchance another boy had hung his travelling bag, containing all his possessions, up there to annoy him because he was a new boy in the middle of term in the middle of the academic year.

He climbed out of bed. He would sneak along and take it down, without any fuss. That would spoil their fun!

Edward let out a shriek of terror. That was no bag! That was a boy hanging from the rafter by a belt around his neck. Next to him were chest and chair to show how he had managed his ascent, but Edward's gaze was drawn to the lad's purple bloated face with its swollen tongue sticking out. He fled from the scene to find a secluded place to vomit and vomit.

CUTLAND

Matthew Cutland signalled to his dogs to come to heel and, with the animals following him closely, began to descend the path to the beach and away from his home, *Tŷ Craig*.

Usually he didn't go abroad when the moon was shining, and an almost full moon was rising slowly in the sky; it looked like it would be one of those nights when shadows would be cast by its ivory light. However, he had to meet with only one of his contacts; no contraband was arriving so he had no fear of a run in with the customs men. The arrangements were to be settled for a week on Wednesday and, if all went according to plan, soon he would be returning to his bed for a few hours' light sleep with the knowledge that before very long his coffers would be full again.

He accepted that he was breaking the law but his conscience didn't trouble him. He had been around the world and met men from other faiths and had decided that church and the Lord God Almighty wasn't for him. He had spent much of his life in the Far East and had dabbled in the religions there; when he settled on Holy Island he had decided to allow fate to take its course. Believing that you had to look after yourself for no one else would, he had constructed a network of contacts who could help him supplement his pile of gold, which was locked away in his vast home.

His priority, when he retired from his job as a ship's surgeon on the '*Homeward bound*', was to find the right property to buy, and *Tŷ Craig* had fulfilled all the criteria: namely physical isolation from the village and an oft-repeated ghost story that kept inquisitive eyes turned away.

Tŷ Craig (Rock House) had been built sixty years ago by an eccentric from Lancashire who had believed that water was good for his health and particularly for his intestines. A bachelor, he had never felt happier than when bobbing about in the waves. He had liked to swim, each day, in the sea and rumour had it that he enjoyed it so much, it was hard to persuade him to come out!

On a visit to North Wales, this individual had seen the ruins of a Roman

Fort, built on an outcrop of land, surrounded on three sides by the sea and he had resolved to buy the land and build a house of his own design there. Using the natural rock for some of the walls and the ancient walls for others, today the house was spreadeagled on four levels, in a higgledy-piggledy fashion with no thought for symmetry. However, it had been built of robust stone brought from the north of England at great expense and it had stood, untouched by the salt and sea, looking as though it would stand there until the end of the world.

In truth, Lord Darling, who was anything but a darling to the local folk, had built his house with all the rooms he had thought important placed first, and only, almost as an afterthought, added rooms in which to sleep. Facing the sea was an immense drawing room, or salon. Oblong in shape, it had a window taking up the whole end of the room, with glass on three sides. Thus Lord Darling had been able to view the water from every angle. He had panelled the rest of the walls in such a clever way that it was hard to find the doors leading to other parts of the house, unless you knew exactly where they were situated.

Originally, there had been a wooden platform extending from these windows which actually hung over the sea. Many people believed that this was where Lord Darling dived into the water. Since the wood had rotted and fallen away, there was no way of seeing that anyone diving from the balcony would have hurt themselves on the jagged rocks below. Matthew had discovered that Lord Darling had never allowed his head to be immersed anyway and the elderly gentleman used to reach the sea by descending a set of stairs that started inside the house, cut from the very rock itself, and continued down to the waves. At high tide, the water was deep enough for the enthusiastic bather to be able to walk straight into the sea, placing his feet on the steps; at low tide, the ocean only licked the bottom step. On these occasions Lord Darling was compelled to wade out for his 'dip'. Matthew found that these worn steps provided an excellent place from which to launch a rowing boat.

When Lord Darling became older he had not liked the cold weather and had built a room at a level below the great salon, on the way down the steps, wherein was formed a deep, marble pool, which could be fed from the sea. If need be, it could also be topped up with hot water to bring its contents to a tepid temperature. Here, the eighty-four year old man had bathed in complete privacy.

On the other side of the salon, and down more steps, clinging to the very side of the small peninsular, were the rooms used for eating: dining-room, kitchen, scullery and various large store cupboards.

At the front of the house was an entrance hall with a, marble floor. Its Spartan expanse was unwelcoming, but Lord Darling had apparently detested visitors. He often had kept them waiting deliberately in this inhospitable place, so the story was told. Matthew had thrown down numerous, brightly-coloured, thick, Chinese carpets and arranged silk screens to give the impression of a much smaller vestibule; nevertheless, very few people had seen inside the house as the present owner valued his privacy too.

Five bedrooms in all sat atop the other levels; one was above the entrance hall, and, being on the same floor as the salon, was reached from one of the hidden doors in that impressive room. Lord Darling had used this particular room for a study, but Matthew had furnished it as a bedchamber to save the necessity of climbing the mean stairs, wooden this time, to the floor under the eaves. Since he and only one servant inhabited the large house, the top floor was seldom used.

Matthew had heard about the house from a second cousin of Lord Darling. When he had viewed it, he decided instantly that this was the house for him. Sometimes he felt he was crossing the oceans, with all the water swirling around the house.

The sea had been his life: his father had been a surgeon before him. He was bequeathed a set of instruments – they remained in his possession – and any common butcher would have recognised most of the set from their own job! Matthew had travelled the world, but had spent his last years in and around China, where he had made his fortune. He had brought back from that far-off land a boat load of treasures, including his only servant. Matthew had heard all kinds of tales bandied about the villages concerning his servant (who never left the house), but he reckoned that the true history of that young person was more peculiar than any that could be imagined!

He had met his servant sixteen years ago. He had been aboard the *'Fair Abigail'* when they had arrived at a remote village to re-stock their water supplies. He had decided to join the shore party in order to stretch his legs – four weeks at sea had felt rather confining. The wind was onshore; thus it wasn't until they had pulled the rowing boats onto the beach that they first realised something was wrong. The stench of death filled their nostrils. Motioning to the sailors to stay, Matthew had made his way into the village. Nothing but rotting corpses. His experienced eyes told him that some plague had struck the entire population; quickly he had retreated, without touching anything. However, just as he reached the sand, he heard a baby's wail – loud, insistent and surprisingly healthy.

Without hesitating, Matthew had followed the sound and there had been a perfect baby, wrapped in some local cloth and laid in an oval basket, with its little arms waving and its eyes aglow with interest. Matthew knew he couldn't leave the little fellow there to die from exposure, starvation, thirst or the illness that had overtaken its community.

His Captain had not agreed with his decision, and had only consented to allowing Matthew to keep the infant on condition it was quarantined in the surgeon's own cabin. Matthew, discovering that the child was, in fact, a girl, had named her Pearl, for her cradle had appeared like an oyster shell, with her in the centre, amidst the putrefying settlement.

During the journey to the next port, Matthew had found out the impracticalities of caring for such a young child, and he had given the baby to the only woman he knew: a prostitute. Leaving money, he had not seen Pearl for another two years. Subsequently, he was only able to visit her when she was six and ten. On the last occasion, he had found her crying over the death of her 'mother', who had perished from some disease caught by her daily contact with the sailors from across the seas.

Matthew had been presented with a weeping child, who had been told mistakenly that he was her father and expected him to care for her. It hadn't taken him many minutes to recognise what her life would become if he left her. Overnight Pearl had become Pete. Ten years after he had saved her, Pearl sailed with him again; no one remembered the baby and everyone assumed simply that the surgeon had need for a kind of valet. Pearl had suited well: she was bright, willing and faithful.

For eighteen months, she was Matthew's personal servant and it had seemed only natural for her to remain with him when he retired and came to live at *Tŷ Craig*. The two of them existed in quiet seclusion after the hectic life aboard ship. Pearl was happy in men's attire, after all those weeks in disguise. Maybe nothing would have changed if Matthew had not caught a fever and been delirious for two days. He awoke, light-headed, to find the girl curled up in bed beside him. When questioned, he had found out that she had tried all the remedies she had learnt from working close to him, but fearing that he was dying, she had lain down to die with him! Suddenly her lithe body, newly-formed breasts and smooth face had set him on fire and he had taken her there and then. Only afterwards had he calculated that she must be fourteen to his three and fifty years, but he had accepted the new arrangement with the same equanimity as Pearl herself.

He smiled wryly to himself while he strode along the path, recalling that Pearl had learnt more from her years with her 'mother' than just how to wash and cook! Yes, he found that the young woman took to her new role with as much self-confidence as she had served him as maid!

Occasionally, Matthew was stricken with guilt and toyed with the idea of keeping their relationship strictly like father and daughter, but he had never viewed Pearl in that light. It had taken his initial meeting with another woman of a similar age to Pearl to stir these feelings in him.

Matthew had never married, and until he had found the baby, would have said that he wasn't paternal at all. But when he chanced upon Mariana watching him move in, he was captivated.

He understood that *Tŷ Craig* had stood empty for many years before he arrived. It had stout, wooden shutters protecting it from entry; however, these were unnecessary, for with all the tales of Lord Darling seen walking around the house at night, the place remained unvisited. Once Matthew had befriended Mariana, he had found out that it had been her custom as a child to climb in through a broken scullery window. She would wander through the silent rooms with the afternoon sun slanting in, casting slivers of light between the gaps in the shutters. She confided in him at a later date that she had not heard the story of the ghost in the early days when she had entered the house and, finding nothing to fear in the unfurnished rooms, and that no one ever found her there, she had made *Tŷ Craig* her hideout.

Thus, when he had espied her, standing on a grassy hillock, legs askance, hands on hips, watching the caravan of boxes, heavy chests and coloured carpet bags being carried into her private hideaway from a small sailing boat tied up at the steps, she was angry and dismayed. She had not hesitated to tell him that she had not expected any new occupants, but his invitation to her to partake of a cool drink on that particular hot summer's afternoon was greeted with a charming smile. Vexation was forgotten, curiosity overcame. Belligerence was exchanged for happy confidences that the house was more agreeable with all his possessions from the Orient. He had appreciated her honesty and valued her trust. Acquaintance blossomed into a relationship that he had never sought or imagined that he needed and now, six years later, he viewed her as a precious daughter.

Pearl did not interact with her; her English was practically non-existent and she had told him that he was all she wanted. Therefore she kept out of the way, whenever Mariana came. However, Mariana knew and loved his black dogs, whose deep barking enhanced their reputation of ferocity. She was, in fact, his only regular visitor. Not a recluse, but a discreet man, he liked his home to be his sanctuary. Needing privacy for his nefarious night-time activities, he let it be known that the guard-dogs were trained to bite any trespassers and he did nothing to disabuse the tale of the ghost. Nonetheless, he was by no means disliked. He preferred to conduct his social life on other people's territory where soon he became popular; he knew about his nickname and encouraged its use. His house might be legendary and the topic for conversation on a dark, rainy night, but he himself appeared to be no mystery. His short, lithe figure, wise blue eyes and weather-beaten face could be found in many houses all across the island. With his natural aptitude for languages, without difficulty he learnt Welsh and mixed well with people from all walks of life. His years as a ship's surgeon made him a good listener and he found a welcome in other people's homes and there seemed to be no hard feelings about him not returning hospitality. He guessed that some speculated on what he was hiding but most accepted his desire for a secluded home – except that lively, intelligent Squire's daughter.

Matthew pushed past the gorse bushes onto the soft sand, looking right and left for the man he was hoping to meet. There he was – standing near the waves. Matthew patted his dogs' heads and lengthened his stride, desire to have the business concluded and to be on the return journey to his safe abode quickening his pace.

EDWARD

Edward stretched his back and flexed the muscles of his leg. He felt exhausted and the image of his hanged room-mate hung before his weary eyes. Thank God those days were long past! He needed to relieve himself but the thought of the effort of dismounting spurred him on.

"Not far to go," he encouraged the horse, and then allowed his thoughts to return to his school days, hoping to forget the more pressing need!

He himself had wanted to hang himself when he had received that epistle from his father after his stepmother's death. Every single word of the angry letter was burned into his mind and, even today, seventeen years later, he could remember certain phrases:

"I rue the day you were born... I'd rather you had died than my own sweet wife... I never want to see you again as long as I live... I won't ever forgive you..."

Now he was a man, Edward could understand better the terrible grief that his father had suffered. Nonetheless, still he abhorred his pater's lack of control, not in writing the letter (for writing sometimes eased one's heart, according to his sister, Pen), but in sending it to him; a young, possibly spoilt, fifteen-year-old.

Until his stepmother had appeared on the scene, he had known that he was the apple of his father's eye, since he was the youngest and only surviving son. His mother did not feature in his memories like his father, because often she was confined to bed giving birth, or grieving the death of one of his older siblings. At least, that was what he had been told when he was a child. His first clear recollections were of a magnanimous father; a spiteful Margaret, who had pinched him when no one was looking and then scorned his tears; a mousy Katherine, who was always too frightened to take his side against her elder sister and a bouncy Pen, who, although she was much younger than Margaret, had defended him, physically if need be, against Margaret's attacks, until the day she had succumbed to smallpox.

One of Edward's clearest remembrances was of visiting his favourite sister who had been so ill. She was lying motionless, her face towards the wall. He had wondered if she was dead, but he wasn't able to touch her to find out because he was made to stand at the door and venture no nearer. He had pulled on his nanny's hand.

"Has Pen gone to be with Jesus?" he had queried in a loud whisper.

"Oh, no, dear heart, and we must all pray that she doesn't."

"Isn't it good to be with Jesus?" Edward puzzled.

"Well… yes, it is good but… but still we'd like… like Penelope to remain with us for a few more years."

"Maybe she'd rather go to Jesus," he had persevered. "You told us that it was lovely to be with Jesus and that nothing horrid ever…"

"Yes, I may have told you that but… but… Anyway, run along dear. Go up to the nursery. It is time for your supper."

Penelope had returned "from the gates of hell", as Ruthie the nursemaid had put it, but she was different. Suddenly Margaret was deemed too old for the nursery, and with her departure and Penelope's protracted quietness, the whole atmosphere on the top floor of the house had changed.

Edward could not remember whether it was from this particular time that he saw more of his father, but certainly Sir William had seemed to delight in teaching his son all that a man should know about life. Maybe it was after Penelope's lucky escape that the older man had accepted that Edward was likely to be his sole surviving heir, for, once Edward was out of petticoats, Sir William had ordered his son to be dressed in miniature adult clothes, often matching his own. This had thrilled the boy and Edward had begun to identify with his father and idolise him. When his lessons were finished each day, Edward was taught to ride and to handle a gun. After his sister's illness, he had accompanied the Squire more and more frequently around the estates. Yes, his life had been filled with his esteemed parent.

As far back as he could recall his mother had ignored him so much that he didn't realise that he had two parents. At nine he had overheard one of the servants say that after each of her children was born Letitia Rowlands abandoned them to the care of others, almost as if they ceased to exist after birth. This had meant he had seen his mother rarely. Never receiving any love from her, he had been unaware that this was abnormal behaviour. After all, he was surrounded by a whole flock of nursemaids and nannies that cared for his daily needs and he could always run to his beloved father. His mother became a shadowy figure, whom he encountered some Sunday afternoons, along with his other siblings, when he was expected to recite some of his lessons to her. Occasionally he would receive a pat on the head after his recitation and he recalled now that the only time she had smiled at him was after he had read the big, family Bible; then she would look really pleased with him.

If he ever did think about the situation in his family, he had assumed that his sisters saw more of his mother than he himself, whilst he, being a boy, was expected to spend time with his father. Thus, he had given his entire child's love to his paternal relative. Wanting to receive approval from this man, he had always listened diligently to what was said and tried his very best. Sir William had seemed to enjoy working with a child who showed such promise and a certain amount of skill at an early age. Thus, with the Squire he was energetic and open-hearted and full of conversation, but with his mother, unfamiliarity led to dislike and he was as distant as she. Although later his tutor had decried Sir William's lack of discipline towards his son within that very son's earshot, Edward himself had grown up in a man's world, revelling in being his father's constant companion.

Yet it had all ended when his stepmother had arrived in their lives. If Edward was honest, he would admit that, initially, he hadn't been desperately hurt by his father pushing him out from the centre of his life. At that time, his own thoughts had been increasingly bound up with this fascinating beautiful woman; indeed he had fallen in love for the first time. It was not until he was looking back from his exile at school that he felt increasingly betrayed by his father's sudden switch from loving him to loving his second wife. He had reasoned that Sir William could and should have loved them both! A dull ache filled in his breast.

Almost permanently angry at being sent away, soon Edward had found an outlet for his sentiments in his escapades under the tutelage of Lucas. Very adept at climbing, both boys had clambered out of the school confines each evening to discover the pleasures of drinking, gambling and the inevitable relationships with women.

It was no surprise that it was another woman who had brought about Edward's further downfall, together with his budding love of gambling. Fortunately the woman involved was not one of those Edward met on his breaking of curfew, although she did play a significant part in his future. He was introduced to Susanna Hopewell by the adventurous Lucas. She was the daughter of one of Lucas' parents' friends who was a judge, and therefore highly respectable. Even so, Edward had gone to Susanna's bedchamber on many occasions, for a rapid ascent up a rope of ivy was no challenge to him!

Edward could picture her even after all these years: soft, fair ringlets, dancing green eyes and infectious grin. It had been Susanna who had said that she wanted to see *his* bedchamber. He had laughed at her request and told her that she did not want to see where he slept, for it was an austere, non-private room with eleven other hard beds, but Susanna had nagged and nagged. Whereupon Edward had explained that girls were not allowed into the school at all and most certainly not into the dormitories except on 'Open Day', once a year. On that occasion, he told her, parents, sisters and anyone else who so desired could be given a tour of all the buildings.

Lucas, hearing of Susanna's request, gave Edward a challenge. The bet was that Edward take his young lady not simply into the dormitories but into the headmaster's office. Edward had never been able to refuse a wager and this time he was sure he could win.

He had borrowed a set of clothes from Sam Baker, who slept opposite him. Since Baker was shorter that Edward, he had no difficulty in fitting Susanna out with boys' clothes, wig and all! Not just into the school, but in broad daylight, and under the very nose of three masters, Edward and Susanna had strolled past the school gates. They had sped up to the bedchamber and then made their way to the headmaster's study. Finding this room empty of people, but containing a long settle on which parents could sit when in conference with the headmaster, Edward had proceeded to give his partner a victory kiss. However, the headmaster, entering unexpectedly to find what he thought were two boys embracing, had lost his temper. Despite Susanna's cry that she was a girl, not a boy, the master was not pacified; and on hearing her father's name, he had turned purple.

Edward grinned at the memory. Even at the time, he had wondered if the Head would die of apoplexy, instead of fearing what punishment would be meted out to him. Eventually the whole story was unravelled. Edward was surprised but pleased that Lucas, learning that his friend continued to be questioned by the tutors, had knocked on the Headmaster's door and confessed his part in the prank and both boys' parents were summoned.

Lord and Lady Lucas, who lived only sixteen miles away, had speedily arrived and decided that it was time their son left school and entered the Navy, which had always been his career. The old system of entry into

The Fleet was for young men to go as apprentices to merchant captains before Navy service, but a new scheme had recently come into being under Charles II. This allowed sons of gentlemen of quality to go to sea in a Navy ship rather than on a merchant ship. Thus, they would receive, besides seaman's wages and victuals, the sum of four and twenty pounds a year Table money. The boys themselves did not usually see this money for it was donated to the captain, who then not only permitted these raw recruits to eat at his table, but generally took care of their education too. Therefore it was arranged for Lucas to travel to London to begin his studies for entry into the Navy of William III as a Gentleman Volunteer.

Of Edward's parents there was no word until Edward had received that stunning letter. Shocked to the core that his loving father never wanted to see him again, Edward had determined to run away from school to a place where his father, even if he ever repented of those hurtful words, would never find him. Edward had reasoned, in his misery, that since Sir William no longer wanted to relate to him then he would not care what happened to him. He resolved to abscond from his lessons and join a travelling fair; there were several of these in the area because of the Easter celebrations. The confused boy fancied that, with a bit of training, he could become a tumbler.

Lucas had tried to dissuade him by suggesting that Edward start with him in his new studies under the patronage of someone other than his father.

"Surely you've got a rich relation somewhere to whom you can repair. Think, Rowly, think! We haven't much time!"

"I don't want to approach any of my relatives. Then my father will know where I am."

"Yes, but you wouldn't suit a fair. You've been used to money all your life and a home and…"

"I understand all that but no one would think of searching for me there…"

"Oh, be sensible, Rowly. Look, I've got an older brother. If I tell him of our plight, he might well help… You'll need clothes, books and maybe instruments. I don't know. Mother was talking on and on about a great long list of things I should take."

"No, thank you, Lucas, my friend. It's very thoughtful of you but if I go to one of your relatives, then it would be like begging… charity. I would rather earn my own living."

"Rowly, you could get a loan…"

"No. Please say no more. I've made up my mind. And, please, when you're asked, don't tell anyone where I've gone…"

"As if I would!" Lucas' scandalised tones rang clear in his mind, despite the lapse of time.

Several nights of sleeping rough, and being refused by two sets of fair people who seemed cautious of strangers (he reflected later that his expensive clothes wouldn't have helped his cause!), had lowered Edward's enthusiasm. He began to see the futility of his plans; nonetheless, nothing would make him return either to school or his father. He had burned with rage against his unjust treatment by Sir William and secretly he had been glad that Mariana had died: for if he could not have her, then why should his bad-tempered unreasonable old father live with her?

Searching around in his brain for alternatives, he had concluded that the only place he could go was to his Uncle Richard in London. Maybe, just maybe, his uncle would know what Edward could do with his life.

Making his way to London with no money proved arduous. It was four weeks before he had arrived, tattered and footsore, on the doorstep of his uncle's house. All of a sudden, he had feared that his uncle might contact his father and he had refused to give his name to the footman; in turn, he had been refused entry to the elegant town house. Eventually he had told the servant who he was but, by now, the footman did not believe his story. If it had not been for the timely arrival of his Aunt Anne, Edward might well have never gained entry to the family home.

Perhaps it was better that Edward had told his story to his aunt, who then regaled her husband with the facts; perhaps his uncle would have been sympathetic anyway. Whatever, Richard Rowlands, catching a snippet of information about the fate of his nephew's confederate in the tale, had settled on the idea of Edward going forward into the Fleet as a Gentleman Volunteer too.

It was a dozen years kept secret before Edward had found out that Richard had written to his older brother a forthright letter castigating him over his treatment of his son. Nonetheless, the first missive did not give Edward's whereabouts to Sir William until the boy had gone to sea, just in case William had interfered. In subsequent messages between the two brothers, as the truth came out, the Squire, who, like his son, detested accepting charity, had sent the money for his heir's entry into the Navy.

Yet, not once, in seventeen years, had he unbent and communicated with Edward himself.

Edward stopped at the crossroads to check the signpost. He felt rather disorientated. Was it tiredness? Or was it being lost in thought so much? He decided that he had to stop.

It was a full quarter of an hour later that he set forth again. Patting his horse on the neck, mumbling a few heartening words, he turned the animal towards the road marked 'Four Mile Bridge'. With the gentle rhythm of the horse's walk and his bladder emptied, it wasn't many minutes before he had abandoned himself to the foregone years again.

With hindsight, he understood that he had pushed down his grief and anger, unconsciously deciding to deal with them at a later date. There were new horizons opening up to him, starting with an animated reunion with Lucas. The two boys had begun to study under a Mr Flamsteed, the First Astronomer Royal, at Greenwich. Lucas found room for Edward at his lodgings in Chamber Street near Tower Hill, although Edward regularly visited his aunt and uncle.

Edward had been brought up in London, dwelling in his father's town house, but never before had he been without supervision and the lads enjoyed exploring the rejuvenated City, which had been rebuilt after the great fire of 1660, when over 9,000 houses had been destroyed. The new stone buildings no longer leaned together as if they were sharing intimate secrets with each other, but there were still plenty of dingy, sordid backstreets for two young men, bent on discovery, to explore.

In spite of the prolonged hours spent under Mr Flamsteed, studying navigation and the modern subject of mathematics, which was not taught in schools at this time, Edward and Lucas were able to find time to visit the taverns and coffee houses of the City as well as to watch the men building the Cathedral of St Paul.

Altogether, with every day full, the six months of learning in London had flown and it was with great excitement that Edward had joined his first ship, *'Leah'*. Alas, he was separated from his friend, but nevertheless thrilled to be aboard a real ship at last.

'Leah' was a third-rate ship, with fifty-six guns. There was a whole host of unfamiliar facts and skills to be learnt and Edward settled in well. How strange it had all seemed at the outset! One of his strongest memories was of his own thankfulness at how easy his life was as an officer compared

with the ordinary seamen – and particularly when he contrasted his lot with the battered, pressed men. They often arrived in rags, bewildered by the drastic change in their fate. Edward's sympathy was aroused with the understanding that there, but for the grace of God, went he! He had hidden from a few violent press gangs during his sorry journey to his uncle's house. He was doubly glad of the backing of his family because he ate at the captain's table and slept alone in his minute cabin. Once over the initial bout of sea sickness, he became accustomed to his ordered life.

Many of his reminiscences of those early years in the Navy were blurred by age now, but the day he realised that he had lost his father was imprinted in his memory forever; certainly his father lived somewhere in this world but he was dead and buried as far as his son was concerned.

During England's war with France, Edward had been involved in numerous battles but there was a single engagement which stood out in his mind. His ship was one of twenty-two third and fourth-rate ships sent to protect the great Turkey Fleet: a magnificent fleet of 400 merchant ships sailing for Smyrna in the Eastern Mediterranean and therefore needing to pass the French Navy.

In the beginning, the squadron, which included *'Leah'*, had been accompanied by 102 men-of-war. However, after seeing the Turkey Fleet safely past Brest, these huge ships returned to Plymouth; it was decided by the Admirals not to risk England's best warships any further. But these top men had not taken into consideration that, in truth, the French were out at sea and not skulking near the coast. All 120 sail of them were waiting eagerly for the English to enter the trap.

Starting with one or two distant masts, soon more and more French sails were seen; and then *Leah* was amidst enemy ships, surrounded on all sides. Edward had felt fear crawling on his skin and sweat break out on his top lip. The cannons began to roar: Boom! Boom! Boom! Edward believed his end had come when shot started flying from every direction.

"Oh, God have mercy on us!" one agitated sailor cried as he knelt up on the poop deck, crossing himself in the middle of the smoke and terror.

"Christ have mercy on us," had come the reply from another man as the first man fell, his head blown into a thousand bloody pieces.

Everywhere was chaos: men screaming with pain and fear; commands shouted and disobeyed; confusion and disorder. Edward himself had rushed hither and thither and then from nowhere, it seemed, like rats swarming over stored barley, the French were among them, brandishing their wicked swords and cutlasses, firing pistols, intent on capturing the vessel.

Now it was every man for himself!

How much later it had been that Edward became aware that the cannon fire had decreased, he could not remember. He learnt afterwards that two stout Dutch ships, part of the squadron, had arrived to rescue the smaller ship, engaging the enemy. Apparently, even the merchant ships with their precious cargoes had fought, and miraculously the battle moved away from *'Leah'* as the English, courageous and determined against the odds, bombarded the French.

With night falling, *'Leah'* was a miniature battleground in herself. Edward had slashed and cut, thrust and parried, his sword arm aching terribly, his back pressed to the mizzenmast. He had lost count of the number of wounded and dead piled at his feet in a groaning, gory pile: all that had mattered was his own survival.

The 100, 200, maybe more, Frenchmen who had arrived in barges and boarded *'Leah'* had been gallantly fought by the 300 or so men who lived and worked on the ship, defending not just their country but their lives too. With darkness had come more confusion, but, by then, only a few of the intruders remained alive. Abruptly, in one simultaneous gesture – almost as though commanded – weapons were laid down. Then prisoners were tied up and the wounded attended to and an eerie silence had fallen upon the ship, only broken by the intermittent moans of the injured and the creaking of the timbers of the vessel, as if in relief.

Soon had come the order to hoist sail and *'Leah'* retreated, leaving the toll of damage to man and ship to be reckoned up the next day.

Edward had worked all night, throwing the dead enemies unceremoniously overboard to clear the decks; carrying the wounded to the quarterdeck where the last remaining surgeon was tending them; giving encouragement to the dying. On and on through the murky air he had toiled, although his own body craved rest.

It was not until he had finally lain down in his cabin, with slumber now eluding him, that he had become aware that his own face and arm were bleeding and that he was covered with dozens of scratches and bruises. However, now he was abed, he could no more have risen again to bathe them than fly. Images of carnage flashed before his eyes and he longed for them to go, and for the blessed oblivion of sleep to enfold him.

Unheralded, his father's face was before him and he heard him say:

"I rue the day you were born. I never want to see you again as long as I live."

All the tiredness of the day, the fight fought and won made him prey to depression; it surrounded him, too heavy to shrug off, wrapping about him like the thick blanket of smoke which had filled the ship's decks earlier. Suddenly, he wished that he had died during the battle. Then he would have been at peace now; no more fighting or struggling; no more feelings and emotions; nothing but rest, everlasting rest.

All those months of hiding his feelings, never acknowledging that he was deeply upset – not just angry, but hurt to the innermost depths of his being – by his father's behaviour had hit him unexpectedly, as forcefully as the French coming aboard *'Leah'*. At that very moment he began to question whether his father had *ever* loved him. For, if he had done so, surely he could not have behaved in such a harsh manner? Yet, if his father had *never* loved him, then he had been gravely mistaken. So how would he ever know when, or if, anyone loved him again? Without warning, he had wanted to weep – weep like a child for the lost love of his father. His mother had never loved him; his stepmother, Mariana, had not known him long enough to love him; only his father had loved him, he had thought, and now, perhaps even that was not true. He felt unutterably, completely alone…

No wonder he had never forgotten that day for it spun him round and round in a spiral of hopelessness.

It was from then onwards, he recalled, that he had found melancholy wash over him, often without notice, again and again. Fortunately, when he was busy and aboard ship, usually he could keep his sadness at bay. But some days, with no premonition, despair would descend upon him. At first, he had allowed himself to sink into gloom and he would bark irritably at anyone who approached him; but when the moods recurred year after year, he would say inside his head, "This will pass; tomorrow I'll feel better". And with this as his only comfort, eventually even his closest friends did not know about these bad days, for he would hide his dark thoughts by being especially full of fun and jokes; or he would turn to drink for solace.

It had taken until the time that he was in hospital, afraid of dying, for him to share with another person his own deep-seated problems. Strangely enough, it had not been a priest, nor a doctor, but a fellow patient who had received his confidences. The man had lost both legs and his sight but remained cheerful. He had counselled Edward to return home and set things right with his father.

"Talk to him, Cap'n," he had advised. "He must be an old'un by now. See if yer can't make matters straight atween yer. Tell him he hurt yer… if he'll listen; but at least go and make yer peace with him."

Sound advice, Edward had thought.

Thus, here he was, about to cross onto Holy Island after seventeen years away. He had no fears that his father would not receive him, but, with his horse's hooves ringing over the bridge, it occurred to him that his stepmother had died while giving birth and so there must be a child. Searching his memory, he could not recall whether the baby had been a boy or a girl. Tactfully, Pen had never referred to either his father or his dead stepmother or the child in her regular correspondence to him. How much of the affair Pen knew, he had no idea himself, for in the early days he had not wanted to discuss it; then, as the months went by, it had been too painful to dig up all the old grievances.

Had Mariana's child been a boy or a girl? Had it even lived? Yes, he was sure of that, for now he recollected his Aunt Anne saying once that the child had grown up "wild and undisciplined". A boy, probably. Yes, his father had replaced him in his heart with another son whom he could teach and advise and love! Edward rebuked his bitter thoughts. He must not allow this kind of thinking to dwell in his mind; rather, he must befriend the lad. Maybe he would be interested in the ships or even the Navy, for hadn't the child been brought up by the sea all his life? Edward smiled. Strange to think that he, who had only visited the coast during the summer months, should yearn for the vast oceans of the world! Not that he would return to sail again. No, he had left the Fleet and was quite a wealthy man in his own right. His father had never intimated that he had cut his heir out from his inheritance, but perchance he had done so when a new son had been born of his favourite wife. After all, everyone knew Sir William had loved Mariana more than Letitia!

How familiar in many ways the whole island was to him! The sun was long gone but the sky was not completely dark, so far west was he. Painted in delicate mauve, with a hint of shell pink surrounded by lemon edges, soon it would have a curtain of indigo, dotted with diamond stars, drawn over it. Its translucent beauty drew Edward's tired eyes. In spite of the fading light, he was able to see the different shades of green in the grass and the knobbly grey of the rocks. Already the breeze of the early evening was getting chilly and Edward calculated that the night air would be cold. Surely he was nearly there?

The dusk made identification of landmarks more difficult but at last ahead, outlined against the mellow sky, was his destination, his home. Of course, the house was not where he had spent his childhood but it was the last of his inheritance – that is, if he still had one– and it was full of memories of sun-filled summers and the warm fragrance of the first woman he had loved.

Edward's horse clattered into the yard and he was glad to see a light burning in the kitchen. Stiff with fatigue, his descent from the roan's back left him in an undignified heap on the unforgiving cobbles. No one appeared to greet him. He manoeuvred himself upright and, pulling a walking stick from one of his saddlebags, limped around the house, his wooden leg beating a jaded rhythm on the path. He felt that the lateness of the hour, together with the occasion, merited a front door entrance.

Several knocks brought no response, so he shouted out and was rewarded with the squeal of stiff locks being unbolted. Then there was an unknown maid, candle in hand, peering at him through the dim light.

"Who is it?" she piped up, the English syllables hesitant.

"It's…" he began.

"Who is it?" This stronger echo was a voice he recalled.

"It's me, Wilson," he proclaimed. "Edward. Don't you remember me?"

Wilson appeared in the doorway and Edward smiled, while he watched puzzlement, followed by recognition, followed by amazement, pass across the older man's face.

"Is it really you, Sir? After all these years?" Wilson paused. "Oh, come in, Sir, do please come in. You must be worn out."

"That's an understatement, Wilson. I've been in the saddle since three o'clock this morning. Up before the cockerels this day! My horse is round the back. Is there someone who can see to her?"

"Of course, Sir. Of course."

Edward saw Wilson register the stick in his hand and the reason for it, when the tap of wood resounded in the hallway. The faithful retainer inquired, "Can I be of assistance to you, Sir?" His tone was tentative. Was he not sure of the reaction the comment would engender?

"I'd be most grateful," admitted Edward with as cheerful a note as he could muster. "I'm still not completely used to this new peg of mine. And… and after a day of constant riding… Well, it's damned sore!"

"Anyone would be tired after a day and evening in the saddle, Sir. Elin, come along girl, show us the way to the library or…" Wilson stopped mid-sentence. "I think the parlour might be best although it is a big room and…"

"No fires have been lit in there today, Mr Wilson," the maid put in.

"Who is it? Who's come?" These words made all three people in the hall raise their heads.

Edward halted in the centre of the floor. Descending the stairs was the woman of his dreams: Mariana. Mariana coming to greet him. His heart stood still. She was as young as he remembered her, eyes aglow with curiosity, with her long, black hair framing a perfect oval face – not a blemish or mark to mar her beauty. He shook his head like waking from sleep. This could not be his step-mother, for even if his family had deceived him and she had not died, she would be a woman in her mid-thirties, not a girl of seventeen. Exhausted though his mind was, immediately he found the solution: the child. Here was the baby, fully grown and the image of her mother. No, he amended this when she reached the foot of the stairs, the candlelight reflecting in her dark eyes and setting her hair glinting: she was more entrancing!

"You must be the child," he murmured in a bemused way.

"Child? What child?" echoed the young woman. "Who are you?"

"This is Sir Edward, Miss Mariana," explained Wilson, standing between brother and sister.

"Sir Edward? Edward, my brother?" proclaimed Mariana at the same time as Edward started:

"Your name is Mariana too…"

They both stopped. Edward felt embarrassed. Was she embarrassed also? What kind of greeting should pass between them?

"I was just taking Sir Edward to find a place to sit down for he has been travelling all day," intervened Wilson, covering the awkward moment.

"How did you know?" muttered Mariana. Her eyes dulled, sorrow replacing curiosity.

"Know? Know what?" repeated Edward.

No one replied. He looked from one face to another and then he knew.

Without warning, he understood why he had been driving himself so hard and why the old manservant was referring to him as "Sir Edward".

"He's not… he's not gone?" he stammered. His whole body sagged. Wilson stepped forward.

"Sir, you must come and sit down. It will doubtless come as a shock to you, as it did to all of us: Sir William passed away in his sleep last night."

"No!" Edward's bellow bounced off the walls. "No, he can't have gone. Not after I've come all this way, after all these years, to make my peace with him. No, it can't be too late!"

"Who is it? What's the matter?" A woman appeared from the kitchen, whom Edward had no difficulty identifying: Mrs Jones. She must have heard his shout. As she passed through the door she was wiping her hands on a cloth, but when she saw him, she threw the striped material into the air and sailed across the hall to clasp him to her ample bosom. "Why, Master Edward, is it really you? After all these years? My goodness, you're all grown up; a real man now!" She rounded on Wilson. "What made you keep him standing here? You must come and sit down, Master Edward. I wondered who it could be, coming to visit at this ungodly hour; but you're no visitor! One of the family, you are. Elin, run and tell Thomas to stable Master Edward's horse. Now, where would be best to sit, I wonder?"

"I'd prefer to sit in your kitchen, Mrs Jones. Like I used to in the old days." He couldn't keep the weariness and defeat from showing.

"Aye, the very place. Come along. I'm sure you remember the way. It's not cold in there like in the parlour and I'll find you a bite to eat. Wilson, would you bring a drink for Master Edward?" Mrs Jones shepherded him towards the back of the house whilst she talked.

MRS JONES

Mrs Jones indicated a wooden chair for the new master to sit on and then made her way on through the kitchen to the larder. It took several trips back and forth to bring out what she considered a reasonable feast for a man who had been riding all day. She wished that Elin would return from the stable; her legs and back ached and she could have done with Elin's help or even one of the younger maids, but they had all been sent to bed many hours ago. She herself had been on her feet late last night with the laying out of Sir William and then just an hour or two of rest before rising at five this morning. Tonight, with a second disturbed night, she was feeling her age acutely; she was nearer seventy than sixty, although she wouldn't admit that to anyone.

Once the food was set on the table, even then, she didn't feel she could sit down because of the master's presence. She leant against the sink and eased off one of her shoes from her foot. Two of the candles were guttering, sending wisps of smoke up and swirling around the room. She was transported back fifty years to the kitchen in her parents' house.

Mrs Jones had been born Miss Kezia Reece and was the ninth daughter in the family. Her father was a very religious man and when the first six of his offspring had died, he had sought refuge in the book of Job in the Bible, equating himself with that saint of yore. From the last chapter of Job, he learnt that the Bible hero had had seven sons and three daughters to replace the children God had taken from him. Thus, when George Reece's wife bore him more daughters he had prayed that his afflictions were over and named them Jemima, Kezia and Keren-happuch, after Job's second set of daughters. Quite a mouthful for childish tongues, especially since his youngest turned out to be a tiny fairylike child. Their mother had called them affectionately: Jem, Kez and Keren. If her father was a disciplinarian, her mother was benevolent and motherly. Perchance Mother felt the need to counteract the rigid rules of the head of the house; perchance Father abhorred her slackness and ordered the household to make up for her lack of order! Kez didn't know but it was to her mother that she ran when she found out that she was expecting a baby.

Looking back, Kez understood that she was rather an innocent; perhaps her sisters were too because her mother had wanted to protect them from the evils of this world, cosseting them year after year. (Keren had been kept in infant clothes and a cot long after she had outgrown them.) It wasn't that Kez didn't know where babies came from, but she certainly didn't think that she was in for anything other than an evening of fun when she had met a bold, Irish lad called Patrick.

She recalled that it hadn't been all that difficult to disentangle herself from her father's stern reins or her mother's gentle grip amidst the crowd of jolly people intent on having a good time at the annual fair. Father had been intent on watching for any and every danger and was looking right and left ahead of the family party; Mother had been fussing and flapping, trying to protect eleven-year-old Keren from getting lost. Thus the young couple slipped away; leaving the noise and laughter far behind they wended their way up the hill to the sweet summer meadows above the town.

Kez was very happy to kiss this handsome fellow who told her that her hair was light as goose down and her eyes as green as the hills at home. At first she did push him away when his hands strayed under her petticoats, but he continued to murmur such delightful endearments that she let him continue and before she knew it, she had given herself to him. Then she awoke from the magic spell he had woven over her! She sat up abruptly, pulling down her skirt and run away, telling herself that no one must ever know what she had done, and especially not her father.

Nevertheless it had been her father who was the second person to find out, one Saturday night four months later. She was able to hear her father's voice across time and feel the sting of the strap on her bare skin in that kitchen, lit by untrimmed candles all those years ago. The heat of the fire; the harshness of her father's reaction; the weeping of her mother; the sickness in her stomach; the shame of it all came together in her heart and she believed she was in hell. But hell was yet to descend.

Five days later, her welts still smarting and her soul in turmoil, she was sent to her elder sister's home in a village on the outskirts of Chester. There, according to her father, she was to stay until the baby was born and then... She was not sure what her future was to be after that hazy event.

Over the weeks, she discovered that daily living could be more hellish than one isolated evening because there was no end in sight. The Browning household put her through not physical beatings but psychological pressures: grim protestations by Jemima who was married but had no children; patronising lectures by Jemima's husband, John; prim recriminations from the housekeeper; whispered sneers from the indoor staff. These verbal lashings had stung her and then there was the rigid control of her everyday life (mending the household linen and a short walk around the garden after dark were considered the best way to make her pay for her sin); her father's regime seemed tame by comparison. Not that she had any contact with Father or Mother or young Keren or anyone outside the house at all. Her world had shrunk. She thought she would go mad; she felt she was being treated worse than the lowliest maid. A housemaid would not be supervised from dawn to dusk and would be allowed to eat at the table with the other servants and visit her family on her fortnightly Sunday afternoon off; Kez had to eat miserly rations in the solitary loneliness of her room and had no time off from her boring routine.

However the seasons did pass, much to her surprise, and whilst her waist grew so did her contentment. She learnt there were ways to alleviate her imprisonment: if she was very hungry she would sneak down to the kitchen at night and make herself some tasty morsel; she could garner scraps of material and thread from the growing pile of mending to make baby clothes for her child secretly. The latter gave her quiet satisfaction.

She continued to feel that she had too much time to contemplate, but something Jemima said made her see that this was part of her punishment – she was supposed to be reflecting on her situation! And at the conclusion of all her thoughts, there was no one with whom to share her hopes and fears. It did not take her very long to work out that she would not be welcome at her father's home, but she came to accept that she did not want to return there. With the passing weeks, she did look to the future. She couldn't – wouldn't – go home and she did not intend to stay at Jemima's either. She planned to keep the child but how? Peradventure she could earn a living sewing – surely there would someone who would pay her for her exquisite stitch work and embroidery! Or the recipes she had learnt to cook… Perhaps there was a household somewhere that would employ a cook who had a baby dozing in a basket by the fire.

The day of the birth came and hardly was she aware of how intoxicated the midwife was amidst all the pain. It seemed like hours before the final gush of fluid released the child between her legs. All of a sudden, from nowhere came Jemima to swoop upon the bloody babe before it made its first cry! Kez watched in horror as her sister laid the child in the cradle and straightaway placed a pillow over the tiny body. She tried to pull herself out of bed but she had no strength left. She called to the midwife to save her baby, but the woman was leaning drunkenly against the wall. She screamed at her sister not to do it and was told that the child was deformed and wouldn't have lived. But, an hour later, when she was alone, she dragged herself across to the cot, uncovered the lifeless body and hugged it – him – it was a boy – to her full breasts. She examined him minutely and could find nothing wrong with his limp limbs, his round, downy covered head, his soft body, his tiny perfect fingers and their nails. No, her sister had cold-bloodedly murdered her completely healthy baby!

Then she had come to a decision – she wanted nothing more to do with this unfeeling family. How dare they condemn her for an illegitimate child and yet condone infanticide! She could not believe that Jemima had acted on her own – her father must have instructed her to kill the child and maybe even to employ a midwife too under the influence of drink to intervene. Her mind was made up – she would leave right away.

Kez had wrapped the child in her own shawl, crept down to the kitchen to pack a half a loaf of bread into a checked cloth, and left her prison. She had buried her son in a shallow grave in a green copse beneath the trees at dawn. She dared not leave a Christian symbol upright at its head, like she had seen in the churchyards, but tenderly she laid a small cross fashioned out of two twigs on the recently-dug earth and said a prayer. Now she would begin a new life.

Thus Miss Kezia Reece set out on her journey to become Mrs Catherine Jones. It had taken her nineteen years to find her way across the miles from Chester and up the scale of jobs to housekeeper at *Trem-y-Môr* – a journey to which she had added respectability in the form of a change of name (Mrs not Miss – she had never married but who would find out?) to her hard learned housekeeping and culinary skills. And, at the old Manor House, at last she had found a place where she felt at home. And she had stayed ever since. Thirty-five years of happiness.

Only on one occasion had the past come to haunt her and that was the day the man who had just arrived as her new master came into the world. She put her foot back into her shoe and went to relight the candles which had sputtered out. Her gaze took in the young mistress, elbows on the table, enraptured by the reappearance of her long-lost brother and Sir Edward himself, the pain creases smoothed out by rest and her food, she hoped. A grown man and she hadn't seen him for seventeen years, six months, one week and two days. Her own dear Edward. She could remember the day that Edward had been born as if it was yesterday.

Mrs Jones had risen at her usual time on that morning and, whilst the kettle boiled, she went out into the yard and around the corner of the house to view the sea.

An almost full moon hung low, nearly touching the land it seemed, away to the west, in a brightening sky. Through her bedroom window earlier she had been able to dress by its chalky light but now it had increased in size and was both the colour and texture of buttermilk. Its daytime companion was filling the horizon with a velvety light which made every blade of grass crystal clear and Mrs Jones smiled with pleasure. A heavenly summer's day was promised in the dawn.

The kettle boiled, Mrs Jones had made a pot of tea for her mistress. Mrs Letitia Rowlands had arrived a fortnight ago, with her husband, Sir William, for a holiday from her other children before she was delivered of the child lying in womb. Mrs Jones had sent up the maid – what was her name? She recalled it was something most inappropriate – ah, yes, 'Charity'. That was the girl's name – Charity – and a less charitable person you wouldn't wish to meet! She had been sent from the village when the Master and Mistress had arrived and Mrs Jones had had the devil of a job getting the lazy girl to do anything. One of her first jobs was to attend to the Mistress with an early morning brew and Mrs Jones sent her up.

Meanwhile the housekeeper sat on a chair by her kitchen table and poured the stewed tea into a cup. She could afford to sit for a minute or two.

"Mrs Jones, I've taken up the tray but my lady says she doesn't want it because the baby is coming."

Mrs Jones leapt to her feet, forgetting to reprimand the maid for her sarcastic use of the term "my lady". All she heard were the words that the child was coming and she knew that the master was away from home!

"Quick, girl, run for the midwife. This baby is two weeks early and we'll need all the help we can get! Go, girl, go! Don't stand there, gaping!"

Mrs Jones threw the kettle back on the fire and then staggered upstairs. She had always been rather stout and her own good home cooking had meant she had gained weight in the last three years at the Manor House. By the time she had flung open the door to her mistress' bedchamber, labour seemed to be well underway. Mrs Jones had barely caught her breath when the baby arrived, with a lusty howl of protest.

"Take it," gasped Mrs Rowlands. "What is it?"

"A boy, ma'am. A beautiful baby boy." And he was. The spitting image of her own lost son. The same silken fair hair, when she washed the blood from him; the same perfectly oval face with no evidence of its squeezing in the birth canal; the same floppy legs and chubby arms. And yet this baby was alive with slate-blue eyes open and questioning; waving hands that clutched her own fingers and a voice that proclaimed he was here and here to stay! Mrs Jones fell in love with the child and held him with all the tenderness of a mother.

"Is he healthy, Jones?"

"Oh, yes." In her absorption with the tiny babe, she forgot to address her mistress properly.

"You must look after him."

"Me?"

"Yes, otherwise God will take him from you."

"Take him from you? What do you mean, ma'am?"

"I mustn't love him. I mustn't. Otherwise God will take him from me, as He has taken all the others."

"Oh, no, Mrs Rowlands, that can't be true!"

"It is true. Why else have so many of my children died? I prayed and prayed and then I understood: God wants me to put Him first. He doesn't want me to love these little ones more than Him."

Mrs Jones stared at her mistress. She saw the lank hair and sweat stained skin. She noticed the wet sheets, the blood and afterbirth, but she focused on the wild, staring eyes. Was her mistress deranged? Or was it just the strain of giving birth? She had no difficulty recalling the pain and upset at her own son's birth. The other woman was continuing:

"You wouldn't understand but I know I'm right, Jones. I'm not mad, you understand. But what other reason can there be? So many babies... So many lost before they are five. And this one is a boy. He must survive, because all my other sons have died. God has taken them from me, as a punishment for... I must spend as little time as possible with this baby. Then God will have no need to chastise me. He'll understand that I don't love anyone more than Him. You must care for this child, as if he was your very own."

Mrs Jones gathered the diminutive form into her arms. Was her mistress right? Was that why *her* son had died? Because God was punishing her for her sin? That sounded like her father speaking! No, what was she thinking of? Her sister had killed her baby.

"My very own," she had whispered. "I had a son once..."

"You had a son. What happened to him?"

"He was... died at birth."

"Oh, my dear woman, I am sorry. What was his name?"

Mrs Jones cradled the baby's head, almost unaware of what she was saying. No one had ever asked her this before; yet no one else had known about the baby since that awful day when her sister had smothered the tiny life spark.

"Patrick," she hesitated. "After his father."

"Well, you understand then. It's not a foolish fancy, you know. I loved my little William too much and he died at nine months... And then the twins at three months and Jane was only two years old. Richard – he was named after my father – he... he managed to reach his fifth birthday. They last longer if I don't love them. Baby Letitia was only three weeks old, you know. So you must care for this one. I'll get a wet nurse..."

"Oh, no, Mistress. Surely you can feed him yourself. God wouldn't be so cruel. He gave you the milk, after all."

Mrs Jones believed the woman was raving – some sort of childbed fever. Best to humour her, she decided. "I'll wash and swaddle him and then I'll help you. I don't know where that wretched girl is with the midwife."

"I must pray more." Mrs Rowlands' voice was weak. "Now God has given me a son, he must not die. William must have an heir. I will pray. Keep the child away from me."

She fell silent – was she praying?

Over the next hour, Mrs Jones watched her mistress carefully. Occasionally she checked the child, for once the bands enclosed him, he had quietened and gone to sleep, but each time she touched him, he was warm and pink. The housekeeper's care of Mrs Rowlands was no less tender. Although she would have said that she didn't know the mistress very well (their visits here were too infrequent and London maids were brought to wait on both master and mistress), she felt a bond with this woman, who had confided in her. She could see that Mrs Rowlands really believed what she had said, and Mrs Jones suspected that she had not told another living soul about her suspicions over why her children died. Mrs Jones' own opinion was much more prosaic: children died from all kinds of illnesses – that's why God usually gave large families. Look at her own family – six sisters lost in ten years!

In fact, with the passing days, reluctantly Mrs Jones found herself remembering her family more and more and wondering what had become of them. Daily, Mrs Rowlands repeated her beliefs until the servant, although not believing the truth of these allegations, at least had to admit that her mistress wasn't suffering from delusions just because she had given birth. There was no fever or other rantings except that the Lord Almighty would take the child if his mother loved him too much. In a way she had to admire the other woman for her piety. But, most of all, simply she revelled in having to care for the newborn child.

She appeared to have gained the mistress' trust. Not only had she dealt with all the necessary tasks for baby and mother in the time it took Charity to bring back the midwife, but she seemed to have a natural talent with Master Edward himself. Even when the nursemaid arrived from London, ten days later, the baby would often cry unless he was in Mrs Jones' arms and she spent hour after hour neglecting her housekeeping duties, to play nursery maid to the young master.

For her, Edward was her lost son come back from the dead. For the next three months, she had lived in paradise, until the family had returned to the capital city.

From that time onwards, Edward had held a special part of Mrs Jones' heart. Whenever the family resided in the Manor House, Mrs Jones would spoil the youthful heir, giving him special cakes and tarts she had made, cooking him his favourite recipes, packing little surprises for him to take on his outings. She loved all the children, especially when they were under a year old, but Edward's place in her affections was assured because of those first few days of his life.

When Sir William had banished his son, Mrs Jones had been starved of news – including why the Squire had fallen out with his only son. It was several months before she found out that Miss Penelope was in contact with him, and she waited with avid interest to hear any titbits of information about the lad. Thus it was that tonight her heart was pounding with excitement, and with her thoughts spinning around her head, she overruled her feverish brain and came back to the present. She should listen to his conversation with Miss Mariana in order to find out where he had been and what he had been doing recently. She'd already picked up that he had been wounded and convalescing in hospital; she would feed him up because he looked quite sallow and thin from hospital gruel. She heaved her tired frame away from the sink and moved towards the table. She must urge him to eat more. No real mother could have shown more concern!

EDWARD

Edward only had a hazy recollection of the conversation which had occurred last night home. He was glad to have chosen to rest in the homely surroundings of the servants' domain. His sister, perched on a chair next to him, seemed to be at ease.

In the beginning, when he sat by the fire, relief flooded through him because the weight was taken off his stump. However, with the passage of time, his muscles seemed to set rigid and every part of his body ached and much of what was said didn't penetrate his pain filled mind. He could recall the words bouncing back and forth between Mariana and the housekeeper – something about "a great brute of a beast". That turned out to be referring to the horse Mariana rode. He had shared how he had wondered if his stepmother's child was a boy or girl. Yes, that was when Mrs Jones had informed him that often Mariana behaved like a boy! Subsequently the comment had come about his sister's behaviour.

Mariana herself had alternated between sadness and enthusiasm throughout the evening. Her eyes had shone when she had told him about the "mystery man from the sea". He was called "Jack" by her, "because he looks like someone called 'Jack'!" Naturally this wasn't the first case of loss of memory he'd come across in his life, but he'd let the girl chatter on. Anything to keep away the occasional tear which rolled down her cheeks when reference was made to their father. He had tried to distract her by changing the conversation. His grief was not raw like hers; he had mourned the loss of Sir William all those years ago.

There were periods of silence too but with no constraint even when they were alone together. Where had the others gone? The maid must have left to fetch the lad from the stables and Mrs Jones was searching in the larder. Wilson was bringing him some ale.

Ah, the food! What a choice he was offered! Cold leg of lamb, pheasant, cooked pork, mutton and samphire, hare pie, anchovies, leeks in Mrs Jones' special sauce, cheese… He'd begged for mercy. It appeared that the housekeeper's motherly instincts extended from her care of Mariana to himself now he was home and when she heard about his convalescence, she'd bustled about all the more!

His sister had been very sensitive to his feelings. She came across as very forthright, not afraid to tackle any issue: she asked how he had lost his leg; why he had quarrelled with their father; where he'd been all these years and fought both the maid and housekeeper who kept nagging her to go to bed! Nevertheless, she had been prepared to tell lies in a *sotto voce* in order to comfort and reassure him, recounting to him how their father had talked about his long-lost son. When he had shaken his head in disbelief, Wilson had corroborated her story. What had been his words?

"Sir William spoke of his own very foolish behaviour towards you; he said how, at the time, he was beside himself with grief and that you were just a young boy. Of course, I'm not saying he talked of you at *first*, but then he ignored Miss Mariana here for nigh on a year. No, but he felt your loss once he had come out of his terrible despair."

Nonetheless he hadn't been able to believe the loyal retainer! For none of this explained why his father had never written, but Wilson had an answer to this too. Something to do with pride and how difficult it is to admit "you are wrong and especially to a man who is younger than you, Sir." Edward had acknowledged that he had been proud too. Letters can go in either direction.

Part of the conversation was about his ability to understand and speak Welsh. That was when the stable lad had appeared with his bags. The boy's faltering English was matched only by his own stumbling Welsh. He hadn't practised it for years.

When he'd finished eating, Mariana had perked up. She had wanted him to tell her about all the places he'd visited. She had jumped out of her seat when he told her he was a captain and seemed determined to romanticise the whole job. Little did she know of all the responsibilities he carried! Even the War she found thrilling and he hadn't enlightened her about some of the sights he'd seen and the horrendous loss of life.

His sister, Margaret, had cropped up too. But that had brought them back to the sad arrangements for the funeral and Mariana had covered her face with her small, slender hands. That time he had been unable to turn the conversation to lighter matters. Instead he had told her that now he was here, he would take charge and she wasn't to worry her pretty head about it. She was far too young to have all this thrust on her shoulders! Of course, Hughes had gone and there was some new Parson, Reverend Owen, who he'd promised to visit today… Today… He sat upright away from the pillows.

Swinging himself out of the bed, he recalled how difficult it had been to get up the stairs last eve and how he had wondered out loud if he would have to make his bedchamber on the ground floor in future. He had been forced to allow Wilson (a man old enough to be his father by his haggard looks!) and the stable lad to assist him. Wilson seemed to think that it was his master's pride which stopped him from asking for help. Pride! After all those doctors had poked and prodded him! No, it was his assessment of the strength of the stooped servant, although he had no concerns about the lad. While they had moved up, with Elin being the light-bearer, Mariana behind and a man on each side, he had expressed his hope that it was only the extended hours of riding which had set him back and not something more sinister. He stretched his legs; yes, this morning he did feel better.

And then there was the final scene of the evening. That stuck out in his memory. The motley group of people had filed along the corridor to the Hall Chamber when Mariana had declared in a shaky voice:

"I'll leave you now, Edward. I'm sure you'd rather be alone. Goodnight, brother, and I'm so glad you have come home."

Edward had freed himself from his human crutches and caught Mariana in a fast embrace.

"Goodnight, my dear, and may thanks for the welcome you've given me," he whispered. That was when he had known. His heart had plummeted, for he became aware that although he had tried and tried to forget his stepmother, he continued to love her; and her daughter's remarkable resemblance to her made him love her too. Yet this love was as impossible as the last, if not more so, for this Mariana was his sister. If the elder Mariana had left his father, or she had been widowed, he might have been able to marry her, but no priest in the land would allow him to marry his own sister. Having barely arrived, he acknowledged, for everyone's sake, that he would be forced to leave again as soon as he could, before he made a fool of himself for a second time!

He reckoned that it was these thoughts which dragged him down into depression. It was scarcely relieved by the light of day. He rose from the bed.

Not much more than an hour later, after bolting down a gargantuan meal, he set off in the farm wagon into Holyhead. He was accompanied by a lanky young man, brother to the stable lad who had helped him last yesterday (Evan was his name), and a large selection of his brothers and sisters, some of whom sat in a line along the tail-plate swinging their legs.

Edward's private reflections turned to his attractive sister once the cart moved off. He had insisted that she stay at home, since he judged it would be unseemly for her to be seen abroad this soon after their father's death. Meekly she had agreed, returning to her own bedchamber with a dejected look on her face. Wilson had explained to him that it was hard for all of them, and not least Mariana, to be with him when he resembled his father to such a degree. That had made him look in the glass but he couldn't see it himself!

At least his leg was much more comfortable after a night of rest. Mrs Jones had produced some marvellous ointment which she used for her arthritis. It was concocted by an ancient crone called Mrs Williams, who apparently knew hundreds of remedies for all manner of ills. Wilson had administered it to Edward, late the previous evening, and now his peg-leg was fitted snugly into place with only one sore spot rubbing.

Trem-y-Môr (he knew it meant View-of-the-Sea) was fortunate to be on the route from Four Mile Bridge to Holyhead and therefore the road, although rutted, was wide enough for the wagon. Edward was aware that the responsibility for the upkeep of the roads fell on each parish. Once a year, the parish vestry appointed an unpaid Surveyor of the Highways who supervised the work. Each landlord was obliged to give a certain amount of labour per year and each individual man in the parish could be asked to give six days' labour every year without any remuneration and was expected to provide his own tools and even horses and carts.

Edward recalled that when he was last here those six days had amounted to something of an annual holiday, at least for the agricultural workers in this rural area. Some men, unwilling to lose their week's wage, sent their wives and children in their stead and thus a merry crowd of all ages would arrive in a jubilant mood, supposedly to work. When Edward was a child, he had joined the band of shrieking children, whose main intent was a game of 'Bear Leader'. One chosen child was the bear (who crawled around on hands and knees with a rope around his neck), whilst it was the job of his blindfolded partner to lead and protect him from all the others.

Edward smiled with the recollection that most of the games ended in a fist fight and maybe that had been the unconscious aim in the first place! Since the adults used the occasion for an exchange of gossip, at the end of the day, the road seldom looked any different!

Edward noticed that the roads hadn't improved much since his childhood; therefore their journey was rather slow. However, their progress was hindered not only because of the state of the pot-holed road after the storm, but also because halfway there, they became stuck behind a farmer driving his cattle along in a sluggish, bellowing mass of flicking tails and fat udders swinging back and forth.

Edward found that Evan was silent for the whole journey. Was his companion overawed by the master travelling with him in a common farm vehicle, or was it the hackneyed problem of language? Neither man was fluent enough in the other one's language. Consequently, Edward allowed his eyes to rest upon Holyhead Mountain, hump backed, alone, marking the end of the land, like a forgotten signpost.

Eventually, the group from the Manor House parted from the cattle on the edge of the village and, after passing an inn called '*The Welsh House*', they wended their way up through the scattered dwellings to the Vicarage.

As Edward stepped from the wagon, a furious shower of rain began. Hurriedly he limped to the grand front door with a wave of his hand to Evan. Providentially, he had already arranged to meet the lad again at the market cross, so there was no need to stand talking in the downpour.

The door was answered by a timid maid, who was very thin with round eyes. She ushered Edward into a spacious hall, where he waited whilst the maid ascertained whether the Parson was at home. Edward shook the raindrops from his cloak, removed his hat, stamped his one boot and glanced around. It was an ill-lit cheerless room, with only one rug near an empty fireplace and an ornate clock.

"The Parson will see you now, Sir," the maid announced, returning through a door to Edward's left. He was irritated that the girl had not asked his name; nor did she take his hat.

He was shown into a dim room, made darker by the overcast sky. The chamber was bereft of all furniture, except for a wide desk which squatted on the uncarpeted floor along with three chairs. One of these was high-backed with no padding and it stood behind the desk. The other two, set side by side, for visitors presumably, were made of plain wood, unadorned by any carving and were likewise without seat cushions. Seeing another empty grate, Edward felt unwelcome for the second time.

The Vicar himself added to the atmosphere of inhospitality, for he was standing, immobile, by the window with his half-turned back towards Edward. In his hand was a sizeable leather-bound book which he was studying. He seemed unaware that someone had entered the room or perhaps whatever he was reading was totally engrossing.

What was wrong with the man that he was behaving in such an ill-mannered way? Edward waited for his host to speak first, but as the silence stretched between them, he grew impatient. After all, he had many other arrangements to make that day.

"Good-day to you, Parson." His voice echoed around the scantily furnished room. "I have come to arrange the funeral of…"

"Have you a body?" The Vicar spoke without looking up.

"I beg your pardon!"

"Has your relative's body been found?"

"Of course it's been found! It was never lost!" Edward snapped. He was still talking to the man's back. No fire, no lights, no drink or refreshments offered, no seat to rest on and now this uncivil man was asking nonsensical questions!

"Never lost, eh? That's very good. Well, the problem is that I'm very busy. Over one hundred lives at the last count were lost from the two ships. **'And that day, one hundred and thirty were killed…'** Bodies are appearing every hour and we are being forced to lay them out in the church until they are identified. So I have been thinking maybe I will conduct a single memorial service…"

Edward drew himself up to his full height and tapped his stick on the floor.

"Reverend Owen, isn't it? Are you suggesting that my father's funeral is conducted amidst a service dedicated to 130 other people, in a church stacked high with makeshift coffins?" His words were strained from the effort of curbing his temper.

The Vicar turned a page in his book and then slowly looked at Edward for the first time.

"I know it is a distressing time for you. Our Lord Jesus was acquainted with grief: **'When Jesus therefore saw her weeping, and the Jews also weeping which came with her, He groaned in the spirit, and was**

troubled.' However, I am just one man with one pair of hands and one voice. I cannot possibly conduct individual funerals after a disaster like this one."

"Individual funerals! Individual funerals! You are insulting my father. I had heard that you had called upon my father recently, yet you now treat him like a drowned sailor. Well, good day to you. I have never been treated with such insensitivity in all my life, and you a vicar! I shall be contacting your Bishop and arranging for another cleric to conduct my father's funeral. Fortunately, the family grave is not here in…"

"Wait, Sir, wait!" The Vicar laid the heavy book on his desk and scurried around to reach the offended man whilst Edward put his hand on the door handle. "I do beg your pardon. I don't… don't seem to have caught your name. Who was your father?"

Edward scowled.

"My father is…was Sir William Rowlands."

"Sir William Rowlands! *The* Sir William Rowlands? Of *Trem-y-Môr*? The Squire? My dear Sir, I do offer you my most humble apologies. I had, of course, heard of the demise of your father. He was a dear, respected friend, but I had no idea that… that he had a… a son! Sir, I was expecting one of his daughters or one of their husbands to come to me. Do please take a seat." Hastily the Vicar reached for the bell pull hanging down the side of the fireplace. "I didn't realise who you were. I shall order some… some… What would you like, Sir? Brandy? I have it sent from Bristol, y'know."

"Nothing, thank you," Edward replied icily. "I neither require your seat nor your drink. I am shocked that a clergyman can treat another fellow…"

"Oh, Sir, Sir, you must forgive me. I have been inundated with relatives as well as local people bringing in more and more bodies and I've seen Mr Lloyd several times and the…"

"I want to hear no more." Edward was finding his anger, now aroused, was hard to pacify.

"Oh, Sir, you must understand I have had no sleep these past few days and I did not realise who you were…"

"Then your behaviour is even more despicable: that you treat people of different rank with different behaviour! I'm sure the good Lord showed impartiality to any…" Edward stopped, aware of his own hypocrisy: he was asking for favours for his family because of their position in society.

There was a moment of complete silence; Edward began to feel foolish.

The other man's anguished face suggested that he was searching for a way out of this awkwardness too.

"Sir Rowlands, I…"

"Captain. I'm a captain in the Fleet and, as yet, am not used to being called 'Sir Rowlands'." His tone was brusque but quieter.

"Captain Rowlands, pray be seated. I cannot apologise enough. It was entirely my mistake. Your father was a dear, dear friend of mine. In fact, as you remarked, I had been to see him only a few days ago. Did he speak to you of the matter about which I called on him? We spoke at some length on…"

"Speak to me? No, of course not! My father was already… had passed away by the time I arrived." Edward made a move towards the door. He would leave right away. He did not like this man, who could turn so quickly from rude to obsequious; hands together, a slight bow in his posture, like an overzealous waiter. What an unpleasant character!

Just at that moment, the same maid who had answered the front door entered the room.

"At last, Jennett! What a long time you have taken to come!" The Vicar was short with his servant. Edward reckoned the other man was castigating himself for the difficult start to the meeting. "Fetch us some glasses, girl!"

"Not for me, Parson. I require nothing."

"Oh, Sir… Captain, please don't refuse my hospitality. There are many things for us to discuss and you will… will want to rest your leg. Did you lose it in the War?"

"You leave my damned leg out of this!" snarled Edward. "I came here to arrange a funeral to bid farewell to my father. I do not, I repeat, *do not*, want or need a drink." Edward frowned at the quaking maid, who shrunk back from him.

The Vicar shooed the girl out of the room with his outstretched hand. Returning to face Edward, his attitude changed again. Much to Edward's surprise he spoke boldly:

"Captain Rowlands, naturally I will be most willing to discuss every detail of the funeral with you, and the very best funeral you shall have. For, after all, aren't I soon to become one of the family?"

"One of the family?" Edward repeated. For the second time he wondered if this man was sane.

"Why, yes. The matter your father and I were discussing, when I last saw him, was the marriage of his daughter to me… and… and he agreed that we could meet again to set a date and…"

"His daughter. Which daughter?"

"His youngest daughter, of course. Miss Mariana."

"Mariana?" Edward's tetchiness vanished in disbelief. "She didn't mention it, although she knew I was coming here." Surely this could not be true! Had she said something last night when his thinking was befuddled with tiredness? He shook his head.

"Ah, she is a well bred girl and she knows it would not be seemly to bring up a joyful subject such as a wedding at a time like this. And she is surely also overcome with grief, I should think. **'And they lifted up their voice and wept.'** Miss Mariana has suffered a double blow. First she lost her… her betrothed and now her father. We will have to postpone the wedding; I have already waited and I can wait a little longer."

"You discussed this with my father and he agreed?" Edward's heart was freezing at the very idea of his winsome, lively sister married to this… this fat toad! Well, snake might be a better description but a snake that had just swallowed its prey!

"Oh, yes, we talked at length. Your father was… hmm… he had… He seemed to know he was near to entering into the heavenly kingdom and he wanted to see his youngest daughter settled."

Edward watched the Vicar's face closely. He was suspicious, although he couldn't have said why. The man's manner kept changing. He'd got rid of the maid and, without warning, was talking about marriage. Was this all a tangle of lies? By his earlier question, he had verified that Edward had had no opportunity to converse with his father even on his deathbed and therefore was unable to contradict him. Yet what would be the point of lying? Edward had no time to think clearly because the Vicar was harping on: "Verily, none of us know the time that God has appointed to call us to Himself. **'But God said unto him, "Thou fool, this night, thy soul shall be required of thee."'** Yes, Miss Mariana wasn't… isn't… my… my wife, but she is as good as… At least, Sir William and I had spoken…"

"Had he spoken with her about it?" Edward's thoughts were still trying to grasp the idea of Mariana and this odd man in any sort of relationship, least of all marriage. What had they in common?

"Ah." The Vicar walked back to the window, apparently in deep thought. Edward could see beyond him to the sky outside. It was a patchy blue but the passing away of the rain clouds had not really helped the gloom inside the house. The Vicar went on: "I wonder if that is why she has not mentioned it to you. At all events though, I do know that Sir William was well pleased with my family and background and present circumstances. My great-grand…"

"Yes, yes," interrupted Edward ruthlessly. He was not going to listen to this fancy any longer, for fancy it must be! He had met men like this one before and had the distinct impression that the Vicar was taking advantage of his own ignorance. He continued to be unable to quite work out where the truth lay – the repeated hesitations seemed to indicate that all was not quite as it seemed, but it could just be the way the Vicar talked. His archaic speech and Bible-quoting did nothing to endear him to Edward.

Edward's mind was spinning. Events were happening too quickly for him to cope with them. Firstly there was the terrible disappointment of missing speaking to his father by just one day. Secondly he had this strange notion in his head that somehow he loved the young Mariana – yet how could he love a woman he had only just met? Thirdly came the knowledge that his love, if love it was, would have to remain unfulfilled because the woman was his sister. Fourthly he had concluded that the consequence of all this was that he would have to make his home somewhere else – but where? Fifthly this: the shock that possibly Mariana was betrothed already to this annoying man! And underneath all these other problems: the responsibility of arranging his father's funeral and perhaps having to take up some duties in the area because he had inherited the job of local Squire. No, enough was enough! He had no time to sort out all his feelings but one thing was sure: he was not going to allow Mariana to marry a man who was old enough to have sired her; that was too similar to the fate of her mother, a circumstance which had already caused him such pain. He would never approve of that kind of marriage!

He faced the other fellow head on and announced rashly:

"I'm afraid I don't want to hear all about your credentials because you will not be marrying my sister."

The Vicar returned his look; steely grey eyes did not waver in his ruddy face. Edward looked away first. Why had he said such a thing? Now he was at a real disadvantage; he had not spoken without thought for many years. Had panic overtaken him or tiredness confused him or… or love? The Vicar took a step towards him; Edward gripped his stick firmly, ready to do battle. Immediately he sensed this man would not give up such a woman as Mariana without a fight. After all, he himself didn't want to! He would have to keep one step ahead of him. He noticed the Vicar was screwing up his eyes, as if assessing him. There seemed no doubt that they would lock swords. The Vicar undid the lowest two buttons of his coat and inquired:

"Might I be permitted to ask why? We have only met once, yet you are prepared to overrule your father's judgement. If it is because of my behaviour at the beginning of our conversation, then I can only reiterate what I said before…"

Edward stopped listening. Already he was regretting his impulsive statement. His opponent had struck the initial blow and it had gone home! Straightaway he could see that he would have to think of a plausible reason to explain his strong dismissal of this man's proposal. For a start, the Vicar was second only to the Squire in the local community and many would consider he was a 'good match' for a chaste girl like Mariana – the youngest daughter in the family. No point saying that he, Edward, was now Mariana's nearest male kin and had taken an almost instant dislike to the man. Any argument about Mariana not being consulted could be easily demolished because he just wasn't in possession of all the facts; maybe Mariana *had* been consulted and simply had not disclosed it. His brain raced on, thinking of several ideas which he then rejected. At last he responded loudly (as if the person with the loudest voice would win),

"Because… because she is going to marry someone else. He's… he is a close friend of mine. She and he met not long ago and he fell in love with her but… but…" Edward's imagination failed. How had he got himself into this mess?

"But there was her love of Mr Wynne to consider," suggested the Vicar.

Edward looked at the bulky man, his figure outlined against the window. Did he know that this story was concocted? Why was he helping him now that his words had dried up? Or did he innocently believe him? The very point which had been raised – that he wasn't well enough acquainted with the Vicar – was working against him. He was unable to read the other fellow's face. He could feel the force of the other man's personality trying to win. Nevertheless, he came back determinedly in his own private argument; there were some hard facts that were true and he did have a certain amount of power. Mariana came under his guardianship and no guardian in his right mind would let his charge marry this man. Why?

The question screamed in his head again. No logical answer came, only a primeval instinct. He wished that he hadn't started the lie but he'd had to think quickly. No alternative offered itself. He persevered:

"Yes. However, when he – Septimus is his name – discovered that Mr Wynne was dead, then he begged me to convey... to convey his wish to marry her. This is the very reason why I came to North Wales. Unfortunately, I had no idea that my father... my father..."

"That your father had, in fact, made other plans?"

"Mariana knows nothing about these plans that my father made with you," Edward insisted, gambling that if Mariana had known and was happy she would have told him when they were sitting at the kitchen table the previous evening. But surely, he reasoned silently, she wouldn't want to marry this pompous man! Septimus was, in truth, dead, but the Vicar did not know that! How had he got himself into this mess? he asked himself for a second time. He was a captain of a ship, used to having to make quick decisions in the midst of combat and yet in this situation he was like a child called up to explain himself to the headmaster. Maybe if he could play for time... Yes, he had to speak with his sister and find out if she was aware of this proposal. He mustn't let this bully overwhelm him. He persisted:

"In spite of the tragic news I found when I arrived yesterday, I was able to tell Mariana of my original reason for coming this morning. Naturally, she had not contemplated marriage with Septimus because... because she loved Mr Wynne." Edward longed to wipe his brow. Did his story sound plausible? Was the Vicar taken in? Why had he started on this discussion? He should have left when he had intended to, half an hour ago!

"David, you mean?"

Edward watched the other man. This must be a pit dug for him to fall into, but what could he do? He didn't know anything about Mariana's betrothed, except that he had died and it was this man who had informed him of this! Had that been a trap too? He had no choice – he was caught in a dead end with nowhere to run! He had better not hesitate any longer.

"Yes, David Wynne." Was that a smirk hovering on the Vicar's lips? "What a tragedy his death was! But Mariana is considering my friend, although, as you said, nothing can be done whilst she is in mourning. She is too upset at the moment. We have agreed that after the funeral, we will spend some..."

"Where does your friend live?"

"Portsmouth."

"And he met Mariana there… or… or here?"

Edward sat down suddenly; he felt exhausted and his leg was aching again. He *must* escape and there was only one way he could do it: terminate this ridiculous conversation.

"Here, my man, where else? I think that is enough talk about my sister. Shall we decide on the arrangements for the funeral? I have a whole host of other things to do today. And, I'm sure, you do too!"

PENELOPE AND ROBERT

Penelope Roberts pushed open the door at the back of her home using her shoulder and stepped down into her kitchen, with a basket of newly-collected eggs carefully held under one arm and a jug of warm milk in her other hand. Slowly she moved across the blue flagstones to the great table in the centre of the room. This oak table, made from one solid piece of wood, had stood in this precise spot for longer than anyone could remember, and some believed that it had been built with the house. Penelope's long beige skirt brushed against its turned legs when she placed both her burdens on its surface.

Quickly, now that she was free of her fragile load, Penelope went to the dresser, which was overflowing with large and small pewter dishes, and caught up several plates and noggins which she then set around the table. Today she was in a hurry for, immediately after serving the first meal of the day, she was away to see her bereaved sister.

"Robbie! David!" she called at the door leading to the rest of the farmhouse, hastening past it on her way to the fire to hang the kettle on the hook. Above the fire, on the mantelshelf, were various Toby jugs, a mortar and pestle and four brass candlesticks, their candles low, the flames spluttering in the hot, melted wax. She stood on tiptoe to blow them out. She had lit these candles when she came down before dawn, ready to go and perform her chores outside, and she had forgotten to extinguish them, such was her haste. This morning, she had kept her tasks to a minimum – just milking the cows and feeling amongst the straw beneath the hens for the brown, speckled eggs. Usually on this day of the week, after her meal, she would be churning the buttermilk to make butter or more likely during this month of the year, beginning the process of making cheese. However, with a death in the family…

Yesterday, she had spent all day washing the clothes, for her maid, Mary, was ill in bed. She made the 'soap' herself by pouring water through the ash from the fire, allowing it to trickle down past the cold white ash to a layer of hay and on to the stones before running out from the bottom of tub. From there it flowed along a groove in a piece of wood and into a bowl – yellowy green and ready to anoint the clothes. Difficult stains were soaked in their own urine, collected from the chamber pots and allowed to ferment. Once the initial processes had started in the yard she had gathered up the clothes in a basket, and staggered down to the river. There she scrubbed and beat, pummelled and rinsed all the materials, enjoying the icy stream pulsing past her bare legs as she sweated at the strenuous task. At least, in the summer, she might meet a neighbour or two doing their monthly wash and exchange gossip. Winter or scant daily washes entailed getting water from the well, and squashing the dirty linen into a wooden tub; usually, on these occasions, her hands, right up to her wrists, were red and raw. She had thrown the garments out to dry on nearby bushes and even on the grass of the top meadow, only to have to fetch them in within the hour, when the rain started. Last evening, she had flung some of the wetter items over the settle and along the wide seats on each side of the massive chimney piece. Nimbly she caught up the dry, stiff clothes and, folding them hastily, laid them in a tottering pile on her own chair, knowing that she would not be sitting on it today. She would have to press some of the more decorative articles of clothing when she returned from her sister's house; the working clothes could be worn as they were – creased and rough.

Spoons and knives, plates and noggins arranged around the table, she stopped her frantic activity to carefully pull a crusty loaf from the oven. Each evening, excepting Sundays, she made up a batch of bread, allowing the dough to rise overnight. Her first duty each morning was to lift the loaves into the oven to cook whilst she was in the cowshed. She loved kneading the dough, hitting its warm, soft body, pulling its sticky, stringy depths, all the while watching her children amusing themselves with homemade toys near the hearth and her husband smoking his pipe and sitting in the big oak chair opposite the settle. Kneading helped to release the frustrations of the day; any pent-up anger or feeling of injustice or bitterness which had sprung up: all such things were relinquished and rolled into the bread. Then, wiping her fingers on a damp cloth, she would leave the dough to rise and would do some knitting, or play with the children, or feed the baby. Then, there was more punching and stretching of the dough until it was ready to divide into the bread-pans, making several loaves and maybe some buns. Once a week, she would bake some *bara brith*, cheese bread or cinnamon loaf: some variation to add to the daily quota of bread which disappeared down her husband's and children's throats. Of course, that was without mentioning Thomas Weller, their handyman and his wife, Mary, and little ones, and feeding any travellers passing by!

Now, placing one loaf in the centre of the table and the others on the window-shelf to cool, she plucked at a wisp of hair tickling her face and tucked it back carefully into the knot tied loosely at the nape of her neck.

"Robbie! David, hurry up!" She repeated her call while the kettle began to hiss.

She gave the flummery or *llymru* a stir when she passed by. She had been given some honey on her last visit to *Trem-y-Môr* and so she added a final spoonful to the gently simmering pot. All her family liked sweet flummery!

The back door opened and in came her husband, pulling his stained, working smock over his head. His feet were stockinged, since he had abandoned his clogs outside the door, in order that the mud and manure would stay in the farmyard and not smear across his wife's flagged floor. He allowed the door to close on the two farm dogs, who sniffed the air, hopeful of some scraps, before lying down, resignedly, on the doorstep, which they did every day.

Robert Roberts, brown-haired with hazel eyes, wrapped his arms around his wife as she reached for the salt cellar on the mantelshelf. He kissed the vulnerable base of her neck beneath her coiled hair. Penelope, clasping the salt cellar in her hand, turned within the circle of his arms and offered her lips to him. Robert held her tightly, his mouth on hers, his body pressed against her smaller frame. At last, after twelve years of marriage, she had accepted that he did not see the awful ravage done to her face by smallpox and she was relaxed within his embrace.

"I love you," he whispered against her pock-marked skin.

"I love you too."

"What is that sticking into my ribs?"

"The salt," she smiled.

"*Mam! Mam*, shall I bring the *baban*?" A child's voice came from the upper floor.

Robert released his wife.

"Are you taking Sarah with you?" he remarked.

"Yes, she would need feeding well before I was back. And you can't feed her! Where's Llewelin?"

"He's gone to check the calf. You know how devoted he is to it."

"Well, he'd better not get too attached for we can't keep…"

"*Mam! Mam!*"

"Hush, Robbie. Don't make such a noise. Is she asleep?" Penelope raised her voice to let her son hear.

"You mean 'still asleep', my love," twinkled her husband.

"She's got her eyes open," Robbie informed them.

"I'd better go," Robert said. "He'll drop her on those steep steps. There's no point in bringing the cot, is there? Hey, you need to stir the *llymru*."

"*Llymru!* Now look what you've done! I've burnt it," cried his wife.

"I like burnt *llymru*…"

"All this kissing when I'm cooking…"

Robert put his finger to Penelope's lips. He gazed at her face with adoration in his eyes.

"Don't refuse me. I can't help it. I love you so much," he breathed.

"Get along," admonished Penelope with a grin, "and bring the little one. Don't bother with the cot today."

There was a thump from above their heads.

"Robbie!" Penelope ran to the door, the flummery forgotten. However, there were no cries of pain.

"It's all right, *Mam*. It was only the pot," shouted Robbie.

"The pot!"

"Yes, I moved it to reach…"

"Leave her, your *Tad's* coming."

"I can manage…"

* * *

"Leave her, Robbie." Robert's voice demanded obedience. Two swift strides later and he was in the cramped hallway between the kitchen and front parlour. Up the ladder to the area above, within seconds, Robert was standing with his head amongst the rafters. He had divided the upper floor himself into two rooms, split by a lightweight, wooden partition. The larger half was his and Penelope's, shared at the moment by baby Sarah; the confined half was where the boys slept, three to the bed, warmed by the chimney at their side.

Both rooms were open to the thatch, with sloping roofs and narrow windows. The boys had a low bed with short legs; thus it could be pushed to the very edge of the angled roof. Robert and Penelope's bed was full-sized and had been built by the village cooper for them, actually in the loft and therefore it could neither be moved up nor down through the hole in the floor. Next to the bed was a sturdy cot on rockers and there, blankets kicked off, blue eyes shining, mouth open in a watery gurgle, was Sarah. Robbie was standing by her side, indignation written on his face.

"I'd have managed," he pouted.

"I know, son," soothed Robert, ruffling the boy's hair, "but you wouldn't have wanted to hurt her if she fell. Is David awake?"

"He is, but he's pretending he isn't."

Robert scooped up his daughter in one arm, including a white blanket, which hung crookedly down and, taking Robbie's hand, tiptoed into the other room. There, amidst a tumble of bedclothes, was a child, curled-up, with just a foot sticking out from beneath the quilt. Robert let go of Robbie's hand and, putting a finger of warning to his lips, bent over and tickled the protruding foot. It shot back under the quilt like a tortoise's head into its shell, and a muffled giggle was heard. Robert squatted down. He put his hand into the hole where the foot had disappeared, grasped the heel and dragged it gently until a whole bare leg and one rounded, bare buttock showed.

"It's time to get up, David," commanded Robert.

"Me… non't… to…" was the inaudible reply.

"You must. *Mam's* got to go and you're to help me today."

Immediately the leg swivelled around and David's brown hair appeared, bent low over his shins, his cheeky face peering from beneath the quilt reminiscent of an old woman from under her shawl. He came face to face with his father's knee and his sister's interested eyes.

"Sarah," announced David. Then, shrugging off the bedclothes, he stood up, his rucked-up nightshirt falling back down to his ankles.

"Get dressed quickly! The *llymru* is ready. Robbie, could you hold Sarah whilst I get down the ladder?"

Robbie beamed.

"Of course, *Tad*."

Robert balanced the tiny body in the arms of his gratified son and climbed through the hole in the floor. He stood on the third rung, his head remaining poked through to the upper room, and reached for Sarah, and then turned and carried her to the kitchen. Robbie was down in a minute, with the agility of a monkey; barely had he sat on a low, four-legged stool when he was joined by his brother, David, with his shirt on inside out and his breeches undone, but nevertheless looking very pleased with himself.

Without thinking, Penelope redressed her youngest son with one hand while she served the meal.

"I think we had better get started. Llew will be all day," she suggested to her husband. He took his place at the head of the table, the baby cradled safely in the curve of his arm. Sarah's rosebud lips broke into a smile whenever she caught her father's eyes.

"Sarah stinky," complained David, climbing on his stool.

"You smelt at her age too, my lad," mused Robert.

"I can't do everything, David, my love," remonstrated Penelope. "I can't wash Sarah *and* make your meal. Do you want milk?"

"No milk. Horrid milk," declared David.

"Milk is delicious," contradicted Robert. He began to shovel food into his mouth.

"Can I cut the bread?" mumbled Robbie, his tone suggesting that he knew what the answer was going to be before he spoke.

"No," answered both his parents firmly at the same time.

"I'll leave Llew's food in the pan. Now, Robbie, I'll cut you some bread." Penelope left the fire, her face red from its heat. "Is Thomas coming in to eat, Robert?"

"No. He's gone to help Mary. Then she can be here when you leave. He says that she is much better today and…"

"Oh, I wish she didn't have to get out of bed but I have no choice. I must go and see Mariana; she must be grieving."

"Don't you worry about Mary. I'll make sure she doesn't do too much. Thomas and I can cope without women for one day, you know!"

"I do know. I just feel torn between…"

"I understand," nodded Robert.

"Would you like me to take Sarah?"

"No, I'm managing. You start your meal; you've got a long journey ahead of you," Robert replied, glancing at his daughter. She gurgled.

"Don't take that much butter, David," Penelope rebuked her youngest son. "Today, you two must be good whilst I am gone and listen to your father."

"Why do you have to go? *Taid* doesn't need you; he's dead, isn't he?" This from Robbie.

"*Taid* dead," echoed his young brother.

"Robbie! David!" Robert's uncompromising voice brought a pucker to David's mouth. "Your mother has to go and see Aunty Mariana. She's all on her own now and I'm sure she's very sad. So, let's hear no more talking. You've started your meal, I hope. All I want to hear is the sound of chewing."

Robert's eyes met Penelope's over the silent children's heads in a question, "Are you all right?"

* * *

Penelope gave a half smile in assent. In the middle of the day, yesterday, with Robert working in the field, a messenger had brought the news about Sir William. She had held inside her feelings, in order not to upset the children; she cried only once she had gone to bed and was in her husband's arms. She had to acknowledge that she had not been very close to her father in these latter years (for Mariana had taken up much of his time), but sorrow tugged at her heart; also she was grateful to him for helping Robert and her buy the farm when they were first married.

Mary, the maid, arrived just as Robert finished his meal. She looked pale but insisted that she was well enough to get up and take charge in her mistress's absence. Her own child asleep in a shawl, she found room for David on her lap, which enabled Penelope to hurry away and change her own clothes and her daughter's too. Within a short time, she was ready to go and the family grouped outside to wish her "Godspeed".

Normally Penelope would sit behind her husband on the broad back of the mighty carthorse, Sandy. However, unlike other farmers' wives, Penelope had learnt to ride as a child. Therefore, if she ever ventured out without her husband, like today, she preferred to ride Sandy rather than hitch him to the wagon and drive along the twisting roads. Across the horse's neck was slung a bag containing a few baby clothes for Sarah, and strapped to Penelope's front, was Sarah herself, wrapped in a cocoon of blankets, fast asleep, full of mother's milk, her eyes tightly closed and her butterfly breath showing misty in the early morning air. At the ready, for the journey would take some time, was Penelope's knitting. She had become very skilled at using her knitting needles when she rode, for her mount never galloped like her sister's horse, Mars. He plodded along with scarcely a change of height to his muscular back. No, her only problem today was that the sky had given birth to a line of black-tipped clouds and she did not want to get drenched.

Robbie, Llewelin and David sat astride the stone wall that separated the yard from the nearby fields. Robert touched his wife's foot.

"Take care. Send her my love. Come back to me as soon as you can," he pleaded.

"It may not be tonight but…"

"I know, dearest. Don't worry about us; we'll manage without you, won't we boys?"

"Yes, *Tad*," chorused the boys.

"Look after my beautiful daughter," Robert instructed.

"I will."

"And your beautiful self."

"Hush, Robert!"

"I shall miss you." This in an undertone.

"And I you. On, Sandy, on."

The horse began to move and the two elder boys leapt from their perch to accompany their mother down the muddy path to the crossroads.

"Me, too. Me, too," shrieked David, waving his legs. Penelope saw her husband lift him down with a warning:

"Mind the horse's feet, little one. Llew, wait for your brother."

"Come on, Shortie," teased the nine-year-old, racing along the path.

"Not short. Me's not short. Me's coming. Wait. Wait," wailed David.

Penelope watched her sons; in the end, David was level with his brothers, in front of the placid horse. He and Robbie were pretending to ride, their legs raised in prancing steps, their voices in unison: "Clip, clop. Clip, clop. Gee-up, Sandy."

Penelope glanced over her shoulder at her husband, who gave an affectionate grin and then turned, whistling the dogs to come to work. Thus she was on her way and she began to enjoy her ride to *Trem-y-Môr*. It was unusual for her to be off her feet at this time of day and the repeated sound of Sandy's hooves blended with the birds singing: thrush, blackbird, and skylark and, occasionally, the raucous screech of the gulls. She breathed in the heady aroma of newly-cut grass and honeysuckle and the sweet perfume from the last of the gorse flowers, over the top of the more natural smell of the land and now the tang of the sea, borne on the wind. Country and sea mixed and mingled together. Her favourite place! On the one side, rural life: slow-moving, round and round, changing with the seasons; on the other side, the busy life of seaports, dependent on the daily tides and capricious weather. Their farm was not within walking distance of the sea; it was near the centre of Anglesey. However, in every direction, were beaches, an easy ride away: expansive, sandy, beaches at Aberffraw; rocky, cliff-bound beaches at Amlwch; the busy harbour at Beaumaris and the tidal creek beside Holyhead. Penelope never ceased to find pleasure at the variety of enchanting places on Anglesey.

Reaching for her needles, and seeing the road empty ahead of her (since it was still early), she smiled with a sense of peace and allowed Sandy to pick his own way through the mire. The road was awash with murky puddles, its edges deep with mud and manure. It was hardly more than a track, being only wide enough for traffic in one direction, and Penelope hoped that she would not meet too many other travellers. Such meetings meant side-stepping into the ditches, and with the persistent rain (and more promised with those clouds!), she would be hard-pressed to keep her blue, woollen stockings clean and poor Sandy would arrive begrimed with dirt, his legs and belly dyed dark brown, his upper quarters the usual sorrel: he would look like some strange painted statue!

Her needles clicking, Penelope kept an eye open for unexpected holes in the surface of the road, fallen trees or even an overturned wagon awaiting rescue, with maybe a wheel shaken off, its axle adrift and its body askew. She would have to guide Sandy around obstacles like that, but he was quite capable of steering a path through the normal sludge.

Finishing a row of knitting, she caught a glimpse of her daughter's downy hair and her heart filled with love. Who would have believed that she, Penelope Rowlands, badly scarred by smallpox, could have found such happiness? She thanked the Lord each and every day for the many blessings He had poured out on her.

How lonely and inward-looking she had been when she had first come out from that awful illness! She remembered, however, that in the beginning, her greatest fear was not scarring, but that she would be permanently blind. She had spent days in bed and, during her lucid moments, had been very frightened to find that she could not see. Twenty-one days without sight had seemed like an eternity to a seven-year-old! Totally unaware of what the malady had done to her face, she had been relieved when she had found that she could see again. Her plump, healthy body had become wasted; her bones protruded through her skin, especially at the knees and hips and elbows. Also she bruised very easily, even after she was out of bed, and therefore she always had purplish skin somewhere on her wizened body. She was told afterwards that she had been believed dead three times. But she was simply glad to be feeling significantly better until one day she had heard a nurse murmur:

"Poor wee mite! Look at her face. It's unrecognisable. She's been positively mauled by the pox…"

Then she began to be frightened again; even so it was not until her return to the nursery floor that she learnt the true extent of her disfigurement.

During the course of her sickness, Penelope had lain away from her brothers and sisters, in a room on the second floor of their London house.

The residence consisted of six storeys, if the lowest floor which was made up entirely of musty cellars was counted, and the top floor which was where the servants slept. The fifth storey above ground was given over to the children and included their bedchambers, nursery, a poky kitchen, schoolroom and various rooms for the nannies and nursemaids.

However, the gravity of Penelope's state meant that she had been carried down to the fourth floor and put into a spare room, with an adjoining dressing-room, where the nurse slept. In fact, Penelope had two nurses, who shared the duties. In this way, the sick little girl had been watched twenty-four hours a day. Later, she learned that her parents believed that it was this constant attention that saved their daughter's life, but she believed firmly that it had been God who had saved her, for amidst the pain and delirium, she had met and spoken with a figure dressed all in white with long hair and a beard and a light that emanated from His being. She believed that this person was Jesus, but she had never told anyone about her vision: at first, from anger, at the way the illness had left her; later from embarrassment.

Unlike her brother, Edward, Penelope had no memories of her life prior to her attack of smallpox, but she recalled vividly the day she was taken back to the nursery floor, for it had changed her life.

She remembered that it was a bright day with a petal-blue sky and a joyous sun. She awoke before dawn because she knew that today she was to return upstairs and she was excited. She had no fear or premonition about the reception by her siblings, since there were no mirrors in her room, and, in spite of what she had heard the nurse say, she had no inkling of the extent of the terrible changes wrought to her skin. All thoughts of her appearance were far from her mind, for she was not a vain child. Rather, she lay in bed and imagined her own familiar bed upstairs with its pretty, yellow curtains.

Soon, she would be reunited with all her toys and especially her dolls. She had been permitted one doll with her during her infirmity, but she had several favourites and she had missed them, particularly when her condition improved. She went through their names, picturing each one in her head. In the last few days, she had become bored and, strangely enough, was looking forward to returning to her lessons and even to doing her samplers, which she hated usually. Also, it would be good to rejoin her brothers and sisters. Altogether, the feeling of anticipation was almost like having another birthday and she wished away the last hour until Barker, the footman, came to carry her up the stairs.

Eventually, the moment arrived, and she felt very important lying in Barker's brawny arms whilst they ascended the stairs. At the last minute, the nurse decided to stay downstairs, saying that she needed to sort out her belongings since her job here was finished. To this end there was no one to refuse her when Penelope begged:

"Please can I go to the schoolroom? Please?"

Barker halted at the top of the stairs.

"Well, Miss, I was told to take you to your own bed. You must be feeling a bit weak still."

"Oh, but I'd like to see Edward and Margaret and Katherine. It's weeks since I've seen them."

Barker nodded his head in apparent agreement.

"Well, Miss, I can't imagine there would be any harm in that. Why don't you just say 'Good day' to them and then I can carry you to your bedchamber." Penelope thought he whispered, "I'm not in any hurry to get back to my tasks under that old scrounger Brown! He may be the butler but he's not my master!"

Penelope plucked at Barker's uniform when they reached the schoolroom.

"Please put me down." She kept her voice low, because she wanted to surprise everyone.

"I'm not sure, Miss. Are you strong enough?"

"Please," pouted Penelope.

Barker let her stand on the carpet in her bare feet.

"I'll be right behind you, if you feel faint, Miss," he assured her.

"Here I am," Penelope cried gaily, flinging open the door; it was an eternity since she had last had lessons in here.

Margaret was up at the front of the room, behind Miss Buckley's desk. In a split second, Penelope realised that the teacher was not in the room and her eldest sister was pretending to be in charge. It had happened many times before. All of them were always restless on days when the sun was shining like today; when the summer air and garden aromas were calling to them to forget how to conjugate a Latin verb and come outside to play.

Edward was not in his seat either, but was pressing his nose against the window pane and looking longingly out over the lawn. Katherine remained seated but leaning under her desk and Penelope saw that she was retrieving her chalk, which had rolled on to the floor.

Margaret turned.

"Now who is this who has entered without knocking?" She gave an excellent imitation of the missing teacher. "Oh! Oh, what has happened to your… your face? It's… it's horrible and… and ugly," she continued in her ordinary voice, all trace of laughter gone from her.

"Who is it?" Edward asked with an air of wonder, spinning round from the window.

Katherine burst into noisy tears, her hands beginning to shake.

Penelope came to an abrupt stop and stood rigid.

"Don't come near me, you hideous monster!" screamed Margaret. "You're disgusting… like a beggar… a leper. Go away! Go away!"

"It's me, Penelope."

"Come, Miss." Penelope felt Barker put his hands on her shoulders. "You'd better get along to bed. Children, where is your teacher? Who is in charge here?"

"Is that you, Pen?" demanded Edward curiously. "Is it really you? It sounds like you, but it doesn't look like you. Can I touch your face? Will it always be like that?"

"Go away!" repeated Margaret loudly, backing in to the corner of the room. "Don't come near me. I don't want to catch smallpox. I… I don't want to… to look like you!"

"You won't catch smallpox after all this time, you foolish girl," proclaimed Miss Buckley, arriving behind Penelope and the footman. "Whatever is all this noise about? I leave you only for a moment to search for a book and look what happens! I have found the book and it explains just what I was trying to say. Excuse me, Barker. Katherine, pull yourself together and stop crying. What would your father say? He told me that he wanted both his daughters and his son educated equally. He doesn't want a family of ignoramuses! I had never taught girls before and I had my doubts and certainly you girls are very fidgety but… Katherine, did you hear me? Penelope is quite…" Miss Buckley marched into the room, her starched clothes crackling with efficiency.

"My God!" The teacher's fine face drained of its entire colour. "It's cruel!" she gasped. "I had heard it whispered in the servants' hall that you were unrecognisable, and it was too heavy a cross for you at your age, but this… It would have been better if you'd died!"

"No!" exclaimed Barker and then seemingly forgetting who he was talking to, continued, "How dare you say such a thing, you unfeeling woman!"

He bent towards Penelope. Realising that he was going to scoop her up into his arms, she twisted and ran. She sprinted along the corridor, down the stairs and back to the room that she had just recently vacated. She slammed the door after her and turned the key in the lock. Collapsing against the solid wood, her breath ragged, her legs began to tremble from her unaccustomed exercise, but no tears fell across her scarred skin.

She heard people thumping down the stairs and swiftly she pulled the key from the door, thrust it into the lock of the entrance to the dressing room and wrenched it around. Then, clutching the key to her heaving, breast, she sat cross-legged on the floor and closed her eyes.

What sort of a god was God that He had allowed her to live when she was a freak? God had spoken to her, hadn't He? He'd told her that she wasn't going to die, but live to be an old, old woman. She had been glad when she'd seen her vision, gratefully turning her back on death and on heaven too (for surely that was where she'd met Jesus?); she had returned to this world and now she had to bear this!

"It would have been better if you'd died."

The words beat a tattoo in her brain.

Rejection! Derision! Long words, which she didn't know at seven, but she would learn in later years, and the fact that Jesus Himself had suffered also; He had been despised by men too.

All she knew at that moment, in her frightened heart, was that no one recognised her and no one wanted her. Yet she herself had not been able to see what her face looked like. What had happened to her? She felt her skin, trying to imagine what she looked like.

Suddenly someone was hammering on the door, calling to her to let them in, but she was not opening the door until she had seen her face. She knew how to see herself: wait until dark and look at her reflection in the window pane. She was competent at lighting candles. Hence, she accepted that there was nothing to do but bide her time until dusk. She climbed on to the bed and burrowed beneath the quilts, with her hands over her ears, to deaden the shouts coming from outside the room. She would not answer until she had found out what was wrong with her.

In truth, her weak reflection, produced by two undersized candles, portrayed a picture much worse than reality, but she did not discover that for several months, since she could not bear to look in a glass for ages. For the present at least, that evening, she could understand her family's reaction, for she could not even recognise her own face in that faint image in the darkened window. It appeared as if she was wearing a grotesque mask like the mummers at Christmastide. She turned back to the bed.

All was quiet outside the door; they had left her alone. Why had they left her alone? The answer sprang to mind immediately: they were hoping that she would remain locked in until she died. Ugly! Disgusting! Leper!

If she had been older she would have seen the foolishness of her explanation. When she grew up, she learnt that it was her father who had suggested that the nursery servants stopped banging on the door. He had reasoned that unless they were intending to actually break the door down (and it had seemed a shame to ruin a perfectly good door), it would be best for everyone to calm down.

During this conversation with her father, years later, she found out that he had heard a jumble of reports of the incident from a distraught Miss Buckley, who continued to be shocked at her pupil's ravaged appearance; an exceedingly angry Barker, who probably recounted the most accurate facts of the whole affair; a stony-faced Margaret, who refused to see that she had done anything wrong; a weeping Katherine, who could not string together an intelligible sentence; and an excited Edward, who was too young to understand and was not sure what all the fuss was about! Privately

Sir William had thanked God that Penelope's mother was in bed recovering from the birth of another daughter. He had sworn the weary servants to secrecy, but it was already too late! The noise of the insistent knocking had aroused the interest of everyone from housekeeper to lowliest scullery maid, and even the butcher-boy, who was in the kitchen at the time. The tale had spread like the recent fire of London, repeated, changed and exaggerated until it was almost as altered as Penelope's face.

Sir William told his adult daughter that he had insisted she be left in peace since obviously she was upset and needed time alone. He had reckoned that a few hours would not hurt her. However, the very nurse who had neglected to go upstairs earlier with Penelope had unpacked her chattels and came to see the Master. She had informed him, in no uncertain terms, that this kind of distress always brought on a relapse and probably the sick child was already insensible. Nevertheless, Sir William had remained adamant. Nothing would be done until later, he decreed, and then, if no response came, Barker would climb up and break in through the window. And that had been his final word on it! He had demanded that the other children return to their normal routine; that the servants go back to their set tasks; that order be restored again and that sanity take the place of hysterics. Only then did he go to tell his wife the most accurate version of the tale, according to the way he understood it.

However, little Penelope knew none of this. She was unaware of the good intentions behind her father's instructions and she cowered under the bedclothes with only her childish thoughts for company. The utter silence spelt out more clearly than anything that she was hated, a monster, and a changeling: unwanted and unloved. She *felt* like the same person she had been before the illness (somewhat more tired maybe, and, of course, thinner), but her hair hung in the same, golden tresses, which had been admired by others, and her hands and feet were hardly marked. It was only her face that was so terribly affected. She closed her eyes in sorrow.

The following morning, Penelope unlocked the door. During the night, she had decided what to do: if she was well behaved and never drew attention to herself, then people would not notice her or her handicap. Although she had accepted, in those lonely midnight hours, that she would never be loved, she hoped to be able to sit on the edge, to be on the fringe of others' lives and, accordingly, be allowed to look in from outside. She would try to be inconspicuous every day. She had a plan: she would not ever be a nuisance to anyone by asking for things or butting into conversations or disturbing them or playing their games. If she stayed quiet, life could be the way it was before and she could be a spectator, at the very least.

To this end, she tiptoed upstairs before the household arose, dressed herself and sat on her bed with her arms and legs folded. She would try to be invisible, like the angels who watched over children. Then, everyone could continue with their lives and she could observe them without interfering. After all, her bedchamber looked exactly the same; her toys were arranged on a shelf; her dolls in a bunch on the bed; insomuch her fears of change were banished. She concluded that everything would be like it had been before yesterday.

However, overnight, the whole of the nursery floor had changed!

Miss Buckley was gone. Officially, Penelope overheard, she had been dismissed for her insensitive behaviour, but Penelope suspected another reason: she could not bear to teach such a hideous child.

Margaret was gone. It was explained that she was too old for the nursery, but Penelope found out that she was locked in her new bedchamber on the fourth floor, until she agreed to apologise to her sister for her deliberate cruelty. Penelope didn't want an apology, she wanted her sister to attend lessons and play with her. No recanting came; yet Margaret was released, but rarely visited her siblings. Penelope couldn't understand the power play between Sir William and his eldest daughter: all she knew was that Margaret could not stand the sight of her misshapen face.

Katherine was gone, at least, from the room that she shared with Penelope. That first morning, she awoke to see her sister, cross-legged on her bed, and burst into fresh tears. From then on, she cried persistently whenever she was near Penelope, and soon moved into Margaret's vacant room. By keeping Katherine away from her sister, Penelope never understood that everyone was at their wit's end with a girl who dissolved into weeping at the mere mention of Penelope's name. From Penelope's point of view, it was clear why Katherine never played with her: she could not endure to be near anyone who was this badly maimed.

Edward was gone from being her close friend. Initially he was comparatively normal. He came and talked to her and brought her toys and books and he asked her questions, albeit in hushed tones "'Cos," he explained, "Nanny says I must be kind to you 'cos you've been at death's door." Penelope didn't reply to him, in keeping with her resolutions.

Whispered queries about whether she had lost her voice in the same way he did when he had a sore throat in the winter still didn't elicit any answers and Edward accused her of being a stuffed animal like the stag heads on the stairway. Then Sir William chose this time to start training his youthful heir for his future responsibilities. Edward did wish her a kind of farewell, when he told her about Father's offer, by saying, "You'll be all right. You've got Katherine and all your dolls and I'll see you in the evenings at supper time." Penelope shed a lone tear when she watched him run after his long-legged father down the garden path. Who could blame him for abandoning her when her deformity was incredibly unsightly?

Penelope forgot that she had seen hardly anything of her mother in the days prior to the smallpox. (Naturally, her father had visited the nursery rarely, except in crises; what respectable father would? The running of that part of his household should come under the supervision of his wife.) No, Penelope's misery multiplied when she noticed her parents' absence from her life for the first time and she worked out that they came so infrequently because they couldn't possibly love such a scarred and grim-faced child.

Even Nanny Caruthers was gone. Customarily she had been there when Miss Buckley had upbraided them and usually she had a spare corner of her lap for one of her old charges. Nowadays, she was only to be seen occasionally, disappearing around doors with bundles of linen and bowls of dirty water. Penelope was aware that another baby sister had been born whilst she had been ill, but that was only one more and she argued inside her head that babies slept most of the day, therefore Nanny could have found time to leave the baby and cuddle her. With a sinking heart, Penelope concluded that Nanny didn't embrace her anymore because she too could not abide to touch such a disgusting, repulsive creature.

Verily, Penelope withdrew into a shell, living in her own private world, speaking infrequently, convinced that if she went unnoticed, eventually someone would come to love her again. Maybe this strange behaviour would have lasted forever if, three years later, Miss Swann had not come to live with them.

Penelope gazed back across the years, accepting what an inward-looking child she had been. Without warning, a splash of rain landed on her cheek; hurriedly she stuffed her knitting in the bag that was slung around the horse's neck. Adjusting the sleeping Sarah to lie more easily, she clicked Sandy's reins to urge him to walk at a faster pace.

THOMAS

Thomas leant against the broom handle and watched his father walk across the cobbled yard. He had been wondering what had happened to his father this morning. Increasingly, Owen Lewis had not been coming in each day to help his son with all the duties that needed to be done: grooming the horses or mucking out the stables or accompanying the Rowlands family on their expeditions to other parts of the island.

Thomas had risen at dawn and had made a good start on the tasks set before him. Today there was extra to do: the roan that Sir Edward had ridden in on last night had to be stabled and cared for and then there was the problem with the carriage wheel. It was a nuisance that the carriage was unavailable for the new master to use since he couldn't be expected to ride again this morning after that exhausting journey from London. However, the farm cart could take man and wheel to Holyhead. Accordingly, Thomas had loaded the broken wheel into the farm cart and had spoken to his brother, Evan, instructing him on where to take the wheel, how to behave with Sir Edward, and explaining that he had to deliver the master to the Vicarage. Thomas had not wanted the gaggle of brothers and sisters, who had tagged along with Evan, to stay and get under his feet when he had several jobs still to do. (He suspected that his father had sent them away from the cottage to give his mother some seclusion.) Therefore, he had encouraged them into the cart, whispering to them to behave themselves and not be a nuisance to Sir Edward. Then he had returned to the stables, but that must have been over an hour ago, and here was his father at last, traversing the worn stones.

In the moment, before either man spoke, Thomas had time to observe the other man. Suddenly he realised that his father had grown old: his hair was streaked with grey, his shoulders were stooped and his gait, always slightly bowed because of all the riding, was slow. How had he, Thomas, managed not to notice all this before? And what had happened to bring about this many changes in such a short time?

"Son," his father called. "Your mother has asked to see you."

His mother, Bridget! Therein lay the answer he was seeking. His mother was gradually dying. Pregnancies, year after year, had taken their toll; now his mother looked permanently pregnant; the dropsy had a hold of her body and never left even when she was not with child.

Thomas placed the broom against the stable wall.

"Should I go right away?"

"Yes. I'll take over whatever you were doing."

"It's all right, *Tad*, I'd nearly finished."

His father reached his side and Thomas took note of the weary eyes, the lines of worry and the down-turned mouth. He wasn't even forty, Thomas calculated, but a stranger might be forgiven for estimating that his age was nearer sixty.

"I'll go. I think you'd better have a look at…"

"Go, son, go! I really do think the end is near."

Thomas shook his head; his father had been saying this for weeks. Was he hoping that by reiterating this statement, it would become truth? Or did he dread the passing away of his wife? Thomas believed the latter, because he knew that they had been happily married for over twenty years.

Thomas ambled to the kitchen. His meal was laid on the table ready for him; usually he would sit down to eat. Today, he gulped down the herb sausages whilst he wrapped the rest of the meat in a hunk of bread which he tore off a loaf in the middle of the table.

"I'm off to see my *Mam*, Mrs Jones," he muttered through his full mouth.

"Is she bad?" asked Mrs Jones. "Tell her I'll send her some of my gooseberry pudding I made yesterday. It probably won't be 'til this afternoon though, with all these extra people in the house. Of course, I told your mother that…"

Thomas turned on his heel, and made good his escape. He wasn't in the mood to listen to the housekeeper expounding on her theories of what was wrong with his mother. He'd heard it all before anyway!

The path to his parents' home led him along the coast path for several minutes and he saw a bank of clouds on the horizon. Rain later, he prophesised under his breath. He turned his back on this threat when he moved away to the right across the fields. He didn't notice any of the familiar landmarks on the way; he had walked this way nearly every day of his life; he was lost in a brown study. His unseeing eyes overlooked the naked tree, its branches lifeless, for it was ten years since it had been struck by lightning. He pushed through the gate which straddled the pathway, unaware of its feeble barrier. With much practised skill he jumped the boggy mud, through which trickled a stream. He didn't observe the dead carcass of a sheep rotting, its ribs sticking out, its flesh half eaten already, such was his concentration.

And his thoughts? He was contemplating what would happen to his father and his brothers and sisters when finally his mother died. He couldn't believe that his father would marry again. Would he sink into a depression and follow his wife to the grave? Or would he just plod along, keeping up his job as head groom at the Manor House, leaving his children in the capable hands of Thomas' eldest sister, Biddy?

Once Thomas reached the cottage, he recognised the farm cart of the Goode family. Well, not the cart but the horse which pulled it: a well-built creature with a wild look in its eye. He saw that one of his brothers, Owen, named after his father, held its reins. With a word of acknowledgement to the skinny nipper, he stroked the nervous animal's muzzle, murmuring nonsense to it, and went to enter the cottage, but he never crossed the threshold, for filling the doorway was a slim, dark-haired young woman.

Thomas halted and gave a mock bow towards his friend.

"Joanna, what brings you here? Everything fair with your family?"

"Yes. I'm afraid if you've come to see your *Mam*, you'll not get in! My mother is there and Aunt Hesther and Mrs Stowles from…"

"That's all right. I'm sure I can wait. Shall we stay outside? I think the sunshine is warm enough if you sit out of the wind. Let's go round the corner away from little ears." He indicated Owen and two of his sisters who had followed Joanna out and were absorbed in making mud pies with small stones, their sticky fingers in the earth under the windows of the cottage.

There was a tense silence whilst the two young people skirted the white walls of the house and then leant against its coarse surface. Joanna closed her eyes with a tiny sigh and lifted her face to the sun.

Thomas watched furtively beneath his own half-closed eyes. What he saw pleased him! A high brow; long, curling eyelashes; sweet red lips; smooth cheeks; a firm round bosom, gently rising and falling, and slender, neat hands pressed against the brickwork. It must be all of two years since he had glimpsed this woman and she had matured since then. What was she doing home? She had gone to work on the other side of Anglesey for a big household, quite a prestigious job, he understood, which her Aunt Sara had procured for her. She came home very rarely – only for Christmas one year and Easter the second year and both these festivals were long past.

She sighed again and he queried:

"Joanna?"

"I've been thrown out."

Thomas stood upright and faced his friend.

"What happened?" Surely she wasn't with child! He'd heard that she could be very distant with any lad who wanted to go further than a swift kiss or cuddle. Had she succumbed in the end to one of the other servants or the master himself?

"It truly wasn't me." She opened her eyes and regarded him. "A bracelet was missing from Mistress Van's jewellery box and I was blamed. I hadn't even been near the bedchamber. The chance would be a fine thing! But I was the newest maid, apart from… Well, *she* was the housekeeper's cousin and, therefore above reproach!"

"Joanna! I'm sorry. When did this happen?

"Last week. It all came out last Thursday afternoon and by Friday morning, my bag was packed and I was walking home. Too quick, by far!" She paused. "The worst of it is that I've got no reference. And… and the humiliation of having been searched, both my belongings and… my person." Her hurt green eyes looked away.

"Your parents?"

"Oh, they seem to believe me, and Father says I should be glad the magistrate wasn't called, but then, that's the point. There was no evidence. I think the Master knew it wasn't me, but they had to find a scapegoat and I… I was the nearest. I almost wish I had stolen the wretched thing – at least I would have been able to sell it and get some money. Mother's all aflutter. She says I can't stay at home and poor Aunt Hesther is working tirelessly to find me another position and Uncle… Uncle thinks it would be best if I found a husband!"

"No!"

"It would solve the problem. A husband would support me, but… but I had hoped to marry someone…"

"Someone you loved?"

"Someone who wanted me for… myself, not someone looking for an unpaid servant. And this is the kind of man who will offer for me after this, because we can't provide much for a dowry. And, then, it hasn't been possible to keep this quiet – you know what small communities are like. Father was visited by Farmer Bowler on Tuesday. His wife's not cold in her grave yet and he's got a brood of children – five, I think in all."

"Joanna, don't do it. Don't let them force you into marriage."

"That's easy for you to say. But what am I going to do? I try not to mope about the house. I help my mother with the tasks and visit… Oh, I didn't mean that visiting your mother is a task…"

Thomas smiled.

"I know you didn't mean that! I wish I could help – find you a place at the Manor House but the…"

"They wouldn't have me!"

"No, I was going to say that there are no vacancies at the moment. Will you…? Can you afford to wait?"

"Possibly. I am hoping that Aunt Hesther can wave her magic wand and find me a new job. She's certainly got contacts all over the place, but I'm wondering if I'm going to have to go far away and I don't really want to leave this area. Everyone I know… everything I know is here."

"I understand. I had that particular dilemma myself a few years ago. I felt I had to leave but didn't…"

"Joanna!"

"That's Mother. I'd better go. Don't come round the corner 'til we've gone or Mother will be getting ideas about you and me. Thanks for listening, Thomas. I'll probably see you at church on Sunday."

Thomas leant back against the whitewashed stone and breathed deeply. Could he help Joanna? She was very comely; he was of an age when he needed a wife. They had been friends since childhood; she was in trouble. And he had recovered from his infatuation with Mariana, hadn't he? But where would he and Joanna live? The stables were all right for a single man but not appropriate for a marriage bed. Could he build them a cottage in one day, from sunrise to sunset? In this manner, according to local custom, it was accepted that the builder became the owner. Or there was that broken-down cottage on Sir William's land. Could he approach the new master, Sir Edward, and ask for it? Maybe the best plan was to go and view the place; it was ages since he had ridden that way and he hadn't given it more than a glance on that occasion, for it hadn't seemed important then, but now…

PENELOPE

Penelope Roberts leant down and gathered up her horse's reins in her hands. In front of her was a line of donkeys, identical it seemed, each one laden with hefty baskets and all wending their way patiently away from Four Mile Bridge. Fortunately she was able to guide Sandy up on to a grassy knoll which was conveniently placed and thus avoid a muddy bath in the ditch. The tinkling of the bells on the harnesses of the donkeys woke Sarah, who gave a grunt.

"Hush, my darling," Penelope whispered. "Go back to sleep." She gave a nod to the man guiding the animals with a knotty stick and twitched the reins for Sandy to return to the pathway. Then she pushed back the blankets from the child's face. The spots of rain hadn't amounted to much and occasionally the sun broke through the clouds; Sarah would benefit from the summer air. She appeared to be staring at her mother with adoration and again, Penelope marvelled at how far she herself had come from that confused, unfriendly child. It had been love that had transformed her life, like the Parson taught from the Bible. And the first person who had loved her had been Miss Swann.

Ironically, it had been through the very person who had hurt her most, Margaret, that Penelope had met Miss Swann, her saviour.

The whole Rowlands family had taken Margaret to visit the Struleys. It was accepted that one of the Struley boys would marry Margaret when she was of age. There, amidst a host of relatives – ancient aunts, screaming youngsters and humourless adults – was someone who sat on the edge of the gaggle of guests, observing and serving: Miss Swann.

Penelope had not heeded Miss Swann the first day because she herself had hidden upstairs; she did not like meeting strangers with their inevitable stares. The following day looked set to become a pattern: Penelope in her room, peering out the window of her bedchamber, secretly longing to join the others, who were gathered in the garden. A crowd were being shown around the magnificent grounds of the castle, for the spring sun had beckoned all but the most frail to stroll under its heat. There, not quite joining in, yet not excluded (Penelope decided from her eagle's nest position) was a tall, slender woman. Penelope knew why this woman was standing just apart from the others; even from that distance, she could see the wrinkled, deformed skin of the woman's face. Noting that the woman was wandering towards the gate, which seemed to lead to an overgrown wood, the girl slipped down the stairs and ran through the vegetable garden to follow this interesting person. And thus they had met, in a bluebell-carpeted wood: scarred woman, scarred child, and immediately they understood each other.

It had not taken long for Miss Swann to get the shy child talking, although normally Penelope never opened her mouth and particularly not to people she didn't know! The older woman had learnt that Penelope believed that no one had loved her since her illness; within minutes, the girl began to pour out all her feelings, which she had held in for three lonely years. It was only at the end of their conversation that Miss Swann had explained that she was blemished not simply across half her face, from cheekbone down to chin, but also along half the neck and upper body too. It transpired that a neglectful servant had allowed her to fall into a pan of boiling strawberry preserve when she was taking her first tottering steps. The puckered tissue had grown with her, but Miss Swann had not been rejected by her family and she was able to reach inside Penelope's damaged soul and help her.

By the end of the week, Miss Swann and a brighter Penelope were inseparable, and when the time to leave came, Penelope had begged her new-found friend to take up residence in London with the Rowlands family. An extended interview, at which Penelope was present, enabled Sir William to comment on how changed his daughter was, and to offer the post of governess to Miss Swann. It was explained to her that Katherine was, by then, too old for lessons (except how to run a household and catch a husband) and Edward was due his own male tutor after the summer; hence Penelope would be her sole charge. Penelope didn't know whether it was the generous wage which persuaded her friend or other reasons, but Miss Swann had travelled back to their town house with them. Soon she was one of the family.

Over the months the new governess had breathed life into the solemn child. Like waking from the dead, Penelope had returned to a more normal personality and her chattering voice, and even laughter, was heard once more around the house. Truly love could bring about miracles!

During her time of withdrawal, Penelope had sought refuge in writing a kind of diary, trying to express her frustrations and fears in uneven handwriting. She had used simple ideas and words and had written her feelings to an imaginary friend called Rebecca, who could not and would not shun her.

Never before had Penelope shared these letters with someone else and Miss Swann had encouraged her in other literary efforts. She introduced her to a harder vocabulary, and found her books to stretch her mind. Although all books were expensive, she asked Sir William to purchase some for his daughter. Subsequently, she had suggested that Penelope write letters to all her relatives, explaining how she felt at their behaviour, but not to send the letters in reality. Penelope was surprised at how just putting down on paper all her emotions, without confronting anyone, eased the hurt.

Over the next six years, Miss Swann became mother, friend, advisor and healer to Penelope, who refused to make the acquaintance of children from other households. In truth, rarely had she ventured beyond the four walls of her home. She had to travel with her parents to their various homes, but soon she found, at each place, her own favourite haunts, where she and Miss Swann could walk undisturbed. And within each house she had her own bedchamber, which became her private retreat.

When Penelope reached an age when most girls would have been thinking about finding husbands, she had spoken to her counsellor, who had never married (and being then in her early forties, said she never would). Miss Swann talked openly to her blossoming pupil about both the advantages and disadvantages of remaining single. Penelope, who had presumed that she would never marry either, found herself relatively undisturbed by the changes in her body and sentiments when she became an adult.

Nonetheless, Miss Swann was not been Penelope's only friend. Penelope had forged a steady relationship with her youthful stepmother, Mariana, who had treated her, from the very beginning, as though she was not disfigured. Like the governess, she urged her stepdaughter to leave her desk and her writing and to go out into the world. Much to her amazement, Penelope found that, with Mariana at her side, she was protected from people's sharp tongues.

Penelope discovered later, Miss Swann was delighted to see her charge spreading her wings under the care of Mariana and she began to withdraw to the edge of Penelope's life. Eventually, having come into a legacy from a forgotten aunt, she retired to a cottage in Norfolk. Penelope missed her governess, but her new life, with her new stepmother, was crammed with busy pastimes. She had very little time to feel the loss of her best friend; instead she wrote regularly, cataloguing all the functions and events she attended in London.

For a few hectic months, Penelope lived the life of an ordinary eighteen-year-old until, during a frigidly polite visit to her sister, Margaret, she had heard the news of Mariana's death. She was overtaken with sorrow and longed to leave the castle where Margaret lived. After all, Margaret's son was well over the smallpox, and had been left with not a mark on him! Therefore her nursing was no longer required, but what pretext for leaving could she give? Three weeks later she was presented with the perfect excuse: her letters to Edward at his school were returned to her unopened. Foreboding overshadowed her grief. She pleaded her brother's disappearance as her reason for departing, grateful that no objections were raised to her leaving.

Using some sisterly intuition, Penelope returned to the London house (after all, her brother was neither with their grieving father in Wales nor at school) with the hope that Edward might be trying to find her there. She had not been told many details, but surely, of all the family, Edward might think of her as his closest ally? She waited, but Edward never appeared.

Finding herself alone again, Penelope turned to her usual solace: her writing. Margaret and Katherine both contacted her with their disapproval of her unchaperoned circumstances, but the one relation who could have forbidden her (her father) was immersed in his own grief.

For over a year, Penelope put off any real communication with her family, making herself ill from worry and chosen incarceration. Without warning, a letter came from her lost brother, assuring her of his good health and his joy in life aboard ship and she surfaced from her solitude. Right on the heels of Edward's missive came an invitation from her dear friend, Miss Swann, cajoling her to pay her a visit.

Penelope could clearly see the cottage in her mind's eye. She turned her head, picturing it sitting, away to the right of her horse, Sandy, beside the road in the middle of Anglesey! It was over sixteen years since she had first explored Norfolk, but it was like yesterday, for once again, by joining Miss Swann, her life had been spun upside-down.

Penelope needed to walk the last half mile to reach her old governess' home, but she did not mind, for it was a mild rosy evening and she only had her light bag to carry. The coachman had promised faithfully to deliver her chest on the morrow. When she saw the small house, she was astounded that it did not float away on the tide, because it perched on the very edge of the north Norfolk coast, built on the rim of the beach, its foundations merging with the multi-coloured pebbles. Certainly Penelope felt a long way from the crowded, streets of London which she had left yesterday. This would be an ideal resting place; she sighed with pleasure.

However, Miss Swann's greeting was hardly a restful beginning.

"Penelope! What have you been doing to yourself? You're just skin and bones. You look more like you did at ten than a grown woman of nineteen! How could you do it? Neglecting your wellbeing for all this time…"

Penelope listened with good-humoured tolerance. In penance, she ate every morsel of the substantial, appetising meals which Miss Swann set before her that evening and every subsequent evening.

She agreed to leave her writing and instead went for undemanding walks through the mellow, autumn sunshine. Soon she developed a taste for living by the sea and her favourite route was along the beach, skirts lifted up, shoes swinging in her hands, gripping the stones with her quickly-hardened soles. Usually she would stroll towards the nearest village, although she never passed into the centre. She would sit just around the corner from the cluster of houses and gaze at the undulating sea, whilst she fingered the cool, smooth rocks. Over the weeks, she chose the prettiest, roundest, most colourful, most unusual of the pebbles and carried them back to her room to lie on her windowsill where she could touch them at her leisure.

One day, near the start of October, when the sun was beaming as hotly as any summer day, she crouched on the hard stones and watched whilst a solitary rowing boat moved past her vision, gliding through the crystal water, leaving rippling bands of waves to fan out behind it. When the boat reached the outcrop of the land, ready to turn up the shallow river which led to the village, Penelope saw the boat's occupant look furtively to right and left, before dropping something over the side of the boat. The manner in which he had deposited his cargo caught Penelope's interest and she rose up, pulling on her shoes, whilst the boat skimmed up the river.

Suddenly, from the direction of the settlement, Penelope heard shrieks of anger and a small child (boy or girl she knew not which, for both sexes were dressed in petticoats until quite a late age) dashed across the slippery pebbles and straight into the water, shouting:

"Not Digger! Not Digger!"

Along this stretch of coast, Penelope had noticed, the land fell sharply away to a deeper shelf only a few feet from the water's edge and the child, wading frantically out, sank beneath the waves in a flurry of bubbles.

Penelope, unable to swim like most of her generation, started to run towards the place where the child had disappeared, without giving a moment's thought to herself. By the time she reached the languid sea, the child had surfaced, spluttering and kicking, and continuing to sob:

"Not Digger! Not Digger!"

Penelope entered into the water and towards the splashing infant and then herself tripped down the step until the waves lapped against her bosom. However, she managed to catch the child before it sank again.

"Noah! Noah!" A voice came from further along the beach Penelope struggled with her soaked skirts to turn to face the land. There, panting across the uneven pebbles at a laboured trot, was a dishevelled man.

Evidently unaware of any danger, pugnaciously the child was trying to strike out to sea. Penelope gripped the squirming, bundle whilst she manoeuvred her feet until she found the ridge. She heaved herself up. Then providentially, she was only knee-deep in the water and the child was kicking, fruitlessly in the air, unbelievably still determined to swim away. Now that she was out of her impromptu bath, she bore the full weight of his sodden body.

The man reached her side and she noticed sweat on his brow and fear in his eyes.

"Oh, how can I thank you? Noah, you must stop kicking. What do you think you're doing? Stop kicking, I tell you."

Seemingly unafraid of the man's stern voice, Noah screamed all the louder:

"Digger. I want Digger."

"What are you shouting about?" countered the man.

Penelope gave up trying to hold this wriggling, fighting boy. She allowed him to slide down her ruined gown and then, tucking her hands under his arms, lifted him clear of the water. Once he was safely ashore, she dragged her heavy skirts out of the sea. Without warning, with the danger over, she felt dizzy and her legs were shaking. She was aware of her clinging clothes. Instantaneously, she wanted to leave this awkward situation and return home.

The man snatched the child up under one arm, and pinned the boy's flailing arms in a pincer grip.

"Noah, Digger is at home. Now that is quite enough! Stop struggling! One more word out of you and I'll take the strap to you." The child went limp and started to cry: large tears which dropped from his face and mingled with the drips from his clothes, on the smooth rocks below.

It appeared to Penelope that, at last, the boy was defeated. The man must have been thinking the same, for he lowered the child to stand on his own feet, just keeping a restraining hand on his shoulder. He said:

"That's better. Let me whilst I speak to this kind lady who was charitable enough to rescue you. Please forgive me." He spoke to Penelope. "The child's dog…"

"I seen him," insisted the boy in a whisper. "He throwed Digger over the side."

Penelope glanced from father to son.

"The man in that rowing boat certainly did throw something overboard." Penelope spoke in a doubtful tone.

"Oh, how can I convince you?"

Penelope found herself staring straight at Noah's father when she heard the desperation in his voice. He was persisting:

"I, too, saw the man throw something over the side but please believe me, it was not the child's dog. In fact, I will bring the troublesome Digger to see you."

"Noah!"

Penelope glanced up. Coming towards them was a buxom woman with a baby in her arms and an older boy trailing at her side. Penelope concluded that she was Noah's mother. Certainly Noah seemed to confirm this since he slipped easily from the man's grip and ran to the newcomers, hiding his tear-stained cheeks in the woman's skirts, clutching the cloth with his fat fingers.

"Oh, Noah," she remonstrated, "you're all wet. You must come back to the house immediately before you catch a fever."

The words were clear despite the small party being afar off. Penelope saw the woman bend to lift the weeping child into her arms, already laden with the baby. Then, without a sign to her husband or Penelope, she turned her back and took her tribe home.

Penelope was annoyed. Nevertheless, she saw this as her cue to go and she began to walk in the opposite direction. She was beginning to feel chilly and shivered.

"Please wait," started the man, striding to reach her side. "I must thank you. The daft child can't swim. If it hadn't been for you, he would surely have drowned."

"It was nothing."

"No, indeed! My life wouldn't have been worth living if anything had happened to that young man! His mother dotes on him."

Penelope did not reply. She could see that the mother was devoted and completely absorbed with the child to the point of rudeness.

"May I escort you home?" the man persisted. "Do you live near here?"

Penelope quickened her pace. She found herself attracted to this man and had forgotten her own appearance for a few moments whilst she was standing with him, before the other woman arrived. She was shocked by her stupid heart's feelings, and denied uncivilly:

"No! I'm all right."

"But you are soaked to the skin. Here, let me lend you my coat." He started to unbutton the garment.

Penelope pursed her lips. Why couldn't he just go and return to his wife? Why was he behaving in this way? Why was *she* behaving so? There was no need for *her* to be boorish. Miss Swann would abhor such ungracious manners, yet Penelope found herself repeating:

"No! No! I don't want your coat."

"Well, at least, allow me to accompany you to your house."

"Leave me alone," stormed Penelope. "I am not a child and I am quite capable of going home by myself. I don't live far from here."

The man stopped abruptly. Penelope's body flushed with embarrassment. She wanted to apologise, but was afraid that the man would come to the doorstep with her. Thus she said, without raising her head:

"Good day to you, then." She managed to speak at a normal pitch, even if her voice sounded distant. "I am glad your son and his dog are safe. Please excuse me…"

Penelope walked away without a backward glance. She was cross with herself for her churlish behaviour. She was unused to dealing with people and she was frightened by the emotions which had been raised in her heart; she had found herself forgetting, for a short while, her shameful disfigurement and admiring this man with his tall stance and apologetic eyes. Usually, when she met a man (and this was becoming an increasingly rare occurrence), she was overcome immediately with the feeling that he was staring at her in pity. She would lower her eyes and slip silently away, hating his compassion, yet hating herself more for still being ill-at-ease with others. However, during the time when Noah had been crying, she had looked directly at this man and what she had found there had pleased her, and he a married man with three children!

She stumbled in her haste to be gone from the situation, sure that the man's eyes were burning into her back. At last she was at the cottage with the door closed behind her. Immediately she had to bear with her friend's exclamations of horror and demands to be told the whole story. Penelope gave a carefully edited account of the incident. Then, while she stripped off her saturated clothing, she was able to steer the conversation into a discussion about the rower's suspicious behaviour.

It was not until she was alone in bed, waiting for sleep to come, that she had time to let her thoughts return to the child's father. Since the man was married, and she would never see him again, she allowed herself the luxury of dwelling on him for one night only.

Imagine her embarrassment the following day when she opened the front door to find this very same man standing on the doorstep. He introduced himself as Robert Roberts, tutor to Noah's elder brother, Stephen. Miss Swann, appearing behind Penelope, asked him in, whereupon he proceeded to invite the mortified young woman to Lockley Lodge, where the children were staying.

Penelope, once she discovered that this man was not, in fact, the father of the children, was ashamed of her imaginations; she felt somehow the others could read her mind and, overcome with humiliation, she stuttered:

"I... I... No, thank you. It's... it's kind of you, Mr Roberts, but I'm afraid I will not... not be able to accept."

"But it's only for a nursery meal. Miss...?"

"Rowlands," supplied Miss Swann, with a half-smile.

"Miss Rowlands. There will only be myself and Miss Walters, the governess, whom you saw yesterday, th..."

"No, thank you. You mustn't think me ungrateful, but I am convalescing and not going out much yet," argued Penelope. This was a broad-faced lie but he couldn't know that!

"Maybe your mother can persuade you. Mrs Rowlands?"

"I'm not Penelope's mother and, although at one time, I could have been said to have some influence over her, I'm sorry to say that she's far too grown-up for me…"

"Couldn't you *both* come?" Robert's eager demeanour was difficult to refuse.

The two women looked at each other. Penelope felt she could read what her old governess was thinking: "Why are you being this obstinate? I know you don't like meeting strangers but you have always loved children." Penelope sighed inwardly. She realised that she could not refuse without being impossibly rude, yet she was frightened – frightened at the strength of her own reaction to this genial man. She had never even looked at people of the opposite sex. Suddenly, overnight, she found her thoughts filled constantly with this man and a shiver of excitement ran down her legs. She must withdraw; stay away from him, for any plans of a relationship must end in disaster. No man would want her with her ugly face – and especially if that man mixed with pretty women with curly, fair hair and a pleasing bosom, like the governess she had seen yesterday. However, she would have to go on this one occasion and then hope that he would leave them alone.

So it was that Penelope and Robert had met and Penelope spent the next fortnight of their acquaintance trying to still her feelings of love – dare she use that word about such a newly-formed friendship? She knew that Miss Swann accompanied her willingly on many outings: jaunts in a carriage to a nearby town; walks on the beach and a trip on a boat along the river – all with Miss Walters and Robert and Stephen, Noah and baby Joseph and the inevitable, barking Digger. Kept busy by the children and not given time to remember her own appearance, unconsciously Penelope allowed her affectionate nature to show itself and it flourished under the attentive gaze of Robert Roberts.

Whenever Penelope reminisced on those weeks, she recalled them as the happiest time of her childhood – if child she could be called – for she let her hair fall down, literally, when she carried children pick-a-back and crawled through the sand or when she paddled in the water, or sang songs in the carriage. Incredibly the sun shone, bright and hot, and the gentle breeze was almost tropical every single day. Although the hours of light were shortening and the nights were cold, the parts of the day when the sun was at its zenith were temperate like summer and the jolly band laughed and played in holiday mood.

Abruptly, their paradise was ruined by the arrival of the children's parents. They were not pleased that their offspring had been careering around the countryside like gypsies, tearing their clothes, returning dirty, but happy, from each day's adventure. Nor were they glad that they were in the company of complete strangers, even though they could see Miss Swann was very genteel. All this was said in one curt interview. There was scarcely time to exchange addresses before the Lockleys were gone – whisked back to Lockley Manor, near Norwich.

Subsequently, as if with their departure, the sun was finished. The days became cloudy, the wind punishing, the light barely conquering the darkness each morning, and the last leaves abandoned the branches of the trees and lay dead on the ground, sad and spent like Penelope's brief interlude of joy.

Once more, Penelope was a single woman with no laughing youngsters clutching her skirts; no runny noses to wipe; no tears to stop; no grazes to rub and no warm, grimy bodies to hug. Surely there would be no chance of it ever happening again. She knew that she herself would never marry and bear children and her nieces and nephews were too well-brought up to run free and wild as the young Lockleys had done. No, she understood in her heart that the last two weeks had been a dream. Bravely she faced that Robert had gone and she would not meet anyone like him once more.

Penelope was jerked back to the present by the sound of thundering hooves. She caught at Sandy's reins and pulled him to a halt, assuming that there was some crisis and it was best if she kept out of the way; but it was only two lads having some kind of race and with shouts and a great beating with upraised whips, the men swept past her and she was alone on the track again.

ROBERT

Robert watched his wife ride away before turning to whistle for his dogs. He strode back to the farmhouse, calling:

"Boys. Don't waste any more time. We must get the sheep to the shearing pens."

The farm boasted twelve sheep and four lambs as well as the two cows and the calf which had been saved from slaughter this year. Penelope had got her rennet from a neighbouring farm. This precious substance, essential to curdle the milk, came from the stomach of a very young slaughtered calf who had never tasted grass.

Yesterday, in a different part of the river from his wife, who had been scrubbing clothes, Robert and his servant, Thomas, had gone waist high into the water and washed the tangled coats of the sheep. No soap was needed to get the dust and muck out – just hard work and the running current. Robert smiled to himself with the memory. Drudgery it was not, on a fine summer's day! By this morning, he trusted the fleeces would have nearly dried with the body heat of the ewes – he knew a ten pound fleece washed after shearing could take days to stop being wet.

Llewelin had stripped off his shirt and tried to copy his elders and manhandle some of the smaller sheep into the stream. The flock seemed to enjoy it when they were in but bucked at the actual moment of entry. Once their coats were waterlogged, the weight had become too much for the lad but Robert was pleased with what his son had achieved.

Halfway through the previous day, the men had paused to down a sheep washers' posset – an ancient recipe which combined hot milk, ale, and breadcrumbs with nutmeg and pepper stirred in. Comforting warmth which they had welcomed for they had found the flowing water cooled the blood after many hours! And the pastries, which his wife had wrapped in a cloth, gave them extra strength to return to the task in hand.

Always with Robert was the need to teach his sons how to run a farm. Long ago, he had insisted that during the winter evenings they were to learn their letters, in the same way he had learnt from his own father. His experience tutoring the Lockley clan made the lessons fun, he hoped, but during the summer months, chalk and boards and books were abandoned and the children were taught practical lessons on every aspect of rural life.

With July just a hop and skip away, Robert knew they were entering the busiest time on the farm and his father-in-law's funeral was an inconvenience that he could well do without! First there was the hay to be got in and this year he had promised his eldest son could use a scythe. An experienced mower would be able to cut his two-acre field in a day, starting at five and taking advantage of the light evenings but, even with Llewelin helping, they would need a couple of fair days. Well, longer, of course, because, after cutting, the hay lay on the ground to dry, being turned regularly before it was raked up and stored in the barn to feed the animals all winter.

For a short while Robert forgot yesterday; his attention was taken up giving orders to his two dogs. Quickly they rounded in his sheep and herded them down the narrow track. Then, with hedges on either side to keep the animals walking in the right direction, and his youngest son astride his shoulders, Robert's worries crowded in. If the hay harvest was essential for winter food for the beast, then the wheat harvest was just as important for people. Sowed last September, farmer and hands had weeded the crop recently. Using a homemade two-pronged fork and hook of wood, they had laboured one grey but dry day to remove flowers and unwanted weeds from between the stalks of wheat. Robert had learnt that such a lot of the success of farming was in the hand of God because he believed He controlled the weather. At least today, rain, if it came, wouldn't be such a disaster.

Their first year on the farm had been a disaster. The ground had to be cleared of stones and roots before planting and with so much carpentry and masonry to be done on the house the land was neglected. He and Penelope had had to dive into their precious reserves of money to buy even the most basic essentials such as flour; they didn't have their own pigs to slaughter for meat or even a milking cow.

Suddenly, Robert was lost in the past.

Robert's father, Francis, was the youngest son of four hearty lads who were born and raised on a farm, just across the English border in Wales. Their proximity to the other larger country meant they were bilingual and when the time came to set up their own homes, all four abandoned their homeland and moved to the western counties of England. Only two years later, due to a calamitous harvest, both Francis' parents joined his eldest brother's family near Shrewsbury.

Francis himself was articled to a solicitor and it took him only three weeks to realise this was not the profession for him. However, two events, which occurred in those three weeks, changed his life forever. Firstly he met his employer's daughter, Susan, and, so the story was recounted, fell madly in love with her on first sight, and secondly, whilst visiting the local squire to discuss the legal papers for the sale of some land, he met a boy called Benjamin. Benjamin was crippled and each day sat outside the dining room windows of his father's mansion to soak up the sun's rays and breathe in the country air. Francis Roberts encountered him whilst being shown by the master of the house the area of land which was to be sold. When Francis announced his intention of leaving his studies, it came to the attention of Benjamin's father and he was invited to tutor the Squire's heir. With his new employment came a furnished cottage and Francis didn't waste any time proposing to his sweetheart.

Robert was the only child who came out of their loving union.

Robert's memories of his early life were rolled into one picture of cloudless days galloping around the Squire's estate with a bevy of other children whose parents worked inside the mansion and without its impressive walls. Whether it was catching the ponies and leaping on their backs, or swimming in the refreshing depths of a pool formed by the dam they themselves had built, Robert could not recall ever getting into trouble or even being reprimanded. Returning, tired and grubby at the end of the day, sometimes as the sun twinkled over the horizon, his mother would greet him with a smile and a plate of homemade food. Of course, he recalled that he was given lessons by his unassuming father but they didn't seem to bite into the hours he had to play and explore the fields, woods and gardens. Surely, as he grew older, he would have been required to learn skills and buckle down to some kind of a job, but his carefree life came to an end when his mother died just after his eleventh birthday. Without notice he found himself a weekly boarder at the local school for Gentlemen Farmers' sons with only the weekends for leisure, and that didn't include Saturday mornings!

Distanced from his childhood friends by grief and his sudden maturity, now, when he came home, he would spend time with his father. Robert's love of the outdoors and his interest in the running of the estate was suppressed, although many hours passed with just the two of them sometimes fishing or walking. The winter evenings were filled with reasoned discussions or reading side by side in front of the fire in companionable silence. Once a year Robert joined his grandparents, uncle and cousins for a rackety fortnight where he could be a lad again, but all too quickly his childhood was over and he had to find employment for himself. Benjamin was eight years his senior but had five siblings who kept his father busy but, again it was Benjamin's family who introduced Robert to one of their relatives. At nineteen, Robert became a tutor himself to the young son of Lord and Lady Huggett.

Some tutors and governesses found themselves caught between the family and the servants below stairs. With Robert, school and his relationship to his bereaved father had swept away the mischievous youngster. He grew up serious and respectful, strangely at ease with most men, whatever their position, but shy with womenfolk because rarely did he speak to the fairer sex.

Robert had not courted any girl seriously before he met Penelope. He was not one whose head was turned by a pretty face and from their first encounter on the beach rescuing Noah, Robert was drawn to the disfigured woman. Brought up by a man who treated the crippled Benjamin the same as any other child, Robert did not notice Penelope's scars; instead her agreeable personality – when it eventually appeared – and her intelligence made him fall in love. Was it love at first sight like his own father? He did not know, and he was unable to hear again about his parents' romance, because his dear pater had passed away three years earlier. All Robert knew was that when, after five years of not seeing Penelope, he received a distressed letter from the woman whose presence never left him he didn't hesitate to saddle a horse and race to see her.

Two days of frantic riding with indifferent hostelries on the way meant he was rather unkempt when he arrived in London. Ushered in to wait in an impeccably clean and tidy drawing room, Robert wished he had thought to wash and change before arriving on Penelope's doorstep. He tried to straighten his curly locks and spat on his finger and wiped away a smudge of mud from his cheek. His heart was thumping loudly and he felt out of breath, as if he had run all the way from Norfolk on his own two feet instead of urging his slow mount to move faster! Where was she? What would she look like? Would she have changed? Would she welcome him?

The door opened and there was Penelope, his own true love. The years had not changed her appearance and, like him, she seemed to have come without freshening up her gown or face. He noticed that there was dust on her skirt and her hair was falling over her shoulder, loosened from its pins. Had he disturbed her in some task, maybe packing? Then he wondered if she was excited at their meeting when she stammered:

"Mr Roberts... I... I..."

"My dear Penelope." He cut across her, his voice high with anxiety. "You don't mind me calling you that? I have always thought of you as 'Penelope', after all the times we shared together."

"Times we shared together? What do you mean?"

"With the children on holiday."

"But, Mr Roberts, that was only two weeks, five years ago. You can hardly..."

"Five years, eight months and seventeen days, to be precise." He stepped across the floor, closing the space between them. He wanted to be near her.

"Mr Roberts!"

"Oh, don't be formal with me. My first name is only one letter less! Please call me 'Robert'. It is almost the same. Oh, please, I have counted the days."

"But, Mr Roberts... Robert, you've only written to me twice."

"Yes, but I have carried your replies around with me all the time – pressed against my heart."

"Please, don't say that! You're embarrassing me."

"But, we are alone." He gripped her hand and stared intently into her eyes. Suddenly the words spilled out: "Say that you'll marry me."

"Ma... marry you! What are you talking about?"

"I love you. I want to have you for my wife." He found himself leaning towards her. What would her answer be?

"You can't possibly love me. You don't know me. Even I wouldn't say that I..."

"Ah, you feel it too. My dear, dearest, most precious Penelope, I want to marry you."

Penelope pulled away from his grasp and walked very sedately to the window. He was glad she could not see his crestfallen features. Would she deny him her love?

"How has it all come about? Why now?"

He reckoned she was prevaricating. He wanted to see her face and read what he believed was there, but she kept her back to him. He took a deep breath to steady his nerves and managed to say calmly:

"I read your letter about… about your changed circumstances and I knew I had to speak right away. I, too, have had news during the last two months. I have been left a small – you might think it a very small – amount of money, by my godfather and I am at last in a position to leave my job and set up my own household. My greatest desire has always been to be… be a farmer and I know that… that it will be hard work, but I'm not afraid of that! If we could find a farm to rent…"

At last, Penelope turned to him, saying:

"Do you know anything about farming?"

"Not really, but I've read some books. Well, I suppose, I do know a little. I was raised in the country. It was very rural where I was born and I had access to the farm on the estate. My father wasn't a farmer but my grandfather was! He had several acres of land just the other side of the border, in Wales. Hence the name, I suppose. I've got Welsh blood in me. Maybe I get my dream to till the land from him. But, whatever the reason, I used to spend every available hour I could in the fields when I was a child and my father and I used to be out in the open whenever we could and…"

"But it's rather different to actually run a farm, don't you think?"

"You don't want to be a farmer's wife." Robert's tone was flat with disappointment. He hung his head. "That's why I've not asked you before. When I discovered that your father was Sir William Rowlands, I decided I couldn't ask you to marry me. After all, I was merely a tutor, and I could not support a wife and children on my wage… But I had hoped… with your father being a squire with his own lands… Well, a farmer… At least…"

"It's not that. I have no particular interest in money. I know nothing about farming, but I suppose we could learn. No, it's just all been rather sudden."

"…*we could learn*…" Oh sweet joy!

"So, you will consider it? You do feel something for me?"

"No, don't put words in my mouth. I… I'm not sure…"

Robert hesitated no longer. He had his reply. He was across the room whilst she continued to speak and caught her in his arms before she had time to resist. He firmly cut off the sentence, without apology, by covering her lips with his.

"Will you, Penny, my dear? Say you will," he whispered against her skin. "I can succeed with you by my side."

"What about my face?" The words were barely audible.

"What about your face? To me, it's beautiful, for it belongs to you. I know you no other way. I love you as you are and I hope you will have me as I am. I'm not very good for you. I bring no money or title…"

"Please don't say anymore, Robert. I don't want money or a title. All I want is… is to be loved…"

"Well, my own Penny, you certainly are that! I know your Miss Swann loves you, but no one could love you half as much as I do. I'm bursting with love for you and I want to marry you right away. The only problem is your father…"

"You leave my father to me. He won't refuse me. He'll be glad to have me off his hands after all these years!"

Robert was catapulted out of his reverie when a shout came:

"Good day, Mr Roberts!"

He had reached the meadow and the noise and bustle claimed his attention. Before him there must have been a hundred sheep gathered from all the surrounding farms. In the centre of the field were five shearers. Robert knew they had been at their task since early morning, for skipping with apparent delight across the grass were many newly-sheared ewes, bleating to their lambs to come and rejoin them. Robert sighed, his worries returning. He was late; his wife's journey had delayed their arrival here.

Robert saw the wooden pens along one side of the field. Slipping David to the ground, Robert instructed Robbie to watch the youngster whilst he concentrated on guiding his dogs to keep his own flock together and into one of the pens.

Once this was done, Robert had the chance to exchange civilities with his neighbours. What a crowd! June was very much the month for the sheep to be divested of their coats. Any earlier and a late spring cold burst might bring illness to the animals; any later and the fleece would be shed naturally, catching on thorns and branches and be wasted.

"I've heard about your wife's loss." The words were said too many times to recount.

"Yes, she's gone today to see her sister," he replied again and again, whilst he tried to watch that his younger sons didn't get burnt by the boiling pots of tar bubbling near the shearers, ready to be daubed on any nicks or cuts on the skin of the sheep. Robert knew the tar sealed the wounds and, in particular, prevented flies from getting in and laying maggots. Robbie seemed fascinated by the shearing scissors themselves and stood watching the men sharpening the blades with smooth stones before expertly snipping wool from the next beast; others would roll the complete fleece up in a bundle. This year, it was Robert's intention to sell all but one of his fleeces – they needed the money more than the wool for the household.

Robert moved forward in the unofficial queue as the sun climbed behind the rain clouds. The shearers, sweat falling from their brows, worked without rest and past midday Robert was informed:

"That Henry Simmons is doing his forty-fifth one."

When he heard this, Robert reassessed his estimation of the number of animals that had been brought together today.

"How many do they hope to do before dark?" he asked the man who had mentioned the shearer Henry Simmons.

"Sixty is by no means unheard of."

Later, Robert had a few moments of panic when he couldn't find David in the laughing, crowd but the child had curled up under the hedgerow and was fast asleep. It was one of his own dogs who discovered the prone figure, sniffing and nudging the child until Robert whistled him away. Robert didn't disturb his son but kept one eye on the blue breeches beneath the leaves because, suddenly, at last, it was the turn of his stock to be released from their heavy coats.

All day, above the drone of masculine voices, the shriek of playing children and the cry of the sheep, came the lilt of the bagpipe and from mid-afternoon other senses were awakened by the aroma of mutton cooking over the fire. Robert spoke with a few of the women, who seemed in charge of the meal, although he knew it would have been the men who had slaughtered the old ewe, once its last wool had been garnered. It was when he had settled his sons, cross-legged on the ground with bowls of stews and an elderflower fritter apiece, that Will from the next farm approached him.

"It's a good day that yon Squire has returned," he said.

"Which squire?" Robert returned.

"At the manor. Your brother-in-law, man. Haven't you heard?"

"Heard? No indeed."

"He's been away seventeen years, I understand. Banished by his late father."

"Do you know why?" a new voice piped up. It was Ruth, Will's wife.

"I don't. My Penelope writes to her brother but they don't talk about the past."

"Hear tell it was over a woman, and your brother-in-law only a lad!"

Robert's face, reddened by the sun, for he had forgotten his straw hat in the confusion of the morning, went a darker hue. He was fond of his peers and more than happy to discuss politics or diagnose an illness amongst his livestock or estimate the price that they might get for the fleeces and whether the wool should be sold to foreign merchants and carried across Europe, but he felt uncomfortable talking about his own relatives. Maybe it was his years of being a tutor – so different from farming where one relied on the goodwill of your acquaintances just to survive the length and breadth of the changing year. He gave what he hoped was a non-committal grunt.

"Can I borrow your horse to move my hay to the cow shed next week, Robert?"

The embarrassed man was rescued by Isaac, his nearest neighbour. He was much more comfortable with this kind of conversation!

"Yes."

"*Tad*, can I take Sandy across to the Lewis farm?" Llewelin must have heard the request.

"Possibly. It depends. I might need you to scythe our own crop, remember, son." Robert gave the lad a friendly punch on the shoulder. "In fact, I think we should be setting off for home. Your brother has fallen asleep again but with his nose in his stew and I am hoping your mother has returned. I'll need you, Llew, to rub Sandy down tonight."

"Yes, *Tad*," the boy beamed his pleasure.

Robert returned the grin, suddenly aware of the exuberance of youth. He was beginning to feel his age at the end of a busy month, but his eldest appeared to have boundless energy. He was astonished a second time when Llewelin and Robbie ran ahead of the bleating mass of animals wending their way home, whilst he and Thomas brought up the rear, cradling a sleepy David in the crook of his arm.

PENELOPE

When the riders had disappeared around the corner, peace descended. Penelope patted Sandy's head and steered him once more into the centre of the road. It wasn't many minutes later that she saw the turning to *Trem-y-Môr* right in front of her; Sandy came to a standstill, shaking his head and whickered as though he was asking her if he was to go down the rutted path. She touched the reins to set the horse walking again. When she reached the stables, Owen Lewis appeared, a bucket in his hand. Hastily he put it down and came to assist her. Behind him, a boy, one of his younger sons – she thought it was Morgan – leant against the stable door.

"Mistress Roberts!" Owen greeted her. "We've been expecting you. What a sad day! There was no warning that the Squire was ailing. Can I help you?"

"Would you take the babe, Owen, please?"

Knowing how many children the groom had brought up in his own home, Penelope lowered her daughter into the man's arms without hesitation.

"My, she's a beauty," admired the servant, holding the baby and smiling at the little round face.

Penelope slid from the horse's back, unconscious of her skirt catching up to reveal her stockings. She felt completely at home with the people who worked for her father and without thinking entered the house through the back door. Ever since her marriage, she had not mixed socially with her own class, but then she had never been one for meeting others; thus she did not miss them! The Welsh language she had learnt was from the local, ordinary folk who, she understood, would never count her as one of them because she was a 'stranger', but who seemed to like her nevertheless. She hoped it was because she never put her nose in the air like some she encountered. Often she and her husband found their house full of an evening; many neighbours came to sit in their warm, welcoming kitchen to discuss any subject from politics, through religion, to the weather or the state of the crops.

In the kitchen at *Trem-y-Môr*, Penelope was greeted with glad cries, which she suspected were more for the arrival of the baby than for herself. However, these exclamations were stifled quickly when everyone remembered the reason for her visit: her father would be laid out somewhere in the house.

Mrs Jones and Elin were busy cooking mountains of food; Penelope presumed it was for the wake before the funeral. People would be coming from far and near to pay their respects. Already piles of cooked food had been arranged in tottering stacks all around the room.

Mrs Jones laid down her ladle and spoon with a bright smile and relieved Penelope of a slightly damp Sarah. The housekeeper hugged the baby to her generous bosom and a tear formed in the corner of her eye.

"Are you going to the parlour, my dear?"

"Now, Mrs Jones, you know I never do that! Once a month I've been coming for… how long is it? Ten years and you surely don't need to be told again that this room is the one I want to sit in. There's such lovely smells in here and so much going on! Anyway, I'm not a visitor, am I?"

Unfortunately, this speech was hardly audible, because baby Sarah did not appear to be pleased to be handed away from her mother and she wailed loudly in protest.

"Oh, the little darling is wanting milk," sighed Mrs Jones joggling the child up and down.

"Yes," admitted Penelope. "You'd better give her to me and I'll feed her. Then you can cuddle her."

"Where would you like to sit? The rocker?"

"Anywhere. Sarah's used to being fed in all sorts of places, aren't you sweetheart? The rocker will be fine."

Once her mouth touched her mother, Sarah's crying stopped immediately. Momentarily, all that could be heard was the vibrant sucking of the child and the creak of the wheel when the dog turned the spit.

"How's Mariana taken all this?" questioned Penelope, beginning to move the rocking chair back and forth. "Where is she?"

"She's in her room, poor mite," explained the housekeeper. "Elin, would you go and tell Miss Mariana that Mistress Penelope has arrived."

Elin shook her hands free of excess flour wiped them on a cloth and left the room.

"Now, run along, you two!" Mrs Jones clucked at Elin's two sisters,

Kate and Peggy. "You can have a short time out of my kitchen. Go and see if those lazy hens have decided to give us some eggs; I need more for this cake. Hurry before the rain starts!"

Penelope surmised that the housekeeper was disposing of all the listening ears in order to be alone with her. She knew that Mrs Jones' health had deteriorated in the past few weeks, although her legs were always swollen because she spent hours on her feet. Recently the old woman's world had narrowed to the house and backyard; even church she had to miss except for special occasions. She had to rely on people who came to the Manor House to keep her supplied with her favourite food: gossip. Sure enough, Mrs Jones lowered her voice conspiratorially. "Miss Mariana's taken it rather badly, although the arrival of Master Edward… I mean the new Squire has…"

"Edward! Edward is here!" Penelope sat up quickly. Her young daughter was wrenched from her supply of milk and bawled her displeasure. Skilfully Penelope guided the child's gaping mouth into place without looking at the baby and settled again in the chair. "Well?"

"Aye, he's here, but he's not here at the moment." Mrs Jones beat butter in a bowl expertly whilst she talked. "Rode in late last night and terrible tired he looked. 'Course, he's changed mightily since I last saw him. He was hardly more than a boy when his father sent him off. Wicked cruel it was! But there, he's come back and a day too late. Missed his father and very upset he was that Sir William was already gone. He's got a wooden leg which Miss Mariana thinks is quite dashing. Not me, though. He's still limping…"

"I know all about his leg. He wrote to me and told me and not before time too! You know, Mrs Jones, I didn't hear a word from him for nearly nine months. He was never the world's best letter writer, but I was very worried that something awful had happened to him, when I didn't hear from him for ages. Apparently, he had been very ill with fever after losing his leg and he was lying in a hospital in Plymouth. However, he didn't mention to me in his last letter that he was intending to come up here. I'm surprised he didn't stop at the farm on his way."

"Probably didn't know where it was. Also he was very late arriving here. We were on our way to bed, but I soon found him something to eat. Talking of food…" Mrs Jones wiped her brow with the back of her hand. "Would you like something to eat? We're having a meal at six, today. We're all turned upside down at the moment. But I'm sure you're hungry, feeding that child."

"Yes, thank you. When I've finished feeding Sarah, I'll give you a hand."

"No, you won't! You sit and rest. I'm sure you deserve a rest, running that great big farm with all those children."

"Oh, Mrs Jones, it's not a great big farm," laughed Penelope.

"Mmh, maybe it is, maybe it isn't, but there we are. Giving all your strength to making milk. I know you don't hold with wet nurses but…"

"Certainly not! I enjoy feeding my own children and anyway, it actually gives me an excuse to sit down sometimes!" Penelope lifted the baby. "There we are, my sweetie. Let's change you over and then we can get you into some dry clothes. Where is Edward then? You never told me."

"He's gone to see the Parson. What with all these shipwrecks, we haven't seen the Parson yet, and…"

"Yes, I heard about the wrecks," rejoined Penelope. "Two in one night!"

"Three, according to Miss Mariana. She saw one sink right here."

Mrs Jones went on to tell Penelope about the stranger upstairs and how his arrival and the demise of Sir William had jerked Mariana back to her senses finally. Barely had she finished telling the tale when her young mistress arrived. Penelope stood up, hastily retying her bodice and held the baby against her shoulder.

"Shall I take her from you?" offered Elin, who had followed Mariana into the room.

"Thank you," Penelope replied, handing the child to the other woman. She allowed a silent Mariana to take the place instead. When Penelope had first met her half-sister, her advances of friendship had been rebuffed, continually, but Penelope (and Robert when he came), had refused to take "No" for an answer. Gradually, Mariana had begun to respond to her sister, especially, it came out later, when she saw that her father did not love Penelope more than he loved her! Although Penelope was almost old enough to be Mariana's mother, their relationship had developed into sisterly affection. During the months when Henry had been at school, Mariana had spent long afternoons at the farm in the centre of Anglesey. And, of course, the two families met for the celebrations at the main religious festivals. However, by no means did the two women confide everything in each other, although, Penelope guessed, that Mariana was grateful enough to have a comforting shoulder to lean on today whilst she shed a few tears.

For the time it took for Mrs Jones to make pastry, roll it out and line four dishes with it, the two sisters exchanged much news; grief was shared; information about the man upstairs, his injuries and Mariana calling him 'Jack' and then the unexpected arrival of Edward and his resemblance to the late Sir William.

Whilst the housekeeper filled the pastry with cooked plums, she regaled the others about Bridget, Thomas' mother, and whether this unfortunate women was indeed pregnant or just swollen with dropsy and if her death was imminent. Mariana had just stolen a griddle cake from a stack of still-warm ones which had been cooked earlier when the door burst open to reveal Kate and Peggy, who was chanting:

"He's coming! He's coming!"

"Ssh!" admonished Mrs Jones. "Don't make such a noise! Who is coming?"

"The pirate with the wooden leg."

"He's not a pirate," interjected Mariana. "He's the new master and you'd better start calling him 'Sir', or he won't be pleased."

Edward appeared whilst Mariana was speaking, his face flushed, and Penelope watched his eyes sweep over the people assembled in the kitchen. She saw him rest his gaze on Mariana, who was spreading butter thickly on to a griddle cake. All at once he looked back across the room and straight at her, as if he had missed her at first!

"Penelope! How marvellous to see you!" he said in English. Immediately he caught her in a tight embrace. "You haven't changed at all!"

"Not changed!" Penelope's voice was muffled against the weave of his coat. She pulled away from him before retorting, "I'm not sure that's a compliment! I've four children…"

"Where are all your sons? And your husband? Is he amidst this throng? I'd like to meet him soon."

"You'll see him at the funeral," promised Penelope. "Did you manage to arrange everything? I assume it will be on Sunday, during the morning service." She was surprised to see what looked like pure hatred pass fleetingly over her brother's features and she saw him glance at Mariana.

"No, it isn't going to be on Sunday. There have been too many deaths with all these shipwrecks. I agreed to have it the day after tomorrow. Friday, that is."

"Friday!" snapped Mrs Jones.

"I hope that is convenient for you…"

"Yes," agreed the housekeeper, flushing. Penelope wondered if all the extra responsibilities had made the older woman forget to whom she was talking. She was speaking again, "I was thinking that it would be on Sunday. However, I can see the sense of it. I'll be able to cope, I suppose, now I know which day it is. That means the vigil will be tomorrow night. Ah, that will keep us all busy! Anyway, for the time being, come, Sir, and have something to eat. We'll be serving the main meal at six, but I've got…" Mrs Jones started to clear a place at the table. Penelope suspected that the housekeeper's whole life revolved around the preparing of meals, serving the food and tidying away afterwards.

"No," her brother answered. "No, thank you, Mrs Jones, I'm not hungry. At least, not if we're eating early. But I'll gladly sit down, for there's news to hear from Penelope."

When he took a seat, the baby gave a cry. Edward looked up in surprise at Sarah in Elin's arms.

"Who's this then?" he asked. "Surely it's not yours, Elin? Your name is Elin, isn't it?"

"She's mine," confessed Penelope, taking the child. "You never heard, did you, that I'd had a daughter? Her name is Sarah. Would you like to hold her?"

"No, thanks. I've never held a baby in my life."

"It's not difficult, Sir," smiled Elin.

"All right, Edward," murmured Penelope. "I won't force you."

"Men don't like babies," stated Mrs Jones.

"My Robert does," disagreed Penelope. "But Sarah is his fourth."

EDWARD

"As I've said before, I am looking forward to meeting this man of yours." Edward spoke quietly. It was the truth, but, at this very moment he wanted, above all else, to converse with Mariana alone and question her about what the Parson had told him. Also, he had decided to search through his father's papers to see if anything was written down about the proposed marriage. He couldn't shake off his tiredness; he felt like he'd been through a battle with the French. His leg was aching again, sending shooting pains through his muscles.

"Give *me* the child," commanded Mrs Jones. "She's a real darling, aren't you, *cariad bach*? Look, she's giving me a smile. Well, Master Edward, what about the coffin? Had Mr Cutlass seen to it?"

"Yes, I saw someone about a coffin. A Mr... Mr..." He was only half concentrating, since he was watching Mariana, who seemed unaware of his scrutiny.

"Mr Hughes, you'll have seen," supplied Mrs Jones. "Good, that's fine. The sexton will know, of course. Sir William is to be laid with his second wife, your mother, Miss Mariana."

It dawned on Edward that this indomitable woman was more in charge than he was! However, she had not finished speaking yet.

"Now, Mistress Penelope, let's get you some food. Kate, fetch me that loaf. Peggy, did you find any eggs? Miss Mariana, if you eat any more of those, you won't want your meal and I'm doing lamb for you. It's your favourite. Master Edward..."

Thomas came through the door and the housekeeper's words petered out. "There's someone to see you, Sir. Mr Lloyd. I've sent him to the front door," announced the young man.

"Oh!" sighed Edward, "who's this then?"

"He's the waiter and searcher," Mariana explained. "He does most of his work at Beaumaris but he pokes around Holyhead too. I'm away then. I detest the man!"

"Well, that's an inauspicious beginning! Penelope, dear sister, you must come with me," pleaded Edward.

"Not me! When I come here, I come to prattle in the kitchen, not entertain guests. Don't let Mariana influence you! He's a pleasant enough sort of man if you…."

"No… No, he's not!" spluttered Mariana. "He's… he's untrustworthy and false-hearted. And he's inquisitive – always on the lookout. He's usually first on the scene when a ship's sunk and he stands guard over the beach, not allowing anyone to pick up the tiniest thing."

"It's only his job," chided Penelope, mildly. "He can't permit cargoes to be stolen. He has to assess…"

"I don't care! He doesn't have to be so niggardly. He's too zealous at his job and he's mean…"

"I'd better go then and see what he wants here," intoned Edward. "I'm used to dealing with officials, but I'm not sure I can be of any help to him. I wonder what he wants."

"He's probably come to offer his condolences," Penelope commented.

"Not him!" raged Mariana. "And if he has, then we don't want them. Father never spoke well…"

"Oh, Mariana, if you feel that strongly, you had better keep out of his way," advised Edward. He was interested to see his younger sister's reaction to his unknown man. Again he wondered what she thought of the Vicar. "Mrs Jones, will Wilson have opened the door? Where is Wilson?"

"He's in Sir William's room, Sir," explained Elin. "He's sorting out all the clothes and… and… everything. Then the room will be ready for you to move into. However, I'm sure he'll have answered the door."

"I wasn't expecting to move into my father's room."

"But you are the master now, Sir!" exclaimed Mrs Jones, rocking the baby to and fro as the child's eyelids fluttered towards sleep.

"I… I suppose I am, but I won't be staying long."

Cries of shock came from all four women.

"Not long, Sir. Whatever do you mean?" The housekeeper was the first to speak.

"You've only just arrived!" protested Mariana.

"Surely you told me you'd left the Fleet," remarked Penelope.

Elin didn't comment in words, but gave a gasp.

Edward scanned their anxious faces.

"I… I… Well, I haven't quite decided yet. What with this threat of another war and… Ah, Wilson, here you are. Have you put Mr… Mr Lloyd in… in somewhere?"

"In the parlour, Sir."

"Very good. Oh, Penelope," Edward entreated his sister, "please come with me. I need your support. I don't speak very good Welsh."

"Oh, no, you're a big boy now! And you're the master of the house, so you'll have to cope with all the social calls that a squire receives."

Edward stood up, straightened his cravat, and followed the butler out of the room, with resignation. His new position in the community was full of complications! In truth, he was finding it very difficult to concentrate on anything since he had heard the Vicar wanted to marry Mariana, even the arrangements for his father's funeral. Above all, he felt desperate to talk to her alone, not only to ascertain whether she knew about the proposal, but also to hear what her feelings were towards the Vicar himself. However, the Manor House was full, and the demands on his time set out, for he was the Squire. Also there was his other sister – he was keen to converse with Penelope, of course. Although they had to exchange only the most recent news, being regular correspondents, he was intrigued by this self-assured, poised woman, who no longer shied away from meeting people. She appeared to have completely conquered her fear of company (or at least, the company of family and servants), and he assumed that the credit went to her husband. Or was it due to motherhood?

There were several relationships, old and new, that he longed to explore and yet no time to do what *he* wanted at all! It was impossible to see people on their own, and he realised that more would be coming – his other sisters and then more distant relatives. He had noted the panic on the housekeeper's face when she had been told that the funeral was on Friday, but feelings of panic were rising in his chest. Too many people to meet, in too short a time, after too long away! Edward allowed his shoulders to sag under all the responsibilities thrust on him. He knew how to run a ship, but run a Manor House, arrange marriages for young girls, hold babies, deal with complete strangers; he felt weighted down with care! He entered the parlour, his thoughts in turmoil.

Mr Lloyd was a man in his late thirties, Edward judged. He was pinched with an angular face and a pale complexion. He had light brown, almost yellow, eyes with bruised shadows underneath. He was biting the edge of his finger. Was he nervous? Certainly Edward towered over him – the other man was a good head shorter than him – and he hoped that would give him an advantage. Why was he needing again to be in control of these encounters? he asked himself. He decided that he just felt overcome by the unfamiliarity of being the Squire.

"Good day, Sir." Edward greeted his guest as warmly as he could, trying to keep impatience and tiredness out of his voice. He continued, "You are Mr Lloyd, I understand. How can I help you?"

"Are you… are you Sir Rowlands?"

"Yes, I suppose that is precisely who I am, although I can scarce take it in. I'm more used to 'Captain Rowlands'. Won't you sit down? Can I offer you a drink?"

"No, thank you. I am extremely busy, because of the aftermath of the storm and all these wrecked ships. I have heard that a man was washed up on this side of Holy Island. I am simply here to ascertain whether this is true or not. If a man was found on your shore, then I want to see him and hear all the details of the ship he was travelling on."

"I'm afraid that will be difficult," responded Edward amiably. He saw the other man bristle. He reckoned that this man was used to a fight, used to insisting on his own way, used to forcing himself into places where people did not want him. All signs of that initial nervousness had disappeared. Or maybe it hadn't been nervousness at all. Edward's face fell – he just couldn't cope with another battle! Not after this morning! He knew that most of the gentry (even those who were Justices of the Peace) condoned smuggling; happily they paid land tax and the Church Mise but they tried to avoid paying duties on imported goods (whether wine or soap or timber) and would consort with smugglers. This man's job couldn't be easy and it seemed to have made him aggressive.

"It's not," went on Edward, "that you can't see him, or that he doesn't exist. It's merely that he's lost his memory."

Edward watched the other man draw himself up to his full height. Edward swore under his breath at the awkward state of affairs. It wasn't his fault that the stranger upstairs recalled nothing, but it must seem like a tall story to this experienced man. Every day, he must come against people evading the issue and surely he would have heard every kind of excuse under heaven before! There were plenty of reasons that Edward could think of why folk wouldn't want this scrawny man to know what craft they were sailing in and what her business was, and what cargo she had in her hold! Edward shifted his wooden leg, conjecturing that very few people escaped this man finding out the truth, however much they tried!

"Lost his memory, eh? Well, I'll see him anyway," Mr Lloyd drawled.

His tone did suggest indeed that he thought Edward was lying. Edward tried to see the situation from the other's point of view. It was no good if he lost his temper or his judgement because of anger, like he had done with the Vicar. This man was not interested in his sister, was he? Could that explain why Mariana had spoken so vociferously against him? Although he felt his hackles rise, Edward took a deep breath and controlled himself, saying pleasantly:

"You may see him, of course, but it's not worth you wasting your time. He remembers nothing." He closed his mouth firmly when he had finished speaking. Then he stared at Mr Lloyd, allowing a silence to grow between them. He had learnt, long ago, that this made others uncomfortable and it was a trick he had used on his officers and men alike. He noticed the man shifting from one foot to another, realised that he was gaining the advantage and smiled inwardly. He let a few more seconds pass before commenting:

"I thought you said you were in a hurry."

"I am… However, I must insist on seeing this man before I leave."

"There is really no need for you to insist. I have already told you, you are most welcome to see him and ask him any questions you like. I was only trying to help you." Edward inclined his head to one side in a gesture of courtesy. "Please come this way. He is still in bed. The surgeon who is attending him has suggested that he stays there for the next week to ten days. At least, that's what I have been told. I haven't actually met him yet. Of course, he may be asleep at the moment."

Edward escorted his spiky guest up the stairs, deliberately taking his time, making Mr Lloyd go at his pace. He made no attempt at small talk, not because he was trying to unsettle the other man any longer, but because of the effort of climbing the steps. He turned the corner of the stairs slowly, but he did not pause for breath until he reached the landing. Here, a balcony ran to his left, forming the upper hall, and leading off this were the corridors to the bedchambers. On his right was a door that opened into a passage, at the end of which was the master bedchamber, the Hall Chamber. He gestured to Mr Lloyd to follow him to the left, past the door to the Parlour Chamber and down three steps into a lobby that gave access to the back of the house and the backstairs. He knocked on the left hand door.

"Come in." It was Mariana's voice.

Edward opened the door. Like where he was sleeping at present, this room had a window overlooking the roof of the scullery and the cobbled yard. Unlike his bedroom, he recalled, there was no view of the sea; he suspected that one could catch a glimpse of the mountain above the village of Holyhead, if one leant against the windowsill. However, the room was much warmer than his, presumably because it was not buffeted by the sea winds and he knew it had a pleasant prospect over the fields.

In the centre of the room was a four-poster bed, in which lay a gaunt man, his face chalky. His hair, although brushed, was lank and Edward's eyes were drawn immediately to the bandage around his head. Propped up by several pillows into a half-sitting position, he was not only awake but returned Edward's gaze with one of apparent curiosity.

Mariana was settled on a wooden chest with her legs curled up like a child, but she scrambled down quickly. He imagined that Lloyd was the last person she wanted to see judging by her wrinkled nose and pursed lips.

MARIANA

Mariana pressed her skirts against the wall, almost unconsciously intending to put as much distance as she could between herself and the man who trod in after her brother. She saw Edward glance around before moving straight to the side of the bed to introduce himself:

"Good day to you, Sir. I am Edward Rowlands, Mariana's brother. I was sorry to hear about your mishap and I hope my household is providing all your needs. This," he waved a hand at the slight man standing at the foot of the bed, "is Mr Lloyd. He is here to question you about your adventure, although I have assured him that you remember nothing."

"What!" accused Mariana, starting forward. "You've come here to pester Jack with all sorts of…"

Her words fizzled out as the full force of Mr Lloyd's reptilian eyes rested on her. She retreated to her post by the wall, her face reddening, a shiver of fear tingling down her spine. She had the strangest feeling, which occurred every time she met this man, that he had a vivid imagination and was stripping off her clothes in his mind. He seemed to be aware of her discomfort and enjoyed seeing her confusion. He had never said anything coarse or suggestive to her. Nevertheless, the feeling was acute and persisted. She hung her head beneath his scrutiny. There was a moment of tense silence. Then he turned to the bed and asked:

"Is your name 'Jack'?"

"No. I can't remember my name."

"Then why does Miss Rowlands refer to you by that name?"

"Because we have to call him something," butted in Mariana. She was surprised to find that anger had chased away her disquietude. "You can't call a guest, 'Stranger!'" Without warning Mariana felt her brother's disapproval focused on her. She was ashamed of her sharp tone and rude words, but truly she did believe that Jack wasn't well enough for an interrogation. She knew she ought to go, but her desire to protect Jack stopped her from leaving.

"I see… ee…" Mr Lloyd's long-drawn out reply suggested impatience. "Then, how did you arrive at this particular name? Did you choose it?" The question was directed at Jack.

"No, my friend Mari… Miss Rowlands did."

"Your friend?" Mr Lloyd's eyes flashed from Mariana. She could feel his probing – he wanted to catch them out, surely! "So, you've met before…?"

"No," Jack countered, his face bland and submissive. "We have *not* met before, but I think someone is your friend if they save your life, don't you?"

"And how exactly did Miss Rowlands save your life?" Mr Lloyd's voice was quiet and slow.

"She dragged me from the sea."

The thin man turned fully to Mariana and said:

"Did she indeed?" Again he stared until she lowered her eyes. "So, would you say, Miss Rowlands, that *your friend* had come from a ship?" He accentuated his words with heavy sarcasm.

"Of course he came from a ship! I saw a ship," she insisted indignantly. Mr Lloyd's disbelief hung over her testimony.

"You saw a ship. Where?"

"Out near the point."

"And what happened to her?"

"I don't know. She sank, I suppose."

"I've heard no reports of other sightings of this ship. What was her name?"

Mariana half opened her mouth in amazement.

"How could I possibly know that? The ship was far too far away. Quite apart from the fact that it was dark and windy." Her own sarcasm sounded lame.

"Yes, of course." Mariana decided that Mr Lloyd's voice was how she imagined a judge would talk to a guilty prisoner. He swung around towards Jack continuing: "Have you absolutely no memory of what ship you were travelling on or even what she was carrying? Maybe you can recall…"

"Nothing," denied Jack firmly. "I'm sorry to be unhelpful, but there it is. I can assure you that there are some facts *I* would like to recall myself – for example, who I am! However, Mr Cutlass, who has attended my wounds, has promised me that, given time, my memory will almost certainly return. Then I will not only know who I am, but also where I live and then I won't have to trespass on these kind people's hospitality any longer and…"

"You must remain here until you're completely recovered," interjected Edward.

"That's very kind of you, Sir."

"No, indeed," urged Edward. "I have seen men lose their memories before. Mostly it returns, but sometimes gradually and sometimes all of a sudden."

"This is extremely inconvenient," stated Mr Lloyd. Mariana fancied that he did not want the interview veering off; he wanted to keep all questions under his control. "I have to write up a report for my superiors and no one except you, Miss Rowlands, has seen this other ship. Did anyone else at the Manor House see it?"

"Well, where else could Jack have come from?" Mariana was able to match Jack's unemotional tone and she was pleased to raise a quizzical eyebrow to add to the effect of calmness. If only she could make Mr Lloyd look foolish. "Surely you're not suggesting that he swam all the way from Ireland, or that he floated around the coast from one of the ships that foundered off Holyhead?"

"I'm not suggesting anything, Miss Rowlands. My job is to find out the facts and only the facts, not some story fabricated to cover…"

"Lloyd!" Edward interrupted.

Again silence, broken only by a distant bleat of a sheep.

"I'm sorry I can't be more help," apologised Jack. "However, as soon as I remember anything, I'll send word to you."

"Hmmrph! Would you like me to investigate if anyone has lost…?" started Mr Lloyd.

"That would be impossible," intervened Edward. "I was with the Parson this morning and he told me that dozens of folk have lost relatives in this storm."

"I could still make enquires and…"

"I don't think that Jack would be able to cope with a constant stream of people coming to look at him to see if they recognise him," declared Mariana, her instinct to protect reappearing.

"Isn't that for the man himself to say?" observed Mr Lloyd bitingly. Mariana got the distinct impression that he would have preferred to conduct this examination alone.

"Maybe in a day or two," conceded Jack. "At the moment, I'm spending most of the day sleeping."

"I shall circulate your description. In the meantime, Miss Rowlands, if you can describe the vessel you saw."

"I can't remember. It was just a ship."

"What kind of ship? A fishing boat, a sloop or a man-of-war?"

"I don't know." She tried not to sound petulant. She wanted to say that she wouldn't help this man even if she could recall any details, which she could not!

"Very well, then. I shall take my leave of you. If *any* of you remember anything, please would you tell me." Mr Lloyd clicked his heels together like a soldier standing to attention. "Good day to you, Miss Rowlands, Sir…"

"Allow me to escort you," interrupted Edward. He signed for Mr Lloyd to precede him out of the room.

Barely did Mariana wait until the door had closed before bursting out: "I hate that man!"

"Why?" asked Jack.

Mariana sat back down on the wooden chest and considered. Her real reason was he was creepy but she didn't want to say that, so she stuttered:

"He's just… just… I don't know. I simply don't like him. Don't tell me you liked him? He's always prying…"

"I can't say whether I liked him or not after such a short acquaintance. However, I am pleased to meet your brother. I had no idea you had a brother living here. You didn't tell me."

"Edward only came late last night."

"He seems to be very hospitable."

"I got the distinct feeling that he disapproves of my behaviour, but I can't help it. Mr Lloyd always… always brings out the worst in me."

"He certainly doesn't put one at one's ease. Never mind, Mariana! He's gone now."

"Yes, but he'll be back, sticking his nose into our business and he…"

A knock sounded.

"May I come in?" Penelope's head appeared around the door.

"Oh, here's my sister, come to meet you," cried Mariana. "You'll soon have met all the family. Penelope, this is Jack. Don't you think he looks like a 'Jack' to you?"

Penelope entered the room and put her arm around Mariana's shoulders, laughing:

"Mariana, dear, you're embarrassing the poor man!"

PENELOPE

Penelope grasped the pieces of straw and pushed them into the end of the twisted 'plait', carefully turning the rope to form the flat base of the basket she was making. Last week she had finished a larger woven hamper which was in use already, full of logs and standing outside the back door ready to be heaved in by Robert, to be put by the stove. Today she was creating a laundry basket since the old one had disintegrated. Beside her lay Sarah, kicking her legs and gurgling at her own inner thoughts. Penelope brushed a fly from her daughter's face, sighing with fatigue. Her arms ached and she was glad to sit on the grassy bank in the shade of the hedgerow, not idle but involved in a non-strenuous task.

Earlier she had exhausted herself beating the butter. May was the busiest month in the dairy. The calf was eight weeks old but milk production continued high and the two cows had to be milked morning and evening. June had pushed May behind it, but Penelope continued to be industrious. Knowing that she would be away from the farm to attend her father's funeral tomorrow, she had worked feverishly in preparation for a day when there wouldn't be time to complete the quota of tasks.

From the top of each full pail of milk, she skimmed the cream, adding it to what she had saved from yesterday and the day before. Gervase Markham's book instructed that you should never keep this nutritious yield for more than three days in summer although in winter sometimes it could last six days. Placing the cream into a butter churn, she had pumped the sturdy handle up and down, beating until she felt the liquid turn sticky and thicken. The length of time it took for this to happen depended on all kinds of circumstances, not least the weather. This morning it had taken what felt like an age and she had wondered if it was her grief over the loss of her father that had affected the process. Robbie had scooped some of the mixture (which came out of the hole in the lid with the movement of the cylindrical stick) into his mouth. Nonetheless, the job was not finished once the cream solidified; the energetic work had to continue until the heavy, stiff texture lightened when the butter separated from its milk. The latter could be used in many ways – her family drank it usually, whilst some farmers fed it to their pigs – but it wasn't unheard of to give it to the poor on occasion. Scooping out the fat with a large wooden spoon, the churn could be put aside; however the buttermilk needed to be squeezed out fully to prevent the product going rancid. Then Penelope had used the wooden fluted paddles, called 'butter hands', to compress the solids, getting rid of the last of the liquid – a motion not unlike kneading – before moulding the butter into pats and adding salt for preservation.

Catching sight of her husband as he strode through the field, with a clutch of boys in his wake, her heart strings were tugged to the past, to that time when Robert was tutor to the Lockley children. From this distance Robert could have been that young man again and she recalled her terrible loss when her newfound friends were whisked back to their ancestral home. Beginning to form the edges of the basket with her skilful fingers, the intervening years melted away.

Looking back from the present, now she saw that she had shrivelled from happy, sanguine woman to quiet, mature, serious writer once more; at the time, she didn't have the perspective and was unaware of the changes. Maybe Miss Swann had observed it because her companion agreed to escort her back to the London house without any of the usual protestations. There they lived in literary peace, their days filled with discussions of the latest book that they were reading, or writing poetry and stories. They were two women cut off from the world, with only a few servants who grew rotund from lack of work and the leftovers of the meals sent back to the kitchens.

Only twice in five years had Penelope heard from Robert: once to say that Noah had died, after falling off a horse; the other letter informed her that Miss Walters had left to be married to her cousin who lived in Ireland. Of himself he said nothing and, although Penelope shed a few tears for the small boy she had rescued from the sea, it all seemed rather long ago and far away and her distress was fleeting.

Not many weeks after her second missive from Robert, to which she had not replied yet (although she had written several drafts and then thrown each away!), her father, Sir William, visited her. Rarely did he make the arduous journey to the great city and, as ever, Penelope was glad to see him and to hear news of the child, Mariana, although she had never seen her stepsister. As usual her father duly invited her to come and stay, but

Penelope felt that his offer was just a duty. He and Mariana lived in splendid isolation, wrapped up in each other's lives and the local life of the island. She surmised that she would feel an intruder and that she would be unable to visit *Trem-y-Môr* without being reminded of her stepmother and her brother, both of whom she had lost. Of course, she corresponded regularly with Edward, but his replies were infrequent and brief; she hoped that one day he would leave the sea, and then, if he settled near her, possibly she could pick up her friendship with him again, but adult to adult. Assiduously she and her father never mentioned the name of Edward; but they did exchange news about Katherine and Margaret.

However, on this particular occasion, Sir William appeared anxious to leave from the moment of his arrival; he had heard that Mariana had succumbed to the measles (an illness that could prove fatal) and he wanted to return to her side. He explained to Penelope that he had only come to tell her that the London house was to be sold – had actually been sold already – because of his shortage of money and could she please vacate it within the month? He tempered this abrupt announcement with an invitation to both his daughter and Miss Swann to join him in North Wales. Then he was gone!

Penelope was speechless with rage, but she had no money of her own to support the town house. She told Miss Swann that she had no desire to go and live with a man who had given no warning of his intentions and seemed to have no notion of the anger and turmoil he left in his wake.

"I suppose we will have to go and live permanently in Norfolk," Penelope suggested, pacing the room.

"No, you're far too young to bury yourself in the country. Maybe you could take up residence at your aunt's house or with one of your sisters. At least, you'd have some lively company in which…"

"I don't want lively company," Penelope barked. It was the first time she had ever raised her voice to her companion and this, more than anything she said, revealed her anguish. "You are my friend and we have lived together in this house for many years. I'm happy with your company and I'll come with you to your house now, if you'll have… have me. You've never complained before about our lives together…"

"No, I haven't, but I have been aware for a long time that I am not the same generation as you and you need to mix more with people your own age and maybe even…"

"Don't say it! Don't insult me by saying that I might find a husband. No one will want… will want me…"

"You're wrong, Penelope, dear. There are many women who marry who never thought they would…"

"No! It's not true. Anyway, you never married."

"That is correct: I never did. But, firstly, I did not spend my whole childhood with my nose in a book and, secondly… Oh, Penelope, I interacted with people other than my closest family and servants. Of course, some people stared at me, particularly the first time they met me, but anyone who wasn't prepared to talk to me because of my scars wouldn't have been worth getting to know. However, I did, in fact, have two proposals of marriage which I…"

"You never told me!"

"Refused," continued Miss Swann as though Penelope hadn't spoken.

"Refused? Why?"

"Because I didn't want to get married for the sake of it – simply for me to become a married woman. I loved neither man. Nevertheless, I was not alone. I met plenty of men in my daily life. I lived in a big household where there was a constant flow of visitors and there were children and people of different ages. I never shut myself away with one old woman for company when I was young."

"I'm not young! I'm twenty-four."

"You're young from where I'm standing, dear Penelope. I chose to come and teach you because… because I liked you and I wanted to help you and I believe I have…"

"Of course you have."

"Well, I'm glad; but I was forty-one when I decided to spend time with your family. I didn't have to leave my home – not because I was thrown out or rejected nor because the house was being sold – I simply chose to. And I chose to leave *you* when you had the friendship of your stepmother and she encouraged you to meet people of your own age and generation."

"But you came to live with me again, after you had left me."

"Yes. I felt London was a better place for you than Norfolk and I realised that you didn't take proper care of yourself – even to the point of not eating for days – when you lived alone, but I never believed that we would be this isolated…"

"You mean you haven't enjoyed living here and you've hidden it from me all these years!" Penelope stood before Miss Swann in confusion.

"No, Penelope. Please be seated. It's hard to talk to you when you're constantly walking up and down. That's not what I said. I have always, *always* enjoyed your company – even when you were a child. I... I love you like a daughter and I could happily live with you for the rest of my life, but you... you might think you would be happy to live with me for the rest of *your* life, but it would be wrong. It would be selfish of me to take your youth and then die, for die I will one day, and almost certainly before you. There's nearly thirty years between us, after all, and then you would be truly alone. Go! Go and live with your family now, whilst you can still adjust to living with others. After twenty years of living with me, or even ten years, you would be unable to fit in with anyone else's routine. Go and be young. I know you don't like large gatherings but you can mix with others in smaller numbers. One to one, even. You can share your life with other people's children, if you don't want to marry and have children of your own. Children are good to be with, for they see life differently from adults. They see everything in terms of right and wrong – black and white. And you... you are good with children."

"I don't want to live with my family. There's no one I can live with. Father and Mariana don't... they don't... I would feel like an outsider. And Margaret! I'm sorry, but I just *can't* live with her. Yes, we exchange letters and news, but I couldn't live with her. I suppose... If I'm honest, I... I never... Well, I can't stand her. She... I've never forgiven her. Oh, Miss Swann, what am I to do? Don't leave me now. Don't *you* abandon me. Don't shun me."

Penelope's voice had sunk to a whisper. The other woman put out her hand to touch her ex-pupil.

"I'm not shunning you, my dearest Penelope. I'm trying to do what's best for you. I love you. I can't keep you to myself any longer *for your sake*. Don't you understand? You don't belong to me. Your life can only be lived once. Go out and enjoy the world..."

"I don't want to," disagreed Penelope. "I like living with you."

"But I won't be here forever. If you can't live with your family, and you don't want to live with a husband, then, at least, find yourself a companion who is your own age – preferably one who will encourage you to go out from yourself. Your writing is excellent. It has helped you to recover and I admire you for writing letters to so many people so regularly, particularly to those who you obviously aren't fond of, like your sister. But you're not living…"

"Please, Miss Swann, don't say anymore. You say I'm not living. What is life? Surely if one is happy with what one's doing – whatever that is – then one is living. Some people love the sea, like Edward, my brother, and they will sail on a boat amidst terrible danger and hardship… I wouldn't call that living, but they do. Is it wrong to spend one's life reading and writing? Surely it's not wrong if I enjoy it?"

"No, Penelope. It isn't wrong." Miss Swann's voice sounded weary of argument.

"So you'll let me come and live with you in your cottage?"

"No, Penelope. I won't. I've tried to explain why and I'll say it again: it is *because* I love you that I'm refusing you. I believe that you would be happier living amongst people…"

"Happier? No, Miss Swann. I'm happy with you. Before Father came to visit I was living very happily, believing that you and I would continue living our comfortable, quiet life together forever. Suddenly all this has arisen. I don't understand why you say…"

"I've told you. It's because I love you and I want the best for you."

"Surely, if you want the best for me, you will allow me to choose what I want. Since I've no money to buy or rent a house here in London…" She paused. "In fact, I wouldn't live in any other house here, because I have lived here most of my life and I consider it to be my home. I'm asking you if I can come and live in your home. We can move our belongings and our lives to the cottage. It will be better really, since we won't have to fit in with servants who keep asking us at what time we want our meals. No, we will be able to please ourselves, like we do during the summer, and we shall be happy together again. You'll see."

Penelope stood up and moved to the door with an air of confidence. She saw Miss Swan rub the scars absentmindedly on her face and heard her sigh and whisper, "I tried. At least I tried."

Penelope did not look back but made her way straight to her own room. She was hurt and bewildered by her companion's behaviour and, espying Robert's letter on the desk, decided that it was time she answered it. Soon, she found herself pouring out all her feelings on the paper: both about her father's cavalier behaviour and her retired governess' unexpected reaction.

Half a week later, without warning, one of the servants came to tell her that she had a visitor: a Mr Roberts. When Penelope entered the room, summoned from the study where she had been packing her books, her heart began to thump loudly. She suppressed an urge to cover it with her hand to still its frantic beating, and instead, smoothed down her dusty gown, in an attempt at composure.

A few minutes passed and then she thought her heart would burst out of her bodice when he proposed to her. She had felt the need to move away from his intense gaze. She walked, as sedately as she could, to the window, desperately trying to control the mad beating in her chest, the thrill of excitement in her stomach, the shivering in her limbs and the joy in her voice.

"How has it all come about? Why now?" She needed composure more than ever before! Then she found herself really interested in what he was saying and they began to talk about farming.

Then had come the expert kiss which had put an end to her arguments! It was the very first time she had been kissed and it did feel rather strange to taste another person's mouth but, since it was her long-dreamed-for Robert, she submitted to the sweet as wine experience.

"Will you, Penny, my dear? Say you will," he whispered.

Doubts remained and she continued to waver, but this time because of her scars. However, he brushed these aside, declaring his love for her in words loud and clear. Suddenly her mind was made up and she proclaimed that nothing and no one would get in their way and certainly not her father, which was Robert's worry!

When the news was related to Sir William, Penelope realised that he was thrilled – absolutely and honestly – that his daughter had found contentment. Immediately he suggested that they start their project on Anglesey on a farm which he had heard was being sold cheaply because the house was badly in need of repair. He offered to help them, using some of the money from the sale of the London house, since he explained that he had a troubled conscience about selling the house without informing Penelope. Also he said that he would use his influence to make sure that they got the farm if they wanted it.

Penelope and Robert had travelled to see the farm and were pleased with its potential. Robert spoke a smattering of Welsh, for his grandparents had refused to speak anything but their native language to him when he was an infant! He told her he was overjoyed to return to the home of his ancestors. Penelope was elated to settle within easy travelling distance of her family, but not to be sitting under their very noses. Her only sadness was that Miss Swann refused adamantly to come and live with them or near them, saying she was too old to move to a new country and learn a new language. However, she promised to visit them whenever she could, once they had settled in. Yet, they were not entirely alone, with no familiar faces around the house, because Thomas Weller and his wife, Mary, who were the coachman and upstairs maid at the London house, agreed to accompany the newly wedded couple. Thus, with a few belongings and all her writings from the last fourteen years, Miss Penelope Rowlands, now proudly Mrs Robert Roberts, moved to North Wales.

MARIANA

Mariana sighed and rubbed her brow. Sweet Jesus, she was worn out! Like all the rest of the family, she had been up all night for the vigil or *gwylnos*. In the centre of the room was her father's coffin and the room was overflowing with mourners. Mariana was seated just to one side of her father. She was fortunate to have a chair; most of the others were standing. People had come and gone, throughout the night, although Mariana had lost count of who was here and who was not. Each person, on their arrival to *Trem-y-Môr*, had come and knelt by the coffin and recited the Lord's Prayer. As they rose from their knees, Edward had given each a cup of ale. Mariana had remained by her father's side for the whole time, although others, wearying of the hours of waiting, had played games in other parts of the house and outside – at least this was the usual practice at vigils.

Mariana had not joined in with any jollity. Instead, whilst various persons had prayed and read parts of the funeral service alternately, she had allowed her mind to recall the halcyon days of her childhood: days of laughter and fun, spent with her beloved, generous father. Somehow she could not find it in her to while away the time in anything other than reflection. She had not even been able to add more than a croaky voice to the hymns and psalms that had been sung.

Now she stared at the coffin, near enough for her to touch, but seemingly miles away. Surely her father was not lying in that wooden box with its three lighted candles atop, burning lower and lower with the passing night? Surely, somewhere, amidst the noisy throng, in some other room in the house, was her father, speaking words of comfort to the bereaved widow, or daughter of the person who was in the coffin! Mariana imagined that, at any moment, Sir William would make his way through the close-packed bodies, and take her hand and squeeze it encouragingly. Mariana gripped her fingers together until the knuckles showed white.

The dawn had pushed back the darkness, with regular monotony, uncaring that her heart was breaking. It appeared, from her position in the throng, that it was a dull, grey morning with mist; but she did not mind what the weather did. All she desired was that today was over.

A change of voice of the person reading made her notice the words. It was part of the Bible:

"Out of the depths have I cried unto Thee, O Lord. Lord, hear my voice: let Thine ears be attentive to the voice of my supplications."

Mariana recognised the resonant tones of Reverend Griffith Owen. She glimpsed the edges of his capacious, black cloak; the rest of him was hidden from her. Had he just arrived? She was sure that everyone else would have willingly, and by tacit agreement, handed over the recitations to him. After all, this was his job! Anyone else would be doing it simply out of respect for the Squire. Was he reading the words, or was he reciting from memory? She was too tired to care. She could easily ignore the actual syllables, because his voice was droning on – a fly battering itself against a window. However, to her surprise, the words caught her attention and gave her some measure of comfort:

"The Lord is my shepherd; I shall not want. He maketh me to lie down in green pastures: he leadeth me beside the still waters."

Moving into the room came Elin, with a tray, collecting the used crockery for what felt like the thousandth time. All through the vigil, homemade wine and ale had been doled out, together with plates of food, from cold meat to mouth-watering cakes, to sustain the mourners during their watch. Mariana had been offered her share but she had refused. How could she eat on an occasion like this?

Suddenly, it was the time to go outside and begin the procession to the church. From a distance, Mariana could hear the tinkle of a bell. Was it an omen of another death? No, it was the sexton, ringing his hand bell to call the people to order. He would marshal the unruly and sad alike into line, ready to walk behind the coffin.

Mariana lowered her eyes to her lap when a gap was opened in the packed room to make way for the four bearers. The candles were extinguished, leaving a trail of smoke and the soothing smell of hot wax. With a heave, the cumbersome burden was lifted on to the ready shoulders. One of the bearers was Edward. Mariana wondered how far along the route he would manage before he had to allow someone else to take his place. Owen, Thomas and even Wilson would all want a turn. She knew that only friends must carry the coffin, in order for the evil spirits to be warded away from her father's soul.

No, Mariana's heart cried silently, when many of the women began to moan and sob. No, don't be dead, Father! Come back! Come back! May all this be a dreadful nightmare! Oh, to wake up and find herself snug in her own bed with her father asleep in the next room and these agonising feelings without foundation! But, no, this was no dream from which to wake – this was reality. The clock could not be turned back.

"Miss Mariana."

It was Elin, urging her to stand up and go outside; she had a part to play. When she arose, she swayed from weariness and hunger. Elin opened her mouth to speak, but Mariana shook her head. There was no point giving up now! She knew what she had to do and she would do it.

The majority of the mourners had already filed out of the house, leaving it forlorn. If it had been a poor man's funeral, everyone would have dropped coins into a dish which would have been laid out for that purpose, but no clinking was heard in the Manor House.

Actually, as people left the house, a reverent silence descended. Many folk were praying, with their heads bowed and their hands together. Mariana paused on the doorstep and gazed at the press of people assembled on the grass; there were so many that some were forced to stand on the nearby beach. Rolling in over their heads, from the sea, was a penetrating mist. She could see wispy strands floating inland. Unexpectedly, the men and women nearest to her seemed to shrink to tiny, doll-like proportions – all in miniature, dressed in their best clothes. She wondered if she stretched out her hand whether she would pick them up. She blinked and they grew again. She frowned. What was wrong with her?

She knew everyone was waiting for her. She stepped towards the coffin, with Elin behind her, bearing a huge dish laden with white bread. Following Elin out of the house was Peggy, carrying two wooden bowls. Beside her walked Kate with the ale and milk which would be poured into the bowls while they were held over the coffin. At the rear, but by no means last, was Mrs Jones. In her hands she held a hunk of cheese from which protruded a piece of silver, reminiscent of the ancient, standing stones erupting from the humpy earth of Anglesey.

Mariana panicked. She recalled that she had to give all these tokens, across the top of the wooden box, to some previously chosen people, but which ones were they? She caught sight of Edward, looking exhausted already, and Penelope, whey-faced, next to her husband. She tried to catch their attention. Then she saw Wilson. He nodded to her and gave a half smile of encouragement. She remembered that she was amongst friends – all supporting her. Wilson's nod directed her gaze to the recipients of the gifts; dutifully she took the food and drink from her servants. She sipped of the milk and ale before handing over all the victuals. She watched whilst the drinks were tasted – now she recollected that only poverty-stricken mourners had been picked for this privilege. Then, with one wave of movement, the whole company knelt and the Parson started the congregation to recite:

"Our Father, who art in heaven…"

Mariana swallowed a lump in her throat and forced herself to chant the familiar words. She kept her eyes closed during the prayer. A suppressed sob made her open them. From where she was kneeling, all she could see was the straight wood of the box, but she was able to feel the mass of humanity surrounding her on every side and from all directions emanated the stink of unwashed bodies, above the smell of dank mist. She felt enclosed. She wanted to be alone, to mourn her father privately. Who were all these people and why had they come? They had not loved him – not like she had! Take Edward, for instance. He would carry the coffin, but he had hated Sir William for years. And Penelope: she had never been close to her father. And… No! Mentally Mariana shook her head. This was not fair of her. There *were* men and women here who had loved him and some had come not just because they loved him but out of respect to him. There were bound to be those here who were curious, possibly wanting to see the family's misery or to find out for themselves what the new Squire was like, but most would attend out of genuine sympathy. It looked as though the entire island had congregated outside; she could not recall if all these people had been crammed into the house. Surely there would not have been room!

Mariana felt her chest tighten. There were too many people here. She wanted to gasp for breath. No one was physically pushing her in the back, since there was a respectful gap of well-trampled grass between her and the others, but she felt the throng crowding in on her. When she got to her feet, after the final 'Amen', she swayed again; she felt ill.

She watched the carpenters shuffling forward to nail down the lid. But before this, salt had to be placed on the body. Salt: such an inconspicuous substance, yet vitally important in life and death: in life, to savour and preserve food and after life, to symbolise incorruption and to keep the devil away.

Mariana had to place the salt inside the coffin. She found herself not wanting to glimpse the face of her father, but she could not escape. She lifted her eyes and saw Meyrick and Elizabeth Parry standing next to Lord and Lady Wynne…

Henry!

She lowered her gaze and when the lid was raised she saw Henry, lying in her father's place, his features serene and smooth. She heard the creak of the wood as the lid was pressed down. Henry was in the coffin. Wait! she wanted to shout, Henry is in there! No, she reminded herself: her father was in *this* coffin, but Henry *had* lain in a tight-fitting box smelling of newly-planed planks of wood and sawdust. Henry! Her precious Henry. She hadn't been to his funeral, for she'd been too distressed. Maybe that was why she had found it so hard to really believe that he had gone.

Now the nails were in place and she could hear the rhythmic strike of the hammer. What was it like to lie down in a coffin and feel the air becoming stuffier and stuffier? She could not breathe! She felt the mist stroke her face, wrapping around her, entombing her. She had to break away; she had to be alone; she had to see an uninterrupted view – preferably miles and miles of unbroken sand, bordered by a tranquil sea, ending in a distant horizon. She looked around her; she must go. Go and run. Run and run. Away from all these people, weeping and sobbing, singing psalms, crying in prayer and the persistent sound of the hammering. Everyone was coming closer, imperceptibly leaning towards her, and hedging her in, confining her, shutting around her. Give me room, she wanted to scream.

At last the lid was down, locking her father in. Soon, so soon, like Henry before him, Sir William would be lowered into the ground and the soil would rain on top of him. Starting with a few handfuls thrown in by relatives, and ending in heavy shovelfuls from the sexton and stamped down for good measure. Then he would be gone forever. She would never see him again on this earth.

Father! Father! Father!

* * *

Mariana opened her eyes. She was lying in her own bedroom, under a light coverlet. She became aware of voices downstairs. Was the funeral over, or was the procession still about to leave? Her last recollections were of the coffin being nailed down. She turned over and concentrated on the murmur of conversation. It was coming from the parlour, not from a crowd outside. The funeral must be over.

Who was downstairs? Who had come back to the house? It was the custom, after the burial, to go to the ale house, yet someone was talking in the room below her. Perchance a select few of the mourners had returned – there would be plenty of food left! She knew Mrs Jones hadn't stinted. Were the mourners gorging themselves again unashamedly on the food so laboriously prepared? Were they drinking down her father's stocks of wine, meanwhile forgetting that they had just seen the supplier of this feast buried six feet under? Was her father's name just a memory even now, and people already discussing other issues: exchanging news of rarely seen relatives; catching up on the latest births and deaths; dissecting the most recent policy passed by the Government or how the Enclosure Acts were affecting Anglesey; wondering if this year's crops would produce a good yield?

Mariana sat up in bed. She could not go down there to the drawing room. She would be expected to balance a plate in one hand, a glass in the other, and mingle with people with whom she had no desire to speak. She would have to listen to bromides and reply with inanities – they pretending that they were devastated by Sir William's death and she pretending to be grateful for their sympathy. No, she did not want others' solicitous questions as to whether she felt better. She no longer wanted to share her grief; she would have to come to terms with her loss all by herself.

Instead, she must get away – away from the curious stares of the other mourners; away, possibly, from the attentive, hands of her maid, Elin; away, certainly, from the clucking of Mrs Jones, who would urge her either to stay in bed or not, depending on who remained in the house, bringing her plates of rich food, the thought of which made her stomach heave. She needed solitude, with no fear of interruption, for, even if she locked her door, someone would come knocking, asking her if she was awake, requiring her to undo the bolt and talk to them. No, she did not want to see anyone, how ever well meaning their intentions.

She knew what she must do: she must creep away, whilst they all thought she was still in bed. She turned back the cover and tiptoed across to the corner of the room where sat a chest. She dug down to the bottom until she found a patched pair of breeches and a smock coat. Several years ago, she had discovered a massive box full of clothes, up in the garret, in the part where Elin and her sisters didn't sleep. One rainy afternoon, she and Elin had raked through the long-forgotten treasures hiding under the eaves: outmoded pictures, stained bath tubs, a high chair with baby teeth-marks in the wood, some worn out carpets, and a fire screen depicting ancient soldiers with spears and two more chests, bursting with costumes. Some of their finds were moth-eaten or chewed by mice; all were dusty. Immediately perceiving the possibility of borrowing some boy's garments, Mariana had directed Elin's attention to a dear old battered rocking horse, which she remembered riding in the nursery. Then, later, without her maid, Mariana had returned to sift through the garments. Some were obviously her dead mother's, but half of one box contained what must have been Edward's clothes, left from when he was banished from *Trem-y-Môr*.

A shirt, two pairs of breeches, a coat, even a short cloak and several hats had disappeared from the garret, if anyone had been interested to notice and Mariana kept them right at the bottom of her own chest. Maybe Elin knew they were there (for it was hard to hide anything from her personal maid), but the other woman wouldn't dare remove them. Pulling on the clothes, she cast her mind back. When had been the last occasion she had used them? She could not recall. Probably late October (and now it was June) or even before that! No wonder the desire to steal away was so compelling!

The garments were creased and musty but it all added to the disguise, for today of all days, she did not want to be recognised. She longed to take her horse, but everyone knew Mars and reports of her clandestine ride would almost certainly reach her brother's ears and who could say? He might search for her. No, it was better to walk with her hat pulled down. Then she could pass, if not for a farm-boy, at least for a travel-stained wayfarer, bound for the port. She hoped that she would not meet anyone; she intended to keep to isolated footpaths. Surely no one would be out for a stroll in this mist!

Whilst she plaited her distinctive hair and tucked it up under the hat, her mind began to think about how she could leave unobserved. It would be no good venturing down the stairs, neither front nor back, for someone would be bound to see her, either visitor or servant. No, the only possible escape route was out of the window in the Back Chamber, where Jack was in bed, and across the scullery roof to the far end. From there, it was only about a six-foot drop to the grass below and then she would be away along the beach. Sometimes, in the past, she had taken the longer drop to the cobbled yard, but she could not land there this morning. The yard was full of the noisy clutter of carriages, stamping horses and attendant grooms. God willing, when she crossed the roof top, the mist would hide her from the eyes of Owen or Thomas or any other people standing below.

Mariana left her room cautiously, looking both ways. There was no sign of anyone, although she could hear voices in the downstairs hall. Obviously the mourners were all over the ground floor of the house – possibly in the dining room and library as well as the parlour. She calculated that there would be no point in locking her door, since, if her absence were noticed, probably some person would break the lock in an attempt to check she was not completely overcome with grief! Let them find an empty bed! Once she had gone from the house, nobody would be able to track her and she would face the rebukes when she returned; for now, the desire to be alone was too urgent to ignore.

She slunk along to the Back Chamber, wishing Jack to be asleep. It was a pity she could not use the window in Edward's room – he had not moved into his father's room yet – but she would have to jump from the window ledge to land on the slippery tiles of the sloping scullery roof and that would be hazardous, whereas she could step out of the window in Jack's room.

Gingerly she turned the door knob of the Back Chamber, warily pushing open the door.

JACK

Jack woke with a start. He opened his eyes and looked around, trying to decide where he was. There was a window to his right with dense green curtains but this wasn't his room – at least not one he recognised in that second between sleeping and waking! Momentarily a hazy memory seeped into his mind – of a bedchamber wallpapered in turquoise blue – and then was gone. Where was he? In some inn perhaps – not on ship for there was no rocking of the waves. Ah, now he remembered: he was lying in bed after being found on the beach nearby this house, which belonged to the Squire who had a very attractive daughter and… and he could muse no more. A pain shot through him in a rigour and he could think of nothing else as his injured body writhed in agony.

The spasm lessened and he relaxed with relief, sweat making his night-shirt stick to the bed clothes. He took a couple of deep breaths and then allowed his other problem to come uppermost into his consciousness: who was he? He had no memory of anything beyond the most recent past.

Over the last few days he had longed to recall something of his life before these hideous wounds had affected him so badly, and in particular, he wanted details of his identity, but to no avail. Nothing! He could recall nothing at all! Every time he woke, he wished that he would have come to his senses and be able to think clearly but, like the glimpse of a face in a passing carriage, he was unable to focus. Then he would concentrate hard, ignoring the throbbing in his head, and try to decipher more information from that fleeting image. Nothing!

Sometimes, he decided, the best plan was not to concentrate at all, but let his mind wander and allow any memories to float through his brain, but, again, this didn't work. Nothing!

The retired surgeon, Cutlass, had assured him that what he was going through was normal, and what he must do was rest. Rest! How could he rest when he was living in such darkness? He *must* get better and soon! He must get up and find out where he came from before that fateful storm.

However, it wasn't just his memory loss that distressed him. His meandering thoughts came full circle to where he had started when he awoke – his physical wounds! The cumulative pain from his head and leg filled most of his waking hours and his body lay weakly, adding to his sense of defeat and frustration. No drug – and he seemed to have been given several cocktails of potions – took away that dragging, gnawing ache and there was definitely *no* cure for the deep stabbing spasms he encountered – though, thank God, usually the latter only lasted a few seconds.

Movements needed to be planned carefully and he found it best to lie perfectly still most of the time. Talking often exhausted him, although it depended on who was conversing with him, and climbing out of bed to use the chamber pot left him dizzy and disorientated. However, he had an overriding desire to be up and about and not convalescing anymore and, to this end, he disciplined himself to increase the range of his movements each day.

In the beginning, he had made himself use the spoon and feed himself (whilst keeping his head motionless), although the effort left him listless; then he would move his head gently from side to side repeatedly whilst he was awake, trying to overcome the swaying of the room. Yesterday he had insisted to himself that sitting up and swinging his legs out of bed must be done without help from others. He sighed. That was yesterday. Today's goal? He decided it was time to see if he could walk a step or two unaided.

He could hear voices coming from downstairs and he knew the funeral of the late Squire was over. He reckoned that no one would bother with him at the moment, since Mrs Jones and the maids would be fully occupied serving the mourners.

He turned carefully on his side and then rested to let the pain recede. Slowly he let his legs slip over the side of the bed. Now, he pushed with his left arm, forcing himself into a sitting position. He exhaled loudly, wondering if he should abandon his plan. His wounds were screaming. He gritted his teeth, and placed his bare feet on the floor. Then, using his hands he brought himself to a half-standing position, trying not to stretch his leg muscle too quickly.

The door opened with a creak. Jack glanced up to see a lad creeping around its edge. Surprised, Jack overbalanced and fell back on the covers of the bed, sweat beading his ashy face, his lips pursed.

"Who are you?" he questioned while the boy exclaimed in a dramatic whisper:

"What are you doing?"

"Mariana! What are *you* doing?"

"Why are you out of bed?" scolded the young woman in her normal voice, shutting the door. "You shouldn't be out of bed. It's much too early. Here, let me lift your feet into…"

"Leave me alone," growled Jack. "I've had four days in bed, and I think it's time I was up and making a move."

"It's too soon, I say. Matthew told you it would take at least a week."

"Damn Cutlass! I can't bear to be abed any longer." He closed his eyes, trying to stop the nausea that was sweeping over him in waves.

With the lengthening silence, he realised that Mariana was waiting for him to lie down and, although frustrated, he gave in to the uncontrollable desire to be flat on his back again. He slumped sideways, paused to let the ache subside, and then moved very slowly from his side on to his back and pulled up his bruised legs. He tried, oh how he tried not to show it, but a grimace of pain screwed up his face. He heard Mariana draw near.

"Would you like me to cover you?"

"Yes." This through clenched teeth.

"Are you all right?"

"God damn you, woman! Why can't you leave me alone? What made you come in at the precise moment I was trying out my strength and now here you are seeing me at… at my worst…" He expelled a long breath of sheer exhaustion but the torment was receding.

"Serves you right to be in pain," retorted Mariana, seemingly not taking offence at his oath. "You're trying too hard too quickly. You should listen to Matthew."

"Yes, madam," whispered Jack. He let himself relax into the softness of the mattress. Ah, that definitely eased the agony. He allowed a faint smile to lend mockery to his words. "You do turn up at the most inconvenient times!"

"Inconvenient! Well, I like that!" bandied Mariana. "Because of my sense of timing you are alive today and not mouldering at the bottom of the sea!"

"Peace, Mariana, peace!" he whispered, gazing at her through slit eyes. "I can't take any more strain today. Of course, you are absolutely right."

He opened his eyes and, clutching at the covers, pulling them up to his chin, he expanded, "I am eternally grateful to you for saving my life and maybe I am even thankful that you entered the room when you did. I had decided to see if I could walk across the room and would probably have attempted it, such is my stubborn nature, in spite of the sickness and dizziness. However, on reflection, when I consider how awful the pain was, just from standing up, it's as well I *didn't* set off away from the bed, for probably I'd have fallen and maybe even hit my head again…"

"Oh, Jack, there's no need for you to hurry out of bed. In fact, really, there is no need for you to leave at all and…"

"There may not be from your point of view, my lass, but I must begin to search and find out who I am." He turned his head, hoping the pillow would give him more support. "Now, before I burst from curiosity, which could be more painful than getting out of bed, what *are* you doing in such a sorry costume?"

"I'm disguised."

"I can see that! I didn't recognise you until you spoke, but what are *you* doing out of bed?"

"How did you know I was in bed?"

"Mrs Jones, naturally. She came up here with some food for me and told me how you fainted at the wake – nearly knocked the coffin off its bier, by all accounts."

"She's exaggerating."

"I don't think so. However, it seems to me that I should be reprimanding you for being out of bed." He caught her hands which were busily patting the quilts and smoothing them over his chest. "Mariana, stop fussing and answer me. Are you…?"

"I'm quite recovered, thank you." She refused to meet his eyes. Instead, she looked towards the window. "It was just that… that I felt… felt enclosed. It was like *I* was in the coffin. I suppose it was partly because there was such a crowd and partly because… because everyone's so concerned about me… sort of cosseting me, like… you're doing now."

"I'm sorry." He released her. "I don't mean to make you feel 'enclosed'. I'm just worr…"

"No, it's not really you. I don't mind you asking. It's… it's… Well, Edward never takes his eyes off me. He watches me all… all the time and… and again and again he tries… asks me if… how I'm faring. And then there's Mrs Jones. I suppose I can't blame her either. She has always alternated between fussing over me as if I was still a babe in arms and scolding me for 'my wild notions'. Am I wild? People say that I am, but I don't feel wild. I just hate to be restrained. There are too many rules: don't do this and you can't do that and you shouldn't go there." Mariana twisted her hands together. "Father was… was never like that." Her voice trembled but she went on, "He never told me to sit up straight or brush my hair. He encouraged me to enjoy life and go out… out with him to places that Mrs Jones reckons I shouldn't have gone. I've even seen an '*Anterliwt*' at Whitsuntide. Of course, it's called an 'Interlude' in English. It's a play, quite harmless really. However, sometimes it can be… well, you know… saucy. It often has a hidden meaning. Anyway, Mrs Jones disapproves of them wholeheartedly. She doesn't know I've been and would be appalled if she discovered I had. You mustn't tell her, Jack!"

"I won't."

"Father treated me…as an individual. He never made me conform. If I wanted to ride, then I was allowed to. I didn't have to eat unless I was hungry. If I wanted something, then he'd get it for me, if he could. But now… now, everyone's crowding in on me. Everyone is very interested in my welfare – how I'm coping. But I'm all right without their care…"

"You did collapse, though."

"Yes, and that was my own stupid fault. I hadn't eaten anything all night, even though there was plenty of food. I didn't want to eat with Father… Father lying there and I didn't feel hungry either. My insides were sore. I couldn't face food. But it wasn't just lack of food. There were all those people surrounding me. I felt I couldn't breathe. They were all watching me and waiting. Nevertheless, I would have been fine if I hadn't started thinking… thinking what it must be like to lie in a coffin and hear them hammering down the lid." She paused. "Of course, I was imagining what it was like if I was still *alive* and… and Father is dead." Mariana faced him squarely before continuing:

"Do you think I'm mad, Jack? Fit only for the Bethlem hospital in London? I used to talk to Henry, you know, after he had… had died. But then, I didn't think he was dead. It wasn't that I *saw* him, but I heard him talking… talking to me in my head. He would tell me what to do."

Jack kept silent, trying to sort out his befuddled thoughts before expressing them.

"Mariana, don't torment yourself. Of course, you're not mad. You're just… just shocked. You've been through too much recently. Too many people you love have… have died in too short a time. Which one of us wouldn't talk to someone we'd lost? First, there was your Henry…"

"I found him myself," explained Mariana, sitting down on the bed. He managed not to show how much this hurt him; instead, just closed his eyes for a second. "On the beach, like you. Actually, I thought you were Henry; that's why I pulled you out of the sea and…" She stopped, her face tinged with pink. "Oh, I'm sorry. I shouldn't have said that. If… if I'd known you then, like I do now, I would have saved you because you're… you're a good person and worth saving."

"You don't know that."

"What?"

"That I'm a good person. I thought you'd painted my past in lurid colours."

"Yes, I did think, at first, that maybe you were a pirate or an escaped convict, but you can't be now."

"Why not?" Jack raised his eyebrow, and then wished he hadn't. Momentarily he lost the train of the conversation as a line of pain sped from brow to wound.

"Because… because…"

He came back to what she was saying, fleetingly realising that this conversation could be crucial to any future relationship they would have together. She seemed to be opening her heart to him. He tried to be emphatic and succinct.

"You don't know me, Mariana. You don't know me hardly at all. You shouldn't trust me. I could be lying about my loss of memory. I could be running away from someone and if I told you who I was, you wouldn't hide me but tell…"

"Are you?"

"Am I what?"

"Lying."

"No."

"There you are then!"

"Mariana, it's only words. I could still be lying. You don't know…"

"I *do* know. I know in here," she thumped her chest, "that you're not a wicked person. Yes, you've got scars, but that doesn't mean you're a criminal. You could have got them in the Fleet. They whip you there, according to Edward, and often on the smallest pre…"

"Ah, but I might still be a rogue."

"Why are you saying all this to me?"

"The reason is: I don't want you to trust me." He continued to struggle to keep focused. Weariness flooded his limbs. "You can't tell what a person is like from their appearance, as you yourself have said. You have got to…"

"Why don't you want me to trust you?" she broke in accusingly.

"Because soon I'll be leaving…" A shiver of resolve clarified his thinking.

"No!" The syllable was surprisingly vehement.

"Yes, my dear. I must. I must find out who I am. I may have responsibilities to carry out and commitments to fulfil."

"But you'll come back?" she pleaded in a small voice.

He made no reply, not this time because of lack of concentration but because he was trying to overcome a sudden desire to grasp her hand and tell her what she seemed to want to hear.

"Jack. Jack, say you'll return to see us."

Her insistence and the longing in her eyes made him say:

"Yes, I suppose I will, in order to tell you who I am and how… how grateful I am to you all for helping me and to you, especially, Mariana, for rescuing me. However, you're vulnerable at the moment and you're too trusting…"

"It's no good." She shook her head.

"What isn't?"

"Trying to stop me trusting you. I already do. Haven't you noticed how often I come to your room?"

"I have." All of a sudden, he wanted her to go. She *was* vulnerable. He must lighten the tone of what he was saying or he'd end up regretting his words. He felt vulnerable too! "I thought it was because you enjoyed inventing a past for me."

Mariana smiled shyly and his heart lurched. God, she was attractive in her very youthfulness! But he mustn't take advantage of her – in fact, it would be crazy to do so in his present unknowing condition. She hadn't taken the hint for she was saying quietly:

"No, it's not that. It's because I feel safe here. I don't quite understand why. Maybe it's on account of you being a stranger. You don't know anything about me, except what I tell you and… and…" Now it appeared that it was Mariana who was struggling to put her thoughts into words. "It's as if time stands still here, in this room, for you yourself remember nothing about your life. Oh, I can't explain it. It's more than that. I feel comfortable with you, for you don't disapprove of me. Take now, for instance, Henry (and Edward, if he saw me) would have been angry that I'm dressed like this, but you're not. Henry used to be great fun when he was a little boy. We used to compete to see which one of us could do the very worst, most dangerous, daring exploit. But when he grew up, he didn't like me behaving like a boy. He thought I ought to be ladylike, I suppose. I was aware, always, when he got older, that I was a girl and he was a boy; whereas when we were young, it was… We were both boys. No, 'boys' isn't the right word. We were comrades – partners. Oh, I think he loved me… No, I believe he loved me and I loved him, but often I had to pretend that I was different… There you are, you see? I told you so."

"What?" The word came out before he could stop it. He should have kept silent for maybe then this flow of honesty would dry up.

"You… you've made me see this… about Henry. I've never realised this before, but it is true. I had to hide my true self. I… He wanted me to behave like a girl – to be maidenly – at a time when my inclination was to behave like a boy. However, I would pretend to be feminine when I was with him. I used to allow him to help me up into the carriage and things like that, but I didn't really *need* his help; I just used to pretend I was helpless.

"Oh, but I never pretend on a horse. I used to race him and he would get cross, especially if I won. No, I tell a lie. He didn't mind who won. It was just that he didn't like me charging off… He said he was worried that I would fall, but… I never fall off. The truth was that he wanted me to behave like other girls, who meekly walk their horses and never canter and certainly don't gallop! I'm not saying that I minded him caring about me, treating me like a real lady. No, not at that time. In a way, it was all so different from what I was used to. I suppose Father assumed that I never needed his help; he trained me to manage on my own. But, I remember, when I was fifteen or sixteen, that I used to be good and behave when I was with Henry and… and then, after he'd gone away or I'd come home, I used to do something really wild to sort of make up for being good. Oh, dear, that sounds very childish."

"I guess you had to allow your high spirits out sometimes." Jack spoke carefully, his tiredness slowing his brain. He couldn't fight her manifest need to talk. He must just let her speak until she had no more to say.

"Henry should have known me better, for we first met when I was only five. He, of all people, should have perceived that I wasn't humble and conforming. Surely, he should have seen that it was all a pretence."

"Yes." Jack could feel the room going round but deliberately he jerked the sleepiness from his tone. "Yes, but some girls are boyish when they are young, and then when they mature, they change. He must have thought that you had changed."

"I'm not sure. He wanted to protect me but I don't need protecting. I can see that today, although at the time... Well, if I'm truthful, I suppose I enjoyed having a beau who... who wanted to look after me. Yes, I did enjoy it, but it wasn't me. If... if I'd married him, in the end, I would have been unable to keep up the charade. I would have needed to go away from him for an afternoon and do something reckless, and that would have made Henry ashamed of me. Oh, this is awful! I shouldn't be thinking like this. I loved Henry. I... still do love him."

Silence fell between them.

"Jack? Are you all right? Oh, I'm sorry, I should..."

"Yes, I'm fine, just thinking. Of course you still love him. And, if I may be so bold as to disagree with you..." He wanted to sketch a mock bow with his head and right arm, but settled for a half grimace. "I think you'd have had a happy marriage. Probably, he'd have treated you less carefully after he'd been married to you for a few years!"

"Do you really think that?" Mariana's tone was sceptical.

Jack smiled.

"Ah," she sighed. "It's all very difficult. Maybe I would have changed as well. Maybe I wouldn't have needed to be... so unruly. After all, I have changed just in the last few months. One thing I've learnt: I want to be... be... *me*. I haven't quite discerned what I am yet, but I hate to... to be bound by others. Especially by ridiculous rules. I'm not much good at being a Squire's daughter and I won't make a very good wife. For example: I don't like sewing or keeping an inventory of what linen and china we've got in the house, or... ordering meat or... or.... Oh, it's hard to think of everything. Just all sorts of housewifely duties. And I don't dote on babies either. I can guess what you're going to say: 'Wait until it's your own household and your own child.' But..."

"I wasn't going to say that. However, it may be true."

"But it may not. Fortunately, I'm never going to find out because I'm never going to have children, since I am not going to marry."

"Why ever not?"

"Because I can't get over my love for Henry."

"Good God, woman!" His voice was strong! He couldn't let a statement like that go unchallenged! "You've just been carefully dissecting your feelings and already you're looking more objectively at them."

MARIANA

Mariana stood up and walked across to the window. She could see nothing but the smoky mist hanging over the wet buildings and grass, like a dirty sheet or a… a shroud. She shivered.

"I'm sorry. I've hurt you." Jack intoned softly.

Mariana did not reply for several seconds and then she spoke thoughtfully:

"No. Possibly you're right. It's only that… I can't imagine marrying anyone else. Scores of men I know… look… well, ogle at me but…"

"You're a beautiful woman, Mariana." His words seemed to be said sincerely.

"I'm not sure about that… Oh, when I stare at the glass, I think that I'm beautiful, but inside… inside I'm not beautiful. I'm often angry and restless and rebellious and…"

"But men will always desire you, for you are quite… quite perfect."

Mariana laughed, turning towards him.

"Oh, Jack! That wound has stewed your brains! Although… although it is flattering to hear such words, but… but there's more to me than how I look! You say that I don't know you and that's true, but you don't know me either. When you say things like that about me, you are looking no deeper than my skin. I believe Henry knew me. At least, I… I thought he did. Yes, he loved me for… myself. Oh, I'm all confused now. You've made me wonder about our relationship. I suppose, I don't really understand myself yet, so how can I expect others? Henry was proud of me. I'm sure of that. He used to… sort of preen himself whenever we were in company – as if to say, 'Look what I've caught!'! And I enjoyed that, for I was… am… am pleased with Henry. He was the man I most wanted to marry and therefore I was glad to be… be shown off. However, there are times when I hope that someone will love me not just because of the colour of my hair or eyes, but for who I am. After all, one day I will grow old and then who will want me? Oh, Jack, I can't explain what I'm trying to say."

She leant against the windowsill, feeling the rough cloth of the breeches rub her legs. She noticed that Jack was pale and he was evidently making an effort to speak but she wanted to hear what he had to say.

"Mariana, you're fretting about nothing. Henry loved you, and part of his love was pride in you. That's only natural. I'm sure that he loved your character too. Remember, he had known you for a long time and he must have seen you in all sorts of different moods. But, anyway, your appearance affects the person you are." He closed his eyes before continuing, "I'm sure your sister would agree with me. You are really a very fortunate person. Some women would... would give anything to look like you, but then you're used to it. Your life has never been any different. You haven't experienced what it is like to walk around unnoticed and unloved. You only know what it's like to turn heads wherever you go. My advice to you is to enjoy being beautiful. But beware... There's a world of difference between desire and love. You can, of course, find them hand in hand, but now you have lost Henry, who had, as you yourself said, been acquainted with you since childhood, you'll be meeting all sorts of men and you must be careful that you don't marry the wrong man on..."

"I've already told you, Jack: I'm not going to marry anyone."

"You say that today and I can understand that. But it's early days and you've just lost your father and..."

"Father was an original! He didn't think I was beautiful. He always thought *my mother* was the most beautiful, most perfect woman in the whole world. He... he simply allowed me to be myself."

"He could afford..."

"What? We're not wealthy..."

"I'm not talking about money. I meant in parenthood. He could afford to indulge you for you were a child and you loved him in return and gave him all he needed just by being you. However, with adults... With two adults there has to be more give and take within the relationship. You can't demand that someone accepts you *exactly* as you are. I'm not just talking about marriage. It's true for friendship too. There's always pretence in life. Think. Isn't it true that when you're with Mrs Jones, you behave in a different way to the way you used to with Henry, for to one you will always be a child, whereas to the other, you were a woman? So it is with all our friendships. We show a varied face to various people. Mariana, I'm going to have to rest now. Could we continue this conversation later?"

"Oh, Jack, how unthinking of me! But what you say seems to make sense and yet how can you speak like this? You sound as if you're married. Are you? Just answer this one more question. Are you married?"

"Mariana, I've told you: I don't remember anything."

"Well, how can you talk like this then if you don't remember anything?"

"I honestly don't know. I just feel that you'll probably never find any man like your father, even an older man than yourself." His words were spaced out as though he was having to think of each one individually. "The relationship you had with your father was unique. So, too, with your husband. He will know you in ways that no one else ever will. And from the day you marry, you will change. You will have responsibilities. Firstly, to your husband, then to your children. And that's not to mention your new role as mistress of your own home, not your father's home. You will have to deal with servants who *don't* remember your first word or tottering step…"

"I don't think I want to get married then. How can I be myself? What about all the things I want to do each day?"

"That's what I'm talking about. You won't be able to do exactly what you want, all the time. Now, when you were a child, your father could allow you to do whatever you wished. You were not his wife! Every adult has had his or her turn being a child. However, once you grow up, life changes…"

"Then I'll never marry!"

"You only say that because you haven't met another man yet. We've talked about the responsibilities, but what about the joys and pleasures? There are advantages in being grown up. For example: you are your own mistress or master. Within the confines of society and your own circumstances, you can choose how to spend your life. So, in that sense, you can be yourself. And if you are fortunate enough to find love in your marriage, which many do, then the gains easily outweigh the losses. Remember how you felt about marrying Henry. You wanted to marry him, didn't you? You didn't get tied up with arguments about whether you would be allowed to do what you wanted to."

"No," Mariana replied, returning to perch on the edge of the bed.

"If you can find love and friendship in marriage, you are in an enviable position. But there are other pleasures, as I've said, like being in charge of land or a house or even what linen or glass to buy for your house!" He closed his eyes, his white lips slightly parted.

For a few moments the room was hushed and then she mused dreamily:

"You must be married."

She had thought he might be dozing but he murmured,

"Why do you say that?"

"Because you talk as though you are. Mmh, that's a pity."

"Why?"

"Because…" She halted. Their talk seemed unreal, for his face was still and it was as if she was speaking to herself. She mirrored his murmur, shutting her own eyes, letting the words trip from her tongue, gently caressing the both of them. "Because I could have married you, I suppose. I mean… I mean that you're the sort of man that I might marry. You could be my friend. You're easy to talk to. Would you marry *me*?" The last question she spoke under her breath, not expecting a reply.

"That's an unfair question." Surprisingly, he kept on responding. Was he really awake? "I don't know who I am or if it's possible to marry you; I may have a wife already, as you have said."

Silence. Peace descended and Mariana decided to tiptoe across the floor. She had overtaxed this man and must be on her way, but she did so want to know what his feelings towards her were and in this half-whispered world where their eyes never met…

"But have you thought of marrying me, Jack?"

"No, I haven't."

"Oh." Now she knew!

She sprang up, the spell broken. She saw him brace himself. Was it against the springing of the bed or her confidences? Gone was the intimacy and, half-offended, she demanded:

"You've thought of… of other things, haven't you? Like bedding me? Why don't you bed me?"

Jack's lips opened as if he was about to laugh but instead he asked,

"Is this some kind of proposal?"

"Why not?" Mariana twinkled, pursing her lips in what she hoped was a sensuous way. How volatile were her emotions today! The tone of their conversation had turned to joking. It was as if they were talking about other people and not themselves.

"Because I wouldn't care to take advantage of such a young girl and…"

"I'm not too young!" She couldn't let that pass! "I know what I'm…"

"*And*, let me finish, because I'm just not well enough yet."

Mariana leant forward and whispered gleefully, like the child she had just denied she was:

"I'll hold you to that… You wait until you're up and about!"

"Oh, Mariana, you're unique!" Jack was grinning broadly, although he kept his bandaged head motionless. She saw there was a tinge of red in his cheeks. "Quite unique. That first day when you came in here and fell asleep on my chest, I decided then that I would never meet anyone else like you."

"Don't laugh at me!"

"I'm not laughing at you." His face sobered. "Truly I'm not. I think you're… there's nobody else like you anywhere, although I don't have any memories of other women I've met. Nonetheless, I have enjoyed talking to you, for you come out with such lovely ideas. What other young woman would speak so frankly to me, a stranger, about subjects like this one?"

Mariana blushed. She perceived that she had allowed herself to break her own rules: not to speak about confidential things with men. She had promised herself never to repeat that embarrassing incident with Thomas. Flirting might be acceptable, but Jack mustn't think that she had no morals or a loose tongue. She must steer the conversation into safer channels. Her grief and loss had meant she had forgotten her vowed intent, or was it this man? Really he was very easy to talk to! He was speaking again.

"I like you, Mariana."

She glanced away. She must think of a flippant reply to show him that she was just teasing him and not serious at all.

"Even, when you look below the skin?" she rejoined, forcing herself to meet his eyes.

"My dear girl! Of course! Have you a mirror in your room? You look like a filthy lad from the stables or at best a runaway schoolboy, but I'm still having a great time conversing…"

"Thank you. I'm pleased that…"

Suddenly there was a noise outside the door. Before Jack could blink Mariana had flung herself beneath the bed and was lying hidden, wrinkling her nose slightly at the odour of urine coming from the chamber pot. From her position, she could just see two pairs of feet at the end of the bed and she recognised one set of boots: they belonged to Matthew Cutlass. Barely had she time to wonder who the other person was when he spoke and a shiver passed along the whole length of her body.

"Ah… er… Jack. Mr Cutland has agreed to let me have a look at you. I was unable to examine you last time I was here, for I was fairly busy, but… Have you been told that usually I am called when a physician is needed?"

It was Mr Lloyd. Mariana tensed her muscles.

"Jack? Jack?" repeated Lloyd in a loud voice. "Do you hear me?" Then, changing to Welsh, he queried, "Do you think that knock on the head affected his sanity, Cutland?"

Mariana felt anger fill her bowels. How dare he talk Welsh in front of Jack, when he must realise that Jack didn't understand?

"Mr Jack." Matthew spoke in English. "How are you feeling today?"

"Much better, thank you," answered Jack, with what Mariana thought was a touch of exasperation.

"Would you have any objections to Mr Lloyd examining you?"

"I suppose not, but I'm perfectly happy to be under your care."

Mariana watched Lloyd's feet whilst he walked around the bed and then the quilts were flung over the end rail in an untidy heap, making her hiding place darker. The conversation lapsed and then a gasp of pain.

"Oh, did that hurt?" Lloyd's tone was guileless.

Mariana began to seethe with rage. Speaking in Welsh seemed a very minor offence compared with hurting Jack! She wanted to do something, but what?

"I see you have no nursemaid today." It was her enemy again, almost as if he was aware of her presence, but his next words belied this thought. "You know, Cutland, this man was well-attended by the enchanting Miss Rowlands last time I came. Now, can you bend your leg? Damned lucky that gash didn't touch your…"

"Thank you, Mr Lloyd," interrupted Jack. "My private parts are not your concern. I really do think that I prefer to be left to the tender mercies of Mr Cutlass."

"But I'm only going to give a second opinion. You've got some bruises spreading here." Again there was a pause in the conversation before Lloyd enquired, "Now, what about your head? Shall we unwind the bandages, Cutland?"

"I'm… I'm not sure. I suppose it will be…"

"Very good, then. Have you bled him? He has some nasty tumours."

Mariana chafed. Why was it taking so long? And why was Matthew agreeing to Lloyd's examination, when it was obvious that Jack was suffering? She surmised that Matthew had to tread warily with this Customs man.

"I don't normally bleed my patients under these particular circumstances," countered Matthew.

"Hmm, well, he's bleeding himself here. God Almighty! That's a deep cut! Yet... I'm surprised that it should lead to complete loss of memory."

"Mr Lloyd, I..." Matthew himself sounded distressed.

"Lloyd, I've had enough." Jack spoke quietly. "I don't know what you came here for, except perhaps you're one of those fellows who like seeing others suffer. However, I've..."

"Damn, no! You're such an interesting case and your inability to remember anything fascinates me. Cutland and I were discussing your condition downstairs and I simply enquired whether it would be possible for me to see you myself. I had no intention of visiting you when I came to the house. After all, there has just been a funeral. Isn't that right, Cutland?"

"Yes, man, but I didn't expect you to set the wounds bleeding! However, I'll rebind..."

"No, no! Allow me. I caused all this 'damage'. If you'd lean forward, Jack... Jack. Now, there's a curious name. Has the enchanting Miss Rowlands thought of any other names for you yet, or does she feel she knows you well enough to simply call you 'Jack'? Ah, but then she has been rather... rather intimate with you – what with dragging you from the sea and dressing your wounds... Sounds a bit far-fetched to me, don't you think? A slight woman like Miss Rowlands wouldn't have that much strength! Why don't you tell me the truth?"

"I remember nothing." There was no mistaking the strain in Jack's voice. Was it pain or controlled anger? She herself would give almost anything to leap up and punch Lloyd in the face, but even she understood that her reputation would not be worth a penny if she appeared from under the bed, especially dressed as a boy!

"Do you believe him?" Lloyd must be addressing Matthew, for once again he was speaking in Welsh. "I think he's hiding something: piracy, spying or more likely smuggling? You know about smuggling, don't you, Cutland?"

"I know absolutely nothing about smuggling. I am a law-abiding citizen and have been one all my life."

"With well-lined pockets, though?" sneered Lloyd.

"I made my fortune in China," returned Matthew stiffly.

"So you say. So you say. Well, you'd better pray that I never find you out in a boat with… with contraband in it."

"You never will." Mariana saw Matthew move around the bed. Then he observed in English:

"I think, Lloyd, that it's somewhat rude of us to be speaking in Welsh in front of our patient. Lloyd was just asking me whether I was involved in smuggling, Jack. As if I would be! I have no desire to bring illegal goods into our country. I understand the need to charge custom duties on some items. Smuggling is to be abhorred, isn't it?"

"Yes." Jack whispered faintly.

"Now, Lloyd, this man needs to lie absolutely still until his head stops bleeding and…"

"I'm sorry to have been heavy-handed," Lloyd began in an exaggerated tone, which nearly made Mariana reveal herself. "Most of my patients are pleased to see me when I arrive, and naturally, I'll not be asking you for a fee since my examination is part of a very thorough investigation that I am undertaking at the moment."

"Yes, I'm sure you are!" Jack's rallying tones heartened Mariana.

"I'll take my leave of you. Please don't forget: if you recall anything, however insignificant it appears to be, send for me."

"Cutlass, may I have a moment alone with you?" requested Jack.

"Certainly."

"Good day to you." Mariana felt Lloyd wanted to linger. "I might just have a word with the new Squire. Now, there's an honest man. No subterfuge in him."

Mariana released her breath. She hadn't noticed that she had been holding it! However, she remained where she was because she did not trust herself to be civil to Matthew, after he had consented to Lloyd's visit to the sick room.

"I must apologise," Matthew announced. "I had no notion…"

"No need to apologise. All I ask is that you will promise me that you won't give him your permission to see me again whilst I am too weak to…."

"No, I *must* say sorry, for I had no idea what he was like with patients. He is very popular around these parts. Well, let's put it this way, folk do call him when they are ill…"

"Maybe it's from a lack of there being anyone better. You ought to offer your services more." A whisper of exhaustion.

Matthew cleared his throat.

"Shall I redo your bandage?"

"No, thanks. I think I'll go to… sleep."

"Very good, then. That's the best thing to do. I won't let Lloyd near you again. There's no doubt he was being clumsy deliberately, presumably in an attempt to break down your resistance! Nevertheless, I do try to keep on the right side of him, for he noses into everyone's business and, if he chose to, he could make life quite difficult for me!"

"Ah."

"I'll say no more. Sleep now. It's what you need. I'll be over tomorrow."

Once Matthew left the room, Mariana pulled herself out from under the bed, using her arms as levers. She bumped her head and appeared at Jack's side, bristling with indignation and cried in a half-whisper:

"How dare he! How dare he molest you like that!" She caught sight of the sick man's face. His eyes were closed and there was fresh blood staining the linen bandage. Her anger expanded until she thought she would pop if she did not release it. Without warning, she realised that she must control her wrath, since Jack would not be able to cope with it, and pity flooded her heart. Then, with new maturity, she saw that she was not going to be her true self for the sake of another. She spoke calmly, "Oh, Jack, you poor man. Are you all right?"

Jack gave no reply and she wondered if he had lost consciousness.

"Jack," she offered, "shall I fetch you a clean bandage?"

"No, leave it. I think I will sleep. That brute has caused enough damage already!"

"I hate him! I could kill him. Maybe I will."

"Most unladylike, my dear," murmured Jack.

"Oh, Jack." Impulsively, she bent and kissed him tenderly on his ashy lips. He opened his eyes in surprise and stared at her.

"Mariana?"

She looked away, muttering uncertainly:

"I'm sorry, Jack. I don't…"

What in the world had made her do that? she asked herself.

"Ssh, don't be sorry," he breathed. She glanced at him and saw a hint of a smile in his clear blue eyes. "If I had an ounce more strength, we could try it again, but if you don't mind, rest is what is uppermost in my thoughts. Are you still going out?"

"Yes."

Mariana gave a final pat to the bedclothes and went to the window. She saw, out of the corner of her eye, Jack turn his head when he heard her open it.

"Mariana, what are you doing?"

"Going out the window."

"You foolish girl!"

"Don't fret. I've done it many times before. It's why I came into your room in the first place."

"Be careful then. For goodness' sake, don't fall!"

"I won't. Now, you close your eyes. Oh," Mariana paused, balanced on the window ledge, "I may return this way later, so don't be too shocked."

BIDDY

Biddy glanced around to check that there was no other servant or any mourners nearby to witness her escape. She had crossed the yard of *Trem-y-Môr* and skipped up an embankment away from the busy bustle. Before her was a thicket of gorse. She withdrew her hands up the stained sleeves of her bodice and covered her face with her forearms. Then she pushed her way through the tough prickles.

It took barely a minute for her to arrive at the bare patch of earth in the centre and, although her hair was pulled, her skin was not scratched. She flopped down on to the dry soil and breathed in the heady coconut smell of the last of the golden flowers. There was no sign of her entry – the thorny branches had sprung back into place and she knew no one would find her here! She often used this hidey-hole.

Biddy stretched her hands out from her sleeves and relaxed back, squirming to make a dip in the dry cinnamon seat beneath her petticoats. Neither mist nor rain seemed to penetrate the foliage – she could always count on not getting wet when she hid here. There were one or two roots sticking out but she knew where they were and avoided them. Just out of arm's length was a hole the size of a saucer – presumably where rabbits came and went, for there were some of their pellets in the enclosed clearing, but she had never actually encountered any of the creatures.

When first she had found this secluded shelter, if she lay down the sky could be seen above her head, but over the years, the bushes had grown and spread out and now she was in a cave of prickles and flowers, but she didn't care. Usually she would close her eyes and doze so it didn't matter whether she had a roof of bottle-green or not.

Oh, she was fed up! Fed up of serving those who had come to the funeral today and fed up of the endless routine of her daily life. She was fifteen – soon to be sixteen – she should be out and about, courting, laughing with her friends, making secret plans and giggling whilst she shared them with her cronies, not caring for her dying mother and numerous younger siblings!

She did have a secret plan, but one she had no intention of sharing with any of her acquaintances. In fact, she was not going to share it with anyone in case in so doing the dream was wrenched from her and thrown in the mud and trampled underneath her feet.

How long had she had this plan? Since… forever! Well, at least, it seemed as if she had been hoping and desiring forever! It had been born – this wonderful dream – when she was just six. She closed her eyes and let the present fade into the past.

She had been sitting on a dry stone wall, kicking her bare feet against the sandy stones and singing; trilling a ditty her mother had taught her. All around her there was noise and confusion for this was one of the most thriving horse fairs of the year. She was accompanied by her father, who was not too far away, but out of earshot. He had been sent here by the Squire to buy a horse but Biddy wasn't interested in the livestock like her brother, Thomas! Not many minutes earlier her father had lifted her to this eyrie above the heads of the crowd, with a whispered warning:

"You stay there, my Biddy, or you might get kicked by one of the animals. I won't be long. The auction is about to start. Thomas is… is around somewhere but I'll keep an eye out for you. Don't move until I come back."

She hadn't minded. She was rather glad to sit since her short legs had struggled to keep up with the long gait of her father and brother when they had walked the four miles before the sun had made its appearance for the day or the birds had started to twitter their morning chorus.

To her breast she clutched a spotted kerchief, which held some bread and cheese for their midday repast. She began to hum. However, the words of the ballad came into her mind and before long they burst from between her lips, dancing on the back of the tune. No one even glanced her way and she realised that she couldn't be heard above the auctioneer's harsh cry; the grunts of the bidders; the stamp of agitated hooves or the vendors' shrieks with cries of "Buy my tasty pies, freshly made today!" and "Bring your horses here to be re-shod" from the blacksmith's glowing booth in the corner of the fair. Not a single person was listening to her!

A smile creased around her lips. She knew she had a clear voice. Sometimes at home she was admonished not to sing loudly in case she woke the baby or disturbed her mother from her rest, but here she could chirp and whistle and nobody was going to tell her to stop.

How she loved to sing! Sing and sing and sing. Increasingly there seemed to be a melody ready to spring forth from her mouth. Sometimes her *Tad* would tease her that she sang more than she talked and it was true. If she felt happy she would converse in a warble rather than the staid sentences of her brothers and sisters. Simple words like "What's for our meal today, *Mam*?" could be fitted to notes she had just made up, but normally she would use familiar tunes and fit the words she wanted to say into verses and even a chorus.

"Well, my pretty! What a nightingale you are!"

Biddy came to an abrupt halt as a stranger touched her bare leg in a light caress. Someone *had* heard her!

"No," he cajoled, "don't stop! What a sweet voice you have? How old are you?"

All at once Biddy was shy. She closed her mouth in a nervous pout and turned her eyes towards the crowd to find her father. She was perched high enough to look right over the man's crumpled hat.

"Ah, I've frightened you, but you've no need to be. I was just marvelling at the harmony and range of pitch of your song. With a little bit of training and my son accompanying you on his fiddle, you could become famous!"

Biddy glanced down. The man was a good foot below her gaze, with a swarthy face and dark eyes. He was speaking Welsh but in a thick accent which made him hard to understand. However, she heard the praise in the intonations. She was thrilled, for she believed that she did have a unique voice and sulked if her family told her to be quiet. She was very proud of the way she could remember melodies and carols, hymns and madrigals! She smiled slightly more confidently.

"Come now, my little robin! Would you give me a few more bars of that tune you were singing?"

She obliged, allowing her legs to swing in time to the music. How well he heard she did not know for suddenly the crowd nearby were cheering on two lads who had started a fight, but her admirer's face broke into a grin and he reiterated:

"Ah, such notes from one so young! If only I could have you live with me, I could train you up! It wouldn't be just tavern folk you could entertain but lords and ladies too! Where is your mother? I would like a word with her." His face radiated excitement.

Biddy's heart thumped rapidly! She had wanted to perform in front of an audience ever since she could remember!

"My father is here." She ran the words up a scale with a lilt. "Over there!" Her finger pointed away.

"Well, let me lift you down, my dove, and let us go and seek him out and ask if he will give permission for lessons to take full advantage of the breath in your lungs and the honey in your voice!"

Biddy allowed the stranger to take her kerchief. He placed it on the grass by the wall before stretching out her arms for him to swing her down. As he did, his jacket flew open to reveal a vivid lining. Biddy gasped with pleasure as pink, turquoise, lemon, lavender and indigo patches glinted in the morning sun. When her feet touched the ground the coat fell flat against its owner's shirt and the rainbow disappeared as if it had never been.

All fear left her with the glimpse of such vibrant hues, for instead of sombre grey material, grubby and stained from daily use, which gave this man a slightly sinister look, she knew that underneath, literally, was a person who loved brightness and joy and life. She longed to tweak the buttons of his jacket to reveal the cloth again or to ask why he wore such a garment, but, instead, she grabbed her bundle, placed her hand in his and pulled him in the direction of where she had last seen her father. This was too good an opportunity to miss!

At first it was rather difficult to make the multitude part to let them through but her determination and the man's height cleared a path. Before long she was at the front of the throng, staring at an empty circle of flattened grass where the horses were being exhibited – cantering round and round with flowing tails and pounding hooves, their owners running ahead of them, pulling at their reins. Once at the inner line of people, a brief glance and she found her relatives, for Thomas was standing there too. Boldly she moved along the crowd's edge, the man still in tow.

"*Tad*!" she shouted. "This man wants to speak to you."

Her father took his eyes off the animals and patted her head rather absent-mindedly. She saw the stranger extend a hand of greeting but she was disappointed that she could not hear their exchange. A child of no more than two was seated on the churned ground bawling at the top of his voice. Biddy strained to catch the words of the men but all she could see was the flash of sapphire and peach as her new found friend produced a leather purse from inside his jacket and then the crimson of her father's stubbly chin as his face flushed.

She had just decided to try to comfort the baby next to her when her father grabbed her by the shoulder and marched her away, roughly pushing her through the heaving masses back to the stone wall. In vain, she twisted her head to catch a last glimpse of the man who was going to whisk her away from the drab surroundings of her home and make her famous.

"*Tad*!" she cried. "You're hurting me!"

"Why did you come and find me? Didn't I tell you *not* to move? What do you think you were doing, coming so near the horses?"

"But, *Tad*, what did the man say? He told me that I had a beautiful voice and I could sing in front of kings and queens."

"Nonsense! He wanted to buy you from me! Some ridiculous story about teaching you to sing and dance! He just wanted to make money from you! What would your mother have said if I had let you go? Come along, now, I've bought a horse for the Squire. Let us find a quiet place to eat."

"But I'd like to play to kings and queens."

"Don't try my patience, Biddy! I've met his kind before. A vagabond! A charlatan! He would have used you to enhance his own lot! You, sing for royalty! What rubbish! Now let's forget all about him and eat!"

Biddy sighed as the memory of that day faded before her closed eyelids. Over the years she couldn't remember what the man had looked like but she would never forget the silken lining of his coat. Not many months later she heard the story of Joseph and his multi-coloured robe from the Bible and had dubbed the man 'Joseph' in her thoughts.

She was convinced that her father had misunderstood the other man. She had found the inflection of his voice hard to comprehend. There had been no underhandedness, surely. He had called her his robin and nightingale and had recognised her true talent.

For several years she had begged both her parents to let her find someone who could teach her scales, to read music and help her to exercise her vocal chords, but to no avail. There was no money or no time and so the dream had taken shape. She would save any pennies or farthings she could and when she was older she would run away from home and go to London where she would find a competent musician who would take her under their wing, for payment, of course, and coach her until she was invited to the Royal Palace to perform.

Biddy yawned. How much longer dared she stay here? Had her disappearance been noticed? There was such a bunch of maids and men servants at the Squire's funeral that she hoped no one would count heads, or if they did, they would not realise she was not around. A few minutes more, she promised herself.

Closing her eyes again, in her mind, she flew away to her own bedroom. Here, behind a loose crooked stone, was her treasure – her saved money. Rarely was she able to count it because she shared the room with all her sisters and they slept beneath the rafters, head to toe, on lumpy mattresses. Last time she had calculated that she had about half a year of her present wage. She was paid for her work at *Trem-y-Môr*, although she was owed money at the moment. Recently she had gone several days to the Pugh household across Holy Island at *Tyddynypandy* to be a maid in a new house. A few more coins had been added to her store. Here, on days when her hands were chapped with chilblains from the cold, red with the damp, or her feet were swollen and aching from the standing up, she would practise her singing, under her breath and allow her spirit to float away towards her dreams. She could almost hear the applause, the wonder in others' tones at how she, just a young maid from the far away country of Wales, could have been blessed with such a rich and deep voice. Who had trained her? they might enquire. Oh, she had taught *herself* until very recently! they might exclaim. No formal training just angel voices to inspire her and a lifetime of dull tasks where she could repeat the tunes and words until her skills were honed and ready to bring pleasure to any audience who were lucky enough to hear her.

MARIANA

Mariana did, in fact, lose her footing on the wet roof. Unceremoniously she slid down the tiles, trying desperately to find a foothold that might halt her progress, and she landed in an untidy heap on the ground. She stood up and tried to rub out the grass stains from her seat but without success.

The mist had thinned. Immediately she perceived that if she went along the beach, she risked being seen by those in the house. Thus, she turned, instead, away from the torpid sea and, after squeezing through a hedge, found a path towards the east of the island.

She strode along the track, enjoying the freedom of not wearing a skirt and petticoats. How easy it was to walk in breeches, for there was no length of material to become entangled in brambles or to drag through the mud! How much better to be a man! Then she would be able to do whatever she wanted and to go anywhere she desired, without a chaperone. A single man could squander away the years in travel before choosing to settle down and marry and have children and carry responsibility on his shoulders; but a spinster had to either marry or be dependant on her relatives. Penelope had told Mariana of how society had shunned her for living in her father's London house all by herself, yet Edward had run away to sea and his reputation, far from being tarnished, was enhanced. Mariana knew that it would be acceptable for her to live with her brother, but what would happen when he married? Certainly his future wife would be in charge of the household and what if she took it upon herself to try to shape Mariana's life? And then there would be babies and, as a spinster aunt… No, she could not see herself living here once Edward married, yet where could she go? *Trem-y-Môr* was her home.

Imagining herself to be a man, she lengthened her stride and swung her arms. Now, if she were a man, she could get even with other men like Lloyd, scoundrel that he was! Did he think that he could torture Jack into remembering? What had Matthew been doing to tolerate the manhandling of his patient in that manner, starting the wound bleeding again? She allowed her anger to dissipate, stamping it away while she marched along the grass; it would be an invisible path to many, but the slim girl was familiar with every way and track around her home. As she moved along, she pictured herself sticking a sharp dagger into Lloyd's back or punching him across the jaw or even shooting him with a pistol. Then she dreamt of disgracing him with his superiors, for she knew that, in reality, she was no match for him physically. Her plans for revenge eased her ire.

By the time she reached the sea near the village of Rhoscolyn, which overlooked the sandy coastline of Anglesey, the mist had vanished – wiped away by an enormous hand – like rubbing a steamy window. Now, there was a cerulean sky and, to her amazement, the beginnings of a sunset. Was it that late? Etched across the heavens were scalloped-edged clouds shining pink and gold: a gigantic shell lying on a blue beach, glittering in the evening sun. Mariana gazed in wonder before, perching on a rock near the brink of the sea. Removing her oversized borrowed boots, she dabbled her feet in the water. She could see barnacles amongst the nut-brown web of seaweed, opening in the returning tide. She rested her bare toes on the serrated rock and curled her sole against the uneven surface.

Gradually, she became aware of someone watching her and there, a mere four feet from her, was a plump, speckled seal, its sorrowful eyes staring at her with curiosity, its whiskers twitching. Smoothly it swam towards a rock, hardly rippling the surface of the calm sea, and with a great effort, heaved itself up on to the shore. It must have decided that Mariana was not an enemy and it allowed its wet fur to be dried by the fading evening sun. Mariana smiled. She was surprised that the somnolent creature could lie that comfortably on such a hard surface, since her own posterior was pricking her. Slowly she stood up to leave, hoping that the animal would not be frightened, but it lazily turned over, waving a flipper, as if in farewell, and closed its eyes.

Retracing her steps homeward, Mariana pondered about what a marvellous life the seal led: a quiet restful evening soaking up the last of the sun's rays, followed by a slow dip in the cooling water to search for a fish or two for supper. It had nothing to think about but what to eat and where to sleep. Then she changed her mind when she recalled that seals had predators, including man himself!

Before long, she was thinking of other matters, and, in particular, whether her brother had a strong temper and, if so, whether he would vent it on her for disappearing. Father would not have scolded her, she decided, aiming a kick at a bush of gorse, for he understood her need to be alone sometimes. Although she had not thought consciously about her father until then, she found her heart was more at peace. At the moment, her main feeling was hunger and, with a bit of good fortune, she might not have been missed. She hastened along the path. It was not far to home – soon she would join the main trail, which would take her past *Trem-y-Môr*. Unexpectedly, she heard voices, English voices, coming from the, as yet unseen, track. Mariana crouched low and, crab-like, went up on to the outcrop of rock overlooking the thoroughfare.

"Pull, Perrin, pull."

There, before her, was a seal. Well, after her very recent encounter with the seal, she was reminded of it! A fat woman, dressed in sober black, was stuck in the half-opened doorway of an overturned carriage. Her face was cherry-coloured, her hair, partially loosened, was falling over her shoulder and her hat was gone.

Standing on a boulder by the edge of the path, her hands vainly clutching the fat woman's out-stretched arms, was presumably Perrin. She looked almost as harassed as her mistress. The width of the trapped woman's hips, possibly made even wider by padding beneath her gown, was preventing her from leaving the broken vehicle.

Immediately, from further up the roadway, came the sound of hooves and a lanky man appeared, leading two horses. Mariana worked out that he was the groom or driver of the crashed carriage, because he was wearing a splendid, maroon livery and he was walking the frightened animals. Certainly, Mariana noticed, the larger of the two horses, a chestnut gelding, continued to roll his eyes. He halted when he saw the coach, evidently believing that this four-wheeled vehicle might once again cause every bone in his body to shudder to a halt and send him to his knees.

"Steady there, boy," the man crooned. Then, raising his voice, he added, "How are you doing, Madam?"

"Gradeson! Is that you Gradeson?" The trapped seal was unable to manoeuvre herself round to see her servant.

Mariana wanted to laugh. No, she concluded, this woman was far too loud to be compared to a seal, although her body was massive – too big for her smallish head. Silently Mariana backed down from her vantage point and joined the track some distance from the catastrophe. She sauntered along casually, her mouth forming a whistle. She stopped, as if seeing the tableau for the first time, unchanged, with the man still at the heads of the horses and Perrin still pulling and pulling fruitlessly.

When Mariana drew closer, a genuine look of shock came to her face – she recognised the imprisoned woman. Surely this was her sister, Margaret? Yes, it was six years since she had last seen her and she had gained weight definitely, although Mariana always remembered her as being heavily-built, but she would have known Margaret anywhere. The urge to laugh swelled within her again. Registering that Margaret would not recognise *her*, she carefully controlled her laughter, and walked right up to the carriage to stand by the mud-stained undercarriage. She saw that, scattered for several yards, in all directions, was her sister's luggage, and what a great number of different pieces there were! Obviously Margaret had come to stay! Keeping her features straight, she stared at her half-sister's overheated face with almost vacant eyes.

"Hey, you! You, can you help us? Can you hold the horses or do you know somewhere we might obtain an axe to break down this door?" Margaret's voice was familiar now Mariana was near, and edged with alarm. She looked very hot and Mariana wondered if she might faint, but her voice was not weak; she was continuing:

"Gradeson? Are you there?"

"Yes, Madam."

"*Do* something," Margaret implored.

"I don't think the lad understands you, Madam. He may be... er... simple, Madam."

"Stop pulling, Perrin. You'll wrench my arms off my body!" Obediently the maid let go and Margaret sank back inside the carriage. She must have lost her foothold for she cried: "Ouch! Now my ankle is twisted. Gradeson!"

"Do... you... speak... English?" enunciated the groom.

Mariana winked at him, forgetting temporarily that she was dressed like a boy.

"Of course I do," she declared in Welsh. "I understand every word you're saying, but nothing would prevail upon me to help you. I haven't seen such a funny spectacle in years!"

"Oh, dear, these heathen Welsh!" wailed Margaret. "What made my father keep his inheritance in such a God forsaken place? Gradeson, you must go and fetch help. There must be a farm near here. Unfortunately, my gown prevents me from leaving the carriage. Go, Gradeson! It's no good talking to that idiot!"

"Should I leave the horses, Madam?"

"Of course! I'm more important than a horse. They won't wander far. Now, Perrin, could you possibly find me a handkerchief? I feel…"

"Yes, Madam. If you could just manage without me whilst I search in one of the bags."

"Yes, yes," snapped Margaret. She placed her elbow against the edge of the door and leant her head on her arm. Mariana watched her begin to pin up her disarrayed hair, almost without conscious thought.

All at once, Mariana felt a wave of pity for her sister; Margaret had not panicked like many would have done! Nevertheless, she didn't offer any assistance. Realising that the older woman was on her way to *Trem-y-Môr* made her see the wisdom of returning hastily. She must be dressed in her own clothes when the party arrived. She might not be able to predict with certainty what Edward's reaction would be to her disguise, but she had no doubts what Margaret would say!

Turning on her heel without another word, Mariana ran up the track and away over the fields to her home. She half-contemplated reporting the accident, but she reasoned that then her masquerade would be revealed. She decided that Margaret would have to find her own solution to her troubles as though she, Mariana, had not chanced upon her.

Before Mariana reached her home, the sun had disappeared below the length of the horizon, and there was an evening breeze floating from the sea to stroke the land. In the gathering darkness, Mariana tiptoed, towards the rain barrel that stood at the corner of the house; it enabled her to climb back on to the scullery roof. However, the barrel had been moved and, since she did not want to go around to the other side of the house because of her need to keep her jaunt secret, she retreated across the damp grass and charged towards the building, leaping high into the air at the last moment. Her hands could find no purchase on the smooth tiles. She sank to the ground despondently. Now she was bound to be discovered and probably she would have to endure a lecture.

"Would you like me to help you up?"

Mariana jumped with surprise, although the question was whispered. There stood Thomas, who must have witnessed her unsuccessful attempt to gain access to the roof.

"Oh, Thomas, would you? I'd be most grateful."

"Take the boots off then." Thomas smiled. "Aren't they an old pair of mine? They're far too big for you!"

"Yes, but I've long since stopped getting blisters from them and you had shaped the right and left feet. The hobnails really grip when it's wet unless you're walking on cobbles! How did you know it was me, Thomas?" Mariana stood barefoot, ready to fit her dainty toes into the man's cupped hands.

"I've seen you before, Miss. I can't say that I approve but there we are. It's not my place to say anything."

"Where's the rain barrel?"

"Round the other side of the house. It was taken there a few months back. Ready?"

This time, Mariana reached the roof easily and she turned to thank her groom.

"Can you throw my boots up?"

"I'll bring them to you tomorrow, Miss. Now, tread carefully, for there are some loose tiles up near the top."

How simple it was with someone to help! It took Mariana just a moment to arrive at Jack's window and then she had clambered in, out of sight. Jack was lying flat, his pillows at the foot of the bed, with his eyes closed. His face was as white as the clean bandage swathing his head. Mariana noticed that beside the door, were the stained cloths and a basin of bloody water. Resisting the urge to wake him, she fastened down his window and crept away.

MRS JONES

Mrs Jones paused at the door of her room and surveyed her own domain by candlelight: straight opposite her was the bed covered with a large black and white Welsh wool blanket and it looked inviting but to her right was a fireplace with a welcoming glow. Who had had the foresight to set match to sticks and coals in all the busyness of the last hour? Elin, perhaps? Almost she moved towards its orange warmth but her eyes were drawn upwards.

Over the glowing embers was a shelf on which stood the housekeeper's favourite possessions: two brass candlesticks in which the candles flickered; a blue pottery jug which she put flowers in sometimes; a pretty shepherdess in a delicate china dress which she had purchased from that fair where she had met Patrick all those years ago; a fold of green corduroy cloth which held a tiny pair of knitted baby boots (which she had shown no one) and her ivory hairbrush. Not much for a lifetime of collecting, but Mrs Jones had come to this house with very little in her bag. Naturally there were other items in the chest-of-drawers in the corner of the room or in the trunk under the bed, but, she was the first to admit that there wasn't much clutter to attract dust in here. Over the years, she had added to her belongings but only when something really took her fancy and she had surprised even herself at how choosy she could be! Hence her estate didn't amount to much – not like what Sir William had left behind!

A compact wooden table stood against the wall opposite the fire on which she kept a cup and saucer and a thick mat on which rested her kettle, which she could place on the fire. This enabled her to have a cup of tea in privacy. But today, although she was gasping for a drink, her priority was to lie down and lift her swollen legs off the ground.

She shuffled past the chair, pushing it slightly nearer the end of the bed but being careful not to allow its legs to be burnt by the fire, and heaved herself on top of the bedclothes with a sigh of exhaustion.

It was over! The whole funeral was over – vigil, burial and wake and the old Squire was no more. Ah, what a twenty-four hours it had been! Not a moment to rest and too much to be done – whipping cream, beating eggs, stirring sauces, rolling pastry, pouring mixtures – again and again – each task seemingly endless.

Behind her closed eyelids she saw the kitchen of the Manor House crammed with meat, breadstuffs, cakes, delicacies and dainties. Food! Oh, she hoped never to have to prepare another dish again! Stupid, of course, seeing as she was the cook, but for tonight and probably tomorrow too, the family and servants could be served up the remains of the feast instead of her and her bevy of maids preparing meals from raw ingredients.

What a madcap system it was! To provide victuals for an indeterminate number of mourners all through the night and then again after the interment! How did these traditions get started? Who decided? And did anyone think of the long-suffering servants slaving over a hot oven or on their feet morning, noon and night? Well, that was it! She was getting too old for this kind of thing! If anyone else died, and God forbid that this should happen, she would not be able to do it again. Elin or Biddy or Kate would have to do the back-breaking job next time.

Next time. She exhaled loudly. There would be no 'next time' for Sir William. What a final thing death was! No going back! No shirking it or postponing it! He was gone – and wouldn't be seen again this side of the gates of heaven. Of course, Mrs Jones believed in an afterlife, but as far as this earthly life was concerned…

The housekeeper shifted her legs, trying to ease the pain. As her body relaxed, the images of the last day-and-a-half paraded through her mind.

Her domain, that spotless kitchen, chaotic, with every dish and receptacle filled with tempting food. Not a spare plate or spoon and all the dirty crockery piling up ready to be washed.

The picture faded and she saw instead the hallway of the Manor House, crowded with people, many of them strangers, piling into every corner – not an inch to spare. How many times had Mrs Jones tried to push her way through with an overloaded tray? Too many times to count or recall! She wouldn't forget the teaming hordes easily!

Her memories narrowed to a single person. Dear Mariana, white as a winding sheet, fainting away with all the strain and sadness. Mrs Jones had wanted to cradle her in her arms but others had reached the supine figure before her and the Squire's youngest daughter had been carried away to her bed. Even now the scene of her forthright young mistress, pathetic and unconscious – her severe, mourning dress grass-stained and mucky – made her half rise. Should she go and check the child was all right? No, for Elin, who had been up the back stairs several times, had assured her that Miss Mariana had recovered and was sleeping peacefully.

And what about her other 'child'? Not that anyone would describe the new master as a child but in her heart… Her beloved Edward, materialised in front of her weary eyes. She noticed again the fatigue written across his creased brow. His peg leg aching, she wondered, or just coping with both the grief *and* disappointment of missing that reunion with his father? Or was it all the onerous responsibilities that had landed on his broad shoulders? How she had longed to draw his head on to her bosom and reassure him that all would be well! Frustration burned in her chest, for she was neither his mother nor even related to him.

Oh, the feelings that tugged at her heart strings! Who would choose to be a servant? Not she! Because all her love had been poured into this family who had no more connection to her than that she was their housekeeper! Did she have a place in their hearts? Unlikely! Who would mourn if she died?

Ach! What was she doing – thinking that maybe she would be the next to go? She had seen many a dead body – and had laid out more than she dared to remember – so why was she in such a maudlin state tonight? Was it brought on by sheer tiredness?

This last marathon of preparation of edibles had made her realise that she was getting too old for this kind of work. Should she be retiring? That begged the question: where to? All she owned was contained in this very room. Although she had salted away several gold coins, which were hidden beneath her mattress, she was aware that her money would not last long and an even shorter time if she had to pay rent. She was aware that this room went with the housekeeper's job and would be needed by her replacement. She had no home of her own.

Yet if she didn't retire, would she just drop dead one day like her beloved master? What did most people do? she pondered. They had sons and daughters who would offer them accommodation in their dotage age in return for… Well, what could she offer a family? Excellent meals prepared and cooked, if the ingredients were available; inestimable advice on many illnesses; help with young 'uns, despite her apparent barrenness. Oh, yes, if she had a family, she might be able to go to them, but it seemed like another life time ago since she had seen her relatives. Where were they now?

Probably her own parents would be long dead and buried, and her sisters? She had no desire to meet Jemima, but Keren? The master's death, more than any others she had known, had made her understand how important family was and how fragile a hold people had on life.

The same thoughts had recurred in her mind over the last few days: death was final and life was finite. Everyone died eventually and nobody knew how many days on this earth were left to them.

Take the Squire – the *old* Squire – he had been here less than a week ago – bellowing out his orders to Owen and Thomas to get the carriage ready or telling her that old Ferguson had brought him a present of some trout and could she cook it just the ways she knew he liked it? Oh, he had never shouted at her – her master of years! He had trusted her with all the running of his household. The best master a servant could have and suddenly he was no more! She knew that his passing on hadn't quite been immediate, according to Wilson, but in terms of life, with respect to the passing of the days into night and back into days, the Squire had been here one moment and gone the next! She tried to imagine him striding through the front door, his boots begrimed, his wig askew, but all she could see was his lifeless body laid out ready for the grave.

Enough! She would ruminate no more! What was the point? Thinking, imagining, even mourning wouldn't bring him back. And yet… if his death made her change the way she lived her life, mayhap there was a reason for her to dwell a little more on the events of the day.

It wasn't just that she could die tomorrow – that was in the hands of the Almighty – but the possibility had given her the idea that she should – maybe could – retire and spend her days a bit more easily. Able to put her feet up whenever she felt like it! Get up and go to bed when it pleased her and not be answerable to anyone else on how she spent her hours and minutes! No, that wasn't what had shaken her daily routines. What she had realised in her meandering thoughts was that time was running out and she ought to make her peace with the ones she loved. Loved? Her family? No, she didn't love her own flesh and blood – she cared more for those who lived in this household, but there was a tie of past generations with her sisters – a communion of mutual ancestry. Unexpectedly, she felt pulled to find out what had happened to them. Surely, they would have husbands and children and grandchildren and, maybe, even great grandchildren and all those imagined people were linked to her by blood – by common forefathers!

Should she travel back to her roots? Would they be living in the same area? Could she find them at all? If she asked Sir Edward for the loan of one of the younger lads and the farm cart, she could investigate. Yes, her aching joints would be jolted up and down but, if she could locate Keren, she could be reconciled with some of her relatives before it was too late. For if there was one thing that death was, it was final! There it was again – the same truth settled in her head, depressing and yet invigorating her simultaneously.

Oh, should she get up and make that cup of tea? The problem was that she knew she had no water in her kettle or in the big jug that was tucked away on the floor behind the table. If only she could wave a magic wand...

A knock on the door roused her from her reverie and there stood Elin and in her hand the longed for cup and saucer on a tray!

"Oh, *cariad bach*, how did you know I was gasping?"

"Because I was too! How are you doing? Are your legs easier?"

"Of course. There's nothing wrong that a short rest won't put right! Sit down. Sit down. Put your feet on that stool. I'm sure you're tired too. Are all the guests gone?"

"Yes, at last. If you don't count Mr Cutlass."

"And Miss Mariana?"

"Dressed with her hair pinned back. She's off to join the men any minute."

"Well, I know black is right to wear but the colour makes her look wan. Her face like a pale moon and her eyes too big for..."

Mrs Jones' words trailed off. She sipped the liquid whilst Elin perched on the wooden chair, turning it slightly in order to face the housekeeper, who had pulled herself up to a half-sitting position on the patterned cover.

"The little ones?" the older woman enquired a few moments later.

"I hope you don't mind but I packed them off to bed. Peggy fell asleep across the dog, her thumb in her mouth, so I woke her up and bundled her upstairs."

"Did I see your *Tad* at the funeral?"

"No, he's stuck at home with a fever, but my stepmother was there, brandishing her favourite stick and wearing a new cap by the looks of it."

"Oh, dear. Are things as bad as ever? How long is it since she married your dad?"

"Too long! I would say she gets worse as the years go by. Thank the Lord she couldn't have children of her own, but she still rules my youngest brothers and sisters with that stick of hers! Whenever I go home, and I go as infrequently as possible, they all clamour for me to find them jobs here. Maybe there will be one or two changes now the new master has come."

"There might be, but what do you think of that strange comment he made about not staying long?"

Elin shifted in the chair and poked the coals. A yellow flame sprang up and two, glowing pieces settled further down at the rear of the hearth.

"I don't know," she murmured.

"He told us he had left the fleet and this *is* his home. Why would he not stay? But then it must be difficult for a man who has travelled to foreign countries to remain in one place and be content. He needs a wife, I suppose, and children. Talking of which, Elin, I've been thinking that I might go and find my sister and…"

"Your sister? I thought you told me all your family was dead."

"Did I? No, no! It's just years since I've seen them. Of course, I won't go soon but maybe in the spring next year. Yes, spring is a good time to travel, with all the flowers peeping up and the wind warm with the promise of summer. I've a hankering to visit. There might be babes for me to cuddle…"

"But who would do your work?"

"Well, that's the problem. We must sort out some help. If we had a new mistress by then…"

"Elin."

The door swung open on a hasty knock.

"Wilson!" exclaimed Mrs Jones splashing tea over her bosom.

"Oh, I do apologise. I had hoped not to disturb you tonight, Mrs Jones, but there is just one last task I need Elin to do. Not you, Mrs Jones, not you. I need young arms and legs. Elin?"

MARIANA

Mariana descended the main stairs, smoothing the front of her gown with her slim fingers. She had been grateful that, although Elin had found out that she had left her bedchamber, the loyal maid had hidden the fact from everyone else, telling them that her mistress remained asleep in her bed. She had laid out one of Mariana's best gowns with its black, stiff petticoats, and she had appeared to help her mistress dress right on cue! Had she seen her return, or was it some sixth sense the maid possessed?

Although Mariana knew that Edward had no idea that she had been out, nonetheless, she paused outside the dining room door. She composed her features and tried to look as if she had spent the whole afternoon and early evening dozing. She touched her head. At her request, Elin had re-braided her hair and twisted it into a heavy, plaited coil on the back of her head. The maid had protested at the style:

"It makes your face look severe, Miss Mariana. Shall I not pull it quite so tightly?"

"No," Mariana had protested, glaring at her reflection in the glass. "I want it away from my face…"

Now Mariana patted the neat strands, recalling her maid's puzzled look of disapproval. How could she have explained that she wanted to recapture that sense of masculinity of earlier that allowed her to feel free and strangely stronger? Also, although she had not formed the thoughts in her mind consciously, she hoped to be less attractive tonight. She found her brother's brooding eyes, which were fixed on her often, disturbing. If he had been anyone other than her brother, she would have said that he desired her; she had had plenty of experience of men's looks, from mildly flirtatious to raw passion. Surely she must be mistaken with Edward. It could not be interest of that nature in his glances; it must be concern for her welfare.

Mariana entered the room and surveyed it. She wasn't fond of this room for mostly it was dark, only lightened by the sinking sun and that only during the summer months. An oak table, capable of seating twenty, dominated the floor and, although the sombre wood was lovingly polished regularly, its depths defied brightness. Pushed back against the wall, almost like a meeting house, were the chairs – old-fashioned, sturdy, unattractive – at least that was what Mariana thought! This was a room where one had to be on one's best behaviour, changed from everyday clothes into evening wear, with the conversation stilted and the feeling of lethargy creeping over one after an enormous meal which sank to the bottom of the stomach! Mariana preferred to eat in the kitchen, but today the remains of the feast for the mourners had been laid out in here.

Much to her amazement, there was enough food to cover the whole of one end of the table. Near the leftovers, she noticed three places set with cutlery. She frowned. Had Penelope not left? Was Jack expected to join them? No. The answer was before her in the figure of Matthew Cutlass, glass in hand, his face redder than usual (had he been drinking all day?), standing half-turned away from Edward, gazing over the sea.

The room had windows in two of its walls, not near the door end (for this wall backed on to the scullery), but in the corner quite close together: one window overlooked the edge of the beach, the other watched over the patch of land where Mariana had landed in such an ungraceful heap earlier. Yet the room was still murky and Mariana was glad to observe Wilson lighting more candles.

Edward came forward to greet her, an amiable smile on his face, his hands outstretched.

"Mariana, how are you feeling? I trust that you are recovered. I must say that you look even more like your mother than usual with your hair like that." He took hold of her fingers.

Mariana blushed and glanced away. There was that look again which disturbed her greatly!

"Yes, thank you. I… I must apologise for…" she stammered.

"No need, my dear sister. It was a very moving occasion and your behaviour was most understandable. All the guests have gone, except Mr Cutlass."

"Penelope?"

"She left earlier. She seemed very tired. Of course, it was a long night. I hardly had an opportunity to speak to either Penelope or her husband, but I've arranged for us to visit them next week, if that's convenient with you."

Mariana nodded and then pulled away from her brother's grasp. She remembered how eagerly she had touched him that first night when they had sat in the kitchen together. She had wanted to comfort him when she had seen his confusion about their father's attitude. Yet, this evening, she herself was confused by the message in his eyes.

"I have invited Mr Cutlass to stay to supper," Edward proclaimed, indicating with a gesture that Mariana should join them. "I'm hoping he will help us finish up some of this food. Mrs Jones certainly did us proud! I've instructed her to go to bed. I said we would cover all the dishes which had any food left. I hope you don't mind. Come, my dear, why don't you take a seat? You haven't eaten all day – you must be hungry."

"I am. Where are you sitting, Matthew?"

Matthew turned to her with his usual expression, but what else did she expect? He could not know that she had witnessed the scene with Jack and Lloyd.

"Have you seen Jack?" she demanded, determined to bring the subject around to her friend sooner rather than later. She believed that Margaret would be arriving at any minute.

"Will that be all, Sir?" Wilson enquired before Matthew had a chance to reply.

"Yes, Wilson." It was Edward who responded. "May I take this opportunity to thank you personally for all you did during the wake and today, on a day that must have been very upsetting for you too…"

"Thank you, Sir." Mariana was sure that Edward was right in assuming that the servants missed her father almost as much as the family, but the butler's face was impassive. "Are you sure you are able to serve yourselves, Sir? I am quite willing to stay…"

"No, Wilson. We really don't need you."

"Very good, Sir. Goodnight, Sir, Miss Mariana, Mr Cutland."

Edward pulled up a chair for his sister and then, waving towards another for the retired surgeon, he proceeded to slide several dishes of food nearer. Initially, he served the others and then Mariana repeated her question about Jack. She was gratified to see the older man refuse to meet her eyes and he said:

"I'm afraid his condition has deteriorated, Miss Mariana."

For several minutes Mariana found herself quizzing Matthew in such a vehement way that her brother intercepted with a rebuke:

"Mariana! Cutland did his best. He has been up since and redressed Jack's wounds and given him some powders to relieve his pain."

"I think that he…" she started forcefully, ready to take up the battle with both men.

"I think we should leave the conversation there, Mariana." Edward's tone brooked no argument. "Jack is fine again. Matthew has made amends. Lloyd has gone. Could you pass me the pie, please?"

Mariana bit her lip when Edward gave her a glare of warning. She stuffed some food into her mouth and chewed noisily. She was aware that she was being unnecessarily hard on her old friend and she couldn't quite decide why she was in such a state. After all, she herself had figured out that Matthew would have to pander to Lloyd to protect himself. She must be 'overwrought' – that's what Mrs Jones would diagnose. She supposed it was because Lloyd, the real culprit, had escaped. She swallowed a large ball of food and felt it heavy on her chest. All of sudden she was overcome with exhaustion. What did it matter anyway? In many ways it was good, for it meant that Jack would be with them longer and, for some unaccountable reason, this thought lifted her spirits.

"Did you have a lot of pain with your leg, Edward?" she piped up. Having decided to let the subject of Lloyd go, there seemed no point in sitting in silence.

"You could say that! The pain was damnable, although the strangest part of it all is the pain I get *now* in my amputated leg."

"Now? I don't understand."

"Well, I feel pain in my right leg or foot and it's not even there!"

"Sweet Jesus!" gasped Mariana, her interest aroused. "That must be awful!"

"It is, but I'm getting more used to it every week. I often want to scratch it too!"

"How did you lose it, Sir?" asked Matthew.

"In the War," returned Mariana.

"No, I didn't," contradicted Edward, "although it's easier to say that I did, for it saves lengthy explanations. I came out of the Treaty of Ryswick without a mark. Well, only a few very small, insignificant marks."

"Where did you go to after the War then?" Mariana asked.

"To the West Indies."

"Why did you go there?"

"The Indies had had quite a rough time themselves. Our English colonies had been seized by the French, the Spaniards and some even by the Germans. The Spaniards and our English settlers started quarrelling because of a few of our Scottish comrades. They were trying to colonise the Isthmus of Darien."

"Where's that?" Mariana questioned, leaning her elbows on the table.

"It is part of the Spanish Main: part of the mainland belonging to Spain."

"So, what did you have to do?"

"Our regular soldiers were very weak with yellow fever, and unable to really control any arguments. It wasn't just the settlers fighting over different pieces of land. You see, all the harbours around that part of the world were – are – infested with pirates who harass all kinds of ships."

"Pirates?" Mariana perked up, her exhaustion forgotten.

"Don't look like that! They're vicious, unscrupulous men and I hope you never have reason to meet any…"

"We have them here sometimes," commented Matthew.

"Yes, I've heard," frowned Edward.

"They have threatened the people of Holyhead in the past. They come ashore and… and… Well, I'm sure you don't need me to enlighten you about what they do." Matthew grimaced.

"They're despicable," agreed Edward.

"Did you ever fight them?" Mariana persevered, unsuccessfully trying to hide her eagerness.

"Oh, Mariana, what a child you are!"

"Don't say that!" pouted his sister.

"It's a compliment, my dear. I'm glad you've never experienced the horrors of war or the likes of men such as some of the pirates who roam the sea. My greatest thrill at that time was that I was given command of my own ship. She was called *Speedwell*."

"What size ship was she, Sir?" interjected Matthew.

"Only a fifth rate, but she had thirty-two guns and she was all mine."

"Who was out there with you?" continued the retired seafarer.

"Benbow. Admiral John Benbow and a mighty fine man…"

"Yes, but what about the pirates?" Mariana didn't want to be cheated of a good yarn.

"Mariana!" laughed Edward. "Yes, I engaged in battle a few times with pirate ships, although I never met Kidd."

"Who was he?"

"You mean, 'Who is he?' He was originally a privateer with a ship called the *Adventure*. It had been fitted out by the Governor of New England himself and Kidd's job, ironically, was to hunt pirates and the French. However, the gain to be had from pirating was too enticing, I suppose, and he turned pirate himself."

"Has he been caught?"

"Not as far as I know."

"So, what else did you do out there?"

"Let me think. We were involved with the actual governors of some of the islands. New governors were always deposing the old ones and slapping them into prison and then, often months, even years later, executing them. There was much unrest on the islands – probably always will be. And the Spaniards! Ha! They were so angry with the Scots that they were hostile to us. In Cartagena, they wouldn't allow our boats to enter the harbour, in order to restock our water supplies. They felt that we English should oppose the Scots. And another time at… Now, where was it? I think it was at Porto Bellow, the Spaniards fired at Benbow because he was flying blue colours which they did not recognise…"

"You mean you had to be on guard all the time," butted in Mariana.

"Yes, indeed. And we had other enemies."

"What kind?"

"Ah, this, my dear sister, you will consider less interesting: yellow fever. Well, there were many different fevers, but yellow fever killed over half the Spanish in the garrison at Cartagena. That was when we first arrived. However, almost all my crew succumbed to it sooner or later."

"Did you catch it, Sir?"

"Yes, Cutlass, I did and I thought I was dying…"

"Did many of your men actually die?" interrupted Mariana.

"Yes, my dear." Edward paused. "Then, of course, there was the inevitable attack from another source. I'm referring to the sea-worm. That is, *teredo navalis*."

"What did it do?"

"They eat away your ship, lassie," instructed Matthew with his booming laugh.

"Yes," added Edward, "often we were a month careening."

"Careening? Is that…?"

"Oh, Mariana, so many questions! You've quite given up eating. Here, have some more…"

"No more meat, thank you, Edward. I will try that syllabub though. That'll be light; I feel full, but I would like something sweet to finish my meal. Maybe I'll just have some fruit. Now, come, tell me more."

"All right, I'll explain whilst you eat. All our ships have a sheathing of tar and hair and, quite apart from the sea-worms, over the months, seaweed and barnacles encrust the ship's hull. Naturally, that makes us very sluggish, which we can do without any day, but particularly if we're involved in a chase. Therefore, every now and then, we dock, and unbend – that means unfurl – the sails, unrig our topmasts and so on. Then the ship lies on her side and we can tackle the hull."

"But, where do the men go?"

"We sleep usually at the nearest inn, but out there we used to camp on the shore in tents. It wasn't a very happy time, I might add, for I used to feel most vulnerable. Aargh! And the heat! It was unbearable. I used to long for the cool breezes of the English hills."

"Did the men scrape the bottom of the boat like the fishermen do here?" Mariana continued to only play with the food on her plate.

"Quite right, my dear. We, of course, removed the guns, cables, anchors, ballast and, most importantly the gunpowder and then the carpenters would scrub the hull and repair any wood. After that the caulkers would work with hot tar. Now that really is a very, very hot job under the midday sun!"

"What about everyone else? Was it a kind of holiday for them?" Mariana went on.

"Certainly not! There's no such thing as a holiday in the Fleet. The cooper would mend the water casks; the sail makers would patch the canvas of the sails; the gunners' mates would check and repair the gun-carriage and the ordinary seamen would splice and trim the rigging and…"

"Yes, yes, I see what you mean."

"It all sounds very familiar," sighed Matthew. "I can picture it in my head."

"But you still haven't told us how you lost your leg," Mariana teased her brother.

"Yes, well, it was all rather embarrassing really. On our way home from the Indies, we encountered dense fog in the middle of the Atlantic and we lost the rest of our squadron. There we were, floundering around trying to find our direction when… Crash! Right in front of us was an enormous wall of ice."

"Ice?"

"Yes. An iceberg. Thirty? Forty? Fifty foot, towering up – a great wall of ice and what with the fog and all the confusion we ran right into it. The look out would have been due for punishment, I can tell you, for these floating islands of ice are common enough, but by all accounts, it simply loomed out of the fog. Anyway, later on I was in no state to care whether the lad in the crow's nest was blamed or not…"

"What happened then?"

"When we hit the ice, the foremast split – right from the step to the partners and…"

"What's the step?" mumbled Mariana.

"It's the block in which the base of the mast is set," explained her brother with no hint of impatience at her repeated interruptions. "The partners is a… a kind of support. How can I explain it? Where the mast passes through the deck, timber is put around to strengthen it. Anyway, a God-almighty shudder ran through the ship from the bow to the stern, and the mast cracked and split almost through its whole diameter. Of course, I had it shored up, but we were suddenly caught up in a squall and the shoring just wasn't strong enough to withstand this new battering. Without warning, the mast collapsed on…"

"Collapsed!" exclaimed Mariana, her eyes a mixture of excitement and horror.

"Onto me and several other men. Luckily, I was shielded by one of my officers who, along with two other men, died instantaneously. Many, many men were injured."

"So did you lose your leg then?" queried Matthew.

"No, although I broke it in more than one place. Needless to say, various other parts of the ship, apart from the mast, were damaged and we were leaking badly by the time the squall had left us. If I remember aright, I was told afterwards, it was as much as nine feet of water awash. However, we still limped towards home. I, myself, was in my cabin with my leg swollen to the size of a tree trunk and a fever raging in my head. I was totally oblivious to our condition and how close we were to foundering. I can tell you though, there was great rejoicing amongst the crew when the soundings showed traces of weeds and mud. Very soon the Scillies were seen. Unfortunately, even when we berthed at Plymouth, we were unable to leave the ship because it was feared we were carrying infection."

"But, if you had your leg then," pondered Mariana, "how did you lose it?"

"Gangrene, I assume, Sir?" supplied Matthew before Edward could open his mouth.

"Yes," came the faint reply. Edward was lost in his own musings momentarily. "And the fever. I was unable to shrug it off for weeks. Terrible dreams I had too." He smiled. "I think I drove my room-mates mad with all the bellowing and screaming. Except Septimus, that is. Now he was in a much sorrier state than me. Two legs gone and he was blind. Poor sod! He's dead now. Couldn't stop the sickness spreading, but… but… but he taught me a lot about myself and it was he who persuaded me to return to make my peace with my father." He banged his fist on the table, making the crockery jump, and Mariana start in surprise. "One blasted day! One day!"

"Edward, don't!" panted Mariana when her heart returned to its normal beat. "Don't torment yourself! Wilson assured you, like I did, that Father had forgiven you. And the will… Remember, he left you everything since you are his only son. Well, apart from a few paltry sums of money to…"

"And you. Why did he not leave you more?"

"I was betrothed."

There seemed nothing to say to this and, briefly, all three were caught up with their own thoughts. Then, just when Edward stood to refill their glasses, the door opened and there stood their sister, Margaret.

MARGARET

Margaret halted in the doorway and stared at Edward. Despite knowing that her father was dead, such was the curl of his wig and the soft candlelight shadowing his jaw, that she imagined he was Sir William and her mind spiralled back down the years to another scene. Oh, it had not been here in *Trem-y-Môr*, but it had been in a dining room lit by dusky candles and there had been three people sitting around the table: her father at its head with a man on his right and a woman on his left! And then, like now, she had felt the intruder with a kind of embarrassed pause in the conversation, an unidentifiable tension hanging between them, slender as spider webbing. Then, she had believed it was because she was late and she had tossed her head insolently and marched to her place at the table, allowing the footman to pull out her chair and glide it back underneath her full skirts. She had arranged her napkin over her lap before looking expectantly at Sir William.

"Father?"

"Margaret, my dear daughter. I am so glad that you have seen fit to join us, for Sir Struley and I were just putting the final touches to the marriage contract between Humphrey and yourself."

"Humphrey?" Margaret's voice was high with indignation and panic.

"Yes, Margaret. Humphrey is the eldest son and therefore..."

"I thought I was to marry Walter." Margaret swallowed a lump in her throat.

"Margaret! Please do not interrupt me!" Sir William turned to his guests. "You must excuse my daughter, Sir Struley. Sometimes she can be rather impetuous."

"Soup, Miss?" enquired the footman.

"No! Father, might I have a word alone with you? In private?" Margaret half-rose from her seat.

"Indeed not! We are in the middle of our meal. We waited and waited for you, but when you didn't put in an appearance we began without you. Now, I suggest that you start on what we are eating. What is it, Cowley?

269

Plaice? Delicious!" He sniffed the dish proffered to him by his servant.

Margaret ground her teeth. What should she do? She could defy her father; she often did and got away with it. For several years she had been a law unto herself, since… since that time when she had refused to apologise to her sister, Penelope. Margaret reviewed her childhood, shaking her head at the servant when he tried to slip the fish on to her plate.

Margaret had enjoyed being the eldest child, and, as it turned out, the only child, for the first four years of her life. She had survived when the next babies did not and she had been pampered by both her parents and staff. Margaret ruled the nursery and when Katherine was born and lived, and later Penelope, they were, after all, only faceless babies and she… Well, she was able to talk and walk and even read and write and embroider and ride a pony! No, they had not threatened her; she had received all the attention – that is, until the day Edward was born.

When young Margaret had peeped initially into his cradle, Edward resembled all the other newborn babies with a round, slightly bruised head covered with downy hair, a toothless mouth which could emit piercing cries, and two button eyes. Another baby. Nothing special. No threat to her supremacy.

However, Edward was something that neither Katherine nor Penelope, nor she was: he was a boy, a son, the first son to be born in nine years. Overnight, it had seemed, her father forgot her, for whenever he visited them, he made straight for Edward's cot.

Margaret became angry and resentful. She had tried tugging at her father's sleeve, speaking in an extra loud voice, showing him her latest achievement, but he used to listen with only half an ear and his gaze would stray towards his son, there to rest. Once Margaret had thrown her small, wiry body on to the floor in a tantrum, drumming her heels on the floorboards, striking out at anyone who came near her, but that display had resulted in a severe beating from her beloved father himself, which had stung her bare flesh and hurt her confused soul.

From that moment, Margaret had come to loathe pain, especially physical pain. She developed into a child who would avoid pain at all costs, whilst simultaneously learning that she could inflict pain on others and not be found out. Her most consistent target was that hateful boy, Edward, who had usurped her position in her father's heart.

Although only eight, Margaret discovered that, when a harassed nurse was running betwixt cradle and cot, she could volunteer to watch the 'older' children. Soon Margaret was pinching Edward surreptitiously on his fat, baby arms, or even shaking him, if no one was looking, and by the time the nurse returned, she would be embracing him, her features wide-eyed in innocence, assuring the nurse that his cries were only due to a touch of colic.

For several years, Margaret had bullied Edward, safe in the knowledge that he was unable to tell anyone about what she used to do, and it might have gone on for longer if Penelope had not set herself up as Edward's champion. Suddenly the nursery had divided into two camps: Penelope and Edward against Margaret and Katherine, who was kept firmly in her place with threats of retribution. Margaret assumed that she would be victorious, since she was twice their size. But the two youngest members of the family did not hesitate to attain victory by the simple method of running to the nearest adult and telling tales. Since physical attack might have led to her receiving pain, Margaret had resorted to verbal intimidation when no adults were around, and insisting on the rights of the eldest child on every occasion.

Her main privilege as the oldest was to spend time away from the nursery, not in the company of her father (which her young soul craved) but with her mother.

Margaret's first memories of her mother were of a laughing woman with dove, grey eyes, who had adored her only surviving daughter and played with her and dressed her like a doll and cuddled her securely in her arms. However, with the passing years, Letitia had become silent and then morose and then, in Margaret's own words, strange. Little Margaret had not wanted to spend time poring over the difficult words in the Bible or kneeling for hours in the chapel on the stone floor in whispered prayer. Thus, in the end, even her supposed treat of spending time with adults led to more bitterness being laid down in a new, hard-setting layer on the foundation already rankling in her heart that her father ignored her.

To her own disgust, when Edward left babyhood, she became fond of him. He was a pleasant boy, easy-going and friendly. Nonetheless, she was jealous of the way he received Sir William's attention, the very thing she craved. Added to this, Edward spent too much time in dark corners confiding with his friend and sister, Penelope. Her regard for him shrank and their relationship remained tenuous.

Over time, Margaret began to loathe her youngest sister. This was not just because Penelope had become Edward's protector, but because she was pretty and vivacious. Penelope had wavy, fair hair falling down her back in symmetrical ripples; clear skin which never reddened or blotched, and melting brown eyes which could be turned upon the nursemaids and nannies alike in order to get her own way. Those cups of liquid chocolate would touch the stoniest hearts and, with the combination of her blonde hair, who could resist her? No one. And she wasn't just a picture to look at, for she had a sunny character too. She was sociable without being pert or cheeky. Penelope was 'a real darling' according to one Irish maid.

Penelope had all this whilst she, Margaret, had straight brown hair which could be seen on the heads of countless other children the whole world over, and it grew very slowly in thin wisps which refused to curl or lie neatly, whatever was done to it. Margaret's eyes were brown too, but dull compared with her amiable sister. Added to that, she was unable to compete with her sister's gregarious personality. Margaret became increasingly moody and resentful. The two youngest were the favourites with everyone, whereas she, who had known what it was like to be the favoured one, was pushed aside. It wasn't fair!

Then had come the fateful day when her sister returned to the nursery, after her brush with death. Margaret tried to be honest with herself and her so-called abominable behaviour. Had she been glad when Penelope had been scarred? No. Even in the hidden recesses of her breast, she would not have wished such an awful fate on anyone. She had not visited her sister whilst Penelope was ill except early on; rather, she had enjoyed lording over the younger children upstairs and, to her surprise, really associating with Edward for the first time. Just as she was beginning to understand that it was not his fault that Father preferred him, Penelope had come back to the nursery floor. What a shock! Yes, her reaction had been one of pure shock and not malice. Truly she had thought that Penelope looked frightful and she had never understood why she was treated in such a severe manner. Why should she have to apologise for speaking the truth? After all, adults were urging her repeatedly not to lie…

Margaret had been locked in her room for days – an eternity it had felt like – but one thing she had known was that, even if she had to live her whole life shut away, she would never, ever say sorry since she had not done anything wrong. Her lovely sister had walked into the room, hideously disfigured, and frightened her. And Margaret had every reason to be afraid for, although barely had she recognised Penelope, she knew that her young sister would be all right in the end. Penelope had such a jolly character, whereas she, Margaret, would shrivel up and die if she became deformed. Margaret was terrified. Already, even at her tender age, she had received some of the harsher side of life. What was to stop her catching this awful disease? No, she had perceived immediately that she could not risk going near Penelope in case she caught smallpox.

Yet the agitation increased when, within a few short hours of her banishment to her room, she had begun to bleed from between her legs. Was this some punishment by an unseen hand? Was she going to die like her sister nearly had? She had felt the trickle begin and had been petrified when it had continued all through that first night of her imprisonment. When the pain had come, during the long, lonely midnight hours, Margaret had tossed and turned.

Margaret was surprised and then infuriated by the maid's complete lack of sympathy when, the next morning, she had wanted to change the sheets in a matter-of-fact manner. The brisk girl had muttered something and politely asked Margaret to vacate the bed.

Margaret had moaned:

"Can't you see I'm dying? Leave me alone." And she had turned her white face to the wall.

The maid had remained for a few moments saying nothing and then left Margaret to her forebodings. The girl had clutched the sheets in her hands and groaned until the maid had returned.

"Go away!" she had shouted without moving. "I've told you already to leave me alone. I want to die in peace."

"Now, Margaret," had come the firm reply. Nanny was at the door and she had supplied her charge with some vague facts about menstruation, of which the only one that had penetrated Margaret's pain-filled mind was that this torment would occur every single month for practically the rest of her life. Margaret was left in clean sheets to curse again the day that she had not been born a boy. If she was a boy, she had wept into the pillow, she would not have had to suffer this indignity and agony and she could have been her father's favourite!

She had discovered two truths during those solitary days in her room.

Firstly, she had stumbled upon the tremendous comfort of food. She had learnt that whether she was angry, excited or sad, food made her feel better. She had developed a gargantuan appetite for meals and a habit of nibbling in between them, for, when she had food in her stomach or her mouth or even in her hand, she became a match for anyone. Yes, it meant she was buxom, she argued to herself, but then she had been big-boned since childhood and was quite tall for her age and if she became too thin she would look like a maypole and hadn't she seen what thinness had done to Penelope? That girl continued to look to be at death's door, years after her illness, with all her clothes hanging on her as though they belonged to someone else.

Secondly, Margaret had learnt the pleasure of winning a battle and how powerless her parents, and particularly her father, were in controlling her. Of course, eventually, Sir William had been forced to release her from her room, especially when he had seen she was quite contented alone in there, eating and eating. She was as unrepentant on the day she left as on the day she had entered.

Once Margaret had realised that her father considered her too old to beat physically, she had felt the throb of victory in her blood. She came to understand that she could bully him in the same way she had bullied baby Edward and once she was out of the nursery (due to her behaviour) she determined to do exactly what she pleased in her daily life. Sir William had stayed out of her way on the whole. Did he understand that she had won? She noticed that whenever they met, he tried to regain the upper hand. At least this was what she reckoned explained his constant verbal castigations of her. Margaret could recall some of their fiercer shouting matches; her father always came out worse off, she believed. With maturity, Margaret began to use her own tongue as a weapon. Habitually she said the most outrageous statements and the only punishment her father could mete out to her was to send her to her room. Nevertheless, Margaret had not cared about this since her indiscreet words could not be *unsaid*. She revelled in the look of scandal on people's faces and watching Sir William's face purpling. Sometimes, if a certain function bored her, she spoke disrespectfully in order to be sent away in disgrace and escape the tedium.

However, on this occasion, with Sir Struley and her father eating their way relentlessly through a leg of pork, neither of these reasons made her speak. She sensed that Sir William had won his first battle against her. Margaret seemed to have misjudged her father's power. She had forgotten that he *did* have the ultimate weapon. He was able (and apparently had done so already) to arrange her whole future life. Margaret pecked at her meat, defeat sinking to the base of her stomach. A dull ache twisted through her but she knew that it had its origins in more down to earth reasons: her monthly bleeding had started tonight. This was the reason for her tardiness. Sitting there sulkily planning what to do, she felt the familiar pain begin in the recesses of her abdomen – completely unlike any other pain she had experienced – quite distinct from the discomfort due to overeating or wind or the gripe from loose bowels. A woman's pain, which only another woman could understand. Margaret's spirits sank lower for she knew the cramp would grow and spread, often right around to the back and down her legs, never letting up its hold on her body until it had finished its course.

The pain made her furious. Damn all men! What did they know what it was like to be a woman! Here they were discussing her future as though she were a cow for market!

Margaret had known the Struley family all her life – that is to say, she was acquainted with Walter and his brother Ralph. In truth she had never seen the eldest brother, Humphrey, who her father was expecting her to marry. The reason for this omission was that Humphrey was weak in the head, a simpleton, and he was kept confined to his quarters in one wing of the castle. Rumour had it that he was still unable to control his bladder consistently and he could not talk in a language other than that of a two year-old, although Margaret calculated quickly, he must be twenty-nine by now.

How could these men, and one of them her own father, be planning to marry her to Humphrey Struley? She had not been ignorant that marriage between the two families would occur, but she had assumed that she was meant for Walter, the youngest son. Walter, who was her contemporary, she liked in a mild way, for he was happy to give way to her more forceful character. Ralph, the middle son, was her senior by ten years, and he was away often when she had arrived at the Struley home. She recalled that even if he was staying at the castle, he would spend the day, from early morning to dusk, astride his magnificent horse. Of an evening he would exchange no more than polite small talk with the young Margaret. In her memories he was tall, even when a boy, with a hearty laugh, and surrounded continuously by graceful girls vying for his attentions. No, Margaret had been contented enough to converse with the equable Walter.

In the past year, circumstances had changed which had made Margaret's hopes rise concerning her marriage to Walter: Ralph had been lost at sea, presumed dead. It had come to Margaret, that, although she was not going to marry the eldest son, she would be doing so, in effect. After all, wasn't it common knowledge that people like Humphrey never lived long? They were prone to illness and then there was the possibility of them killing themselves since they combined all the dangers of a nursery situation with the strength of an adult! And Humphrey was not expected to marry and certainly not be capable of siring children. Therefore, Margaret had complied happily with the plans to join the Rowlands with the Struleys; she could see a pleasant future as Walter's wife.

What had gone wrong? Had she been mistaken about the bridegroom? Had it been decided eons ago that she would marry the eldest son since she was the eldest daughter? Or had her father misled her deliberately in an attempt to pay her back for the numerous occasions she had humiliated him?

Margaret stared at Sir William, but his features were unreadable and he was deep in conversation with his guest. She noticed that neither men took any notice of Walter's mother, who sat mutely by their side. Suddenly Margaret came to a decision. She stood up, wilfully knocking over her glass, to catch their attention. She had sat placidly too long!

"I shan't do it!" she shrieked. "I won't marry a madman. He ought to be locked up and the key thrown away!" All the anger of the past years against her father burst out. "I shan't do it…"

"Margaret! BE QUIET!" bellowed Sir William. He could be overpowering when he chose to be; the words were a trumpet blast. After he had silenced his daughter he commanded her, in a more normal voice, to leave the room.

"I won't." Margaret was shivering with emotion and her own tone remained loud and belligerent. "You'll have to carry me from the room. I want you to promise that I won't have to marry that simpleton. You can't make me do it. I won't say the vows. I won't. I won't. I won't…"

Her father left his seat and was around the table in a trice. For only the second time in his life he hit his daughter – a stinging blow to the side of the head, which left her speechless, with the room dancing around in duplicate and she felt a surge of blood leave her body between her legs.

Margaret glared at her father. Then, as majestically as she could, she turned from him to depart, saying in a deadly whisper:

"You shouldn't have done that! This isn't the end of this."

* * *

Margaret came back to the present with a bump and barked:

"Well, what's all this then? A merry family reunion? Where have you come from Edward? Where are Penelope and Katherine? Is this your husband, Mariana, or an old friend of Edward's?"

"Margaret…" began Edward, rising from the table. "What a surprise! I thought…"

"What do you mean? A surprise?" broke in Margaret irascibly.

"I mean that we had quite given up hope of you arriving. Do sit down. You must excuse us but we've sent the servants away…"

"That's strange," ranted Margaret. "One opened the door to me. Ah, here he is. Wilson, isn't it?"

"I've brought you some eating utensils, Mrs Struley. Won't you please be seated? I've given some victuals to your maid and I'll have some sent out to your groom…"

"That won't be possible. He isn't here. He's coping with the carriage. We had somewhat of a mishap…" Margaret started to recount her journey when she heard what sounded like a giggle. She turned stern eyes on her younger sister. "Mariana, I see you are the same as ever. Father never taught you any manners."

"I beg your pardon, Margaret. I'm afraid I've been drinking too quickly and have the hiccups."

Margaret narrowed her eyes.

"You look familiar to me," she sniffed. "I suppose it's your resemblance to your mother. Although I'll say this for your mother: *she* had impeccable manners. Now, Edward, I don't recall you introducing me to this gentleman."

"This is Mr Cutlass… Cutland. He is our closest neighbour. Cutland, my sister, Lady Struley."

"Not 'Lady' anymore, Edward. Didn't you hear Wilson? I'm plain 'Mrs'."

"Really. Why is that?"

"It's a long story." Margaret pursed her lips. "Not to be told tonight!"

"As you say, Margaret. Allow me to help you to some meat."

"I can do it, Sir," countered Wilson, appearing with a plate laden down with various foods to tempt a tired traveller's palate.

Margaret almost snatched the plate. She needed no tempting; she was desperate to eat to revive her flagging spirits and cover her disappointment over the reappearance of her brother. She needed money, dear God, how she needed it! And here was her brother, sitting at the head of the table, as if he owned the place, which maybe he did! Swallowing her first mouthful, she chided herself not to lose hope. It was her understanding that her father's will had not been written recently. Edward might well have been excluded if when a lad, he *had* made advances to Father's beloved Mariana, as rumour told it! Everyone knew Sir William had been besotted with his second wife!

"So, when is the funeral?" Margaret asked.

There was an awkward silence.

"I'm sorry… sorry, but… it was today," confessed Edward.

"Today! You mean to tell me that I've come all this way for nothing! Couldn't you have postponed it until my arrival?"

"I am very sorry, Margaret," repeated Edward, "but there's been a tragedy in our community recently…"

"I'm not interested in your excuses. I am very, very upset."

"I didn't think you were that fond of Father," murmured Mariana.

Margaret glared at her stepsister.

"You *are* as bad as ever! I remember you when you were a child – you were forthright then! I see you haven't changed. My relationship with my father began years before yours did, my girl."

"Maybe," flashed back Mariana, "but you were never close to him."

"Mariana, I think that is enough…" Edward advised.

"What do you know about it?" stormed Mariana, jumping to her feet. "None of you have lived with Father for years. You, Edward, were actually banished. Yes, banished from this place and you… you, Margaret, haven't set foot near us for years and years. But you've come now, haven't you? Now, that there's something to be had! None of you care… I mean really care that he's gone… dead. None of you loved him like I did." She stamped from the room.

"My, my, what a fiery child!" Margaret observed mildly. Mariana's outburst had cleared her own emotions and the food was giving her strength. "I assume she is still unmarried and I can see why. She may be a beauty but who'd want such a bad-tempered pup around the house?"

When nobody spoke, she went on:

"Ah, Wilson, may I have some more of that delicious dish there? Yes, that one. I do love the taste of parsley. Now, are arrangements being made for a bed for me?"

She noticed the servant look from her to Edward, but before he could reply Mr Cutland remarked:

"I think, if you'll excuse me, I'd best be going, Captain Rowlands. I've enjoyed your company. It's made me pine to be aboard ship again. Anyway, I'll be back tomorrow to see my patient."

"Yes… Yes, Cutlass," responded Edward absentmindedly. "Please forgive our family. Everyone is tired and feelings are… are sensitive. Mariana is still distraught after last night."

"Don't apologise for Miss Mariana. I've known her a long time and, if I might be permitted to say, love her like a daugh… a niece. She's a special friend of mine and I'm used to her open ways. I'm just glad to see her out of that trance she's been living in since the death of Mr Wynne."

"Yes, that's true. Shall I show you to the…?"

"No. No. You've got to arrange who is going to sleep where and such matters. I would offer you a room in my house, but I'm afraid, my lifestyle doesn't cater for house guests very often and…" Mr Cutland stood up whilst speaking.

"You mustn't worry." Edward smiled.

"I don't see what the problem is," Margaret complained. "There's plenty of bedchambers here, aren't there?"

"May I escort you to the door, Mr Cutlass?" Wilson inclined his head at the old surgeon.

"We have another guest staying with us…" declared Edward once he was alone with his sister.

"Who's that then? Katherine?"

"No, we haven't seen or heard from Katherine yet. No, our guest is a man who was flung up from the sea a few nights ago."

"But there's still…"

"Yes, yes. It's just that I haven't moved into Father's room yet. It doesn't seem right somehow."

"Did you see Father before he died?"

"No. Unfortunately, I arrived a day too late."

"Sounds familiar," rejoined Margaret *sotto voce*.

"Maybe *you* had better sleep in Father's room…"

"No, indeed! That definitely would not be right. I'm sure Wilson and some of your maids can carry your belongings across. Surely Father had more servants than Wilson? I remember a woman… the housekeeper… Mrs…?"

"Jones. Yes, but though it may seem strange to you, we had sent them away before you came. They have been on their feet all day and all of last night for the vigil."

The door opened behind them and Wilson returned.

"Your room is ready, Madam, when you want to retire. Your maid can be put up in the garrets with our own maids, if that's all right with you, Madam."

"No, it isn't all right. Perrin will sleep in my room. I have her near me always; I suffer from terrible headaches and need her at hand."

"I will explain that to Elin, our maid, then, Madam. If you'll excuse me?"

"I didn't know you suffered…" Edward started to speak but his sister cut him off rudely:

"You know virtually nothing about me! Now I shall go to bed. I am very tired. I haven't slept well these past four nights – too many bedbugs. I trust there are no bugs here."

Edward stood up when she left the table. Margaret thought she heard him say:

"Not in my bed, there aren't, my dear sister. Not in my bed!"

EDWARD

Edward closed his eyes and leant his elbows on his desk, allowing his forehead to rest on his upturned palms. By God, he was sapped by the trivialities of every day life at *Trem-y-Môr*! There had not been any peace in the house for the last seven days and it was almost entirely due to Margaret's presence.

The very first night she had offended the maid, Elin, by declaring that the bed was not made up to her liking, then further insulted her by demanding that Elin showed a more respectful face and attitude to her. Margaret seemed to have no concept of what all of them had been through that day and the previous night.

Before Edward had even arisen the following morning, Margaret had set up the hackles of Mrs Jones' back by criticising all sorts of household matters from too much dust under the beds to too little salt in the stew and surely the dog had fleas! Edward had been bewildered by her monologue of complaints.

Mariana's temper flared whenever she caught sight of her sister and Margaret, instead of leaving the girl alone, perpetually admonished her for slouching at the table; leaving her clothes flung on the floor in her room; wearing her hair loose; visiting a single man in his bedchamber; spending time with the servants and talking Welsh to them... The list was endless! Edward could not keep track of everything that Margaret thought was wrong with her young half-sister. All that Edward knew was that there would be an explosion of ill feeling between the two warring parties ere long!

He recalled that from the initial moment of Margaret's arrival – on the evening of the funeral – he had felt the need to try to pacify both women. Yet he wasn't impartial in any mediation, for, he admitted to himself, he was on Mariana's side. At her best, Margaret patronised the younger woman and at her worst, she was downright vicious! If only Margaret hadn't come. At that meal with Cutland, he, Edward, had hoped that Mariana was making a few tentative steps towards overcoming her grief – her curiosity about his time in the Fleet showed her to be a caring and interested person, but he had not seen that side of his youngest sister ever since.

Margaret herself had been in what was apparently a good mood, especially after hearing the contents of the will. Sir William, although leaving the house and lands to Edward, had left small, but satisfactory, sums of money to all four of his daughters. In the beginning, Edward remembered with another sigh, Margaret had been cross that Wilson had received over one hundred pounds.

"It's too much," she had complained. "He'll only squander it. Servants don't know how to handle money."

Edward could hear her voice now. However, when she had understood that Mariana had not received any more money than herself (even though Mariana had been the favourite daughter, Margaret had informed him), she had forgotten Wilson and swept around the house as if she had won some private victory. She had immediately written to her sick husband (whom Wilson had told him had a problem with drink), and then announced in an exulting voice that she was very comfortable here and would be staying to sort out the household. Edward had groaned then and he groaned again now.

The appearance of Jack from his room yesterday had eased some of the undercurrents between the brother and sisters, but he had noticed that Margaret always treated Jack as though he was a misplaced servant. Edward smiled grimly. Last evening Margaret had upset Mariana again by berating her for ogling at Jack. Because Jack was present, there was a charged pause before Jack replied that he liked exquisite women staring at him. *That* had annoyed Margaret. Edward could see her outraged face in his mind. He leant back in his chair with a cheerful grin.

Exquisite women! Was Jack falling in love with his charming young sister? Which reminded him of the Parson, a man who claimed he loved Mariana. *He* had called every single day this week on some pretext or another! Fortunately, Edward knew that he had been unable to see Mariana without Margaret being present. This was not just for reasons of propriety but because Margaret had struck up a close friendship with the Reverend Mr Owen. She always appeared from nowhere whenever he was announced!

Edward guessed that by this time the Vicar would have told Margaret about his plans to wed Mariana. Strangely, Margaret had said nothing. Had she spoken to Mariana yet? Surely not, or he would have heard about it! Were Margaret and the Vicar putting their heads together literally, plotting? He found it hard to believe on such a short acquaintance – although why did she spend so much time in his company?

Come to think of it, Mariana seemed to be avoiding not only Margaret but himself also. He could not figure out the reason for this, since he had been very careful to hide his growing feelings of love for her. Perhaps she wasn't avoiding him but simply keeping out of her sister's way. Still he had not been able to speak with Mariana alone – at least not without making an issue of seeking her out and he was not inclined to start any conversation under those circumstances. Yet how could seven days have passed with no opportunity to speak to her privately? He had begun to wonder if unconsciously he was avoiding finding out answers. Was he a coward in fact, or had the passing days helped him see the futility of worrying about the Parson and his proposals? After all, he himself was Mariana's nearest male kin and since he would never give his consent to such an ill-matched marriage, even assuming that his sister was content to marry the Parson, why fret any more? And he hadn't been completely idle but had searched amongst his father's papers. However, he had found nothing concerning a marriage contract between Mariana and the Parson. Nevertheless, today, he *must* speak with her, for, today, several more problems had descended which affected his own future.

He could hardly believe it was only ten o'clock in the morning! This was why he was sitting in the library behind a locked door. No more bad news until he could sort himself out over all that had happened already today!

Edward clasped his hands behind his head, leaning into the back of the chair and recalled all the people who had come to see him.

Mrs Jones had put in an appearance early. One fact that had emerged when going through the late Squire's papers was that he owed wages to all his servants. Mrs Jones alone was due twelve pounds for four years of service. He had mentioned the money to the housekeeper when she had entered the room, before she had time to explain her reason for coming, and she had declared:

"I'll take all that's owing me then, Sir, and I must tell you that I am resigning today!"

Edward had opened his mouth on the word "Why?" but was overridden by a garbled tirade, much of which he couldn't remember. The crux of the matter was that he had to decide between his housekeeper and his eldest sister. He knew about some of the trouble between the two matrons but he was unprepared for the vitriolic torrent that flowed from Mrs Jones' lips. He had no time to reply before she had marched from the room leaving her ultimatum – "Me or her, Sir. You must choose!" – almost palpably on his desk.

Now he decided that he would have to stiffen his backbone and face Margaret and tell her to pack her bags. He could not afford to lose such an efficient servant as Mrs Jones. Elin seemed a very capable maid but she was young and if Edward had to go away again (and it looked almost certain that he did because of the other news he had heard today), then he would need Mrs Jones' experienced hands here to run his home. He would have to speak to Margaret and, although he was a grown man and used to fighting the French, the thought of confronting his eldest sister made him quiver. She was formidable.

He closed his eyes, recalling his next visitor. Barely had the door shut behind the bristling, affronted housekeeper, when Owen Lewis, the head groom, had knocked timorously. Edward had spent nearly half an hour listening to him, paying his back-pay and his wife's (for her work in the kitchen and dairy before her illness). He assured him that if there was anything he could do, Lewis wasn't to hesitate to mention it. Lewis had received the money, apparently gratefully, and tucked it carefully into his pocket. Edward guessed the other man was thinking that the coins would help affray the cost of the burial. The groom slipped from the room as cautiously as he had entered it.

It was after his departure that Edward had gone back to peruse the books. Guiltily, he had discovered that no less than four of Lewis' sons were outdoor staff at *Trem-y-Môr*. Thomas and Evan he had met but Morgan and another Owen were a fodderer and gardener respectively. There were also a carter and two ploughmen to pay and… Edward groaned despondently. He had noticed several men around the yard, but he had not discovered their names yet. What a headache it all was! Fortunately the indoor staff seemed to be confined to Mrs Jones, Elin and her two sisters, and the sick Bridget, wife of Lewis. There was another child, a girl, who helped. Was she another sister of Elin? She earned five shillings a year, according to the books, and her name was Biddy. Yet he had not encountered her in the house. He must ask Mrs Jones about her. Peradventure she had been dismissed but her details not erased from the books. So many servants! So many new faces! And there were his tenants too. He had met a few of them this past week, but he could not put names to faces. Wilson had been a great help to him. Wilson… Wilson…

It had been today also that Wilson had spoken to him, although earlier than the others, for he had been dressing when the valet asked for a word with him. Wilson had told his master that now Sir William had left him some money, he would like to retire from service. Unashamedly, Edward had begged him not to leave. There were too many responsibilities to be learnt, he had explained, and he needed continuity. He had exhorted Wilson to stay, even offering him a wage increase. This latter the old retainer had refused stiffly but he had agreed to stay a little longer. Edward wondered if he had not seen a glint of relief in the other man's eye with the decision made!

Edward shifted his chair nearer the desk and fingered the two letters laid before him. He had settled in this very seat – after placing the account books back on a shelf – with the intention of writing to his sister, Pen, who had sent him a note yesterday to request him to postpone his visit. Apparently the Roberts had found some blight on their newly shooting-up crops, although Edward had been unable to read the precise nature of the problem. Penelope's writing became almost illegible when she was agitated. Edward knew he must reply this morning. He had just re read Pen's letter when a sharp knock at the door had come. Expecting another unhappy servant, he had called a "Come in" and Elin had entered, bearing two letters which had been delivered by the post-boy. Edward took the well thumbed paper, surmising that the post-boy was lingering on the premises, probably settled in the warm kitchen, enjoying a hearty exchange of news with Mrs Jones even as he himself received the missives!

Edward stared at the letters lying open on his desk. One of them was a threatening letter – oh, not frightening to him, more like a tiresome fly that needed swatting – but its intention was to arouse fear. It was written by a letter-writer, obviously, for the author was an illiterate prostitute from St James Park. She was promising to seek compensation from him if he did not send her some money for the pregnancy which had made her lose her job. His child! His child! What did she take him for? A nincompoop? Nevertheless, if he was travelling to London – and the contents of the second epistle made him realise that he would have to go – then he might as well visit this slut and tell her she had chosen the wrong man to blackmail!

Women. What a curse they were so often! He remembered the night he had gone to see… What was her name? He glanced at the black writing. Annie. Yes, Annie. He had been slightly drunk and they had laughed together at his inability to hold his own with her! Eventually, he had succeeded in taking her and he had wept on her shoulder, explaining it was not the drink that had hindered his performance, but his sorrow, for he had just lost his wife.

Of course, Alicia had not been his wife in name, but she had been in all else. Alicia, or Ally, as she had called herself. What a frightened little shrimp she had been – bright ginger hair and a handful of freckles scattered across her snub nose! She could not have been more than fourteen, maybe a year younger, when he had first met her. She had been soliciting and very unsuccessfully if he remembered aright! He could see her now in his mind's eye.

"Well, Cap'n, would yer like to take me 'ome?" she drawled. He was not a captain, but the slight tremor in her voice caught his attention and a glimmer of something else.

"What do you want from me? Go home to your mother!"

"I haven't got – ain't got no mother."

Edward had meant to pass on but he stopped and spoke with her. Within a few seconds he was accusing her of not being a prostitute at all and when it was obvious she needed money, he had slipped her some coins and urged her to get herself some decent employment.

"Thank you kindly, Sir." She bobbed like a housemaid and sped away with his donation clutched in her hand.

Much to his annoyance, he saw her the following day trying to interest another sailor. However, the man brushed past her and Edward grimaced. There was something about her which declared that she was not what she appeared to be – not in her dress, since she must have copied some of the more experienced women, and not in her voice, if she remembered the accent and to drop some of her consonants, but something else which made men wary. Was she a runaway heiress or the daughter of a judge? he asked himself, crossing the street to her.

"Excuse me, Miss," Edward entreated, coming up behind her. "I'd like to…"

She turned to see him and had the grace to blush.

"Oh, it's you, Sir."

"I thought I told you to go home," he rebuked her. "Where is your home?"

"I got no place to go, but I'm willing to come to yer rooms, Sir, and oblige yer. And when I save enough money, I can rent me own rooms like…"

Edward opened his mouth to tell her once again that she was too young to be trying to find customers and startled himself by saying:

"You'd better come back with me."

He saw her swallow nervously but she trotted along behind him obediently, like a faithful dog, whilst he cursed his own stupidity. What was he going to do with her once he reached his rooms?

Before he had time to close the door to his rented room in 'The Humped Bridge' inn, she was undressing her underdeveloped body.

"Wait!" he gasped. "What are you…?"

"But, Sir, yer won't pay if I don't… and… and…"

"Now stop slurring your words like that. I can tell it's put on. You need to practice more if you don't want to make mistakes."

"Oh, Sir," she shuddered, lowering her head. Edward noticed a tear drip from her cheek. Agitatedly her fingers plucked at the fastenings of her bodice.

"You'd better sit down and tell me who you are. What's your name?"

"Ally. Alicia, Sir."

He soon had her story. She was the daughter of a clergyman – a curate from Kent. When her father had died, she and her mother and two brothers had come to London to look for her mother's own brother, who was a merchant. However, when finally they had reached his house, they discovered that her uncle had died recently and his widow had married again without delay. The new husband was unwilling to support this brood of relatives. Alicia and her family had found themselves with nowhere to go but the backstreets of the capital city. Verily sheep thrown to the wolves! thought Edward.

Soon their meagre money had gone on renting filthy rooms whilst Alicia and her elder brother, Christopher, searched for jobs. The shock of her changed circumstances had left Alicia's mother ill and depressed, and, despite her and the lads' best efforts, within four weeks, Alicia was burying her other parent. The young people had changed to even cheaper accommodation, but Alicia had been forced to remain at home to nurse her sensitive youngest brother through a fever which took him to the grave also.

Alicia and Christopher had agreed to give up their room to save their money for food. For several months the two had slept in alleys and under arches, not managing to find permanent work to support them. As Alicia walked around the streets, she explained shyly to Edward that she had seen that there was profit to be earned if she would sell her body, yet her early religious life forced her to reject the life of a street woman. It was only in the last week, when she had lost the last remaining member of her family to the hand of death, that she had decided to copy the other prostitutes.

"You must understand, Sir, that I tried. I really tried to get other jobs, but someone else always seemed to get there before me. Every job I went for had dozens of applicants. When my broth… when Christopher died, I knew there *was* something I could do and…"

"You haven't found a customer yet, though, Alicia, have you?"

"Yes. Yes, I have."

"No, Alicia, don't lie to me."

Edward heard the swallowed gulp of air whilst she turned her face away. A whisper:

"No, Sir. I must be doing something wrong. No one… No one…"

"Like all jobs, it's not as easy as it looks! Come on, cheer up! You should be glad. You're too young to be selling yourself."

"Oh, Sir, if you could… could…"

"No. No. I had no intention of taking you to my bed. I'm not sure why I brought you here, but now I've heard your story, I'm even less inclined!"

Alicia stood up, pulling her cloak around her slim shoulders.

"Thank you, Sir. Thank you for listening to me. It has helped to talk to someone… someone who speaks the language I used to hear."

"What are you doing?"

"I'm going now, Sir."

"Where to? You told me you had nowhere to go. Is there nobody else you can turn to before it's too late? Another relative?"

"No. I can't even get work as a maid in a big household without a reference…"

Edward rose quickly.

"You can't go. I'll try to help you get a job. I've many acquaintances around the docks. Maybe I can find…"

"No, Sir. I can't expect you to help me. You don't know me. Why should you help me?"

"Because I've sisters whom I would hate to see reduced to… to what you have been. Please wait here. I've a plan. No, on second thoughts, I'll lock you in. I don't want to return, having found you a place, only to discover the bird has flown, from a mistaken sense of pride or whatever. Consider the alternatives: you'll get a customer in the end who won't mind that you have no experience. Once that has happened, there'll be no turning back and you will never have a chance to marry even a poor man who is respectable. Few want a woman who has shared her bed with dozens of different men."

Edward could have bitten off his tongue when he saw her flush. He turned smartly on his heel and left. By the end of the afternoon, after a brief consultation with Widow Aitken about the best opportunity for a girl like Alicia, Edward returned with details of sweaty employment. She was to work in the kitchens of a nearby inn, which, he told her triumphantly, included a narrow low bed under the rafters.

He towered over her, pleased to see that her serene face gave no evidence of tears or anger, and smiled with kindness. The next moment, his smile turned to a frown. Courageously – he had to admire her courage – her small, steady voice explained to him that she would only accept his help if she paid for it. Gone was the quivering child; in its place an almost confident miss who was disrobing once more. To his dismay, she stated adamantly that if Edward refused her payment, she would not work in the kitchens but disappear into the murky alleys of London and begin a new career with any men who wanted her.

Edward stared into her determined face. Instantly, he knew she would win, for his compassion could not let her go and, he reasoned, lying once with him would not ruin her life, if she was sensible in the future. Yet… Exasperated, Edward almost told her to leave. Here he was trying to save her and obstinately she was offering herself to him!

With petticoats and bodice discarded, her revealed breasts made desire rise within him. Arguing silently in his head that with his shore leave ending he had no time to dissuade her, and marvelling at the workings of the female brain, he perceived that it was better for Alicia to learn from him than from some of the customers she would find before long. Cursing again his impulse to interfere in her life, he allowed his own sentiments to override his common sense. *And,* a persistent voice whispered inside him, it was several days since he had lain with a woman and this one was, after all, a virgin. Thus he gave himself up to the sensations of the next hour, surprised at how delightful it was to teach someone else.

The following morning, true to her word, Alicia, or Ally as he now called her, left him to begin her job at the inn.

How could Edward have known that he would miss her pert face almost as soon as she had gone? How could he have predicted that his heart would lighten when she had come knocking at his door late that evening? How could he have perceived that picking up Ally from the street would so change his life?

A pattern was set. Whenever he was ashore, Ally left her lonely garret bed and joined him. On each occasion she had enough vigour to fulfil his wishes and he enjoyed her honest, uncomplicated appraisal of life. He never told any of his family or mates about Ally, but he found he used to look forward to seeing her on the homeward journey. She never demanded anything from him, never pestered or nagged him. In return, he made sure she did not lack for everyday comforts, and accepted when she insisted that she wanted to stay working in the kitchens and earn her own wage. He decided that he could allow her some independence as long as she was always there when he came home. He never doubted that she was faithful to him, and, if he saw love in her eyes, he ignored it. When she told him, shyly, that she was with child, he knew the babe was his. Immediately he set about finding her better lodgings. He would provide for his child in the same way he provided for the child's mother.

However, he was not prepared for the strength of his feelings when he held his son in his arms, five months later, but he did not express them. Nonetheless, he found himself looking at Ally with a new respect, as she sat back proudly on the bed. Some would have felt the first stirrings of love if they had held a weeping woman in their arms the following day when the child lay dead in its cot. With hindsight, Edward hated himself for so dreadfully letting down Ally. All he could recall of that awful day was his surprise at how their shared grief united them in a way he would not have thought possible. Still, it wasn't then that he had made a move to bind them together legally in marriage.

How many years had passed until he was lying, sick in hospital, close to death, and had time to think about his mistress? There he began to appreciate all that Ally had been to him. When he was well enough, he wrote to her, telling her about his leg and that he had something to ask her, but he wanted to say it to her face, not write it in a letter. He was not too surprised that she did not reply, because she had never answered his letters (sent from around the world), but he must make haste to visit her, before travelling to be reconciled to his father.

The determination to set right everything in his life, after his near encounter with death, spurred on his recovery. Trapped in bed, day after day, he acknowledged to himself that he had used Ally and now he would make it up to her by proposing marriage. She had been loyal to him for many years and borne his son, even though the baby had died. She came from a respectable family. If he took her to Anglesey with him, no one would know that she had spent years working as a serving wench in an inn. He knew he did not love her, but he felt very comfortable with her and she was very familiar to him, and he felt her loyalty deserved some reward. He was thirty-three years old, and it was time he was married.

Edward screwed up the letter which lay on the desk in front of him, recalling the torment he had felt when he had discovered that she had gone! No wonder she had not replied – she had never received his note. He had stood in front of the wife of the landlord of 'The Bear' inn, shaking with fatigue and frustration, rolling that barren epistle, which had just been thrust into his hand, into a ball and throwing it into the nearby fire.

"When did she leave, woman?" he growled.

"Nigh on six months ago, Sir. Did she not write and tell you? The child and she…"

"The child! What child? Speak up! Don't keep me waiting!"

"Oh, Sir, it was your child – a boy like. She never went with anyone else, Sir. She kept herself to herself. Working here, morning 'til dusk, never saying a word of complaint. She was happier once she had her other room and not her bed at the top of the stairs. It gave her somewhere to go away from here but I'm sure she had no visitors there. Oh, are you all right, Sir?"

Edward slumped on a nearby bench, his leg aching, his head spinning.

"A child," he murmured. "Another son. Oh, why didn't she tell me?"

He didn't realise he was speaking out loud and therefore started when the landlord's wife replied:

"She waited for your letters, Sir. Fairly hankered after them. On the days when one came, she was a different girl, smiling and laughing and working twice as fast. There's no doubt she loved you, Sir, and that's why I say the child was yours, if I might be bold enough to say it, Sir. She had hoped... you know, after the other one... when the other one... Maybe, a wedding band. Not that she said anything, mind, but you could tell, in her eyes.

"'Course, she'd moved up from the lowest of the low but you know that, don't you, Sir? She worked behind the bar and everyone respected her. All the customers knew you couldn't fool Alicia. I think she must have put something away but I never asked. None of my business really. But when the child – the second child – was born, she seemed anxious. Not about the baby's health but about... about you, Sir. You were in the West Indies, weren't you, Sir? She knew when you were coming back. Nine or ten weeks' journey, if the weather was bad. She counted the days but you never came. Then one morning she didn't turn up for work. She wasn't behind the bar by this time – Lily did that but I had her in the back – helping out – with the babe in a basket then. I sent Mary to see if she was feverish or the little one but Mary said she'd gone – disappeared – no note – nothing for us or for you. I'm sorry, Sir. It must be such a shock for you. Sir?"

Shock? How could such an inadequate word describe his feelings of remorse or sadness? Edward had been filled with guilt at his careless behaviour. What had driven his common law wife to disappear with his precious son into those dingy alleys and dirty cobbled lanes near the Thames? She, of all people, knew how futile it would be to try to find work, and with a small child... What hope? Surely, she wouldn't have to resort to doing what he had saved her from all those years previously? Urgency was replaced with frenzy. He had combed the drab houses, the lively markets, the jostling inns for a ginger-haired woman with a babe in arms. But no one had seen her or, at least, no one was prepared to confide in a tall sea captain with one leg and a look of anguish and sorrow on his face. And, thus, he had fallen into the arms of the willing Annie, sobbing out his grief and fears.

Edward smoothed out the crumpled sheet of Annie's letter and then, crushed it between his fist and aimed it at the embers of the fire in the library – unlit but ready to be used if the weather turned chilly.

Edward sighed unhappily. He had failed. Failed. Failed to find Ally and failed to reach his father in time. And now, in less than a sennight, Ally's features had been replaced by a pensive, oval face with seductive eyes, promising lips, and a mass of silk, jet black hair. Mariana. Mariana. Mariana, *his sister*.

Edward shut his eyes and tried to picture Ally. It was over three years since he had last seen her. What had happened to her? No clues had been left at the inn or the room he had rented for her. Surely she had no money and though she was experienced in work, who would take her with no reference and a crawling youngster? Yes, the landlord's wife at 'The Bear' had employed her but they had known and trusted her; others would not be so kind. She must be dead. Her colouring was too distinctive for her to pass unnoticed and his search had been as thorough as any man could have done who had just risen from an amputation and weeks in bed. If she were alive, someone, somewhere, would have remembered her.

What if she had become ill like her family? Would a landlord care to find out who she was and if she had relatives? Unlikely! Surely his thoughts would only be along the lines of how soon he could get rid of the body in order that the next tenant could move in!

Oh God, don't be dead, Ally! For if you are dead, then your son, our son, my son will be…

Edward opened his eyes and shook his head. He must rid himself of these morbid thoughts. He had much to do. The other letter he had received from the post-boy assured that!

He picked up the dog-eared piece of paper. It seemed to have taken several weeks to reach him, having gone to the hospital first. The delay called for an immediate reply. It had come from no less a personage than Admiral Humphries and stated that simply the Admiral wanted to see Captain Rowlands to discuss a special, secret voyage. However, Captain Rowlands was asked to oblige Admiral Humphries and travel to London directly.

Edward was torn between a desire to write back, declining the offer (with the explanation that he was not fully recovered from his leg), and the desire to use this as the perfect excuse for leaving *Trem-y-Môr*. If he went away, he hoped he might be able to put his sister out of his mind. She dominated his thoughts all day and half the night; images of her danced before his eyes; even in sleep he was not free of her, for he dreamt of holding her in his arms. Why did he always love the unattainable? First his stepmother and now his half-sister.

He sighed for what felt like the hundredth time. How could he leave his estates with his father hardly cold in the grave? He knew that an absent landlord led to laziness. How could he supervise the harvesting, insisting that his tenants gave of their labour as their contracts stated, if he were not at home? Already, he had been approached about becoming a Justice of the Peace. Nobody waited long round here! Mayhap he would go for a ride. That might clear his thoughts.

He found himself putting the Admiral's letter next to the other in the fire-grate and setting them both alight. Watching the smoke curling up the chimney, he wondered why he had destroyed them. In particular, the important naval letter had not included details, presumably deliberately. He shrugged and, reaching for his stick, made his way to the stables.

Margaret

Margaret paused in her violent rubbing of the dining room table and narrowed her eyes. There, marching across the short grass outside the window, was her half-sister, Mariana, boldly leaving the house. Where was she going at this time of the morning? Why was she not inside, remaining to receive any guests who might come to offer their condolences? She could wait for them, sitting meekly in her bed chamber, embroidering her initials on a cushion cover, or getting out her canvas and paints and...

Margaret snorted in a most vulgar way at the unlikely picture of her youngest sister doing anything according to the customs of the day, and then glanced around to check no one had heard her. However, she knew there was nobody nearby for she had told the housekeeper that she would be in the dining room polishing off the spots she had noticed on the table last evening and she didn't need any assistance! She had hoped that the tone of her voice had shown that she was doing a job she considered beneath her, but who else was there to ask? What sloppy housework! This establishment was under staffed. If she were in charge...

She folded the cloth between her hands and closed her eyes. There *had* been a house where she had been in charge – well, castle and entire estate – three times the size of this Manor House – maybe four times larger – but no longer! She had lost her position to a usurper and all through ill luck! Why did it dog her so? When would fortune smile on her? How had she ended up in such a disagreeable position? It had all been her father's fault. She allowed her thoughts to dwell on bygone days.

Margaret found her mind returning to that time when her father had struck her in front of Sir and Lady Struley after she had refused to marry their eldest son. She had made that threat with menace in her voice:

"You shouldn't have done that! This isn't the end of this."

Nonetheless, she had realised soon afterwards, that her words were meaningless for her father had seen her married to Humphrey Struley, simpleton and infant, and only Margaret herself knew the reasons for her capitulation.

After that heated battle between father and daughter there had followed a year of crackling tension. Margaret was not locked in her room, like on that earlier occasion, but she was imprisoned within the oppressive walls of her family and she ate and ate until her weight made it hard for her to breathe. "Baggy Maggy", Penelope had called her and she knew it was true. As the difficult months passed, the desire to escape burgeoned; surely even marriage to a madman had to be better than this household.

Walter had helped to persuade her.

"You ought to meet him, Margaret," he had urged. "He's absolutely harmless. Like a child. He's happy as long as he's got all his toys around him and a plate of sweetmeats by his side. He wouldn't disturb your life at all. He would remain in his own chambers and you would, of course, have a whole suite of rooms to yourself. You could do whatever you wanted with each of your days and you wouldn't ever have to see him, although he's so friendly... Once... once he got to know you, he'd be thrilled if you played with him for a short while occasionally. I *do* and... and I find it's quite fun... sometimes. And... and I live in the castle too, y'know, and I would be company for you and... and if... Well, if anything happened to Humphrey... y'know... If he... Well, I'd marry you then. Please think about it, Margaret."

Margaret did think about her future. Increasingly the picture of a complete set of rooms all to herself and each day to do with as she willed, appeared attractive to her.

Then came the final blow which broke down the last of her resistance – her mother died. It wasn't that she was close to her mother, but she had found comfort in her mother's private chapel during the past year. Sitting in the cool, tranquil room with the sun tingeing the stained glass windows and breathing in the smell of beeswax and the scent of flowers which were arranged daily, she felt at peace and this was the only place she experienced it.

She had talked to her mother sometimes, when that distant lady had not been engrossed in prayer. She hoped the other woman would be able to influence her father's decision, but it seemed not. Usually her mother had not answered her comments but spoke in unrelated sentences as if she wasn't listening. Words like:

"You're getting too fat, my love. You'll die if you're not careful."

"Marriage is a good thing for a woman, although the Lord God of heaven can be very cruel."

"I hope you don't have too many children."

"Do what you think best, my daughter."

Margaret wondered if her mother understood that she was to be married to Humphrey, not Walter? Did she even remember that Humphrey had never grown up? How could one really know what went on behind those folded, praying hands and doleful eyes? Margaret found it hard to give credence to the fact that her father still sought out this woman to provide her with more children, although Margaret herself did not have any idea what the act of marriage entailed. Yet, as she became reconciled with the idea of marrying Humphrey, she knew that it did not matter that she was ignorant of these things, for she would not be expected to be intimate with her daft husband.

Thus it was that Margaret admitted defeat and married the eldest Struley son, Humphrey. He was not able to say his vows beyond, "Yeth, yeth" – his baby lisp. He could not sign the register but marked an uneven cross in the appropriate place. Margaret thought her own tidy handwriting looked ridiculous beside it, but when she signed her maiden name for the last time, she felt as though the gates of her prison had been opened. At last she was free from her father's power! Now she was a married woman, she could do what she pleased since the particular husband she had agreed to marry would have no say in her life.

However, Margaret discovered that she was not free yet. Sir Struley, a widower by now, who looked at her with the grateful eyes of a spaniel whenever he met her, had other plans. He insisted that for the first night of their married life together, the couple must be given the master bedchamber where he and his wife had spent their wedding night.

Cautiously Margaret entered the echoing chamber to find that her new husband, who had only met her three times before, was sitting on the floor, large tears falling from his eyes. It seemed, from his repetitive moans, that he was weeping for his familiar servant, John John. Margaret knelt beside him and tried to comfort him. She dragged up memories of her younger brother and sisters and how to cheer them up. After a fruitless hour she gave in, and called for John John. She watched whilst John John rocked Humphrey, singing to him as if he was truly only a babe. Once Humphrey was asleep, John John retired and Margaret dozed fitfully on a chair.

The next day, it was Walter who approached Margaret to explain that his father was anxious for a grandchild and could she and Humphrey… oblige? Margaret met Walter's embarrassment with anger. She was tempted to reply that it had been Walter himself who had promised that she would lead a separate life from her spouse. Yet something in the young man's eyes prevented her from speaking and she calculated that it would not be such an arduous task since, who would ever know what she and Humphrey did behind closed doors? She agreed to spending each night with her husband, but passed her days in her own rooms which were as spacious and pleasant as she had been led to believe.

By the third evening Humphrey appeared to recognise her and was content to be left in the master bedchamber with Margaret and dozens of toys to amuse him. Thus a pattern emerged: Margaret would play with him, surprised at her patience. Then, when Humphrey's eyes began to droop, she would tuck him into bed. There was not even the need to undress him since John John had seen to that task already. When she was absolutely sure that her husband was in a deep sleep, she would lie down, fully dressed, on top of the covers beside him. She refused to admit to anyone that she had no knowledge of what she was supposed to be doing with Humphrey in order to produce the long-awaited grandchild. She simply gave, by a nod of her head, the impression that all was well between them and they were doing their best.

Her acquiescence was rewarded when, after only ten days of married life, Humphrey succumbed to a summer fever and it was agreed that Margaret should sleep in her own bed. There the matter rested, and during the two years of her marriage to Humphrey Struley, she never spent another night in his company.

Margaret resumed her fierce polishing of the table in *Trem-y-Môr* but her eyes were unseeing and her thoughts were stuck in the past. She recalled those halcyon days when she was in charge of Struley Castle, issuing orders to a bevy of servants, controlling the redecoration of various of its dingier rooms, organising a few occasions when very select guests were entertained and arranging bigger parties of relatives to visit for several days. Oh, yes, despite her youth, Margaret was convinced she had brought fresh vision to her role as new mistress.

Her father-in-law and her husband died within a week of each other; the former passed away in his sleep one night and the latter fell prey to a particularly virulent form of his perennial fever.

Good to his word, Walter waited until the designated time of mourning had passed and then proposed to Margaret. Thus it was, with an elated heart, anticipating that at last, she was going to beat fate and get what she wanted, that Margaret bounced down the aisle on her second wedding day. She had managed to lose some of her weight by careful eating and Walter declared to her, in a stage whisper, that a man could not wish for a lovelier bride.

How could one's heart turn from sugar to iron in a single brief moment? As the bride and groom exchanged the first kiss of their marriage, the door of the church opened to reveal a burly man with a handsome woman on his arm: Walter's elder brother, Ralph, not lost at sea at all, but shipwrecked off Greece and now returning with his own bride to claim his inheritance.

Gall pumped through Margaret's veins and entered every part of her body even unto the extremities and there it lodged.

Life was cruel! Life was hard! Walter was the younger son and they had nothing!

"Not nothing, Margaret, my dear," Walter denied that evening when the couple had retired after the rousing celebrations which encompassed the homecoming of the long-lost heir as well as the wedding feast. "We shall be comfortably off, if we're sensible."

"Sensible! Who wants to be sensible? We won't have the Struley thousands! That woman is already proudly bearing your brother's son."

"It won't matter," promised Walter benignly. "We have each other and we've had to wait years for today. Humphrey is dead and…"

"More's the pity!" his wife spat acrimoniously.

"Margaret!"

"Well, at least I had the money and the title then!" She saw the colour drain from her husband's face, but now she had started she was unable to stop. She had kept the rankle inside too long and she continued relentlessly, "In the end we could have come together, I'm sure and produced a son and…"

"I thought you despised Humphrey."

"I did, but…"

"So you only married me because you thought I was heir to all that money? Is that the truth, Margaret?"

There was a desperate plea in his voice for her to deny his questions. Margaret made no reply.

"I see." Walter's tone was angry. He drew himself up to his full height. "Well, you'll just have to do your best with me for a husband. It may interest you to know that I have been fond of you almost from the start and, during the last two years, when I have actually resided in the same place as you, I would say that I have grown to love you. If you'd only stop believing that fate is against you and accept what you have in life, we could be happy together. So, now we shall go to bed and…"

Maragret blanched. She felt the blood drain from her cheeks.

"Go to bed?" The trembling whisper came.

"Yes." Walter's words were hard-edged to her ears. "We'll do what you were so sure you could do with my simple brother, Humphrey. He may have had a man's body, but I'd be very surprised if he could knew what to do!"

"What do you mean?"

"Have you ever seen a naked man before, Margaret? I doubt it. I don't suppose you saw Humphrey with no clothes on, but, if you did, I don't suppose you saw him look like this!" Walter threw off his robe and stood unashamedly before her. She opened her eyes in horror. "Just as I thought, Margaret dear. This is what you see in a man when he is ready to take his wife on their wedding night."

"Take his wife," echoed Margaret faintly. She was beginning to feel sick.

"Yes, Margaret." His voice was firm. "Now you must remove your clothes too."

"What… what are you going to do… to do… with…? Oh, Walter, I'm sorry. Don't make… don't…" Margaret started to cry in panic.

"It's all right," Walter spoke softly. He paused. "I'm sorry too. You made me very… I was… Look, it will only hurt the first time and I'll be very careful. After the first time… well, you may even come to enjoy it. Some women do, so I've been told. Please take your clothes off. It'll be… er… easier."

Margaret stood rigid, unmoving, except for tremors travelling from head to toe. Walter stepped forward and began undoing all the buttons, fastenings and bows on her elaborate dress. Barely did she hear what he was muttering:

"It will be all right, my dear. Why did your maid not help you undress before I came? My valet had laid out my night clothes for me. Come, lift your arm up and help me. How do you women move in so many layers of clothing?"

Margaret could feel him trying to lighten the tone of the occasion but she could do nothing but shiver. At last she was undressed but, in spite of the fire roaring behind her back, she was covered with goose-pimples and had to clench her teeth to stop them rattling. He took her chin in his hand and forced her to focus on his face. No anger, just pity.

"Oh, Margaret, don't be frightened. It won't hurt *that* much. It's what men and women do, y'know. I'll be as…"

"What? What are you… you going to do?" she stammered, staring again at his excitement.

"Do you really not know? Margaret, you should be full of… of joy yourself, not all this anxiety. This… I should bring you pleasure. Do you really have no idea?"

She shook her head within the circle of his fingers and turned her apprehensive brown eyes on his puzzled blue ones. She was filled with anguish about what kind of pain she was going to suffer.

Walter sighed, releasing her, stepping back and pulling his robe to cover himself. She remained where she stood, pale and nervous. A short explanation later and she was begging:

"Could you… could we leave it for tonight?"

"I've already thought of that but I honestly believe that it will be worse if we leave it. By tomorrow night, you will have allowed your wild imaginings to overwhelm you and you won't even have the courage to come to this room. And I… I'm not sure I can even… Here, lie down…"

Walter encouraged his wife to stretch on the bed, but she did not relax. She lay, eyes closed, a rabbit in the sights of a hawk.

"Oh, Margaret, if only we… I want to please you too, y'know. I don't want to be a brutal husband. I love you. I had hoped you loved me too. I want to enfold you in my arms and teach you how you can…" His words petered out and he covered her still body with his own.

Margaret opened her mouth and howled with pain.

Walter leapt back in horror and before leaning forward to clamp his hand over her lips.

"Quiet!" he begged in a fierce whisper. "There are servants about."

She could hear the anger in him returning and even she felt the shame of others knowing what had gone on between them. She resolved not to cry again, however bad the agony, whilst he assured her that he would be as quick as he could. This time he placed his hand over the lower half of her face – did he not trust her? She met the bewilderment in his expression and then allowed her own thoughts to blot out what was happening to her.

Margaret sat on the dining room chair shakily. All these reminiscences had made her feel ill. The polish and cloth were abandoned when she put her fingers over her reddened cheeks. She admitted to herself that she had never recovered from her initial distaste of the intimate side of marriage, although Walter was right in that it grew less painful.

However, with the expectation of the suffering of lying with her husband haunting her most days, she was pleased when the monthly agony of menstruation stopped. It was Walter who had to explain to her that the changes in her body were due to her being with child. He appeared thrilled with the prospect of a son or daughter and told her that he would not be coming to her bed again until she was delivered. Margaret could hardly contain her delight. What a relief! What a boon! If carrying a baby freed her from the nightly torture of enduring Walter's embraces, she decided that she would spend the rest of her life producing children just like her mother before her. After all, pregnancy did not hurt – she encountered no sickness or discomfort – that is, until the day the child decided to enter the world.

Then Margaret knew that the pain that women had to bear was far, far worse than she had ever imagined. For twelve hours she felt as though she was being broken in two and she openly wept and screamed. Never again! Never again would she allow her body to be used by a man for his satisfaction, and it came as no surprise to her that when the baby finally emerged it was heralded as a male. She turned her face from the mewling bundle the midwife was holding and wept, this time with relief.

For nearly six months, Margaret ignored her son whilst she argued and argued with her husband. She understood now that their coming together produced children and she alternated between weeping disconsolately and shouting at Walter that he did not know how excruciating it was to give birth and she never wanted to repeat the experience. After all, she pleaded, she had given him one son: the tiny Walter, named after his father.

Her husband spent most of the conversations trying to hush her voice, reminding her that they didn't want the whole household to hear about her undutiful behaviour. Of course, he said caustically on more than one occasion, all the servants *did* know and all the members of his family too.

He tried to reason with her, cajoling her and even bribing her, but all to no avail. Margaret's aversion to pain made her intractable.

Eventually, he had resorted to threatening her. He chose the one thing she could not live without – not the freedom to move from room to room like her father had done – she suspected that he knew this would not influence her for she seldom mixed with Ralph and his wife – no, Walter chose food to be his weapon. He denied her any meals and she yielded after only three days, ungenerously – all these years later she knew she had been mean – laying her body on the bed with no attempt to please him, but with a resigned look on her face, her muscles hard in anticipation, and her entrance dry and tight.

Once Walter had left his seed and another child was growing inside her, he repeated his behaviour and vacated his place in her bed. Immediately, Margaret worked out that she had several months in which to think of a way to prevent him from returning to her after the baby was born. The first answer that sprang to mind was to run away, but she acknowledged that she had nowhere to run – not least to her unkind father – and surely Walter would search until he found her.

Her mind kept busy, day and night, exploring possibilities – it had to be a foolproof plan. With the passing weeks her spirits sank lower and lower whilst she rejected more and more ideas. Finally, she reasoned, the simplest solution was to kill herself, even deducing that if she did so before the birth, she would save herself the torture of delivering the child as well! She shared her bleak reflections with no one, although it took her several weeks to settle on what was the easiest and least painful way of ending her life. She had no inkling, at that time, that her mind and reason were being affected by the disturbances occurring in her body due to the baby – how could it be true when she had felt so buoyant when carrying her first child?

After much deliberation, she decided to jump from the tower of the castle. She had noticed that the moat had risen after the unceasing rain of recent weeks – fed by the mountain stream – and Margaret reckoned that if the fall did not kill her, she would drown instead.

However, even in death, fate was against her. The water seemed to cushion her fall, her petticoats ballooning out and slowing her descent. Her heavy body sank beneath the icy water just as chance saw to it that Ralph was riding by. He flung himself unhesitatingly into the turbid depths as the waves washed over her head.

She never even lost consciousness and remembered his tirade on the muddy grass where he heaved both himself and her:

"How dare you! How dare you do this to Walter and our family! You deserve to die for your ingratitude but I shall tell everyone that you were overcome with dizziness and fell accidentally. You're a wicked woman and…"

Margaret listened no more but clutched her abdomen as the birth pangs began.

Walter and Margaret's second son, Henry, was born a month early and being half the size of his brother, slipped easily from his mother's loins after only two hours. Her husband was allowed to visit once the child and she were washed. He entered the room, glanced at the cot and hurried to her side, twisting his hands in agitation.

"Oh, Margaret, I'm so, so sorry!" He seemed to be almost in tears. "Ralph told me what you did, although we've spread it around that you slipped and fell. Oh, my dearest, if only you had told me how dejected you were. To… to contemplate… To even think of killing… Oh, Margaret, Ralph has advised me to…. I won't make you… I won't come to your bed again, but please get better soon. Be at peace now and regain your strength."

Margaret stared at him with exhausted eyes. Could it be true? Did he really mean that she would never have to submit to his attentions again? Certainly he appeared sincere and she gave him a wan smile. She nodded, muttered something about resting and, after sleeping the clock round, woke refreshed, all depression gone, ready to begin a new life.

Much to her surprise she did have seasons of happiness, she recalled. Of course, there were days when she suspected that the core of rage and negativity pressed down deep inside her might resurrect itself if life became harsh again, but, on the whole, without the troubles of her initial time at the castle, the years flew by.

Now, picking up rag and polish, and resuming her task, Margaret let a picture of her two sons – long-legged and personable – fill her mind. Walter, her eldest, the image of his father when she had first known him, was engaged to be married and she wondered what it would be like to be a grandmother. His betrothed was fiery-tempered…

Margaret came out of her reverie as the door of the dining room spun open.

"Miss! Miss!" It was one of the children – Peggy or Kate – she didn't know which one was which. Undisciplined and unruly – not a credit to any training they had received from the housekeeper, if they had been drilled in their daily duties at all!

"My name is 'Mrs Struley'," Margaret barked.

"I know, but Mrs Jones says I was to tell you that there's a visitor to see you."

Margaret whipped off her apron, flung it and the cloth into the girl's roughened hands, patted her coiffure and hurried from the room, all thoughts of the past and her husband banished from her mind.

KATHERINE

Katherine gazed at the rolling fields beyond the carriage window. Nearby, the verdant undulations, with dots of sheep and untidy stone walls, were quite discernible as pastures with their tree-edged borders, but further off the grass green changed to slate blue – almost grey – as the South Downs stretched away into the distance. Sussex – her home for twenty odd years – spelt contentment, peace and beauty and she had no desire to leave this delightful land for the wilderness of North Wales, even for a short visit.

She knew that she should go to her father's funeral and she had intended to join the rest of the family but now the message had come about Phoebe's illness, what could she do but command the carriage to turn around and return? Thank God, she had not reached London or even further into Wales itself. She should be back at *Little Oaks* before the sun set today.

What if Phoebe was to die? How would she cope? She had Daniel, of course, but Phoebe… Phoebe was her baby. She pulled the leather strap and released the window.

"Can you go any faster, Wade?" she called to the coachman.

"It's a going as fast as I can," came the reply.

Katherine leant back in her seat and surveyed the sky – azure with tiny puffs of clouds. What Daniel would call 'children's clouds' for they looked as though they had been painted in the heavens by a group of children – regular, fluffy, standard. She smiled. Ah, all that Daniel had taught her about art! What nonpareil! What joy he had brought into her life! It wasn't that he had educated her in technical skills – the use of colour, the different brushstrokes or the accuracy of her portrayals – no, he had encouraged her to abandon the formality of her canvases and paint not what her eyes saw but what her heart envisioned!

She, who had loved all things beautiful from the time she had tottered on infant legs across her parents' lawn and touched the delicate petals of the purple rhododendron flowers, was able, under Daniel's excellent tutelage, to express some of her greatest dreams.

Oh, how she had sought out all that was good and clean and pure in life! From the first gently pressed plants, to the symmetry of the threads of her embroidery, on to the cadence of the spinet played in the drawing room and the ecstasy of words in poems printed and read, Katherine had revelled in elegance and loveliness. Not for her the boisterous nursery games, or dirty romps along the paths or sand, which her siblings engaged in! Instead, Katherine would trail daintily behind her brother and sisters, careful not to let her new shoes become splashed with mud or her petticoats besmirched with leaf juice. And those early formative years became a pattern for her adult life, although she didn't realise it at the time.

Katherine, second surviving daughter to Sir William Rowlands, sailed through her days, deliberately avoiding trouble, anxiety, rudeness or argument. If any of these nasty occurrences impinged on her, she would turn away deliberately and feast her eyes on the creamy dome of the sky, or the sway of the tree trunk, its leaves a silvery sheen, or the detailed, swift stroke of the artist's portrait or the gloss of a dust-free bevelled chair or the refinement of the peacock blue cloth of dress or jacket. Her ears closed to brash conversation, to raised voices, to tense tones and she would listen to the blackbird's song, the steady chime of the clock, the wind rustling the hedgerows and the rattle of a child's stick against the railings.

Katherine lived in a splendid world where pretty girls smiled bashfully at dapper men; where lively dogs skipped with bright-eyed children; where summer sun seduced a rosy earth; where all was well and nothing terrible ever happened.

This unrealistic bubble might have been burst when Katherine attained adulthood, except that she met and married a man whose love for order, seemliness and refinement barely outdid his love for his youthful, comely wife.

Alexandre Barnsley – half Dutch, half English – found in Katherine a porcelain doll of great worth. He spoilt her with rich brocades and soft velvets; he adorned her with polished jewels and startling head dresses. He never disabused her of her ideals but indulged her craving for charming things, filling his own house with all she asked for and allowing her to while away her days in seclusion.

Katherine closed her eyes against those misty clouds and sighed, allowing her body to move with the rhythm of the rocking coach. Dear, sweet Alexandre – forty years her senior, not just husband but father, advisor and saviour to her. Yes, they were man and wife but he said from day one of their wedded bliss that all he required of her was to warm his bed and gladly she had entwined her slender ankles around his icy feet and hugged his grizzled head to her shapely breasts. Katherine knew nothing of the consummation in the marital bed and was unaware that she had missed out.

Travelling to the continent before the War, the couple had indulged their common interest in the noble and lovely. They had inspected long-lost treasures hidden in dark shops in narrow side-streets and walked hand in hand along Parisian streets strewn with fallen pink blossom. They had gazed at the great works of art hung on huge walls (he admired Durer's watercolours but she favoured the miniatures of Nicholas Hilliard!) and attended opera and dance, concert and play, indoors and out. Keeping away from prostitution, street brawls, poverty and degradation, they had searched and found all that was pleasant, agreeable and witty until it was time to return home to *Little Oaks*.

Alexandre's fine house, where the little oaks were sturdy and gnarled by now, boasted original Elizabethan architecture surrounded by rose arbours descending to neatly kept lawns which swept down majestically to the lake where a rushing stream wended its way through leafy woodlands to cross the road in a ford.

Here, Katherine's days were undisturbed by disorder or untidiness. Each day she would partake of a light meal to break her fast, followed by one or two turns of the hour-glass working on her latest project – on canvas or cloth. Alexandre always praised her efforts and called them masterpieces. In the middle of the day the couple picked at a cold repast spread on the table in the conservatory where sometimes they would read out alternately the latest poetry written, printed, bound and sent to them, hot off the press, from a friend who lived in London. A gentle laugh and a rewriting of some of the badly metered verse saw them through most meals. The afternoons stretched invitingly before them and could include a short meander to the water's edge, where Katherine would dangle her fingers through its weedy margins, watching for shiny fish slipping through the emerald depths. In summer, there might be cinnamon biscuits or lemon cake on the terrace before it was time to change for dinner and then often Alexandre arranged for a musician to accompany their slow dances or elegant whirls around the tan floor in the ballroom.

Each day was a pleasure – unhurried, unstressed – unmarred by distasteful tasks or strife, confusion or turmoil. How did she live such a life of contentment? Could it be that the minutes she spent in quiet contemplation – before she met her husband coming from the library and linked arms with him in the doorway to the dining room – were these solitary minutes responsible for her serenity? For Katherine had learnt that the mystery and mystique of religion had a certain beauty of its own – a balm which quietened any restless thoughts or desires she encountered. Once she left her father's household she had adopted the more popish practices of the Roman Catholic Church rather than her mother's Protestant ways, for in the candles and incense, the regular words of the services, the cleansing of the confessional and the artistry of the churches, Katherine had found peace.

Peace. She had no peace this afternoon, with her dearest Phoebe ill in bed, nigh on death mayhap. She fidgeted on the cushioned seats and remembered the day she had been called to set out on this aborted journey.

Daniel had been there, his easel set in the sunlight pouring through the long, wide windows of the gallery. He said that light was the medium he used when painting and the June days this year shed brilliance across the room. He had planned his portrait of her with great precision, seating her against a length of shimmering silk, cobalt blue, to highlight her fair skin and hair. He had gone through her wardrobe choosing eventually a dress of yellow – almost gold – with bodice and fastenings of deeper buttercup, which, he said, brought out the hidden depths of her own gold tresses. He had not only suggested that Phoebe sat on her knee but insisted that the delicate dog curled there because, he stated:

"I always think of Phoebe on your lap. I can imagine her nowhere else!"

And he was right, for, whenever Katherine sat down, a lift of her hand and the light-boned creature would spring on to her and with a single turn settle comfortably to snooze away the hours.

Katherine's thin fingers were stroking the velvet grey fur when Phoebe had lifted her jaws and sneezed with gusto. Katherine cupped the curve of her pet's back bone to prevent her slipping off her knees but the spell was broken and Daniel put down his brushes and stepped towards his subjects.

"Shall we finish there? I've done enough for today. I am continually amazed at how still you can sit – you are the calmest model I have ever had! How do you do it?"

Katherine lifted Phoebe on to the floor and stretched her slim arms above her head.

"I have much to think about."

"Are you praying?" he teased her.

"Sometimes."

She rose gracefully, shook out her full skirts and glided across to see his work. Daniel never demurred or protested like some artists she knew, who would not allow you to see the canvas until all the strokes were done.

She tipped her head on one side and gazed at what she saw: a shapely woman, with a slender neck, her translucent skin unlined, her blonde hair caught in a tidy roll at its nape. The narrowness of her waist, the pertness of her bosom, the delicacy of her fingers – all were exact, including the sleeping pet on her lap with its sleek coat and refined muzzle – no detail was inaccurate and yet hardly did she recognise herself, for the whole picture gave the impression of youth and she was in her late thirties.

"How do you do it, Daniel?"

"What, my sweet angel? I've told you – you must paint with your heart – with your imagination – not with your eyes."

"But it's so different to that one." She pointed at a portrait with a heavily gilded frame hanging further down the room. This had been commissioned by her husband when they were newly married. The artist, she couldn't recall his name after all these years, had caught her kneeling in chapel, her face upturned, her hands folded, her eyes closed. There was the light behind her – the glow of candle or ray of sun – but there was not the same quality of liveliness in her as there was in Daniel's creation. Nonetheless, she acknowledged, though different, both canvases were magnificent since her radiance shone through and her good looks would be kept for future generations to see and admire.

Katherine moved her gaze to study the man in front of her. He was beautiful – yes, she would use that word rather than the more usual tag of 'handsome' which described the male sex. His unruly curls surrounded an unfurrowed brow and smooth, clear cheeks and accentuated his straight nose. His mischievous hazel eyes, his incredibly white, even teeth and the tilt of his nose made her wonder if someone somewhere would not one day fix his likeness in marble or wood and display it as bust or full statue in a hallway or museum.

How wonderful this man's arrival had been! The very same day, nay hour, she had kissed her husband farewell, longing to lie next to him once more and chase away the coldness of death, she had met this god of a man. Sensing in the servants' manner that perhaps she would be wise to leave the laying out of Alexandre to them, for death had a messy side, she had descended the vaulted stairs of her home and wondered how she could drive away the unpleasantness and smell of illness and passing away.

She had learnt all those years ago, when Penelope, her sister, had skipped into the nursery, that when ugliness and gloom presented itself, it was possible to overcome by an effort of will and ignore discouragement. Later, her crying on seeing Penelope back in her bed clutching her ragamuffin assortment of dolls, did not really show the depth of her distress at being presented with such disfigurement. Nonetheless, her weeping *had* brought about her removal from the situation and she had swiftly recovered. This had taught her to run away, sometimes literally, from any situation which upset her. That day, when she had left her husband's sick room, she had intended to go into the garden and smell the scent of the early roses and there had been Daniel – young, vibrant, very much alive and seemingly as serious about the pursuit of the sublime as she herself and her late beloved Alexandre.

Of course, she had discovered since, that Daniel had a side which neither she nor Alexandre possessed. Daniel had a fascination with things which were not spotless and stylish. She knew that he would go into the nearby village and sketch scenes that she would never contemplate observing, let alone preserving on paper! He had dropped his artwork one morning, on his return, and she had glimpsed a drawing of a dead badger, its leg half eaten by some other beast... and there had been other horrific depictions – a crippled child on crutches and a wizened cow, a dilapidated cottage and a tree struck by lightning – which Daniel had picked up and shuffled into place with a muttered apology. She didn't understand his need to record such monstrosities but deliberately she closed her mind to what her companion did when away from her as long as he shared in her desire to seek out everything perfect and enchanting in the time they had together.

A disturbance at the door broke her assessment of her friend's superb good looks and she surveyed a mud-bespattered lad push his way into the room whilst her butler, Cooke, tried to prevent his entrance.

"Madam, I..." Habitually unruffled, Cooke was the colour of a tomato.

"Let me go!" The boy's voice was menacing. "I must speak to the lady.

Are you Mrs Barnsley? I have a message for you. I would have been here earlier but…"

Katherine closed her eyes against such a foul sight. With this untimely interruption Cooke had let her down and usually he was such an excellent servant! Day by day, it was his job, with the help of Mr Steel, her lawyer, and her housekeeper, Hoddy, to protect her from the unsavoury side of life; so how had this uncouth man gained entrance? She took a step backwards whilst Phoebe cringed against her full skirts.

"Daniel," she sighed. "I don't want…"

"Now look here, whoever you are…" started the artist.

"I have come from North Wales, Sir. I would have been here days ago if my horse had not been stolen. The lady's father is dead, Sir."

Katherine gasped and turned away. Daniel's arm went to support her but she was not dizzy, only repelled by this stained traveller and the unexpected and unwelcome news he bore.

"Go!" instructed Daniel, as, at last, the butler managed to manhandle the lad towards the door. "Give me the letter."

With the departure of the lackeys, quietness descended and Phoebe sniffed at the French window to the terrace. Katherine pushed open the lock and followed her pet outside, unseeing when the dainty creature squatted on the lawn and then hurried back to her mistress' side. Katherine headed for a set of chairs and table sheltering in the shade of one of the oaks, like a woman in a dream. Barely had she seated herself before Phoebe was pressing her damp nose against her with a low whimper. Katherine stroked her mouth and stubby whiskers absent-mindedly and began a soliloquy, unaware of Daniel taking his place at her side or the arrival, not many minutes later, of one of the under-butlers with a tray of refreshments.

"What a wonderful man my father was! How sad that he should have passed away. A marvellous father – not over familiar with us children, but you wouldn't expect that from a great man. He was strict but always fair. He spent much time on his various estates, keeping his affairs in order, but he used to come to the nursery whenever he could get away from his duties. An esteemed man and many will miss him dearly. He was kind and sympathetic when I told him I wanted to marry Alexandre. I know Margaret said he was a bully and forced her into an unhappy marriage. But he never bullied me. And Margaret has two well favoured sons so my father was proved right in the end. My father was an attentive husband too and my mother always spoke highly of him.

"I remember when my mother passed away. That was a great loss too. She was an exemplary mother. She arranged for us to have the best upbringing we could want with benevolent servants and well-educated teachers. She introduced me to religion too. Much of the comfort I find in God is because I observed her and her private prayer life. She never shut the door of her chapel on me and, as long as I was respectful, which, of course, I was, I could spend as long as I liked in there.

"Margaret could be a bit overbearing, especially when I was small, but she just had a forceful character. She seemed to know what she wanted and went out to possess it. I listened to what she used to say and mostly went along with her because it avoided arguments. She was also very clever and would help me with my lessons.

"I didn't know the younger two as well as Margaret. Edward was just a baby and then he was being trained to be the heir and he did all kinds of manly things with my father. Penelope... Penelope was a dear, sweet-natured child but after her illness... Well, her gruesome disfigurement repelled me... I didn't go near her much but graduated from book learning to being taught how to be a lady. That's when I really started to appreciate painting..."

Katherine looked up, noticed that the dog had crept on to her knee surreptitiously, and that Daniel was offering her a slice of treacle tart. On his lap she could see the tatty letter but she had no need to peruse it.

"I suppose I ought to go to the funeral."

"I would think that might be over now, my angel."

"Yes, but Mariana... Mariana is my half-sister, half my age and... and I have only met her a few times. She's an unruly..."

"Eat your tart, Katherine, and we can talk about the arrangements when I have consulted Cooke and Steel."

Katherine came back to her present surroundings as the carriage bumped over a pothole in the road. Daniel had been as good as his word and it had taken only twenty-four hours before she was on her way and now she was nearly home – she could see the farmhouse which belonged to *Little Oaks* sitting at the next bend and her tenants working in the fields nearby. Not long, she crooned, before she could embrace Phoebe, check her condition and make sure that a doctor had been called!

Katherine gathered up her bags and sat four-square on the seat whilst the vehicle turned into the beech-lined drive. Here were the woods, here the glimpse of the sun-dial on the terrace, here the curved sweep of the forecourt and here was Daniel and… and Phoebe.

Barely had she climbed out before the fastidious dog had bounded up to her, emitting sharp excited barks. Katherine bent to pick her up and the noise stopped.

"Phoebe, my darling, you're better!" she cried.

"She revived as soon as she heard the wheels of the carriage. I think she was pining for you. She fled to her bed once you had gone, refused to come out and turned down all food, even the tastiest morsels Mrs Marsh could concoct…"

Katherine allowed Daniel's words to soothe her agitation. Everything was all right again. She would write to her family tomorrow, explaining that she was unable to get away at this time but wishing them all the best. For the moment, she would send for Marsh and instruct her on how to prepare Phoebe's favourite dish: lamb's liver in gravy.

EDWARD

Edward entered the stable yard and stopped abruptly, his thoughts skittering to a halt also, for the images in his mind jumped into reality. There, before him, just mounting her horse and looking magnificent in a black costume, which accentuated her delectably slim waist and upturned breasts, complete with riding hat, her hair loosely caught back from her forehead, her eyes eagerly scanning the mountain, was the woman who had haunted his life for the past week: Mariana.

"May I ride with you and save Thomas the trouble?" he called, striding forward – if his gait could be described as a stride with a crippled leg causing him to limp.

He saw her glance undecidedly towards her groom and back. What looked like irritation flashed across her face before she smiled her assent.

"I'm sorry, Sir," apologised Thomas a few minutes later, leading a horse across the cobbles, "but we haven't a good mount for you. Sir William's stable has become rather depleted lately. You'd better buy some new stock at the next fair."

"This one looks fine. I shan't be staying long enough for it to be worthwhile setting up a stable."

"Not staying, Sir?"

"I've had news today which makes it imperative for me to travel to London." Edward acknowledged to himself that, although he had thought a canter would clear his head, he had made up his mind already. Did the vision of Mariana have something to do with the decision? "Now, before we go, may I say how sorry I was to hear about your mother, Thomas."

"Thank you, Sir. She's been in bed for many months." The younger man assisted his master into the saddle. He adjusted the stirrups before enquiring, "Is that comfortable for you, Sir?"

Edward nodded, his gaze on his sister.

"Which way were you going, Mariana?"

"I don't really mind which way we go."

"Let's head towards the mountain then."

Mariana wheeled her horse around and they left the yard together. Whilst they crossed the grass to the sand, Edward noticed that his companion was keeping her restless mount restrained.

"Do you want to let him have his head?" he enquired.

"No, but…"

"Oh, Mariana," he laughed, "even I could do with riding faster than at this snail's pace!" He urged his own steed forward. He was confident that she would pass him, for he had heard of her horsemanship and he hated to see both stallion and rider so frustrated, especially when he sensed that he was the reason for the slow walk. His expectations were realised when, he was overtaken and the impromptu race began. When he caught up with her, Mariana's eyes were shining.

"Poor beast!" she twinkled at Edward, leaning across and patting his mare's lathered neck. "You're pushing her too hard. She's an old lady!"

"And I'm an old man! Thanks for waiting."

However, Mariana did not continue their ride but clutched the reins tightly, keeping Mars at a standstill.

"Are you really going to London?"

"Yes."

"What news have you had?" she went on, scanning his face. "Must you go?"

"I thought you'd be glad," muttered Edward, hope rising irrepressibly in his heart. Had all the strain and worry and longing shown naked in his features? Surely she did not feel his love and returned it! No, that was ridiculous! his reason argued.

"Of course not! What made you think that?"

"Nothing in particular." All of a sudden, he wanted to end the hidden tension between them that seemed to emerge whenever his future plans were raised. Should he propose they return home? But they had barely started and the horses were by no means tired. Thus he asked, "Do we go this way?"

He indicated a path along the broken edge of the cliff. The width of the beaten sandy surface suggested that they would have to go single file. He was relieved that conversation waned. Mariana was lost in her own private thoughts also and he gave himself up to his surroundings.

He could hear the waves rhythmically patting the rocks on his left, although he could not see where sea and land met. Nonetheless, his eyes observed the glistening surface of the topaz water stretching, ruffled by the wind, boundless to far horizon and he felt released from the anxieties which had dogged the last week.

The sunshine of latter days had encouraged new growth to the plants and prickles and shoots brushed against the animals' flanks. Edward was aware of the resistance but the view ahead caught his attention – standing proudly against the pale blue sky was their destination, Holyhead Mountain. Speckled with heather and gorse, its lower slopes adorned with lush fields and decorated occasionally with white washed dwellings, it beckoned the riders to climb its height.

"Do you think we'll be able to see Ireland today?" Edward broke the spell of silence.

"I shouldn't think so. The horizon looks hazy to me. It has to be absolutely clear, but we can go to the top to look. Are you coping?" Mariana glanced back over her shoulder. "This track opens out soon. This stretch isn't well frequented, as you can see. It's too near the cliffs and there is a shorter path linking the road to the cottages. I prefer it, though, because of the views. What do you think?"

Edward did not reply, hoping the query was rhetorical. The distance between them, the rustling of the undergrowth, the snorting of the horses and the call of gulls on the wing made any interchange difficult but once they were riding abreast, he longed for the previous solitude for Mariana's first comment was:

"I wish you weren't leaving." It was as if there had been no break between the two conversations.

"Why?" he asked, trying to still the unwelcome increased beating in his chest.

"Because I shall be left alone with Margaret. Why does she behave so? Why must she always scold me? And others too?"

"It seems to be part of her nature. She was domineering when we were children too. But you're not going to be left alone with her. I've seen Mrs Jones and she has given me a choice."

"Oh, she did it, did she? She's been threatening for days but I managed to persuade her not to come and see you."

"Why?" Edward repeated.

"Because... because she's part of my life and I've had enough changes recently. First Henry, then... Father... Father died. Then you came and Margaret and... and even Jack. Nothing seems the same. My whole life has been turned upside down. But, can you answer me this, Edward? Why is Margaret staying? Why doesn't she go home? The funeral is well over and..."

"I suspect she's enjoying lording it over all of us! Oh, yes, she frightens me sometimes. I understand, from various snippets of information, that she doesn't get on with her sister-in-law."

"Why doesn't she set up her own house?"

"Not enough money, I should imagine. Walter is the younger son and the money Father left her just wouldn't stretch that far."

"I know that," groaned Mariana. "I worked out that I wouldn't be able..."

"What are you talking about? Your home is *Trem-y-Môr* and your inheritance is for when you find a husband."

"I'm not going to find a husband. I'm never going to marry."

"Oh, my dear! How can you speak with such finality? You'll get over Henry eventually."

Edward stopped speaking. Ahead was a small knot of people. The men raised their hats and he acknowledged the gesture with a smile, although he did not recognise them. Were they his tenants? Momentarily, he was distracted from his sister by the thought of what his life would be like if he did not go to London. He would meet his tenants and others' tenants, not just on occasions like this but at every village activity and all the local social events. He knew that there were many gatherings throughout the year, many of them on Holy days. After church, he would be expected to stay and cheer at a football match when his tenants might play against a neighbouring parish or he might have to judge a dancing competition between the girls or... He frowned. One thing was sure – he would meet that forelock-tugging parson at every event.

"Mariana?" he questioned once they were alone again. "Talking of marriage. Did Father ever speak to you about a proposal of marriage he had on your behalf recently?"

"No."

"I thought not." Relief soothed him.

"Who was it from? Not Nathum Parry of Llangefni? He's always casting his sheepish eyes in my direction, but I couldn't bear to marry him.

I have this terrible desire to slap his stupid face whenever I see him and he's permanently got his mouth half opened…"

Edward's laughter halted her description and she laughed too.

"I'd like to meet him. I can imagine him quite well, after what you've just said. No, it wasn't him." He paused. "It's the Parson and he…"

"The Parson?" Mariana jerked the reins.

"You didn't give him your permission, did you?"

"Of course not!"

Mariana released her breath in a long-drawn out sigh.

"I couldn't bear to marry him either. In fact, I think I'd prefer Nathum any day to him! The Parson's so old and always speaking as if he himself wrote the Bible…"

"Old! Your mother married Father when she wasn't much older than you."

"That's true. I hadn't thought of that. Oh, Edward, let's not talk about the Parson. Tell me, what was my mother like? Really like? Penelope's told me some stories – how much fun she used to be – but what do you remember of her? What made her marry a man twice her age and with grown-up children?"

"I don't know. Look at Katherine's husband, although he didn't have any children when he married her. Why do people fall in love with anyone? Your mother was fun to be with, but she had a serious side and sometimes, in the brief time I knew her, I caught her looking troubled. But, whenever she thought anyone was watching her, she'd smile her bright, friendly smile and all traces of sadness would be wiped away. She never told me about her life before she came to us. I think, maybe, she had an unhappy past."

"Where did she come from?"

"No one knows."

"But didn't she…?"

"It's no good, sister dear! I'm not a very good source of information. Penelope was better acquainted with her than me. I only knew her for a few months. Didn't you speak to Father about her?"

"No, he was too upset about her death. He never got over it. They say…" Mariana drew ahead to circumvent an overgrown bush in the way before she said, "They say… they say that you loved her. Did you?"

Fussily, Edward adjusted his hat to cover his embarrassment, grateful of his sister's half-turned back.

"Who can say? I think the answer's 'Yes', but I was young – only fifteen. She never returned my love. I'm afraid she only had room in her heart for one person and that was Father. If Father hadn't lost his temper and sent me away, I suspect I'd have soon recovered my own senses, but, as it was… um… for years… I idolised her. She became almost a saint in my eyes – a Madonna."

Mariana allowed him to draw level with her, sympathy in her expression.

"You are very like her."

She blushed, denying the compliment, saying she was no saint. He tried to explain but she rushed in with a question about *his* mother. He was not able to furnish her with much more information about his own dam except with a statement about Letitia's interest in religion. This brush with theology brought them swiftly back to clerics. Mariana's tone reassured him when she declared:

"Don't mention the Parson! I won't marry him. If only Father hadn't died, I wouldn't have had to get married at all!"

"You don't *have* to. No one is going to force you. Most people *want* to marry. Why don't we say that we'll not rush into any contracts at the moment? In fact, why don't you come to London with me?"

Edward cursed his own loquacity. He must think before he spoke, but surely his heart was dictating his speech rather than his mind at the moment. He held his breath whilst the silence continued. Dear God, that God whom my mother served, don't torment me and let Mariana assent! Yet his soul longed to see her lips form the syllable "Yes".

"No," she murmured eventually. "It's tempting."

He grimaced at her choice of words with all the impulses that were swirling around his head. He opened his mouth to reply but she hadn't finished.

"But I think it's too soon. I don't want to leave the island. My world has shifted too much already. I want some routine and…"

"I can understand that!" He tried to keep relief out of his voice. "I am longing to settle down."

"Then why are you going?" she puzzled.

"Ah, the plain truth, is that I'm curious. Some sort of secret voyage has been hinted at, but you mustn't mention it."

"I wouldn't tell anyone!"

He wondered if he had offended her for she pushed ahead and

dismounted. But she spoke levelly when she informed him:

"Here we are, nearly at the top. We'll have to go on foot from here. Can you manage?"

Edward's reply was with action and by the time he was standing beside her both horses had started to crop the wind-battered grass. Mariana turned towards the sea and shielded her eyes but she claimed not to be able to see Ireland, although her finger pointed in the direction of the Wicklow Hills.

"That almost looks like them," he remarked, following the line of her outstretched index. "But, it must just be clouds." He caught his hat and gasped, "What a wind! It's almost gale force! I'd forgotten how strong it is up here. You don't really feel it until you come around that corner. Shall we go right up to the top?"

A brief discussion followed about how his disability might affect this decision, which ended in him taking her proffered arm. He was adamant that he did not intend to come this far and not reach the summit!

They stumbled up the steep path, silent now from concentration and breathlessness. The last section was almost vertical and quite rocky – no place for a man with only one leg. Edward was just beginning to regret his impulse when without warning they arrived. They stood pressed together, their clothes flapping in the violent gusts.

"This is one of my favourite places," shouted Mariana. "You can see so far!"

Edward tried to agree but the words were snatched from his mouth and he contented himself to look around.

Before them, on three sides, was the sea, enclosing Holy Island in a tight embrace. Behind them, glinting in the sunlight, Edward could just discern the tidal estuary at the Rhoscolyn end of the island. It was not quite possible to make out the path of the sea, but it was obvious that the water completely surrounded the land. He observed tiny ships in the creek, dolls' houses strewn about the patchwork earth – ribbons of golden sand at the edges mixed with green meadows and darker woodland areas. In the distance, across another larger island, Anglesey, were the Snowdonia mountains, a fine backcloth of everlasting humps stretching down the Lleyn Peninsula: never-changing, sturdy, comforting but mysterious. What a viewpoint indeed!

Pressure from a small but firm hand on his sleeve made him lean once more on his sister's frame and descend the slope. Almost immediately, an outcrop of rock sheltered them from the full force of nature and Edward exhaled.

"That's better. It's like being in the crow's nest up there."

"Not so frightening!"

"True. Would you mind if we sit for a moment?"

"Not at all. Let's go another few yards. I remember there's a flattish shelf of stone where we can sit. One thing I do like about being up here is that you feel kind of safe, for no one can approach you without you observing them. Not that there are many people around today. Look! Those figures working in the fields are the size of ants."

Momentarily Edward wondered why his sister had need for safety but the breath was still knocked out of him, so he followed her example, marvelling at the vista and drawing her attention to a toy-sized carriage slowly wending its way to Four Mile Bridge. Mariana identified for him *Carregfan*, where she said her friends lodged when they were in the area. She showed him where the Vicarage stood and many other individual houses in the village. With a bit of squinting, they reckoned that they could even see a corner of the roof of their own Manor House but Cutland's house was hidden behind a fold of the land.

"I shall miss the island," Edward said, "even though I've only been back just over a week." The sentence was out before he realised that he himself had broached a subject that he had intended to avoid!

"But you're not going away for long, are you? You are the Squire now. Have you arranged for a steward? Father never bothered, but he was rarely away for more than a fortnight. At least, that was true in recent years."

"I hadn't thought of that. Yes, I must arrange it."

"You are coming back, aren't you?"

"Yes, I hope to return…"

"You don't sound very sure. What you need is a wife! Shall I play matchmaker? Let me think. Who can we find for you? Seeing *Carregfan* over there reminds me of the Parry girls. Yes, what about one of the twins? They're the pick of the four anyway. Esther is married already, although you wouldn't have wanted Esther. She's too like Margaret and…"

"How old are these twins?"

"Fourteen."

"Fourteen! My God, they're mere babes!"

He remembered Ally and he clearly saw her piquant face. Something must have shown in his own expression because his sister, who had been gaily listing other possible matches for him, ceased chattering before saying:

"You've got someone, haven't you?"

Gone was the teasing tone; she placed her fingers on the cloth of his sleeve and repeated her question. For a moment, he resisted her pleadings and then he whispered:

"I do love someone, yes."

If he had hoped to stop her pestering, he was mistaken, for she would not let the subject rest. Even whilst he rose slowly, and began to move towards the horses, she carried on, trying to winkle out of him the name of the person he had claimed he loved. She even suggested that he might be pining after her mother after all these years. The light in her eyes, the sensual curve of her red lips, the line of her determined jaw, her voice high and excited, set him alternating between anger at his own foolishness and a deep longing to shout from the top of this mountain that it was she whom he loved. But, his knowledge that such a declaration would frighten her and drive her away, kept him resolved and uncommunicative. He tried to distract her by asking her to search for a suitable stone for him to use as a mounting post, but the interrogation continued. Eventually, he admitted that he loved a woman called Alicia, who had died before he had been able to marry her. Only then was her curiosity satiated and she swung herself into the saddle and led the way at a sedate pace, with no more than the occasional comment.

By the time they reached home, Edward's leg was aching and he was desperate to sit in a low chair with a tot of rum in his hand, but as he and his sister entered the kitchen, he knew there was no chance of his wishes being granted. Margaret was standing in front of the dresser surrounded by what looked like every single piece of china which had originally stood upon it. In her hand was a stained rag. Leaning against the table was Elin, who appeared close to tears. Of Mrs Jones there was no sign.

"Ah, you've returned," began Margaret, carefully stepping over the piles of crockery at her feet. She had an enormous apron wrapped around her well built figure, and Edward was surprised at how much less severe she looked. He felt that she was really enjoying herself. She met his eyes. "I'm just doing some late, late spring-cleaning."

"There's no need," mumbled Elin. "We did all this very recently."

"Well, then it needs doing again," scolded Margaret tartly. "Not only was there dust on these dishes, but flicks of grease too."

Edward ground his teeth. It was obvious that he could wait no longer to confront Margaret, but she was very reluctant to leave the kitchen even though he asked her politely for a few moments alone with her. She offered to meet him later and when he declined she stated that she had heard he was leaving.

"That's what I want to talk to you about," he asserted.

"Very well, then. While I am away, girl, you can start washing these dishes," instructed Margaret, tossing her work garment over the nearest chair.

She waddled from the room without a backward glance, which was fortunate because Edward witnessed mistress and servant imitating her slow walk. He smirked himself with amusement and then waved his hand at the two girls motioning them to desist. Oh, how he wanted to laugh out loud – really Margaret did ask for ridicule!

Edward passed into the cool, calm depths of the empty hall to find his eldest sister had already disappeared into the parlour. He would have chosen to go into the library where he felt like the master and he could have gained presence by standing behind the wide desk, but Margaret's pre-emptive choice made his flagging nerve fail.

Edward paused outside the parlour door, imagining its contents and gazing longingly at the stairs. He knew that the parlour was very sparsely furnished with all the furniture, which consisted of a set of chairs and table, arranged around the edge. What it needed was to be inhabited by a crowd of boisterous children again like when he was young, where the family had used the parlour as a dumping ground for their personal possessions! Nowadays, Edward found that the bedchambers were the best furnished rooms in the house but he would never ascend the stairway with his awkward leg for what he hoped would be just a short interchange. Had Margaret chosen this room for similar reasons – all that weight must be difficult to get up to the first floor? He straightened his cravat and entered the lion's den.

MARGARET

Once more, Margaret was surveying the scene outside the Manor House. This time she did not see anyone, not least her sister, Mariana. Immediately she heard her brother come in the room, she seized the advantage by demanding:

"Now, what do you want to say, for I haven't much time?"

"No, indeed, you haven't!"

Edward's tone was as forceful as her own had been! Ah, it was going to be a fight then – with words for weapons she decided! In her youth Margaret had watched the thrust and parry between two swordsmen. Although she had never tried with real blades, she reckoned all the verbal sparring with her father had been good practice for this skirmish with her brother! She stood fair and square to her opponent when he told her that she should be preparing for her departure.

"What are you talking about?" she replied, knowing full well that this was the subject Edward had intended to. "I understand it's *you* who is leaving, not me."

"No, Margaret. You are coming with me to England until the road leads north and then I go south to London."

"No, I'm not!" The swords were clashing – she could almost hear metal on metal – the initial bout had begun! "I've only just come and I'm not setting off again in that uncomfortable carriage. My bones feel as if they've been shaken out of my very body. Can you explain to me what all this is about?"

"You… you are upsetting my staff."

She noticed the hesitation – one nick on his skin – one tiny drop of blood already!

"Upsetting your staff! Hah! Those parochial simpletons who have no idea of how to…"

"Margaret! That's enough! You have no right to criticise them, nor to give them orders."

Ouch! The truth hurt her! *Touche!*

Edward pressed on: "You came here for Father's funeral and that is over. You have stayed a week and, frankly, you can't stay any longer, for I have urgent business to attend to, which necessitates me leaving. I cannot afford to lose servants who not only run this house quite adequately with no help from you, but also have been doing it for years. We've managed quite well without your interference."

Margaret didn't hesitate. The best form of defence, even after a small wound, was to attack.

"Well, that's gratitude for you! It's been such an age since this house has had a mistress that it's come to accept slovenly standards."

Edward showed no sign of retreating, not even a bead of sweat on his brow. Margaret drew herself up – she had an undeniable point which she hoped would make him surrender, or, at least, tear his weapon from his hand.

"However, you have overlooked one thing, little brother." The sarcastic caressing endearment seemed to catch his attention. "And that is that you cannot leave a young, single woman (and certainly not one with an impetuous nature like Mariana), alone in a house with a man, unchaperoned and unchecked. Especially…" She paused deliberately, for effect. "Especially with an unknown man. We have no idea where our 'guest' came from, let alone who he is. He is probably a charlatan. Mariana's reputation is already tarnished, from what I can make out, and, if we both leave, her chances of marriage would be ruined forever. I assume you don't want that!"

Margaret folded her arms whilst Edward sat down abruptly in a nearby chair, his weapon spinning across the room by her concerted and well-reasoned argument. It was obvious to her that she had found his weak spot and almost she could see the clicking of his mind, thinking and rejecting alternative plans. Like the wooden cogs turning in the flour mill near the Struley castle, she watched him acknowledge that servants were not sufficient chaperones; calculate whether the man upstairs was well enough to move; realise that if their acquaintance was to be put up in another house, whether that wouldn't cause more scandal, wondering if something had occurred between Mariana and that man. Margaret even thought she saw Edward admit to himself that Mariana was undisciplined, imprudent and giddy, and their father had allowed her too much freedom so that the younger woman was known for her wild ways. She could predict the conclusion of her brother's quick reckoning before he announced that still it was *she* who should go and he would cancel his journey.

Margaret strode across the room and deliberately towered above him. The first round may be over but the fight wasn't finished yet! She used a tactic – a trick – which she had learnt when a child. It had been useful then and easy to execute since her extra years gave her added height.

"Don't be ridiculous!" Again she struck, without warning, a counter statement. "You, yourself, have said that your business is urgent. Just leave me here. I'll keep everything in good order."

Edward arose and said drily:

"That's what worries me. Excuse me."

It was Margaret's turn to yield, since his frame topped her by several inches. She took up her station again by the window. Time for her to regroup. He was insisting that it was she who had to go but she allowed his voice to fade whilst she considered possible manoeuvres.

Overthrown momentarily she accepted that, at one time, she would have been able to beat him, but now they were strangers. Yes, his sword might have gone but he could pick it up again or produce a sharp dagger from the folds of his clothes! Familiarity and regular practice could teach you your enemy's weaknesses but he and she had lived apart since he was scarcely more than a child. Also, she must proceed carefully, because she wanted to stay here intensely and she did not want to alienate him. Her delicately spun plans required for *her* to remain in the Manor House and for *him* to go. If Edward settled into a new life of being a country squire, how could she suggest that her husband, Walter, became his steward? Or how could she prove that, once installed, she and Walter were a treasure too precious to be lost? She had intended, one evening, to mention the need for someone capable to be appointed to that position. Best to keep it all in the family, don't you know? She'd even rehearsed what she was going to say. Of course, she was aware that Walter was not a suitable candidate for the job but *she* would be right behind him and there to help and advise him. She believed that *she* was the best person to manage the estate. Yes, she could see herself as mistress of *Trem-y-Môr* without too much difficulty.

Yet, how to win today? The ancient cry of generals and admirals the world over! Weapons had been lost on both sides but a respite in the battle had enabled her to retrench. What about a different approach? Sometimes men would respond to subtlety – a bit of flattery maybe?

"You are quite right," she soothed. "Sit down, Edward dear. You must be tired after your ride. I didn't mean to undermine you. You are the master here and this is your home. What you say must go. It was just that I had hoped to take some of the strain from your shoulders. You have had all these new responsibilities thrown on to you and obviously you still have some ties with your life in the Navy. I can't carry everything for you but I can help with Mariana. Being an older woman, it was my hope, after I had had time to assess the situation, to guide and help our dear, motherless sister. She is spiky towards me, but, I believe, she does respect me. And, this gives me the courage to suggest that there is another way for the dilemma to be solved."

Up to this point she had kept her eyes studiously staring at the carpet. Now, she ventured a glance to see if he was falling for her new ploy. What she saw made her founder, for the lines of his face were set in suspicion. Her counter plot had turned out weaker than she had thought. She decided that she would try one last strategy – occasionally the unexpected could turn the tables where a show of strength had failed! She took a deep breath and carried on:

"If Mariana was to plan to marry, then she would not need a chaperone on every occasion and we would no longer need to worry about her reputation. There are one or two suitable candidates, but what do you think of the idea of letting Griffith Owen court her?"

"Who's that?"

Margaret could have screamed with frustration. Why was he being so obtuse?

"The Parson, of course!"

In a split second, Margaret found all the ground she had gained lost. She had miscalculated and made a mistake which might cost her the triumph. She bit hard on her lips in defeat.

"The Parson!" Her brother leapt up, his cheeks cherry red and his voice irate. "No, Margaret! I have told him that he won't be able to wed Mariana and now I am telling you the same…"

Margaret gathered together the last shreds of her dignity. Was it too late? She must prevail – too much was at stake. Her life in the castle had become intolerable. Walter's drinking habits were well-known and her brother-in-law, Ralph, had told her, in no uncertain terms what had caused it all. Formerly he had tormented her:

"It's all your fault and your rejection of him. What man can stand to be dictated to by his wife? You and your refusal to let him come to your bed. He went somewhere else at first – a sweet, young maid called Hannah, who I introduced him to, but you attacked his manhood – the very core of who he was! He couldn't even control his own wife – what a termagant you have become! Why couldn't you have shown him some kindness? Why rebuff him in season and out?"

She had refuted Ralph's accusations, claiming that *he* had been partly responsible, with his larger-than-life management of his father's estate. Why couldn't he have given Walter a house of his own? Maybe, if they – she and her husband and two boys – had moved away from the success of Lord and Lady Struley and their boisterous lifestyle, they might have been happy. And, now, so near and yet so far, Margaret had found an opening for that new beginning. Of course, she wouldn't bring her sons to Wales, for they seemed to regard their uncle and aunt as their true parents and mixed with their loud cousins, copying mannerisms and vocabulary, more and more with each passing year. The Manor House seemed ideal for her to regain some semblance of marriage – quiet but not too deadly. There would be plenty of work to interest Walter and drag him away from the bottle and then…

Margaret felt tears prick behind her eyelids. She was lonely. So lonely. That was why she craved the company of the Parson – he was such a sympathetic man, full of tenderness, and he didn't despise her. How she pined for the old Walter back, who had been her friend and confidant, who had respected and… and loved her! But the man who sat most of each day in a drink befuddled daydream did not interact with her and she desired to see him drawn out, weaned off the alcohol and return to the man who had helped her in her youth.

These prognostications raced through her mind, and she decided to pour in a broadside. Keeping her tone low and steady, she argued:

"I have been told that you refused the Parson's offer for Mariana's hand. A story of someone called 'Septimus' or something like that. I haven't heard that name mentioned by anyone in this house, least of all Mariana herself. Tell me, what have you against the Parson – I'd like to hear?"

"How dare you encourage that man!" Apparently Edward's wrath had not assuaged. "Listening to his tale of woe, plotting to…"

"Now, Edward dear, don't get into a rage." She stretched out an arm in a gesture of pretended peace. "You'll topple off that pin of yours if you shake anymore. Reverend Mr Owen and I have done no plotting. He mentioned to me just once…"

"Once! Once! He practically lives here! Hasn't that given the gossips something to talk about?"

"Of course not!" Although Margaret barked the words she was careful to keep a strict control on her sentiments. In her experience once you lost your temper you lost the battle! She began to hope that she had gained the upper hand again when she saw his skin painted a deeper crimson. She allowed her voice to drop. "He has very properly been visiting a bereaved family, and incidentally, has been a great comfort to me. After all, he was a close associate of Fath…"

"Well, I'm glad he's been a comfort to someone, for I can't tolerate the man and neither, can Mariana. That is why he won't be marrying her."

Edward's flash of fury seemed to pass almost as quickly as it had arrived. For a second, Margaret forgot her aim of victory and asked with genuine interest:

"But what is it that you both have against the Parson? He's polite and gallant. He comes from a good family and he has a reasonable living. Granted, he talks in a quaint sort of way, but better Bible verses than swear words. He seems the ideal sort of husband for Mariana. He's attentive and forbearing and, being more mature he'll be able to settle her. He's been married before and…"

"Margaret!" Edward's eyes glittered a warning. "You, of all people, should know what it is like to be forced into a marriage you don't want."

The woman raised her shoulders and straightened her neck and chin with a haughty sniff.

"I don't know what you're talking about."

"I may have been young when you married Humphrey Struley, but I wasn't deaf! Father arranged the marriage and you didn't want to go through with it."

Margaret was cornered. Edward's obviously clear memory of the situation and the fact that she had been soundly beaten by her father on that occasion made her feel small. She had a crisis of confidence. She recalled seeing the red deer rut one November, down in the New Forest. Hundreds of years ago William the Conqueror had planted this expanse of land for hunting. A gamekeeper had explained to her, whilst she watched two magnificent stags lock horns, that the animals only sensed when the wrestling match was over, when one deer had been pushed back a considerable distance. Should she surrender? She didn't reckon she could bluff her way out of this tight spot – better give him a single point but bounce the ball back to him by sound argument.

"My marriage to Humphrey was completely different. Reverend Owen is not an imbecile. Yes, he's a few years older than our sister, but who else is there? And I'll say this…" She pressed on to gain a greater advantage as Edward's face appeared to register the truth of the shortage of eager suitors for Mariana's hand. "He really wants to marry her. He tells me he loves her and you know, with time, love can grow between a couple, particularly if one of them…"

"No! No!"

Edward's bellow made her jump.

"Enough of this nonsense!" His tone suggested that he had finally lost the slender thread of patience he had, if he had had any at all! "You won't ever persuade me. I can't find out if Father did agree to the marriage, as the Parson claims, but he must have lost his wits just before he died, for anyone with an ounce of sense would see that Mariana would shrivel up and die married to that religious freak!"

"Edward! Now you *have* shocked me. He is a man of God."

"I'm not prepared to discuss it anymore."

Purposefully her brother moved towards the door. Margaret took one last shot – a gamble but if it led to victory…

"I know," she proclaimed in a throaty whisper.

He swivelled on his one boot, a frown furrowing his brow.

"What?"

"You know what I'm talking about! You may try to hide it but I've seen it. And that means others may have seen it too."

"What are you referring to?"

Margaret smiled. Vulnerable underbelly indeed! She had witnessed a fleeting look of fear flit across his features. All she needed to do was leave the threat of exposure in the air and she might be able to twist him round her little finger.

"You understand what I am talking about. And it explains fully why you are so against this marriage. However, as you won't admit it nor change your view, I suggest that the best plan is for me to stay here…" She saw him open his mouth and rushed on: "Wait! Let me finish. I will promise to keep out of the kitchen. In return, I will require Mrs Jones to come to me daily with suggestions for the menu."

She stopped, reviewing if there were any other terms she wanted in this tenuous truce or was it a peace treaty or… or even in a complete triumph, for hadn't she got what she had wanted?

She laid out a request for her maid, Perrin, to have her meals on a tray in the bedchamber – the poor woman was isolated by the other servants speaking Welsh and excluding her. She threw in permission to visit some of the tenants. Surely this would strengthen her position here, and let everyone see that she was a considerate and caring mistress. What about taking Mariana with her? Could Edward not understand that it was time that their youngest sister settled down, stopped charging around the country with barely even a groom in attendance and learnt how to run a household? However, at this last comment, he drew the line. He acceded to the other points, agreeing to her remaining here either until the stranger upstairs left or he, Edward, returned. He seemed unconcerned whether she paid house calls to the villagers but then he tinged the taste of victory by reading her a homily of his own!

"You may go out wherever you please. As you have already said, this estate has lacked a mistress for a long, long time. However, you are to leave Mariana at home. She resents your interference and although, unlike Mrs Jones, she can't threaten to resign or retire, I wouldn't put it past her to run away. What you say about her housewifely skills is doubtless true, but that only reinforces what I say: that she would not be a successful vicar's wife. We all admit that she has been allowed too much licence to do what she wants. Nevertheless, there are men who will find that a refreshing change from some of the simpering misses who are ready for marriage. There is a single stipulation I ask for…"

Now, he really did sound like a captain of the Navy addressing his midshipman or her father lecturing a daughter or her brother-in-law passing judgement on a woman, and she pursed her lips in anticipation.

He went on: "All I ask is that you will write to me immediately if there are any crises – not the milk turning sour or the dog escaping – but if any of the household, from yourself to the youngest servant, is…"

She could bear it no more! She informed him that she understood what he meant by a crisis and would not bother him with trivia. When he urged her not to aggravate anyone, she agreed meekly, her eyes cast down. For, suddenly, excitement was racing through her. She had taken him on – giving as good as she got and she had won! She had won! The primary part of her plan was accomplished – more than the primary part – several important points had been attained. Edward was departing and he would be searching for a steward shortly. She would say nothing right this minute, but wait for an appropriate opportunity to throw in her husband's name as a possible solution. She watched her brother leave the room and, when the door had closed, clapped her hands with delight.

EDWARD

Black, black, black!

Everything was black!

He was drowning in a sea of black depression! He couldn't breathe, and if something didn't happen soon, he would not be able to overcome this wretchedness. Yes, a minute part of him realised that he was not being rational – that there *was* a solution – and that he would come back up to the surface of his suffering and overthrow the darkness, but he didn't seem to have the strength to do it and he feared for his sanity.

Wearily, Edward climbed the stairs in search of his manservant. Had he made the right decision in allowing Margaret to stay? He should have insisted that she left and he remain here. His heart clamoured not to leave, but his intellect urged him to put as many miles as he could between himself and the attractive woman who was his youngest sister.

And then there was Admiral Humphries and his command to attend a meeting with him. Was he never to be free from the demands of the Navy? Had he not given the best years of his life to His Majesty's service, even to the point of losing his leg?

But, what was he going to do about Mariana? If only there was someone suitable, he could encourage her to marry and then she would be unattainable to him.

Ally and her son flashed before his eyes. What had happened to them? He had spoken out the words to Mariana this morning that they were dead, but were they? Would he ever marry himself and bear another son or a darling daughter?

Pushing in on this heart-cry, an image of his sister bearing his child broke in. Surely it wasn't simply desire that was driving him? He believed he loved her, truly loved her, and, as he had said to Margaret, her difference, her unpredictability, her very wildness attracted him. She was a Greek goddess, her mind not filled with mundane subjects such as how much flour there was in the bin or had they enough wool to make garments for the winter? No, rather, she was up and involved in some new idea or scheme, a flighty, out-of-the-ordinary project. He loved her just as she was, and he would not like to see her changed by Margaret, or anyone else, even if it meant she was more prepared to be a wife!

Round and round relentlessly his problems chased each other. No order or reason. Jostling to be uppermost in his thoughts, shoving and pushing, until he wanted to scream out his anguish or throw himself from the top of Holyhead Mountain just to get some relief!

Reaching the penultimate stair of the Manor House, the pitch dark cloud enveloped him again, blotting out Mariana's beauty and the adoration of Ally's freckled face; the craftiness of Margaret's arguments and the authority of Admiral Humphries. Oh, he had to get away, throw off this melancholy before he suffocated in its clinging depths!

Mariana's shining eyes and blown-back hair – as he had seen her on the beach that morning – swam before him and he half groaned. How he loved her! What should he do? Strangely, he felt no guilt about loving his sister. Only in the first instance, after he had admitted to himself his desire for her, had he felt shame. How could he want to bed his own sister? his conscience had demanded. Immediately, he had perceived that he could not govern his feelings towards this woman, since she was a stranger to him and not recognisable as a sister, a blood relative. He had never met her before that first time when she had descended the steps to the ground floor on the night of his arrival. He had no shared memories of childhood with her. Only in the likeness to her mother did he have any memories, and that simply increased his ardour, since he had loved her mother before her! No, guilt did not keep him silent – if they were the only two people left on earth he would make a declaration! Rather he hid his passion because of what others would say and how Mariana herself would respond – surely she would be repulsed if she knew!

Yet… he pondered, pausing in the corridor. Yet, had he been unsuccessful in concealing what was in his spirit? Was that what Margaret had been hinting at?

He reached his bed chamber and gripped the door handle, mouthing silently to be released from the torment. He accepted that the best solution would be to leave and hope and pray that without Mariana's fascinating presence he would be able to forget her, in the end. Logic marshalled his confused thoughts. He was not going to come back ever, unless either he or his tempting sister was safely married. Otherwise, one day, he might be unable to restrain himself from proclaiming his love.

The grain of the wood of the door, mellowed with age, reassured him that time passed. He resolved to stick with his decision and go tomorrow. Which thought reminded him of why he had toiled upstairs! He must seek out Wilson and talk to him about finding a head steward. It was a matter of urgency if he was not going to return soon.

He opened the door and stood on the threshold. Over the days, he found that this was the most impressive room in the whole house, commodious and airy. His depression receded slightly with his observations. Dominating the floor sat a massive oak bed covered with a thick quilt, woven locally in a complicated pattern in mustard yellow and brown. Despite the size of the bed, there was still ample room for an expensive rug in gold and saffron from far off Persia, to be laid on the polished floor. An opulent chest of drawers, hand basin and two embroidered chairs constituted the rest of the furnishings but the very lack of furniture gave an even greater impression of space.

Edward had found that the room was sunny usually and today was no exception! With three windows facing south and west even the faintest glimmers of sunshine were caught and reflected from wall or glass. Nonetheless, despite the brilliance his soul plummeted again.

Did this sadness flow from the spirit of his dead father? But he had not died in his bed but in the library, according to Wilson. Edward moved across to the window, wondering if in associating this room with his father he was reminded constantly of the fact that he had missed being reconciled with him. Did this aggravate his grief? Or was it just that he had not experienced anything other than inner turmoil here? How could he expect to find peace or happiness within these four walls?

Edward leant his head against the edge of the window alcove. Despair engulfed him! What was wrong with him? The hopelessness of his position weighed him down. No, it was more than simply being overwhelmed with defeat – he felt forlorn and dejected. Why? He struggled to understand in order to lift himself up from its depths.

It wasn't just the inappropriateness of his love for Mariana or that there was no chance of it coming to fruition – it was that all his dreams were lying dead on the ground, autumn leaves spent and finished!

He had built up such aspirations in his conversations with Septimus: he would marry Ally; he would return to the welcome arms of his forgiving father – not a prodigal son, for it was he who had been sent away – but a wonderful family reunion, complete with slain fatted calf! Oh, his imagination had left nothing out – he could smell the crackling almost and then… nothing! A stillborn child! All the expectations – all the pain and nothing! His father had not even been dead for years, but had passed away only the day before. And, as if the crushing weight of lost dreams was not enough, there were his own feelings of remorse – the knowledge that he could have done more with mending his relationship with both Ally and his father – and, then, one final blow, this growing love for his sister, which could never be declared or realised. God, he couldn't dwell a moment longer in this living hell!

"Sir?"

Edward started when his valet appeared from the dressing room.

"I am just finishing your packing, Sir."

"And yours too, Wilson."

Edward felt a lessening of the poison grip on him while he explained that he wished for his servant to accompany him to London. He discovered that Wilson hailed from that city and he went on to probe how much Welsh the older man understood. His brooding blurred. When Wilson stated humbly that he only knew a few odd phrases, Edward challenged him, teasingly, accusing him of being a fraud! Reluctantly, the servant admitted that he understood almost everything but conversing in a foreign language was more difficult and very tiring. To this end, he asked Sir Edward to keep this truth a secret.

The Fleet captain nodded his assent and settled himself on the wide window ledge, gazing, unseeing at the sea. The thickness of the stones, making up the walls, provided an excellent seat in each window indentation and Mrs Jones or someone had placed sheep's wool filled cushions which eased the ache in his leg. He relaxed.

Incredibly the pain in his heart seemed to have eased also and his spirits lifted. Was it just the distraction of conversation or was it the company of this particular man? Edward acknowledged to himself that he liked Wilson. The other man never appeared to disapprove and even seemed wise to Edward. Was it the age difference or the dissimilarity of their lives? Certainly, one of the servant's most appealing qualities was his ability to listen much and speak little! Edward launched into his speech:

"Wilson, I need a steward. Can you recommend one? I have tried to think who I might get but I've come to no conclusion! You have lived here for eighteen years – and you know more than you let on." He raised a quizzical eyebrow. "So, please will you help me?"

There followed a lengthy discourse, covering a variety of diverse men, ending with two possible candidates: Penelope's husband, Robert, and Mr Cutland. Apparently choosing his words carefully, Wilson explained that he thought Edward's brother-in-law would refuse the position because of his responsibilities on the farm and the distance between the Manor House and his own property. Cutland, on the other hand, might accept but would not want the position permanently, Wilson reckoned. He ended by saying that the problem was two fold and lay in the uncertainty of the length of the Squire's absence and the urgency of his departure.

On reflection, whilst Wilson folded three shirts – maybe the neat task helped sort out his ruminations – he recommended Owen Lewis. He backed up his suggestion by stating that he had found the groom to have a capable head on his shoulders and although phlegmatic was shrewd and knowledgeable, being born and bred locally. Also that Owen Lewis could read and write because his father had been a merchant and taught him his letters.

Edward returned his own concerns: perhaps Lewis' personal troubles – with his dying wife – might prevent him from doing a satisfactory job and it was too much to ask at this distressing time. However, Wilson seemed to know the latest on this and explained that it was expected that the sick woman would pass away at any moment. He went on to ponder the idea that rather than grief inhibiting the groom, it might well help Lewis through the weeks of mourning. However, Wilson added that this last was only speculation and he could not be sure. He urged his master to ask Lewis himself, informing Sir Edward that the Lewis family lived in a nearby dwelling.

On hearing that Mrs Jones had fled Margaret's interference to visit her failing friend in this very same cottage, Edward stood up, saying that he would go and find the head groom and housekeeper and impart to them the date of his departure and talk to them about the proposed ideas. He told Wilson that he was going to offer Lewis the post as an interim measure, until he knew better what his future held and he could appoint a suitable man to be a permanent steward. On enquiry, Wilson assured him that there was even a house, not far hence, which could be made habitable for a family, if the man had one! Of course, if Edward chose not to return, Wilson explained that the vacancy would be filled better by an overseer rather than steward, since even the best tenants needed supervision! He went on to advise his master to mention the dilemma to his own peers in the coming days.

Edward thanked his valet for his counsel, admitting ruefully that he knew nothing about farming but was much more experienced in running a ship or even executing battle plans. Wilson denied that the role of Squire was beyond his master's capabilities, then observing that Edward seemed to be suffering from his wound, he offered to rub his leg, which led to a further conversation about how Edward was intending to travel to London. Edward explained that he had thought already that it would be no use him arriving needing a week's rest when Admiral Humphries had been so insistent on him going at his earliest convenience! But, if they took the coach, which of Lewis' sons could be spared to drive it? Edward limped away, regretting that it was necessary to ask such sacrifice from this single family when the mother was nearing death.

In the event, Edward found it impossible to speak to either Lewis or Thomas (whom Wilson had recommended as the best choice to take his master on his journey), for, when he arrived an hour later, the cottage was full of people.

In the corner lay Lewis' wife, Bridget, he assumed, bloated to enormous proportions added to by the number of quilts placed over her. By her side sat Mrs Jones silently. Edward wondered whether his housekeeper was pensive from the impending loss or because of Margaret's bullish treatment of her.

Edward's attention was caught immediately by Mariana, who was perched near to Mrs Jones. Beside them, Bridget's children, ranging from crawling stage to grown-up, like a display of how the human being develops, were standing or sitting around the crowded room. Edward could not actually count individual heads, because of the lack of light seeping in through the windows. It appeared that the entire brood were present and, dotted between them, were several women – come to help or mourn, he could not discern. Seeing how many strangers were there made him wonder briefly if he had been wrong to assume that all the children here belonged to his head groom – maybe some were visiting with their mothers

– but this was hardly the time to enquire!

Edward noted all this from the doorway and, when he stooped to enter the room fully, his peg leg sank into the mud floor. He was stuck and he looked from left to right anxiously. His sister was the first to notice his plight and poked a finger into Mrs Jones' back, presumably to bring to her attention the presence of the Squire.

Immediately, the housekeeper arose and wove her way through the closely-packed group with Mariana in tow. Edward watched as their places were taken by others who pressed forward to be near Bridget. Barely did he have time to realise that there was no sign of the men he was seeking before Mariana was indicating that he should retreat. Edward tugged at his wooden leg and moved outside, blinking in the sunlight.

"There's hardly room to breathe in there!" Mariana gasped.

"It's the woman I pity," mused Edward.

"Which woman?"

"He means Bridget," supplied Mrs Jones. "But there's no need for pity. She's in no pain."

"I didn't mean that. I simply hope that when I'm dying, I'll be left to die in peace."

"Master Edward!" Mrs Jones' scandalised tones caused two curious children to poke their heads out of the door.

"I think I'll be going," announced Mariana. "Are you coming Jonesey?"

She began to walk away and Edward and the older woman followed through the gateway as Mrs Jones exclaimed:

"Not if that woman is still in my kitchen!"

"She isn't," assured Edward. "And I've had it from her own lips that she won't enter it again."

"God be praised, Sir! Is she going home?"

"She can't yet, but she has promised not to interfere with your job again. So there's no need for you to resign, Mrs Jones. That's what I came to tell you."

"Good day, Squire, Miss Mariana, Mrs Jones."

A new voice came from the path. They turned to see Matthew Cutland with the groom, Lewis, by his side, his skin grey. Edward saw that beneath Lewis' eyes were purplish, half-moon shadows and his shoulders were drooping. Edward reconsidered the words he had been going to say to his servant. The man looked exhausted and beaten.

A query from Mariana told them that once again Cutlass had been chosen over Lloyd to attend the sick woman. There was a spark of determination in Lewis' face as the two men passed them and disappeared into the gloom with a backward assurance that Cutlass would bring Edward a progress report.

"*Bechod*! What a waste! All those children and look what's been done to her," burst out Mrs Jones. "I've always wanted a family but there shouldn't be a child every year!"

Before Mariana or Edward could reply another person joined them. The Parson must have overheard the housekeeper's exclamation for he said:

"Owen Lewis was always a lusty lad, so I've been told. How is… now what is her name? Betty?"

"Bridget, Parson," put in Mrs Jones. "Yes, I remember tales of Owen behind the choir stalls and even once or twice in the graveyard. Oh," she blushed red, "what's come over me speaking like that, with a young woman here? Miss Mariana, you're being too quiet, my girl, and hearing things you shouldn't!"

"I know… know all about these matters," stammered Mariana, indignation written in her stance. "I'm not a child anymore."

"Young maidens like yourself…" began the Vicar.

"Mariana, I trust what you say isn't true." Edward could not refrain from letting the disapproval show in his own features.

"Enough!" chided the housekeeper. "Well, Parson, have you come to pray with Bridget? She's been calling out for you all day."

"Have you been here all day, Mrs Jones?" Edward asked incredulously before the cleric could open his mouth.

"Yes. Jonesey brought over food this morning," butted in Mariana, watching the Vicar, "much to Margaret's disgust."

"Hush, child!" advised the servant, familiarity lending authority to the words.

"Surely you are not referring to your sister?" The Vicar seemed to tower over Mariana. "'**She stretcheth out her hand to the poor; yea, she reacheth forth her hands to the needy.**' Mrs Struley has told me of all the works of charity she and her husband have done for the needy near her home and she tells me that she is going to start visiting the poor and helpless of this Parish soon."

"It must be a miracle then, Reverend Owen," rejoined the young woman, "for just this morning she was saying…"

"Miss Mariana!" admonished the housekeeper. "The Parson will soon have to remind you not to spread tales about others. Now, come along with me. I shall return to see Bridget later, but, at the moment, I have a list of tasks to do in my own kitchen. Thank you, Master Edward, for what you have done. Good day to you, Parson. Sir."

Mrs Jones, gripping Mariana firmly with her strong baking arm, dragged the girl away from the two men as if she was not sure what her outspoken mistress might say next. Edward watched their progress fleetingly and then turned back to the Vicar who was speaking.

"It's so hard for the young when they compare themselves to mature folk such as Mrs Struley. I say this: **'She openeth her mouth with wisdom; and in her tongue is the law of kindness.'**"

"She sounds like a veritable saint. And she is full of praise for you too!" The Vicar smiled.

"She's a very good woman. The Lord has blessed your family with three good women. But you have another sister, don't you?"

"Yes, her name is Katherine."

"If Mrs Struley and Mrs Roberts and Miss Mariana are anything to go by, then this Katherine too must be a help to all around her. Now…" The Vicar cleared his throat. "I'm glad I saw you here, for I had hoped to have a quiet word in your ear."

Edward was hit by heartsickness again and despair burst through his dam of will power. Mariana and the dilemma of his love – Margaret and her manipulating attitude – even the hurried journey to London – washed over him, swirling and pushing, surging and pulling – threatening to take away the air from his lungs and the life from his body.

He wanted to shout at this man that nothing in the whole world would persuade him to allow Mariana to wed him! Nevertheless, he carefully schooled his face and pressed his lips closed – he had no intention of allowing this man even a glimpse of the dejection he was experiencing!

"Mrs Struley and I," the Vicar began, "were wondering if you would allow us to put up a plaque in memory of your father in the church. There's a Vestry meeting this week and I could…"

Edward ceased to listen. He expelled the air he had been holding unconsciously, letting some of the tension seep out from his doleful thoughts and gave up fighting the clinging, leaden depression – at least for the moment. Let the despondency carry him without resistance! When he escaped from the droning of this man, he would try again to swim against the current and win against the whirlpool of his care-worn emotions.

MARIANA

Mariana sat on the beach, her petticoat and gown pulled up to her knees. Her bare feet were pressed down until they had disappeared beneath the soft, cool particles. She caught up handfuls of the sand and let it trickle through her open fingers, finding comfort from the fine texture and evenness of the grains.

She stared out over the rippling water. The waves were breathing languorously against the land. The sky was a spring bluebell gown with a flounce of grey cloud along the hem of the horizon. Sketched across its surface were puffs of pink embroidered stitching which caught her eye – the last reminder of a sleeping sun.

Mariana shifted her feet to allow her toes to peep out and then, stretching her legs before her, she leant back and gazed at the mellow heavens above her head. Soon she must go indoors, but she was enjoying being alone for the present: she wanted to think.

At supper, Edward had announced his intention of setting off for London on the morrow. She felt hurt by his imminent departure; he was deserting her. She did not understand his haste in leaving. Letters from the Fleet indeed! He had told her he had left the Fleet. What right did they have to command him to travel all that way?

Mariana let her head fall backwards and her untied hair caressed the sand. No, she decided, it must be an excuse; he must have some private reason for going. She was cross with herself that during the meal she had been unable to persuade him to stay. And, it was not just *her* feelings. How would her father's estate run without him?

She brought her head upright again. In her heart she knew it was not the management of the Manor House that was worrying her – it was her own predicament. It was because of Margaret! Anger sprang in her throat when she thought of her elder half-sister. She was beginning not simply to avoid Margaret, but to actually hate her. Who did Margaret think she was, ordering her around and upbraiding her every time she saw her? Her mother? But her real mother would never have behaved like Margaret, for her own sweet mother would have loved her. Why did Margaret stay? Why did she not go home to her husband and sons? According to Edward, Margaret had promised not to upset Mrs Jones anymore. Mariana's top lip curled in a sneer. How long would that last? Until Edward's carriage had ridden over the brow of the hill behind the house!

Mariana squared her shoulders, chiding herself inside her head. Surely she was able to cope with Margaret's nagging tongue? After all, Edward's presence had not protected her from that up until now! She could shout back at her sister if she so desired or keep out of her way for most of the day or… No, it was more than dislike or even hatred she was experiencing. It was fear – she admitted she was frightened of Margaret. Frightened of Margaret's power over her life. This very evening, she had been upset.

"The Parson is going to have you, my beautiful sister, and I'm going to assist him," Margaret had hissed when they had met on the stairs. Ridiculously a tingle of panic had run down Mariana's spine. Was Margaret a witch casting a spell over her? She had sounded different.

"What are you talking about?" she had rejoined, standing perfectly still on the step two below her sister. She was determined not to show any consternation on her face. She forced herself to meet the other woman's gaze and had retorted with as much scorn as she could muster, "You can't force me to marry, you know!"

"That's what you think!" Margaret screwed up her eyes. "You're such an innocent. But there are many reasons why you should and…"

"Give me one!" Mariana lifted her head erect, disquietude dismissed by courage.

"No, I won't spoil the surprise. You'll find out soon enough."

Margaret had turned away and plodded up the stairs purposefully.

Now Mariana recalled her feelings of terror. Why was she so alarmed? Margaret's threats meant nothing. She had no hold over Mariana's life. Yet, those few short sentences had unsettled Mariana and fanned her hidden anxieties about her future into a burning flame. There had been something unearthly about her sister, when they had met earlier. It was not just her threats but the way she had leant towards Mariana with menace and confidence of victory nakedly displayed. What exactly did Margaret believe she could do to force her younger sister into accepting the Parson's proposal? Mariana could not imagine and this made her flesh creep.

If only you hadn't died, Father! The cry wasn't whispered but it was deeply felt. Through unshed tears, Mariana saw an evening star begin to twinkle in the darkening sky.

Suddenly she leapt to her feet. She would go and find Edward and ask if she could accompany him to London. He had made the offer on their ride. Elin could pack some clothes for her this evening – it was still early enough. That way she would ruin Margaret's schemes, whatever they were! Full of decision, she brushed multi-coloured particles from her clothes and headed for the house. Marching in through the front door, which had been left ajar to allow the refreshing night air to waft in, she heard voices coming from the library. She stepped towards that room and pushed against the polished wood, standing on the threshold.

Edward and Jack were sitting either side of the extensive desk, a glass of amber liquid apiece. Spread between them were some cards and Jack's hand fingered one of the upturned pictures. They were laughing.

"Edward!" Mariana's voice caused both men to turn towards her. "I've come to tell you that I've changed my mind." She walked across the room and stood near to Jack's chair.

"Changed your mind, my love. What about?" smiled Edward.

Mariana frowned, looking at her brother. He had never called her by that endearment before! Was he not thinking clearly? Had he been drinking too much? She set aside these reflections and poured out some of her ruminations from the beach in a garbled manner, begging Edward to let her come, confusion adding desperation to her tone. She ended half on a sob, breathless from panting.

She watched the men exchange a glance and then Edward was before her, his stalwart hands enclosing her shaking ones.

"What is it, Mariana? What has upset you?"

"I'm frightened."

"Frightened? You? Never! I though you were afraid of nothing and no one, my brave little sister!"

"Don't mock me, Edward!"

She pulled herself from him and moved towards the window. She felt a single tear roll down her cheek and brushed it away impatiently, hoping it had not been seen.

"What or who are you frightened of?" Jack asked.

She heard Edward limp after her and he enjoined her to answer.

Hesitantly, she spoke of Margaret and their unnerving interchange on the stairs. Edward tried to reassure her that he was the one who had the power to agree to any marriage contracts and he would help her find another husband than the Parson, notwithstanding she persisted with recounting her apprehensions, insisting that Margaret behaved as though the marriage was already decided – a prophecy almost!

Again, she begged to be allowed to go to London, or could Edward cancel his plans? She explained how she thought that once he was gone, Margaret would put her schemes into practice. Her voice and hands trembled together in time with one another and she kept her back turned away, grappling with dread-filled thoughts.

"Don't fret, dear Mariana," soothed Edward. "She's deliberately trying to make you scared – maybe so that your resistance is lowered. Truly there is nothing she can do. You can come with me, if you like, but it is late now and everything looks worse at night when you're tired. What do you think, Jack?"

"Stand up to her, Mariana. She's a bully – trying to panic you into thinking that you have no choice. What exactly did she say to you?"

Mariana shook her head, denying that she could remember but trying to describe Margaret's sinister voice.

"Do you recall this morning?" Edward queried. "When you and Elin were making fun of her? Try to see her as someone to poke fun at. She has no power, after all."

At last Mariana faced the men again. She could hear that Edward still did not understand her fearfulness.

"I'll try," she whispered, making a considerable effort to control the fluttering of her heart. Then more strongly, "But, she's like a spider – a great, fat spider – weaving a web. She wants you to go, Edward. She wants you, Jack, out of the way. She wants me… married. Why is she doing all this?"

"Have a drink," urged her brother. He went to pour her one. "Don't puzzle over it anymore. If you are really worried, then I'll promise to come back again before… before… Look, Mariana, I promise you that I will never allow you to marry that stuffy, strait-laced man. Does that help? I'll write to you and let you know my lodgings, just as soon as I know myself. And, don't forget, Jack is here with you whilst Margaret remains. If he goes then she will lose her reason for staying. So, you have nothing to fear. Come and sit down."

* * *

Mariana stood at the entrance of a hole. A tawny mouse with a white, furry front. She twitched her whiskers; she could smell danger. There was something waiting for her. Then she saw it. Two pairs of eyes: one set were bright olive green, shining in the semi-darkness and the other set were smaller, bead-like, with coal black glistening depths. She shivered. It was a rat – the size of a puppy dog and the green, glowing, eyes, belonged to a cat.

Mariana darted back into the recesses of her hole. She watched as a dark paw slid in through the door of her home. It reached in all directions, patting and prying, hoping to grip her thin tail or even her quivering head with its extended claws. Her body was tense in anticipation and she strived to press herself against the wall. The paw disappeared only to be replaced by a bewhiskered nose, sniffing with interest. She could just see the corner of a jet eye.

Mariana started to shiver. She was trapped and one way or another they were going to capture her, even if they starved her to death! She was beaten.

Mariana sat up in bed with a jolt, ready to run, sweat making her shift stick to her back and front. She was soaking wet with fear. She caught her clammy hair away from her neck and allowed her feet to drop to the cold floor. Her mouth was dry. She was thirsty. She must go and get a drink from the kitchen.

She knew the rat in her nightmare was Margaret because of its gigantic proportions, but it took her a moment to recognise the Parson in the cat – rotund, sable and sleek.

Now she was awake the contents of her dream faded, but she could not rid herself of her beating heart or the heat of terror on her body. She was ready to run, literally, and she did feel trapped in her waking state – a defenceless mouse in truth!

Padding across the darkened room, she pulled the sticky material of her light shift away from her skin and made her way to the stairs. She could breathe normally again and felt a draught of a cool breeze bathe her hot, tight skin. However, when she reached the kitchen, her heart contracted again, for there was a shadowy figure sitting in the rocking chair.

"Oh, Elin!"

The maid sprang to her feet. Mariana noticed her cheeks were moist with crying.

"Elin, are you all right?"

ELIN

Elin rubbed her tear-stained skin. She was angry at being found out and by someone who would be able to tell if she was lying! But how could she speak out the truth? What good to say that she loved Sir Edward and she was weeping because of his departure?

Elin had never wanted a man before like she craved for Sir Edward. She had met scores of lads at the Holy Day celebrations and the fairs and even outside church, but no one had ever touched her heart like her master had done. She accepted that there was no chance of an equal relationship, but she did not care. She would give herself to him, and not worry about the consequences, if only he would notice her, but he never even saw her, it seemed!

From the first night she had gone out of her way to make his life comfortable, although at that stage she was working unconsciously. She had found out his favourite foods and then slyly suggested to Mrs Jones that they had not made chicken and leeks in a sauce for a long time, or how about soaking a summer pudding with raspberries until the juices ran red and rich?

Nevertheless, Sir Edward either had not detected the change in menu or, if he had, he had thanked Mrs Jones fulsomely, saying fancy her remembering that he adored cinnamon butter biscuits or quails stuffed with a mixture of breadcrumbs and herbs, or Rhoscolyn oysters freshly cooked or…

No, Sir Edward looked at Elin no more than he did at her younger sisters, Peggy and Kate! If she had not known better, so closely did she watch him, she would have said that he had eyes only for Miss Mariana, but she would not contemplate that the man she admired could desire his own sister.

In the last week, she had resolved that she would be happy just to stay near him, even if he overlooked her every day. And then had come the news that he would be leaving and, from kitchen gossip, she had learnt that he was intending to appoint a steward, which surely meant he had every intention of being away a prolonged time.

Elin brought her brown study to an end and stared at her mistress, wondering again what story she could use to explain her tears. Fortunately, Miss Mariana herself came to Elin's rescue by declaring:

"Are you upset by my sister? You can tell me. I'm as mad as fire with her myself!"

Elin hid her face with her flowing hair. Usually she wore it, tucked up for convenience, not dangling in her eyes when she went about her duties, but tonight she had loosened it before getting into bed. She made no reply still, hoping that Miss Mariana would take her silence for agreement.

"Yes, I can see it is. You know, I'm never ever going to make it to heaven, Elin, for I hate too many people. One of the first persons I remember hating was that awful nursemaid. What was her name? Of course, you wouldn't remember because you weren't here then. No, I can't even recall her name, but I used to kick her on the shins and bite her hand. She was dismissed in the end. Nowadays, I hate all kinds of people like... like Lloyd, for instance. I hate him so much that I often imagine fighting him – punching him in the face – and I'm sure thoughts like that are wrong. But, recently, my hate of Lloyd has paled into insignificance compared with what I feel for Margaret. I burn with anger and hatred for her – it's almost a physical pain in my chest! Oh, Elin, don't let her upset you. She's a... bully. Tell me what has she done?"

Elin sighed inwardly whilst Miss Mariana chattered. Really her mistress could be remarkably naive sometimes! Did she honestly believe that a woman like Lady Struley – or Mrs Struley – or whatever her correct title was – could upset her? No, Elin was used to taking orders from her betters, although she did resent being called "Girl!" or "You!" Nonetheless, there were plenty of ways a servant could get back at someone like Mrs Struley. The best way Elin had found was to talk Welsh in front of her. Nothing seemed to annoy the woman more! Elin had seen the large matron holding her breath with what Elin assumed was suppressed wrath as if she was ready to burst, like a bottle of fermenting wine.

Also, there was Mrs Struley's servant, Perrin. She had confided in Elin that her name was Ellen, too, with the English spelling, of course. Elin screwed up her face when she thought of Ellen Perrin. Elin could not relate to that dried-up old stick of a woman, for the maid servant was much older than Mrs Struley and had the figure of a man! Absolutely flat-chested she was! Elin acknowledged that she could not hold this against her, since it was hardly her fault that no babe had sucked at her breasts, but the wizened body of the other servant served as a symbol of her very person. Elin reckoned she was neither man nor woman and, presumably, was similarly unattractive to both! Ellen Perrin seemed to have a querulous nature when she was away from Mrs Struley and would complain, in a squeaky voice, against the life she had led. Her features appeared to reflect her attitude to her circumstances, for she had a multitude of deep lines either side of her prim, bloodless lips.

Elin brushed back her hair behind her ears. No, she did not like Ellen Perrin and she had perceived quickly that to upset Ellen Perrin was to upset Mrs Struley. Elin had seen that Mrs Struley was fiercely protective of her servant, though Elin could not understand why. Ellen Perrin had informed her that she had only come into Mrs Struley's employ after her marriage. So, it wasn't as if Ellen Perrin had been with her mistress since childhood, like Wilson with Sir Rowlands. All Elin knew was that if Ellen Perrin retreated to her room in floods of tears, Mrs Struley would bellow at any servant who was nearby.

Elin's introspections concluded that neither of the two newcomers upset her, but it was easier to allow Mariana to believe this was her reason for crying.

"I had hoped she would be going," Elin responded evasively.

"Me, too, but Edward won't send her away."

"Can't."

"What do you mean?" Mariana questioned.

"He… he… can't send her away."

"Oh! She's so domineering! Apparently she was the same when she was a child. Edward told me that. I'd have loathed to have had her in the nursery with me! I'm glad she's only my half-sister and I'm glad…"

Elin let her attention fall away from her mistress' words. That was a close escape! She would have to learn to be more careful with Miss Mariana. How easy it had been to defend Sir Edward, but she must not show her feelings to anyone. Tears pricked at her eyelids and she admitted to herself the real reason she was tearful: she was angry with herself and her lack of quick thinking! She had missed an opportunity of a lifetime and it had only been a few minutes ago.

Over the days, Elin had not thrown herself at Sir Edward, despite considering this course of action initially. Instead she had stayed up late, particularly tonight, hovering just within earshot, in case he called. His impending departure had made her bold. This evening he had remained in the library long after both Miss Mariana and Master Jack had retired to bed. Even Wilson had been dismissed from further duties because of the early hour of starting on the morrow, but Sir Edward had seemed reluctant to go upstairs.

Elin had tried to think of excuses to enter the room, but the only one she had been able to undertake legitimately was to replace a few candles that had reached the bottom of their wicks. She had opened the door to see the man she loved sitting with a glass of whisky in his hand. Noiselessly, she had gone about her task, hoping he would speak to her but, from the corner of her eye, she had observed that he never even looked up from his contemplation of the empty grate.

Eventually, Elin had retired herself. To do more would have been inappropriate and embarrassing. However, she had been unable to sleep and had tossed and turned, until she had heard Peggy begin to move too. Her young sister was a light sleeper and Elin did not want her awake and needing to be amused. Thus, she had decided to tiptoe out of the room.

Believing everyone to be asleep, Elin had descended the main stairs, barefoot and wearing only her shift. Rounding the top of the stairs, she had met Sir Edward.

She had come to a standstill with shock.

For a few seconds they had regarded each other and then he had lurched forward and, much to her surprise, embraced her. Before common sense could take over, her pulses were racing! Her dreams were coming true! Instantly she admitted to herself that she would go with this man to his bedchamber without hesitating.

"Is it really you?" he had whispered against her unbound tresses.

Very slowly Elin had lifted her arms to return the hug. She kept her eyes closed and raised her lips to his searching ones. Maybe, if she did not look, she could keep this fantasy from fading. He must have noticed her after all!

Elin's joy evaporated! Tasting the alcohol on his breath, she realised that he was far too drunk to know who he was kissing. The next minute, delight was resurrected because here she was, wrapped in his arms, sharing a deep kiss with the man she loved, whether he was unknowing or not!

However, she was wrong about his befuddled senses, for he had pulled apart from her and stammered:

"No, it's not… You're not… Ally. You've got far too much flesh on you. Ally was always a slim chicken. And her son. I wonder what her son was like? Are you Annie?"

He had peered at Elin's face in the darkness and then shaken his head, asking:

"Who are you?"

She had tried to say her name but her voice would not work, such was her disappointment. So, *still* he had not noticed her!

"Must go to bed." He had staggered against the wall. "I've a tiresome journey to make in the morning, but it's for the best."

Elin had put out her hand to steady him and her hair had brushed his skin.

"Damned soft hair you've got! Thank God for women!"

Before Elin could stop him, he had tottered down the corridor to his room.

Elin had wanted to plead with him that she might not be Ally or Annie but she was here tonight and would give him what he needed: a place to lay his head and a welcome which he would not find this side of London! But she had stood without saying a word, the tears starting then as a release for all the days of held-in emotion. How she had longed for him to hold her! And now the moment had passed! Almost… almost… Why had she not kept him? she castigated herself. Why had she not gone with him, followed him? Why had she turned to descend the stairs to enter the kitchen? The opportunity had been wasted and might never come again. She was weeping with frustration at her own stupidity in not seizing the day.

Mariana's words broke into her reverie:

"… I was wondering if we could make her life here so horrible that she would go anyway. What about, snakes in her bed or frogs in her soup or…?"

Elin regarded her mistress in horror.

"No, Miss. You're much too old for those kind of pranks!"

"Henry told me once that if you balance a full chamber pot on top of a…"

"Miss Mariana!"

"Well, what *are* we going to do then? We must get rid of my sister."

"Just bear it as…"

"Elin! I thought you, at least, would be on my side."

"I am, Miss, but there's no need for childish tricks. It's far too late to be planning what we can do. It's past midnight. Let's go to bed and we can talk about some more practical ideas in the morning."

"What like?"

"I don't know. Pretending there's a plague in the village or…"

The two women made their way upstairs, whispering against each other's ears.

In any event, when morning came, neither servant nor mistress was in the mood to devise ways of sending their enemy back to her home. When the household gathered to watch the coach depart Elin saw reflected in Miss Mariana's eyes the same red rim of despair which she guessed was on her own face.

The servant had to be content with giving a silent farewell to the man she loved, gazing at him when he climbed into the carriage, trying to imprint his image into her mind. She restrained herself from flinging herself at his feet and begging him to take her with him. When she saw her mistress follow the track out of the yard and up to a small knoll not far from the house, she stepped along hastily, wanting to catch a last glimpse of the carriage. It seemed that Miss Mariana had similar wishes for she heard her murmur:

"Come back. Where are you?"

Elin could hear the wheels squelching in the mud and the leather creaking, but the equipage was lost from view. Then it reappeared and Elin crept closer to her mistress who was muttering:

"I won't be afraid! I won't! There's nothing she can do to me! Oh, come back, Edward! Margaret is too strong for me! And I don't know what's she's plotting. It's all very well for you to reassure me to 'Keep my chin up!' but you've gone now! What will happen?"

Elin glanced up at the sky. It had started to drizzle; fine rain which was leaving a net of shiny beads on the hair of her mistress and trickling down her smooth skin. She saw Miss Mariana blink away the water from her eyelashes and wondered if there were tears mixed in with the droplets from the heavens. Or was Miss Mariana like her – not able to weep anymore? She allowed her vision to focus in the distance, waiting for the carriage to appear one more time.

"You must write, Edward. You promised but you mustn't forget. I'll be watching every day, until a letter comes."

Elin leaned towards her mistress, ready to put out a hand to steady her and then the coach rose into view. Sir Edward's shadow was visible from this distance. Or was it Wilson's silhouette? Elin had seen him climb in beside his master. Thomas, hauling on the reins, was alone outside, but Elin understood that he wasn't sad at going away, despite the fact that he wouldn't see his mother again this side of eternity. He had been filled with a young man's excitement at leaving home for the first time and seeking his fortune in the big city, even if he was under the authority of a master.

"They've gone, Miss," she intoned.

Elin sensed someone behind her. It was Mr Jack, pale but determined. Walking any distance seemed to continue to take its toll on his strength. Gladly she surrendered her mistress into his care, for his eyes were scanning Miss Mariana's anxious face.

"What are you doing out in this rain without a hat on?" Miss Mariana demanded.

Elin heard his reply whilst she retraced her steps.

"Mrs Jones' words exactly about yourself! She told me to fetch you in before you catch your death." Her mistress must have moaned because he continued, "Now, Mariana, be brave! Margaret is not a sorceress. She's only your strong-willed, elder sister and, besides, I'm here and I give you my word that I'll protect you."

Elin glanced back to see Jack clutch his hand dramatically to his chest with an exaggerated sign of allegiance. He slipped his elbow through his companion's arm and steered her towards home. Elin was relieved to hear her laugh.

"Oh, Jack, what would I do if you weren't here? Thank you. Come. I'm worried about you getting wet. Matthew would read me a lecture if you get ill again."

Elin strode ahead, disturbing thoughts running through her mind. The scene she had just witnessed had an intimacy which upset her. This was because she herself would give much to have a man who would comfort her in her loss, and also because apparently her mistress was becoming all too familiar with this stranger in their midst. His memory had not come back. No one knew who he was or where he came from. And, surely, he would be leaving himself soon and then she and Mrs Jones would have a very disconsolate mistress on their hands. Oh, why had God created love? What a mess people got themselves into! Elin sighed and pulled her shawl over her own wet curls.

MARIANA

Mariana closed her eyes. Nothing! No one! Not the faintest jingle of reins or the crack of wood which might herald a messenger – if not a carriage, then a horse or perhaps a lowly donkey. Not a sound, except the faint bleating of sheep and the dawn coo of the pigeons nesting over the stables. Mariana could not even hear the sea, although the waves were not far away.

How many times had she halted, like this morning, before her ride, to squint into the distance in the hope of a communication from Edward? Seventeen days. Seventeen days since he had left and not one letter nor a verbal message carried by a person travelling from London to Holyhead! What could have happened to him? He had *promised* her. In their final exchange of words he had said that he would send her news.

Mariana ground her teeth together. At first, she had been worried that some accident had befallen him, but she reasoned that it was unlikely that both Wilson and Thomas had been rendered incapable of sending tidings – whether good or bad! Consequently, with the passing days, she became increasingly angry at her brother's lack of consideration, his lack of care and now, for certain, his complete lack of love for her.

By some miracle, and not thanks to Edward, she had survived the time remarkably well. Margaret had kept to *her* promise not to interfere with Mrs Jones' domain. Instead, her sister had spent most of each day out in her carriage visiting people: from the meanest cottage on the estate to Lord and Lady Wynne at *Plas Hyfryd*. Mariana understood that she had called at the Vicarage on numerous occasions and had been to see Penelope and Robert too. However, Mariana was not really interested in Margaret's whereabouts as long as her sister was not pestering her!

Mariana had to acknowledge that it had been Jack's presence that had made the last sennight more than bearable. She had made a friend and, with the relationship deepening, her grief had been assuaged in a way she would not have thought possible.

A week after Edward's departure, Jack had decided that he must either learn or reacquaint himself with the skill of riding. Matthew Cutlass had been dubious about the wisdom of this, not just because his patient had only arisen recently from his sick bed, but, more importantly, because Jack still suffered from bouts of dizziness. Mariana smiled ruefully, recalling the argument which she had witnessed between the two men. Yes, Matthew had agreed, Jack had made remarkable progress, better than any could have imagined, but if he insisted on pushing himself, he might find himself, flat on his back again and undoing all the progress he had achieved thus far! Jack had dismissed this possibility. He reasoned that he would have to ride one day, if he was to travel and find out who he was and where he came from (since no one had 'claimed' him or recognised him). Thus, saying with a laugh, "There's no time like the present", he had set forth merrily.

Mariana had allayed Matthew's fears by assuring him that she would escort Jack at first, whenever he went out. To her private disappointment, her new friend had no need to be *taught* to ride, which suggested he was not an impoverished man. In fact, she had to admit that he had a very good seat and soon she was challenging him to a race. He had refused, claiming it was too painful to gallop, but his health was improving at such a rate that even Matthew had to admit that he had been wrong! Each day travelling a greater distance, Jack had marvelled that they had gone to no place more than once. He had wondered aloud if Mariana had explored every inch of the island. Mariana had been surprised herself at the pleasure of these shared rides, since she would have said that she preferred to ride alone.

Each afternoon Jack rested, whether from genuine tiredness or from a desire not to offend the retired surgeon further, Mariana did not know. Lately, he had left his bed for these siestas and stretched his spare frame in a chair. If the weather was clement, he moved outside where he would fill the time by reading some dusty volume borrowed from Sir William's bookshelves or exchanging conversation with anyone who was passing, which often meant his companion of the morning: Mariana. Together they "put the world to rights" – those being Mrs Jones' words. Jack had smiled and assured the housekeeper that they were far from doing that. Yet, many of their discussions were serious, especially when they began philosophising on the point of life; reflecting on whether another war with France was inevitable; debating if Wales should have its own government; bickering over the merits of teaching children Latin and Greek from an early age and if they should be whipped for their misdemeanours; deciding that it was unfair that some folk were fabulously wealthy and others poor unto death.

There seemed to be a never-ending supply of opinions waiting to flow back and forth between man and woman. Although Mariana had to tell Jack about recent happenings in Wales and England, he had no difficulty in theorising over all sorts of issues. Once in a while they had argued until the tension was stiff around them. Often, they had lazily tossed ideas out into the warm sunshine without bothering to disagree. Mariana recalled that nearly always they had laughed together and, incredibly, Margaret had not objected to their budding friendship. Maybe no one told her sister that after the midday meal Jack and Mariana did not go their separate ways although she was aware that they rode out each morning.

Even the evenings were passed in each other's company, since, from the beginning, Margaret had retired early to bed, with Perrin in attendance, and she had not changed her habits once Edward left. Consequently, the couple were allowed to stroll along the sand to watch the oystercatchers paddling in the shallow water or the gulls fighting over a dead fish or do battle on the chessboard or play cards long after the moon rose.

Of course, they were not alone on every occasion, for others would join them sometimes: the gardener if he was working nearby; Elin, when her chores were done; even the cattle-drover had contributed to one debate. Yet, Mariana acknowledged to herself, she had found contentment being with Jack and had often wished the others away.

Those had been sunny, pleasant, idle days with long, pink-tinted evenings cradling a sleepy, sinking sun – a circle of burnt orange winking at them, reassuring them that tomorrow it would rise again to watch their relationship grow and their friendship develop.

All had been benign, that is, until three days ago. Then the sun had refused to appear and instead had hidden behind a curtain of thick, coal-black clouds, which showered an everlasting torrent of water from the sky. Abruptly Margaret, Mariana and Jack had been forced to remain indoors. It had not taken many hours, with Margaret as an awkward third person, for tempers to flare between the two women. Now the old Margaret returned, finding fault with her sister and everything she did!

Naturally the talk had turned to Edward and what might have happened to him, and Margaret had not bothered to hide her contempt. She reminded her sister that Edward had happily spent nearly eighteen years without setting foot over the threshold of *Trem-y-Môr* or communicating with any of his family except their sister, and Margaret could vouch that even Penelope had not heard from him this time. Margaret suggested that Edward must have forgotten their existence. Mariana had risen to her brother's defence, although she was beginning to believe herself that what was being said was true.

Mariana recalled that Jack had been a witness to herself and Margaret in a fury, each shouting louder every sentence. Her intention had been to silence Margaret and she wondered if her sister was trying to do the same. Finally the man had banged his plate on the table. Margaret had swept from the room, declaring that she could feel one of her headaches coming and calling for Perrin in a distressed voice. Mariana was left feeling deflated. She laughed, almost like a madman, once left alone with Jack, in an attempt to release her frustration.

One, then another and then a third full day of unremitting rain and today, just when Mrs Jones had feared that a murder would be committed between the two sisters – so Elin had informed – a day of complete calm had dawned, promising to be hot.

The sky was bright blue with joy at the reappearance of its god – Mariana turned her face to bask in the rays. She felt that even the plants must be delirious with glee at feeling the sun's warmth and they were raising their flowers to get the maximum light and heat. Mariana had noticed that others – mostly servants – had begun to hum or whistle with seeming delight at a return to summer and determinedly set about getting everything dry, from wet washing to soggy byres. Each living thing appeared to be giving a sigh of relief that the rains were over.

With the fair weather, Mariana had chosen to mount her horse and ride out to the knoll to stare at the fields and blink towards the high mountains of Snowdonia for some sign of a missive from Edward. All she could see was a straight line of smoke floating upwards from Owen Lewis' house, where remarkably Bridget had taken a turn for the better, halting the constant flow of interested spectators until she should sink again.

Mariana cursed her brother for his lack of thoughtfulness. For a second, this morning, at the meal-table, her forebodings had returned when Margaret had announced:

"Mariana, you and I have been invited to dine with Mr Reverend Owen on Tuesday. I have, of course, given our assent, so may I ask you to make sure you are not gadding about the countryside on that day? Jack, do you think you will still be with us then? Next Tuesday, that is?"

"I don't quite know what my plans are yet, Margaret." Mariana noted that he used her Christian name for the first time. "But, I do realise that your own plans are affected by mine. So, I will tell you immed…"

"What are you talking about?" Mariana saw that Margaret was at her most condescending.

"Oh, I beg your pardon, but *I* was given to understand that once I left, it would no longer be necessary for you to remain here."

"Yes, well, as long as Edward has sent no address or instructions or information about his return, I feel honour bound to stay with Mariana. For all we know, Edward is no longer in the country and I feel Mariana is too young to be left friendless and…"

"Friendless!" Mariana had exclaimed. "What a stupid notion! I've lived here all my life and am surrounded by friends."

"Yes, but there is no one quite like family," Margaret had contradicted firmly, although Mariana had expected to be admonished for her interruption.

"But there's Penelope and Robert only a stone's throw away."

Mariana remembered that at this point in the interchange, Margaret had patted her lips with her napkin, rising from her chair and added:

"Let me be quite plain about this, my little sister. I have no intention of leaving in the near future. So, if you will excuse me, I must prepare to go out. I suppose it is useless to ask you to accompany me, Mariana?"

Mariana had not even bothered to reply but had put as many pieces of braised kidneys into her mouth as she could manage. Instantly she had regretted this action for, suddenly, she had felt very nauseous, recalling her encounter with Margaret on the stairs. She had swallowed painfully and watched her sister sail from the room, nervousness rising in her again. How could she have forgotten Margaret's threats? Only by being engrossed in her new friendship with Jack! How dangerous! She had turned for reassurance from him but not expressed her thoughts in words.

Now, she allowed a shiver to run down her body, but, before the insubstantial terrors could take hold she heard another horse approaching. Looking over her shoulder she saw Jack riding up the track. Deliberately shaking off her suspicions about Margaret's plots to see her married to the Parson, she called in a playful voice:

"I'd just about decided you weren't coming this morning."

"Not coming? Not coming on a gorgeous day like this? You're jesting, Mariana. I am late because I have been preparing a little surprise."

"Surprise?"

"Yes. Not very exciting but definitely one to lift your spirits after all the rain and to stop you looking longingly for a message from your brother! Don't try to deny it! I know why you pause here most mornings. Therefore, I have been pestering Mrs Jones to pack some treats for us so that we can go out for the whole day. And, as long as we are back in time for the evening meal, we have Mrs Jones' blessing."

Mariana smiled, marvelling at her friend's perceptiveness. She observed him whilst he approached her. His appearance had changed to such an extent he was hardly recognisable! That first glimpse of him lying in a puddle of water on the kitchen floor was an image long gone. Then, she would have described his face as gaunt, possibly emaciated, but after several weeks of eating wholesome, carefully cooked, home-grown food, he had put on flesh. Today, his features were craggy, but attractive; if he gained a little more substance to his cheeks, she might even say handsome. His startling blue eyes – which no one could fail to notice and which had touched her grieving soul – had been sunk deep into the hollow of his skull, but currently they sat beneath his dark eyebrows, an almost permanent amused crinkle around them.

Her lips broke into a grin of greeting, for she had discovered that Jack was good-natured and placid, tending to see the funny side of situations; the lines around his eyes and mouth gave the clue that he was often laughing.

"Mariana?" Those quizzical eyebrows rose with the question.

"I was just thinking what a sorry scarecrow you were when I found you." She reflected that his chin was less severe, his skin a healthy brown and even his lips had filled out. She found herself wondering what it would be like to kiss him. She had brushed his mouth quickly the day of her father's funeral but to be held in his embrace and really kiss him… Sensibly she kept these thoughts to herself and asked: "I wonder what your real name is, Jack. Who are you? Do you still remember nothing?"

"Nothing. I have avidly scanned books and listened to conversations in the hope that some name will shout out at me calling, 'You are mine!', but they never have yet!"

"Maybe you're reading the wrong sort of books!" The ready banter which existed between them sat comfortably whilst they turned their horses towards the track. With a click of his reins to set the animal to walk, Jack replied:

"Maybe. Which way are we going today?"

"I have a special place, but it's quite a long ride…"

"Another special place? I thought your favourite hideaway was up on the mountain."

"Yes, it… it is," she stuttered. "I… I run there when I'm frightened." Her brow furrowed with an exclamation. "Oh, I wish I'd never shown it to you! If you're going to mock me, I…"

"Mock you! Mariana, I wouldn't dream of mocking you."

"No, I've changed my mind. Let's go to the Bay. There's that beach and…"

"Mariana!" He put out a hand towards her. "Please, please can we go to your special place? I'm sure…"

"No. It's too late." She shook her head, causing ripples to flow along her hair. "You shouldn't have…"

"What must I do? Go down on bended knee?

Mariana threw him a mischievous glance.

"Oh, all right. I'll take you but only because you never told anyone else about my little cave. However, if we are going, we must ride fast. Otherwise, there'll be no time to spend there and no point in going."

"Lead on! Lead on!"

JACK

Jack watched Mariana jerk the leather between her fingers and then she was away, galloping along the path, leaving a spray of mud behind her. Jack urged his mount to follow. Along the tracks, over several fields where the startled sheep fled in panic, past low-slung, cottages, scattering chickens and children alike who were scratching in the dirt, the two horses flew until they reached the edge of the island.

Mariana plunged Mars straight into the receding sea, wading in until the water reached the horse's belly. However Jack halted. He waited on the bare beach, keeping an eye on his friend to ascertain just how deep the sea would come. He concluded that Mariana must have made the crossing many times before, because she had judged the depth accurately and Mars' feet never left the shifting bottom. The current in the centre was strong and Jack felt a moment of concern when he saw the huge creature being forced sideways, but, with a word of encouragement from his slim mistress, and a pat on the side of his well-bred head, the sturdy horse was back on course.

"Hurry up, Jack," Mariana entreated when she reached the other side.

"I'm coming," he responded. What a remarkable woman Mariana was: very courageous, almost too daring when it came to challenges on a horse, and yet so very frightened of her sister's threats!

Jack eased his mount into the water. He was increasingly unsettled with his continued loss of memory. He had hoped that Cutlass would be correct and that he would remember, given time. Since his physical strength was returning he was anxious to be away from *Trem-y-Môr*. Not that he was not happy there, especially in Mariana's company, but he had to find out his identity. The last few weeks had been an interlude, a journey to another land: paradise, unreal, unjudged by his own standards, for what were his standards? What measure of life could he use when he knew not who he was, nor where he came from? He did not know how to relate to anyone and particularly not Mariana. Their relationship was subtly changing from brotherly affection to something deeper – from gentle teasing to flirting.

But what if he already had a wife and possibly children? Was it fair to encourage this stunning young woman? No, it would be better if he left before she was hurt. In the last couple of days he had found himself thinking in French but he had bitten off any phrases which came to his lips. He was conscious that England's alliance with France was crumbling.

His mind was wrenched from his reverie to the present situation when he felt water flow into his boots. His mare was shorter than Mariana's stallion. The beast hesitated. Jack realised he must concentrate. He held the saddlebag containing their food above his head when the sea drenched his breeches.

Mariana was laughing.

"You knew, you wretched girl!" he cursed as he reached the beach.

"Of course."

"Now I understand why we didn't go across the bridge."

"Oh, no, that wasn't the reason. It's much, much quicker to come across this way. It'll give us more time there."

"I don't believe you. Wait until I catch you!"

Mariana laughed again and, pulling Mars until he reared, with his front legs pawing the air, she set off at a furious gallop, her hair streaming out behind her.

Jack did not even try to chase her. His mount was no match for Mars. Tomorrow, the groom had promised him a new steed, which would be capable of long distance travelling, but today he would have to be satisfied with Sir William's elderly hunter.

Jack noticed that the countryside was becoming wilder, not flat any longer but with definite hillocks. He found the up and down ride tiring and exceedingly difficult to check which way Mariana had gone. Enchantress! Where she went he must follow!

He noticed the characteristic rock outcrops which were common on this side of Anglesey, as if the earth had outgrown its green grass coat and was bursting out of its clothes. Away to his right, a constant companion, was the sea.

Mariana seemed to know ways that avoided villages because Jack passed no more dwelling places. Just when he thought he really had lost her, she appeared from the shadow of a rock.

"Are you dry yet?" she enquired saucily.

"Yes, thank you. And I'm hoping either that we're nearly there or that you'll slow down for me."

"I'll ride at your speed because, from now on, we're leaving this busy path and going across country, where we won't meet anyone except maybe a shepherd or a lonely old woman collecting…"

"Busy path! I haven't met a single person!"

"Well, sometimes it can be very busy. Here's where we turn off."

They walked the animals at a gentle pace.

"Mars is a splendid horse," Jack commented. "Where did you get him?"

"Father saw him when he was in London. Mars was completely savage, unwilling to take even a halter. So Father bought him for me."

"Surely he didn't let you tame him! You must have been just a young girl!"

"No! He didn't go to London with the intention of buying a horse but when he saw Mars he was reminded of me, I suppose. 'Untamed, y'know!'" She mimicked what must have been her father's voice. "Thomas broke him in to take the bit and after that the halter. However, I was the only one to ride him. I went bareback at first. He didn't want to accept a saddle!"

"Did you ride astride?"

"Yes, and Father approved of me wearing breeches for that. Of course, once Mars was used to a saddle, Father expected me to return to a side-saddle."

"Does Thomas ride him?"

"Very occasionally. Mars really only tolerates me." She paused. "And it's best with no saddle at all."

Jack smiled.

"Has he sired foals?"

"Yes, a few times and very fine they are too."

"Did you own the mare too then or…?"

"Yes, we had a mare. We haven't got her anymore. She… She had to be shot."

"I'm sorry."

"Father was out riding her one night and accidentally ran her over a cliff. Only a shallow one. Father wasn't hurt but Favourite broke two legs and... and…"

"I'm sorry to have mentioned it." Jack apologised.

Mariana shook her head before saying:

"We must turn and go through here."

"Where? I see no path."

"Here. Through these bushes. We must dismount. Watch your eyes as the branches spring back."

"Can Mars make it?"

"He's done it before. If I left him tethered this side people would wonder where his rider had gone. They might search for me and then everyone would find the way to the beach. So I usually force him through the undergrowth and that way no one even knows I'm here."

"So this really is like your private beach then."

"It must... Ouch! Be careful, Jack, these twigs are sharp. It must belong to someone, I suppose. There we are. It's all right, Mars, my boy, we're all through now. How are you doing, Jack?"

"Fine! My coat's torn. My breeches, having barely dried, are now in tatters. My hat's gone and the poor horse is practically bald!"

"Jack!" Mariana turned around, watching him emerge. "Oh, Jack, there's not a mark on you!"

"Well, at least I understand why no one ever comes to this particular beach; one needs to wear a coat of chainmail to reach it!"

They were standing on a half-circular stretch of over-grown grass which dipped in the centre. The bushes behind them were as effective as a stone wall at hiding the secluded cove.

"Let's leave the horses here," suggested Mariana.

"I'm sure they'll be grateful. Are there any further obstacles we must pass through?"

"None, but beware of snakes. There are adders here."

"Thanks!"

Mariana set forth across the green, her skirts rustling in the grass. Walking behind Jack saw that the springy heath sloped downwards towards the sea, ending in a length of sand flanked on both sides by rugged, perpendicular cliffs.

"Does no one really know this...?" he began.

"Oh, no! You can see it if you stand on the headland there." She pointed away to her right. "But few people go to the headland, for it leads nowhere. Anyway, who's stupid enough to be scratched from head to toe just to reach a bit of sand when, barely a few feet from here, there's a beach that runs as far as the eye can see, complete with village and river?"

"I understand. Well, shall we eat?"

Jack sat down and opened the saddle-bag. He withdrew two pristine white napkins and laid them out with a flourish.

"Your tablecloth, Ma'am."

He began laying out the food, dividing it equally between the two cloths, and ended by producing a small hip flask.

"Wine, Ma'am?" he continued in his butler's voice. "It may be warm but it'll wet your gullet." He finished in his normal voice with a glimmer of a smile.

"Oh, Jack! You've thought of everything!"

"Not me. Mrs Jones or even the young girl… Kate, isn't it? She packed it, but I did put in a few suggestions."

For a while there was no sound except their munching.

When Mariana had finished she picked up the four corners of her napkin and, tying them together in a knot, tossed it away from her.

"All gone and it was delicious. Thank you, Jack. Ooh, it's hot, isn't it? If course, you can only feel the wind here if it's coming from the sea. My, I'm much better for that food! It's been a long ride. I think I'll lie down to let it settle."

"Wait! Have my coat. It's far too warm for me to wear and it'll save you getting sand in your hair."

Jack stood up, removed both his coat and waistcoat and then placed his clothes on the baking ground.

"Those are fashionable clothes," complimented Mariana. "Is it the one the tailor made for you?"

"Yes. Your brother lent me the money. I hope to be able to repay him in the near future."

Mariana reclined on the makeshift bed. As she did so, she caught her hair up and it spread out like a peacock's tail above her head in an exotic headdress. She closed her eyes.

"You're leaving, aren't you?" she breathed softly.

Jack made no reply whilst he gathered up the remains of his meal and then, stretching out on his side, his elbow propping up his body, he conceded in a gruff voice:

"Yes, I am."

"When?"

"Tomorrow."

"Tomorrow!" Mariana's eyes sprang open and she gazed at him. "Oh,

Jack, so soon. Is that why you arranged this outing? You knew it was your last day. Oh, why do you have to go?"

"Because I'm living suspended in air. I don't know my past or my future. I have been living in the present and… and I have thoroughly enjoyed it, but it can't go on forever. Whilst my body has been mending, a kind of lethargy spread over me, but now I'm better I *must* find out. You do see, don't you?"

Mariana turned her head and looked straight at him.

"Yes. It must be difficult for you… not to know. Where are you going to?"

"I thought I'd go to Chester and then on to Liverpool. Both are ports. Maybe I can find out what ship I was sailing on. I… I've got to start somewhere and, I guess, that's as good a place as any. Nobody around here seems to have seen 'my' ship, so I'd better search elsewhere."

Silence descended. What more was there to say?

He watched the lids of Mariana's eyes flutter shut. He had observed her countless times before and her face was both familiar and endlessly bewitching: her nose straight and dainty; her eyelashes long and curling back to touch her smooth skin like a fancy ruffle; her dark, sometimes mournful eyes, which could melt the heart; her pointed chin, which jutted out when she was angry; her soft petal cheeks…

He reached out to stroke her damask cheek – to feel for himself its rounded curve and in that action he knew what he was going to do. Perhaps if she had reached up and caught his hand then or moved away or spoken he would have been pulled back from her magic power which called him, but she lay motionless and silent, whilst he caressed her cheek. He ran his fingers down her graceful neck to the pulse he could see beating in the hollow of her collarbone. He traced the edge of her brave chin and when she kept her eyes closed, he allowed his fingertips to brush along her nose to those butterfly lashes.

Very slowly he began to unlace the ribbons on her bodice and to open the fastenings and she lay like marble with only the throbbing pulse giving the lie – showing that she was a real, live woman and not a statue.

ELIN

Elin started, dropping the towelling rag she was holding, when Mrs Struley marched into the kitchen demanding:

"Where is she? Where is that little hoyden?"

Elin continued wiping several pans. At least there was plenty of water fetched from the well by Peggy earlier. The housekeeper was cooking the evening meal and had used a great number of dishes; accordingly, she had asked Elin to rinse some of them out since there were more courses to prepare. Privately, Elin felt that enough food was laid across the table and lying in the cool larder to feed three times the number of people who were going to eat tonight, but she knew better than to contradict Mrs Jones. Now she was grateful to be able to turn her back on both women without being accused of incivility.

"Who are you talking about, Ma'am?" Elin wasn't fooled by Mrs Jones' question. Both she and the housekeeper knew the answer before it came!

"My sister, Mariana. I haven't seen her all day and the visitor who has just left…"

Elin heard the back door open and half swung around to see her mistress step inside the room. Her hair was tangled and untidy; her skirt was crushed and covered with horse hair and her bodice was creased. Elin was surprised to see her so dishevelled after a ride, albeit for an entire day. The maid sighed. There would be a lot of endless brushing and cleaning to be done tonight!

"Here we are!" Mariana announced. "I'm sorry we're late."

"You're not late, *cariad bach.*" There was affection in the housekeeper's voice. "*We're just about to finish the vegetables. Elin, are you done yet?"

Elin reached for a clean cloth and with a quick wipe placed the copper pans on the kitchen table within easy reach of the housekeeper, who was sitting on a stool, her sleeves rolled up, her complexion ruddy with the warmth from the fire. Only then did Elin dare to glance at Mrs Struley, who seemed to be swelling to double her size. Her face was puce and her bosom was heaving in agitation.

"May I have a word with you, in private, Mariana?" she demanded breathlessly.

"No. Anything you want to say to me you can say in front of Jonesey and Elin. They've known me all my life, haven't you?"

Elin lowered her gaze, feeling uncomfortable, and began to peel carrots with a passion. Mrs Struley had not been in the kitchen for many days – each morning she had ordered the carriage and been out until late afternoon – but during the last week Elin had overheard some very heated discussions between the two sisters and she did not want to be witness to any confrontation today. If only she could go somewhere else, but unexpectedly her legs wouldn't work. Oh, why had this domineering woman come to wreck the peace of this household? The object of her thoughts was continuing:

"I think it would better if I spoke to you alone. Not… not for my sake but for yours."

"Oh, hurry up, Margaret, and say your piece! Jack and I have been out all day and we've ridden far and I'm hungry and tired. I've already apologised for being late and I want to get changed and…"

"Very well, then." Mrs Struley's voice seemed high. Was she struggling to keep her wrath under control? Elin knew she had a temper. What could have happened to upset her like this? It wasn't as if Miss Mariana and she had been kept indoors by the rain, in each other's company, like the previous three days!

"I have had a visit from a Mr Bowen of Lan… Llan… Llanfair… Well, it doesn't matter where he comes from."

"I've never heard of him," returned Miss Mariana. Elin shrank inside and bent her shoulders over her task. Why did her mistress need to be rude?

"You may not have heard of him, my girl, but he has heard of you and your madcap rides across Anglesey. However, what he saw today made him get in his carriage and come all the way to see me."

Elin squinted at Miss Mariana from under her eyelashes and was surprised to see the other woman hang her head. What had she been up to? Something that even she knew she shouldn't have been doing, if her cowed posture was an outward sign of inward mortification. Then she tossed her snarled mane of hair and said defiantly:

"And what did he see, Margaret?"

"He… He saw you in the sea… entirely… utterly naked… bathing with no clothes on." Mrs Struley caught her breath but Elin couldn't decide if it was with embarrassment, indignation or choler.

Yet her mistress' response was puzzling, for Miss Mariana looked up with a faint smile on her lips. She seemed to have recovered some of her poise for she proclaimed:

"Poor Mr Bowen. Did it offend him to see me naked? Why did he watch then?"

"Watch! Watch! He was riding home from market and happened to glance down at the beach and there you were – parading your body for all to see. I'm disgusted…"

"You're wrong, Margaret! He couldn't possibly have been on his way from market. I was on a completely secluded beach and there's only one place you can see it from – I know for I have checked before – and that place leads to nowhere. No, I think that Mr Bowen is a man who likes peeping at others when they're…"

"Mariana! Have you no shame? No remorse? Don't blame Mr Bowen. Blame yourself for your very, very foolish behaviour. Where was your groom?"

"He wasn't with me. It was such a hot day, I chose to go to that very beach in order to swim and cool off. Anyway, if that's all, can I go and change now? Elin, will you come with me? When are we eating, Jonesey?"

Elin stared at her mistress. She had not been alone today. Yes, she had been without a groom, but Mr Jack had been with her. What had she been thinking to go bathing without any clothes on? It didn't surprise Elin to hear the accusation – she was aware Miss Mariana got up to all sorts of high-jinks – but not in male company. Had Mr Jack been swimming with her? And, if so, why had this Mr Bowen not observed him? Mrs Struley was angry enough and she didn't seem to know the half of it. Had she forgotten that Miss Mariana had told her already that she and Mr Jack had been out all day? Elin put down the vegetables and wiped her hands, ready to go and help her mistress dress for the evening meal, but she jumped again when Mrs Struley thundered:

"No! That is *not* all!" She blew out her breast like an angry cockerel. "Fortunately for you I managed to persuade Mr Bowen not to tell anyone else about your wanton behaviour, but I assured him that *I* would punish you and make sure that you didn't do it again."

Elin stepped towards the other young woman to put a restraining hand on her arm. She guessed that this comment would raise Miss Mariana's ire but she was too late for the shout came:

"Punish me? Punish me? I'm not a child and you, Margaret, are *not* my guardian." Miss Mariana took a deep breath before continuing in a steady voice, "So, if you will please excuse me."

Elin cringed when the older woman bellowed that she would not let her sister go. Why couldn't she perceive that tempers were high and things were going to be said that might be regretted? Mrs Struley was standing solidly between the table and fireplace. Was she not going to let the mistress past? Elin flung a plea-laden look for help to Mrs Jones but the housekeeper appeared to be totally engrossed in her cooking. Elin was surprised, for it was many a month since the senior servant had not had an opinion on a situation and expressed it forcefully!

"I have tried." Mrs Struley's tone was not conciliatory, although she was speaking less stridently. "I have really tried to turn a blind eye to your headstrong behaviour. I understand that you had no mother to guide you, but you did have a father – the same father that I had! I remember that he was always very strict with me. Therefore there can be no excuses for you to behave not simply like a hoyden – charging around the fields with no chaperone – but like a harlot – a prostitute! Baring her body to…"

Elin placed her hands on the table to steady herself from the shock. What was Mrs Struley doing using these inflammatory words? Yes, maybe, Miss Mariana should have been more careful in her choice of places to swim but to call her these specific names… This was going too far! Miss Mariana mirrored her thoughts when she commented, but now in a deadly calm voice.

"Harlot? Prostitute? I was only swimming in the sea."

Elin wanted to scream herself at this interfering woman, who had taken over the running of the Manor House unbidden, to stop the discourse there and then. Mrs Struley might not know Miss Mariana but *she* did and that quiet, controlled sentence spelled much more danger than any raised voices. However, Mrs Struley was ploughing on relentlessly:

"Yes, harlot! Flinging yourself at every man who you see, from… from a complete stranger who could… could be a common thief or murderer to… to your own… *And* you've ignored the man who loves you and would…?

"Harlot, Margaret? Why are you using that exact word? I thought harlots were women who…"

"I know what a harlot is! I was grown up and married when you were in your cradle! Yes, you're a harlot – a prostitute – a whore. Take your pick of which one you want! A whore who is prepared to give herself to anyone… Even her own…" Mrs Struley hesitated and Elin noticed that her eyes rolled upwards before continuing in a sly voice, "brother."

There was a moment of stunned silence.

"Brother?" Elin saw her own bewilderment reflected on her mistress' face. "I don't know what you are talking about, Margaret."

"I saw you." Margaret's hiss was spat across the room. "I saw you throw yourself at him and you with not a stitch on."

"Not a stitch on?" echoed Mariana. She took her eyes off her sister and encompassed Mrs Jones and Elin in an almost blank, ashen gaze.

"Well, only a thin shift between you. There was Edward, tired and… and a little bit drunk, but you weren't drunk, my girl! You knew what you were doing. I saw you rub your body against him, like a harlot, putting your arms around him… kissing him on the mouth."

"No!" shrieked Mariana. Her cry covered Elin's own whimper. Mrs Struley must have seen her the night *she* embraced the new master. "It's lies. Wicked lies! I never went near him! I wouldn't…"

Again Miss Mariana glanced around the kitchen from her sister's triumphant face to Mrs Jones' frightened one. Elin had felt all the blood run from her own cheeks and she stood motionless, battling with herself. She *must* own up and tell everyone what she had done. How she had met the master on the stairway and allowed herself to be embraced *and* how indeed she had returned his befuddled kiss. But she couldn't speak up. She couldn't confess. It wasn't just that she might be dismissed; she didn't want to share such a precious memory, hear it raked up and analysed and… While she was struggling to open her mouth and speak, her mistress moved a step towards Mrs Struley, saying almost inaudibly:

"You're a liar! I would never… I have never kissed my own brother like that! Why are you telling such tales?" She pushed her sister, apparently trying to pass by.

"It's no good denying it." Mrs Struley stood tall, her feet placed apart. "I saw you with my own eyes. On the last night he was here. But, it doesn't surprise me. It's just history repeating itself. I saw your mother too. She was kissing a man, in a corridor, in the dead of night, and it was not Father!

A bride of a month and there she was… with someone else. That's why I call you a harlot. Like mother, like daughter."

Elin watched in horror as Miss Mariana leapt at her sister, hitting at her with clenched fists and kicking.

"No! No! Don't you say that about my mother!"

Elin stood transfixed. One part of her mind knew she ought to go and pull her mistress away but another part of her was glad that this spiteful woman, who had upset Miss Mariana and all the servants, was getting what she deserved! Mrs Struley fell to the floor with the first rain of punches; either the unexpectedness of the attack or the weight of her slight sister half-flying through the distance between them had caught her off-guard.

Elin came out of her reverie at the same time as the other young woman. Maybe it was the blood bubbling from Mrs Struley's mouth – Elin understood Miss Mariana wasn't comfortable around blood still – or maybe her mistress had simply come to her senses. Elin sped around the table even as Miss Mariana ran from the room.

Elin was bending to help the injured woman who lay with her legs kicking like a beetle writhing on its back when Jack entered. He heaved Mrs Struley up and seated her on a chair.

"Elin, please fetch Miss Perrin." There was no doubting his authority. "Mrs Jones, have you a cloth?"

Elin moved nearly as fast as her mistress, skimming up the stairs two at a time. What was going to be the outcome of this? Mrs Struley was just one of many who had accused Miss Mariana of being a wild child and this latest blunder, for blunder it had been, only confirmed the accusations! She was a child! She had behaved worse than one of Elin's young brothers in a fury of frustration when he was denied something he wanted! She was wild! In fact, her behaviour had not been far from that of an untamed animal! Oh, what had happened today to make Miss Mariana lose her self-control like this?

JACK

Jack took the rag from the housekeeper and acknowledged the shrewd look he received with a nod. Mrs Jones' expression clearly said that she had known that the two sisters' different personalities would all end in violence.

He approached Margaret and gently pressed the scrap of linen into her shaking hands. Her whole body was trembling, her eyes were glazed and her lip was bleeding profusely. Jack recognised shock, but his pity was reduced by anxiety about Mariana. Impatience flared. Where was that wretched servant, Perrin?

"There, there," he soothed and was relieved to see the unspoken question answered. The skinny woman rushed to Margaret's side, disapproving clucks coming from under her breath.

"Here's Perrin," he went on, refraining from exclaiming "At last!" "Perrin, your mistress needs to rest. If you can take one arm, I'll take the other."

"I can manage her by myself," Perrin insisted haughtily. Jack noted, not for the first time, that the maid never addressed him as "Sir". He understood that both Margaret and Perrin were convinced he was a nobody! And maybe he was! If only he could recall the details of his past life.

"Very well," he responded politely. He was relieved. He was released to go and search for the other protagonist in this fight. He had overheard some of the conversation between the two sisters and privately felt that Margaret had asked for a beating. She was not badly injured, just stunned, but Jack was worried about Mariana and what she might do when she calmed down. It had been an exciting day for her and to come home to such charges would have made anyone lose their head!

He took the stairs, his strides jumping over every alternate step, with as much haste as Elin earlier.

His thoughts were filled with Mariana. She had given herself to him so willingly, so passionately. From the moment his lips had touched hers, he had lost himself in the moments which followed. Even when he pulled away from their embrace to whisper to her to remove her petticoats, when it should have been possible to break the spell, he was unable to overcome the enchantment. Yes, it flashed through his mind to stop, but when she rose from the sand, effortlessly, in one fluid movement to allow the rumpled materials to fall to the ground and to stand disrobed before his hungry eyes, his resolve melted! That was why he didn't move back from her or lift the yards of cotton to cover her. Instead he watched her rearrange her undergarments to make a more comfortable bed and then stand, just within his reach, her raven hair swaying below her waist, curving around her slender hips, peeping between her arms and body, wrapping about her like a cloud of silk. He feasted his eyes on her sensuous curves, desire coursing through his veins. Yes, he remembered, he had closed his eyelids fleetingly against this vision but she was imprinted on the inside of his eyelids. He must discontinue this madness, he had chided himself, but his will was no longer his own.

"Mariana," he murmured, "what a tiny waist you have! Look, I can put my hands right around it!"

He spread his strong, brown fingers across the taut softness of her belly and rained kisses on her velvet skin.

Thinking back, he recalled that she had appeared to know exactly what to do, although it was her first time! It wasn't many minutes before he was carrying her from the plains of desire to the hills of satisfaction and beyond to the very skies of ecstasy. What a willing pupil she had been to learn what heights of joy could be experienced by a man and a woman!

Only when they had flown to eternity together, only then had he reopened his eyes and for a brief second, his heart sounding against hers, their gaze interlocked, he had fixed the memory in his mind of their oneness. After that, he came to his senses abruptly and pulled away, re-buttoning his clothes hurriedly.

He tried to apologise but she would not hear of it. He sensed her rising to her feet behind him and she moved past him to walk to the glistening sea, with the grace of a cat. A black panther, naked and unashamed.

"Thank you, Jack, thank you." The breeze brought the words to his ears whilst he watched her go. She stood in the shallows, braiding her hair into two long plaits which she tied up together on the top of her head in a loose knot. Her bare behind and slender waist beckoned him again. He closed his eyes and groaned silently.

He shouldn't have done it! Now his desire was spent, he acknowledged that he shouldn't have done it. She might have told him that she had enjoyed it and she blatantly had (surely her body had been made for men to caress!) but he should have known better. He had taken women before (he understood that without having any individual remembrances) but she had lost her most precious possession and she didn't seem to care that it was gone! He should have paused and taken breath, being the older and more mature. One day she would marry and then would she regret today and would she learn to hate him for what he had done?

Jack stood up, smoothed out his crumpled clothes, and walked slowly to the other end of the sand to sit on a rock, lost in recriminations, cursing his stupidity and lack of control.

After her swim, Mariana had dressed and then slept on the coat he had left spread on the ground. He was aware of her, out of the corner of his eye, but he refrained from looking at her directly. Only when she had lain motionless for a while and he heard gentle snores did he, himself, venture into the sea. Swimming long and hard out from the bay had eased his conscience a mite.

Afterwards, he sat near her and he admitted to himself, as he watched her sleeping form, that he could never have resisted her womanly charms. Nevertheless, he tried again, when she awoke, to express his concerns. He stretched out a hand to assist her. Pulling her upright he kept hold of her fingers and enquired:

"Are you all right?"

She gazed up at him. Then, putting his bent knuckles to her lips for a light affectionate kiss, she remarked:

"I should be asking you that! It wasn't me who was ever upset."

"I hope I haven't spoilt you…" he began.

She placed her fingertips on his lips.

"Never, Jack," she flashed back with a grin. "You've opened a whole new world to me. And, now, when you go tomorrow, I shall always have this special day to remember you by. A seal to our friendship, eh?"

Jack had shaken his head then and he shook it again as he reached the door to her bedroom. What an unusual woman she was! And, yet, her assault on her sister gave the lie to her being unaffected by what had happened on the beach. After all, she was only young.

When a knock on the door brought no response, Jack turned the handle and entered the room. It was empty, but he saw, strewn on the floor, the clothes which he had removed so carefully earlier in the day. Immediately it came to him that she had dressed as a lad and gone. But where? He had better go and check the stables.

Whilst descending the stairs, he met Perrin, flattened beneath Margaret's ample form. Hardly could he believe that they had not reached the bedrooms yet; losing himself in his recollections appeared to have slowed time. He was forced to wait at the landing and watch their belaboured pace.

"I'm sure you'll feel much better once you're lying down," he remarked kindly, although it chafed him to be kept waiting.

"She won't get away with this," muttered Margaret.

"Are you thinking of going home?" asked Jack.

"Certainly not!" Apparently Margaret had recovered enough to be her usual tart self, he mused. He noticed that her lip had stopped bleeding but her dress was stained with brown. "I intend to write to Edward and inform him of his sister's behaviour. Quite obviously she needs to be disciplined. I would say a governess if she were a bit younger, but I myself have two grown-up sons and I know all about young people. So, when I feel better, I shall put my considerable experience into finding a solution to the problem, and come up with some way to change her ways."

Jack opened his mouth to exclaim that could not she see that she was only aggravating the problem, but decided to keep his opinions to himself. Mariana and her whereabouts were much more important than arguing with this obdurate woman.

On entering the kitchen, Elin and Mrs Jones both chimed together: "How is she?"

"She's not there, I'm afraid."

"I knew it!" Mrs Jones was the first to speak. "*Cariad bach*! She's run away to hide for a while. Elin, do you know where she goes?"

"No." Elin shook her head. "Thomas might have known but he's not here."

"Don't you worry," reassured Jack. "I'll go and have a look for her. She can't have got far."

"She must have slipped out the front and along the beach." Mrs Jones heaved her bulky body up from the chair with a moan.

"I'll just check the stables. There's no point setting out on foot if she's on horseback," reasoned Jack, walking towards the pantry. Elin followed him out, whispering, "Are you aware Miss Mariana sometimes dresses in boy's clothing?"

"Yes."

"Oh, Sir!" the maid exclaimed. "You're a good man! Find her and bring her home. That wicked woman shouldn't have said all those things. Miss Mariana loved her mother."

Jack was surprised to see the stable-yard exactly as he had left it, untouched by the fervour raging inside the Manor House. He crossed the cobbles he had recently traversed to find Evan in the process of feeding the horses. He saw that Mars was in his stall.

"Everything in order?" he checked with the lad.

"Yes, Sir." Evan gave him a questioning look.

Jack gave no reply but strode from the stables. He had a fair notion where Mariana had gone: Holyhead Mountain. However, it was quite a step from here and he had only ever been on horseback, but surely she couldn't be far ahead of him. If he hastened he would catch her…

Yet, there was no sign of a slight, scruffy boy in the near or far distance. Of course, Jack realised that there were several paths and he couldn't be sure which one she had taken. He was forced to follow the way they had ridden on previous occasions.

He covered the miles at a fast pace, but was dismayed to see how quickly the sun was heading towards its demise; it would soon be dark. Nevertheless, he comforted himself, the light might remain because the sky was cloudless. He was hungry now. It had been a long while since their meal on the beach. Mariana must be famished too.

With the passing journey, his wounds began to ache and he cursed himself for not bringing a horse. Then, when he found her, they could have ridden back together. He hesitated but then decided that he had come too far to go back and collect a ride.

He remained convinced that Mariana must be heading for the mountain, even when he enquired of a lone woman and later a group of children if they had seen a lad pass this way and all had shaken their heads in reply. He was certain she would have gone there, for he had only been talking to her about her hideaway this morning. The earlier part of the day seemed a lifetime away!

Once he reached the lower slopes of his destination, he slowed, shortening his strides to adjust to the ascent. Still there was no evidence of her. She must have raced along for him not to have caught her up or maybe, he thought, she had travelled along a different route.

When he arrived at the summit, he was assaulted by the wind. Strange, he mused, there had been no breeze earlier. He paused at the top to scan the view. The quiescent sea was lilac, reflecting the colourful sunset. On its flat surface was a small fleet of fishing boats out for the night and near the shore he noticed a ship with her enormous sails flapping lazily in the new air currents: a schooner bound for Ireland, perhaps. He felt a stirring of memory but it faded when he acknowledged it and he turned his mind to find his quarry.

Suddenly he had to be careful not to fall, for the dusk tricked his straining eyes. There was no path this side of the headland and it was difficult to see where to put his foot on the pitted ground. He hoped he could remember the exact place Mariana had taken him. He knew he would not be able to see her, if she was here, because her shelter was a narrow cave, facing west with a sloping roof which hid it from above. Then he recognised a peculiar boulder shaped like a human skull. Yes, he was going the right way. He climbed past it and lost his footing, sending a shower of loose pebbles bouncing down the slope into the sea. He clutched at a nearby outcrop and steadied himself. He must go slower and watch he did not topple over, because the cliffs descended in a perpendicular drop to the rocks and waves below. No one would survive if they fell.

"Mariana," he called. Without warning he was fearful for her. Would she have fallen? No, she was too surefooted but she had been distressed. Would it have made her careless? "Mariana, it's me, Jack."

There was no reply except several shrieks from gulls flying overhead.

Jack scrambled the last part partially on hands and knees, but it was not until he stood right at the entrance of the hollow that he saw the object of his search. She was huddled against the very back of the cave.

"Go away!" She greeted him with a scowl. "Leave me alone. I want to be alone."

Jack stepped across the final granite and bent down. The hidey-hole was no more than four feet high and about the same width. He suspected that Mariana could almost have lain down in it lengthways, but he wouldn't have been able to do so. More a shelter than a cave. He knelt and stretched out a hand towards her but she slapped it away. He turned around carefully and sat next to her, not touching her, his knees bent, his spine to the stone face. He was glad to have found her safe but said nothing.

"What do you want?" Mariana mumbled finally.

"I'm not going home without you, so I thought I'd wait here, in the relative warmth, away from the wind, until you are ready to return. Do you mind?"

"Yes, I do," she growled. "I've told you. I want to be alone."

"Well, one can't always have what one wishes in life."

His companion turned away from him, folding her body into a tight ball, her face buried in the cloth of her breeches, her forehead pressed on to her knees.

Jack closed his eyes. By God he was hungry! He hoped she would be prepared to come soon. The minutes passed and the last of the light disappeared.

"It's not true, you know." Mariana's voice was muffled.

"Pardon. I didn't catch what you said."

She lifted her head and repeated herself.

"I wasn't there, Mariana, so I'm not sure what you're talking about." Jack wanted her to express her feelings out loud.

"She'll have told you... told you why I ran away."

"No, sweetheart. She, if she is your sister, doesn't even know that you've gone."

"She deserved it. The things she said."

"What did she say?" Jack wasn't going to admit that he had heard some of the argument.

"You must know," she persisted. "Mrs Jones... Mrs Jones will have told you and Elin... and they will have embroidered it all, to paint my face blacker."

"What a mixture of metaphors! Nobody has told me anything." He explained how he had found Margaret, helped her up, handed her over into the servant's care and then, discovering Mariana's bedchamber empty, had worked out that she had fled and pursued her here. "I assume that you attacked your sister physically instead of verbally this time. However, you, yourself, will have to enlighten me as to what exactly passed between you."

Whilst she related the nasty accusations about her mother that Margaret had thrown at her, he took the opportunity to put his hand on her knee, in sympathy. She placed her small, pale, cold hand on top of his and let her fingers slide between his to grip them. Thus entwined, he encouraged her to say how she felt and wasn't surprised at her hostility towards Margaret. He did hush her when he heard wild emotion rising in her voice and was glad when she said drily:

"She called me a harlot too, but, strangely I didn't mind that, for it seemed funny that... that she didn't know. She didn't realise that we... we'd ... what we had done together. Some prim old man had seen me swimming in the sea with no clothes on. When she began her lecture I thought she was going to say that he'd seen us... us together. But he hadn't! He must have come along too late for that! He didn't even see you. It's quite droll really. At first, I just wanted to burst out laughing that she was so upset that I was naked. If only she'd known what... what... But then she said that I'd kissed... kissed..."

Mariana halted before continuing in a rush, "She said that I had kissed my brother, Edward. You know, a proper kiss. But I hadn't! Never! I wouldn't! He's my brother! It's horrible to think of that. She'd made all that up to... to..."

"To what? Why do you think she accused you of that?"

"Oh, Jack, I don't know. I really don't know."

"Shall I tell you a secret?"

"What?"

"No, I'll only tell if you come near me."

"Near you?"

"Yes, it's been a long time since I felt you near me and I've missed you." He spoke deliberately in a bantering tone. "Anyway, it's damned chilly now."

Mariana slid sideways until he had his arm around her. He pulled her closer, saying:

"That's better. You feel different in boy's clothes. I think I prefer you as a woman."

"Am I a harlot?"

"Certainly not! I didn't pay you, did I?"

Mariana gave a nervous laugh before demanding to hear his secret. He explained that Edward had mumbled something about meeting an angel on the stairs on his way up to bed on his last night at the Manor House. He reckoned Edward must have met Elin, and Mariana quickly agreed, telling him that her maid had been downstairs in the kitchen crying that evening. He had to reassure his young friend that he didn't reckon that the tears could have been because Edward had hurt Elin. Then he clarified why he thought Margaret had made the accusation.

"You don't look alike in the daytime, in your usual dress, but, at night, with your shifts on, your hair loose, in the darkness, anyone might be mistaken."

"Yes, it must be true."

"But, wait, Mariana. We don't know for sure! You'd better not badger Elin for details. Leave it be. She may even come and tell you herself."

"Poor Elin. She must have been very frightened when she heard my sister say that. But, what about Margaret? I must tell her it wasn't me. I must convince her and the only way to do that is if Elin admits…"

Jack spent the next few minutes advising her not to try to clear her name. He argued that Margaret would never believe her, even if witnesses could be provided. And neither of the other women were likely to repeat the story. Even when Mariana brought up Edward, Jack effortlessly dismissed the idea that her brother would even remember the incident. Subsequently, then Mariana turned her worries to her mother but Jack replied that it was his understanding that her mother's reputation was far too irreproachable to be affected by Margaret's libellous charges before warning:

"You must look after your own reputation. You have no need to defend your mother. It's obvious that Margaret is watching you and is determined to upset you. Now, please, can we go? My insides are rumbling and it's just about dark. We must be very careful we don't fall."

"Oh, Jack!" she cried. "I can't face Margaret tonight."

"You won't have to. She's gone to bed."

Holding hands, they climbed from their hole. Immediately they were buffeted by the wind and they squinted in the darkness. They were particularly cautious until they reached the top of the slope and were past the danger. They paused briefly to watch the very last smudges of light towards Ireland and then they set off done the path, remaining aware that they could slip and sprain an ankle, but somehow relieved that they were not above a sheer drop to the rocks. They smelt the heather and the salt blowing from the sea as they hurried towards home, hunger driving all thought from their minds.

Once they reached their own private beach, Mariana stopped.

"I can't go in," she whispered.

"Now, Mariana, I've promised you. She's in bed."

"There's a light from her window. She's still awake. What if she comes down?"

He shook his head but before he could speak, she entreated, "Oh, Jack, don't go in the morning. I can't face her tonight, but I can't face her in the morning either. Not on my own."

"I have already considered that I might not depart tomorrow. However, when you meet her, whether tomorrow or tonight, hold your head up high. Her accusations were unfounded. Let her feel your strength. She's too used to beating you. You've got strength inside you – let it out – show it. I don't mean in bad temper. No, put away your childhood. You did that today, anyway. Treat her with disdain – as though her denouncements are so non-believable that they're not worth troubling with. Don't let her see…"

"Can I go in alone? Then I can pretend… Wait! What am I thinking of? My clothes! I must climb the roof."

Jack grinned.

"I'd forgotten too! Yes, go up and pretend you've been in your room all the time, if you meet her."

"Do I have to apologise?"

"I would, if you possibly can bring yourself to do so. Just say that you forgot yourself and are really sorry. She'll *have* to forgive you then, at least outwardly. Then it'll be her turn to apologise to you for all those horrible things she said."

"She'll never do that!"

"Probably not, but your conscience won't simply be clear, people will also be on your side. If she doesn't say sorry, you'll be the wronged person but if *you* don't, then she'll have been wronged. Do you see? Sorry, I didn't mean to lecture you!"

"Oh, you're so clever. Please don't leave me tomorrow! How will I cope without you?"

"Very well, I should think. You've got plenty of character inside you. Strong character. Anyway, I must go to pick up my new horse first in the morning. Then we shall see. No more talk. Remember that you are easily a match for your sister, but you don't have to prove it by fighting with your fists. You once said to me that you wanted to be yourself. Well, be yourself. Be strong. Be determined and courageous. Don't let anyone bully you. You are a grown woman. A woman, not a child."

"Jack?"

Mariana slipped within his arms again. He returned the embrace but didn't speak. Silently he handed her up on to the roof and made his way around to the kitchen to assure the anxious servants that the prodigal had returned.

CUTLAND

Matthew Cutland began to curse this day. He had travelled to Bangor on a coach, not soon after sunrise, but there had been no return carriage and he had been forced to climb out at the village on the edge of Anglesey, instead of being carried to Holyhead where he had made his start. Now these last few miles were proving tiresome; his boots were soaking wet and beginning to rub and his chest ached.

He couldn't blame himself for the state of his boots; he had not expected to have to use them for a prolonged trek and he hadn't considered the state of the roads for walking! It had not rained today – his entire journey and sojourn in the town had been bathed in sunshine and tonight the sky remained clear with the promise of more good weather tomorrow, although there were a few wisps of cloud high above him. Nonetheless, because of the previous three days the tracks were filled with puddles and treacherous mud and it was hard to find any dry earth to tread on. It would be good to arrive home, have Pearl pull off the sodden leather and then he could place his feet on the fender of a welcome fire!

All the same, he was surprised that he felt so extremely breathless because he would have described himself as a fit man, walking everywhere and the road was straight and flat ahead of him. Therefore why was he out of breath as if he was climbing a hill? His knowledge of medicine meant that he knew the answer but mostly he wouldn't admit it even to himself: he was getting older and his heart was weakening. He had noticed his ankles swelled and he had a persistent cough that wouldn't shift even in the summer months.

Of course there had been other factors today that could be causing this pain. Apart from having an early start and journeying over thirty miles to reach his destination, he had been angry and disappointed this morning. In fact, he had come quite close to reproaching the man whom he had contacted, whom he knew only as Frideric from the city of Cologne lying on the River Rhine in Germany. He knew that reining in his temper would not help his condition. He sighed. What he ought to do was return to his house, *Tŷ Craig*, and encourage Pearl to cook him his favourite meal – mutton and rice – whilst he put his toes to the warmth of the flames and then rest in bed until he felt better, but he still had tasks to do. He wouldn't even enter his home but take his small boat out on the water straightaway.

Many months ago, his intelligent brain had registered what his body was trying to tell him, although he pushed away its gloomy prognostications when he was active. It was only when he was tired and bruised from relating to others that the truth of the situation would conquer his self control over the denial.

If he didn't slow down and rest more then he wouldn't be for this world much longer. He wasn't worried about what occurred after death; he knew all that happened to the body from his years of being a ship's surgeon but the soul… He had learnt what many of the religions taught but he found himself hoping in the belief in the transmigration of souls – reincarnation. He favoured coming back in a higher form, hopefully. He had tried all his life to help others, surely he wouldn't return as an ant or a worm! No, his anxiety was for Pearl. What would happen to her? She would have plenty of material wealth but she had no one who could live with her. No relatives and certainly no friends apart from himself! Would she return to her native country or would she live in splendid isolation here in North Wales? Would she be happy or would the loneliness get to her in the end? She seemed very content during the hours he was out of the house – busy with housewifely tasks – but he believed that there was a big difference between filling the time until the one you loved came back and living completely without others' company. He *must* address this matter in his own mind and then talk to her about the future; he was being rather selfish not to mention it but it was all part of his denying the facts that…

Matthew's thoughts skittered to a halt as his aching legs did the same. He stood in the middle of the potholed road and squinted. What was that in the shadows just ahead? Someone crouching, ready to spring out at him and rob him? He had his answer immediately when he heard:

"There was a bold lass from Llanfair…"

He knew that voice! It was Owen Lewis from the Manor House and it sounded as if he had downed one too many pints. Matthew shook his head; he hadn't known that Owen couldn't hold his drink. The quavery music came from the supine man who was waving a glass jar that glinted in the moonlight.

Matthew moved forward. He would help him; it wouldn't do him any good to stay out lying on the soggy ground all night, even if there were no clouds to wet him again! But, what was he doing here, several miles away from his cottage? Perhaps he had not wanted to visit the local public house in case he was recognised. Yet, here he was, unable to traverse the distance home. He had put himself in danger – albeit unwittingly. Matthew had always believed that the groom at the Manor House was steady and reliable.

Of course, Matthew acknowledged to himself, Owen's circumstances might call for a need to dampen reasoned thought; he could have been drinking to forget his daily life. The man's wife was not just dying but had been on the brink of departing for months and months and that might drive anyone to the bottle! Matthew had been sent for many times with a "Please come 'cos she's taking her last breath!" Bridget's now famous last breaths appeared to be normal breaths for her! Surely this continued waiting meant that there was no closure for Owen and his children in the situation. Week by week, day after day, Owen would have to continue to do his regular jobs whilst living on tenterhooks that today might be the day when his wife of twenty years would leave him. Even if their love was ardent – and Matthew understood that it was – there might be a feeling of needing to get the death over with just to relieve the tension; in order that he could start to grieve and learn to live without her. Matthew had heard that recently he had been asked to be the young Squire's steward – maybe it was this that had pushed him over the edge and why he had faltered by the side of the path with only an empty bottle for company.

Matthew had seen scores of men fall prey to the poison of alcohol. Perhaps the first drink was taken to overcome despair, low self-esteem, or a trauma. Of course the lift of spirits and feeling of being in control and full of hope and optimism – all self-doubt fading – truly happened and the second glass was quickly ordered. The sweet juice could beckon seductively. Soon the person would be free of inhibitions and convinced that all was well, so why hasn't anyone called for another round? Hard on its heels comes euphoria and sentimentality descends and the coarse jokes and songs begin and here was proof of it, lying in the ditch in the prostrate form of this sorry part of humanity. Of course Matthew had seen many turn aggressive and belligerent when the alcohol depressed those enthusiastic beliefs of wellbeing of an hour ago. With buoyant spirits lowered, often the drinker would reason that, rather than quit, the best solution was to down another pint! Ah, but the repercussions would come in the morning, or earlier if a fight started. Better to get Owen home and safely in his bed before anyone else found him and cuts and bruises were added to any the fall had incurred, or hurtful words said, causing long-lasting wounds of the soul – so much more difficult to heal.

Matthew strode towards the other man and pulled him from the ditch whilst several saucy verses of the song rang out into the night. They were sheltered here by a bluff of land but Matthew had felt the sharp wind earlier.

He coaxed the weak man to his feet and put an arm around him to support him. It was several minutes before Owen had finished his drunken ditty and said with a slur:

"Much obliged to you, Mr Cut… Cut… Cutlass. Seemed to have lost my footing back there. Got to get back and see to Bridget. She's not well, y'know."

Matthew spoke gently to him and urged him not to drag his legs, but their progress was slow and it must have been past midnight before he had delivered his charge into the tender care of his son, Evan, and trudged back to his own house.

Matthew hesitated at the door, tiredness almost overwhelming him, debating whether to go in and sleep for a couple of hours before rising and sailing out to the little cove a mile off. However, shaking himself back to wakefulness, he resolved to get his task done before retiring for the night. He guessed that his young common law wife would already be abed and it wouldn't be fair to disturb her twice.

The boat launched, he clambered in, rearranged the oars and began to row out from his own harbour to the open sea, where he hoped the canvas would catch the breeze and save his fatigued arms. The moon's brightness was hidden behind crocheted strands of pearly cloud but the wind high up kept the holey blanket moving along and Matthew could see quite clearly.

With half an ear cocked for the arrival of Lloyd, he had just paused to catch his breath when he heard the creak of another vessel. Quickly he turned his dinghy towards the shelter of the jagged coastline of rocks, feathered his oars and peered out across the water. Coming from the direction of the Manor House was a boat, heavily laden, lying low in the water. The single oarsman seemed to be struggling to make headway.

Barely did Matthew have time to wonder where this craft was going when another man sat up with a groan which was clearly audible across the distance. Matthew hunched over but no one appeared to have observed him, despite a flash of broad moonlight when the wisps of clouds parted.

Matthew could make out that both occupants were stockily built and the rower had a beard, but their clothes were not easily identifiable as fisherman's smocks. He decided they looked like common sailors and the second crony, who had been lying down, was now clutching his left arm and moaning. The breeze carried their words and Matthew heard him say:

"I'll help."

"Don't be stupid, lad! I can manage."

"We'll never make it! The bloody sod took too long to show up," complained One Arm.

"Don't you worry! The Cap'n won't leave without us for this cargo's special."

Matthew heard no more because the boat disappeared behind a bluff of rock. Nevertheless his curiosity was aroused; what was this 'special cargo'? With his tiredness magically gone, he dipped the oars into the waves and skimmed powerfully in their wake. He decided he dare not hoist the sail; he didn't want to be detected. On the other hand he didn't want to lose them. After all, he knew that there were plenty of narrow creeks in this area where a small shallop could hide! He had explored many of them with the purpose of eluding that fox Lloyd!

Skirting the corner, he felt the pull of the current give added speed to his chase. Fortuitously they weren't too far ahead; their progress was ponderous. He glanced over his shoulder warily. Now he feared that he might catch them up. He held back, resting momentarily. He trusted that the sculler would be concentrating too hard to notice him; One Arm had his back to Matthew but presumably he was too preoccupied with his injuries to turn around.

Along the coast they went. Matthew conjectured that this yawl had a rendezvous with a larger vessel and he could guess where the latter was berthed! There was only one inlet where a tall masts could disappear from view and it was only about a furlong further. A good navigator was needed to keep the ship from going aground in the restricted entrance but Matthew had chanced upon a few vessels moored out of sight.

Aware that he would be discovered if he went up the creek itself, he moored his own craft a short way before the hiding place and crept, half bent, across the rocks and up a rough sandy hillock. He was in time to see the boat reach its mother ship. A rope was thrown upwards to be caught by willing hands and secured and wood scraped wood.

Matthew knelt in his vantage point and pulled his coat around his shoulders; the wind had picked up again. Fortunately there was light coming from the decks of the ship and he observed with interest. Was the 'special cargo' in boxes or sacks? he mused.

Much to his surprise the first thing unloaded was neither of these but another person – male by all accounts wearing breeches and shirt – unconscious or dead – limp and quite difficult to manhandle. No wonder the oarsman had struggled so much to propel them along and it explained why the yawl had lain low in the water. One Arm was pulled aboard and then two sailors climbed down to help manoeuvre the body up the barnacled side and into the arms of several other seamen. Matthew's surgeon eyes noticed the dark patches on the pale clothes of the injured man, clearly visible. Surely the fellow was still alive (although they were bumping him upward unceremoniously) or they would have ditched his body sooner and lightened the load in the boat! Confirmation came with the words:

"Watch his head, Bancroft! We don't want him dead!"

Matthew sighed. His hands itched to go and attend to the stricken man. He wished they would hurry up and bring forth the 'special cargo'. There must have been quite a fight to secure it with two of the party succumbing to such horrendous wounds. Matthew surmised that a blade or two had been drawn from beneath the cloth of jacket or trouser belt. And what could have happened to the hapless individual who had not wanted to part with the 'special cargo'? Probably he was lying somewhere, fatally wounded or dead already.

Matthew stood slowly, using the nearby rock as a lever. He kept his head bent and hurried back to his own boat. He was none the wiser despite the strenuous work of following, but at least now he could use the wind to carry him to his own destination before the entire night was over. He sighed again and wearily hoisted the familiar sail.

MARIANA

Mariana looked up from the food on her plate at the two other people who were in the room. They were absorbed in conversation and, not for the first time, Mariana wondered why it was *she* who had received the proposal of marriage.

Abruptly the Vicar and Margaret stopped talking.

"Miss Mariana?" frowned the Vicar.

"Is your food all right?" Margaret asked, taking a massive mouthful of pheasant herself.

"Yes, quite all right." Mariana nodded. "I simply have made my decision about… about… I have an answer for you, Parson, and the answer is 'Yes'."

She spoke in a quiet but clear voice, although her heart wept at the announcement. She could hardly believe that she had just agreed to marry the Parson. Oh, Jack, where are you? Why did you leave me?

Mariana ignored the uproar her words had produced and allowed her thoughts to float back to the day after her argument with Margaret. So many momentous events had happened that day that she could scarcely take in that it had only been six weeks ago. Yet the event that overshadowed everything else concerned Jack.

Jack.

Jack. Was it really six weeks since she had seen him? What marvellous truths he had taught her during his brief stay at *Trem-y-Môr*! Henry's death had changed her; there was no doubt about that. Her father's demise had brought her to her senses but, looking back at the past year, she had to acknowledge that it was Jack who had changed her the most. It was he who had introduced her to the delights of passion and it was he who had urged her to be herself. She had tried to take his advice and that in itself had made her a different person. However, more than these new experiences, he had given her something that would alter the whole course of her life.

When she had arisen the morning after that disturbing day, she had had no idea of what was before her. Yet did one ever know what lay ahead?

No. She had not divined that Henry was going to die, although she had experienced a feeling of dread when she had seen the storm approaching. Several months later she had not anticipated or worried that her father was on the threshold of heaven. She had not foreseen what her relationship with Jack would do. Was God really in charge, which was what the church taught, or was it all chance or fate?

She submerged herself in memories.

* * *

Mariana stretched her arms above her head and then in one movement threw off the bed covers and leapt out of bed. She would go for a ride and trust that she could get out of the house before Margaret made an appearance. Probably Jack wouldn't accompany her – he would be busy with his preparations for buying his new horse. She slipped down the back stairs, certain she would not meet her sister on the way, and flung open the door to the kitchen.

The room was still, with no Mrs Jones bustling about with pans cooking the first meal of the day; no Elin preparing bacon patiently; no Peggy running and fetching for the housekeeper; and no Biddy carrying water. Everyone appeared to have absconded, including the mongrel (who should have been trotting on the wheel to turn the meat), except for young Kate.

Soon Mariana discovered that Owen's wife, Bridget, had died during the night. All thoughts of riding fled from her and she determined to visit the cottage herself. However, she bumped into Elin when she turned to leave and just behind her came Hugh, the post-boy.

Hugh the Post, as he was affectionately known, came often to *Trem-y-Môr* and he was no boy but a mature man in his fifties. Sir William, the old Squire, had received many letter and packages, but Mariana understood that, more importantly, with the Manor House being on the main road to Holyhead, Hugh would often call in empty-handed, to pump Mrs Jones for gossip.

Mariana was aware that Hugh was a widower, whose only daughter lived twenty miles away, and that possibly he used his job to put off the moment of returning home to what Mariana guessed must be stark and empty rooms. Mariana didn't begrudge him time in the bustling kitchen on a cold winter's day or a refreshing glass of ale on a hot summer's morning. She suspected he knew all about her strange behaviour of talking to Henry. Of course, he had met Jack and had been regaled with the circumstances of the stranger's arrival, the extent of the wounds and subsequent convalescence. Mariana was sure that Hugh hadn't stayed long to chatter the morning of Jack's arrival and the demise of her father! She speculated that Hugh might have been reluctant to pass on any more than the bare facts of the Squire's death, because of his respect for Sir William, but a mysterious man who had lost his memory... *that* story could have been embroidered from household to household, with more and more embellishments with each telling! Notwithstanding, Hugh had set up his own private investigations about the identity of Jack; all had yielded nothing.

When her brother had ridden in, with his lost leg and tales of the war, Mariana understood that tongues had wagged and who better to supply both fact and fiction of Edward's youth, and his infatuation with his beautiful stepmother, than the post-boy! Hugh had a sharp memory and anything he couldn't recall, Mrs Jones would be sure to fill in the lost details. Of course, Hugh had been one of the few who had met Edward before his hasty departure to London a couple of months ago and would therefore be in a position to answer questions about the new Sir Rowlands. Standing just outside the kitchen one morning, Mariana had overheard Hugh repeating what might be a common statement: "It's a wicked shame that the manor has been left in the hands of that Lewis! What does he know about stewarding?" She could see that this was a widespread opinion! Yet, Owen Lewis had been doing such a steady job. How would his wife's death affect his concentration? The question flashed through her thoughts.

And then there was her sister, Margaret, and the frequent visits of the Vicar to the Manor House. Mariana had no difficulty believing that this had generated much speculation. It was true that in some parishes there was a close friendship between the incumbent and the lord of the manor but not in *this* parish! Mariana understood that a rumour had gone around that Margaret was a widow but Hugh would have put everyone right about this. Mrs Jones wouldn't have held back in telling the post-boy all about Margaret's sick husband, Walter, and probably how disruptive her sister had been to the housekeeper's domain and routines! Mariana surmised that Hugh the Post knew more than one cared for him to know about all the households he visited and the Manor House was no exception! And here he was with the long-awaited letter from Edward. At least, that's what she hoped it would be; she couldn't quite make out the handwriting from this distance.

Mariana took the travel-stained paper, and disappeared upstairs to her own bedchamber, leaving Elin, no doubt, to give the man all the information about Bridget's passing away. Mariana reassessed her plans: she wouldn't ride today, after all. She flung off her habit, impatiently surveying the worn paper all the while. She supposed she could have saddled her own mount – surely all the stable boys would be supporting their grieving father on this sad day – but she was desperate to read what her brother had written and she needed privacy and time straightaway before she was interrupted. She did pause to choose a dress that she liked but then hastily dressed whilst her mind whirled round and round.

She saw that the letter was addressed to both herself and Margaret, but since her sister had not come downstairs for the day yet (if she had, Mariana was sure that her voice demanding attention would have been heard all over the house), she would open it and take any consequences of this flouncing of courtesy by explaining that she had been unable to find her sister. This excuse meant it would be circumspect to leave the house altogether in case, with the irregularity of the servants' behaviour today, Margaret came knocking on her door.

Mariana fled to the beach. During the time it took to walk right to the end of the sand, she reflected on the news about Bridget. If she was honest with herself, she wasn't that upset, only perchance for the relatives left behind and in particular the smaller children. Not only had there been too many deaths recently but this one had been expected and long overdue and this seemed to dull the grief.

Mariana sat near the water's perimeter and stared at the writing on the letter resting on her knees. It didn't look like Edward's hand. She tore open the seal and confirmed that the name at the end was indeed that of her brother. However, he had penned no more than ten lines and she frowned with disappointment. To have waited an age for such meagre information! It started with an apology for the length of time he had taken to tell them where he was staying in London. It went on to say that he had been dangerously ill with fever. That at least explained the handwriting! He gave his address and wrote that so far he was no further in finding out about his orders from Admiral Humphries because he had been too weak to visit him. He sent his love to all in the household and said he would write again when he knew anything more.

Mariana looked up from the single sheet. What did I expect? she scolded herself. He had promised to inform her of his whereabouts, which he had fulfilled, and the illness explained the delay and made her ashamed of all the cursing she had done about him, believing him to be unfaithful and callous. She shook her head, recalling the days of waiting and fretting, peering into the distance for the arrival of Hugh the Post or anyone else. All this time Edward had been languishing in his sick bed, conceivably tossing and turning at his inability to contact his family, rather than selfishly getting on with his own business with all thought of his sister and her fears forgotten!

Mariana allowed an image of Edward to settle before her and then she refocused on fine sand, her eyes perceiving something left on the beach. What was that? A bloody rag lying on the golden grains. Mariana slipped the letter into her pocket. She was wearing one of her favourite outfits: a pale, buttercup yellow gown. She knew it suited her and it gave her confidence to wear it. She needed to feel indomitable this morning since she had to face her sister. Suddenly she was glad that the message from Edward had arrived today – it could be her excuse to visit Margaret's bedchamber. Then she could mumble her apologies swiftly and be away.

She stood up and walked towards the object that had attracted her attention. It was indeed a blood stained rag. She picked it up and fingered it. How had it got here? It could not have been washed up by the returning tide because the red stain would have soaked away in the waves. It looked more like a piece of a petticoat or shirt, not a handkerchief – its edges were too uneven. It was a torn piece of cloth but hardly a pad to be used by women once a month or in the kitchen for the pans! Who had been prowling on this beach, leaving parts of their clothing here? Mariana tossed her head and dropped the cloth; then she bent to retrieve it. She would ask some of the others; someone else might have seen something. It went in her other pocket.

Plodding back to the house, she rehearsed what she was going to say to Margaret. It wasn't the first time she had done this; she had lain awake for part of the night thinking about her outburst. She accepted it was wicked to have hit her sister and therefore she would have to seek a pardon if she was ever going to relate to Margaret again, and herein lay the rub. Yes, the crux of the matter was that if only she could *never* see the woman again then there would be no need to apologise. She felt that she had been sorely provoked and there might even be a case that she and her mother had been wronged. She really hated her sister and her dear wish was to run away or avoid meeting her in the Manor House.

Where could she go? She had pondered and pondered. She had thought about Edward and then about Penelope but rejected going to them – not least with respect to the former since last night she had no idea where her brother was living! She had wondered briefly if Margaret would be affronted enough to pack her bags and return home but concluded that her sister was far too stubborn to abandon any plans she was devising because of her younger sister!

No, Mariana's common sense had told her that it was impossible to dream that she would never see her sister again. Therefore, she must face reality and beg her pardon. Initially this course of action had offended her and, after much tossing and turning, she had determined that she would say the words with her lips but not in her heart. Years of attendance at church had taught her that this was a sin, but what could she do? After all, she hated the woman and that was a transgression too!

She had come to the end of her inner turmoil by deciding that to make life bearable for everyone in the household she would say sorry. Notwithstanding, in the meantime, she would revive her efforts to force her sister to leave. Her friendship with Jack had lulled her into thinking that there was no need for Margaret to go, but now there was no excuse for her to stay, with Jack's imminent departure. Mariana found the anticipated sorrow in losing Jack was alleviated with the thought that Margaret would be losing her reason for remaining at *Trem-y-Môr*.

Also, in those quiet night-time hours, Mariana had resolved never to allow herself to be in a position where someone could make her lose her temper like that again. The consequences were too humiliating.

In truth the actual moment of contrition was not as bad as Mariana had imagined. Margaret's face was blue this morning from the bruises that Mariana herself had inflicted on her and her lip was swollen, red and ugly. Mariana's remorse when she first saw her sister enabled her to speak the words without stumbling or stammering. Added to this the look of surprise on Margaret's face eased her embarrassment; clearly Margaret had not been expecting an apology.

A second to hand over Edward's letter and she was on the brink of escaping. Margaret's eyes blazed briefly – presumably because the missive was already opened – but nothing was said and then miraculously Mariana found herself outside the room with the ordeal over. She fancied that the next time she encountered her sister would be easier and each subsequent time would put her one step further away from both the fight and its inevitable necessary penance.

At last Mariana was at peace. She made her way to Jack's room and knocked. She did not expect him to be there since he had told her that he was going to fetch his new horse, but she wanted to relate to him how she had acted upon his advice. A glance around the door confirmed the room was empty. Why had she not thought to ask if she could accompany him? She stood in the doorway. Laid across the quilt was his coat. How strange that his bed should be made already! She had never known him pull up the sheets, and surely no servant had started in this chamber on a morning such as this! Had he not slept here? Had he gone into the village to find… not a woman, please God? Yet what else would tempt him to stay away all through the dark hours? He had spent every night here as far as she knew. Of course, usually, she would be in his company for the evening but last eve Elin had brought up some food for her on a tray; afterwards she had blown out the candle and tried to sleep.

Mariana quitted the desolate room. Thus began an anxious journey around the Manor House. Elin was questioned after Mariana had to wait whilst Perrin bore away a substantial repast for Margaret to consume upstairs. More precious minutes were lost whilst she had to wait to answer Elin's tentative questions about whether the letter said that her brother was returning to North Wales soon. Crossing the yard, Mariana decided that she should write to her brother and inform him of Bridget's death. He wouldn't get here in time for the funeral. It might make him realise that the estate needed him here. Then her thoughts returned to Jack and his whereabouts. She checked all parts of the stable and was on her way to Owen's house when she met the housekeeper. Mariana had to enquire after the grieving family before she could interrogate Mrs Jones concerning any sightings of Jack.

With hindsight, Mariana wondered why she was suspicious about Jack's disappearance from the outset. It was just so unlike him not to be near at hand; she had become accustomed to talking with him about sundry matters and the more she searched the more intense was her need to confide in him.

When it was obvious that no one had seen him since last night, she decided to saddle Mars and go to the farrier, but Jack had not collected his new mount. Some inner caution kept her enquires discreet but she rode home disquieted.

Returning to where she began her search she flung herself down on the bed in his chamber and faced the unsavoury fact: Jack had gone from their lives as abruptly as he had arrived.

Immediately she acknowledged that she was tremendously hurt by his lack of farewell but she covered her own feelings with anger, even though she was alone. How dare he not tell her when he was going! The words reverberated around her head. After all their hospitality! And her friendship. She had spent hours with him. Could her sister have been right all along? Had he been a charlatan? Was his memory loss faked? She recalled questioning his views on marriage. How could he expound on being married if he had no memory? He, himself, had told her that she had no proof that he was telling the truth and that she should not trust him. Had he been trying to warn her that he was lying?

Or was it what had happened yesterday? A half smile fleeted across her lips as she recalled their intimacy. She sat up slowly. Had he got what he wanted from her and then fled? Without warning, her stomach turned cold.

Then she remembered her own shame when she had heard that Edward had been ill – there had been a reasonable explanation to why he had taken weeks to write. Was there a reasonable explanation to where Jack was?

She castigated herself for her treachery. How could she be so disloyal barely twelve hours after she had last talked to Jack? He must have met with some misadventure. She could not have been so mistaken; they had fraternised deeply in the last fortnight. Margaret's unpleasant opinions had been declared before any of them were acquainted with him; Margaret had judged Jack without evidence. Yet, she, Mariana, had been absolutely certain that he was a good, trustworthy person. They had shared so much together, not least their physical union yesterday. Was it only yesterday morning that she had lain in his arms? It seemed like a lifetime ago. Tears filled her eyes.

She tried to recall what he had said when they had travelled back to *Trem-y-Môr* last evening. He had definitely told her that he had reconsidered leaving today. Had it been another lie? Had he wanted to deceive her deliberately?

No! She screamed the answer silently from her lips. She knew him well enough to know when he was lying, did she not? But did she? Was their whole relationship a fraud? Only she had glimpsed the ship that he had been travelling on. Had he allowed everyone to think that he had been shipwrecked whilst remembering all along where he had come from really and who he was? Confusion suffocated her ire; misery descended.

She longed for certainties and then said out loud:

"But your injuries were real enough, Jack. They weren't faked!"

She walked to the window, still hoping that she might catch sight of him in the distance. She did not want to believe that she had been duped by him. Could she have simply missed him in her search? Had he taken a different path to the farrier? But, then, she argued with herself, why had no one else seen him today?

Moving around the room, she listed everything she saw. Here were the suits he had ordered from the tailor. Well, one of them and the coat of the other! Why leave the coat? Here his personal articles which Edward had loaned him. Of course, these weren't strictly his, and he might have decided to leave them behind, reasoning that it would be stealing to take borrowed articles. But the clothes were his, albeit paid for with money lent by Edward. They wouldn't fit anyone but Jack.

Mariana scoured the room. Why, if he had gone, had he left everything? The more she looked, the more she realised that nothing had been taken. But then, her stubborn mind said, these were not his belongings – they were simply all the possessions he had accumulated whilst he had resided here. After all, he had not brought anything with him, so why should he take anything away? He had vanished as surely as if he had never come into their lives all those weeks ago in the storm.

Jack, where are you? her heart cried. She could not believe that he had disappeared. He would have told her. He would have bid her farewell and she could have wished him 'Godspeed'. He might have kissed her, especially after yesterday.

Mariana sat back on the bed and sighed. Not Jack, please not you as well. Henry and her father had abandoned her, through no fault of their own, but nonetheless they had gone. Not you too, Jack. She had always known that he would go, but she had assumed that he would keep in touch.

"What has happened to you, Jack?" she asked the empty room. "Where are you?"

There were no answers to be found here. She stroked his coat and held it to her face. It smelt of him and she was reminded of the previous day. Could it be true? Had he used her? She shook her head. Even if he had, she still did not regret it. She decided that yesterday's outing had been perfect. Too perfect! Mariana closed her eyelids on the unshed tears. No tears! No regrets! Jack was gone. Gone!

Mariana's musings lasted barely a minute and she returned to the present. A lump in her throat choked her and the Parson's look of incredulity blurred. She mustn't cry! Margaret had risen to her feet and was chanting:

"A toast! A toast! We must have a toast! This is marvellous. We must tell everyone. Oh, there's so much to do. We…"

"No," contradicted Mariana. She had not arisen and the Vicar had half stood up and then perched on the edge of his chair. "I am happy to marry the Parson…" May God forgive me, her heart mourned. "However, I do have one or two conditions… er… requests. I want a quiet wedding and… well, as quiet as we can. And, I think it would be best if we arrange it for as soon as possible. Would this week be too soon, Parson?"

"This week? Hrrmph! No, indeed! I think people will understand your request for a quiet wedding. After all you are still griev…"

"This week!" butted in Margaret. She sat down abruptly, catching the table with her arm and making the dishes shake. "Why?"

"I…" muttered Mariana.

"It doesn't matter, Mrs Struley," intercepted the Parson. "Let God be praised! Nothing else matters. I'll get a special license. There's no time for banns…"

"If you'll excuse me." Mariana pushed back her chair. "I don't wish to break up the party but I have a headache and I think I had best lie down."

"A headache? You!" Margaret's face was full of suspicion. "It's usually *me* who has the headaches. However, I'm sure the Parson won't mind. He and I can finish our meal whilst we discuss any details."

Mariana nodded. She must away or the tears would fall. No one must know. No one must suspect that she was unwilling. Now she had decided she must pretend, for she *had* to marry the Parson. She had to marry the Parson.

"Miss Mariana… er… Mariana," stuttered the Vicar as he left his seat and moved towards her.

Mariana halted. How much longer would she have to stay?

"Mariana, may I just say, 'Thank you!'?" The Vicar swallowed anxiously and glanced at Margaret. It was almost as if what he wanted to say he did not want to say in front of her sister. "Goodnight, my dear. I hope you feel better soon." He stretched out his hands to her, but she gave him a half-hearted smile. Then, with a nod, she left the room.

Better soon! Better soon! His words rang in her ears whilst she ascended the stairs. She had no headache and what she did have would not be better by the end of the night!

BIDDY

Biddy strode along the edge of the track, her head bent watching for potholes, her left arm swinging but she kept her right arm crooked for she was carrying a bundle of her belongings.

She had done it! She had left home and was on her way. It seemed almost impossible that it was nearly two months since her mother had died but her life had been one long drudge and now, at last, she was free. Free from screaming babies and snotty infants; free from washing all her brothers' shirts; free from building and tending the fire through the heat of the summer; free from spending all day preparing and cooking, only to see the meal disappear in a trice; free from being at the beck and call of all and sundry with hardly a moment to herself.

Sweet Jesus, she was as hot as if she was bending over that fire and the sun had only risen about an hour ago! What was it going to be like when it reached its zenith? But then she was wearing far too many clothes because she had reasoned that it was easier to wear her petticoats and two bodices than to carry them. However, she had reckoned without the intense weather.

The sun had bounced over the faraway Snowdonia hills and raced upwards, spreading its rays over glassy sea and heathery heath. Over to her right, down towards the Lleyn Peninsula, there was a light covering of clouds, almost like the thin ice which formed on the ponds in winter, sprinkled with fresh frost similar to the sugar icing she had seen on some of Mrs Jones' sweet desserts. Oh, if only it was cold today – if only she could rub her face against the frozen water! The thought of icy water made her thirst intensify.

She hitched her bundle higher and marched on, her thoughts reviewing the last days and weeks. What a commotion when her mother had finally passed away! Yet Biddy hadn't shed a single tear. She was glad – although she kept this to herself – she was glad the old hag had gone, for when had she ever done anything for Biddy? Year after year her mother, Bridget, had lain in her bed, huge from pregnancy, only getting up to drop another baby and then returning under the blankets. How had she managed to produce so many offspring? And why?

Biddy pursed her lips. She wasn't going to be caught like that! A yearly baby and ill health dogging your footsteps. She knew all about how babies were made – living in a single room didn't give any privacy and when her father had climbed on top of her mother on a regular basis, Biddy would turn over and put her hands over her ears. In later years, she and some of her sisters had graduated to the low space in the loft but she could still hear the panting of her parents and it disgusted her.

If her father had shown some restraint, she argued inside her head, then she wouldn't have had fourteen siblings whose care had been thrust upon her without a by your leave just because she was the eldest girl! Yes, she had been caring for them during her mother's last illness, but the full responsibility had descended on her bony shoulders from the moment her mother was found cold and heavy in the early morning.

In death, as in life, her mother had been the centre of the family. Privately Biddy wondered if her mother hadn't enjoyed the situation and kept to her bed in order to have everyone running around after her. She had made a fearful fuss just getting up to use the chamber pot and had needed help to do this most intimate of tasks. Biddy had hated assisting her but what she hated most was her mother's tongue.

Cries of pain, snippets of advice, showers of complaints and the orders… Biddy shuddered unconsciously. Orders had been shouted out from cockcrow to twilight and her mother had expected immediate obedience. For years Biddy had felt more like a servant than a daughter. She had been expected to look after several young children (Adam, Hanna, Peter, Francis and Mary), keep the fire going, cook for the entire family, wash clothes, go to market *and* keep up the tally of work in the Manor House, although she had been excused this last once her mother had gone. She assumed that her father could see that she didn't have a spare second to lend a hand in Mrs Jones' kitchen, let alone venture further afield.

Of course, she was glad not to have to go and work under someone else's authority but it meant she had lost all her independence and the small pile of coins (hidden from prying eyes) had remained the same week after week, never increasing.

What had rankled the most? The loss of the hope of saving enough money to train as a singer, or the feeling of being taken totally for granted?

She couldn't decide.

If only her father had been at home more, but he had changed overnight after the day of the funeral. Rising near dawn herself, barely had she time to say a couple of words to him before he had left the cottage. Left to perform his duties as steward for the Squire, riding one of the Squire's horses, not returning to the crowded cottage until it was time for him to fall into bed. It was as if he had soared above his family – almost, Biddy felt that he looked down his nose at them. Was it his new status or did they remind him that much of his lost wife? Biddy didn't think so! All she saw was that her father had gained the freedom of being cut loose from his wife's sickness and the responsibility of his large family – the freedom she herself longed for! He didn't seem to even mourn his loss, although her brother, Evan, had told her that such was the depth of their father's sorrow that the only way he could cope was to work from sunrise to eventide in order that he did not have any time to dwell on his privations.

Hah! thought Biddy. That was a convenient excuse! He was not taking his obligations seriously. After all, he had fathered all this brood of children!

When she had dared to voice some of her grievances her father had looked away and told her that her contribution to the housekeeping money was no longer needed since he had a steady and increased salary. He hadn't taken any notice of her grumble. She felt used. In fact, it was as if she hadn't spoken. How could she explain her loneliness and lack of status? Over the years, at the Manor House, she had graduated from one of the lowest maids with their humble duties and now Peggy and Kate were set to clean the fires or scrub the chamber pots. However, in her own home she felt no better than a dog, since she had to tackle every kind of job.

Nonetheless, it wasn't just the daily drudgery – there were her brothers and sisters themselves, who, having been raised by a woman who could not get out of bed and keep them out of mischief, were unruly and rude. They did not recognise Biddy's new authority. The youngest, Baby Benjamin, had to be tended every hour and seemed to do nothing but mewl; the younger ones had to be watched so that they didn't injure themselves or others; the older ones were reluctant to carry out any of the jobs Biddy asked them to do. At first, it was she who not only rose to light the fire but also collected the firewood. Within a few days she had tried to delegate firewood collecting to Owen (named after his father) and John, who usually played truant and disappeared to the stables whenever they could. She had persevered, even allowing the fire to go out and offering the boys cold broth for their meal, to try to make them see that she couldn't do everything and be everywhere at once. It was a continuing battle and she felt the loser!

The task of fetching water from the stream she gave to the girls, Mary and Maggie, because it was nearer the cottage but they were lazy too, preferring to play their make-belief games than to take their obligations seriously. They were no more malleable than their brothers! And Martha – she was the next eldest after herself – would wander around the countryside, collecting flowers and then want to use the fire in the cottage to concoct homemade medicines. She hadn't taken any of the burden upon her shoulders and seemed impervious to Biddy's pleas for assistance.

Biddy had nearly been broken by the washing for such an extended family, because without the hot tubs used at the Manor House it could take four days of the week simply to get the clothes washed and that didn't count drying them. This was possible if the sun shone, but on rainy days she couldn't move in the cottage for wet washing!

She missed the fellowship of Elin too, although Elin came whenever she could. The day of her mother's death they had lost the stranger from up at the house – Mr Jack.

Miss Mariana had told Elin, who had relayed the gossip to Biddy – although not until a week after her mother's funeral – that Mr Jack had been walking to pick up his horse, ready to depart and find out who he was and where he came from. A carriage had pulled up behind him to ask directions and a man had stepped out who had recognised him.

Elin had explained that Mr Jack had a large estate in Scotland but his servants had not been searching for him because they hadn't known he was missing. The vessel he had been travelling on was his own ship and his family thought he was sailing on the other side of the world and they weren't expecting him back until next year. However, it transpired that his wife was in childbed and Mr Jack had hurried to be there for the birth of his child.

Elin had confided in Biddy, whilst she beat her brothers' dirty breeches against the stones by the river, that she, Elin, and Mrs Jones had been rather hurt that Mr Jack hadn't even bothered to come and say his farewells, but it turned out that this was Miss Mariana's fault. She had urged him to leave immediately since he had such a long way to travel and… Biddy had stopped listening.

What did she care what people like Mr Jack did? He wasn't trapped in a situation not of his own making, carrying the burden of bringing up children that weren't his own, with the future stretching endlessly off into the distance! He had his own estate; servants to look after the fruit of his loins; money to put bread on his table; a soft bed at night and time to pursue his own leisure, whether to sail across the wide oceans or shoot and hunt with his friends. His world was a million miles away from hers, but what she coveted most of all was his freedom. He was truly master of his life whereas she was imprisoned, a slave to her family's demands.

Each day the tiredness of her young body grew; each day the hopelessness of her daily life increased and each day her dreams sank a little further into the earth and dirt under her feet in the cottage where she served from the darkness of the pre-dawn hour to the gloaming. She sang no more. She didn't even hum a tune whilst she worked. All pleasure was driven from her by the aching burden of each hour.

That is, until yesterday. And yesterday something had snapped. Maybe it hadn't been Mary's fault that the food she, Biddy, had spent all afternoon preparing, ended up spilt, but it had seemed like a deliberate act of destruction. Francis and Peter had started to scrap over some difference of opinion, which she neither knew nor cared about, right in the centre of the room. She had screamed at them either to stop or take their troubles outside but she had been ignored. She had stepped between them to separate them and that was when it had occurred: the pot had overturned and juice and vegetables had landed on the soil of the floor, ruined and wasted.

How had it happened? She hadn't seen, but neither of the boys nor herself had been near the pot. It was that bastard Mary.

Biddy halted on her journey in the middle of her reminiscences. "Bastard." That was a word she shouldn't be using because her Catholic mother had taught her that swearing was wrong but Mary, at six, was a bastard. She was a sullen, shy little girl. She would pull the hair of the baby and then point the finger literally at one of her other siblings. She would slope off to walk by the sea even if she had been asked to run to Mrs Jones to beg some borrowed flour or deliver a message to one of her brothers; she would spend hours watching for her father to arrive and then press her thin body against his knees, sucking her thumb and looking up adoringly at him. Biddy had come to despise her and this last act seemed to be full of spite.

Biddy lost her temper. She banged the boys' heads together; she scooped the baby up away from the fire; she shooed Mary and the rest of the children out the door and then she fled upstairs and flung herself down on the bedcovers and cried. Yet, in that first outburst a tiny seed of an idea had come to her. She had always intended to leave, so why not follow her dreams? No one could stop her. She had her savings and if she left early one morning, without being seen, she could put lots of miles between her and her squabbling, noisy, ungrateful family.

Hence her haste today. She might feel as if she was going to faint with the heat, but nothing would make her stop and rest. She hadn't even eaten anything. She toiled on, overcoming the discomfort by imagining herself singing to a distinguished audience, the applause filling her head. It was such an age since she had been able to indulge her fantasies that it sprang on her with the freshness of a new idea and lent joy to her journey.

Barely an hour later Biddy was delighted to accept a lift on the back of a farm cart bound for market. She climbed on the tailgate, rearranged her layers of petticoats, letting a small breeze fan her skin; the tops of her legs were chafed from the unaccustomed walking and the sitting down (and allowing a gap between her upper legs) relieved the discomfort.

Now she had time to survey her surroundings. She noticed wayside flowers: the purple pink of mallow, the shapely cups of the yellow foxglove and the waving heads of the blue devil's bit scabious; even the smart regular shape of the common speedwell. She knew some of their names but she didn't know their healing properties like her sister who was just a year younger than her. Martha had learnt much about herbs; how ground ivy could be used as an infusion for loss of appetite or for a winter cough; the effectiveness of raspberry tea for menstrual pains or garlic mustard which made a poultice for ulcers and cuts. Biddy had listened politely but not bothered to identify and collect the plants – it was music she was interested in – how to lift the spirits with a song or gladden the heart with a melody, not how to boil leaves to ease digestion. And more recently, she would have preferred Martha to have cooked meals instead of brews and potions!

Biddy parted from the morose farmer when they reached the Menai Straits. A grunt was all the farewell she received but she was glad – she hadn't wanted any questions about where she had come from or where she was bound for! Standing on the ferry the midday sun was fierce and she screwed up her eyes against the blaze. Much to her embarrassment she was sweating profusely, which caught the attention of her fellow passengers who gave her strange looks. She decided she must remove some of her layers soon; she didn't want people to remember her and describe her to any of her family if they came asking after her. Not that she believed they would. Martha would be expected to take her place and once she had ordered the daily tasks, calmed the little ones and fed the men folk, she, Biddy, would not be missed. In fact, the more she thought about it, the more she decided that she had done everyone a favour since Martha would make a better mother than she ever would have! Martha didn't have aspirations to become a famous singer; she had wanted to become a wife ever since she was four years old.

Biddy hesitated once she reached the mainland. One track along the edge of the water was flat but busy with traffic; the other track wound its way up the hill, and no one was travelling along it. She chose the latter since it seemed to continue straight east (which she understood was the way to London) and she had journeyed in that direction across Anglesey. Yes, the path must go through the mountains but Biddy preferred a less frequented route. However, she was shocked by the gradient of the hill that climbed away from the fast flowing channel she had just crossed. She had never been this way before and had not expected to struggle this much. A bout of dizziness made her surroundings swim before her eyes and it was then that she remembered that she had not partaken of any food since yesterday morning. She must stop and eat some of the provisions she had brought with her in her pack.

On she plodded, hearing a cuckoo far away. She paused to look but it was hidden; yet, because she stopped, she observed a tiny orangey brown bird with a black head, which flew from her, in shallow swoops, making a noise of banging two pebbles together. She wished she had wings and could ascend the hill with as much ease as the little creature! It went in front of her, pausing on the top of dry stone walls or the broken stump of a tree struck by lightning. Later she heard the croak of raven and observed two black shadows circling overhead. She shivered despite the warmth of the day. She knew the stories of these clever birds, which were considered prophetic. Was there a graveyard or a place of execution near here? Then she remembered tales of wolves living out in the wilds. She shook these anxieties from her mind, trying to focus on more pleasant things, and walked on.

On both sides of the thoroughfare rocks rose from beneath the grass in gritty grey layers and she was reminded of the puff pastry Mrs Jones would make for guests, filling the dainties with cream and custard. Oh, she was hungry! Hungry. Hungry. Beneath one of these outcrops sat a sheep and its lamb, not newborn but clean with the even texture of its first full fleece. Sensibly, mother and baby were settled in the shade and made Biddy long to rest in a cool overhang. Two horsemen rode along and she stepped on to the grass, nibbled by those sheep and their comrades, liberally salted with their droppings; she bent her head until the men had passed.

On and on she went until, at last, the track levelled out. In the distance she could see several mountains and she assumed the path went between them rather than over their tops. Behind the right hand one was another peak shaped like the hat a Chinaman had worn at the fair last summer. Suddenly she became aware of the trill of a stream. She brought her vision back from the far distance. Without hesitating, she turned off the rutted road and was enchanted to find a woody dell, shaded and delectably chilly and empty of other travellers. She had not encountered anyone since the riders and decided that it would be safe to undress, even though she was in the open air. She cast off the bodices and all the petticoats and bent to drink from the rushing water before dipping her hand in and rubbing the clear liquid over her reddened face and neck. She wet the cloth of her skirt, hanging down to her feet now it had lost the support of the under garments.

She cast about and saw, nearby, a patch of livery green moss, slightly damp but she welcomed its freshness and lay down. Almost before her eyes were closed she was asleep!

Biddy dreamt of the man at the fair with the rainbow coat, who had showed such appreciation for her singing. He met her in the woodland and invited her to join him and come to London with him, winging her over the hills in a coach of maroon with a golden crest painted on its side. She could not make out the lettering on the coat of arms nor did she question how such a lowly man could own a magnificent vehicle like this one, but she had just stepped up inside its plush interior when she heard a voice say:

"Hey, what a beauty we have here!"

She awoke with the realisation that the words were not part of her dream. She lifted her hand to shade her eyes peering through the dappled shadows of the slanting sun through leaves. The speaker was a lad not much older than her, dressed in the soiled smock of a field worker – a hedger or ditcher possibly. His greasy locks hung to his collar and his voice boomed as he continued:

"Come on Rees, don't hold back. Let's have some sport!"

Biddy scrambled to her feet, dismayed to see her discarded garments flung beneath the trees. What must these men have thought? She was surrounded by four men – well, three and a simpleton. Each was as unkempt as the next except the poor fool who gazed vacantly at her – his clothes were slightly less creased and cleaner – maybe because he did not work but watched from the sidelines. Biddy put back her shoulders, standing tall and stated:

"Have you seen my brother? He went to fetch us some food and will be returning any moment."

"Brother?" sneered the first man who had towered over her. "There's no one here but us and what's this?" He picked up one of her discarded petticoats. "Were you going to bathe? We'll stay around and watch, shan't we? Eh, Morgan? What do you think?"

Biddy moved to gather up her belongings. She noticed that her bundle had been opened. The group must have been here for sometime. She felt vulnerable, being in a state of undress and having only just awoken, and she was frightened too, but hearing that one of the lads was called Morgan reminded her of her own brother. She took a deep breath and tried to assure herself that these lads wouldn't harm her. They must have mistaken her for a trollop, dozing in the day instead of labouring hard to earn money for a husband or father.

With her clothes and bundle safely clutched to her bosom as a kind of shield she spoke again:

"So you haven't seen my brother? Well, never mind! I'll just have to go and find him."

The first man barred her way. Her back was to the stream and she doubted that she could make a quick retreat across its stony bubbling depths.

"Not so fast!" he cried and grabbed her wrist, twisting it and forcing her to drop the things she held.

"Let me go!" she retorted, anger replacing fear momentarily. "You'll have my brother to answer to! And he's twice your size!"

"You hear that, Rees? This saucy girl has a brother bigger than me!" He wound some of her auburn hair around his stained finger.

Biddy half turned to the other men, even though her left arm was being held tightly. They had said nothing and, although they formed a loose ring around her, she hoped that they might be reasoned with, even if the leader was intractable. She was glad her money was hidden beneath her waistband. She wasn't going to give them any of that unless… would they accept a bribe and release her? Would that satisfy them? Or would they take her savings and then continue with what they were planning? She tried to size them up. None of them, except her captor, was stocky, and she was strong after her heavy manual work, but surely she would never overcome all three! She wanted to appeal to the other men, but neither would meet her eye and the simple one had wandered away and was sitting on a rock by the edge of the water, staring straight ahead.

"Look, what's your name?" She addressed the man who held her. At least he was concentrating on her. She determined not to show any trepidation. She knew that wild animals would often pick on one of their weaker brethren if they smelt defeat. She forced herself to just think of him as one of her insubordinate siblings – after all, she'd had eight weeks of trying to order her family. "I'm sorry I don't know your name. If you'll just let me past I can be on my way. I have to visit my sick mother who is dying. I've come from Amlwch and have a few more miles before I get there. That's why my brother went for food. He really will be back any moment and he's got a temper you know. Red hair and a fiery temper! And our mother was… is Irish."

She knew she was chattering but she couldn't help herself. Despite her best efforts terror crawled over her skin. Images flashed before her eyes. She had wandered from the main thoroughfare, but even if she was by its side, she would find no help there – it was such a lonely path. Why had she chosen the road into the mountains? Hadn't she heard stories of robbers hiding in caves in uninhabited places? And she had seen the ravens. Had they been an omen? She forced herself to meet the man's intense gaze; he didn't seem to have been listening to her, caught up in his own imaginings, but he must have, because when her brave words dried up he spat:

"Irish? I might have known it! You're a tinker – ripe for the picking! That's where you get your green eyes and your brazen ways! Now, if your brother is coming then we'd better be quick. Let's have a look under here," he flicked the wool of her skirt, "and then you can be off to see your dying mother."

The man pulled her by her arm until she was touching his filthy smock and she could smell his breath and feel his stubble against her cheek. His other arm he flung around her shoulders to grip her close and then he tried to kiss her. Biddy was petrified. She pushed against him and struggled to be freed but he held her fast. Then, without any warning, he hooked his foot around her ankle. She lost her balance and fell back on to the bed of moss which had been so inviting earlier, with him lying atop her.

Biddy began to scream. His weight was crushing and the knowledge of what he intended to do made her panic. She tried to kick him but he pinned her down. With one grimy hand across her mouth, he silenced her and with the other he felt beneath the lacings of her bodice and then his fingers moved to her lower body. Her cries turned to a whimper as she felt her breath squeezed out of her and she started to retch. Inside her head the scream went on for her father or Thomas, Evan or Morgan or anyone… anyone who would come to her aid.

She heard the crack before she felt her attacker stiffen his chest and legs. She opened her eyes to see a colossal man standing over them, in his hand a shepherd's crook, which he appeared to have used to beat the lad. With one movement, the shepherd dragged her tormentor away from her by his neck. Hastily she tidied her disarrayed garments and tried to sit up. She was shaking from head to toe, rigors of fear and relief simultaneously.

"Be gone!" The shepherd wasn't frightened, but then he would have had to tackle fiercer animals – even those prowling wolves, which she had thought of earlier – who preyed upon his flock. Biddy was half aware of her assailant readjusting his breeches and she thought she heard a snarl of rage but of the rest of the group there was no sign. A moment later she was being offered a hand to help her to her feet.

"There, *cariad*, are you all right? I trust I came in time. Can you stand? Are you alone? Will you come back to my home with me? My wife will help you. What's your name?"

Biddy made no answer. It was taking all her concentration not to fall over. The shepherd gathered together her belongings whilst she suddenly became aware of someone staring at her. But it was no person but a shaggy grey dog, who, when it realised it had been noticed, shambled up to her, head down, tail wagging and licked her fingers.

"Don't be frightened of *Bach Bach*. He won't hurt you. As you can see he's not small any longer but he was a tiny puppy – the runt of the litter

– but a finer sheep dog you couldn't find anywhere in the country. Can you walk? Would you like to lean on my stick?"

Still Biddy couldn't get her tongue to move but she took the gnarled wood and, with the other hand clutching the back hairs of the friendly dog, she followed her saviour.

Using all her self will to prevent her from tripping, she wasn't aware of the distance they travelled. It was not in the direction of the track she had climbed but tucked away in the fold of the hill above the wooded glade. More a lean-to than a cottage, she did notice. The shepherd called out when he went through the door and then turned back to urge her to enter his home.

The dog sat down on the threshold. She struggled to get the staff she was using through the low doorway but the shepherd dipped the stick and pulled her and it into the room. For several moments Biddy could see nothing. Then, when she became accustomed to the darkness after the glare of the sun, she stared in disbelief for there, sitting in a row on wooden stools, were three identical children.

"Oh, don't you worry about them," smiled the shepherd. "That's Jacobus, Johonnes and Charolus – named after our great grandfathers and an uncle – and you're not seeing double, they are triplets, and it's difficult for me and the wife to tell them apart. Peggy?"

He lifted his voice to a shout: "Where are you, woman?"

From the corner, and she must have been there all the time since it was a single room, came the shepherd's wife. In a few short sentences, Biddy's plight was explained and Biddy found herself led to the fire. The shivering, which had lessened, started again with the recounting of the scene in the copse, but with gentle hands the shepherd's wife bathed her cuts and bruises, crooning with sympathy and calling her by baby names, and the three solemn boys watched without a sound.

Biddy herself was silent. It was as if she couldn't get her voice to work. Without warning exhaustion struck her and she wobbled. Then she was sitting on a three-legged stool which had been grabbed from beneath the bottom of one of the triplets. Biddy allowed the shepherd's wife to minister to her, sleep sweeping over her. It wasn't long before she was tucked up in the family bed. Her last reflection was that maybe it would have been better if she had stayed with her own family, because although she had had to work they would have protected her from dangerous wolves – yes, her overwrought mind reasoned that those men who had preyed on her were easily as dangerous as ferocious animals – wolves like she had met today, and the shepherd's wife had been kindness itself… maybe mothers' constant care was something she had taken for granted.

MARIANA

Mariana watched the Parson furtively, out of the corner of her eye. It was done! The deed was done! She had survived today and the noisy chatter of the *neithior* or wedding feast. She just had to live through tonight and all would be well. Her secret would be secure forever. She was a married woman now – at least legally, even if the agreement had to be finalised in the bedchamber.

She held her cold fingers up to the fire and breathed deeply, trying to still the pounding of her heart and the nausea in her stomach. She suspected every bride was nervous on their wedding night and she was certainly anxious, but not for the normal reasons – Jack had taught her the joys of intimacy between man and woman – but because so much was at stake – her reputation and her family's too, she supposed.

She felt as if she had been holding her breath ever since that day when she discovered what had happened to Jack and the subsequent decision to enter into matrimony with the Parson. She found herself lost in memories.

When she had finally understood and accepted that Jack had vanished, she had sought a way to cover her own embarrassment. If Jack had duped everyone, then those at the Manor House had been the most deceived; and of these, she had been the most hoodwinked. She had cursed herself, even whilst determining that others wouldn't see her foolishness. It was too soon after her childish loss of temper. People had viewed her as a child for too long! Thus, she had invented a tale, with as many details as one of Hugh the Post's best! This story was told to all – from Margaret to the smallest child in the road.

Of course she had known that Jack was leaving, she had stated. Hadn't they all known that? It was no secret that he had ordered a new steed from William Phillips; he was due to leave the very day he left. Surely that was no surprise to any one.

There was the problem of the horse; it was never collected. Hence she invented the fable of the passing carriage with the old friend in it who had recognised Jack. Why, she asked, would he need a mount when he was riding home in a carriage?

"So, who was he?" This was the question on many lips. Forget the horse, who was Jack?

Details of Jack's identity had not been easy to fabricate. It had to be plausible, but also she wanted him to be *someone* in order that folk like Margaret were proved wrong. Therefore, she had created a title for him and an impressive estate far away in another country, so that no one could see through her lies.

It was straightforward to explain that no report of him missing was circulated since it was his own vessel that had sunk, and his family believed he was the other side of the world.

Once started, Mariana had found the story tripped off her tongue readily; hundreds of particulars she manufactured for those hungry for gossip. She assured them that his memory had not returned before he had left but his friend had filled in all the details that he needed to know.

Elin and Mrs Jones had been the most difficult to convince, for they had seen her dismay that first morning. Mention of Jack's wife in childbed seemed to explain the haste of his departure and his apparent rudeness in not staying even long enough to wish them all farewell. Mariana had even dug into her own reserves of money to leave in Edward's study with the words, "Jack wanted to pay my brother back for his loan." Fortunately, Bridget's death had kept those at *Trem-y-Môr* busy and Mariana had escaped reasonably lightly from her servants.

Margaret was too concerned with her own welfare to cross-examine Mariana. Her main concern had been whether Jack was ever returning! When she heard that he was married, she breathed a sigh of relief and sank back on her pillows. Mariana guessed that she was already counting to see how many more days she could stay in bed receiving sympathy after that unprovoked attack by her half-sister.

The final question for Mariana to answer was his name. She had found this one of the most difficult facts to invent, but finally had chosen "James Daniel Burns", having heard her father (many years previously) talk about a family of this name from the western coast of Scotland. "*Sir* James", she always emphasised. Not a single person queried her choice and in the Manor House, at least, he was still referred to as "Jack".

Mariana had done well; she had found the initial days a strain, but she was amazed at how quickly the others lost interest. *Only* she seemed to be upset by his departure, and she had to bear both the loss of Jack and the worry that maybe something awful really had happened to him. Had he been set upon by thieves? Had he gone for a walk that evening and fallen and hurt himself? Had he…? Her fertile imagination conjured up picture after picture of calamity. Common sense reasoned that if this kind of thing had happened, then he would have been found. Since this hadn't occurred, then he must have left after cold-heartedly deceiving her for all those weeks. Round came the argument again and again – the one that she stubbornly clung to – that he was a genuine person, not capable of such depths of deceit. Yet, if this was true, then where was he, and why had he left under such mysterious circumstances? The kindest explanation she had thought of was that he was a spy (working for the government) and had been required to hide his identity; maybe he had decided that it was best if she did not know where he was going to or his time of departure. With that she had to be happy until a fortnight ago. Then all her former worries had revived. Mariana's reminiscences focused on that particular life-changing day.

* * *

It was a cool morning with a brisk offshore breeze. The sky was full of dirty ragged clouds which had hidden folds of grey; some were shaded with dark pewter. She suspected that it would rain later and urged Mars towards the mountain. She wanted to have her ride and get back before any downpour.

She had barely left their private beach when she was overcome with sickness. She dismounted and stepped away from her horse to vomit behind a bush. There wasn't much in her stomach, since she had arisen early and had not eaten yet, but she gagged miserably. When the spasm had passed, she sat on a hump of coarse grass and stared at the slate sea. She reached into her pocket for a handkerchief on which to wipe her mouth; instead she pulled out the scrap of bloody cloth, which she had found on the day that Jack had disappeared. Forgotten was the sickness as she pondered the material.

"Mariana! Have you fallen?"

It was Matthew Cutlass. A moment later she saw him striding towards her along the windswept grass.

"Mariana, are you all right? I saw Mars without a rider and I thought you had been thrown."

"Matthew. What a pleasure to see you! It has been a long time. Where have you been hiding?"

"Are you all right?" he repeated.

"Yes. I just felt sick and got down before I… Poor Mars would have been most offended."

"Sick? Are you ill? Have you actually been sick?"

"Yes, over there. But, never mind that! What do you make of this?" She made to rise, but the man restrained her with a hand on her shoulder.

"Have you been sick before?"

"Honestly, Matthew, I'm fine now. It's passed. I feel better now. I'm just puzzled by this. I found it on the beach recently and…"

"Have you a fever?"

"Matthew! I tell you, don't fret! It's nothing. I have been feeling sick occasionally for a few days but I'm not worried and you shouldn't be either. It must be something I ate. However, this… this is dried blood, isn't it? But whose blood?"

"It's an old rag, my dear. Nothing more."

"No!" Mariana leapt to her feet. "It's Jack's. It's Jack's shirt. I remember the feel… I remember his shirt. He had a shirt made of this material, because he asked me to choose between two different bolts of cloth from Ambrosius the tailor. Blethyn, his wife, helped me choose this one because it was softer. It's hard to see the weave because the blood has ruined it, but… Oh, Matthew, what has happened to him?"

"What do you mean? I thought Jack was borne away by a friend to his wife…"

"No," shuddered Mariana. "That was only a story – a fiction." She closed her eyes with shock. How could she have been so blind all this time? She should have recognised the material when she had first picked it up from the sand.

"A story? It can't have been. I heard it from the very best authority. How can you be so sure?"

Mariana turned to catch her horse, which was sniffing the grassy tussocks between the sand.

"I must…"

"Wait!" Matthew caught her yellow sleeve. "Please explain why you are upset."

"Oh, Matthew, it's all my fault. I… I made up the story. It was me."

She crumpled the rag in her hands. What had she done? Because of her stupid pride, she had allowed everyone to believe that Jack had left of his own free will, but he must have been injured, and now it was too late. Because of her he must be dead! But where was his body?

"Mariana, my dear child." Matthew slipped his arm through hers and led her gently down the path. She was too confused to notice that they were walking away from the Manor House. "Will you please tell me what this is about?"

She sat down and told him then – all about her foolish behaviour and her suspicions. The tears came before she had finished but she didn't care. She had caused the death of another.

"My dear girl, I wish I could reassure you. I wish I could tell you are mistaken, but, now you have explained all this you have made me remember an incident that happened a few weeks ago."

Without delay Matthew related the events of the night, just before Bridget's death, when he had followed the rowing boat and how they had unloaded an unconscious man. Mariana remained motionless and, after a few minutes into the telling, he put his arm around her. She neither shrank away nor leant against him; she did not want comfort – she was consumed with guilt and recriminations. Even when her friend assured her that he believed that Jack – if Jack it had been – was not dead because of the way he was lifted over the ship side and the comments of the sailors, she remained silent.

"However, my dear, I can't say categorically that it was Jack who was taken on board. I didn't recognise him and I would have thought I would have. I tended him enough times and…"

"It was Jack," she intoned under her breath. She stared at the rolling sea with glistening eyes. "I knew he wouldn't go without seeing me."

"Now that you have told me that he disappeared without trace, I must conclude that it was Jack," acknowledged her companion. "At the time, I assumed he was a third member of the crew and that they had been in some kind of fight. Afterwards, I listened out for gossip but no one reported any local person missing. Some abortive smuggling attempt, I concluded. I decided the 'special cargo' was in their pockets or somewhere like that for they certainly didn't unload anything else. I almost stayed to watch them sail away. Oh God, Mariana! If I'd known, I'd have gone after them or, at least, tried to find out who they were and where they were going to."

Without warning, Mariana swung away from him.

"I'm going to be sick," she groaned.

Matthew held her head as she vomited the foul, yellow bile. When she had finished, he offered her his own handkerchief to wipe her mouth before holding her trembling body to his chest.

"Mariana, I'm so sorry. Look, I'll do my best. I'll try and find out what I can. I didn't see the ship's name, but I'd know her if I saw her again. Let me walk you home. You can't ride. You must go to bed. I'll bring you some…"

"No." Mariana shook her head resignedly, her hair brushing his coat. "We mustn't tell anyone about Jack. There's no point anyway. They all think he's gone and no one seems to miss him except…"

"Mariana, can I ask you something? As your physician?"

"Oh, Matthew, the sickness doesn't matter!"

"It does, if you are with child," he replied quietly.

Mariana drew back from his supportive embrace and stared at him in horror.

"Can you…? Are you sick…? Is that's what's wrong with me?"

"Some women do experience nausea during pregnancy. But is it possible? Do you understand?"

Mariana swung round and ran towards Mars. He whinnied when he saw her approach, but didn't move. Before Matthew could stop her she had grabbed the reins and flung herself into the saddle and raced away.

It was on that unheeding ride back that the notion to marry the Parson had entered her mind. She hadn't been too concerned when her monthly bleeding hadn't arrived, but with that and the nausea, and now Matthew's counsel there seemed no doubt that she was with child. In the following week, she had only seen Matthew once and he had no news about Jack. She had not stayed to talk to him because she did not want to discuss her condition. She had rather hoped he would have forgotten, although the look in his eyes told her otherwise. Nonetheless, she comforted herself, she had not admitted openly that she had lain with a man, so, at least, he could not broach the subject with her easily, physician or not! Once she was married, all would be well. Anyway, if there was one person she could trust to keep his mouth shut, surely it was Matthew Cutlass! As far as she could ascertain he had not recounted the truth about Jack's disappearance since she had spoken with him. When they met he informed her that he was going away for nearly three weeks and she had hidden her relief. Steadfastly she wouldn't allow herself to answer the question of why she should wish one of her only friends not to be near her and help her at this time!

The evening after she had agreed to the Parson's proposal and hastened upstairs she did some more serious thinking. She decided that on the morrow she must put on a bright, cheerful face to the whole community since word of her betrothal would have spread by morning. She must be particularly careful with Elin, for the maid had been with her for over five years and appeared to be able to read her mistress' every mood. Thank God that the Parson appeared to be so relieved to be marrying her that he was content to hurry the preparations! Would Edward have time to come? Margaret would definitely to write and tell him of her victory. And her other sisters, Penelope and Katherine? The latter she had never met, but Penelope was her confidante, wasn't she? Could she not tell her what had happened? She suspected that her half-sister would be rather shocked and might disapprove; Penelope was rather old-fashioned in her views. In which case she must make sure that Penelope did not guess that she was unhappy with the marriage.

This conclusion meant that she would need to concoct a suitable reason for her sudden announcement. But what possible explanation could she give since the truth could not be said?

Another night of tossing and turning had ensued. Keep it simple, she had urged herself. She was tired of subterfuge; it had exhausted her creativity to make up the full yarn of Jack and his whereabouts. Perhaps she could say that it was nothing more than that, as she had become acquainted with the Parson over the last few weeks, she had perceived that matrimony to him would be pleasant. Or perhaps she could say that they had talked of marriage before, but only recently had decided to go ahead. That would explain the Parson coming often to the Manor House.

Mariana returned to the present. What a hectic week it had been! There had barely been time for the *gwahoddwr* to chant the verses and Elizabeth Parry's sewing woman (who had adjusted her ball gown all those months ago) had been working every day and half the night to finish Mariana's wedding gown. Mrs Jones had organised the feast and the Parson had arranged for the harpists to come. The dancing and the singing had lifted everyone's souls except Mariana's, but she had pinned a smile on to her face eight days ago and it had stayed there ever since.

Nevertheless, inside, and especially when she was alone, she was prone to self-pity and fanciful plans of escape. Her instinct was to flee but she knew she must not. No more wearing breeches and climbing along the roof so she could run and hide! She had made the decision to marry the Parson of her own free will and she must go through with it. No! argued her heart. It was not of her own free will. She did not want to tie herself to this man for the rest of her life, but she had had no choice. It was not her fault! It was not her fault!

It was your fault. Mariana had heard the words as though someone had spoken them. Yes, she admitted, she had chosen to lie with Jack and consequently she carried his child. Some would say that she had been unlucky to get caught after one occasion, but no one would say that it was not her fault. That is, if they knew and they never would. She had married the Parson and, if the infant came early, he or she would simply be a big baby, despite not having reached full term, and all would believe that the child was her husband's. Surely they would! They must do! Time and again she had reminded herself what happened to unmarried mothers: people scorned and shunned them; some hounded them out of the village with stones. She recalled one girl called Rachel. What an uproar there had been! Rachel's own father had beaten her until she had revealed who the father of the child was, and then the whole community had ganged up on the lad and insisted that he marry the girl.

But there would be no point in beating *her*. Even if she did say that Jack was the father, Jack had melted away, disappeared without a trace. Thus, she had resolved that no one was going to find out; none would see her shame. And now, at last, she could relax! She curled up her fingers and then stretched them out, smoothing down the creases in her gown.

She glanced again at the Parson. Parson! Parson! This was her husband and she would have to get used to calling him "Griffith". He too seemed lost in thought. Was he nervous also? she wondered.

GRIFFITH

The Parson rubbed his hands across the seat of his coat whilst he warmed himself at the fire. On this auspicious day, when finally he had attained his desire, to marry Mariana, he had ordered fires to be lit in all the rooms in the Vicarage. Usually he never allowed fires until November, but, even though September was just around the corner, he had told his housekeeper what he wanted, for the nights were growing chilly. If he had been on his own, at this time of the evening, he would have been kneeling in prayer. With his mind on higher planes, he would not have been aware of the cold seeping through his body, but gloriously he was *not* in prayer. He was *not* alone. His bride was here. His wife was here. He wanted to welcome her into his house, his life and soon his bed.

He moved fractionally away from the fireplace and appraised his wife surreptitiously. She was sitting with her eyes fixed on the dancing flames. Her black hair was shining, reflecting the light, and her small hands were clasped in her lap, as white as the gown she wore. No one, anywhere in the land, could have been granted a more beautiful bride! She had been solemn rather than radiant during the celebration, but many young brides were full of qualms. He knew that, because he was a cleric. They were nervous of tripping over their skirts in the aisle or worried about getting their tongues twisted on the vows or even fearful of what was expected of them on their wedding night.

Had Mariana been nervous? Was she anxious still? When he had seen her in the church, he had felt that her usually sparkling eyes were dull. Maybe he should have agreed to her riding to the church, as many girls did. They would come escorted by their friends who would be trying playfully to lead the maiden astray from the church whilst the guiders endeavoured to bring her to the ceremony. However, she herself had said that she didn't want to enact this ritual.

Griffith had been pleased when she had made her vows so sincerely, quietly, but without a tremor. No, it had been he, unaccustomed to being the groom, who had stuttered the words, for he had been trying to recite the part of the service which the clergyman usually said! What a fool! Nevertheless, hopefully, no one had cared and before long they had been at the church door where a rope of flowers was held across the porch. By then, he had noticed, Mariana's face had reddened to a misty pink.

If she had not been pleased with all the arrangements she gave no sign. He had been surprised that the Squire had not attended the wedding, but relieved. Sir Rowlands was the member of Mariana's family who he least liked. Her sister, Penelope, and her husband and children had supported Mariana, and, of course, her eldest sister, Margaret, had been behind it all. He knew he had her to thank, not just for the details of the wedding plans, but also for the fact that Mariana had agreed to marry him at all.

He recalled that he had been completely taken aback when Mariana had made her startling announcement at the table last week. How had her capitulation come about when she had seemed so aloof to his attentions? Margaret had explained that she had talked to the girl about marriage and, presumably, being an older woman, had put Mariana's misgivings to rest. Also, it had been Margaret who had faithfully encouraged him to go to *Trem-y-Môr* often in the last few weeks in order for him to meet with her young sister. Margaret had told him that she was sure that when Mariana became better acquainted with him she would change her mind and see that he would be a good husband to her. And she had!

Dear loving Margaret! What a faithful sister she had been! Even with all her own worries about her sick husband and the grief over her father's death and helping run an unfamiliar estate, yet she had found time to help him. Margaret, it was, who had paid for the exquisite gown (which his bride was still wearing). She had even offered to lend her sister some of her jewellery. She had told him that herself. He understood that she had contributed of her money and time. **"Who can find a virtuous woman? For her price is far above rubies."**

The Parson moved to the small table where Mrs Beacon, his housekeeper, had laid out some wine and glasses. It was not that Mariana needed anything to lend colour to her cheeks at the moment, for the heat from the fire had polished her skin like a rosy apple, but Griffith himself felt in need of support. At last he had this gorgeous creature all to himself! She belonged to him legally.

How he had fretted that this time would never come! He should have trusted the good Lord. **"Be careful for nothing; but in everything in prayer and supplication with thanksgiving let your requests be made known unto God."** He had prayed and prayed and here she was – all his!

He allowed his mind to go back over the past few years. How many times had he knelt in prayer on the bare boards of his study floor to cry unto his God? How many times had he ignored the pain of the wood on his cramped knees and the hunger which gurgled in his stomach as hour after hour went by? The anguish in his heart had consumed him. He had a need, which ravaged him day and night. So much so that he had begun to neglect his parish duties. He had started not to attend the festivals and wake days, the dancing competitions and games, in favour of time spent praying. Soon, if he were not careful, complaints would start. The thought of Mariana slipping through his fingers (maybe to an upstart like that fellow, Jack) had increased his fervour. The more he agonised that his thirst would never be assuaged, the thirstier he became. He coveted her. Countless hours were spent with his body motionless but his lips silently moving, calling on his God to release him from the torment. Yet God had remained inscrutable and he had despaired that he was being punished for his lust. But no! God had just been testing him. Now, at last, tonight had come.

Fleetingly, he remembered his first wedding night. What a farce! Tonight would not be like that! His first wife had been a shy, timid little bird of a woman who had no more aroused him than a sparrow in the garden, whereas this young woman had a figure which none could match and hair the colour of a raven and skin like… like… He cleared his throat with embarrassment with the notion that Mariana could read his mind. No, he would have no problems on *this* wedding night!

"Would you like some wine, m'dear?" he offered the woman of his thoughts. He was glad to see, when she put out her hand to take the glass, that she was not shaking, but he was concerned. She had said hardly a word to him since they had been alone.

"Are you tired?" he asked. "Would you like to go to bed?"

Mariana's eyes flew to his and then back down to her lap. He could have bitten off his tongue. Had he glimpsed fear? He was not sure. Suddenly he wanted to suggest that they sleep in their own respective beds tonight. It would give her a chance to recover from the busy week and… No, if he was truthful, it was not her he was concerned about… It was himself. It was *he* who was apprehensive. What if he failed again? Maybe it would be better to postpone the consummation. If he did not try then he would not have to face failure again.

Then he caught sight of the arch of Mariana's neck; it was slim and pearly and his gaze travelled down the edge of her robings to where the cloth stretched across her bosom

"'**Thy two breasts are like two young roes that are twins, which feed among the lilies'**'," he murmured.

Mariana looked up at him.

"I beg your pardon. I didn't hear you."

"'Twas nothing. Are you ready? Are you ready to go upstairs?" He could hardly keep the excitement out of his voice. How could he have contemplated not taking his bride tonight a moment ago? There was no need for guilt anymore. No need for prayer or fasting. This was his wife, by legal right. The hour had come to make her his wife not only in name but also in truth!

"I'll go up and… wait," she whispered.

"You know your way, don't you? Mrs Beacon has shown you your room and I instructed her to leave candles alight on the stairs."

"Yes, I know my way."

Griffith watched her go. He had not expected her to be this placid; he always thought of her as fiery. Yet, somehow, he was comforted by her tranquillity, for he felt it was seemly in a young maiden on her wedding night. Also it gave the lie to the rumours about her wildness. He would not give her too long to prepare, for already he could feel the blood coursing through his veins. Images of her undressing sent shivers of anticipation along his body. He strode from the room. Speed would be important if he was to succeed, he reasoned. He climbed the stairs two at a time.

Mariana was seated on a low stool, brushing her hair. Her clothes were dropped on the floor, ready for her maid to pick up in the morning. She was wearing a long shift which allowed only a glimpse of her marvellous curves but he was enthralled by her hand moving, with rhythmic strokes, over her luxurious, shining locks.

"Will you take off your… your shift so I can look at you?" he stammered. His voice sounded croaky even to himself and too abrupt, but immediately she arose and laid her silver hairbrush down. Then she undid the fastenings with shaking fingers and let it slide to the ground in a shimmering pool at her feet. Now her hair was her only covering and she looked, not at him, but seemingly at a spot on the wall behind him. He held his breath. She was as magnificent as his imaginings – a princess – a goddess.

Whilst the moments ticked by there was silence between them except for the crackle of the fire and the wind rattling the window. He couldn't have said how long they stood there before she said:

"Parson… Griffith? Are you all right? Can I get into bed? I'm cold."

He heard her voice from far away. His body was rigid but his hands hung loosely by his sides. He could feel sweat on his brow and running down his back. How could he answer her? How could he tell her that after years of wanting her, now he had her, he was no more able to lie with her than he had his first wife? He knew, even with the image of her naked femininity dancing before his eyes, that it was no good. He had been so sure, so convinced that with this sensuous creature he would be able to enjoy his marriage properly, but his body told him otherwise and he cursed himself and his father.

Turning from Mariana, he stamped from the room and down into his study, bolting the door behind him. Once he was alone, violent shivers took hold of him. Waves of anger and frustration rode through him and he gripped the solid wood of his desk in an attempt to stop them whilst his mind swung back through the years to when he was five.

He was an only child and lonely with it. For his entire childhood he had been in awe of his father and worshipped his mother.

"**'He that spareth the rod hateth his son: but he that loveth him chasteneth him betimes.'**"

That had been his father's maxim, although Griffith had been such a quiet, conforming child that the mere threat of a beating sufficed on all occasions. That is until the night that had haunted him for the rest of his life. It was two weeks after his fifth birthday, but the memory never seemed to dim.

Although he had a nursemaid from the time he was born, his mother had spent many hours holding him and talking to him. He was told that she had waited ten years for him and she believed, rightly it turned out, that she would not have another child. She soon dismissed the nursemaid as incompetent because, he learnt later, she wanted him all to herself.

What a wonderful mother she was! She had taught him his letters and how to sing whilst she played the harp. She had crooned over him and cuddled him until she became the centre of his world.

Then he overheard the servants saying that, because his father reckoned that his son was growing up pampered, he had arranged for him to have a tutor who would arrive soon after his fifth birthday. Griffith lay awake at night in trepidation. He didn't understand the word 'effeminate', which the maid had used. What did it mean and why did his father's concerns of him growing up 'effeminate' mean that he and his mother should be separated? His response to his father trying to keep him away from his beloved mother was to increasingly seek her out, often in her own room, where he would sit on her lap and smell her heady perfume which he associated with her. Mama. Dear Mama.

The day he had his first beating was the day he met his tutor for the first time. Mr Macdonald was a gaunt man with a stammer. He came from Scotland and appeared to listen closely to Griffith's father expounding on the strict standards he required, whilst Griffith cowered in the corner. The teacher seemed very tall and unfamiliar to him and his terrors intensified. He began to weep for the tender arms of his mother.

"Mama, Mama," he sobbed repeatedly.

His father demanded that he stop but he was frightened of his father too; both men filled him with apprehension. Finally his father fetched his stick and hit his son twice on his buttocks. It was not very hard but the boy bawled all the louder and twisted from the room and ran straight to his mother's room.

"Come back!"

Griffith could hear that his father was even more incensed. The man's footsteps sounded loud and measured as he trod down the corridor and Griffith sought refuge behind his mother's skirts.

"Go to the schoolroom!" The words were roared and Griffith saw his mother put her hands over her ears. He wanted to do the same but panic made him cling to the soft, reassuring folds of his mother's clothes.

"Leave him, Father," advised his mother. "He's only a baby and he's upset now. Let him stay with me until he's calm. I promise you that I will personally bring him back to the schoolroom and settle him into his desk. After all, my dear, it is only his first day and Mr Macdonald is unknown to him. Don't you agree, Mr Macdonald?"

Griffith sank to his knees when he saw his father swell with rage. How could his mother have been brave enough to stand up to this ogre? Had she no fear? Even the tutor's face was pale. Was he afraid too?

"No!" came the retort. Without warning the boy was scooped up, away from the safety of his mother's protection, and carried under his father's arm. But Griffith wasn't prepared to go without a fight! Foreboding added strength to his kicks and screams.

Once the schoolroom was reached, his father caught up the stick and beat him until he lay on the floor, his whole body on fire. His crying subsided to dry sobs, which racked his thin frame. He turned his face to the hard wood, certain that he was going to die.

"Get up, son." The command was said quietly but to this day, Griffith was never sure if there was remorse in the tone. Painfully he pulled himself upright but he kept his eyes lowered. "Now you will begin your lessons. I am paying Mr Macdonald to educate you and he is going to start today. If I see any more of this babyish behaviour in you I will beat you again until you learn to grow up and be a man."

Without a backward glance he swept from the room.

Griffith cringed once more when his tutor approached him but the stranger spoke slowly and kindly:

"Well, Griffith, I think we'll start with some reading, but I expect you'd rather stand than sit."

With hindsight, after a stringent daily regime was established, Griffith recognised that his tutor had taken pity on him. The lessons were kept lighthearted and fun, but for the small boy the hours were an anguish, not simply from the agony of his rear end but from a desire to see his mother again. He wanted to be held to her breast and assured that she would protect him from his vicious father. He willed the day away.

However, when finally he was released from his studies and he was free to visit her, he found her door locked. To his knowledge it had never been barred before and his anguish increased. Had his father beaten her too? He climbed the stairs to his own bedroom high up under the roof, with wretchedness in his heart. He flung himself on to his bed, miserable and sore, to fret away more hours.

In the middle of the night he woke in a sweat. He had been dreaming about bears. He had seen a dancing bear at a fair once and, in his dream, there had been a whole string of huge, brown animals. They were joined together by heavy chains and were lumbering towards him. Without warning they reared up on their back legs and, from nowhere, came sticks and their faces changed to his father's face, duplicated along the line. He awoke with his heart thumping, scared and disorientated.

"Mama," he wailed. "Mama."

Yet his mother didn't come. Where was she? He must find her. He tiptoed downstairs and to her room, his bare feet making no sound. Silently he opened the door.

There was his father in bed, lying on top of his mother and coming from between his legs was a short stick. His father was beating his mother again and again and she was crying out in pain.

Griffith stood and watched, transfixed, torn between a desire to leap on his father's back and make him stop, and the need to creep away and pretend he had seen nothing.

Suddenly his father turned. If Griffith had thought that his father was angry earlier, it was nothing to the rage that encompassed him in that moment. All the boy could do was to stand and stare at his father's naked body with its stick waving dangerously in the air. Then he was being thrashed again.

* * *

The Reverend Mr Owen closed his eyes and sank to his knees. How clear was every detail of that dreadful experience, even after all these years! Of course, in adulthood he had understood the scene in the bedchamber. Yet he himself was unable to perform the same duty to his own wife, such were his feelings of terror remembered from that day.

He was aware that people thought his first wife was barren, but how could they have known that she had remained a virgin? Was it all going to be repeated? Was he to fail with Mariana too? He shook his fists in the air and silently called on God. How cruel He was! Now the Parson understood why the woman who had filled his mind continually had been allowed to marry him. So that she could sit at his table, walk in his garden, lie in his bed each and every night and torment him forever with his failure. What excruciating torture God had planned for him. He was in hell!

EDWARD

Edward half-leaned out of the carriage window. He could smell cut grass! Oh, to have left behind the stench of the city and be journeying towards the scattered village of Soho! He was finally off to meet the Admiral. He was not sure how formal an interview this was going to be, but he was glad to see the countryside as they drove to Sir Humphries' Tudor home. It was set amongst green fields away from the soot-stained grime of the city. Thomas had emitted a whoop when he saw the farms and tilled land, and Edward had wanted to echo the exclamation of joy! Edward knew the lad had been missing his home and, if he were honest, he was homesick too for his own windy corner of Anglesey. He would like to walk along the misty coast or ride across the sandy beaches. Most of all he ached to see Mariana.

Edward leant back into the carriage seat – it was too uncomfortable to press all his weight on his one good leg and also slightly embarrassing to be hanging out of the window like a child excited to arrive at the place of destination. He closed his eyes and let his nostrils remind him of where he was and when he shut out the visual stimuli, his thoughts returned to the events of the last few weeks.

What a strange time it had been! He had left *Trem-y-Môr* with a heavy heart. Even the possible prospect of a new command, in charge of a secret voyage, had not raised his spirits. On the journey to London he had found Wilson a surprisingly entertaining companion. The old servant was perceptive and the two men had talked well into the night on several occasions about Sir William and Edward's real mother and his stepmother. What a mine of information Wilson had turned out to be! He had lived with the family for such a long time that he was really one of them. Yet, Edward reckoned, that his lack of involvement and not being on an equal footing with the people he served, enabled him to observe and he was able to make canny assessments of each of them. When Edward had exhausted the subject of his relatives, *he* had regaled Wilson with tales of his seafaring days and they had laughed together. The only person whom Edward did not talk about, although he would often turn Wilson's conversation towards her, was Mariana. However, he wondered if this very omission meant that Wilson had an insight into the real situation. He hoped not!

Edward's first task on reaching the busy capital was to find lodgings. He chose the 'Wishing Well': an inn where he was unknown; he was very conscious of the confidentiality of his summons by Admiral Humphries.

Once he had been shown his rooms (which consisted of a bedchamber and an adjoining parlour which overlooked the walled garden containing the old well itself) Edward had left Wilson unpacking. He had passed Thomas standing apparently awestruck in the yard, seemingly astounded by the bustle and noises of a hectic city inn. He had decided to go and see Annie (the prostitute who had sent him a letter) and get that unpleasantness behind him, and then tomorrow he would visit the Admiral. By the following day he trusted he would be feeling a bit more rested after the journey!

He had found Annie's lodgings with some difficulty. He concluded that he must have been rather the worse for drink when he had come here before. He was shocked by the steep climb up four flights of stairs. How had he managed that with his leg? Even months later, with his stump healed, he was breathless and tired when he reached the highest landing. He had knocked on the door and, hearing no reply, he pushed it open. He had no intention of coming again if the woman was out.

Annie's room was on the top floor of an old tenement. He could picture it now as the carriage swayed and shook. Annie's quarters must have covered the entire top floor of the building but, because she lived under the eaves, the sloping, damp roof took away the majority of the space since no one could stand upright except in the very centre of the room. Also, he recalled the prostitute's room was full of clutter and dust with only one filthy window, which didn't look as if it had been wiped for years; the untidiness and dimness increased the wretchedness.

Initially Edward's senses were assaulted by the stink of vomit and illness, but more than that there was a feeling of hopelessness pervading the air. Was death lurking in the corner? Edward halted. He wanted to turn tail and leave. His own fragile emotions could hardly cope with taking on board another person's problems.

Was Annie even here? He peered into the gloom whilst he raised his hand to cover his nose. Then he heard a groan and he saw, beneath the rags which served as blankets, Annie. At least he assumed it was the woman who had written to him because so thin and wizened was she that he did not recognise her at all. Had he really laid his head on those shrivelled breasts? No, she had been young then with a roundness which asked to be squeezed and, although her face had been painted, she had been clean. He did not remember this room. Was he at the right place? Yes, he recalled the low roof, for they had laughed when he had banged his head against it again and again. But the bed was different. There had been red satin sheets on it. He clearly remembered them for at the time he had thought them out of keeping with the rest of the impoverished furnishings. Nevertheless, he had concluded, her bed was her place for work; thus, on his last visit, he had dismissed the sheets and turned his attention to the woman that they held!

"Annie?" he queried, moving cautiously across the room, careful of his head with the roof and of his feet with the mess on the floor.

The emaciated woman sat up. He saw the pain etched on the face when she pulled herself upright. The covers fell away to reveal yellowed skin and an enormous bump. The baby! How could he have forgotten the child? It was the reason for his coming. It seemed obscene against the frailty of the rest of her skinny body. To his eyes it looked as if it might arrive at any moment. At first the woman's gaze was unfocused. Was she about to faint? he wondered. Then she clutched the stained edge of the covers across her flattened breasts and said:

"I ain't got no more. Yer can't take no more, 'cos there ain't none."

She spoke remarkably strongly for a sick woman, he thought. However, when she had finished speaking, she began to cough and the cough turned to vomiting. She spewed up black bile which ran down the side of the bed to the floor. Edward looked around for a basin or receptacle which he could hold up to catch the disgusting liquid, but he could not identify anything quickly and she had finished and was lying back, wheezing for breath, before he could move.

"Annie, it's me. Captain Rowlands. You wrote to me. Remember?"

"Ah." There was remembrance in her eyes. "Yer too late. I'm a goner and so's the babe. No." Feebly she held up her hand. She seemed visibly weaker after her coughing fit. "Don't come no nearer. I'm mortal sick."

"But can't I do anything to help you?" Edward offered. He had intended not to part with a farthing of his money to this conniving woman and now he found himself filled with pity. He was contemplating finding someone to visit and clean up this dump and nurse Annie in her last few hours. After all, she had been a help to him all those months ago in his hour of need! She had comforted him not just with her body but with true sympathy. "Look, can I get you food? Or money? Shall I leave you some money?"

"No need, Cap'n, though it's kind of yer to offer. Nothing fer you to do. I ain't got long."

"I'll tidy up a bit…"

"No!" She actually managed to shout, but it appeared to take her strength. "Don't come near else yer'll get it. Go! Go! Just to see yer has helped. Yer came."

Edward hadn't the heart to say that he had come to tell her to leave him alone, that the child could not possibly be his! What did it matter now? In a few hours she would be dead and she was right: the longer he stayed here, the more likely he was to catch her illness and the smell of the room was upsetting him increasingly with the passing minutes. He felt queasy already.

"I'll give you some money," he told her.

"Don't yer come near." She coughed twice before croaking, "Throw it."

He was touched by her concern for him. Taking two sovereigns from his pocket, carefully he threw them on to the bed, where they sat gleaming for a brief second, incongruous against the dirty rags. Then her claw-like hand grasped them and tucked them out of sight in the confines of her bed.

"Ta."

"It was nothing." He had never meant to give that much but compassion had overridden common sense. "I hope… hope that you feel better soon. The baby is…"

"The babe is dead," she enunciated despairingly and closed her eyes in farewell.

He stood for a full minute, undecided as to what to do further for her. Then slowly he turned and picked his way back to the door. Only then did he notice some of the contents of the room: piles of filthy garments (were they hers?), a chair with one leg missing, an overturned cooking pot (that would have served as a basin earlier), a cracked mirror. Suddenly from nowhere, scuttling before his slow stride, two furry, fat rats appeared, possibly foraging for food. He glanced back one last time at the dying woman.

"I'm sorry," he remarked softly. "So sorry."

Then he hurried away.

Even when he reached his own lodgings he could not rid himself of the melancholy which had settled on him in that dreadful room. The memory of the broken-down whore filled his thoughts. Wilson, on hearing the account of the visit, insisted that Sir Edward give him all his clothes to be cleaned, including his wig.

Reluctantly Edward changed his coat, shirt and breeches and then sat down to pen a letter to those at the Manor House. However, he found that his head was aching and a black cloud had descended on his spirits. He would write tomorrow after he had been to see Admiral Humphries.

Edward opened his eyes and put a hand out to steady himself when the carriage hit a particularly deep rut. Were they nearly there? He hoped not because he was lost in the past still. He had never sent the letter the next day because, by the morning, he was vomiting also, and he was too ill to care whether he lived or died. He did not think to instruct Wilson to contact the Admiral or to write to his sisters; he was sunk in a world of pain and fever. He discovered subsequently that Wilson didn't have a spare moment to think about the rest of the family; he was busy making sure that his master did not tread the same path as the woman who had given him the illness.

For nearly eight days Edward had lain, alternating between a hazy state of uneasy sleep and violent vomiting. Wilson cared for him with the tenderness of a father. By the time Edward was alert enough to dictate a note to be sent to Admiral Humphries it was too late. He heard (by return post) that the job had been given to someone else. Remarkably, this unfair treatment had jerked Edward out of his misery and languor; he was determined to go and protest at being pushed aside. His pique had spurred on his recovery, although his body was so weakened by the illness that he was unable to rise from the bed for a further ten days.

Nevertheless, during his enforced bedrest, he had written to the Admiral, insisting on an audience, and had been informed that he could call whenever he was recovered. He presumed he was being made welcome because no one in the Fleet had any idea why he was requesting an interview. He had kept the true reason for seeing his superior until the day he should meet him face to face. Maybe they thought he was going to ask for a new command! In fact, he was furious at their cavalier treatment of him. How dare they summon him all the way from his estates, only to give the mission to another? Initially his anger had raced around his brain whenever he thought of it, but his body would descend into tiredness. He decided that he would compose a suitable speech when he was stronger. No one was going to push him around! He was still a captain, not an invalid whom people could step on! One leg or two!

During those days, when he was in his right mind but his pitiful body needed building up, he had remembered his sisters and that they did not know where he was staying. He had written to them forthwith. Once he had sent the one-page missive, he found himself brooding about them, especially Mariana. Through the hours of boredom he would recall the time he had spent at *Trem-y-Môr* and, in particular, images of his beautiful young half-sister danced before his eyes. He longed for a communication in return to hear how she was faring.

How he had wished that he could rise up from between the sheets, but Wilson turned out to be a very strict guardian and no amount of pleading from Edward could persuade his servant to allow him to get up before he was ready. He had sent one or two notes to his friends but he had dissuaded any from coming to visit in case of infection and he had whiled away the time by sleeping and dreaming of his love. Soon he would be able to see her again. He was surprised at how much he missed her and his own resolve not to mention it to anyone increased his loss: he would give anything to glimpse Mariana for just a moment!

Nonetheless, at least, he reckoned, the change in his circumstances meant that it would not be long before he could return to his estates. Since the confidential command was cancelled, he resolved to travel to Anglesey directly he had seen the Admiral. Thus, alongside the desire to speak his mind to his superiors, was the need to be healthy enough to attempt the journey back to North Wales. Both inducements aided his recovery and brought a relieved look to Wilson's face.

At last the chafing had ended and, apart from having to wait for a suit from the tailor (made because he had lost so much flesh during his illness) Edward was better and able to pick up his life where he had left off. Finally he had set forth to meet the Admiral and make his complaints. He had been in London just under four weeks. What a waste! If only he had known what his visit to Annie would do, he would not have gone to see her. In all possibility by now, she was dead, and, according to Wilson, he was lucky not to be dead himself.

Today, feeling the best he had for a month, he had dressed in his new clothes and climbed into the carriage. He opened his eyes again, to ascertain if the journey's end was in sight. Away to the left was a grand house, which he presumed belonged to the Admiral. Sure enough, the horses turned and the entire equipage passed through two brickwork pillars and along a sandy drive.

The past faded as the carriage slowed. He took a deep breath, straightened his cravat and began to rehearse the biting words he had prepared to give to his superior.

Actually Edward had several more minutes standing in a draughty hall to prepare his speech before the self-important butler ushered him into the presence of Sir Humphries. At the other end of the room from Edward the man he had come to meet was sitting at a table that could have seated a whole ship's company, but that nevertheless looked dwarfed against the dimension of the room in which it was placed. This was no dining room but a ball room! Between the table and Edward stretched perhaps sixty feet of floor, highly polished by some lowly housemaid until it was as slippery as a frozen lake. To a fellow with one leg it was a fearful prospect, even with the aid of a crutch. Edward gripped his stick fiercely. He was determined not to fall. That would be too embarrassing and would rob him of the poise he would need to express his indignation! Gingerly he trod towards the table.

The Admiral was partaking of midday repast and he seemed unaware of his guest's difficulty. He began firing questions at Edward the moment the butler had announced:

"Captain Rowlands."

"Ah, there you are Rowlands. Are you better? Glad to see you are. You've been hiding yourself in the backwoods somewhere. Where is it? Some God forsaken hole in Wales, isn't it? What made your father keep all his lands out there? Too far, by God! Heathens! That's what they are! Come and sit down. Would you like something to eat? Beef? Cheese? Fruit? I'll call Courtney to get you a plate. No, maybe not, for what I have to say to you is private!"

Since the older man had been bellowing in a voice which would have made the laziest seaman jump to attention, Edward suspected that the entire household would have heard his every word. However, because he was concentrating very hard on completing the last few steps he made no reply. The Admiral did not seem to need any answer anyway; he might have been talking to a stuffed animal, for all the real notice he was taking of Edward. He continued to shout. Edward sighed a silent prayer of thanks when he reached the table without even a slip of his foot. Briefly he stood behind one of the row of dining chairs which were neatly pushed beneath the gleaming polished surface and allowed himself to catch his breath. He did not even begin to think about the return journey. Sufficient that he had arrived within speaking distance of his superior. However, apparently he was expected to go even closer.

"Hurry up, Rowlands! What's keeping you? Come and sit down. Here, near me. No need to stand on ceremony with me. We've a secret to share, after all! Oh, it's your leg, is it? How is it? Are you used to it yet? Is it made of good, solid oak? How long is it since you were at sea?"

Edward made his way to where the other man was sitting, using the backs of the chairs to support him. He was wondering how he would manage aboard the moving deck of a ship if he was this unstable on land! Perhaps it was propitious that he had been turned down for this voyage. If only the old fool would stop speaking, he could begin his prepared speech.

"Rowlands, sit down, I tell you! Have you lost your tongue? I don't remember you as being so reticent. Sit down and listen. I've a task for you. The question is: will you be able to do it?"

Edward sank gratefully on to a chair three along from the Admiral. He had imagined that he would stand confidently before the man and say his piece but he had reckoned without this ordeal. He was out of breath. How humiliating! Had Sir Humphries planned it so? No, for he was talking about a job for him. What was he going to be offered now? He had better listen and then he could refuse. That would show them! He was not going to take orders from anyone after the way he had been treated!

He looked at his neighbour. He was a short man with a protruding stomach covered with yards of lace neatly arranged to show between the open sides of his silk waistcoat. His coat's sleeves had turned-back wings for cuffs, which reached up to his elbows and were extravagantly furnished with oversized, decorative buttons. Edward shook his head in wonder. When had this revered leader turned into such a fop? His buttons were trailing in the butter dish as he reached for more food. On his lacy shirt were crumbs and stains from his meal. Edward knew Sir Humphries had a formidable record of bravery in his youth, but today he looked like an infant learning to eat! How the mighty have fallen! Yet his voice was as booming as ever.

"Well, are you willing to do it, Rowlands?"

"What exactly do you want me to do, Sir?"

"Didn't you get my letter? Isn't that why you're here? The secret voyage. What's wrong with you, man? Your injury was to your leg, wasn't it? Not your head."

"I... I thought the post had been taken. You wrote and told... told me that someone else had got the job." Edward frowned. Had his recent fever affected his memory? Or was his companion becoming forgetful in his dotage?

"Oh, that! No, no. Protocol. Secrecy. Misleading others. Can't have anyone else knowing your business, can we? What I have to say to you is very, very secret. Come on, Rowlands, eat something. Don't just sit there. I find myself, if I don't eat often, my stomach rumbles and rumbles. Wind, y'know. Bad problem with wind. Do you have the same? Now, enough of that. Where was I? The question is: can you go?"

"Go where, Sir?"

"To Portugal." Finally Sir Humphries lowered his voice to a conspiratorial whisper. "How out of touch are you? Do you keep yourself abreast with the latest news? The French, man."

"I know that there is talk of another war, Sir."

"Yes, yes. Let me explain the position. I must ask you not to tell any of this to anyone else at the moment. Of course, you were highly recommended for this assignment. You would not be here now if you were known for blabbing! Louis XIV is wanting to unite France with Spain and his plan is to put one of his *own* family on the Spanish throne."

"Very clever, Sir. The Spanish king has no children himself, does he, Sir?"

"No, Rowlands, and, more importantly, he's ill too and may die at any moment. So Louis will have to work quickly. In fact, there have been too many delays already. What with your illness and finding a suitable ship. However, you were asked for specifically and... there we are." His tone suggested that he himself had not thought the wait worthwhile but his superiors had overruled him.

Embarrassment reddened Edward's face; therefore he replied lightly:

"It would certainly be an extensive kingdom if King Louis can succeed. After all, Spain has many colonies in the New World too."

"Indeed! Indeed!" The Admiral resumed his hearty manner. "You don't need to tell me that! So, to what we want you to do. Our own King, God bless him, is wanting to form an alliance with as many countries as he can in order to enable us to resist the French." He paused. "I don't think it would take many guesses to see some of our allies. What do you think, eh?"

Edward watched his companion closely. Was it a rhetorical question?

"Well," Edward began haltingly. "There's Holland and…"

"Yes, yes. No need to list them all. Your only worry is Portugal, for that is where we want you to go."

"Portugal, Sir? She's not very big, but…" Edward stopped, enlightenment dawning. Life would be very dangerous for Portugal if France was able to join with Spain. If she sided with the French then England's fleets would attack her, but if she chose to be an ally of the British, then she would have a war on her hands situated next to Spain as she was!

Before Edward could continue, the Admiral stood up. Edward rose himself. Was this the end of the interview?

"Sir? What do you need me to do?"

"The King wants you to go to the Portuguese Court and deliver some secret letters."

"Sir!" Edward couldn't keep the incredulity out of his voice. "This is truly an honour. When does he want me to leave?"

"Soon, man, soon."

KATHERINE

Katherine raised her eyes from the paper on her lap and gazed between the lattice panes of glass out of the window. If she squinted she could see the sunken rose garden where she loved to walk and sit. There would be no one there at the moment for the full heat of the noon-day sun was upon the earth but maybe later she would visit it and find the peace it held for her in the velvet softness of the pale petals and the fragrance of the flowers themselves.

Katherine raised the paper to eye-level, glad she continued to be able to make out these strokes of the pen; she hadn't told anyone that her eyesight was failing. She read what she had written quietly under her breath, revelling in the metre, enjoying the words, marvelling that this had come from inside her:

> "The water crashes upon the shore,
> White horses galloping along the tide,
> Never ceasing; they ride for evermore.
> Their raw strength pounds the sand on the beachside,
> Changing the landscape as they both collide.
> Ebbing, flowing…"

* * *

Ah, it was pleasing to be writing again. She had not done much creative work since the loss of her husband but this morning the words had sprung into her mind and she knew she must set them to paper before they eluded her. Once they were safely written down, she might change a word or two, but she had found that her initial thoughts were usually the best and if she tweaked the verses too much they lost some of their charm and originality.

Was there more inside her head? Not now, because crowding into her thoughts came the events of the past week. Who could have foreseen that she would be staying here and not arrived at her half-sister's home on the isle of Anglesey? And who could have imagined that she would have two proposals of marriage in the same number of days? Oh, to be a bride again, sweet and innocent; brave and beautiful.

She had started the journey to see Mariana in good faith, albeit after a few days of procrastination. She had known that it was her duty to call upon her relations, but she had delayed and delayed the departure, using the inclement weather as her principal excuse. In truth, her reluctance came from the sheer enormity of the distance she was going to have to travel and the years of separation; she had never actually met Mariana and it was hard to go such a great many miles to comfort someone she didn't know or really care for.

She had entreated Daniel to accompany her, even though she was aware he had a prior engagement. Each summer, he would visit the houses of the wealthy and paint the bonny baby of the family or the comely wife of an ageing lord or the champion horse of the landowner. Whilst he remained with her at *Little Oaks* he had no salary. She paid for all his living expenses since he was her companion, but it was her understanding that these summer expeditions – and he could travel as far as the northern parts of England – gave him coins in his pockets to cover any expenses and for his private needs. She knew it was unfair to ask him to forgo this. Nonetheless, she had enquired whether he could postpone his first commission until her return from Wales. He had looked distressed, presumably that he couldn't comply with her wishes, but had told her that the dates of this particular appointment could not be changed because the family were going abroad within the month. Thus he had abandoned her, with a promise to return in the autumn, and left for an estate just thirty miles north of London to paint a series of pictures of four well-favoured daughters of an earl.

Katherine had surmised that the empty house would encourage her to depart but a lethargy had descended on her and several days of thunderstorms followed by weak patches of sunshine enabled her to convince herself each day that today wasn't the day to set off.

Then had come an invitation to a select gathering at the home of an old friend of her husband's, Oliver Whiting. She calculated that this was not far off the route to walk and she had figured that she and Phoebe could cope with a single day's journey to Chelsea Castle – nowhere near the old village of Chelsea which was now very much part of the city of London, but south west of the capital, set in breathtaking grounds beside a picturesque village.

With her personal maid, Tanneke, who had been sent from her husband's maternal home in Holland a good decade ago, travelling with her in the carriage, and her dog sitting on the seat beside her, Katherine had begun her journey, after many remonstrations to the butler, Cooke, and the housekeeper, Hoddy. It was many years since she had left home.

The first leg of her errand of mercy had passed without a hitch, but she had found the jolting of the carriage gave her a headache and Phoebe had become listless. Thus, when she had entered the echoing hall of Chelsea Castle, dark and chilly even in the late afternoon sunshine, to be met by Oliver, she had begged to be excused and asked to retire to her room. She couldn't face meeting any of his other guests until she had recovered.

The next day, she had descended the wide stone staircase in search of the dining room and, without the hurry of yesterday, noticed the furnishings of the hall. Several suits of armour caught her eye and a huge bearskin rug, which some ancient predecessor of Oliver had shot and brought back from Russia. These she recognised from previous visits but no longer were there colourful flowers to brighten the dreariness of the room and, of course, no fire was lit in the empty grate, because it was summer. She shivered, remembering a cameo of the time she and Alexandre had attended for a Twelfth Night party. Then the space had been filled with laughing merrymakers in fancy dress (Alexandre had come as Henry VIII and she as Anne Boleyn) and the warm wine and festive jollity had driven away the coldness of the thick stone walls and the aged wooden rafters in the recesses of the draughty roof way above their heads. The Minstrels' Gallery had been keeping up to its name with a group of musicians and Katherine had smiled and danced with her beloved husband until nearly dawn. Now, her footsteps reverberated and she stood at the bottom of the stairs and tried to recall which door led to the dining room. A gusty bellow of laughter suggested the way and she pushed open the heavy oak door to survey her host and another man who greeted her with a cry of delight:

"Katherine! How wonderful to see you again!"

She looked at this be-wigged stranger in confusion.

"Don't say you don't remember me! We met a few years ago and I am an old school friend of your brother."

"My brother?" Katherine was no nearer to recollecting his name and threw a glance at her host.

"Beg pardon, my dear," Oliver acknowledged her plea. "Where are my manners? This is Captain John Lucas."

"Yes, I have known your family for years. I am sorry to hear that you have lost your father."

"You have seen Edward?"

"No, but I have heard from him. He is in London recovering from a fever caught from a… well, caught, as many of our summer illnesses, from the very streets beneath our feet. But you'll be glad to know he's just about recovered and off on a secret voyage for the Admiral, lucky bug… lucky man!"

"Please sit down, my dear." Oliver indicated a chair near to himself. "I hope you too are recovered from your journey. What will you have to eat?"

Katherine asked for some fruit, and selecting an apple from the bowl, she proceeded to cut and core it before slicing it thinly whilst the men tucked into a more substantial meal of what looked like venison. She considered the creamy slices and, deciding they were too big to put in her mouth without filling it too much, she quartered each slice and arranged the pieces in a neat pattern on her plate.

Silence was kept for a few minutes before the other guest enquired:

"And how is your clever husband? We spent a happy hour discussing mathematics last met we met. Is he going to join you?"

Oliver coughed twice into the painful pause.

"Alexandre passed away…"

"Oh, my dear Katherine, how uncouth of me! I had not heard. I hope you are…"

"I am improving slowly," murmured Katherine, touching Phoebe's head for reassurance and comfort. This man was too loud for the morning table!

"I, too, have lost my wife of ten years. Letitia was taken up during the pox epidemic last year and I have found…"

"My mother's name was 'Letitia'," commented Katherine. She had decided that she didn't like this man, and once she was finished with her fruit she would think of an excuse to return to her room. She was relieved that there was not a large party being entertained, although it might just be that others would come down later. She must hasten away soon. But to be able to chew and clear the plate, she must not talk and therefore she asked politely:

"Are you home on leave from your ship, Mr Lucas?

She didn't listen to his reply but ate quickly and then made her escape to the sunken rose garden after enquiring on directions from her host on how to get there. This gem she had discovered on one of their previous sojourns here and it came as no surprise to learn that Oliver's late wife had spent many happy days in this superlative part of the landscaped gardens.

Katherine took advantage of the sun breaking through the charcoal indented clouds, and sat and let the welcome rays bathe her, allowing the tension of the meeting with the enthusiastic Mr Lucas soak away through the stones underneath her toes. She would forgive him since he had such a round, jovial face, beneath his curly wig, and bright blue eyes. He behaved like a young man, although, if he was Edward's contemporary, he couldn't be more than a year or two younger than her.

It was later that same day that Katherine met Mr Lucas for the second time, and much to her own amazement she found herself changing her judgement of him, and it was poetry that caused this reappraisal. She discovered that through his wife he was familiar with many of her favourite poets and she saw a gentler, more modest side to the assertive Mr Lucas. There followed several days of budding friendship, and if his hearty laugh punctuated their intimacy, she noticed it was usually after he had drunk a glass or two of wine and she excused him because she believed that his grief over the loss of Letitia was more raw than he had led her to believe at first.

It was on her fourth day at Chelsea Castle, when her conscience was pricking her that she ought to be leaving to make that postponed visit to her half-sister, when she saw a familiar figure come around the lily pond. The man's arrival set Phoebe barking excitedly and her own heart fluttered with joy: it was Daniel.

"What are you doing here?" she called whilst he marched around the pond. "Don't fall in! And, you, Phoebe, be quiet, you silly thing! Don't you fall in either! Come here, my baby, come away from the water."

Neither man nor beast succumbed to her fears and she flung out her hands to grasp Daniel's capable fingers.

"What are you doing here?" she repeated. "Did you hear me above Phoebe?"

"I did hear you but felt I wouldn't shout my answer to the whole world! Oh, all right, you little darling, I have noticed you."

There followed a few moments whilst the dog squirmed and wriggled under Daniel's comforting stroking. Thus Katherine did not hear the explanation of his appearance until they had traversed the stone steps up through the shrubbery.

"It was some spotty rash which had not been identified yet by a physician. I wasn't even allowed into the place, although I would have liked to see what the daughters of an earl looked like with spots. I was shooed away, spent an uncomfortable night in an inn and was riding back to *Little Oaks* when I remembered you were on your way to see your sister and that now I can accom…"

His words petered out when they were joined by another.

"Oh, Daniel, this is John Lucas, who is staying with Oliver. I assume you have met my host, Oliver Whiting. He knew my husband, but John was at school with my brother. John, this is Daniel …"

Katherine's words dried up as a flash of what appeared to be hatred sped between the two men.

"Have you met before?" She was confused by the depth of feeling in the air.

"No," growled Daniel.

"I haven't had that pleasure." John gave a watery smile and extended a hand. "Who did you say you were?"

"I am a fr…" began Daniel at the same time as Katherine replied:

"Daniel is a distant cousin of mine. He is staying as my guest at my home and we…"

Once more her words died. Why had she fibbed? Some womanly intuition about why these two men were eyeing each other like rival dogs fighting over a female. This is ridiculous, Katherine chided herself. She must be wrong. Daniel had never been proprietorial before and she had only been acquainted with John for four days!

Notwithstanding, that initial assessment returned to her again and again when she watched the men relating. She found it very distasteful and looked for an opportunity to speak to Daniel but she was never alone with either of them because she found herself with raging headaches which started in the morning and barely shifted by noon, only to return when the candles were lit with the fading light. She spent time in her own bedchamber, hardly touching the food that was brought to her, and was alarmed when a knock came at her door one evening. Gratefully she saw the full figure of Oliver on the threshold and willingly welcomed him in. The conversation which passed between them relieved her anxieties and she woke the next day feeling refreshed, with all forebodings gone and a sense of peace.

She was able to spend time in prayer and then instructed Tanneke to fetch her most becoming gown. She had decided to forego the first meal of the day and take Phoebe for an early morning walk. The mint green gown had a tight-fitting bodice but no robings; its rounded neckline ended in a tucker. The front of the bodice, one with the skirt, wrapped over itself and Katherine fastened it with an emerald brooch – a present from her mother-in-law sent from their Dutch family home with Tanneke. She knew the gown suited her and the new-found peace lent roses to her often pale cheeks. She set forth confidently.

Her solitude was broken by John, fortuitously alone! He informed her that he had been for a ride but there was no sweat on his brow or crease in his shirt and she discerned that he had washed and changed before he had sought her out, for that was what he said to her:

"I came to find you."

"Find me? Is all well?"

"Indeed, never better. Shall we sit awhile?"

He seemed rather serious and for one terrible moment she feared that he was going to propose to her, but he talked about his retirement from the Navy next year and surprisingly confided in her about how much he sorrowed still over the baby daughter who had died at three days old. He admitted that he told very few people about his grief because he felt embarrassed that he should continue to be upset five years after the baby's death. Katherine understood and sympathised, although she had never lost a child, not only because Alexandre was no longer with her but she could imagine how devastated she would be if anything were to happen to Phoebe.

Soon John lightened the conversation by offering to accompany her to North Wales. He explained that he would love to see 'Rowly's' home – "That's your brother, Edward. I used to call him that at school." He went on to say that he hoped they could spend some happy hours reading poetry on the journey and ended by flattering her. The compliments that he paid her made her blush and she said that she wasn't sure when she would be setting off again but she would consider his kind offer. With this he had risen, bowed over her hand, brushed it with a kiss and withdrawn.

Hard on his heels and much to Katherine's consternation came Daniel.

He appeared to have dressed in his best clothes too and had been looking for an opportunity to talk to her. Had he watched John walk away across the dew-covered grass? Without further ado, he had dropped to his knee, grasping her left hand in his and asked her to be his wife.

"Don't be ridiculous!" she had exclaimed. "You're far too young!"

"I'm twenty-two, my sweet angel, and I hope that the difference in our ages will enhance our relationship, not hinder it!"

"I'm old enough to be your mother! Get up, Daniel! People might see you."

"I don't care! I love you and I want to marry you. I thought we could visit Venice on our honeymoon and then return to *Little Oaks* in the spring."

"Daniel, get up! I refuse to discuss this any further unless you stand up."

"All right," he acceded, "but I just wanted you to know that I am serious. I have loved you for as long as I can remember and I have just been looking for the right time to speak to you and…"

"Hush, Daniel! Come and sit by my side. I am really touched by your declaration but I can't accept it because…"

"Please don't say it's because I am too young. My father married my mother at twenty-two and I'm sure we can get along together because we have had all these months…"

"Hush, I say! I can't accept your proposal because I have already agreed to marry someone else."

Daniel leapt to his feet with a cry:

"I knew it! That Lucas! He got here before me! I should have spoken to you earlier – before you ever met him. You can't love him. He's…"

"Daniel, I have told you to be quiet. Please let me finish. It is not Mr Lucas who has asked for my hand in marriage. It is dear Oliver. He…"

If she had hoped to calm him with this information she was mistaken. He howled as if in pain. She stood herself at this, dismay and apprehension churning inside her. She had never seen him like this; usually he was so equable and… and accommodating to her wishes.

"Daniel?" She twisted her hands in agitation. "Daniel, please stop. You're upsetting me."

He had paced away from her with that cry of anguish but now he strode back to her and gripped her by the shoulders and she saw deep into his hazel eyes. There was real torment and she could not bear it. She jerked away from him and he released her without trying to prevent her moving.

She saw Phoebe cowering under the stone seat and she gathered her pet into her arms, tears falling on to the soft grey fur.

"I am so sorry," she whispered. "I didn't know. I thought we were friends. Why didn't you say something? Tell me?"

"Because I was waiting. Waiting for you to come out of your grief. I loved you. I didn't want to upset you. But when you called me your cousin… How could you? Why did you? I thought then that…"

"I don't know why I did it, dear Daniel. It just slipped out. I felt something between you and I… I'm sorry. I shouldn't have said it. I should have just told John that you were my dearest and best friend. And it's the truth, Daniel. You *are* my dearest and best friend! But, that's all. When I agreed to marry Oliver, I didn't think of you…. I just assumed that you would follow me and live here or if Oliver and I live at *Little Oaks* that you would remain there, going away on your summer jaunts, but that we would still be friends. I suppose, at the back of my mind, I imagined that you would find a buxom young wife and you would come to me and ask if she could join our idyll and I would say 'Yes', but I never thought – I didn't realise – I didn't know you loved me. You know, as a man loves a woman. I'm sorry. What will you do?"

The tears were flowing fast now, down her cheeks and on the back of the dog and splashing on to the ground. Suddenly Daniel was at her side. Briefly she wondered if he was going to embrace her but, to her surprise, he went down, not on one but two knees. He pressed his head against Phoebe's fur and the little dog turned and began to lick his face. Were there tears on his skin too?

"Don't cry, my sweet angel. I can't bear to see you cry. We will work something out. If only you will let me stay. I need to stay near you. I want to be able to look at you and draw you and put your image down on canvas – your beguiling smile, your tender lips, your peaceful eyes, your slim waist and your glorious hair. Don't tell Oliver that I love you. I won't ever mention it again. I will keep in it my heart and treasure it there, if you will agree to me staying by you forever."

Katherine released the slender animal into his arms and allowed both pet and man to lean against her full skirts.

She had promised that he could make his home with her and she had agreed not to mention his love for her to anyone else. She had stroked the top of his head with a caress not dissimilar to that which she gave to

Phoebe and she had believed that all would be well.

And today, just twenty-four hours later, that sense of wellbeing had not left her. In fact, the new arrangements for her future suited her so much that she had been able to start to compose this poem. She touched the silky head of Phoebe, recalling the feel of Daniel's hair, and smiled softly to herself. All things would work together for good.

EDWARD

Edward stood up as swiftly as he could with his awkward wooden leg and limped across the sumptuous room to the graceful woman standing near the window.

"Is it true, Aunt Anne? Is it true?" he implored.

"Edward, would I lie to you? Of course it's true! I have – somewhere – a letter from her to me. If you like, I can go and search for it, but it will take a little time because I keep *every* letter sent to me. Over the years I have accumulated quite a few, so I will have to look through them all for this particular one."

Edward gazed into the eyes of this woman who had become like a mother to him. Her face was tired and lined with wrinkles but her smile was the same as it had always been and her gentian blue eyes invariably held a welcome for him.

She was dressed in the fashion from twenty years ago: a gown of fawn beige with a gathered open skirt which had been drawn up and back and pinned to the waistline of her bodice to reveal a beige and pink striped top petticoat. Edward guessed that assisting the numerous petticoats she wore under her skirt, to spring out from her still narrow waist, would be a hip pad, unseen, but giving her extra poise. The full sleeves of her damask bodice were pulled by drawstrings to form a forth of frills about the elbows. The bodice had been cut to reveal the V-point of her corset at the front waistline and around her neck was a string of polished stones. These were beige with a pinkish hue which enhanced her gown.

Delightfully and expensively dressed as usual! Edward understood that his uncle never stinted on her clothing allowance. Her greying hair was covered by a cap of lace which had several pleated frills sewn on its face edge. These developed into streamers or lappets which fell right down to her bosom. It was this style of cap particularly which Edward remembered his aunt wearing consistently, and which now younger women were discarding for the latest style, as fashion dictated. Yet his aunt did not look either old or frumpy. At least not to him. The cap suited her and somehow was comforting to him. He felt she would live forever, never changing and, during a season when much was new and different, he liked to come and visit her.

Now, here she was, standing there looking exactly as she had a few moments ago, and yet what she had told him had altered his entire life. His whole world had shifted beneath him, opening unexpected avenues for him to travel down and making him feel as if he was walking on air. Did she realise what this information meant to him? He suspected that she did, for she was shrewd and knew him well – maybe better than anyone else in his family. He had been so cut off from all his relatives for all those years, except his dear aunt and her husband. Of course he had written to Penelope, but Pen, when he had seen her recently, had herself changed. She had developed, from caterpillar to butterfly, under the love of her husband and the respect of her neighbours, into a stately, young matron, wise for her years, honest and friendly. Where was the introverted girl he remembered? She had gone.

However, his aunt had remained the same each time he had returned from foreign lands. She had been ready with a cordial smile and a listening ear on every occasion. Yes, that was her strength. She listened. Indeed, she was an ideal mother – certainly by his standards. He was intelligent enough to surmise that it was probably the very fact that she was *not* his mother that enabled him to have such a good relationship with her. How appropriate that it should be she who had told him the news which had revived him!

He reached for her hands and smiled down at her.

"Aunt Anne, I believe you. Like you say, why should you lie to me? But, if you could find the letter from Mariana, it would be… Well, it would really help me… to see it written down, you know."

"Of course, I understand. You love her daughter, don't you, my son?"

"Oh, Aunt, yes I do."

The woman leant forward to kiss him on his cheek.

"You seem taller with that peg, but you can't be. Please, take a seat, for I may be a while. Pull the bell if you require anything."

"Thank you. Don't worry about me. I can wait now and… and dream."

Whilst his aunt left the room, her skirts swishing, Edward sat down and blinked in the afternoon sun. He tried to still his racing pulse and control the excitement bubbling up inside him. This news was like finding a chest full of treasure! He could hardly believe it!

First that amazing request from the Admiral. He could hear the words ringing in his head!

"The King wants you to go to the Portuguese Court and deliver some secret letters."

Edward rubbed his upper thighs. His bad leg seemed to be aching much more after this latest illness. Nonetheless he tried to hide the pain. He did not want to have to forego such an important venture due to bad health. A job for the King himself! To think he had gone to Sir Humphries' home intent on speaking his mind. Thank God for that shiny floor! That had so taken up his concentration that his anger had evaporated and he had kept his mouth shut. Thank you, God! What an opportunity to have missed through his own ill temper! A whole week had passed since then and he had been sent no further orders. It allowed him time to fully regain his strength, but since yesterday the hours had begun to drag again and he had decided to come to visit his relatives. He knew that his old friend, John Lucas, had gone into the country and he didn't seem to have the patience to renew acquaintances with people he knew less well.

First the King's orders and now this! Strange how everything was happening at once! To think that only yesterday...

The door opened and his aunt entered.

"Ah, Edward, here I am. I can't believe it! The letter was in the first place I looked!"

"How wonderful!"

"Do you want to read it?"

"Could you just tell me how it started, please? Then, yes, I should like to read it. I'm completely overwhelmed. I can scarce take it in."

"Where shall I start? What do you remember of your stepmother? I recall clearly the very first time I saw her. It was in this very room. I was shocked, I must admit. Your mother, Letitia, was... Well, Mariana and she couldn't have been more dissimilar. Mariana was beautiful, of course. Not that Letitia... Oh, dear, I shouldn't have put it like that! Letitia was... was ordinary, but Mariana was out of this world. And it wasn't just how she looked. She was beautiful inside too. You never missed her when she was in the room, even if it was crowded. Not that she pushed herself forward so that everyone would notice her... No, she was almost shy, but without that awkwardness shy people often have. Oh, I don't know how to describe her.

You *knew* she would never say anything to upset you. She had impeccable manners, but it was more than that. She was a joy to be with. She put you at your ease, even though she was so young. You wanted to be near her."

"I remember that, although I was only a child," Edward chimed in softly. His mind was flooded with pictures of his stepmother. What a pity she had to die at such an early age!

"Yes, she loved children in particular. No, she loved everyone. I never heard her say anything nasty or unkind about anyone. She always saw the good in a person. But, most of all, she loved your father. Her love for him shone out from her face. Even on that first meeting, when they stood in that very doorway over there, I knew. I knew what William had come to tell us. Of course, at that time, he was a regular visitor here. He and Richard would often argue, but only with words. They were just like lads scrapping together. More a discussion really. It wasn't until you... It was over you they fell out irrevocably. Richard could not accept the way that William had treated...

"Anyway, you know all that. William brought Mariana to meet us and I knew that he was going to announce their betrothal. It was in both of their eyes. I must say, though, that I was worried about what Richard would say. There was such an age gap between them and she was very different from Letitia. But, Richard was enchanted with her too, from the moment he saw her. If it hadn't been for me, I think..."

"Aunt! You don't mean that!"

"No, I don't, I suppose. Richard and I have always had a close relationship, but... but there was some quality in Mariana which attracted men. It wasn't that she was conscious of it. She had a kind of 'little lost girl' look that just begged them to help. By all accounts, her daughter is the same..."

"Oh, no! No! No one could say Mariana is helpless. She's wilful and strong-minded. She says what she thinks but, having said that, she does have something which... which catches the eye. Maybe it's her looks. Maybe..."

"Maybe you want to tame her?"

Edward laughed.

"It's no good asking me. I'm biased. I love her. I think she either instils love or hate in one. She certainly stirs you up. She and Margaret don't get on well though and there's at least one man whom *Mariana* hates. I assume he is not attracted to her. Lloyd, his name is. But then, some say that he's an unpleasant individual and…"

"I'm not surprised that she does not get along with Margaret," interrupted Anne. "Margaret and Mariana's mother… I'm sorry to say it was Margaret's fault. She fair bristled whenever she saw Mariana, but then Margaret was always a spiky child. Jealousy, I think. She adored your father. She was the first born in effect. William did not seem to notice her. Then, when Mariana came along…" Anne sighed. "Even though Margaret was grown-up… Still, all this is beside the point. Your father and Mariana were married very quickly, if you recollect. I suppose people thought…"

Anne cleared her throat and looked away.

"It's all right. I understand." He grinned at the expression on his companion's face. "I do know about these matters!"

"Yes, well… It wasn't true though. Mariana was an innocent. They only had a short betrothal because there was no reason to wait. They loved each other. They were both adults. They did not need anyone's permission."

"Had she no family?"

"Not that she ever mentioned."

"I remember no one represented her at the wedding. Didn't… didn't Uncle Richard…?"

"Yes, Richard took her family's part." For a moment Anne was silent, apparently lost in thought. Then she burst out:

"It all started at the ball. You surely remember that!"

"Of course! I wasn't allowed to participate but I came right at the beginning for a short while. I can remember Mariana very well. She was so elegant. Her gown was lilac, wasn't it?"

"Yes, now I come to think about it, it was! What a good memory you have! You were only a child!"

"Well, I can admit it now: I was half in love with her myself. Calf-love, but very intense. A great deal about Mariana is imprinted in my memory – almost every detail – yet other things have faded. I got a terrible shock the first time I saw her daughter."

"Is she really like her?"

"Ah, Aunt, I've already told you, I'm biased. She's… she's more beautiful, in my opinion. But, maybe my memory of her mother has been distorted over the years. Who knows? I'll bring her to see you soon. She'll like you. And she's never been to London."

"Thank you. Now, where was I? Yes, the night of the ball. It was only a few weeks after their marriage and your father had been flung into all that business about your grandfather's debts. What a nightmare! What a start to their marriage! However, it did not seem to matter to them. They were so much in love, as I have said. I recall that he had been away for a week before the ball. Mariana was staying with us. She was… sort of subdued. I'm sure she was missing your father. He'd told us he'd only be gone a day or so and a whole week had passed. She tried to hide her feelings. In fact, she did very well, because I did not notice anything was wrong until I saw her when William returned. Then I realised just how restrained she had been before. She sort of woke up, when he returned. Came to life. I can see her now. She flung herself into his arms when he alighted from the carriage and she was normally so well-mannered. I think she just forgot herself. She was little more than a girl, after all.

"He came the actual afternoon of the ball and they hardly had a moment to themselves before the guests started arriving. They were the guests of honour and were caught up in talking with practically everyone and then there was the dancing… Yes, there was plenty of dancing! Mariana was never without a partner, but I suspect that her eyes were constantly on your father.

"As the night wore on, I'm sorry to say your father became drunk. So drunk that he started to get aggressive… He began to shout about your grandfather and the wicked way he had lost all the money. And… he had to be carried away to his own room. Richard always said William was abusive in his cups."

"That's rather unfortunate," commented Edward. "Yet it happens to many men. It's almost as if they are different people. Better if you are a person who sinks into a kind of stupor!"

"Indeed! However, what you have just said may have been the problem that night. Remember, Mariana was barely acquainted with your father. They were married very quickly. It was certainly the first time that she had seen him… er… drunk. Well, reading between the lines of the letter… I think she was rather upset… and disappointed…"

"I see. She had so looked forward to the return of her husband and what a performance, by the sound of it! Poor woman! It must have been a shock. Strange, though, how children are shielded. No one told us about Father and how he had to be carried to his own bed. I've never heard this before.

What happened that night then?"

"Nothing, at first. After he had gone, she continued to dance. I saw her several times. I remember her heightened colour. I suspected she was upset, but I couldn't get near her. She was always dancing. Then, when I wasn't looking, she disappeared. I assumed that she'd gone to William…"

"But she hadn't?"

"No. When the letter came, it explained that she had gone for a walk in the gardens and there had met, by chance, another of the guests. She did not know his name and even from her description of him, I could not identify him. He could have been one of several men. All that mattered was he was young and handsome and… and he was there when your father wasn't…" Anne trailed off into silence.

"You don't need to say anymore. I can easily guess what happened. What's puzzling me is why she wrote and told you about it?"

"Mariana was not yet twenty, I shouldn't think, at that time. She was stricken with guilt. She discovered that she was with child and she wrote to me for advice."

"How could she be so sure that it wasn't my father's? She must have…"

"Because," insisted Anne firmly whilst looking away from her nephew, "the following morning William left for Caernarfonshire. He was away for many weeks. Over a month, I'm sure. She knew, Edward, my son. She knew." Anne finished in a whisper, almost as if she was imagining her sister-in-law's remorse all those years ago.

Edward was silent too, thinking again of the implications of all this.

"I can't believe it," he marvelled eventually. "Mariana's not my sister, after all. I can't believe it. Oh, Aunt Anne, I can't tell you how relieved I am. To find… find yourself attracted to… to your own sister! I felt awful initially. I was aware that it was impossible. I decided that I had to get away. I was so frightened that someone else would see. But now…"

"What are you going to do?"

"Why didn't she tell Father?" Edward ignored her query. "Didn't he suspect?"

"No, he didn't recollect any of that night and… He could not recall if… Anyway, I advised against telling him. There was no point. What was done was done. She hadn't set her cap at the other man. He'd simply caught her when she was tired and confused and upset and maybe a little disillusioned. She had seen a side of William that she did not know existed. She never saw the man again. Probably she would not have recognised him if she had…"

"I am still very surprised. For Mariana… *Mariana* to… to… She loved Father so much."

"Oh, Edward! It was a foolish mistake! Don't condemn her! We all make mistakes. It was just a shame your Father went… went away… had to leave so soon and for so long. Otherwise dear Mariana would never have questioned who the baby's father was."

"I'm not condemning her. How could I? This news has changed my life – for the better! If it hadn't have happened or… or if she had not written to you or you had not told me or… Nonetheless, I'm just glad that Father never doubted… As it was he rejected baby Mariana nigh on a year, in his grief. But, I'm glad that I discovered before it was too late."

"Too late! What for?"

"I intend to marry her."

Anne stood up hastily, wringing her hands together.

"Edward! Is that wise? I would never have told you if I'd thought… I just hated to see you so miserable. I thought it would put your heart at rest. You can't marry her – not unless the whole world knows about her mother's infidelity… And there's Mariana herself. Does she love you or does she think of you as a brother? Is it wise to tell her now, that… that William wasn't her father? She's barely over her grief at his death and…"

"Wait! Wait! I haven't thought through all the details yet myself. All I know is I must tell her of my love. I had already decided that I would return to *Trem-y-Môr* eventually. I'm the Squire and I've all my tenants and lands to supervise. All I can say is that I will try to get to know Mariana better… sound out her feelings for me. She's already had a proposal of marriage from a man old enough to be her… her father. Well, it's not like Father and Mariana. There's no love between them. I thought… I suggested to her before, that she come with me to London. Then I changed my mind because I was worried that I might declare my love for her and, until today, that would have mortifying for both of us. All I've resolved thus far, is to invite her to accompany me to London to meet you and Uncle Richard and Sarah and all the others. Then, when I've got her away from… from… I mean, when we have become better acquainted, I can gently tell her the news about… about her parentage. I've thought no further than this, Aunt, but…"

"I'm worried, Edward. It'll come as a shock to her. She's not actually related to any of us. We know nothing of her background – neither her mother's nor her father's, as it turns out. In fact, we don't know precisely who her father is even! I did make one or two discreet enquiries after I had received Mariana's letter, but then I reasoned that if I had advised her to forget it, then I must too. But you should understand that she won't like to be told that she is… illegitimate. All these years it has been hidden. I nearly burnt the letter, but…"

"I'm glad you didn't…"

"Why not?"

"Because this is my proof. To Mariana, if she doesn't believe me."

"No, Edward! You can't have the letter. It's mine. My personal property. I've held Mariana's secret for over eighteen years. I've mentioned it to no one. No one. Not even my husband. Oh I wish I hadn't told you. You can't tell anyone now. It's too late. It all happened too long ago. You mustn't…"

Anne walked over to the window to stare through the glass. Edward was sure there must be tears in her eyes. He watched her whilst trying to sort out his own confusion.

"I'm sorry, Aunt, but I can't honestly say that I wish you hadn't told me," he confessed over the ticking of the clock. "I'm sorry to upset you, but, with or without the letter, I will do as I say. If I were to keep this knowledge to myself, in the same way that you have all this time, then, at least, I don't need to feel guilty about loving my own sister. However, I want more than that from life. I promise you that I will speak to nobody until I have spoken to Mariana and tested her reaction. If… if she reacts badly or if I never feel the time is right I will never tell her, but, please see that I must try. I have… I have never felt like this before about any other woman. Even… no, especially not her mother. I didn't love my stepmother. I understand that now. I was only a lad and I was infatuated by her. I… I have had women. In fact, I've… I've even had one woman in a close relationship for several years and I have… had a ch… But, I didn't love this woman. Mariana is the first woman I have ever loved and until I spoke to you, I believed there was no hope for my love, but now…" Edward stood up and appealed to his aunt.

"Aunt, you must understand. Mariana is my reason for living. Don't think badly of me. You… you love Uncle, don't you? You know what it is to love. Don't ask me to keep this… this information to myself and not to act on it. I can't. I must at least try to win her love."

Still there was no reply and then Anne said, with what sounded like defeat in her tone:

"Where would you live? You couldn't live where people knew you."

"I have money. If… if she will have me, we can go and live elsewhere – perhaps abroad. The New World possibly. I don't know. I haven't had time to make plans. Oh, please don't turn your back on me."

"It's all right, Edward." Anne faced him as she spoke. "You are right. Why should I expect you not to grasp at happiness? You can have the letter. All I ask is that you are sensitive to the fact that this is a private letter which… which has details in it that can… can shatter people's lives. You must make sure that it doesn't fall into the wrong hands."

"Oh, Aunt, please trust me. I know what it is to suffer. I have been right to the doors of death and back. I no longer want revenge on… on my father. He's dead after all. I wanted to make my peace with him… And I would have, if I'd arrived sooner. I want to put the past behind me now. If I didn't love Mariana, I would not spread it around, but, as you've said, if she agrees to marry me, we'll have to give some explanation to… to the other members of the family, at least. Fortunately, both my stepmother and my father are past caring what happens is this world. But remember, it may be that it won't work out… I'm… I have to go away for…"

"Away? Where to?"

"I can't tell you, but within the next few weeks I shall be sailing on a very important voyage. A commission from the King no less! I'll do nothing until I return. That'll give me time to think. Please smile, Aunt, and let me see that you aren't angry with me, for I'd find it difficult to leave if I thought my favourite aunt was cross with me."

"My dearest Edward, I'm not angry with you. I just hope you know what you're doing. You were treated so abominably by your father and I would never want you not to be happy now. In fact, I've hoped for a long time that you would find yourself a wife. I just hope that what I've told you today doesn't bring you even more trouble."

***

"I had prayed to God that He would bless us with a child, but that first week when my dear William was gone from me, I knew that I would have to wait longer for God to answer my prayers. How despairing I felt and then when I saw him again how my heart leapt for joy! For I knew that now he was back he would administer comfort to me and soon I would have a child of my own. What sorrow I feel now that I have discovered that I am with child and it is not my dear William's! Oh, may God forgive me! I know not whom to turn to but you, my sister Anne. I feel I must make a clean breast of it to my husband, for I have deceived him and my soul is…."

Here the writing had faded and Edward raised his eyes from the letter. He was glad to stop squinting for a moment or two. His stepmother's writing was very small and indistinct. Poor woman! What remorse she must have experienced! Yet she had recovered from her guilt because Edward recalled how contented she and his father were. She had been so lighthearted with him and his sister, Penelope. No, he contradicted himself. If one had caught his stepmother unawares, there would be a look of sadness in her eye often. He had assumed it was because of some event in her past life, before she met his father; today he wondered if maybe it had been because of the child.

He glanced at the paper and then laid it on the table. He was seated in his own bedchamber in the inn. He reached for the glass of wine that Wilson had left for him.

What should he do? He could not travel to Anglesey to converse with Mariana because he had to await his orders from the Fleet and this was something that should be broached in person. He had promised his aunt that he would test Mariana's reactions before imparting the truth. He must wait until he had time to see her and talk to her. Yet how long would he be in Portugal? What if Mariana found herself another suitor? Jack? Even the Parson? Suddenly he recalled Mariana's words to him on that last night before he had left. It was five weeks ago, but he could still hear her voice:

"She's like a spider – a great fat spider – weaving a web. She wants you to go, Edward. She wants you, Jack, out of the way. She wants me… married. Why is she doing all this?"

Dread clutched at Edward's heart. He had heard only once from those at

Trem-y-Môr and that had been from Margaret herself. Mariana had never written to him. Her silence seemed ominous. What was happening there? Had Jack gone? Had Margaret manoeuvred Mariana into marriage with that pompous Reverend Owen already? No! Surely Mariana herself would have asked for his help if she was frightened. No, Jack must still be there and protecting her. Nonetheless, he must write to Mariana and make sure that she did not marry anyone else before he had a chance to declare himself. Yet, how could he do that? How could he, without explaining why, urge her to remain unmarried? He was her guardian. Maybe he could simply remind her that his permission was needed. But was it? If she was willing…

No, it would be best if he went to his superiors and enquired whether there would be time for him to return to his estates briefly before his departure. After all, the Admiral had led him to understand that he would be leaving immediately and already days had passed. What was the delay? If there were time, he would race home. It would be preferable to kicking his heels here and he had been wondering what to do with Wilson and Thomas. Wilson was too old to adjust to life aboard ship and there was no need for him to do so, for Edward had decided that this voyage really would be his last. Thomas would choose to return too. Neither servant would want to remain in London whilst he was away. Thomas, after his initial wonder at all the sights of London, was longing for home. Therefore, if Thomas and Wilson were travelling back to *Trem-y-Môr* in the carriage he could accompany them, couldn't he? Even to have one day with his love. Even an hour. Just to see for himself that she was all right. Letters were no good. People could hide behind the polite sentences. Even if Mariana wrote and said that all was well, it would only take two minutes in the kitchen of the Manor House for him to ascertain whether his sisters – nay, his sister and his love – were at daggers drawn or not. Also he would not mind seeing Holyhead Mountain with its wind-wrapped sides ablaze with the purple heather and breathe into his body the pungent scent of the salt and sea. More than that, he was desperate to see a small, slim woman with a magnificent mantle of raven hair and magical eyes. Yes, he would go home for a quick visit…

There came a knock on the door. Wilson opened it and announced a Mr Barrett. Edward hardly had time to rise to his feet before his visitor was telling him that he must set sail.

AUTUMN

ELIZABETH

Elizabeth Parry stared at the woman who rose from her seat and came to greet her. This couldn't be Mariana, the motherless girl who she had tried to cherish all those years ago; the child whose behaviour had set the entire Parry household a-twitter; the imp who had disrupted every lesson in the nursery; the enchantress who had turned men's heads wherever she went!

Yes, Mariana was wearing a cap which befitted her married status and not a single strand of her silky hair could be seen beneath it, but the donning of a mere cap couldn't change a person that much! Elizabeth would have said that the girl's beauty would have shone out even if she was wearing a sack, and on closer inspection it seemed to Elizabeth that Mariana was dressed in something that resembled a sack! Grey, dull, coarse. A cursory glance and the older woman began to understand what had happened. She saw that not only was Mariana's gown hanging badly from her shoulders but it was so obviously completely out of fashion that it must be that the Parson had dressed his new wife in his first wife's clothes.

Elizabeth's indignation rose like bile in her throat. What was the man thinking to allow such a magnificent creature as the youthful Mariana to be seen in such ugly clothes? She knew the Parson was careful with his money – his sermons often praised thriftiness – but this was taking penny-pinching to the limit! The parsimonious parson! And who on God's earth had sewed the garments? One of her daughters, when they were aged eight, would have done a better job! She must lend her sewing woman, Anne, to the Vicarage household for a second time.

A few weeks ago Elizabeth had been astounded with the news that her adopted daughter – for that was how she thought of the old Squire's youngest child – was to be married to the Reverend Mr Owen. She had travelled that very day to *Trem-y-Môr* to offer her servant to help with the bridal dress and to say that she would give any other assistance that might be needed with such a short betrothal. There had been no bright light of excitement in Mariana's eyes on that occasion but Elizabeth decided that the girl had been positively alive compared with the present! Not a spark of interest in the day's events showed on the face of the thin, drab woman standing in front of her. What had happened? There was an air of defeat in the room.

Elizabeth took a deep breath. Whatever might be said about the colour and cut of the new Mrs Owen's clothes; however poorly they had been sewed to fit their slimmer, younger owner, the question which sprung to mind was: why did Mariana put up with her current wardrobe? Where was that fiery spirit which used to send her galloping across the countryside not even accompanied by her groom; where the restlessness which meant she would not sit still for her lessons; where that independence which meant she followed no rules but her own? Elizabeth noticed a lacy shawl thrown across the back of the chair Mariana had just vacated. Was this bright item all the girl could muster in rebellion to her husband's commands, or had some thoughtful maid encouraged her to wear it to alleviate the awful plainness of her appearance? Yes, she had never hankered after the latest designs from London but to appear in the front parlour and greet guests dressed like this! Pity jostled with scandalous shock in Elizabeth's breast.

"Mariana, my dear." Elizabeth embraced the skinny figure. The girl's fingers were icy and her cheek cold and pale. Elizabeth held Mariana at arm's length and looked into her expressive eyes. Misery dwelled in their dark depths. What had occurred to create such anguish? Was the Parson cruel to her? Elizabeth had come once before, a week after the marriage, but had left after only a few minutes, driven out by the arrival of a retired surgeon, a Mr Cutland, but she was not going to go home today without finding out some answers. She released the other woman and her hostess suggested they sat down.

Whilst Elizabeth chatted about ordinary matters, filling in the latest news of her own family, her mind feverishly sought answers. She'd heard the rumours, of course; she was by no means the only visitor to the Vicarage. It was her understanding that many of the townsfolk had called on the Vicar and his new spouse. These people might say that they wanted to congratulate the couple but Elizabeth suspected that they came out of idle curiosity. They might want to inspect the Reverend and his young bride to find out whether Mrs Owen had made any changes to the dowdy furnishings of the Vicarage. Some might have turned up to investigate more the tales which were circulating – on a one to one basis. Naturally Mrs Owen was seen when she attended church, but there she seemed to be almost guarded by her husband; usually she stood right beside him and his beady eye and well-known strict standards defied intimacies with his wife. Maybe some, like herself, Elizabeth mused, simply wanted a conversation alone with Miss Mariana. No, she was no longer a miss – a single woman – but Mrs Owen, and a different person.

During the opening chit-chat Elizabeth found herself longing to encounter the reckless Mariana of yore, with her loose hair, a curtain of silk down her back and an adventurous gleam in her eye before she set off on some madcap scheme. Elizabeth wondered if she was the first to think this and decided it was unlikely. Any who had known this young woman from childhood would not welcome the change. Surely they, like she, would agree that if this was what marriage had done, it would have been better if Mariana had remained a spinster! Her husband had not simply curbed her but driven the very life out of her!

Elizabeth and her husband, Meyrick, had found the Vicar and his wife the subject of gossip at their own dining table and it appeared that the vicar's nuptials were the talk of many a home. The main opinion was that the girl should not have been allowed to make her own decision so soon after her father's death. Yes, they all acknowledged that no one had forced her into marriage, but older folk said that her grief might have distorted her view of the situation.

Where was that brother of hers? Elizabeth had heard this question asked. Had he been consulted? Certainly he had not made an appearance at the wedding. A few were heard to pronounce that it was a wicked shame to tie a spirited young colt like Miss Mariana to a staid elderly carthorse like the Parson! Elizabeth had kept her mouth shut when this was repeated to her. The speaker, a Miss Dawkin from the village, had gone further:

"I know the Parson is very regular with his visits but he doesn't know the meaning of having a good time! Yes, he loves his food and isn't averse to a glass or two of wine but my sister and I agree that he always puts a damper on any party he comes to. You go and see if I'm not right, Mrs Parry. He's put a damper on the Squire's daughter, yes he has. Where's that merry laughing face she used to have? I think…"

Elizabeth allowed the remembered comments to fade whilst she scrutinised Mariana. The other woman was talking but there was a listlessness about her and her sentences seemed to peter out. Was she finding it hard to concentrate? What *was* the matter with her? Was she pregnant? That had some very peculiar side effects! Craving coal or being tired day and night. In fact this was the other rumour which was circulating. Miss Dawkin had declared:

"What the Parson's wife needs is a babe. That would put colour back in her cheeks and rouse her to life again, for at the moment she looks like death – death before its time!"

"Are you with child yet?" Elizabeth asked. She didn't mind getting straight to the point. Time was passing and she had not found out anything to answer her unspoken questions. She must try to winkle out as much information as she could before another caller interrupted her, like on the previous occasion.

The lass blushed but shook her head and then managed to steer the talk away from herself by enquiring:

"Speaking of children, how is Esther?"

Elizabeth admitted defeat momentarily – Mariana was telling no secrets. She might have only been wedded three-and-a-half weeks but it was not uncommon for fertile women to get pregnant on their wedding night! Her eldest, Esther, had married in April and conceived that very month; at present she lived on the outskirts of Cardiff – a short carriage drive from the family home.

"Esther? Well, that's what I've come to tell you. My husband and I and the girls are leaving for the south tomorrow. Not only does my husband have some business he wants to finish but, also, we heard last week that Esther is struggling now she's getting bigger with the unborn child. I'm going to spend a few weeks with her. She's not alone, of course, but it would be lovely to see her after the summer months and hear all her news. She's not a regular letter-writer, which is incredible when you remember how proficient she was at her lessons. My, how time flies! It just seems like yesterday since you were all in the schoolroom and here you are getting married and having children of your own. I assume that the Parson will be delighted to have a son. His first wife was barren, you know."

Mariana gave no reply. Elizabeth cleared her throat before continuing:

"We won't be back for Christmas this year, so there'll be no party at *Carregfan*…" Elizabeth stopped. Why had she mentioned that? She must not have been thinking straight, or was she unconsciously hoping to jolt the other woman out of her silence? "Oh, my dear, I am sorry…"

"It's all right, Aunt Elizabeth, it seems as if it happened such a long, long time ago."

Elizabeth leaned towards her hostess.

"Are you really happy, my child?" she implored.

"Happy? Of course I am!"

"I was so surprised when I heard and…"

"Why?"

It was her turn to blush.

"Well, it was quite soon after… after dear Henry and your poor father…"

"That was one of the reasons I accepted the Pars… Griffith's offer. He is very different from Henry. There have been no comparisons and… and I have settled in very well here."

There was something in her tone which said the subject was closed, but Elizabeth wasn't going to leave it there. After all, the girl was as good as one of her own and there was no Mr Cutland to interrupt her this time. Maybe she could draw her out by sharing some of her fears.

"Mariana, my dear, I am really glad. I was worried that your sister… You know, she's such a forceful person. Margaret, I mean, not Penelope. I hope that she's going back to her home soon! There we are. That's just my opinion. However, if she had tried to make you marry against…"

"No, Margaret had nothing to do with my decision." There was a glimpse of the old Mariana in her rallying tone.

"I had heard," Elizabeth persevered, "that she comes here often. She's not advising you on how to…"

"No," interrupted Mariana but her voice sounded jaded again. "She is Griffith's friend and she used to come here even before the marriage. I… I don't usually see her. She comes to consult with my husband. Now, that's enough talking about me. How are the twins? They have not come near me since my marriage and they can't say that it's the three-mile journey which prevents them."

"No, my dear. They were all set to come today but I told them that I wanted you all to myself. You see, my dear, I have been worried about you. I do hope that you feel that you could confide in me, if you had the need. I think of you as a daughter, you know. After all, you shared my children's lessons and all those visits when you came to our house. I trust you felt welcome and part of the family. We certainly considered you as one of the family. Is there anything that you want to say? Or can I help you in any way? In fact, I came to offer my… our assistance."

Mariana shook her head, looking away, and Elizabeth wondered if her direct speech had brought the shutters down. Would the girl have confided if she had not spoken out but just waited and listened? She would never find out now! Best to persevere! She went on:

"Well, there is one thing I think I ought to tell you. The housekeeper here, Mrs Beacon, has she been kind to you?"

"Kind? She is… is as a housekeeper should be, I suppose."

"I suspect she won't hand over any responsibilities to you. And this is what you need to know: she is the Parson's wife – first wife, I mean – she is her cousin. She was older than Barbara and quite protective – maybe slightly overbearing. She was widowed when Barbara was a young maid and so was free to move in. She came to the Vicarage soon after the marriage, which some thought was unwise but the Parson didn't seem to mind. Of course, she was devastated when her cousin died. I understand that she's quite protective of the Parson these days. I'm not saying that she's not an excellent housekeeper but she might…" Elizabeth paused. She felt she was babbling. Mariana had a blank look on her face. Why was she bothering? The girl obviously didn't want or need her help. "Well, I just thought I would tell you in case no one else did. Don't let her upset you."

It all sounded rather lame. What exactly was she trying to warn her about? She wouldn't have minded if Mariana had framed the question but her look remained vacuous.

Elizabeth understood that Mariana had brought two of her own servants with her – the one who had accompanied her right into the hallway at *Carregfan* on that fateful night when Henry Wynne had drowned, and another girl who had run away from her father and returned shame-faced a few days later.

"You have your maids with you, haven't you? From *Trem-y-Môr?*" A nod was all the reply she got. "Well, I'd better be going. There is much to do with the journey tomorrow." She wondered if she should embrace the child. Child? Mariana was no longer a child or under her care. She had a husband now!

Elizabeth was sorry that Henry Wynne had perished in the storm. She was sad that Mariana had lost her father, but the Squire's death could hardly be described as untimely. She was appalled at the new bride's attire and demeanour but, she acknowledged to herself, it wasn't any of her business actually.

"Farewell, and remember my offer. Anything… anything I can do to help," she stammered. She felt a fool. She had imagined all sorts of trouble and herself as confidante and the young woman opening up to her, and it had all come to nothing.

Elizabeth glanced up the stairs on her way out, again wondering what lay behind the closed doors of both house and marriage, and then she was stepping into her coach. Of the Parson there was no sign.

Settling herself in her seat, her mind was in turmoil, persisting in trying to ferret out answers to the reason for the tremendous change she had witnessed in her young friend. She did not observe the lacy clouds drawing across the pale sunshine; nor did she register how the hedgerows were on fire, starting on a single branch with flames of burnt ochre and crimson, or tawny and gold which gradually spread across the staid green of summer; she saw not the lone tree with its bunches of brick red berries masquerading as leaves. She did not hear the trill of tiny bird on the wing about to leave for winter or question why an owl should hoot at midday. Her thoughts were reviewing the strange conversation she had just had and how her fosterling had turned into a dressmaker's dummy.

It wasn't until the horses pulled through the gates of her own house that she was jerked out of her reverie. She saw, on either side, that the mountain slopes were swathed in lavender heather with an occasional stripe of candy pink bell flowers swaying in the wind. By the side of the road was hawksweed – a dusty yellow. She shook herself, deliberately leaving her own musings and disturbing anxieties behind and began to think of all the various tasks she had to do before the morrow. Mariana was *not* her daughter, after all, and she must attend to her own offspring. Lately, she had become restless with the estate in North Wales – even the garden held no peace – for she longed to be near her eldest daughter. She had grandchildren by her sons' wives but this precious babe would be borne by Esther – flesh of her flesh and she wanted to will the days away until the arrival of the infant. Yes, she must concentrate on her own kin and leave Mariana to the care of her new husband, or even the young Squire, whenever he returned.

EDWARD

Edward leaned on his stick and watched as the *'Dart'* moved slowly away from the wide expanse of ocean and sailed along the edge of the land. Portugal – his destination. He had decided to anchor in the Caiscais Road, not far from the Castle of St Julien, and they were nearly there now. However, instead of allowing his vision to rest on the distant hills or his senses imagine the delights of port that he would be able to sample soon, he noted the heavy fortifications on this particular stretch of coastline. He would report all this when he returned to England.

Lisbon sat at the mouth of the River Tagus, but any ship had to pass by several minor forts with any number of guns. Some appeared to have as many as twenty, Edward counted, whilst the *'Dart'* glided on her way. If a vessel was not attacked or stopped by the firing of these cannons, she was faced with the eighty guns set in the walls of the castle. Edward looked with interest at the castle. His keen eyes noted immediately that not every gun could be pointed at any one ship at one time, but if thirty or so artilleries all fired simultaneously a vessel would be badly damaged! Edward was impressed with Lisbon's defences. It would be hard to slip by unnoticed. Pray God that Portugal would side with England!

"Ten fathoms, Sir," a voice piped up and Edward signalled for the anchors to be dropped. Presently only a skeleton crew would be left guarding the ship; however, most of the men and officers would climb into sturdy rowing boats and make for shore. Some of the crew had tasks to discharge, such as refilling the water barrels and replenishing the stores of food, but the outward journey had been fleeting and hopefully the return voyage would be accomplished with as little trouble; therefore there was not much restocking to do. Really Edward had been very pleased with how easy everything had been thus far. Hardly a challenge to an experienced man like himself, but the weather had been kind and the wind had blown as if specifically to carry them to Lisbon.

Edward watched whilst some of the excited men lined the decks ready to disembark. Before long they would be seeking the nearest tavern to assuage their thirst: both for drink and women! He, though, must go and write up the log before gathering up his private documents from his strong chest and setting out in search of the British Envoy: a man called John Methuen.

As Edward made his way painfully back to his cabin he sighed. He was grateful for the briefness since it had made him see the problems of captaining a ship with one leg. He had known another disabled man who had managed but maybe his injury had been less sore than his. All he knew was that, although the ship's doctor had helped him to the best of his capabilities, he had missed the regular massage which Wilson gave him as well as the daily anointing with Mrs Williams' special ointment. Edward felt old and tired. He wanted to settle down in retirement now and leave the fighting of another war to the eager young men who were waiting to defend their country. He had deliberately savoured the journey for he accepted it would be his last command.

He caught sight of Hall and Smith and Davies, three Gentleman Volunteers, who were starting in the Fleet in the same way he had done all those years ago. They were dressed very smartly, ready to impress the Portuguese ladies, and Edward smiled to himself. One pastime he would not be indulging in on this trip was courting ladies! He was too anxious for news of Mariana. In fact his soul brooded on her too often and his sleep was haunted by her. How was she and would she welcome his advances when he returned? He had kept his aunt's letter with his other secret letters but he had only reread it once for he had found that it brought home to him the truth of what he had discovered and then his heart had begun to thump with fear that something would happen to prevent him from attaining his desire. The timing of his father's death was fresh in his memory. It was better not to dwell on the matter.

"Good evening, Sir." This greeting was from Hall, who was a massive sixteen-year-old who seemed to have grown even bigger on this short journey. "We are able to accompany you ashore, Sir, when you are ready."

"Very good, Hall. I'm nearly ready."

Edward opened the door to his cabin and limped to his desk. Now that he had arrived at Portugal he had no inclination to go ashore. It was not simply the effort of getting into the yawl over the side of the 'Dart', but rather the thought of mixing with company. Almost certainly he would be asked to stay at the Methuen residence and suddenly all he wanted to do was to hurry back to see Mariana, king or no king.

By the time Edward did reach the home of John Methuen, his black mood had enveloped him. He hid his ill temper behind a stiff front and gave terse replies when his host questioned him. His conscience chided him – there was no excuse for his rudeness, but he did not seem able to shrug off his melancholy.

Over the next few days, he learnt that Portugal's allegiance to England was by no means settled. Methuen was of the opinion that the King of Portugal had already allied himself to the King of France. However, it appeared the common people were not supportive of their king: they did not want to align themselves with the French.

There were delays concerning Edward's own secret task. It was not a matter of delivering his letter and setting sail for home; he had to await a reply. Edward was aware that his own dourness didn't help the tension in the house. He felt that Mr Methuen was trying to ease the situation when he exhorted Captain Rowlands to enjoy all that Lisbon had to offer.

Edward found the thought of spending time amongst the crowded streets of Lisbon with noisy people, whom he did not understand, or making stilted conversations with strangers of his own rank, was unappealing and he asked if he could be provided with a horse. For the first four days of his enforced wait, he rode into the surrounding country, alone with his thoughts, travelling long distances in an attempt to ease his wretchedness, not even halting during the blistering heat of the midday sun when all the local inhabitants dozed.

On the fifth day, the Envoy had to warn him that his solitary rides were arousing interest and there were murmurs of spying. Edward stared in horror at his host. He had not been a good guest at all! Hastily he apologised for his boorish behaviour with an explanation that his estates had been left in turmoil after his father's death and he had been engrossed with his plans. Much to his relief, Mr Methuen appeared quite willing to forget Edward's impolite actions and he began to entertain Edward – presumably with what he had originally intended.

One of Edward's first visits was to view the Portuguese fleet in the company of the Envoy. The fleet, consisting of eleven ships, lay above Belem and Mr Methuen explained that each one of them was fitted for service and ready for sea. Edward saw that most of the vessels were the equivalent of the English Fourth Rates. They were manned with forty to sixty guns, but moored alongside them were three French Men-of-War. Privately Edward agreed with his host: the King was interested in, and maybe had already, sided with France.

Whilst they stood there they were joined by another man who was introduced as Mr Lyndon. He was lean with an enormous, beribboned wig, and much to Edward's surprise he did not leave after the initial formalities but rather tagged along with them, interrupting their conversation repeatedly. What was wrong with him? thought Edward, exasperated by the man's persistent talking. His voice grated for he sounded as though he was speaking through his nose and not his mouth at all! This was just the kind of person Edward had no patience with at the moment. Irritatingly, Mr Methuen gave the impression of being unaffected by the newcomer. When they turned away from the fleet, which was rocking gently in the waves, Mr Lyndon cleared his throat noisily.

"Please excuse me for interrupting," he drawled. Edward scowled at him. That was how this tiresome man prefixed all his sentences but he plainly was not really sorry. "It's just that I wondered if I could ask a small favour of you, Captain Rowlands, if you don't mind."

Edward turned on him in disbelief. They had met but half an hour ago and already the man was wanting something from him! He knew Mr Lyndon was a merchant and also, from his speech, that he had decided opinions on every subject under God's sun, but what could he be wanting from him?

"I had heard that you will be sailing for England soon, Sir. Would it be possible for my daughter to travel home with you?"

Edward stared at the shorter man. *Now* he understood. Mr Lyndon had led them to believe that he had just chanced upon them, but it was obvious that the meeting had been contrived. Edward lifted an enquiring eyebrow at Mr Methuen, who made no comment, but simply led the way down some narrow, uneven steps.

"I don't usually carry women on my ship," Edward replied tightly, half concentrating on the stairway. "Would she be travelling alone or are you wanting passage too?"

Mr Lyndon did not appear to take offence at his negative intonation.

"Oh, no Sir. I'm only asking on behalf of my daughter. I am unable to leave Portugal at this time but I am worried…"

"Worried? What about?" accused Edward. Why had he taken such an instant dislike to this man? He could not exactly identify the reason, but he kept his voice discouraging.

"I am worried about a war, Sir. You know, between ourselves… That is the English and the Portuguese, Sir."

"War? I see. And your daughter is too…?"

"Captain Rowlands, Sir," intervened Mr Methuen. His tone suggested that he did not understand Edward's attitude and Edward could hardly blame him when he didn't understand his own reaction to the merchant. "Mr Lyndon is not alone in his desire to see his daughter safe. Several women and children want to leave. I am sure that this will be the first of many requests you will receive from people wishing to travel home. Have you no room?"

"I have room. It is not usual for a Navy ship to carry passengers and I would be very uneasy to have an unaccompanied woman on my ship. But, if…"

"My daughter will be no trouble to you, Sir. I will tell her to remain in her cabin at all times."

"I haven't finished yet!" rebuked Edward. "If there really are many women wanting to come aboard then the whole situation will be quite different. I assume, in the event of war, or the imminent start of a war, I would be allowed to take civilians on board."

"I'm sure, Sir," soothed Mr Methuen, "that there will be a family who could take Mrs Sa…"

"Sandleigh," finished Mr Lyndon. "She is to be known as 'Mrs Sandleigh'. I must tell you, Captain, that my daughter married a Portuguese man without my approval. She is a widow, and when she arrives in England, I have told her not to use her Portuguese name. Especially, if we are at war with Portugal. People…"

"Maybe it would be best if the Captain met your daughter, Mr Lyndon," broke in the Envoy.

"I…" started Edward.

"That would be excellent. Tomorrow night. If you come to my house, I will provide you with the finest meal you can have in the whole of Lisbon." Mr Lyndon was gone before Edward could protest.

"That's good then," smiled Mr Methuen. "Now if you would just follow me, the carriage is around this corner."

Whilst walking he explained to Edward that he knew Frances Sandleigh personally and was sure that she would not be a nuisance on board. She was a very sensible and clear-thinking girl and certainly not one to flutter her eyelashes at rough sailors.

Mindful of his behaviour on his arrival, Edward kept silent. The prospect of a whole evening spent in the company of Mr Lyndon did not interest him, but the Envoy assured him that Mrs Sandleigh was a lively companion and Edward schooled his face along agreeable lines. It didn't really matter what he did with his time here. It was all wasted. Soon he would be able to return to England and from there to North Wales.

Nevertheless, Edward's mind was jolted out of his constant reverie about Mariana when, on the following evening, Mr Methuen's carriage drew up outside a palatial one-storey bungalow overlooking the estuary and out to sea. He had not expected an ordinary merchant to live in such a grand style. Perhaps the daughter's late husband had owned the house.

Edward had become enchanted by the graceful buildings built in Portugal. With such a fierce heat (and he had been assured that the present weather was as nothing compared with the real heat of summer), lasting most of the day, the houses always offered a cool, refreshing change from the outside, with their quiet, dark corridors along which glided quiet, dark servants.

This particular house had a well-tended garden stretching down the hill towards the brilliant sea. Near the entrance were flower beds covered with exotic flowers whose names were not familiar to him, but whose riotous colours stunned his eyes. When he stepped towards them their powerful scent accosted his nostrils. Such glamorous plants and quite different from their staid English counterparts! No one could walk past and not notice them!

At that moment, something moved at the corner of Edward's vision and he glanced up. A woman was wending her way amongst the neat rows of vegetables which ranked along the lower slopes of the garden. She must be the gardener's wife since her long skirt was enveloped in a capacious apron and her head was protected by a floppy straw hat.

Almost he called, "You have a spectacular garden," but then he realised that probably she wouldn't understand. He could see that her bare hands and forearms were dark brown, tanned by the ever-present sun, and the strands of hair, which were escaping from beneath her hat, were black. She was Portuguese; she might speak a little English but his knowledge of her mother-tongue was non-existent. Whilst he stood and watched, she walked down towards the water, not heeding him, and he spotted that she was carrying a basket. It was conceivable, he pondered, changing his mind, she was the cook or a maid sent to fetch some produce at the last minute for the evening meal.

Edward limped towards the vast wooden entrance and pulled the bell. Almost immediately a native man opened the door. He conversed in perfect English and ushered Edward in with as much composure as any servant in England.

From the second Edward stepped over the threshold of the house, he was astounded at the wealth of his host's furnishings. The place was exquisitely decorated and the extravagant rugs and furniture were tastefully arranged. Mr Lyndon's wife must be a remarkable woman. Yet he had not mentioned a wife and neither had Mr Methuen. It was not just the opulence of his surroundings that caught his attention. The more he looked the more he saw that everywhere, from hall to salon, were shelves and tables supporting rare and original objects. Ancient figures jostled for space with modern sculptures, and meticulously painted vases and golden goblets stood tall above miniature ornaments and silver crucifixes. Just when Edward felt that he had seen the most expensive of them all, his eyes would alight on some new piece which outclassed the others. Mr Lyndon was more than a merchant! He was a collector of fine art and evidently had no money problems to curtail his interest!

Edward stood admiring each piece until he was drawn to the window ledge by a jet horse which reminded him of Mars, his sister's steed. Its clever maker had left the animal permanently prancing in the air. One could almost hear its snort of impatience to be away for a gallop.

He lifted his focus from the statue; his heart contracted with homesickness. Instantly he noticed, through the window, etched against the evening sky, black rain clouds. Damn! A storm was brewing and he was so desperate to set sail. If it harried the sea, he would be foolish to set off amidst the angry waves dancing to the tune of the slate heavens above.

When he had arrived at Mr Methuen's house late this afternoon, ready to prepare for this occasion, he had been informed that the letter he was waiting for would be ready tomorrow. His spirits had lifted; his enforced stay was nearly over. He had to survive this evening only and then he could return to his ship. But not if this blasted storm raged for long! Perchance it would blow over, his miserable heart begged whilst his experienced gaze saw the truth.

"Ah, Captain Rowlands." It was Mr Lyndon. "You are early. My daughter will join us in a minute."

He clapped his hands and a servant appeared bearing a tray of drinks. Lazily Edward noted that this man seemed to have quite a few servants – another sign of his wealth? When the attendant withdrew, Edward found himself praying that he wouldn't be left alone a long time with his host. The memory of the previous afternoon was too fresh and he allowed his contemplations to turn to Mr Lyndon's daughter. Did all these treasures belong to her perhaps? What kind of woman was she to have been able to stand up to her father and marry against his wishes? He concluded that she must be similar to his Mariana – wild and untamed. Young and full of life and insisting on her own way. Yet, now she was a widow. How had her husband died?

Edward had no more time to think, for his host was talking to him with his nasal twang. How Edward hated the sound of his voice! He nearly smiled, reflecting that he was getting like Mariana with his instant dislikes of people!

"I see you were admiring my pieces…" Mr Lyndon was saying.

"No," contradicted Edward. Somehow he did not want to feed this man's pride. He sensed that he had been invited here not just to meet Mrs Sandleigh but to see this man's assets. "No, I was watching the storm clouds and, if I'm not mistaken, the arrival of more French ships."

Mr Lyndon's face blanched. What is he so afraid of? wondered Edward.

"My God! There's… there's one, two, three… twelve of them. Twelve Men-of-War!"

"Fourteen, I think," corrected Edward, "and those smaller ones are fire-ships. When…"

"Oh, Captain Rowlands, have you made up your mind yet? My daughter is a sedate, well-mannered woman and I can assure that you will not regret taking her. I can pay…"

"As our Envoy predicted, I have had several requests…"

"Ah, here is my daughter. Frances, come and meet Captain Rowlands."

Edward swivelled to see Mr Lyndon's daughter standing in the door of the room. It was the woman from the garden! At least, he felt sure it was her, although she had changed her gown and her hair was neatly arranged in a bun on the back of her head. She was not beautiful, but her oval face was smooth and her drawn-back hair revealed a high brow. Her expressive brown eyes spoke of sorrow, not fun. Not young, as he had presumed, but her upturned nose gave her a look of innocence. Despite his recent musings, he concluded that she did not resemble Mariana; she was sylphlike and poised and manifestly used to being the mistress, for she came forward immediately.

"Captain Rowlands," she nodded confidently. "I'm delighted to meet you. Have you counted the increased fleet, Sir?" Her voice was low and pleasant to the ear after her father's aggravating tone and the smile she gave Edward lifted her features from ordinary to comely. When Edward bent to brush his lips against her hand, he saw her too-brown skin and decided that this was definitely the woman he had observed amongst the flower beds.

Mrs Sandleigh stood by him at the window.

"I am pleased to make your acquaintance," responded Edward. She was standing close enough for him to smell her clean skin, and he was surprised at his reaction to her. It had been an age since he had mixed with his equals. That is if a merchant's daughter was his equal. Her father was very wealthy even if he had no title.

She did not blush under his scrutiny, but pointed at the ships.

"More French, I see, Captain. I wonder what the King is playing. Some deep game, I'm sure."

"I wouldn't know, Mrs Sandleigh…"

"Oh, you mustn't call me 'Mrs Sandleigh'. Call me 'Frances', please." She turned towards him and she was only a few inches away from him. He saw the lighter creases in her bronzed skin around her eyes. He judged she was in her thirties and found himself wondering whether she had any children.

"I am really hoping that you will allow me to travel to England with you. My father said he had asked you. I have always wanted to travel and in particular to visit the country of my origin and it would be a great honour to go aboard one of His Majesty's Fleet."

Was she mocking him? No, her face was serious. She seemed very eager to depart. All the same, she did not strike him as someone who would cockle up in war conditions.

"Can you be ready by tomorrow? I know ladies are notorious for their baggage…"

"I am ready now, Sir. I only require space for two medium-sized chests and a carrying bag. Are you fully laden?"

"No. Will you be bringing a maid with you?"

"No, Sir. I could not ask one of the local girls to leave their country. I… I won't be coming back."

"Even if there is no war or when the war is over?"

"No, Sir," she repeated. Edward waited for her to expand on her reasons but she did not enlighten him.

"Ma'am, if I am to call you 'Frances', then you mustn't call me 'Sir' but 'Edward'! Where in England are you bound for?" he enquired.

"She is going to my family, whom she has never met." It was Mr Lyndon. Edward had forgotten that he was in the room. "Once my business here is finished, I shall be joining her and we shall purchase our own residence."

"Are you happy to go?" Edward saw father and daughter exchange a glance when he formed the question but he could not understand its meaning.

"In many ways I would rather stay," Frances acknowledged. "I have lived here all my life, but I understand the dangers and my father is most anxious that his most precious possession reaches England."

Edward felt a current of feeling pass from the woman to the other man. Obviously she did have rebellious thoughts sometimes. Widowhood had not stamped that out of her! What possession was she talking about? Herself?

"Dinner is served," a servant announced.

"Would you follow me?" Frances led Edward through into another spacious room no less filled with ornaments. This room also boasted several oil paintings, one of which must surely be Frances' mother. The resemblance was unmistakable. Edward was nonplussed to learn later that the portrait was in fact of Frances' grandmother.

Edward discovered that this shapely, sun-tanned woman who sat next to him was able to banish the deep-seated depression which lurked, ready to overcome him. It was the first time he had relaxed in any measure since his arrival in Portugal. The British Envoy had tried to arrange outings and meetings to amuse him, but it was Frances who enabled him to forget Mariana and the difficulties which lay ahead in his private life. It was not that she was witty or jovial, nor did she make him laugh, but she was intelligent and shrewd. Edward was amazed at her knowledge, not just of politics but of nautical matters. It was then that she told him that her grandfather had been in the Fleet and she pointed out to him her grandmother's portrait. She described how her grandfather had been pressed into the Fleet but had risen up through the ranks over the years. When he had retired to Portugal, his only son, the ingratiating Mr Lyndon, had come with him, bringing his wife too. Frances explained to him that she had been born in Portugal and had never been abroad.

Throughout the meal Mr Lyndon did not bother to join in with the conversation or to comment on the different subjects in the same way he had done with Mr Methuen yesterday. Had it been the Envoy he had aimed to impress or did his daughter's intellect daunt him? Whatever the answer, he was engrossed in his own reflections and barely said a word. Unexpectedly Edward found himself dominating the talk and extolling the delights of England.

By the end of the evening, he was glad that Frances Sandleigh would be travelling with him. She would be stimulating company at his table. However, he would make sure that there were other female passengers. Of her mother no mention was made and Edward assumed that she was dead. Frances was apparently the only child and must be the favoured possession which Mr Lyndon wanted to save from the possible conflict. Edward gave it no more thought. He simply found himself looking forward to having discourse with the charming Frances and he was relieved that she was not being accompanied by her father.

He mentioned his assent as he was leaving and watched while Mr Lyndon released a drawn-out sigh and wiped his forehead with his handkerchief. Frances' reaction was different: Edward reckoned he caught a glimpse of fear flit across her face before it was hidden carefully behind a courteous word of thanks.

Tomorrow! Tomorrow, they would set sail. Edward's heart quickened with excitement on his return to Mr Methuen's home.

However the storm did not pass by. Therefore Edward had to postpone his departure and then further unforeseen circumstances delayed him even more. He received a command from the Royal Family: the Queen Dowager had requested his presence.

Hence, while the rain beat furiously on the window panes and the sea battered the shore and two ships moored in the river gave way under the force of the tempest and sank to the muddy bottom, Edward drummed his own desperate tattoo of frustration with his fingers as he waited in a lonely corridor, with Mr Methuen, for entry to see the Queen.

Edward had dressed in his best clothes, since he had never met royalty before, but after a four-hour wait he felt his creased appearance was no longer fit to grace the Queen's apartments. Fortuitously a polite courier explained in rapid Portuguese that the Royal lady was unable to see them that day and both men should go home and await another summons. Rather than relief, Edward was incensed and when he was told he replied to Mr Methuen in an irate voice that he would wait only until the weather conditions were right for setting off and if he never saw the Queen Dowager then so be it!

"Please, Captain," entreated Mr Methuen, "could you keep your voice down? English is understood here. We… we are all representatives of our country. It's not only me who is an envoy – all of us are envoys in one sense and at this particular time…"

Edward closed his mouth. What Mr Methuen said was true and he flushed red at his unfortunate outburst. By a supreme effort he curbed his impatience for a further two days.

It was whilst Frances was with him that he was informed that again Her Majesty was able to receive him. Frances had come down to the 'Dart' with her baggage; Mr Lyndon had escorted her to supervise the loading. He seemed to be his old self today, full of vociferous advice, and Edward promptly invited Frances to his cabin whilst her father called out orders concerning the chests. It was amidst this chaos that the Royal messenger arrived with Mr Methuen and Frances' eyes lit up when she heard the news.

"Would you like to come too?" asked Mr Methuen urbanely.

"I would very much like to. I've seen Her Majesty on several occasions but I've never talked to her. Will it be all right? Do you think that she would mind?"

"I'm not sure," returned the Envoy with the ghost of a smile. "You can accompany us to the Court and we shall see. Captain Rowlands and I discovered the other day that it's not our decision. We have no influence or authority there."

Edward was delighted that when they arrived they were ushered straight in and they did not have to sit in the corridor, even for a moment. Notwithstanding, the room they entered was crowded with people. Edward could recognise that they were all speaking Portuguese but he heard at least two conversations which were being conducted in French.

Mr Metheun marched straight into the crowd, following the courtier, but Edward hesitated whilst he glanced at the floor. It seemed very slippery to him.

"Would you like to take my arm?" suggested Frances.

"Thank you."

Edward kept the crown of Mr Methuen's hat in view whilst he and Frances pressed their way through the babbling throng. Were all these people intending to see the Queen Dowager too? He was relieved that he did not have to join the end of a queue.

When he reached the other side of the room, the Envoy had halted beside a low door and he gave a shallow bow to them both. No one challenged Frances' presence and she kept her arm through Edward's.

"Shall I come?" whispered Frances to Edward. He nodded and she went on: "Now that I've come this far, I really don't want to miss this opportunity!"

Thus it was that Edward and Frances came face to face with the Queen Dowager. Incredibly, over the threshold, there was a secluded walled garden and when the door shut behind them, peace descended. Not as much as fifteen feet away from them sat the Queen, not on a throne, which they had imagined, but on a settle. She was incredibly fat, possibly due to a dropsical condition, and, despite the heat (which had returned in the wake of the storm), was dressed entirely in black. She was flanked by her ladies-in-waiting, all of whom were silent, watching the newcomers with disdain.

Edward realised that he was staring and he pulled away from his support and awkwardly bowed towards the royal party. Meanwhile, he noticed that Mr Methuen was whispering to a servant who was wearing a luxurious blue livery. Although the Dowager and Edward had already exchanged glances, protocol demanded that he be announced. For a few seconds no one moved and then Edward heard his name being called. Not sure what to do, but seeing the Queen's chubby, bejewelled fingers proffered, he bent to kiss her hand.

"Your Majesty," he murmured.

"Who is the woman?" demanded the Queen Dowager. "Is she your wife?"

One of the Queen's servants – a pompous looking man who seemed to believe he was important and maybe he was because he was translating the Royal phrases – told Edward what the Queen had asked. Edward saw the startled expression on Frances's face out of the corner of his eye. She looked as if she wished she hadn't come, after all! The Envoy had flushed the colour of beetroot when the words were first spoken, since he understood Portuguese. Yesterday he had told Edward that it was not wise to upset Royals and now he too looked like he regretted inviting Frances to accompany them.

Mr Methuen spoke rapidly to the Queen and she replied but no translation was given and Edward glanced from one to the other in confusion. He noticed a stain of embarrassment on Frances' cheeks and was frustrated that he could not speak the language. What *was* the old lady saying? But, there was no time to think because almost immediately the Queen was speaking but this time amazingly directly at Edward. Mr Methuen and Frances withdrew a pace or two.

Edward felt the strain of the situation. His leg was aching but he knew he could not sit down in Her Majesty's presence and his head was throbbing. It was easy to relate how he had lost that very leg which was bothering him, but he was wary when he was grilled about what England's intentions were concerning Portugal. He was not sure how tactful the interpreter would be – the Envoy might have omitted any blunders Edward made with a paraphrase, but he had no idea how his words were being translated. Edward had to use all his strength and think carefully before he opened his mouth.

This was the reason that he lost patience when he was eventually apprised of what the Queen had said to cause such consternation to his companions. Without warning, the Queen had waved her hand and a courtier had ordered them to leave at once. There were more bows to execute and Edward followed Mr Methuen's lead and then they were back in the crowded room and the audience was over.

"Thank God!" exclaimed the Envoy. "Thank God that she seemed to get tired of us and thank God that it was all a whim!"

"What are you talking about?" Edward couldn't keep the irritation out of his voice.

The others broke into cackling laughter.

"When she wanted to know was whether Mrs Sandleigh was your wife. I thought we were in real trouble…"

"I shouldn't have come," giggled the topic of his conversation.

"It was my fault," laughed Mr Methuen. "I don't know if I'm going weak in the head by allowing you…"

"But what did she say?" Edward was not enjoying all this frivolity, despite the fact that it was the first time he had seen a grin on Frances' face.

"She said that if I wasn't your wife, then you should marry me."

"What a damned cheek!" roared Edward, causing one or two bystanders to gape. "Who does she think she is?" Edward stared whilst both his companions shook with laughter.

"But that's the whole point!" Mr Methuen was able to control his voice first. "She's royalty! She can say whatever she likes. If she wants to play matchmaker she can, can't you see? You should be thanking God, as I am doing. I thought we might be clapped into prison for bringing Mrs Sandleigh with us. I'm sorry, Frances, but…"

"No." Frances was sober at last. "It was entirely my fault. Such a foolish notion of mine to come. I am sorry that…"

"Don't apologise. I should have known better but I really had no idea that the Queen Dowager was behind that door. I thought that we were being taken to her and would have to wait in some sort of anteroom." Mr Methuen laughed again. "Still, what she suggested is not such a bad idea. You're not married, are you, Captain Rowlands? Royal Decree, no less. I've heard of stranger beginnings than that! I'm quite glad you didn't understand though because…"

"I'll choose my own damned wife!" retorted Edward. Then he remembered Frances. "Oh, beg pardon! It's nothing against you. I… I…"

"It's all right." Frances' tone was light, although her mien belied her indifference. "I understand. I was rather taken aback myself. I wonder what made her say it. Such an odd thing to say."

"Goodness only knows!" exclaimed the Envoy. "I'm just glad that is what she meant. When she demanded 'Who is that woman?' I presumed we were going to be punished for bringing an uninvited person into her pres…"

"It's just," went on Edward as though Mr Methuen had not spoken, "that I hardly know you and… I have someone at home."

"Please, Captain Rowlands, Sir, don't… there's no need to… I haven't taken offence. In fact, as you can see, I am highly amused."

She turned quickly from him and Edward released his breath, hoping that would be an end to the awkwardness. What an afternoon! He was desperate to leave and was delighted when Mr Methuen recommended:

"Let's go before anything else untoward happens."

He led the way back through the mass of people and Edward found his mind returning to its usual furrow – he imagined his love – his sister who wasn't his sister – Mariana. He hadn't been telling a lie when he had told Frances that he had someone else.

BIDDY

"Watch out!"

Biddy jumped in surprise at the strident voice! She felt the jug slip through her fingers to land with a crash on the newly washed flagstones of the Vicarage kitchen floor, powerless to stop it. Pieces of china flew in all directions but before she could bend and pick them up she received a stinging blow to the side of her head.

"Get out!" screeched Mrs Beacon. "Get out of my sight! I told you to be careful and now look what you have done!"

Biddy clutched her burning cheek and turned from the fuming housekeeper. Standing behind her were both the cook and Jennett and her smarting skin stung afresh when the blood of chagrin flowed through her veins. Why did both of them have to witness her humiliation? It wasn't her fault that the jug had slipped! It was all the shouting; it made her nervous.

Out the door and across the cobbled yard she half ran, still holding her face, her own fingers over the handprint the slap had left on her pale skin. She slipped behind the stables and squeezed through the gap between wall and hedge before she was on a common path which ultimately led to the sea. However, Biddy had barely traversed a yard or two before she reached a gate. Pushing it open, she headed towards the hen house and then she was inside with the smell of hay and the comforting clucking of the birds. At this time of year, the chickens were moulting and producing fewer eggs. It was Biddy's job to collect them and she had found only three this morning. She guessed she was safe from inquisitive eyes since no one else came looking for eggs. She gathered up one of the hens – she called it 'Lisbeth'. The bird was used to her, but struggled to be released and when Biddy let it go, it perched nearby. Biddy began to stroke it with unseeing eyes as the tears started to flow. Letting them bounce down past her mouth and chin and flick from her apron, she was unheeding such were her reflections of the past.

Biddy had woken in the low bed of the shepherd and his wife several hours after the attack and was disorientated momentarily. She recognised that she wasn't at home but where was she? Once she remembered the events of the afternoon, the shivering began again and it was all she could do to say that her name was Biddy and that she came from Anglesey. Even warm soup and a hunk of dark gritty bread didn't quiet her spasms and she fell into an uneasy sleep only when everyone else had nodded off – the shepherd was snoring gently – and she could remain awake no longer.

By the morrow her body was still but she felt weak and nauseous and gave no protest when the solicitous shepherd offered to take her down to the Menai Straits where he placed her in the care of one of his relatives who was crossing the teaming water to the island where she lived. All thoughts of travelling to London were gone; all she craved was to return to the cottage where she had been born and to see the faces of her relatives she had so carelessly abandoned the day before.

Thus began the strangest week of the young girl's life. Passed from family to family, each person seemingly kinder than the one before, Biddy travelled the thirty-odd miles to her home. She knew not what tale was told to explain her lack of speech or her trembling hands but she cared not. She was hardly aware of where she was or sometimes even who she was. It was only when she saw the well-worn track which led to the Manor House that she came out of her introspection enough to thank her latest saviour and whisper that she could manage from there on. There was surprise in the man's features and, for a second she wondered if it was because she had spoken for the first time in his company, but he willingly left her and she walked into her old home with a sigh of relief. Everything would be all right now!

However, the cottage was in gloom, no fire lit and not a single person, young or old, to welcome the prodigal daughter. Biddy stood in confusion and then tried to summon her voice to work. She cried in a hoarse whisper for her father and brothers and sisters but no reply came.

What had happened? Had there been a plague? But there was no smell of sickness in the room or unwashed bed linen. Had everyone gone to a fair? But she could recall no festival at this time of year. Was there a shipwreck to which all had been summoned to help? But the weather was fine and the skies clear.

All of a sudden, her legs wobbled and she fell into the bed her mother had vacated not many months previously, pulling the familiar bedclothes around her hunched shoulders and sucking her thumb without realising what she was doing. She closed her eyes because it was only in sleep that she got away from the images which haunted her thoughts, although some nights she woke in a sweat with the feel of the cruel man who had assaulted her, on top of her and the taste of his lips upon her mouth. Yes, she sighed, everything would be all right now she was home!

Yet it was no dream which awakened her but the rough pull of her father's hand and his growl.

"Biddy! What are you doing here? I was worried sick about what had happened to you and then today at Miss Mariana's wedding, I heard where you had been. What impudence to return and sleep in my bed as though nothing had happened! Get up and get out!"

Biddy found herself hauled to her feet and the habitual shaking began. She wanted to scream and shout, to protest that it hadn't been her fault that she was set upon by a gang of youths, but the only sound she could muster was a whispered plea of "*Tad*! I…"

"No, none of your stories! How could you do it? Run off with a lad without leaving any kind of message for us. And now to come back! What are you doing here? You may have thought you could go of your own free will but you should have stayed with him. You're not free to come back. Where is he? I should punch his face in and force him to marry you. What am I to do with you now you are soiled! No one will want you for a wife and the whole village has heard about you! And when the Squire returns… I am Sir Edward's steward and I can't let any of my children bring this sort of shame on me. I daren't lose my job at this time. Oh, the shame! My dear departed father will turn in his grave!"

It was many months since Biddy had seen her father this animated, although he had stopped shouting by the end of his tirade and covered his face with his hands.

Refutations rose in Biddy's throat but remained there unuttered. She was aware of a row of eyes watching her – her siblings whom she had longed to see time and time again in the last week. She felt their gaze but kept her eyelids lowered. Almost immediately the fight went out of her and she found that she didn't have the energy to state her case: that she was innocent and not de-flowered. What did it matter anyway? Her father seemed beyond reason!

"But where is she to go?" This from Owen, bewilderment in his tone.

She felt tears of gratitude rise in her throat; at least one of her brothers was speaking up for her.

"I don't care!" spat her father. "Just as long as it's not here. Your mother, God rest her soul, would agree with me. To think that you are our eldest daughter and to do such a thing to us! It was bad enough to run off but to come back and think that you can take over your old job. Oh, the shame, the shame! Go, I say! Get out!" Her father was repeating himself in his agitation!

Biddy's belongings had fallen by the hearth where she had dropped them and resignedly she picked them up. The cottage had no fire lit and only two rushlights to show her the accusing faces of her relatives but once outside, in retrospect, the interior was heaven compared with the sharp wind and the unwelcoming cloud-filled night. Disorientated, she paused near the pigsty and that was when she heard the recommendation:

"Why don't you go with Elin? I'm to take her to the Vicarage. I'm sure Miss Mariana – Mrs Owen, I mean – will find a place for you. Follow me."

It was another of her brothers – Evan. Biddy had obeyed his advice and crawled gratefully on to the bare boards of the farm cart before curling up in a ball and pulling her shawl around her head. She was cold and lonely and confused. She could hear the conversation and was aware that Evan was pleading her cause with the older girl, but it was difficult to hear what Elin replied. Therefore, it wasn't until they reached their destination and she was standing next to Elin that Biddy discovered that it had been agreed that the senior servant would ask her mistress if Biddy could be taken on at the Vicarage. Biddy had turned and given her brother a grateful smile as he clicked the reins and disappeared into the darkness.

She had slept that first night in one of the outbuildings at the edge of the Vicarage garden. Elin had explained that she dare not introduce her to the housekeeper that night. If Biddy had known about the hen house then she might have snuggled in beside the chickens that first eve, because she hadn't got much sleep that night and her heart had thumped anxiously through until morning.

Biddy didn't know what Elin said to her mistress or what rumours had reached Mrs Owen's ears but she was ushered into the warm kitchen just after sunrise the next day. A brief moment of relief and then she had met the dragon! That was her private name for the housekeeper, Mrs Beacon.

From the very beginning the two had clashed – girl and woman – despite

Biddy's broken spirit! She had found that this housekeeper was completely different from the kindly Mrs Jones of the Manor House. It made no difference how hard she strived, Biddy did not come up to the standards Mrs Beacon demanded. She kept her head down literally and tried not to show any emotion on her face, keeping her tears until she could be alone. She spoke very rarely and lived in a kind of half-light of fear – dazed and worried, starting at the slightest noise. That was the reason she had dropped the wretched jug today. Being criticised and put down increased her nervousness and this meant she kept dropping things which appeared to enrage the housekeeper even more! It wasn't that she was expecting anyone, least of all the perpetrator of the attack, to abuse her, but she found herself sinking beneath the forebodings which appeared to be an aftermath of her terrifying experience and there was no improvement even when the days turned into weeks, until she had two chance meetings.

On her seventh day, she had fled the lash of the housekeeper's tongue, frightened that the threatened words would turn into action and she would be thrown out on to the street! Mrs Beacon had boxed her ears for good measure before she could escape. She had been castigated for not emptying the slops in Mrs Owen's bedchamber and she had hurried up the back stairs to rectify the omission. The old Biddy would have chafed under the sheer drudgery and injustice of her new life, but she couldn't seem to find her way out of the maze of horror she lived in permanently. The inevitable weeping began as she ran up the back stairs. She flung open the door and headed straight for the bed to find the chamberpot. Seconds later she realised she was not alone; her mistress was seated near the window, gazing out through the glass.

"Why, Biddy, what's the matter?"

She tried to gulp back the weak tears and shook her head in denial. Miss Mariana – she couldn't get used to calling her by her married name yet – rose and came around to touch her hand. She repeated the question.

"I'm all right, Miss," she muttered.

Miss Mariana put her finger on her burning ear.

"Who did this? Was it Mrs Beacon? I must speak to her."

"Oh, no, Miss! It was my own fault."

Her mistress enclosed her with a comforting arm and led her back to the chair she had just vacated.

"Has this happened before?"

Biddy tried to resist sitting down but the pressure on her shoulders was impelling. She began to tremble again and tears rolled down her cheeks. She didn't remember this woman as being tender and sympathetic. Strange to think their ages were not that dissimilar. Only four years stood between them!

"It *is* my own fault. I am so clumsy at the moment and I can't seem to stop crying."

"What happened when you went away? I've heard various stories but only you can tell me what happened! Were you hurt? Where were you going?"

Biddy looked into her mistress' eyes which were level with her own, for Miss Mariana was squatting by her side. She saw compassion and what appeared to be real concern and interest in the truth. Words came tumbling out – jumbled and confused – about her desire to go to London to learn how to sing and how that opportunity had passed and she would never go now. She couldn't bring herself to repeat what had occurred in the woodland but she did say that a shepherd had rescued her from the four lads and helped her back to the Manor House.

"I can't stop thinking about it, Miss… Mrs Owen."

"I'm not surprised. What a terrible thing to go through! What was your father's reaction when you told him?" Biddy looked away. "He doesn't know, does he? No one knows and, least of all Mrs Beacon. I think I will have a word with…"

"Oh, please, don't, Miss!" Biddy was shocked at how loud her voice sounded but she was desperate. "It will make it worse. She will think I've been telling tales to you…"

"I see. Well, maybe I can suggest that I want to have you as my personal maid. I could say that I wanted to train you." Miss Mariana stood up and walked across the room whilst she talked. "That would get you out from under her feet, at least, for some of the day. Elin could instruct you on how to do my hair or choose my clothes. Unfortunately there isn't enough work for both of you, but if Elin was the teacher and you the pupil, then it would explain why I needed both of you. What do you think, Biddy? Would it help? And don't worry about London. I have money which I don't need which my husband gives to me. Next time, you can buy a ticket on the stage coach or you can travel with my brother when he next goes. After all, your own brother, Thomas, went with him last time. Cheer up! Your dreams may yet come true."

Biddy opened her eyes and rubbed the last of the tears from her blotchy skin. Lisbeth, the chicken, had settled. She had come closer and was now snuggled next to Biddy's leg, quietly clucking, whilst the other birds were going in and out of the door as if they were checking on what the girl was doing in their domain! Fortunately there was no sign of the noisy cockerel. He spent much of his day herding his lady friends around the pen and could create quite a scene if he or his mates were upset. Biddy crooned softly to the females. She knew she shouldn't stay here much longer – she was supposed to be driving the Vicar's two pigs out into the nearby woods. The acorns, beech masts and even hawthorn berries were free food which could fatten up the animals ready for slaughtering in a few weeks' time. It was quite a responsible job and the swineherd had to be careful not to let the pigs gorge on too many acorns or their insides might explode – at least that was what some say. Biddy had taken her own family's pig out in the autumn and understood the problem of finding the right balance between too much discipline (which meant the pig got frightened and ran for cover) and too little (which made the animal not move at all but snuffle for ages under the fallen leaves). She had found flapping her skirt or an occasional pat was the best way to control them but her brothers had used a stick if the pig got a taste not just for juicy crab apples but for freedom! Biddy didn't mind being out in the open air and she could go without returning to the scene of the broken jug but her mind was drawn irresistibly back to the recent days.

Yes, her life had improved after her conversation with Miss Mariana and with it the shock of what had happened to her had begun to fade, although there remained many menial tasks which the hateful housekeeper found for her to do. The dragon seemed to delight in finding the lowest jobs and ordering her to undertake them rather than the other maid, Jennett. Even some of the outside jobs, which her brothers would have been given at the Manor House, were done by the inside staff. The Vicar ran a very small ship! Just one groom and the gardener, both of whom lived in the village and the dragon plus the cook, Mrs Thomas (who went home to her husband each evening) and Jennett (who called herself the parlour maid but actually did all kinds of duties). The ranks had swelled to nearly double with the arrival of herself and Elin! Mrs Beacon hadn't decreased the number of her duties. Nevertheless, the precious hour spent with her mistress most days gave her hope. In the privacy of the bedchamber she was treated with consideration and she found that the whole time she was following Elin's instructions, her thoughts were taken away from dwelling on her terrors. Very rarely did she tremble at all in those hours of intimacy with the two other women.

There was another reason she was getting better, and that was because she had found another friend. The first time she had met him was when he had come with an older man to put new thatch on to the cow byre in the neighbour's field. Biddy had seen the roofless building when she had first arrived. Rafters had been secured with wooden pegs and green hazel rods had been woven in to make a base for the roof. She had observed the farmer and his three sons working even in the rain, preparing for the appearance of the thatcher. One day, when she was feeding the hens she had noticed that the whole family was bringing back loads of cut bracken from the lower slopes of Holyhead Mountain. Again and again they came. It seemed that they were going to use the foliage to line the area before the straw was bound to the rods with hemp twine. In the past Biddy had aided her father with a similar task, although she remembered that they had dried the bracken first. Maybe the neighbours had run out of time. Surely the roof had to be on before the ice of winter descended and the cows became sickly from the cold! Seeing the increasing piles of twigs and leaves, Biddy had calculated that the cut undergrowth would probably have filled the whole building and yet it was all going on the rafters. She heard the cough of the children as spores from the fallen plants were sucked into their chests and the occasional cry when a thorn tore at the skin.

Then, the thatcher and son had arrived, bringing the sheaves of standing wheat stalks which had been harvested recently in the nearby fields. Tied with their own twisted straw, the boy threw armfuls up to the man balanced on the roof. Speedily and efficiently, using a huge needle, twine was threaded under the bracken and the thatch was tied on. Biddy watched with fascination as eaves were made, the straw bundles hammered into place using a wooden mallet, and an overhang was left, presumably to shoot the water away from the walls of the cow byre.

The day of the incident she had been close enough to hear the man instructing the boy.

"You've got to get the thickness right. Don't let it 'gully out'. If one part is thinner than the rest then it will wear quicker. Use the mallet like this. If you keep the density even, then no weather will reach the undercoat and the bracken will never have to be replaced, only the top coat of thatch and that not for many years yet. No bird can pull it out if you tie the twine tightly and the wind will not get underneath it. Then, those cows will be snug all…"

The first stone hit Biddy on the shoulder and was followed by two more which struck her head.

"Ouch!" she exclaimed, wondering if the shower of small rocks had somehow originated from the two workers on the nearby roof, but when she turned she was confronted by a crowd of dirty children, some of whom she recognised.

"Whore! Me *Mam* says you're a whore!" The words were accompanied by more sharp missiles.

Biddy put her hands over her face. Where the pebbles hit her clothes she hardly felt them but when they struck her bare cheeks and hands, they drew blood. Now more urchins joined the jeering group and many more voices cried out against her, using more vicious names. Although most of the assailants were younger and shorter than herself, in unison they posed a nasty threat. Without logical thought, she crumpled, sinking to her knees and bowed her head to protect it.

"Hey!" It was a man's voice. "Stop that!"

Immediately the pelting ceased and she sensed a parting of the crowd and then she was being lifted up with a firm grip under here arms. It was the thatcher's son!

"Are you all right? Here, let me help you. My name is 'Edmond' and you must be 'Biddy'."

"How… how do you know my name?" she stuttered.

"I've seen you before and I asked my cousin who you were. Let me take you home – you only live over there. Oh, you're bleeding. Have you a handkerchief? Mine is dirty."

The cut wasn't very deep but Biddy couldn't prevent the trembling beginning and she couldn't get her legs to move. Edmond didn't remove his support but, with a wave to the thatcher, he helped her along the path toward the Vicarage. Of the taunting children there was no sign.

"It's not true," she whispered when they reached the gate. "I don't know what you've heard. Do you live here? I've not seen you before you started the roof."

"I come from Bodedern and I saw you when you were with Morgan Jones. You stayed with his sister last week. Actually I come originally from Dublin but when my parents died of fever four years ago, I was sent to learn a trade from my cousin – well, he's my second cousin, really. He's thatching the roof, even as we speak."

"Here we are. This is where I live. I have a job with the Vicar. His wife is my old mistress."

"I've heard. Has your cut stopped bleeding?"

"Yes, thank you. I'm all right now, but I wouldn't want you to think that those children were telling the truth. I was… was attacked…"

"Ssh! You don't have to tell me. Can I meet up with you tomorrow? What time do you finish work?"

Biddy shook her head.

"Too late to meet you, but I might be able to slip away at midday. Do you stop to eat…" The words dried up. Biddy felt embarrassed. How could she have been so forward? The rumours about her would be true if she wasn't careful! And she hadn't whispered at all but her voice, albeit initially shaky, had worked normally. And the tears, which had started when she was caught in the middle of the crowd, had dried at the sound of his voice. She had behaved much more like she used to before her mother had died.

"No," she continued. "I can't come out in case…"

"Those little beggars corner you again! They won't do that if I'm around. You could chance it just to the field. I will keep an eye out for you and chase them away if they come near you again! Please Biddy. My cousin and I usually eat when the sun is right overhead. If you could sneak out… I'd like to hear your story and… become friends. Would you come?"

Biddy glanced up at Edmond. He was thickset with muscular shoulders, a head of sandy hair – you might call it a thatch of hair on his head – and a pair of dark blue eyes. His nose was slightly crooked as if he might have broken it in a fight and if today's intervention on her behalf was usual then this might be the truth. Talking of which, his mouth seemed to say that he was an honest man. Irish, but with Welsh relatives. He spoke her language fluently and hadn't hesitated to shout at the young ruffians. To think many of her accusers knew her and she had known some of them from babyhood; one or two had played with her own brothers and sisters. What terrible lies were being repeated about her in the community? Was it time to refute them? She was feeling better all of a sudden.

"Yes, I'll try to come."

Perhaps Edmond would be the first to hear her side of the story. Peradventure he would be able to speak up for her in the same way he had defended her. How could she have been so frightened of little children? She should have stood tall and faced their accusations and even thrown some of the stones back…

Biddy roused from her nest in the hen house. She had met Edmond three times since that day he had fulfilled her expectations and more! First the shepherd and then Miss Mariana and now Edmond. Maybe the world wasn't such a grim place as she had believed!

FRANCES

Frances paced up and down the empty quayside one last time and then sat down on her chests with a sigh of frustration and a twinge of trepidation. Arranging her dusty skirt neatly around her ankles, she asked herself for the twentieth time: Where is my uncle? Initially, she had been concerned for her baggage with the throng of disembarking passengers flowing around her and she had kept one hand on the top trunk of the pile and clung tightly to the smaller bag whilst she peered into the crowd. She had never met her uncle before and was not sure what he looked like; she observed every gentleman of about her father's age who strode towards her whilst his gaze scanned the people; some strangers held wide their arms to embrace weeping women and others scooped up wriggling children to bear them away to the waiting carriages; no one had queried her presence, asking if she was Frances Sandleigh! When the mob had dispersed, she relaxed her hold on her belongings and smoothed out her hair and tried to make herself look presentable and not worried and undignified. Her uncle would be here soon, she comforted herself; possibly he had delayed pushing through the noisy rabble to preserve his own dignity! Gradually, the press had subsided and only an occasional person trod towards and not away from the ship; slowly the din turned to silence until she was the only one left, unclaimed. Her anxieties bubbled up again. Had her father not told her uncle what day she was arriving and which dock to come to? She glanced around, aware that the evening sun was sinking fast behind the bare masts of the resting berthed vessels and soon it would be dark. There was a chill in the air and she shivered, reassuring herself that it was cold and not fear that was making her shake. What should she do? Wait a little longer? Momentarily her thoughts turned to the last few days.

How could she have known when she met the tall one-legged man that he would be her saviour and her imprisonment was about to come to an end? Earlier on that day her father had told her that he was expecting a guest, but this was not an unusual occurrence. She had liked Captain

Rowlands – secretly she called him 'Edward' as he had asked – from the first, finding his conversation stimulating and his knowledge deep, and he had treated her with respect and deference, incredibly different from her father's cruel attitude towards her. When she had discovered that Edward was to be the one who would provide her with an escape from the confines of her father's dominion, she had warmed to the seafaring gentleman even more. But it wasn't until the unfortunate encounter with the Queen Dowager that her emotions had burst to the surface of her consciousness and she had found herself acknowledging that here was a man whom she could desire and marry. She had mourned for years for her dead love and it had never entered her head that at the age of eight and twenty she might find her stomach fluttering with anticipation or her heart singing or her hopes rising whenever she saw a broad-shouldered peg legged man!

The day after Edward and she had met the Queen Dowager, they were able to set sail and excitement had chased away any fears or sadness she might have felt at leaving her homeland. Frances had real reasons for rejoicing but she was surprised to overhear many of the sailors saying how glad they were to be departing until she remembered that there was a taut atmosphere in Lisbon itself and she guessed that if one was a foreigner, one might have felt vulnerable. Before they sailed, Edward had confided in her that none of the crew had become embroiled in fights of any kind, either with fists or words, but, with the sails raised, Frances imagined that she heard an almost audible sigh of relief with the widening gap between land and ship! From the outset the sailors sang heartily their homeward bound songs as they pulled on the ropes or washed the decks. There was no doubt of what they were feeling to be leaving!

Only the passengers were found looking back wistfully at Portugal and not all of those were doing that. Frances herself was not among those who strained to catch a last glimpse of Portugal; she was below decks helping with the children and some of the women, who were suffering already from seasickness despite the settled weather and the calm water. Even in the dank confined spaces down there some folk were weeping, presumably because they knew that they would never see all these familiar landmarks again and, for most, beloved husbands and fathers were left behind. Frances didn't cry; she felt nothing but relief. At last she was free! For a moment even the thought of being on the same ship as the man she found both attractive and mysterious – with his plaintive eyes hinting of some tragedy – was forgotten in the euphoria of leaving her father and her lonely life of servitude.

Frances was told by one of the mariners that the Captain had ordered a sumptuous meal for their first evening on board, and she had smiled to herself. Maybe Edward was hoping to distract the passengers from their homesickness but it wasn't the time or place to question his motives when she met him a short while later. It appeared he had come to check personally that the accommodation provided for them was satisfactory. He whispered to Frances: "I am praying that the voyage won't be prolonged. The men don't work well with women aboard," and then he was gone.

If Frances had expected to see Edward on the crossing or even that she might be singled out for special favours, because of their shared experience of meeting royalty, she was wrong. During the meal on that first night, and on subsequent nights, she was not given a seat near the man who sent her pulse racing. One or two snippets of his words reached her ears:

"I am particularly thankful to be past those guns on the estuary and heading for the open sea," and "If we are as lucky as on the outgoing journey it won't be many days before we're sailing up another river – the River Thames." Her conversations were with the First Mate and even the young Gentlemen Volunteers who were seated far from the Captain's eye.

In fact, apart from the meals, barely did Frances catch a glimpse of the man who often filled her unruly thoughts. She chided herself. A captain must have a multitude of duties keeping him busy and, after all, she was just one of many, albeit that she had been the first to be granted safe passage from the imminent war! He had made it very clear that he was displeased with the Dowager's suggestion that they marry and that he had someone he loved in England. She shook her head at her own foolish musings and busied herself with serving her fellow passengers.

In spite of her common sense, disappointment had swept over her when the ship pulled alongside the stone quay in London and she was unable to bid Edward farewell since he was surrounded by others who wanted to thank him. She had no intention of saying out loud (especially in such a public place) from what degradations his agreement to take her on board had released her, but she decided that she did want to shake his hand and express her own gratitude before she was whisked away by her relative and never saw him again. In vain, she waited for the crowd to thin but, eventually, she remembered that she ought to be supervising the unloading of her baggage and she had descended the gangplank without a final word with him.

Which brought her back to the present! Nevertheless, her mind continued to linger on images of Captain Edward Rowlands – his straight shoulders, his square hands, his deep brown eyes with a sadness that he couldn't quite disguise, his gruff voice and his wooden leg. The last had caught her attention from the very beginning but she was too polite to ask where and how he had lost his leg (surely it must have been in the war and its loss wasn't the reason for his melancholy!) and now it was too late. Everyone had gone, abandoning her, and she could hear the sounds of seamen scrubbing the decks, see the flicker lanterns being lit and smell food cooking on the fire, although she wasn't sure it came from the direction of the ship she had just left. Soon the mariners themselves would disembark. Were they waiting for their captain to descend the narrow gangplank before them? Did he remain in his cabin, writing up the log? He had not passed her. Should she go and ask for his help? No, for she was in his debt already. Yet, she couldn't move an inch without help – she had too many chests and they were too heavy for her to drag along. Anyway, she rebuked herself, she had no idea of where she was going! Surely her uncle would appear soon! Best be patient! She bowed her shoulders, shrugging her cloak around her to keep out the ever-strengthening evening breeze.

"Frances." It was Edward, hurrying towards her, a giant to lean on, like in her imaginations. "My servant told me you were still here, sitting on your baggage, forlorn and lost. I never thought to see you like this – you always seem so in charge of everything. It has come to my ears that you have been an angel with some of the women who were sick! Has no one come for you?"

Frances blushed at the compliments and chose to reply to his final question.

"They're just late, that's all."

"You should have come back on board…"

"Oh, no! I wouldn't presume on you anymore," she answered.

"Who exactly are you expecting?"

"My uncle. Father sent a message to him once the arrangements were made."

"Well, one's thing's for sure, you can't sit here. I was about to find myself somewhere to stay for the night. Let's leave word on the '*Dart*' as to where you've gone and let's go to an inn. I know one near here which serves the most delicious mutton stew with dumplings." He paused. "Or, if... My aunt... No, we'll say close by. I'm sure he'll be here within the hour. We did make very good time. Maybe your... did you say, 'Uncle'? Maybe he didn't expect us 'til tomorrow."

Suddenly her circumstances were turned around and she was no longer alone with night falling. Instantly, the captain ordered his personal servant to hire a carriage. When it arrived Edward was all for climbing in and leaving her luggage with his servants but she insisted that her chests were lifted on to the back of the carriage. She felt she ought to give an explanation for her uneasiness, especially when he teased her that they might contain the Crown Jewels, but with a ragged group of the '*Dart*'s sailors standing around, she decided she couldn't confide in him yet. She was sure she could trust a gentleman with the truth but not ordinary seamen! She shook her head, feeling a red stain spread beneath her brown cheeks, and was glad when the captain handed her into the musty interior of the carriage. Her companion hadn't registered her agitation for he proposed:

"I think that we had better book you rooms for the night. After all, even if your uncle appears in the near future, it'll be too late to set off again tonight."

Frances leant against the hard cushion of the seat. Everything would be satisfactory now she was in the capable hands of a Captain of the Navy!

"Bowler," he shouted as the equipage moved away. "I'll be back, when I've eaten, to collect my luggage. Make sure it's ready. We'll be at 'The White Horse' if you need me."

"Very good, Sir."

Frances settled her skirts either side of her legs, and studied Edward. All the recent disquietude had fled. She was recovered enough to announce:

"There'll be no need for me to stay, although something to eat would be welcome."

"The rooms are courtesy of Captain Rowlands, Ma'am. And I'm not taking 'No' for an answer!" He smiled and then persevered, "You have no money?"

"I... I have a very small amount. My father said I wouldn't need any. But, if you will give me your home address, my father will reimburse you."

"There's no need for that, Frances. I was intending to spend a night here anyway and now I shall have the company of a beautiful young lady to while away the evening. This is your first time in England. Allow me to introduce you to the diversions of an English hotel."

Frances blushed for the second time.

"I am neither young nor beautiful…"

The conversation lapsed but almost at once the carriage pulled up outside the inn. Light streamed from its paned windows and beckoned the exhausted travellers inside. Frances felt like a child again. Effortlessly Edward procured two separate rooms and provisionally booked a third for her absent uncle. "Just in case," he whispered whilst the innkeeper showed them into a secluded parlour. Shortly afterwards they were seated either side of a square table partaking of a meal.

For several minutes there was silence and then Frances exclaimed:

"Oh, that's much better! Who would have thought that food could change one's outlook?" And the fellowship of a handsome man, her heart mocked her! "When I was sitting on that chest, it all seemed rather hopeless and…"

"You did look rather sad."

"I was feeling homesick and a bit apprehensive of the future, I suppose."

"And now you're not because of some meat and dumplings and the anticipation of pear pie and cream!"

"No, it's not just the food. Your kindness was… is most welcome. I *will* pay you back soon. I guess, during the time I was waiting and imagining that my uncle was never going to come, it felt very much as if I was in a foreign land. I was in the great city of London! My imagination conjured up all kinds of unknown hazards and even customs which I hadn't encountered before. At least I can speak the language. But when you came along… I'm not usually helpless. I am not inexperienced and, up until now, have been able to cope with most situations. It's just that England is very different from what I had expected."

Edward laughed, creasing the lines around his eyes.

"You've hardly seen anything but the docks."

"And the inside of a very comfortable inn. Were you really coming here?"

"Well, I might not have stayed at this particular one, but I've stayed here before and very…"

"Oh, you shouldn't have changed your plans just for me!" she cried and then continued solemnly as possible reasons dawned on her: "Ah! You couldn't have taken me to the place you were intending going to, could you?"

"Precisely, m'dear. Will you have anything more to eat?"

"No, thank you. I've had enough and I do feel better for food. I'm so grateful to you for…"

"Will you please stop thanking me? I wouldn't have abandoned anyone to sit on that tawdry dock, especially with daylight fading, man or woman. Nonetheless, as I have said before, I enjoy your company. I don't want to hear any more thanks."

"I suppose my uncle must never have arrived, otherwise one of your men would have notified me."

"Indeed. So, what are you going to do?"

"I don't know."

"You must send him a message."

"Yes, but I can't stay here whilst I wait for him."

"Frances, I will leave you adequate funds…"

"No, Sir! I won't allow that."

"Lend, then. I will lend you some money. I am not staying in London for long. I must…"

"Ah, your letter for the King. Does he see you in person?"

"No." He grinned. "Not like the Queen Dowager of Portugal."

There was a pause whilst Frances recalled that unusual encounter for a second time that day. Edward was quiet too. She hoped he wasn't angry again. Purposely she changed the subject.

"So where are you bound for? Did you tell me you lived in Wales?"

"My estates – not that you should get the impression that they are large. Rather, my home is in North Wales."

Frances took a deep breath.

"And your… friend? Is she betrothed to you?"

"I really think…"

"Oh, forgive me. I shouldn't pry." Frances gave a dry cough. What had possessed her? Perhaps unconsciously she had wanted to remind her weak heart not to get too relaxed with this man.

"Frances, I have known you for a week or two and I look forward to our conversations, but I learnt long ago not to bare my soul to anyone. I have a dark side to my personality…"

"Please don't say anymore," intercepted Frances stiffly. "I spoke out of place."

"And I have family problems that would make your hair stand on end."

Edward completed his sentence as though she had not said anything.

"They can't be as bad as mine," Frances replied softly, standing up. "My father hates me."

She saw Edward frown and acknowledged, in that moment, that she was going to tell him everything!

"He gives no sign of it."

Frances hesitated when she heard his jocular tone. She suspected that he did not want shared intimacies but her need to talk overpowered her reason and pride.

"Oh, no!" she sneered strongly. Anger rose and nearly drowned her. She marched to the window, struggling to control the swirling flood. "No, he's much too clever for that!"

She turned and pressed her back against the windowsill, her fingers tightly gripped together, halting again to calculate what would result from sharing her innermost thoughts and then gave into her need to unburden herself.

"Do you want to know a secret?" she demanded but before he could reply, she stammered, "The reason... the reason why I've been guarding my luggage as if they contain the Crown Jewels? Well, they do, in a way. My father's crown jewels! I have, in my chests, two gowns and one shift and only one set of petticoats. All the rest of the space is filled with my father's treasures!" She almost spat the last word at Edward.

"Treasures?" She recognised curiosity. Was he interested, possibly in spite of himself?

"Yes, he told me not to tell anyone, but I no longer care. I don't want them anyway. They're blood money."

"What do you mean?"

Frances folded her arms across her bosom.

"He worked for... well, never mind who he worked for. He... he murdered certain people and he was rewarded. Very rarely was he given gold, although sometimes he was. No, he would come home with valuable objects. I didn't find out exactly where he got them from – whether he was given them or he bought them or stole them from his victim's house – whatever the explanation, he had hundreds of them. You must have seen them all around the house, when you came. He should have kept them locked away, but he couldn't bear not to display them and boast about them. He did keep the most valuable ones locked away... and, the reason why I'm... I am here is not for my safety. Other fathers have sent their daughters away so that they are safe, but my father... He... I am here because of his treasures. He understood if war was to break out his fortune would either be stolen or confiscated and..."

"How much exactly are you carrying around with you?"

"I'm not sure. Some of his pieces are... are priceless."

Her confidant let loose a hearty laugh.

"And you have no money to pay for a room!"

Frances couldn't help a tiny smile curving her lips; the anger was beginning to ebb away.

"Why have you told me? I might rob you!" He seemed serious now.

"You can rob me if you like." She strived to pitch her voice normally. "I don't want it. I'm not concerned what happens to it. It's not mine."

"It'll be yours one day for..."

"No! His will excludes me."

"Why? You are his only daughter, aren't you?"

"Because I hate him and he hates me." She knew the venom was back.

"Then, my dear, why did you do his bidding? Why did you leave Portugal? Why did you not report him to the authorities or whoever? And what are you supposed to do with it all? And why did he trust you not to disappear forever with it? And..."

"So many questions! The first and the last have the same answer. He has something which I want. Not valuable in the sense of money, but valuable to me. In answer to what I am supposed to do with it all: nothing. I'm not to breathe a word of this to anyone. No one is going to suspect a woman leaving the country when there might be a war. And no one did. No one wanted to see what I was loading on to your ship. This plan worked. I am to pretend that my baggage consists of... of feminine articles of clothing and reside quietly at my uncle's house until my father arrives."

"What if he doesn't?"

Frances couldn't prevent her lip curling.

"He will. He always does."

"But what if war breaks out and he's trapped?"

Frances shook her head again, stepping towards the fire. She put her hands up to its warmth. All of a sudden, thoughts of her father sent a shiver of ice running through her blood.

"He would never be trapped. He'd come overland if necessary or stow away or… or any other plan. He's known as a merchant rather than a mercenary, so he can move around reasonably easily without being questioned. However, his respectability was all a cover. You say you have a darker side, but my father is a devil. He will do anything for a price. Just name a satisfactory price and the wicked deed is as good as done!"

Edward arose and walked to her side.

"How did he produce such a fine, honest daughter then?"

"Don't patronise me!"

"I'm not," he denied. "The little I know of you suggests you are honest and…"

"Please…" Frances turned from him and gazed at the shimmering depths of the burning logs. Oh, God, what shall I do? she cried silently. Should she share the truth with this man? He seemed solicitous and compassionate and yet… The only sound was the crackling of the fire and then she whispered:

"He didn't. I am not his daughter." This would be the test. If he moved away now, she would know she had made a mistake. She glanced up at him but could not read his reaction. Therefore she went on, saying with a mocking lilt, "You don't think he'd let a daughter of his travel unaccompanied, unchaperoned to another country? No, my real father is… was Portuguese. He… That barbarian, whom I call 'Father', killed him. When he found out who my father was, he went straight out and killed him."

She saw despair flash across his face! What a strange reaction! Part of his dark side? What secrets burdened him?

"I'm sorry! I shouldn't have told you. You must have enough problems without me loading mine on to you. Forgive me." She closed her eyes to stop the tears from coming. He was not the man she had hoped he was – her obvious rage, confessed loathing and now illegitimacy must have disgusted him.

"Not again! This can't be happening!" The words were a mere whisper.

Frances blinked. Had she heard right? She stared at him and saw nothing but concern and consideration.

"Go on. What happened to your mother?" he asked blandly.

Frances stayed silent. She had been dragged out of her own trouble by his words. She wished she could ask him what he had meant, but politeness held her back *and* his comments earlier about his refusal to share his personal life. As he had pointed out, their friendship didn't extend that far!

She had chosen to reveal some of herself to him but she had no right to expect him to confide in her. For a second, she regretted her confidences and contemplated telling him that she did not want to talk about it anymore, but part of her was detached from how much information she'd imparted to him and part of her understood that she couldn't leave him with half the story. She strangled her own curiosity and stated:

"My mother is my reason for being here." She stopped, trying to collect her muddled thoughts. "She… she left him when… when I was three. She returned to England. He tracked her down. You asked why I don't skip off with his treasures. Because he'd find me. Wherever I run to, he would come. He has people who gather information for him everywhere."

"He didn't strike me as an efficient, clever person. A cold, ruthless murderer, you say?"

Frances screwed up her face with repugnance; ire burned in her throat like bile. "That was why he was… is so successful. No one can believe it of him. He pretends to be an ordinary merchant, fussing over details of insignificant transactions. He can pretend to be obsequious, but it's all a disguise."

"But what happened to your mother? You say she is why you've come to England. Where is she?"

"I don't know!" she croaked softly. It was a cry of despair as impassioned as the man's had been a few moments ago. "I know she is somewhere in England but that's all. *He* knows. He holds the information which I want. I don't think he himself has seen her in twenty-five years, but he has watched her all that time. And… and that's why I did this 'job' for him. He says when he comes he'll tell me where she is."

"And you trust him?"

"No!" Frances stormed. "No, I shall hide his treasures and try a little blackmail myself. Once I have found my mother, I'll return his possessions to him."

"So, it's good that I have no intention of robbing you, after all. You need to keep it." Edward reached out and cupped her chin in his hand, turning her so that she was looking straight at him. "I'll keep your secret, Frances, but why did you tell me?" He let his hand fall.

She shook her head, her heart thumping uncomfortably.

"I haven't decided. You're the first person I've… I've trusted for ages. I find your comp… you are… I suppose I can see you've had your own troubles, I hoped that you would be sympathetic to me." She shrugged her shoulders. "Whatever makes people confide in others? I've had my problems for years and there's been no one to tell. You told me earlier that you are the same. You carry worries in your soul which you do not share. But you can't hide it always. I've seen it in your eyes sometimes. I guess it's to do with a woman. I understand. I loved a man, once. I loved him with all my heart and I couldn't have him. He was never... never my husband, but I lived in his home and called myself by his name."

"And did your... your father stop you?"

"Yes. Whilst he was away I left my home. Hah! Home! It was my prison. I lived no better than a servant except when my father entertained. But I kept abreast of what was happening by reading and talking to the other servants. Then one day I met Ferdinand. He was riding past our house when I was in the garden. He stopped... and our friendship blossomed. We used to talk in the garden and then we used to... to kiss. My so-called father found us kissing. He forbad me to see Ferdinand again. I shouted at him. He shouted at me. Then he told me who... who my real father was and why I was brown skinned and why he had allowed me to work in his kitchens and... and everything. He told me that my mother was actually alive when he had told everyone that she was dead. I was desperately upset. To... suddenly discover that... All the foundations of my world shifted." She shivered with the recollection. "I wanted to get away. I could not bear the thought of living with him anymore. He had betrayed me. I had always made allowances for him and what he did because he was my... my father. But he wasn't.

"So I waited meekly until he had gone on one of his.... trading journeys and then I went to Ferdinand and we ran away together. We travelled to the mountains. We had seven glorious months until he... came. He found us and he... he shot Ferdinand right in front of my eyes."

"Frances." She was completely lost in the past and did not anticipate what Edward was going to do; he pulled her into his arms and she hid her face in his coat, barely aware of who embraced her.

"There was blood everywhere," she mumbled. "Everywhere – spurting out from his chest and he was dead within... immediately." Her words petered out.

He held her against him and she tried to clear her mind of the terrible images and regain some composure. His voice was soothing.

"Frances, don't tell me anymore, don't tell me anymore. It's too painful for you. Come and sit down."

She raised her face to him and their eyes met. It felt like a dream. Very slowly he moved his lips to hers and she did not pull away. It had been so long since she had kissed a man and she trembled. How long since he had kissed a woman? She suspected that it had not been many weeks and she drew away, cursing her fragile heart. Returning to the table, savagely she picked up her glass and gulped down the remains of the wine in one swill. No more pathetic, ill-advised, desperate urges! This man was not for her! He had his own betrothed or lover!

"I fought him then." She spoke loudly. "This supposed father of mine – over the body of the man I loved, but he was stronger. I swore I would never live in his house again, but where could I go? I had no husband and no money. We told everyone that I had been married and my husband had been killed in a hunting accident and we returned to Lisbon. There was nothing else I could do. However, I determined to leave him and find my mother, but he would not tell me where she was. I had nothing to use against him. I could hardly report the murder of Ferdinand. He murdered all the time. So I waited and waited until a chance should come when he would need me or something. It was miserable in the house, but he was away often. Eventually my chance did come. Three years of controlling myself and hiding what I truly felt! At last I could go, for he needed me to carry his possessions out of Lisbon."

"I see now why he was very anxious for me to agree to take you. What would he have done if I had refused?"

"Found someone else. Nothing ever daunts him. He can overcome any pit fall. Never underestimate him."

Edward joined her at the table and poured more wine for them both. He sat down and picked at the remains of the food whilst she admitted:

"If I didn't hate him so much, I would admire him. His disguise was perfect. No one suspects him. But sometimes he seemed frightened. Of those who gave him orders? Who can say? I have no intention of delving into his life. What puzzles me is why my uncle didn't arrive. My father is meticulous over every detail usually."

"It'll be some completely ordinary occurrence such as the wheel of the carriage coming off or a horse losing a shoe."

"Yes, I suppose you're right. Adverse circumstances never prevented my father from fulfilling his plans, but my uncle isn't him, is he?"

"Have you ever met your uncle?"

"No. None of the rest of my family. My father never returned to England. At least, not to visit his relatives. Not that he's estranged from them. He sends them gifts sometimes. Meagre gifts they always were too. He did not seem to want to boast about how wealthy he is beyond Lisbon. I should say that was his only weakness. He could not resist displaying his collection. Maybe he craved people's praise. He didn't have many friends."

"Are you going to tell your family about him?"

"No. I don't care what happens to him or his fortune. Once I have found out where my mother is, I shall leave him."

"Do… do you think she'll want to see you? Oh, I'm sorry, Frances. I shouldn't have said that. It's just that she left you all those years ago, when you were a helpless child…"

"I understand what you are saying. I wonder myself sometimes why she left me. I have never met her nor written to her… I can hardly remember her at all. Yet, I'm compelled to find her and talk to her so that I can find out the true facts. If she doesn't want me, I shall live alone for I will never live with my fath…"

The door opened and the innkeeper entered.

"Was everything to your liking, Sir? Madam?"

"Yes, thank you. You may clear the table now for I must away to the ship to collect…"

"And I must retire to bed," put in Frances, stifling a yawn. All of a sudden tiredness swept over her; the see-saw of her emotions had left her drained.

"I think we can safely assume that Mrs Sandleigh's uncle has been detained. We shall only be needing the two rooms tonight. I'm sure we'll hear from him in the morning."

GRIFFITH AND MARIANA

"Do you realise that we have been married for one month exactly today, m'dear?" said the Vicar.

He looked along the length of the polished table which stretched between himself and Mariana, but she made no reply. He reached out for more bread but he faltered when his hand touched the fresh loaf because he noticed that his wife had not begun her meal. Then, taking the crust and spreading it thickly with butter, he continued:

"You're not eating. Are you not hungry?"

Unexpectedly he wished that they were not sitting in such a formal setting. Usually he felt pride and satisfaction that he had a wife ensconced at his very own dining table, even if it meant he had to raise his voice to converse with her. Yet today, he wished she was sitting next to him and then he could have placed his hand over hers and observed her more closely. However, even from that distance he could see her pallor. Yes, she was looking very pale, more than usual, but it wasn't her paleness which concerned him as much as her listlessness. Take now, for instance, she had not replied to his questions. Biting into his bread, he recalled that she had been like this since... since when? Since her marriage to him. She had never been a quiet woman when she had lived with her father, and she had always had a hearty appetite when he had dined at the Manor House. Therefore, what was ailing her now? Was she unhappy? Had she not wanted to marry him? Had she been coerced into marriage? No, for she herself had agreed of her own accord on that momentous night. It was not even that he had posed the question that night. Indeed, he could not be sure he had ever asked her seriously, to her face. She had known that he wanted to marry her; it must be that his love for her had shone out through his eyes. And, of course, there was her sister. Yes, he had spoken to Mrs Struley about his desire to wed Mariana. Had she insisted that Mariana consent? The answer must be No. Mariana was too wilful to be told what to do...

No, that was not true. She had a reputation for being untamed but he had encountered no difficulty with her since she had resided in this house. In fact, the more he thought about it, the more it came to him that the last month had been remarkably calm, considering his choice of bride. For most of the time, he had been unaware that he was again a married man. He admitted that he had been very busy. Too busy to notice what Mariana did with her moments. He must watch her. It wouldn't be proper if she wasted away. Yet, wasn't that the origin of the problem? He did not *want* to observe her, for that only reminded him of his heartache and failure. He was not inclined to accept that the reason he had been increasingly busy was because he had needed to have his mind full of other matters in order not to think!

Nevertheless, to all outward appearances, his hasty marriage was a success. There had been no raised voices or arguments. He had not been forced to forbid her to do anything – least of all ride that great beast of a horse of hers unaccompanied. She had barely ridden at all! In truth, she had hardly left the house except with him. No, she had conducted herself with a new maturity as befitted his wife and the mistress at the Vicarage. It was what he had told Sir William all those months ago: young girls needed the security of marriage.

Actually, many of his friends had congratulated him, over the past fortnight, on the outcome of his marriage. Yes, they all told him that he had done very well for himself to have such an attractive young woman in his house. He guessed they meant to say "in his bed", but he was pleased secretly with their jealousy. If he was aware that he spent every night lying awake in his own lonely bed, counting the hours until dawn, no one else was privy to this information. To those beyond the Vicarage's walls, they were a happily married couple.

If he, as her husband, did not know how she spent her days, well, what husband did? He had a demanding job and he was expected by the community to visit people and be seen around the parish. Also, there was the time he spent in his study. Every vicar must spend time in prayer and meditation and preparing his sermons. Folk avidly assessed his sermons. If they were protracted he might get complaints, but if the message was too shallow or he used an old sermon, then no one minded speaking their mind to him about it! Once a fortnight, he prided himself in delivering a measured, well-thought-out talk from the pulpit. If he found that one service was not enough for him to say all he had written, then he would carry it on two weeks later. No, he had to have time to study and plan his speeches.

It was not his place to check on what his wife was doing whilst he was working. He had trained his servants not to disturb him if he was in his study. He had drilled into them that God came before all else, whether his own meals or sleep or trivial, below stairs problems. He had explained this to Mariana. His study was sacrosanct. Now, fortunately he had a wife who could cope with the servants and she had them to keep her busy. Running a house took many hours; she must have to give much of her time to that task, he reckoned. She was doing very well, for he had not noticed the slightest tremor of change in any aspect of his household since his marriage. It was similar to what it says in the Bible: **"She riseth also while it is yet night and giveth meat to her household, and a portion to her maidens."** A good wife. Yes, Mariana was a good wife.

He could not actually list all the jobs Mariana did during the day, and he had not seen if she had made any alterations to her own bedchamber because he had not been in it since their wedding night, but many couples lived separate lives. Life demanded it! There was much to do each day. Which reminded him. He should not be sitting here musing over his relationship with his wife; he ought to be putting down his initial thoughts for his next sermon. It was a very important sermon for it was the Harvest Festival and the church would be full.

He hoped there would be no fighting over the setting up of the seats in the church. It was unseemly and it created a nasty atmosphere during the service itself. He accepted that the country families should be given preference, but they had the Chancel. It was the tenants and their benches who caused the most trouble with people removing others' benches and then the first ones moving those again. It was ridiculous! Surely there should be some decorum and reverence in church. Anyway, he would try not to get involved in the petty wrangles. His job was the spiritual feeding of the flock, not a Justice of the Peace choosing between quarrelling factions. Yes, his place was to provide a challenging sermon and he ought to be in his study now, praying over it and preparing what he was going to say.

* * *

Mariana's thoughts were also taken up also with analysing her new situation. Griffith's remark about the date had set her reviewing her days. In many ways she could not remember a time when she had not been married, such was the pattern of her waking hours. It seemed another world since she had galloped across the fields with Jack. And yet, in other ways, it was as if she was not married at all, for she saw very little of her husband and he had never come near her bedchamber after their wedding night Momentarily, she recalled the evening of her wedding. She had steeled herself to receive her husband when he came into her bedchamber and had removed her night attire without too much hesitation. However, she was unnerved when he had remained staring at her. Embarrassment had flooded her under his lengthy scrutiny, not least because he remained dressed whilst she was not! Glancing up at him she was filled with the need to run and escape. She did not want to see this man, this *old* man, this *fat* old man with no clothes on! And she did not want him touching her! She wanted Jack.

She moaned inside her head a prayer of sorrow because her love was gone. Jack, dear Jack, who had taught her the pleasure of passion, was gone. This man, with whom she had joined together in Holy Matrimony, aroused nothing in her but a desire to run. What was he doing? she wondered. What was he doing, standing there, staring? She observed that there were beads of sweat on his forehead and that his hands were moving, rubbing the side of his coat. She looked away again when her heart urged her to flee. No! Deliberately she quietened her thoughts. No, this man was her husband and there was no escape. Jack had not been her husband and now she had chosen to allow this man, who was gazing at her, to have his way with her. Yes, she had chosen her path. She must keep to it. No one had forced her to marry the Parson. For her sake she must go through with it. She must not show any fear or disgust or, for that matter, any knowledge of what he was about to do; she must be calm and relaxed in order to save herself from disgrace and… and the child too. For the first time she understood that she was carrying a child – another human being. For his or her sake too, she must go through with the next few minutes. Then the child would not suffer the stigma of illegitimacy.

Mariana had faced her husband. He was standing motionless. Surely he did not expect her to make the first move! No, his eyes were shadowy. What was wrong with him? He seemed upset and as tense as herself. Was he ill?

"Parson… Griffith? Are you all right? Can I get into bed? I'm cold."
She spoke quietly in order not to alarm him. His hands were at rest now; he
was in a kind of daze but his body was rigid. She stepped towards him but
he turned from her and marched from the room.

Relief and confusion had flowed equally through her veins. What had
been the matter with him? Maybe the strain of the day had overtaken him.
Maybe he had gone to down a glass of fortifying spirits and he would
reappear presently. She had lain awake through the darkness, ready for his
return, but he had not come back that night or any night since then.

She was astonished that the intimate side of their marriage was
non-existent. Did men desire to visit their wives so infrequently? That was
not what she had thought when she had been a single woman! If it had
not been for the baby, she would have been thrilled not to have to endure
a physical union with the Parson, but she *was* with child and if Griffith
did not come again soon to her room, she would not be able to hide her
mistake. Fornication, Griffith would call it. Such a forbidding word for the
delights of lying once with Jack! There had been no word or sign of Jack,
since she had last embraced him on the beach. He had truly gone and she
believed in her heart that he was dead.

She had slipped into her new life remarkably easily for the simple
reason that there was nothing for her to learn, no new skills to persevere
with, certainly not any tasks to tax her concentration. She was prepared to
go further than that and say that there was nothing for her to do – nothing
she *had* to do. Yet Margaret had lectured her on housewifely skills and
even Jack had told her that she would have duties when she became a wife.
Nonetheless, no demands were made on her. At least, not within the house.
She was expected to accompany her husband to certain functions in the
parish, but she had no work as mistress in the Vicarage.

The morning after the wedding, Griffith had handed her over to Mrs
Beacon, the housekeeper, who supposedly was going to show her around
the house and give her some of the keys which hung at her waist. To begin
with Mariana had been fascinated by the number of keys the matron carried.
What were they all for? Nowadays, she was grateful for them because their
jingling gave warning of the stiff housekeeper's arrival wherever she went.
And Mariana needed to know when Mrs Beacon was approaching for she
had discovered, at that initial meeting, that the older woman did not like
her.

From the outset, Mariana had seen disapproval written all over her face. "This new wife of the Parson is not up to the same standards as Griffith's first wife." These words might have been scrawled in black ink all across her forehead.

Mariana could almost hear the housekeeper saying: "Now, Mrs *Barbara* Owen was a real lady and a hard worker – not a flibbertigibbet like this new one!"

Mariana could guess at the kinds of thoughts Mrs Beacon harboured behind her tight brow or muttered in the ears of Cook:

"I've heard all about that Squire's daughter and I'm not going to lower myself to befriend *her*… I don't think there was any need for the Parson to remarry. Why did he do it? Of course, I'll have to be polite just in case the minx has a say in the Parson's decisions and he dismisses me for insubordination. Although anyone with a half an eye can see that he and his wife don't allow their lives to overlap much! They're hardly ever in the same room! Why did the man marry such a chit? It's not as if he's found his youth again and takes her into his bed every night… I don't understand why he bothered to woo her in the first place… I'm determined not to allow the new mistress to tread on my toes. No, without any help from that girl, I shall order this household as efficiently as I've always done. The Parson shall have no cause for complaint. His wife can amuse herself. After all, she's very accomplished at that kind of thing. If the tales about her behaviour are to be believed, then the Vicarage is in for a very rough storm!"

Mariana knew it was only conjecture, but not a single smile of friendliness made her think she had judged the head servant incorrectly.

Mariana had been shown all over the house, by a scowling Mrs Beacon. It was made very plain to Mariana that she would not be welcome in the housekeeper's domain and certainly not in the kitchen at any time. Servants did not mix with their betters, even if she suspected that Mrs Beacon did not want to admit that Mariana was her better! Mariana had read and understood the message and from that day had not ventured near the widow's kingdom.

Soon Mariana had learnt that there were not many rooms in which she was welcome! She was told that her husband's study was out of bounds also and often locked. She had had a glimpse in there on one occasion, but it appeared even more bereft of homely comforts than the rest of the house and she had decided that she did not mind being kept out from it. The parlour was where she could entertain visitors (if she did not want to see them in her bedchamber), but she was not expected to remain in there once they had departed and the atmosphere in the air when a meal was finished (and the maids were clearing the table) was not conducive to sitting idly chatting in the dining room. Naturally she had never knocked on her husband's bedchamber at night and she had not seen inside that room. Therefore, usually, Mariana found refuge in her own chamber. If she had been her old self she might have felt constrained by the walls of the room, but she did not seem to be able to shake off her tiredness, however many hours she slept.

Her long days had developed rapidly into a pattern. Although she was told that Griffith rose with the sun, she herself was woken by Elin at a much more civilised hour. She recollected that Elin had readily offered to accompany her to the Vicarage, but Mariana could not honestly say that she found her presence there a comfort. Whenever she saw Elin she was reminded of *Trem-y-Môr* and mostly she wished that she could forget her previous life. Then, like Jack, with his memory loss, she would have nothing to compare this new routine with.

The first event of the day, where the mistress mixed with others, was morning prayers, said by the Parson, which the whole household was expected to attend. Mariana regularly spent this time trying to control the nausea which would not leave her. Fortunately no one was allowed to contribute anything, other than the Parson, and Mariana's contemplations were her own.

Promptly then husband and wife would walk to the dining room to the beat of the brass gong which Mrs Beacon would strike to announce the meals. There was very strict timekeeping here and Mariana would have found this difficult if she had not felt incredibly lethargic, but her only emotion was mild surprise at how the clock ruled the home. Punctuality was essential and there was a grand clock in the hall which seemed to have been put there in order that everyone could be on time. The clock chimed at quarter-past, half past, three-quarters-to and then played a short tune on the hour, before striking. Since it could be heard in every corner of the house, no one had any excuse for tardiness.

Once the meal that broke their fast was over, the Parson would disappear back into his study.

"He's like a rat going into its hole," Elin had said to Mariana, teasingly. "Do you remember when Mrs Struley…"

"I'm sorry." Mariana was only half listening.

Blood had rushed to her maid's face and Mariana had touched her arm with a half-smile of reassurance that she was not offended by the words. Elin had hurried away but Mariana was sure she heard her whisper:

"Is it only a couple of months since we were mimicking Mrs Struley and the Squire rebuked us? Two young girls laughing together."

Mariana herself felt ashamed that her circumstances had changed to such a degree that she and Elin never made fun of others. She couldn't be bothered to ridicule her husband; she was just glad that she did not to have to interact with him straight after the morning meal and heaved a sigh when he retired into his study, like a rat or not.

Yet, Mariana's mornings were not generally spent in her room alone. She had received many calls over the weeks since her marriage. She did not suspect any ulterior motives until she overheard her maid once again, after a group of visitors had departed. Elin was muttering angrily:

"We congratulate you, Mrs Owen. Hah! You came out of idle curiosity. I might as well offer guided tours for a half penny. Nosy neighbours you all are! You only come to see if my Miss Mariana has changed. Well, she has and I can't understand why!"

Mariana had given some thought to her maid's comments. She was used to folk talking about her – being the Squire's daughter had meant apparently that she was of interest to the community – and sometimes, she admitted to herself, she had played up to their expectations. But, surely now she was a married woman not a single person expected her to behave without decorum! She acknowledged that if it weren't for her maid, she might receive her callers in her shift, because she just could not find it in herself to care what she wore or what she looked like. Occasionally she wondered if it was the babe who was sapping all her strength, but it was not as if she was large with child. Nothing showed, except a slight filling out of her belly. If anything, she had lost weight because of the sickness. Mostly she did not try to understand her lack of enthusiasm.

However, if Elin was right, and people were coming out of a desire to find juicy gossip, then they must be disappointed, because Mariana had determined to behave with perfect propriety. Yes, her smile was false but who knew that for certain? They would not discover any evidence of marital disharmony from her!

Mariana shook her head, considering her reflections. Elin must be wrong. True, she herself had noticed that those who had been used to talking with her after church now avoided her, but that must be because her new appearance made them think that she wasn't interested in their lives or problems anymore. Nevertheless, if anyone came to see her, she would listen and nod and let them know that she continued to be concerned for them. She was inundated with visitors at first, and to this day had never fathomed why people seemed to avoid her after the Sunday services.

She had flushed red that time when she had seen her old friend, Matthew, arrive. She had not returned to the Manor House in the last month, and, although her sister, Margaret, had called briefly on several occasions (leaving her with a headache from the strain of making polite conversation), the sight of Matthew made her perceive how unhappy she was here. When Matthew told her that would have been an alternative solution, she had found herself wanting to fling herself into his arms and beg him to take her away. Almost immediately, the sentiment had passed and she was able to assure him she had no regrets.

"Oh, Mariana, don't lie to me!" He had not tried to hide his anger and frustration. "I've known you too long. I can see with my own eyes that you are miserable."

Again the urge to confide in someone was nearly overwhelming, but she denied any misery out loud and only allowing herself the luxury of crying when he had left, with a pledge to her of his continued support.

Once the socialising was over, it was time for her and Griffith to meet again for a light meal. Sometimes she ate this meal alone, but whether the Parson was there or not, she only ever picked at the food. She never felt hungry. Griffith did not seem to notice that her plate went away with nearly as much food on it as when it had arrived until today! Occasionally, when he had seen a carriage depart, he would enquire as to her callers. She had found that she had to be careful what she told him for, **"Even so must their wives be grave, not slanderers."** He had quoted that verse from the Bible to her one day when he had felt she was gossiping. She was permitted to pass on any useful information about the parishioners to him. Despite having to watch her tongue, Mariana preferred it when her husband was present at the midday meal; otherwise she could feel Mrs Beacon's reproachful eyes burning into her back.

The afternoon was the time to return any calls she wanted to make. Several of her visitors had urged her to come to their homes. She assumed that also she should be making visits to the poorer houses of the parish. There was a regular collection taken each Sunday for the poor of the parish, after the Sacrament, to which Mariana had always contributed, but there were other kinds of help available. Many families were encouraged just by the Parson arriving on their doorstep. Mariana appreciated that her husband was a diligent man; he was always willing to travel to see those in need. Also, Elin had informed her that Mrs Beacon kept a chest full of items which could be given to those who were in trouble: mostly clothes and blankets but pots and pans too. Mariana had not been allowed to peruse its contents. Periodically, Mrs Beacon herself would order food to be delivered to a house where the wife and mother had been taken ill. Mariana admitted to herself that she was confused; she was not sure if she was supposed to be doing any of this. Was this another part of the housekeeper's domain in which she had no business to interfere? She did not dare find out.

Mariana might have chafed over such an existence where she had no purpose. Of course, she thought nothing of relinquishing the daily running of the Vicarage to the haughty servant; after all, Jonesey had supervised all that at *Trem-y-Môr*. It had never interested Mariana how to pickle vegetables or brew homemade ale. It did not hurt her pride to be excluded from those pastimes, although she would have preferred a friendlier person. Certainly she missed Jonesey. No, up until her marriage, she had pursued outdoor activities: riding, swimming, striding across the heather; she had not wanted to learn an instrument or paint or write poetry as other girls did. She had been fortunate in growing up under a father who advocated individuality. Recently, she knew, her eldest sister, Margaret, had fretted over her lack of womanly accomplishments, but all for nothing! For, again fate had been kind to her and provided her with a most efficient housekeeper who did not require her advice and a hard-working husband who was not aware that she was not taking charge. Thus, the afternoon was hers and, often, she would return to bed for a nap or sit doing nothing for hours.

There was that day, she remembered, when Elin had bullied her down to the stables.

"Your horse is in a stall next to the Parson's mare, Miss."

Mariana continued to gaze out the window.

"Come on, Miss! Wouldn't you like to ride him? I'm sure he'd be thrilled to see you! Here's the skirt you used to wear. I'll help you change."

Mariana had allowed herself to be coaxed into the riding costume and down the stairs. She realised that she had never visited the stables here and she *did* feel a flicker of excitement when Mars greeted her with a whinny. All the same, she had not enjoyed the subsequent walk along the lanes with a groom behind her – even at such a sedate pace, memories of wild canters across the island with Jack made her sad and downcast – and Elin had not been able to persuade her to repeat the outing.

For the evening meal, Griffith did require something of his wife. He expected her to have changed her gown and be willing to grace his table for their guests. The Parson had company over often before his marriage, but the table had been an all-male domain. Now, it was her understanding that he wanted to flaunt her youthfulness. Again, it was only thanks to Elin that Mariana was suitably attired. She had caught the maid weeping and when asked she was told it was because of the mistress' appearance.

Griffith had made it clear, from the beginning, that his wife had to be neat and demure, as was fitting for a married woman and the wife of a church leader. He had intense views on what his wife should wear. He had said: **"Wives…. whose adorning let not be that of outward adorning of plaiting the hair and of wearing of gold or of putting on of apparel; but let it be the hidden man of the heart, in that which is not corruptible even the ornament of a meek and quiet spirit, which is in the sight of God of great price."**

It didn't take Mariana many days to gasp that her husband always kept a strict eye on the cost of everything. He had suggested that some new gowns be made for his wife from stouter clothes which would last for several seasons and along less frivolous lines than she had used to wear before she had donned mourning clothes. Mariana had told her maid that the Parson was prudent with how his money was spent and she could see the sense in wearing clothes which did not need replacing each year.

Elin had started crying after the Parson had ordered the housekeeper to fetch some of the gowns which had belonged to his first wife. He had explained to Mariana, in front of her maid, that, with some clever sewing, they could be made over for his new bride.

Once they were left alone, Mariana had found it hard to understand the stuttering words of Elin:

"How can he do it?" she had raged. "You are so pretty, Miss. And those awful dowdy gowns. I won't do it! I won't alter them for you."

However, apart from shaking fingers, Elin *had* sewed the old-fashioned dresses, much to Mariana's relief. Although one part of her could sympathise with her maid, she found that actually she didn't care what she wore. Her primary aim was not to offend her husband; she had reasoned that meekness might entice him into her bed and she *must* do that soon! The knowledge of the growing baby inside her increased her agitation.

After the evening meal, the Parson would entertain his guests without his wife. There would be drinking and playing of cards and male conversation often until the early hours of the morning. Accordingly Mariana was free to retire again to her room.

Each day was identical. Husband and wife would spend no time together and their conversation would always be within earshot of servants. Maybe if they had slept in the same room, they would have talked there, but that was the least likely place where they would meet! Mariana was not hurt that she was not invited to remain with the men. She did not want to have any more contact with her husband than was necessary; she just wanted to be left alone. Sometimes she even became weary of Elin's falsely cheerful comments. Certainly she would have found it very difficult to remain awake until four in the morning as occasionally Griffith and his guests did. All she desired at the end of the day was to climb into bed and fall asleep.

* * *

Griffith's own reflections at the meal table meant that, once again, he was not talking to his wife. It had come to his attention only yesterday that his wife was spending most of her waking hours in her own bedchamber. He might not have been alarmed if his bride had been anyone other than Mariana. But, he was well aware that her life of spinsterhood had been busy and full of outdoor activities and mixing with others and for her to be cooped up in the Vicarage day after day... which brought him full circle – why was she so listless?

He considered whether he should alter some of his habits to divert Mariana. Should they could go out in the carriage together or even ride side by side. But not today – not this week – with the Harvest Festival looming. He could try to converse with her more – draw her out and listen to her opinions and even share some of his own thoughts. But not today – not this week – when every night he had arranged for some of his friends to come around for supper and to stay for an informal social gathering. He didn't need to talk to his wife; he had these men and God Almighty Himself if he needed to unbosom himself; he had not wanted Mariana as a confidante; he had lusted after her as a bedmate. Now that he had failed to consummate the marriage, there seemed no point in reminding himself of the agony by constantly seeing her. Yet, this was selfish. What about her? What if she needed him?

Finishing his meal and noting how colourless his wife looked, he wondered if he had been neglecting her too much. Was Mariana being too accepting of her new status? Was all this quietness strange in one who was renowned for her headstrong ways? Was her meekness a sham? Would she burst out suddenly and upset the household? Or was she ill? He did not know the answer. He refused to even acknowledge that, buried deep down in his heart, was the hope that, one day, he might see some sign of the old Mariana who had attracted him in the first place. He was not prepared to face such emotions yet.

"Are you going anywhere today?" he questioned his wife.

"No," she answered.

Griffith wiped his mouth with his napkin and stood up.

"Well, if you'll excuse me, I must go to my study. We have visitors this evening. I just want to say, that I do appreciate you playing hostess to my friends. I am very proud of the way you entertain them with such poise. I have had many compliments concerning you. You are remembering, my dear, that tomorrow is the letting. The harvest is gathered in and we are thanking God for His many blessings to us on Sunday. We will praise Him for His kindness. **"And ye shall rejoice before the Lord your God, ye and your sons and your daughters."** Of course, my tithe has been brought to me and we will not have to wait until Sunday to be able to see how God has blessed us this year. I hope a good crowd come to bid."

"Yes, I'm remembering."

Mariana's voice was a mere whisper for, without warning, she knew she was going to be sick. It was several days since she had actually vomited, but she could feel the urgency building. She had discovered that by eating very little she could decrease the number of times she vomited, although the queasiness never left her, day or night. Copying her husband, she pressed her own napkin to her lips whilst praying silently that he would hurry up and go! She must reach the privacy of her room.

Mariana waited only until his back was turned before leaving her seat.

With her napkin in her hand she hurried to the door. She must not be sick here. She could imagine the look of horror on Mrs Beacon's face if she was! And here was that very same person, her mouth tightly pursed, presumably in anticipation at seeing the waste of food left on the plate.

"Every day, this girl barely eats a morsel – practically the entire meal has to be thrown away! Why doesn't the Parson reprimand her for such terrible waste? There must be a Bible verse concerning that!"

Again, Mariana believed she could read the housekeeper's thoughts from her facial expressions!

Mariana observed that Mrs Beacon's eyes were darting already towards the dirty crockery, and hopefully had not noticed her mistress' anguish. Without a word the young woman was out the door and climbing the stairs, two at a time, with her skirts clutched in her hands.

By the time she reached her room she had begun to gag, and if Elin had not been lifting the washbasin ready to empty it downstairs, Mariana would have ejected the contents of her stomach on to the floor. As it was she just managed to grip the basin in time.

"Oh, Miss, Miss," cried Elin, holding the china steadily.

Mariana should have been concerned that Elin had witnessed her bout of sickness for, up until today, she had managed to hide everything from her maid. It had meant emptying basins herself discreetly, but she had felt unwilling to let anyone see her plight until her marriage vows were fulfilled. She knew servants well enough to know that sleeping in separate bedrooms would not go unnoticed, but it seemed Elin suspected nothing for she was saying:

"Oh, Miss, I'm so happy for you. You must go and lie down. I'll put a wet cloth on your forehead. Oh, how exciting! A baby! A tiny baby! Now I understand why you haven't been eating and why you haven't the heart to do anything and why you've given up riding and…"

"Enough Elin!" ordered Mariana. "Please don't go on and on!"

"Miss, I'm sorry. How insensitive of me! Here, let me pull back the covers. Now, you just stay here whilst I wash out this basin. Oh, I can't wait to tell…"

"No!" Mariana gasped. "You mustn't tell anyone yet. Absolutely no one! I… I haven't even told my… my husband. I've been waiting until I'm sure, with all the pressures of the next few days, I think I'll leave it until next week. Do you understand, Elin? No one. Can you empty that basin without drawing attention to it?"

"Yes, Miss." Elin looked bewildered but Mariana hoped that her loyalty would demand that she asked no questions. "Don't you give it a second thought. It'll be our secret. You can count on me. Please, lie down and rest. You must look after yourself now that you've got a baby to consider. I'll tiptoe out with the basin."

Mariana laid her head on the pillow and tried to breathe deeply. She *must* shake off this tiredness and think! She must decide how to lure her husband into her bed. Surely it could not be that difficult!

Her thoughts turned to the visit of Elizabeth Parry last week. That had been a nightmare, with the older woman pushing to find out if she was with child yet. It had been relatively easy to lie to her guest but what would happen when the baby started to show? Other folk might not be surprised but her husband certainly would!

Even if Mariana had been delighted with her pregnancy and keen to share the news, she was not sure if she would have told this woman first! She had known the matron for her entire life and yet she could not think of her as someone to confide in and certainly not as a mother, which she knew was how Elizabeth Parry thought of herself. Yes, she had seen the maternal gleam in her eye on many occasions. Mariana suspected that she ought to be grateful that the Parry family had welcomed her into their home and allowed her to share the children's lessons, but she could not find it in her heart to feel gratitude. She had not wanted to be mothered and certainly not to spend her mornings stuck inside at boring lessons!

Strangely, Elin's comments about the forthcoming baby had cheered her. Elin had assumed immediately that her listlessness stemmed from the baby's presence in her body. A baby! Something to remember Jack by. Already she was hoping for a boy. No! Her spirits plummeted. What was she doing thinking like this? She ought to be praying that this child was lost before its time, before anyone knew about it, for it would bring torrents of trouble pouring down on her head. Why, in God's name, did her husband not come to her bed? What was wrong with him? What had been his problem on their wedding night? It was not as if he was a nervous youngster who had not been married before, yet he had been shaking. Could it have been too much to drink? Then why had he never tried again? It was not *she* who was refusing him; she was willing. At least, she must force herself to be willing.

Mariana was feeling no better when she met her husband again at midday. Their hope of conversation upset her further. Griffith told her that John, the groom, had been to see him and had recommended that Mars be sold. The groom had explained that it was a cruel to keep a healthy animal without exercise.

The Parson went on to ask if Mariana thought she would ever ride again regularly, for, if not, then they could not afford the upkeep of a horse such as Mars. The beast would fetch a good price at the auction tomorrow.

Mariana gulped down some wine. This would have been the moment, if their marriage had been a normal one, to announce the news of the child. It would explain her lack of appetite and tiredness and many a husband would advise *not* to ride during the next few months, but it was impossible for her to speak the truth.

"I... I... was... had been thinking I would go out this afternoon," she stammered. She was panic-stricken. She had always believed of Mars was her property, but now, she supposed, everything she owned belonged to the Parson. Another thing she had sacrificed on her wedding day!

"Very well, then. But, I must stress that I do agree with John. Horses need to be ridden. If he would take another rider... But John says that he has tried and was thrown."

"Oh, I'm sorry. It's all my fault. I must apologise to John..."

"No need for that. He is only the groom. That's not what I meant. I've no objection to keeping a horse for you to use, but we're not wealthy and now I've all the expense of a wife."

Mariana did not reply. She should have been angry at his remarks about the cost of looking after her, but her mind was on the horse. She was never going to sell Mars; he was her friend. Possibly one of the few she had left. Even if she was tired this afternoon, she would have him saddled and go out.

It was as she was ascending the stairs after the light repast that she heard someone arrive at the front door. She halted half way up the stairs out of view. Jennett would answer the door. Whoever it was, she did not want to meet them. Then she heard a voice she knew she recognised.

"Of course he's in, you foolish girl! And I won't let you stand in my way. Be gone! Unless you want to actually witness your master's murder."

Edward! By God, it was Edward and in a towering rage! Mariana ran down the stairs. By the time she reached the dining room, Edward had grasped the Parson by his cravat and was turning the material around and around, squeezing the life out of her husband. The Parson was already dark purple.

"Edward!" shouted Mariana. "What are you doing? How dare you! Leave him alone!" Her outraged words went unheeded so she screamed, "EDWARD, LEAVE MY HUSBAND ALONE!"

Her brother released the Parson, who sank to his knees, coughing. Edward swung to face Mariana. He seemed perplexed. She watched his confused face, realising that her hair was pulled back and fastened beneath a white linen cap and her slim body had shrunk with lack of food, leaving her dull brown gown to hang from her shoulders. Her reasoning seemed confirmed with his words:

"Mariana, is it you?" he barked, stepping forward to clutch her into his arms.

Mariana put her hands straight out in front of her to prevent him from embracing her. The scene she had just witnessed had jolted her from her perpetual fatigue. Blood was rushing round her head. She was angry. Angry with her brother. What was the meaning of this atrocious behaviour? Presumably he was furious about her marriage, but he had not been here to advise her. When Jack had disappeared and later she had discovered that she was carrying his child, her brother had been on some secret voyage across the other side of the world. He had not bothered to come and support her on her wedding day. She had written to him at the address he had supplied in London and told him about the forthcoming marriage but she had heard nothing in reply. He had promised her on the evening before his departure that he would never allow her to marry the Parson. How dare he come barging in here today, when she had managed without him all those weeks ago! With no help from him, she had faced her problems and decided what to do and now he arrived and did this!

Yes, everything had not quite worked out to plan. Her husband was not claiming his marital rights, but she was not going to let Edward know that! No one must find out that the child was not the Parson's. If Matthew Cutlass ever queried it, she would deny it. Yes, she would deny to the whole world that the Parson had not fathered her child, if only she could get him once into her bed. Until then she was not going to share her worries with anyone, least of all her brother who had abandoned her when she most needed him!

"Of course, it's me," she responded haughtily. "What is the meaning of this intrusion? Excuse me." She brushed past Edward and bent to help Griffith. She was aware that Mrs Beacon and Jennett were standing in the doorway, so she stated in her best governess voice:

"Ah, Mrs Beacon. Would you be so kind as to fetch the Parson a drink? He's choked on some food."

EDWARD

Edward stared at Mariana, his love, in shock. He could not believe it.

He had left London after seeing Frances Sandleigh into the hands of his aunt (for her uncle never did appear), and hastened to North Wales. Still reeling from the coincidences of some of Frances' revelations, on the journey, he had pondered about the facts he had learned about this woman who had managed to jolt him out of his usual train of thoughts! Not long after Frances had begun to talk, he had recognised the seriousness of what she was saying and had tried to lighten her musings. He had hoped that this woman would not share any more details of her past with him; he did not want their friendship to grow any deeper and he had learnt that shared intimacies nearly always led to closer ties. And, he had argued inside his head, there was no room in his heart for further entanglements at the present – Mariana and his complicated relationship with her was enough of a headache for him! On the other hand, Edward sensed that what Frances was about to say stemmed from her need to talk and not from her wishing to involve him personally. Almost anyone would have served to listen. Certainly she had sounded very irate! Curiosity had got the better of him and he had urged her to continue until she had told him about not being her father's child. Then he wished he had stemmed the flow at the beginning, as common sense had suggested, for he had felt depression descend. He could not prevent the whispered words from escaping his mouth:

"Not again! This can't be happening!"

Not another affair which produced a bastard baby! After all, it hadn't been that long ago he had heard from his aunt about his Mariana's parentage. No wonder he had felt despair, although he had seen the irony too. Initially he had thought that Frances was akin to Mariana and now he had discovered that they were more similar than he had first imagined! With his aunt's news, his heart had leapt with joy, but with Frances he had felt his mood sink. Yet some instinct made him realise that his reaction to what this woman was telling him was vitally important. If he turned from her or allowed his confusion to show on his face, she would not understand and she might feel rejected, and he guessed she had been rejected too often in her life. He had schooled his features and asked:

"What happened to your mother?"

How odd that the dialogue with Frances remained with such clarity! Nevertheless, with the shortening of the miles to Holy Island, he had forgotten Frances Sandleigh and focused on his love, Mariana. He had arrived at *Trem-y-Môr* bursting with anticipation. Soon, he had sung inside his head, he would see his beloved.

He had asked for Mariana's whereabouts when he dismounted. The groom said that she was at the Vicarage. Just then, much to his surprise, Margaret had appeared from inside the house ready to climb into her carriage – he had assumed that Mariana and Margaret had gone to the Vicarage together. No, came the reply from Margaret: Where else would Mariana be since she was married to the Parson? Edward's head had exploded with outrage and barely pausing to shout, "You interfering bitch!" at his older sister he had galloped towards Holyhead.

The three-mile ride had not calmed him. He was ready to kill the Parson and damn the consequences!

Now here was Mariana, all grown up and mistress of the house, looking like a spinster aunt, but nevertheless in control, ignoring him! What had come over her? She had been so vehement that she did not want to marry the Parson. How had the marriage come about? He had decided, on the road, that Margaret and the Parson had connived to make her agree to marry, presumably dragging her to the altar, and that when he knocked on the door of the Vicarage, he would find her a prisoner, locked in her bedchamber. But this! He could not cope with this! He sat down abruptly on the nearest chair and pulled at his own cravat.

Mariana was helping the Parson to get up. She lent him an arm and led him to another chair. He saw Mariana glance at the door. The indoor staff had gone.

"I think," Mariana enunciated coldly, "that an apology is due, Edward." She began to fuss over the Parson. "There, there, Griffith, let me loosen your clothes. Really Edward, brawling like a brat in the street! Have you been drinking?"

"Mariana," her brother pleaded in a whisper. "What have they done to you?"

"Done to me? What are you talking about?" She left her husband's side as the housekeeper returned, bearing a glass. "Thank you, Mrs Beacon. That will be all. You had better leave the clearing of the table until our visitor has left."

"Might I see you alone?" hissed Edward when the door closed behind the servant.

"Certainly not! I'm waiting for you to apologise to Griffith. How are you, my dear? Has the water helped?" The Parson made no reply.

"But he had no right to marry you…" started Edward.

"He had every right," argued Mariana. "I agreed to marry him."

"Told you so," muttered Griffith faintly. "Told you to ask her. She came to me willingly."

"But… but you said to me, Mariana…"

"That's enough, Edward. I decided, without being coerced into it, to marry the Parson. What I want to know is why *you* did not come to the wedding? Had you gone from England by then?"

"I was never invited! I knew nothing about it until I arrived at *Trem-y-Môr* only…"

"Never invited? Margaret *must* have invited you. She sent all the invitations her…"

"Well, she did not send me one," interjected Edward grimly. "And I know the reason why: she knew that if she told me, I would forbid it. Oh, Mariana…" Edward's voice trailed off in despair and he covered his eyes with his hand. His Mariana was married! His love was married! How callous could fate be! No, it was not fate. It was his scheming sister who was to blame. Margaret! Margaret! He would deal with her later. For now, he had to see Mariana alone. No, his heart cried. It was too late! He had arrived too late again! Oh, God, must You torment me forever? Mariana was a married woman! She and this lily-livered cleric were joined together…

Indignation returned. He must not think about it; he must not stay here. He clenched his fists. If he did not leave he might murder the Parson yet. His rage would not be quieted. It was like his father all over again. He must leave. He must leave!

"I must go," he informed her. He did not add, "Before I finish what I started." Instead he proffered:

"I am glad to see you looking so well, Mariana."

That was a lie! She looked thin, too thin, and her face was white with bright spots of red on each cheek. She looked like a scarecrow. Not beautiful like he remembered her, but damn! He still wanted her! He should have had her! He had been cheated again! If only he had not gone to London. Yet, if he had not, he would never have uncovered the truth about her – that she could be his because she was not his sister at all! Now there would be no point in telling her because she was a married woman and she was gone from him forever. His throat stuck on the words, but he managed to say:

"I'm sorry, Parson. Cong… Congratulations to you both."

Then he limped slowly from the room.

Edward knew what he was going to do: he was going to get drunk, blind drunk, dead drunk. But first he had one more person to see: Margaret. He was going to get rid of that viper from his home. Whatever Mariana said, he *knew*. He knew that Margaret was behind all this. Where was Jack? Where had he been whilst all this was going on? Edward calculated that it must be nigh on three months since he had left *Trem-y-Môr*. He presumed that Jack had made a full recovery and had set off to find his identity. Or maybe his memory had returned and he had gone to his own home. Edward felt very out of touch.

He had sent Wilson and Thomas to North Wales without him before he had set sail. What was the point of paying for their upkeep at 'The Wishing Well'. He had settled his bill with the innkeeper before leaving for Portugal and had not returned there. On his arrival back in England he had spent a couple of nights at 'The Anvil' whilst he arranged for Frances to remain with his aunt until she could find her family's whereabouts and then he had made the journey here. He had received no letters or news from his sisters. Certainly his aunt had not told him about Mariana's marriage. What *had* been going on here whilst he had been working for the King?

Ultimately it did not matter. He could imagine what had happened! Jack had left Mariana alone with Margaret who had seized the opportunity to put her plans into action. Why had she been so determined for this marriage to take place? What did she hope to gain from this? He could not understand her motives. Nonetheless, what difference did it make if he understood or not? He was too late. Margaret had succeeded in getting her own will at the expense of other people's happiness and he was going to send her packing. He admitted to himself that Margaret would receive all the anger that he felt towards the Parson, but so what? She deserved it. She had not exactly been innocent in the affair – of that he was sure. Maybe if he and the Parson could have had a man-to-man fight, he would have felt cleansed, but the Parson had just stood there like a quivering jellyfish. No, his acute resentment at the unfairness of life was fanned by his frustration at not being able to attack the man who had taken his Mariana.

Edward did not waste any time. He could see immediately on riding into the yard that Margaret had not gone out, although such was his unassuaged wrath that he would have sought her out willingly in someone else's home and shouted at her there. He found her in the dining room of the Manor House, eating. He began his tirade without preamble.

"Get up!" he growled. "You can leave that food – my food, paid with my money – and go and pack your bags."

"Edward, are you joining me?" Margaret appeared to ignore his words. "Get out!"

"My dear brother, it is quite impossible for me to leave at this precise moment in time. I have so much to do here. Anyway it takes time to pack. Perrin only has one pair of hands and…"

"You will go to your room now and instruct your maid to begin at once. I will give you until the morning to be out of here, since I don't want to be left with any of your belongings. Until then I don't want to set eyes on you. In fact, I hope never to set eyes on you again – ever!" Edward wondered why he did not just grab her by the throat as he had the Parson. Great fat slob! She was still eating, apparently only half listening!

"Oh, Edward, surely you're not really asking me to leave that soon? I do so love it here and I was hoping that Walter would be joining me in the next month."

"No!" bellowed Edward. "Why didn't you tell me? Why didn't you write and invite me to the wedding? Because you did not want me present. You wanted me out of the way whilst you wove your wicked webs. So now you can go home to your husband and practice your schemes on him."

"Schemes? What are you talking about? Why don't you calm down and we can discuss this rationally? I did write to you and tell you about the wedding, but you did not reply. I assumed that you had already departed on your secret voyage." She did not hide her derision. "But, I don't see what you're getting in a state about. *You* didn't try to find your youngest sister a husband as was your duty. That was left to me and, as I've said before, I can't understand what you've got against the Parson. I would have thought that you should be congratulating everyone. Whilst you have been involved in your own business with the Fleet, the Parson has made a very good job of that young girl. She is much more... more mature. She behaves as is befitting of her station – not simply as a wife but as a clergyman's wife. She no longer gallops around the countryside, and entertains with excellent manners and..."

"She may do!" Edward ground his teeth. How had this sly woman got him into this conversation? She had led him away from the salient fact: her departure. If he was not careful she would not go at all. She was clever at getting her own way, he recalled. "This is neither here nor there. Though, I will just say this to you because it needs to be said: you did a great disservice to your sister. The girl – woman, you say – that I saw at the Vicarage did not resemble Mariana in any way. You and your plotting schemes have destroyed..."

"What histrionics! She's just grown up at last. And about time too, I might add. Sit down, Edward and stop scowling at me. I honestly can't fathom out what all the fuss is about. You're behaving as if you were her suit..."

"What are you doing, criticising my reaction?" Edward was shouting again. "Who the devil do you think you are? Coming here for Father's funeral and trying to take over the household. Mariana's marriage was none of your business, but it is my business..."

"What *exactly* is your business in all this?" Margaret sneered. "Your only business in this affair is to find a suitable partner for your sister. That has been done! Mariana is all right. No, I believe you're upset because you had plans of your own for your... your sister. You're standing there in judgement of me and my so called 'schemes' but your scheme is called 'incest', so I think..."

"No!" Edward moved forward, but his sister did not flinch. She didn't seem afraid of him. "No, Mariana is not my sister and I... I intended."

Edward stopped. Oh God, what had he done? In his anger he had betrayed his promise to his aunt; he had told someone else the truth.

"What do you mean?" Margaret's face had blanched. At last she had abandoned her eating and he had her full attention.

"Mariana is not my sister, nor yours." Edward lowered his voice to a weary whisper. "Does that upset the plans for your future? Mariana is not Father's child. No one knows who her father is but..." Edward's voice became menacing. "But I warn you if I hear that you've repeated this information to anyone, I, myself, will make sure that you never speak again."

"Is it true?" There was a satisfied gleam in Margaret's eye. "Of course it's true. I witnessed it. Mariana, Father's precious Mariana, was embracing another man! She was a shameless hussy! She had barely been married a month and she had found a lover! I knew Father should never have married her. She cast a spell over him and she was nothing better than a harlot!"

"Shut up! Don't you ever use that word again about our stepmother."

"Ha!" retorted Margaret. "What a mess you've made of your life, Edward! You loved one man's wife and now you love another man's wife! Well, I'm glad Mariana is married, for I wouldn't have been able to hold my head up if my own brother had run off with his sister. Say what you will. Who's going to believe all this? *I* do, because I saw it, but there's no proof. No, I'm glad…"

"Get out! Go now and damn your packing! I'll personally gather all your belongings and throw them out into the yard. I want no reminder of you here. Ever since you arrived, you've caused trouble. No, it's more than that. You've caused trouble all your life. I remember when you were a child… with Penelope. Well, go! Go from this house and take your filthy tongue with you! And, I repeat, if you try to slander either Mariana's name or her mother's I'll kill you!"

"Don't worry." Margaret was on her feet by this time. "No one will know that the woman you lust after is a bastard. Yes, that's what she is, so there's no need to look like that! I won't tell anyone, but only because it would break Griffith's heart to…"

"Griffith! Griffith! God curse Griffith! You criticise my feelings towards a woman who turns out not to be my sister and at the time was unmarried. If you had not interfered we could have… But you! You are a married woman. No, my sanctimonious sister, you are prepared to – maybe already have – commit a sin with the Parson. Adultery is…"

"Ooooh!" Margaret's breath escaped from her body in an evil hiss. "How dare you! How can you say such things about a man of God? Griffith and I are friends and that's all. I shall not wait here a moment longer to be insulted by you. I shall go of my own free will, and like you, I hope never to set eyes on you again!"

Edward waited until she had marched from the room before he poked his head around the door and roared:

"Wilson! Bring me a drink! I need a bottle of whisky!"

MARGARET

Margaret stood trembling by the window in her bedchamber. Tears fell. That was the second time she had been attacked in this house. Last time she had been physically hit, but Edward's slur on her relationship with the Parson hurt more, and to say that she had always been trouble was brutish. What did he know? What did he know about not being loved? Did he know what it was like to be turned aside for another, which was what had happened to her when a long-awaited son had been born? Her wounded heart refused to acknowledge the thought at the back of her mind that, in adulthood, Edward had been treated just as badly by Sir William. No, all she could register in her bewilderment was that everything in life had conspired against her.

Everything she had ever wanted in life had been denied her. First there had been her father's love. Was it too much to ask to be loved by one's own father? No, most children experienced the joys of that and certainly Edward had basked in his father's love. Then there had been marriage. Was it too much to hope for a husband with a title and some wealth to his name? No, many women found contentment when they managed their husband's estates. Yet she had never been mistress of anywhere and they had no money. Walter had spent all that on his drink. It was not as if she had set her sights on a husband with whom she could share love. No, she had not been so foolish as to seek love from her husband. That was all romantic nonsense. She did not believe that she had asked too much from life. Once she had accepted that her father would never love her she had settled down to make the best of her situation as a grown woman. All she had sought was somewhere to call her own, where she did not have to sit under someone else's wife, and one who was a foreigner at that!

When she had first arrived at *Trem-y-Môr*, something of the ancient Manor House had caught her imagination. It was much smaller than the castle but it was more homely – less cold and unfriendly – and she had become attached to it from the start. This was the kind of house she would like to live in. It had not been the people in the house who had attracted her. Who would have predicted that her own flesh and blood could be so difficult and unwelcoming towards her? And it had not been the service she had received here which had made her want to stay. No, the servants would have to go if she ever ruled here. They would be dismissed and replaced by sensible English ones of her own choosing. It was not even the furnishings, since much of the furniture and curtains and carpets were very dated. Already she had picked out what new materials and wood she would prefer. Possibly she would even change the name of the Manor House to some proper English name. She understood that *Trem-y-Môr* meant *Seaview* – how ordinary! No, it was the very stones of the house and the feel of the rooms which had made her resolved not to return to the castle. She had never felt at ease at the Struley estate and she had expected to send for her husband in the very near future.

Once she had admitted her dream to herself, she had gone about her plans painstakingly. She had decided to cheat fate one last time and she was determined that she would win; her plans needed to be foolproof. She had come to stay and she did not intend to lose out on a chance of happiness again.

Unfortunately, there had been one or two people standing in her way, but she could cope with them. Whatever others might say about her (she knew that they poked fun at her fat body behind her broad back), no one could say that she was not an organiser. As the eldest she had learnt to take the lead. Then, when she was married to Humphrey Struley, she may not have been in charge of the whole household, in reality, but her suggestions had brought about one or two changes which had helped to smooth out the running of such a large estate. Yes, she was aware she had organisational talents. But all that had gone when Ralph had returned with his Greek wife. There was no place for Margaret at the castle and her heart had hankered after her own domain where she was truly mistress. When she had fallen in love with the Manor House, she had decided this would be the very household where she could reign.

Edward had not been a problem. He was a bachelor and, even if he did marry, by then, she would have planted her foot firmly in the door. Anyway it might be possible to persuade him to settle elsewhere. In London maybe. After all, this had never been his home. No, she had only needed him to go away all those weeks ago because of his influence over Mariana. His presence undermined her power, for he was the Squire. Also, if she could encourage him not to stay here, she would have the perfect excuse to suggest her husband for the job of steward. Even when he had arranged a temporary steward she had not fretted. She and Walter would be the obvious choice before long.

Mariana had been the real problem to the realisation of her dream. Margaret needed her young sister out of the way, not because she was in truth the mistress (she had no idea how to run any establishment) but rather because she was the mistress in name. She had been the only female here since she was a child. All the tenants thought of her as the lady of the Manor House. Quite apart from this, Margaret had been genuinely shocked by her sister's unruly behaviour. That kind of thing ended in scandal and, in Margaret's mind, the only solution was a husband for Mariana. Add to that, Edward's desire for his sister, which she had witnessed, and Margaret was glad to see her brother go and had sworn that the girl should be married by the autumn.

Unlike others, Margaret had weighed up the possibilities of the Parson as a suitable suitor when she had first met him. Immediately she had liked him. He was such a sensible man, and wise too. She took pleasure in his company. She would not admit that she found herself attracted to him, although she had wondered, on several occasions, why Walter could not be like Griffith. She understood that her husband's only interest in her had been to warm his bed; she had not forgotten their wedding night. Over the years, she had found it difficult to meet her spouse without picturing him ready to claim his marital rights. She had tried to erase this image, but it would not go away even though Walter had never been near her since the birth of her second son. No, she was coming to believe that Walter had only one thing in his heart when he saw her, whereas Margaret never detected that faint glow in the Parson's eyes. No, indeed, Griffith was a true friend to her. Increasingly she had looked forward to meeting Griffith whenever she could.

The need for Mariana to become acquainted with the Parson allowed her to invite him to come often. She wasn't bothered that eventually it would be Mariana who married to him. That kind of thing with the Parson did not appeal to her, which was why Edward's words cut her very deeply. The aspect of her relationship with the Parson which she most appreciated was that he treated her as an intelligent human being. She could not recall anyone doing that before. Her husband had only wanted her body and her brother-in-law always behaved as if she was some kind of a joke, and she did not mix with her Greek sister-in-law. Her parents had never really acknowledged her acute mind. Her children had not been able to relate to her as an equal, and now they were growing up they did not spend much time with her. Needless to say not a single person at the Manor House had tried to get to know her! No, Griffith flattered her; he listened to her opinions and respected her views. She really liked him.

So why then did people resist the idea of Mariana marrying the Parson? Since Margaret had perceived Edward's attraction to his half-sister she could understand why *he* did not encourage the Parson's suit: he craved Mariana for himself. But what about the intended bride herself? Presumably she was too young to appreciate the Parson's good qualities.

Nonetheless, with the passing days, Margaret was certain that Griffith would make an excellent husband for her sister. Their age difference would be just what was needed. An immature man would only allow Mariana too much freedom.

Finally Margaret had anticipated that Mariana herself would be grateful to her for her far-thinking help in encouraging marriage to such a man as the Parson. Margaret remembered what it was like to have rebellious thoughts. She herself had disliked authority when she was a child, but once an adult, she reasoned, everyone had to conform, and who better to help Mariana than Griffith Owen?

Margaret turned from the window when her maid came in.

"Perrin, we are leaving," she informed the other woman, not concerned that the servant was witnessing her distress. "Pack my belongings. I am going to the Vicarage and I will send Gradeson back for you and as much as you have been able to put in the chests within the hour. We will leave for home from the Vicarage. I know we won't get far tonight, but I'd rather sleep in a flea-ridden inn than stay here another minute!"

Margaret swept up her cloak and descended the stairs. There was no sign of Edward; she left by the front door and walked around to the stables. She was neither willing to see any of the other servants at the Manor House, nor to wait indoors whilst the carriage was made ready for her. She could not bear to be near her brother another second.

Of all the ungrateful men! He was just like her father! She had stayed here, whilst Edward gallivanted all over the country, supervising his tenants and servants and arranging the marriage of his sister, which was his job, and what thanks did she get for it! Granted she had harboured her own reasons for staying, but he wasn't aware of that! He was just bound up with himself and his unnatural desires! Well, it was better to be away from him. She would never have been able to associate with him if he had achieved his aim. God only knew what he would do now! What had he done already? She must go immediately to the Vicarage.

The Parson, who was one of the kindest men she'd ever encountered, would not have understood Edward's anger. She was worried. Griffith would not have lifted a finger to defend himself if Edward had struck him. Had Edward hurt him? She had seen violence in her brother's eyes when he had been talking to her and that had been after a fast ride from Holyhead. What had he done to the Parson? She must go and check that her perverted brother had not killed him. To think that when Edward was a child she had been fond of him! Look how he had turned out! No good saying Mariana was not his sister *now*! He had lusted after her freely when he had thought she was! What terrible punishment would God mete out if he took Mariana away from her husband? She must make haste and warn Griffith.

"Gradeson!" she cried shrilly. "Gradeson, get the carriage ready. I'm going out. Hurry up! I must go immediately."

Fortunately, the carriage remained in the courtyard from her previous aborted journey. When she had seen Edward the first time, she had abandoned her visit to take food to the poor. She suspected that her brother would seek her out but she had not imagined that he would banish her.

All the way to the Vicarage, Margaret was in a fervour. Obviously Edward had been given short shrift when he had been to see the Parson, since he had come back boiling with anger against everyone, but Margaret wondered exactly what had occurred between the two men. Had the Parson stood up to Edward? Verbally, if not physically. Or had the Reverend not been at home when Edward had called? Her brother's anger could have been kindled by frustration. Could it be that Mariana herself had told Edward to leave her alone? Had he broken the news to her that she was not their sister? Surely Mariana was the only one who could convince Edward that everything had turned out for the best.

Margaret shook her head at the injustice of the situation. How dare Edward order her out of his house! Her motives had been pure: to arrange a respectable marriage for her stepsister. Why had she not justified her actions to Edward? No, as with Penelope all those years ago, Margaret could see no reason to explain her actions. She had not done anything wrong, after all. If her brother was not so caught up with his own emotions, he would have been pleased with the outcome. He was beholden to her for releasing him from the guardianship of Mariana. Especially since the girl had such a reputation. Who else would have taken her on?

By the time Margaret was ushered into the quiet depths of the Vicarage, she had convinced herself that she had received the rough edge in this affair. Both Edward and Mariana ought to be thanking her, and when Mariana appeared eventually – after what felt like a rude delay, she was very disgruntled.

"Margaret! Oh, it's you!" She sounded surprised. Margaret did not pursue it but demanded:

"Have you seen Edward?"

"Of course we have seen Edward. He set upon Griffith like a mad bear."

"Is he all right?"

"How should I know? He left."

"Not Edward. Griffith."

"Oh, Griffith. He's resting now and can't be disturbed."

"Well, that's a pity for I had hoped very much to see him." Margaret sighed. She could hardly say that secretly she had hoped that she would be invited to stay at the Vicarage rather than go home. Suddenly she felt nervous. Mariana looked more like her usual self. Seemingly her neatly arranged hair had become loosened during the past hour and her eyes showed irritation. Surely Mariana did not blame her for Edward's behaviour? Whose side was Mariana on? Margaret believed that the Parson would have been sympathetic about the way she had been treated by her own brother, but he was not available. Margaret pressed her head with her hand. Already she could feel pinpoints of pain starting on either side of her temples: one of her terrible headaches was coming. She must remain calm and, if possible, lie down, but it was doubtful that Mariana would ask her to stay.

"I'm afraid that the purpose of my visit is to bid you farewell." She spoke resignedly.

Mariana's reply only served to reinforce her feeling of being unwelcome.

"I should think you're glad to go," remarked Mariana. "You must be missing your own family. It must be…"

"I had hoped to see Griffith... to say..."

"I'll tell him you called. He's sleeping."

"Mariana, did... did Edward tell you what he was planning to do?"

"Of course not! We didn't make polite conversation. I had my hands full keeping him from attacking Griffith again."

"Well, you be careful."

"Careful? What do you mean? Do you think that he will come again? He can't be that uncivilised? He lost his temper, that's all. I assume he had only just discovered the news, but I told him he had no right to complain since I was not coerced into my marriage..."

Margaret smiled, despite her headache. Mariana was not against her! She accepted the responsibility of her decision to marry the Parson.

"I am pleased that you told him that," declared Margaret. "He would not listen to me. He..."

There was a knock at the door.

"Come in," instructed Mariana.

The maid entered.

"There's a gentleman to see you," she announced.

"I beg your pardon, Jennett!" flashed back the mistress of the house.

"Oh, sorry, Madam. There's a gentleman to see you, Madam."

"Don't forget again, Jennett. You'd better show him in and find out his name." When the girl left, Mariana turned to her sister. "We're going to have to replace her. I'm not sure if she's dim-witted, but she can't remember the simplest of tasks. And it's very awkward when she doesn't tell you who is calling."

Margaret stared at the other woman in disbelief. Mariana had scolded a servant and one not much younger than herself! She had been right to tell Edward that Mariana had matured! She stood up; she did not want to meet whoever had just arrived at the Vicarage. It was Mr Lloyd who entered the room.

"Good day to you, Mrs Owen, Mrs Struley. The weather has turned cold, hasn't it?"

"Mr Lloyd, I beg you not to think me discourteous," Margaret told him, "but I was just leaving. I have a long journey ahead of me. Did you see my carriage on the drive?"

"No, I didn't, but wait! I can hear someone now." He moved to the window. "This looks like your carriage. Are you going far?"

"Home, Mr Lloyd. I have neglected my husband and children for too long."

"Well, may I wish you God-speed and I trust we might see you again sometime."

"Thank you, Mr Lloyd. So, Mariana, it's time for me to go. You'll send my regards to Griff… the Parson and tell him… remember that I'll write to him… both of you. Good day."

Margaret did not hug Mariana. She may have decided that her sister was on her side against Edward, but their fragile relationship could not support such displays of affection. There was no point in staying if she could not see Griffith, especially if there was no chance of seeing him alone. She must preserve her strength to cope with the pain of her headache. Maybe she should order Gradeson to take her to Penelope's farm. Yes, they would welcome her. She nodded at Mariana and her visitor and with a few final words of farewell, she left.

ELIN

Mariana laid down the small silver-backed mirror and looked at Elin.

"What do you think?"

"Oh, Miss, you look beautiful."

Quickly Elin began to pick up the clothes which were scattered across the floor so that her mistress would not see the tears in her eyes. She was not lying. She did think that the other woman looked beautiful again. During the last month, slowly Mariana had returned to normal. No, not normal, Elin decided, because she no longer lived as vigorously as she used to at *Trem-y-Môr*, but, thank God, she had recovered from the mopes which had ailed her during the first few weeks of her marriage. No longer did she vomit, although she had told Elin that nausea sometimes overtook her. She ate, if not with a hearty appetite, then enough to feed a woman with child; she was already regaining some of the flesh that she had lost.

Mariana had started to ride again, which had concerned Elin in the beginning, because of the baby, until the maid had seen her mistress return with colour in her cheeks and new life in her eyes. Therefore Elin had not mentioned her fears about the riding and since Mariana had not told anyone else (as far as Elin could ascertain), there was no one to question the rides.

Best of all, Mariana had started being interested in the gowns she wore. They had spent one grey afternoon sorting out her wardrobe. Mariana had stood critically in front of the glass and, to Elin's delight, had rejected many of the dresses. She had told Elin that she would keep as many as she could bear, for the sake of not offending her husband, but she had instructed Elin to brighten them up. Elin was glad that she no longer needed to provide her mistress with suggestions since Mariana thought of them herself! She had accompanied her maid to the market and bought many small additions to her clothes. They had even laughed together when they were out alone on these excursions and on one of these outings Elin had seen Mariana almost her old self. Elin cast her mind back to the day of the Harvest Fair.

The day had started with a service in the church and then the congregation had spilled out to enjoy themselves at the fair. It was at the very end of the day when the encounter occurred. Elin and Mariana were standing at the edge of the stalls looking at a group of shaggy horses, which a weasel-faced man was trying to sell. Whether these sorry looking beasts were the ones he had been unable to sell by this time of the day, or whether all his livestock had been of this poor quality it was hard to tell, but Mariana's love of horses had made her exclaim in anger. Elin put a restraining hand on her mistress' arm. There was nothing they could do.

The two women were holding an assortment of articles which they had purchased and now they were waiting for the Parson. Elin guessed that he had no interest in perusing the wares which women wanted to buy; he had left them whilst he went to judge a vegetable growing contest. Elin had heard that there had been many bets laid, over the months, on who would grow the biggest vegetable, but it looked as if a magnificent, over-sized potato, from the Parson's own garden, might win. However, Elin assumed that the Parson would choose someone else's vegetable for he could not pick his own produce to receive the prize surely!

Mariana had told her husband that she wanted to buy some linen and woollen cloth as well as a new pair of shoes and they had managed to get some bargains. Now Elin was tired and reckoned that her mistress was too. Both of them were wanting to get home but first Mariana was expected to attend Evening Prayer. Where was the Parson? If he did not hurry up, the service would start late. Already the sun was low in the sky, and the air was cooling.

The only restrictions which the Parson had put upon his wife that day was that Elin accompany her and that she hide her small reticule containing her money. Elin had heard what he had said. Nonetheless, unbeknown to the women, the Parson must have told John, his groom, to follow at a discreet distance because Elin had noticed him halfway through the afternoon. After all, there were many strangers here and much drink was being sold. The Parson would not want his bride molested by any who did not know who she was! Elin reckoned that Mariana's beauty was still eye-catching even if she was too thin and pale.

Elin and Mariana had enjoyed browsing. They had been surprised at how few faces they recognised. Maybe all the locals were at the Best Vegetable Contest, they had giggled to each other! They had haggled with peddlers from as far away places as Holland and Germany. They had watched whilst some craftsmen actually worked on their wares before selling them: ironware and carpentry and some distinguished hats. They had filled their pockets with handkerchiefs and lace and had been persuaded to buy delicious delicacies to consume immediately. They were no longer hungry and hoped that Mrs Beacon had not ordered a large meal for tonight. They had smiled at curious young men who had admired them, although Mariana had refused to enter into conversation with them. They had avoided the fortune-teller's tent because Mariana did not think her husband would approve, but, apart from that, they had forgotten who they were for several hours and behaved like young maidens again. Elin noticed that once or twice John appeared to feel the need to step nearer but she knew her mistress would want to deal with any unwanted advances by herself. Hopefully John, like Elin herself, would be encouraged to see Mariana enjoying herself.

However, now, whilst they stood with their backs to the stalls, Elin watched an enormous man running towards them. Then she saw John move, although she suspected that John could not see what she could see, which was that the man was chasing a small child. The infant was looking back over his shoulder whilst he fled from his pursuer. Such was the child's haste that he tripped and ended up right at Mariana's feet. He buried his face in the hem of her skirt, crying in terror. Perhaps it was Mariana's recent concern over the plight of the horses, which remained fresh in her memory, which caused her to react immediately to another living thing being hurt, but Elin watched her stoop to pick up the child. Whilst John strode towards his mistress, Mariana faced the goliath with no fear in her face. Nevertheless it was not she who halted the man but a lithe young woman with a blaze of red hair who appeared from nowhere and flung herself at the man.

"Ma," wailed the child. The man caught the woman a hard blow on the side of her head with a growl of rage.

"You can't protect that bastard this time," he barked, "for I seen his thieving hands pick up me knife meself."

The woman fell to the ground, but wrapped her arms around the man's leg in an attempt to stop him reaching her son. One kick of his heavy boots and her lip was bleeding and the aggressor had reached Mariana.

"Give us the child," he ordered. Then he paused. Elin wondered if it was the burly presence of John or simply that her mistress was standing tall with a determined look in her eye.

Mariana shook her head. Already a crowd was forming and, at last, Elin recognised familiar faces. Elin was sure that no one would allow this bellicose man to touch the Parson's wife.

"Leave him, Tom," panted the woman while she tried to stem the flow of blood from her mouth. "He's only a baby."

"It were him. I seen him. He snatched me knife and I'm going to give him the beating of a lifetime!"

"How could he have stolen your knife?" A new voice was heard. It was the horse dealer, pushing through the people. He stood between Mariana and big Tom. "Didn't you lose that knife in a bet last night with Old Wheldon?"

Tom raised his fists at the horse dealer.

"Let's have the child…"

"No, Tom. You've forgotten but there are plenty of witnesses who will tell that Old Wheldon is now the proud owner of your fine knife. You're forgetting what you did. Too much ale, I'd say!"

Tom made a rude gesture at the horse dealer and turned, muttering to himself. The crowd made a path for him when they saw him give the woman in the mud another kick. No one else wanted to get in his way.

Elin watched Mariana look at the child for what must have been the first time. Momentarily child and woman stared at each other, and Elin saw shock register on her mistress' features. The child seemed mesmerised for an instant too and then he wriggled free and ran to his mother. The red-headed woman was dusting down her clothes whilst she held a bit of cloth to her lip. She grabbed her son in her arms with a sob of relief.

The horse dealer spoke to her:

"When are you going to leave that man, Rosie? He'll be the death of one or other of you one day."

"Now!" retorted the wench. "I'm leaving him now."

"Where will you go?"

"Anywhere. It makes no difference. As far from him as possible."

Mariana stepped up to the woman.

"Would you like to work for me? As a maid?"

Elin and John both gasped. What had made their mistress make such an offer? Elin pondered. Employing young Biddy was one thing; she had been part of Mariana's childhood, but this stranger – and after such a violent first meeting! The Vicarage establishment did not need a maid and certainly not one whom they knew nothing about and who had no references. She was just a gypsy!

"Er… yes, Madam." The woman flushed. "And can I say 'Thank you' to you, Madam, for rescuing my son. Say 'Thank you' to the lady, Ted."

The child hid behind his mother's skirts.

"Don't worry. He's only a baby," reiterated Mariana. "Have you any belongings?"

"I shan't be a moment, Madam. Joshua," she turned to the horse dealer, "look after Ted. If *he* sees Ted, I…"

Mariana swung around to face her astonished servants.

"Elin, you must stay here and tell the Parson that I have gone home and will not be coming to the service. John, you had better accompany me, in case we meet up with the pugnacious Tom!"

Elin shook her head in remembrance. What an uproar Mariana's quick decision had caused! She glanced at her mistress now as she sat in front of the glass. Elin could not help but smile. She had been thrilled to know that Mariana had some part of her old self inside her, but sometimes she wished that it had shown itself in another way.

Mrs Beacon had become unbearable since Rosie had been employed. In all fairness, Elin mused, it was not Rosie's fault. Far from it; already the woman had learnt all her duties and more, and she was very conscientious. No, it was the housekeeper who was irritable. Initially she had refused to accept Rosie's presence in the house until she had consulted the Parson. Nor did she like it when Mariana had announced that Rosie was to replace Jennett. (That silly girl had burst into noisy tears, as if that would help matters!) No, Mrs Beacon had retired to her room until the Parson returned. Then she had demanded an interview with him, presumably in order to confront him with his wife's behaviour. She had insisted on seeing him in the privacy of his study. No one knew what had passed between them, but Rosie stayed and Jennett was relegated to share some of Biddy's jobs.

Nor could Elin complain about the child. He seemed petrified of Mrs Beacon and spent most of his time with John in the stables. Rosie had told Elin that he had a passion for horses and had been very attached to Joshua, the horse dealer. John had informed Elin that the child had hid for days amongst the straw until John had taken him to the field where the fair had been held to prove to him that everyone had gone, including his father.

No! Elin was aware that the hateful Tom was not the child's father but Rosie never said whether Tom had been her husband or not. In fact, although friendly, Rosie did not speak much about her past. It transpired that she had worked in a Vicarage before, since she was able to answer the door and take messages and cope with the parishioners' needs with an ease which spoke of experience. She had even learnt a word or two of Welsh! The Parson was pleased with her, as far as Elin could tell, and Mariana seemed content with the situation.

Apart from this once, in no other way, had Mariana challenged Mrs Beacon's authority, and she did not interact much with Rosie or the boy. Elin could not puzzle out why she had taken on the woman, and Mariana kept her thoughts to herself. Elin herself was happy that Mrs Beacon's ill humour was further diluted and naturally, she found the child adorable. Elin loved all children – so many siblings probably accounted for this – and she had started to give Ted extra sweetmeats when he made his way back to the stables after the meals. The child reminded her of someone but she could not think who! Elin concluded that it had been a blessing that Rosie had come, for Mariana was much more lively and today was no exception.

Elin managed to control the tears of joy and turned back to her mistress' reflection.

"Oh, Miss, you look beautiful," she repeated.

"Where is Biddy? She usually likes to be here for…"

"She's in trouble with Mrs Beacon and Rosie took her to dust the parlour with her, so she could keep out of the housekeeper's way."

"Is Biddy all right? She's not…"

"Oh, no, Miss. She's found a champion in Rosie and sort of follows her around most of the day."

"That's good then. Otherwise I'll have to speak to my husband about Mrs Beacon and I'd rather not! Well, Elin, I must go or the gong will be ringing. Maybe one of these days I'll rid the house of that!"

MARIANA

Mariana stood up. She turned from Elin, wondering if her words sounded too exuberant? She was nervous. Recently she had begun to feel buoyant and energetic. It had all started when she had found Edward attacking her husband. Listlessness had flown out the window when she had gone to his aid. Once her brother had left, she had helped Griffith upstairs to his room, effortlessly fending off Mrs Beacon who had been hovering nearby. Although this was the first time she had ever been in her husband's bedchamber, she had given it no more than a cursory glance, noting that it was as austere as the rest of the house.

What was racing through her relit mind was that here was a possibility for her to become close to her husband since he was shocked still from his near-strangulation. She had closed the door firmly, quietly bolting it against intrusion, whilst Griffith walked towards the bed. She had helped him to remove his coat, waistcoat and shoes. He had seemed unaware that it was his wife who was administering to him. Without talking she had half-drawn the curtains and then sat on the edge of the bed whilst he lay down. So far so good, she thought. He had not asked her to leave. This was the most intimate they had been since their wedding night; perhaps, within the setting of a bedchamber, Griffith would...

However, he had fallen asleep. She had remained with him. One could never guess what might happen when he re-awoke, she had reasoned. And then she had heard a knock on the door and was told that her sister had arrived. She was cross at being summoned; Griffith would probably stir whilst she was away from him. She had convinced herself that the aftermath of Edward's loss of temper might be her last chance for a long time. Every day counted, for the baby was becoming harder to hide with the passing weeks.

Nonetheless, her re-found energy had not diminished when she descended the stairs. In fact she had surprised herself when she had scolded Jennett, the maid. Up until Edward had come she had not bothered with anything in life and suddenly she felt like the mistress of the Vicarage. If only, she had wished, if only she could get her husband into her bed, she could establish herself and, perchance, even have Mrs Beacon taking heed of her orders! Yes, it was good to sense power, albeit only towards one of the lower servants. Her spirits had risen. She had felt in charge of her affairs again. She reckoned she was able to meet anyone with her head held high – anyone in the world. And then she had looked towards the door and seen the identity of her visitor whose arrival Jennett had just announced. It was Lloyd! Not him! She could not deal with Lloyd!

Her sister had only stayed a few minutes and then she was left alone with the man she hated and… and feared most! To think that she had been frightened by Margaret earlier this year; that was as nothing compared with the dread rising in her breast at that moment! Lloyd had been to the Vicarage several times since her marriage but she had never been left to entertain him on her own. Her mind recalled the confrontation whilst she left Elin and made her way downstairs.

"Have you come to see my husband?" she enquired, longing for someone to enter the room – even the unlucky Jennett. She wanted to move and stand behind a chair in order to feel defended against him, but, she chided herself, there was nothing he could do to her here in her own parlour.

"Have you been in bed?" Lloyd replied with another question.

Mariana blushed to what she felt was the roots of her hair. The horrible man had managed to undermine her newly found confidence with a single sentence! Coherent speech failed her, but he was speaking again.

"It's only that your gown is crumpled. I had heard that you rested most afternoons."

Mariana kept her own counsel.

"Are you well? It's unusual for a woman of your age to need to retire to bed during the day. If you need any help or advice from me, I would be only too happy to oblige."

"I don't need anything from you." Mariana hoped that the tremor in her voice did not show. She was struggling to control the antipathy rising within her. "I think it would be better if you came later to see my husband. He is not…"

Lloyd took a step towards her.

"If you like, I could examine you now. Is it your head? I could feel it for bumps or…"

"Mr Lloyd!" Mariana's heart was pounding so loudly she thought he might hear it. "I think you should go. I'll ring for the maid to see you out."

"Oh, it's too soon for me to go. I've only just arrived. Why don't we sit down and talk? Is it said that you have become quite the best hostess in the area. You could describe your symptoms to me…"

"There is nothing wrong with me and nothing for us to talk about. We…"

"Oh, but there is. I've discovered that your precious Jack was not found by his friend and he did not return to his home in…"

"What? What have you discovered? Is he alive? Where is he?"

"You seem very interested in what I have to say now, sweet Mrs Owen. But, there is a price to pay for the information."

"A… a price?"

"Just a few kisses. I've seen you looking at me over the years and I can guess what you're thinking about. Of course, you know all about how to charm a man now that you're a married woman!" Lloyd stepped up to Mariana and caught at her linen cap. It came away in his hand, dislodging some of her hair; several long strands of black fell across her shoulder.

"Ah," he crooned, whilst Mariana stood immobile. Why was she standing here? she cursed herself. Why didn't she scream for help? Her limbs would not respond.

"Ah, my dear Mariana, what soft hair you have!" He picked up a curl and wrapped it around his finger. "Why do you tuck it away now you're married? Is it the Parson? Is he very strict? Why did you marry him? You could have married me. I know how to treat a woman. I would have set the blood singing through your body. I could still teach you a thing or two. Not here or now, for that beady-eyed housekeeper of yours or the maid might come in unannounced, but we could arrange a tryst. You could ride out on your horse and chance upon me. By the old mill, perhaps. But for the moment, if you want to know what I have found out, then one kiss will suffice until our rendezvous."

Mariana willed herself to find her voice and call for one of her servants, but still she couldn't move. She watched Lloyd lean towards her. When his lips touched hers she heard a familiar sound: the jingle of keys. She was aware that Mrs Beacon never bothered to give more than a token knock before entering a room and in an instant, she realised that Lloyd would not have a chance to step away before the housekeeper came bustling in. Immediately she sprang into life. In a split second she was away from the threatening man as the older woman entered. Had she seen them? wondered Mariana and then she noticed her cap. Lloyd still had it. Mariana caught up her hair and pushed it back into the bun which Elin had fashioned for her that morning. She could not prevent her cheeks flushing vermilion. What must the servant be thinking?

"Dear God!" The outraged expletive made Mariana's heart sink.

"Here you are, Mrs Owen." Lloyd's tone was unruffled and respectful. He stretched out his hand and proffered the offending article to her. "You should use more pins to keep your pretty cap on. My sister always recommends not less than eight. You would not lose it then. I hope it hasn't got dirty on the floor. Well, if the Parson is not in, I'll call again later."

Mariana snatched the cloth from Lloyd's cold fingers and fled from the room without meeting the housekeeper's hostile eyes.

Yes, her heart had beaten with real fear that day but mostly she had a dull ache of anxiety about what she was going to do with her pregnancy advancing and her husband's continued absence from her bedchamber. Mariana had spent many hours trying to reason out her husband's lack of interest in her. Eventually she had decided that Griffith did not find her attractive. Since she was used to catching the eye of men all over the island, she had concluded that Griffith was different from other men because he was very devout. Unlike most men, who liked a glimpse of ankle or a low-cut bodice, Griffith (if his recent choice of gowns for her was anything to go by) preferred women who did not show off their charms. Subtlety. That was what was required. It was hard for her to imagine herself from Griffith's point of view. She strived for a way of dressing which was sober enough not to offend his puritan principles, yet not so unalluring as to make him not notice her at all. That must have been her mistake at the start. She had stood naked before him, albeit at his request, and offended him, and then she had worn such dowdy clothes that he was not interested in her!

Mariana was determined to get Griffith between her sheets and it must be soon or no one would believe the child was his. Sometimes she laughed inside her head at the irony of the situation. If anyone had told her that she would be struggling to arouse her own husband's interest (and he a man twice her age!) and not encouraging a younger lover, she would have ridiculed the notion. What Lloyd had wanted was more what she might have guessed would have happened, although not with Lloyd! She had spent several days after that mortifying experience afraid that the housekeeper would tell Griffith, but her husband's behaviour towards her had not changed. Had Mrs Beacon not seen as much as Mariana had supposed?

Tonight, in desperation, she had resolved to really set out to charm Griffith. She had chosen one of her own gowns brought from *Trem-y-Môr*: a rich, dark red material with black borders. She was pleased that it still fitted her. Her waist had thickened but her previous loss of weight meant that the gown clung snugly to her waist and hips. She had placed a white cap over her carefully brushed and pinned hair and she was satisfied with her reflection in the glass.

Downstairs she found Griffith in a mellow mood himself. She had perceived that when he relaxed he used fewer Bible references, which made him easier to understand. Tonight, she heard hardly any and that meant that he was more approachable than usual. However, whilst the meal progressed, she despaired of a way to ensnare him. Apart from boldly asking him (and she was sure he would not respond to that!) she saw no opening. Scraping the last of her apple pudding from her plate she knew feelings of defeat descended, but when Griffith rose from the table he piped up:

"Are you tired, my dear, or would you be interested in a game of chess?"

"That would be pleasant," she rejoined, giving him a wide smile. This would prolong their evening. Did he sense her plans? Customarily, he did not spend time with her; if they had no guests, like tonight, he would head for his study once the meal was over.

They made their way into the parlour. Mariana was not very good at chess and it brought back memories of evenings spent with Jack, but she buried her recollections and concentrated on Griffith. Jack was dead and she must forget him.

The Parson, with his clever memory, excelled at chess, but Mariana did not mind losing, for her husband's victory meant he unbent further.

As they finished their first game, Mrs Beacon came and asked permission to visit a sick relative. Somehow, knowing that the housekeeper had gone from the house, made Mariana believe that tonight was the night. Every circumstance pointed towards her achieving her aim.

She waited until they had played another game and then, when Griffith stood up to refill their glasses, she arose too. As if by accident she caught her foot on her skirt and tripped, landing in her husband's arms, whilst chessman flew through the air. Did he suspect anything? Mariana leant against him. She felt him tighten his hold.

"Mariana," he whispered, "you should be more careful."

"Yes, but you were here." Tentatively she returned the embrace and raised her face to his, allowing her cap to fall askew. He buried his nose in her fragrant, soft hair.

Mariana's face was pressed against the cloth of his coat. Fleetingly she felt panic fill her. She could not go through with this, but she must, for herself and the baby and even for Jack. She did not love this man, nor did she find him desirable, but she needed his seed within her and she must endure. She closed her eyes and swallowed hard.

"You have the most glorious hair," he murmured. "May I?" She felt his fingers lift off her cap and feel for the pins clipping her hair in place. He loosed it from its restraints and, as it tumbled down her back, Mariana experienced a flush of freedom. She recalled the sweet pleasure which Jack had given her and she lifted her lips to Griffith's. All thoughts of going back had disappeared. It was months since she had felt excitement in her loins! Her spine tingled in anticipation whilst her husband stroked her glossy locks.

"Shall... shall we go upstairs?" she breathed against his chin and he nodded. He was silent but Mariana was glad; nothing must break the atmosphere. He kept his arm around her and she fancied that he did not want to let her go. Leaving the chessman scattered on the floor unnoticed, they left the room. Not wishing to shatter the tentative feelings between them, Mariana did not speak either on their journey upstairs. They met no one.

Once they reached the bedchamber, Mariana shivered. The room was chilly and unwelcoming.

"I could light a fire," she suggested in a quiet whisper. "It wouldn't take long. You light the candles."

In the grate a fire had been laid already, for the nights were growing cold. Nevertheless, the housekeeper, who would have ordered the fireplace to be filled, would know that the Parson would not use his fire yet. Mariana had been informed by the chief servant that fires were not lit in the bedchambers before All Saints' Day – November the First. Griffith had given no such stipulation to his wife and he gave no contrary orders now. He set about lighting just a few candles.

Mariana knelt by the fire and expertly lit the kindling. Then, as if there was warmth to be felt immediately, she put her hands in front of the tiny flames. These flames, like the feeling between herself and Griffith, were precious, she mused. They had to be nurtured.

The Parson stood behind his kneeling wife with his eyes shut. Mariana turned and rose up. She noticed his pose and wondered if he was praying. She put her hands on his chest and he placed his fingers over hers.

"Oh, Griffith," she sighed.

She guided his hand to her breast, feeling that he was the novice, but he made no objection to her taking the lead. He sniffed deeply and Mariana was thankful that she had washed her hair only this morning. He opened his eyes and gazed at her.

The small flames of the fire were bright with the burning wood and she suspected that her silhouette would show against the orange and yellow. Again she rejoiced that the growth of the baby wasn't visible. For a second she remembered her wedding night and how he had fled her presence, but then she banished the picture. That night had been a disaster and tonight was going to be a success.

Her husband began to recite.

"Behold, thou art fair, my love; behold thou art fair, thou hast dove's eyes within thy locks: thy hair is as a flock of goats, that appear from Mount Gilead."

"Thy lips are like a thread of scarlet, and thy speech is comely: thy temples are like a piece of pomegranate within thy locks."

"Thy two breasts are like two young roes that are twins, which feed among the lilies."

"Thou hast ravished my heart, my sister, my spouse; thou hast ravished my heart with one of thine eyes."

Mariana listened with surprise to what he murmured whilst he nuzzled her breast and kissed her neck and ran his fingers through her hair. Why was he saying all this? she asked inside her head. Was it the Bible? It did not sound like the Holy Scriptures. No matter, if he was at peace... She gave herself up to his worship and luxuriated in the increasing heat of the fire behind her. Yes, tonight was going to be a success.

Not many minutes later she lay on the bed, frozen with shock. Her husband was not ready to consummate the marriage!

"Griffith," she whispered, putting her hand on his arm. Disappointment and frustration battled with pity. Pity won. She acknowledged that she had been so caught up with her own feelings that she had not considered of him. Forgetting that she was supposed to be innocent of this subject, she asked, "Are you all right?"

Her husband seemed lost in a terror of his own.

"I… can't… can't…" he stammered eventually.

"Oh, Griffith," she soothed, setting aside her constant fretting. She pulled his head towards her breast. All of a sudden, she felt the older and wiser. "Don't worry. It's been a tiring day. There'll be other times."

"No." His breath caressed her skin. "I… I've… I've *never* been able to…"

"Sweet Jesus!" The exclamation escaped her before she could stop it.

"I'm sorry, Griffith," she continued. Was he offended? She put her hand on his head but he lay without replying. She saw him visibly relax and decided that the confession had helped him. She turned on her back beside him and stared at the canopy overhead. Part of her was overcome with sympathy for her husband, but, as his breathing became shallower and he fell asleep, she realised what this meant to her. He would know the child was not his! What would he do to her? Worry kept her awake through the dark hours of night. She began to wonder if it would be better to explain that she had been ravished against her own inclination, but that was such a travesty of the truth, she rejected this idea.

The next day her disquietude was no less. She was not even amused by the thought of the housekeeper finding her in her husband's bedchamber for the first time, although she did note Mrs Beacon's pursed lips. She was consumed with her problem. She *had* to have help, but who could she turn to? Elin was the same age as herself but she was unmarried. Margaret had gone, but then she could not have spoken to her about the situation, and Margaret would probably have told Griffith! There was Cutlass – he was a doctor. But how could she share this with him? It was all so embarrassing and perplexing. Strangely, she would have gladly talked to the very person who had caused her all this trouble; she would not have needed to be shy with Jack, but he was dead. She grasped now why he had been upset after they had lain together. He had known how serious were the consequences of a few moments of pleasure, whilst she had not… then!

Mariana continued reviewing her family and friends. There was only one other person with whom she could bear to discuss her predicament:

Penelope. She was a woman, and married too. She was her sister and her elder. She must have more experience of this kind of thing than her! Although, maybe the best solution was not to mention the pregnancy yet. Unconsummation: the reason for annulling a marriage. Everyone knows that! She might just have the courage to tell Penelope if she was alone.

On the way to her sister, Mariana observed a cloud exactly shaped like a bird's wing covering the pale sun. She wondered if it was some kind of an omen and her hopes rose. When she arrived at the farm, a few splatters of rain fell and she slid from the horse's back and led him quickly into the stable. She was relieved to see no sign of Robert's horse, Sandy. Robert must be away from home. Barely had she crossed the yard where the rain was already bloodying the cobbles before the skies opened.

"Oh, what a downpour!" she called, entering Penelope's kitchen. It was months since she had paid a visit to the farm. Nothing seemed to have changed except herself.

Penelope was standing by the fire. She turned from the pot which she was stirring.

"Mariana! I wasn't expecting you. How lovely to see you!" She dropped the spoon and came to embrace her sister.

Mariana saw that Penelope's arm was bandaged.

"What's happened to you?" she frowned, concern in her voice.

"Oh, it's nothing. Just a sore which has turned nasty. I have put ointment on it, but it won't heal."

"Who has been treating it?"

"No one but myself. I had some ointment left over from last year which I'm using up."

"But how are you managing with all your work?"

"Sit down, Mariana, whilst I take this pan off the fire. Most jobs I manage to do…"

"Let me carry that. It looks heavy. What's in it?"

"Just tomorrow night's meal. Thank you. You can put it there. Now, let me have a look at you. How are you? I had heard that you were staying indoors much of the day. Are you ill?"

"No, Penelope. I see that news travels fast. I was simply adjusting to my new life…"

"Don't tell me my little sister is running her own establishment now!" Penelope trilled, a twinkle in her eye, whilst she put the kettle on to boil.

"Don't mock. I don't think I'm doing badly."

"No, indeed! Would you like a drink?"

"No. I don't want to make work for you. Sit down and talk to me. By the way, I don't think I've really had an opportunity to thank you for the marvellous wedding presents." Penelope had given an embroidered tablecloth and two generous cheeses. "How do you do such dainty stitches?"

"Practice, my dear. You still don't like sewing? You'll have to learn now you're married and especially when a baby comes."

"Don't say that!" begged Mariana.

"Oh, all right. I won't tease you. I know how you hate needlework."

Mariana bit her lip, wondering if she ought to correct her sister and tell her she had been referring to having babies. No, she had only just arrived. It was too early yet.

"So....o," drawled Penelope, sitting down opposite her sister. "How are you enjoying married life?" She cradled her bandaged arm.

"Is your arm hurting?"

"Yes, but don't tell Robert. He frets too much already."

"Where is he? Sandy wasn't there."

"He's taken the boys to help Luke King with his harvest…"

"Harvest! It's all gathered in around Holyhead."

"Yes, it is rather late, but Luke's fields are the last. I would have liked to have gone, but it's no good with my arm."

"And it's your right arm too. Dear Penelope. You can't afford to be ill, can you?"

"Well, fortunately, Luke will be incredibly pleased to see our horse turn up and he won't care that I haven't come. Sandy is in great demand. Too few farms have horses."

"Did you have a good harvest?" enquired Mariana, recalling that the Parson had not been overjoyed with the tithe he had received, but many reckoned there had been too much rain this year and everyone was suffering. She had not heard any news from her sister in recent weeks.

"Are you paying Luke King back?" she went on before any reply came. She was referring to love-reaping or *medel gymorth*, which entitled each farmer to call upon his neighbours to help for one day. Scores of farmers had such meagre holdings that they could not manage to pay harvesters, even for a single day.

Penelope shook her head.

"Our... our wheat failed this year."

Mariana stared in horror at her sister. This was a real disaster. How could she have been so selfish not to have come before to see how this family was faring! She had been too diverted with her own plight. First Griffith and then this!

"Oh, Penelope, I'm sorry. I didn't know... Is there anything I can do?"

"Well, it's certainly been quite a hard few weeks. My arm is the last of a series of difficulties we've encountered. Widow Evans was saying to me it must be the *tylwyth teg*."

"The fairies? Do you believe in that kind of thing?"

"No. I believe in God, as your husband does, and He won't fail us. We've had our bad times before."

"Will you manage?" Mariana was surprised at how marriage had increased her ties to her sister. Surely their bond was closer because of the similarities of their status. Penelope was talking to her in a way she would never have done earlier in the year. This realisation gave Mariana the hope that she would be able to broach the subject of her own worries soon. A thought flashed through her mind: maybe her situation was less pressing than Penelope's. The loss of crops could be a life and death situation.

"We have... have Father's inheritance, but we had put that away for times of trouble. I haven't decided yet whether this is a serious enough crisis to dig into it. Well, how did we get on to this gloomy subject? You never told me how you are managing at the Vicarage."

"Where's Mary?" Mariana answered with another question. Should she speak now?

"She's gone to Luke's in my place and taken Sarah. I find it too painful to carry the babe around all day and if I'm holding her with one arm, then I can't do anything with my other!"

"So, you're all alone?"

"Yes. Which reminds me. You are too. Where's your groom? What's his name? John?" Penelope stood up when the kettle hissed its readiness. "You will have something to eat? I'm not preparing a meal for the family tonight because they'll have had food at the King's. However I baked today. I can't manage kneading dough at the moment. Mary's having to do the bread. Robert complains that it's not as tasty as mine – only jesting of course. I'm thinking, if my arm doesn't heal soon, I'll call in Rose from the next farm. She's thirteen and would be a help. She's been unable to find work elsewhere. There's the question of payment, but I'm sure we can work something out. Well?"

"Well, what?"

"Mariana, you're daydreaming. Will you eat with me?"

"Yes, but only if you are intending to eat too. I'll prepare it. You sound as if you could do with a rest." Mariana prayed that whilst her hands were busy, it would be easier to speak of intimate matters. "I... I wasn't daydreaming, I was thinking. I'm glad you're alone."

"Are you? Is everything all right?"

"I... I... Well, yes and no."

"If you can reach the plates, you can sit down and tell me. Everything else is on the table. Tell me what's troubling you."

Mariana felt the blood rushing to her cheeks. Where should she start? She remembered the baby and her eyes filled with tears. What was she going to do?

"I... I don't know how... Oh, Pen, it's awful."

"Mariana, my dear-heart, don't cry." She stretched out her good arm across the worn wood of the table. "Try to tell me. It won't seem so terrible if you share it. Is it... a baby? Is that why you're crying? It's not like you! Is it a baby?"

"No!" shrieked Mariana, making her sister jump. "Oh, if only it was just that!"

"Is it the Parson?"

"Yes," confessed Mariana.

"Is he... he cruel to you?"

Mariana glanced up, confused. Why did people imagine that her husband was cruel to her? Did he give that impression?

"Oh, no," she reassured Penelope, relieved that her weak tears had dried up. "He... he can't... can't... He and I... We aren't able to... to make babies." She finished lamely, willing her sister to interpret her stammerings.

"Can't make babies?" repeated Penelope. "Do you mean you are not with child yet? I see..."

"No. The Parson... My husband can't..." Mariana looked away from her sister. She did not want to meet her eyes.

"Oh, the problem lies with him. He can't perform his marital...?"

"Yes. I wondered if... Do you know... know of anything I can do? I thought... that it would pass, but he tells me he couldn't... couldn't with his first wife either."

"My dear Mariana, how distressing! And your husband too. Let me think now." Penelope took a bite of cooked ham. "I do read many books but I'm not aware of any book that includes information about this issue. But, there must be some kind of medicine or something. I must say, though, that I'm very surprised. After all, you are an exceedingly attractive woman."

Mariana blushed.

"I... I..." she stuttered. "I had thought it was me, but when he said that he had never... consummated his last marriage, I knew that..."

"Listen, my dear. Will you leave your worries with me? There must be some remedy. People recommend spa water for all sorts of complaints. Don't you let it get you moped. Remember, it's early days yet. Instead, let me tell you some good news. You recall how I'm always talking about my friend, Miss Swann. I wrote, or rather I dictated a letter for Robert to write – the arm stops me holding a quill – asking Miss Swann to come and stay with us. Of course, with her travelling all this way, she will have to remain with us the entire winter, but she has agreed. I'm very excited about seeing her again. It must be all of... twelve years since I last saw her. We've written to each other but it's not the same, is it? I'll not want her to feel obliged to work, which is why I'm considering of Rose but..."

"Where will she sleep?"

"Good question. The barn is next door and we've been planning for ages to knock through the wall. So, if there's time, Robert and Llew will make another room above the floor. It's already got a wooden platform for storing hay and the apples we've picked from our small orchard, but we don't need all that space. Anyway, we'll see... If it can be done, we would put the boys in the barn room and... Wait! I've just thought of something. Yes, this could be the answer. If the room isn't ready, Robert can sleep with the boys and I and Miss Swann can share a bed. Now, why didn't I think of that before?"

"Because you knew that Robert wouldn't agree?" reasoned Mariana wryly, smiling at her sister.

"Yes, you're right there. We'll sort something out. Did I tell you I had Margaret here, wanting to stay? But one look at our narrow entrance to upstairs and she knew she could not climb up. She had her eye on the parlour but..."

"God's bones! Who does she think she is? It's one thing to settle in at the Manor House. We've got plenty of bedchambers, but to expect to…"

Penelope laughed.

"I'm afraid there's much more to it than that, as you can see with my attitude to Miss Swann. I can rearrange the room to welcome her, but I couldn't bear to have Margaret living here indefinitely. She and I aren't close…"

"No one's close to her! Margaret does not seem able to live at peace with anyone. She's overbearing. How did you get rid of her?"

"I'm not quite sure. I think she didn't like my boys – they can be very noisy sometimes and with it being not a very large house, there's nowhere to get away from them. And I don't think she could really cope with sleeping in the parlour. It's hardly private there! So she ate a meal with us, hinted at some dark secret and left. I suppose she slept in some inn nearby. I haven't heard from her, but I assume that she got home safely."

"Well, I'm overjoyed she's gone. I didn't like her. In fact, I would go further and say…"

"Yes, she is very difficult to like."

"Have you any idea what her secret was?"

"No."

"Never mind! I'm not all that interested. I'm just relieved that she's gone. The more miles there are between her and me, the bet…"

"*Mam*! *Mam*! Eat rice pudding and oatcake. *Mam*…" The door was flung open and Penelope's youngest son ran in.

"And he was sick he ate so much," concluded his older brother, Robbie, a mere step behind him.

"No, me weren't… me weren't…" David reached his mother's side and buried his head in her lap.

"There were others there who ate and ate and ate." The voice of Llewelin made the two women look towards the threshold. Being the eldest, he had been given charge of his sister, Sarah. She was fast asleep in his arms.

"Oh, I am pleased that you've all eaten your full," replied Penelope with an indulgent grin. "Come along, boys, greet your Auntie."

"Good day, Aunt Mariana," chorused Robbie and Llewelin.

"Now, David, give me some room to take Sarah." Penelope tried to stand up, but her son burrowed deeper into her skirts. "Come on, my love…"

"I'll take her if you like," butted in Mariana.

PENELOPE

Penelope stared, open-mouthed, at her sister. Never once had she shown any interest in Sarah and certainly she had never wanted to hold her before! Marriage had changed her... If she hadn't just shared about her husband's condition, Penelope would have presumed Mariana was expecting a child. No time for conjecture. The racket was increasing as the boys vied with one another to recount their day.

In truth Penelope could have ignored their tales. She had been to many harvesting days and the subsequent feasts. She was familiar with the event. The boys were shouting to tell her what they had eaten. Penelope could picture it in her head. Initially there would have been mountains of barley bread, placed in earthenware basins and served with warm buttermilk poured over them. This first course was meant to fill the hungry stomachs before the meat was brought. There would have been salt beef offered and sometimes pork, if the winter's pig had slaughtered. Then, to round off the meal, enormous rice puddings, sweet and stiff, were cut into oozing slabs and served almost like cake. There might have been beer to wash it all down, but certainly all the reapers would have been presented with more buttermilk; this time with water added.

Penelope smiled to herself as she saw the remains of the pudding on Robbie's smock. Apparently her sons had enjoyed their victuals. It was given in payment for the work and she wondered how much actual time her sons had given to the task. She guessed that they would have become distracted very quickly and run away to play with the other children. As if in reply Llewelin boasted:

"I used a sickle, *Mam*."

He turned to box Robbie lightly on the side of the head just to prove that he was his brother's superior. Penelope did not scold them. She understood their bickering, as much as David's shyness, stemmed from healthy tiredness.

"And very proud of him, I was," came the deeper voice of Robert.

"I made the stacks," whooped Robbie, fending off his brother and running around the table to escape further torment.

"Ah, but you were too small to lift the stones," mocked Llewelin. "*I* managed to carry them." He was referring to the stones which were placed over the low stooks to prevent the wind blowing them down.

"Robbie did very well," interposed Robert, when he saw his middle son's face. "You were eight once! David, what's come over you? *Mam's* not going anywhere."

"Is Mary coming in?" questioned Penelope, managing, at last, to disentangle herself from the boy's grasp. She rose to re-boil the kettle.

"No. She's too weary. She and Thomas have gone home, but she said she would come across later. It's been a busy day. We didn't stay to the dancing."

"It was red, *Mam*," chimed in David, following his mother to the fire.

"What was, my darling?"

"Man sang with it," David added enigmatically.

"He means the fiddle," explained Llewelin. "I wanted to stay."

"Yes." Robert ruffled his hair. "I know what you wanted. Because you used your sickle so skilfully, you were hoping to be offered some beer and a piece of 'baccy like the other men, weren't you, Llew?"

Llewelin flushed redder than the fiddler's instrument.

"I... I..."

"Maybe he wished to dance," twinkled Mariana.

"No. I don't like the company of girls."

"You won't think that soon," countered Robert with a laugh. "Now don't get upset, son, we were all your age once and a long time ago it seems now!"

"You haven't told me about '*Y Gaseg Fedi*', boys," interjected Penelope intending to draw attention away from her sensitive eldest son. At eleven, he was growing tall and strong, but he did not like to be teased. Even David understood what his mother was talking about: it was the last tuft of corn cut in the field. All faces turned towards Penelope when she asked, "Who cut it?"

"Old Thomas, of course," returned her husband. "He has to sit in the place of honour anyway, doesn't he?"

"Didn't they try to get it into the kitchen?" continued Penelope, her eyes sparkling with amusement. This custom entailed one of the reapers trying to bring the last brushes of corn past the servant girls, who were armed with buckets of water, right on to the kitchen table. The corn had to be completely dry or the reaper had failed. Penelope recollected last year when her Robert had managed the test successfully right here. They had even hung all the last ears of grain from the ceiling but it had not brought them any luck!

"Yes. We's were wet," announced David.

"David did rather get in the way," mused Robert, "but never mind, darling, you're dry now."

"Didn't the rain catch you?" exclaimed Mariana.

"No. We've had none. Has it rained here then?" Robert answered her query.

"Yes. Just as I arrived. It must have been one big, black cloud right overhead!"

"It's a pity you weren't able to stay for the merriment," remarked Penelope. "However, now you're home, I think a wash is called for. Boys, go out into the yard and clean yourselves. You, Llew, look as if you rolled in the field before you left, and you, Robbie, dropped half your meal down your front. Were you thinking of eating it later?"

Solemnly the boys shook their heads. Penelope gave David a slight push towards the others and responsibly Llew took his hand and led him out.

"I must be going," Mariana declared, standing up. "Otherwise Griffith will be home before me. I've had to learn to be punctual at the Vicarage." She handed the baby to her brother-in-law.

Penelope stepped towards her sister and embraced her with one arm. Penelope meant the hug as a farewell and the promise of help for Mariana's predicament.

Penelope mused over her sister's quandary later whilst she rocked her daughter in the crook of her arm. Her kitchen was full of people; the women were crowded near the fire whilst the men stood and sat around the wide table. Every woman but herself was knitting and some of the men had needles too. Several men were puffing on pipes whilst they all contributed to the topic of the evening. Someone, Hugh Pritchard, she thought, had queried earlier:

"Why, if God is just, does He have favourites?"

Immediately several voices had expressed their own personal views but as host, Robert had demanded order. He had suggested that each man take a turn at speaking.

Penelope peeped at her husband, leaning back in his solid oak chair with its hole at one end supporting the rushlight. Tucked between his lips was his special Alderman pipe. Penelope's eyes crinkled with love at him but he did not notice, so deeply engrossed was he.

Meanwhile, the assembled women were competing in a knitting competition. Next to Penelope sat Mary, with her sleeping baby at her side. Martha and her older sister, Rose, were cross-legged on the floor at the foot of their mother. Also called Martha, mother and daughters had walked from their nearby farm to join the social gathering. Completing the circle were the two Evans cousins, both widows, who now resided in the same house for company: Esther and another Mary. In the centre of the women was an untidy ball of wool from which came equal lengths of yarn which had been knotted together. Each knitter was aiming to be the first to reach the knot.

Penelope would have joined in usually, but her sore arm prevented her and she was contented to sit with her Sarah and watch. The sound of clicking needles, mingled with the crackle of the flames, provided a continuous backcloth for the brightly coloured stitches of conversation which each person provided. Esther, her knitting stick firmly stuck through her apron string on one of her needles, was obviously going to win the contest. She matched the lightning rhythm of her fingers with the movement of her tongue. At the moment she was telling the women about old Mrs Williams, who was an ancient crone living on the seashore near Holy Island. She had long since been labelled a witch, but not in a derogatory or fearful way; rather they respected her and held her in awe. Her potions (as Penelope herself knew) were very efficacious and some said that she cast spells and even raised spirits from the dead.

Penelope observed that Martha had ceased to knit and was staring, round-eyed at Esther, as if Esther herself had magical powers. Esther was describing of how Mrs Williams had called up Esther's husband from the grave.

Penelope smiled. She had heard the story dozens of times, but it managed to send a shiver down her spine on every hearing. She allowed her ears to pick up the men's discussion.

Seated on the right of Robert was Hugh Pritchard, Martha's husband, and on his left their own Mary's spouse, Thomas – a Londoner, of course, but nonetheless very much included. Lounging with his back to the wall and nothing in his hands was Benjamin, a fifteen year old who worked for Hugh. Along one side of the table sat the three King brothers and opposite them were their other brother and their father, Luke. Near the women was Penelope's own son, Llewelin. Penelope's two middle sons were abed already, exhausted from their exciting day.

"But I still think it's unfair. What if you're not one of the 'Chosen Ones'? How many of us here are chosen?" It was the eldest King son, Evan, who like all in the room, was speaking Welsh.

"All of us, Evan. We all go to church and…" insisted Hugh Pritchard firmly.

"That doesn't mean anything," informed Thomas. Penelope knew he had mastered everyday Welsh years ago. "Some folk sitting right in the pews may not be chosen. It says in the Bible that God allows the wheat and the tares to grow up together and only separates them once harvesting comes…"

"No," interrupted Hugh. "I still think we're all chosen. We all believe in one God, Father Almighty and so on, and we all worship Him."

"Not everyone goes to church because they believe in God," persisted Thomas, apparently not wanting to be contradicted. "Many people go to…"

"No! No!" Hugh spoke so vehemently that his spittle flew across the table. "Everyone who goes to church on Sunday because they believe…"

"Ah," put in Robert, "but the problem here isn't simply how do we know if someone is chosen or not and should we use church attendance as our criterion, but rather is it fair of God to choose some and not others in the first place?"

"God is completely fair and all loving," Benjamin stated. Up until now he had been silent. He was resented, but Penelope had found, over the years, that this young man thought profoundly about everything.

"Then, how can He reject some people?" enunciated Robert softly.

Luke King leant forward and declared:

"I believe everyone goes to heaven. God couldn't turn anyone away, especially children."

"I see." Robert was smiling. Penelope knew her husband enjoyed these discussions and often deliberately took another side just to see how the others would react. "But what if someone doesn't even believe in God or… or what if they sin and are never sorry? Many preachers urge people to repent. The implication is that everyone *needs* to repent – to be put right with God. If, as Luke says, all people are on the road to heaven, then we could all go out and have a good time and do whatever we want, however wicked. Mm... that sounds like a good idea."

All the men laughed except Luke, who disagreed:

"No, I can't believe in hell. What sort of a God do we believe in, who sends people to eternal damnation?"

For a moment there was a hush, and Esther's voice, like a discordant note, was heard saying:

"There he was, dressed in white with..."

"You'd better watch your tongue with notions," warned Hugh. "The..."

"The Bible says that there's a hell," proffered Benjamin.

Thomas must have been considering an earlier question because he stated:

"Luke, the kind of God we have is a fair God."

"Precisely." Robert's tone was firm. "God isn't a weakling, full of sickly love. He's just too and the rules are that if you sin, you must be punished. If a man poaches on another's land, would you let him off punishment, Sir?"

"It depends on why he's done it. These bloody magistrates," ranted Luke, "don't know what it's like to see your wife and children starving as... as I did." Luke's wife had died ten years ago from fever, but years of poverty and undernourishment might have been the real cause of her death.

"Yes," intercepted Robert gently. Penelope guessed her husband didn't want Luke to become melancholy. "But what about murder? You couldn't say murder was ever right. What about the commandment which says, 'Thou shalt not kill'?"

Penelope's eyes rested on her son when Luke took up his argument still further. Her ruminations blotted out Luke's words whilst she studied her first born. How fortunate she had been in childbed! She had not lost a single baby and now she had another child growing inside her. Would it be a boy as fine as Llew? She approved of Llewelin staying up and listening to the men talk. Rarely did he contribute anything himself, although, sometimes he and his father would discuss a topic on the following day. He was sitting in respectful silence whilst Luke spoke bitterly about the terrible punishments meted out in today's courts. Suddenly Penelope realised that her son was not paying any attention to the men's debate, but was eavesdropping on Esther's monologue. He, like his peer, Martha, was fascinated by the talk of people returning from the dead.

Penelope shifted her position and lifted Sarah's drooping head along her arm. Should she take the baby up to her cot? Her slight movement brought the women's attention onto her.

"You're very quiet tonight, Penelope," clucked Esther. "What do you think of Mrs Williams? Have you ever been to her?"

Have you ever been to her? Penelope's heart jolted. Of course she had! She had asked her for ointment to help Robert's back which he had injured when he had slipped on the icy yard one winter. The lotion had been marvellous. Why had she not thought of Mrs Williams before? The beldam could help Mariana. Yes, she must go and see the elderly woman herself, for she could not expect young Mariana to go and broach such an embarrassing subject.

"Mrs Roberts?" entreated Susan, bringing Penelope's mind back to the circle of women.

"Yes. Yes, I've been to her and I think she's just a harmless old hag who's very clever with herbs and medicines."

"Ah, but not everyone can talk to the spirits," persevered Esther in an important tone and all eyes turned back to her, leaving Penelope to her own reflections.

MARIANA

Penelope would have been surprised to know that she was wrong about her sister: Mariana was desperate enough to visit Mrs Williams herself. Riding home from Robert and Penelope's farm, Mariana had reached the conclusion that the ancient witch might be the very person to seek out. She waited only until she had a legitimate reason for going to see Mrs Williams. She felt it was judicious that no one suspect that she was asking advice from the wise woman; tongues wagged enough about all that happened in the Vicarage.

However, only two days after her conversation with Penelope, it came to her ears that the dame had suffered a fall on the beach near her home. What better excuse than that the Parson's wife desired to care for a member of her husband's flock? Mariana could check that the sick woman did not want for anything. She did not consult Mrs Beacon or the chest of articles for the needy. Rather she ordered Elin to gather up some of the discarded gowns for her to take and she set out accompanied by John, the groom. She even told the Parson where she was going; he seemed pleased that she was taking her duties seriously.

Riding towards Four Mile Bridge, she tried to calm herself. She had been so sure that marriage would hide the baby, but since Griffith had told her of his problem, she was frantic. Her mind had whirled in circles trying to find a solution and, with the passing days, it had dawned on her that the easiest way out for her was to get rid of the baby. Then it would never matter if the Parson could not be cured. In fact, it would make her marriage much more pleasant if she did not have to be intimate with her husband. Although, originally, she had thought to ask Mrs Williams about Griffith, she resolved to ask for something to stop the baby coming. Was it possible? She did not know.

While she rode and the bright October sunshine touched her face, she found herself thinking about the child within her. It was a child, a life, part her and part Jack. It was all she had left to remember Jack by. Could she bear to… to kill it? She had told Jack that she did not like infants, but the sight and feel of her niece, Sarah, had made her feel warm inside. Holding her sister's baby had made her imagine what her own baby would be like. After all, Sarah had started in the same way as her child: in her mother's womb. Mariana was not sure if she was strong enough to take a potion which would bring about the death of her baby deliberately. Over the weeks, she had begun to come to terms with bearing the child and yet she was contemplating killing it! It was not as though she had never dreamt of killing people before. Many times she had wished she could shoot Margaret and even Lloyd sometimes, but, she reminded herself, she hated those people, whereas this unknown baby growing inside her brought only love, not hatred, into her heart. She argued round and round inside her head whether what she was planning to do was murder. She had no answers; all she had was anguish.

Could the old sorceress help her with Griffith? No, she put this idea out of her head. She must beg for something for her condition and not mention her husband's impotence. She felt nervous, not in case Mrs Williams revealed her secret – the gammer was known for being discreet and not divulging why people visited her – no, rather it was her ignorance of these matters and her own distaste for getting rid of the baby that made her stomach contract. She must bear the responsibility just as she, herself, had decided to marry the Parson. Oh, God, why did You give me a husband like this? she cried under her breath. She had never heard of anyone else who had this condition. What was wrong with Griffith?

Mariana glanced at the china blue sky. The cold wind was chasing woolly sheep clouds across the sky like an obedient sheepdog, and the smell of wet seaweed, borne on the breeze with the receding tide, engendered elation. The feel of the broad back of Mars beneath her uplifted her spirits. If only she could solve this she would be able to settle down. Her marriage was hardly days filled with joy and love (she would not have chosen the Parson if there had been anyone else whom she could have courted quickly), but it could be worse… he could beat her, as some husbands did. Yet, if she had known that the marriage would remain unconsummated, she would never have chosen this existence! The presence of the child had rushed her decision. However, there was nothing to do about it now. She had to accept that she was a married woman and make the best of it. Once the baby was gone – if she could only brace up and do it – then could her life be bearable? Yes, if she was allowed to spend time riding each day in the same way she had in her spinsterhood. After all, she and Griffith did not interact for many hours of the day and she had all her old friends still. She could travel to *Trem-y-Môr* and talk to the servants there – her brother wasn't residing at the Manor House at the moment. Yes, she must accept the decision she had made!

Thank God, she thought when she crossed the bridge, that she was not pining after another man – at least not one who was alive. More and more she found she could barely remember what Henry looked like; instead, her mind was filled with pictures of Jack. Was there any possibility he wasn't dead? She might go and talk to Matthew again. No! No, she was married! Even if Jack was alive she could not meet with him; Mariana suspected that Griffith would be a jealous husband. No, she must deal with the baby and then try to be content. Her heart sighed. Was life this meaningless? Was she never to be allowed happiness except to look forward to a daily ride? She did not feel as young as she had a few months ago, but she knew that probably she would have many, many years ahead of her. She had lost so much of her wayward nature recently and she suspected that others would approve, but what about her? Was she meek enough to live the rest of her days with the Parson? She hoped she could, for the sake of… whom? When first she had realised that she was with child, she had tried to take the right path for the sake of the baby and here she was riding to buy a potion to kill it! If the child was dead, would it matter if she scandalised the community by leaving the Parson? But did she really want to leave her husband? Where could she go? Was her everyday routine so miserable? She shook her head. It was too soon to be asking herself questions of this kind. She must deal with the child and only then could she look to the coming days.

She could not do it! This child – *her* child – had never had a chance to savour life. No, it was not even going to be given an opportunity to be alive apart from her, its mother. There was no one to speak up and defend its survival except her and she had no choice!

Was there no other alternative truly? she asked herself, for the thousandth time. No, for time had run out. Griffith had not been near her since that evening together. Already when the baby was delivered, some might question its early arrival – and chief amongst these would be her husband! He would know the child was not his and he would reject the child and her. Would he punish her? He would assume that she had committed adultery.

He was a deeply religious man with high principles. He would not be kindly disposed to her or her babe. No, she must act today whilst it was still possible. But was it still possible? She did not know. She must seek out Mrs Williams' advice.

The wise woman's cottage nestled amongst the tough grass of the seashore and the old crone was as sturdy as the sod itself. She clung to her existence with the same tenacity as the roots of the grass sought a hold on the shifting sand. Reputedly she was over one hundred years old and had lived in this cottage since birth. The stones of her home were battered by the wind and sand and she had boarded up two windows, which faced the fierce sea, presumably in an attempt to keep out the persistent wind. With the passage of time, the roof had allowed the grass seed to take root, until the whole of one side of tiles was covered by the grass, giving added protection and warmth.

Coming from behind the cottage, Mariana was unable to see its precise whereabouts until she rode over the last sand dune practically on to the roof itself. She had been here on several occasions, but never quite remembered the exact location. The beach looked different each time and the hills of sand moved with the tide. Today the strong wind had whipped away the smoke from the chimney so that there was no sign of the dwelling from afar off.

From the very doorstep the sand lay in golden waves to the sea with grains dancing in the wind like pockets of mist. By now Mars' feet were sinking into the soft ground and Mariana dismounted and led him to the door.

"I won't be long," Mariana shouted at John, the groom, above the roar of waves and wind. Already she had told him that she had heard about Mrs Williams' fall and since Mrs Jones, her father's housekeeper, had been greatly helped by the witch, Mariana felt honour bound to visit!

Mariana's firm knock at the rough door gave no hint of the turmoil inside her. Even at this very moment she wanted to turn back, but never had she been cowardly and in her innermost being she accepted that she had to go through with this. When there was no reply, for a brief interlude, her heart leapt for joy. Mrs Williams was not at home! Was this an omen? Fate or God taking a hand in the events?

No! The door opened and there was the elderly woman dressed in a shabby, black gown with her back bent. Upon her balding head she wore a dirty cap and she looked at Mariana with rheumy eyes.

"Who is it?" she sniffed.

"It's Mariana Rowlands from *Trem-y-Môr*," Mariana intoned, without thinking.

"Nay, it can't be. She's married."

Mariana smiled. Mrs Williams might be ancient and hunched, but there was nothing wrong with her wits!

"You're right, Mrs Williams, but I thought you might not know me as Mrs Owen."

"'Course I do. Come in and sit down."

The inside of the cottage was completely dark once the door was closed and Mariana stood, willing her eyes to adjust to the gloom so that she could identify somewhere to sit. To her left she was able to discern orange embers glowing faintly beneath a pot or kettle hanging above their meagre warmth. She focused her gaze on the fire and soon could make out the receptacle was a soot-encrusted pot. If Mariana had been made of weaker stuff, she might have fled at the sight of the witch's cauldron, but she had known Mrs Williams since her childhood and the scruffy beldam held no fears for her.

"I've brought you some clothes. I hope you can find some use for the material." Mariana thrust the package into her hostess' hands and stumbled towards three-legged stool near the fire. There did not appear to be a proper chair. She squatted down, enquiring after Mrs Williams' health.

"I did have a fall, but I broke no bones. So, what can I do for you? It's a baby, isn't it?"

Mariana lifted her head in surprise. How had the witch known?

"Yes," Mariana started, trying to keep her voice equable. "I want to be rid of it."

"It's not your husband's." It was a statement, not a question.

Mariana began to feel cold despite the stuffiness of the cottage. The chimney was not drawing well and billows of smoke kept wafting across her face. Whatever was cooking smelt unappetising and she felt sick. This decrepit woman could see too much! Maybe she should not have come after all. Did Mrs Williams know everything? Marina had the uncanny feeling that she did!

The girl shivered when the hag shuffled from her side and disappeared into the depths of the darkness. Mariana strained her eyes to no avail. Then she heard the old crone's voice; it seemed to be coming from faraway. She shivered involuntarily.

"How far gone are you?"

"I... I've missed two of my..."

"You mean three, don't you?" corrected the elderly goodwife.

"Well, yes, it is three. It's hard to count for I have never been... been regular." Mariana coughed when more smoke belched from the fireplace. She could have said the exact date the baby started to grow inside her, but she was afraid that it was already too late to stop the child. Yet if Mrs Williams had second sight why was she asking questions at all?

"You've left it late." The other woman reappeared and crouched down next to Mariana, who found suddenly that she had to force herself not to shrink away when a gnarled hand stretched out and touched her. "I'd advise you to keep it."

"I... I can't," mumbled Mariana.

"I know. Why don't you let me help you with your problem?"

"My problem?"

"My child, *I know*. You can't deceive me. I know about the Parson. I might be able to help you, but you would have to remember my instructions carefully. Can you do that?"

Hope rose irrepressibly in Mariana's heart. She did not need to kill the unborn infant, after all! But what if Mrs Williams was mistaken? If she continued to wait for her husband to come to her bedchamber...

"I think... it would be better to get rid of the... the baby," she whispered with a lump in her throat.

"No, it's very late to be tampering with nature. You should have come earlier. Let me help you with your husband. It'll work and he'll never find out. Trust me, child." Her fingers gripped Mariana's frozen hands tightly, imprisoning her. "You do trust me, don't you?"

"Ye... yes."

"Very well. Here is the liquid." She produced a small bottle from the depths of her gown and pressed it on Mariana. "You must give it to your husband not sooner than an hour beforehand. Have you a clock in the house?" Mariana nodded. "Of course you have. A tiresome piece that's always chiming, isn't it? No sooner than an hour and he must not drink any wine or spirits after he has had it! Do you understand?"

"But how do I administer it?" Mariana peered at the bottle. "Don't I put it in his drink?"

"No. No wine or spirits. Food is best. No more than five drops. Five drops. No sooner than an hour beforehand. But there is more…"

"Oh, I hope I can remember all this," muttered Mariana with a sigh. She was beginning to feel faint. The smoke and her own fears had made her head spin.

"You will, my child. The last instruction is that you must be at your alluring, your most charming. You must do your very best to help him. Can you do that?"

"Yes. I… I do so very much want…"

"Well, at least it is not a requirement that you love the person!" Mrs Williams laughed at her own humour. Mariana stared at the other woman. The laugh was a deep, jolly sound; Mariana would have expected a cackle.

"Now, it won't work after the hour and the potion won't last longer than a month. If you leave it longer than a month, it will not work and it will make him sick. Do you understand?" she repeated.

The woman stood up and poked the fire. Mariana felt as if she had been dismissed.

"I… I would like the other… other one too. I assume a month from now will be too late to be rid… of the baby and if I can't… can't… I want to keep every door open. I can pay for both," she finished lamely.

"You foolish child!" scolded the witch. "You don't need the other. Trust me, remember."

"Please," pleaded Mariana. "I can't come again to you. People might be suspicious. If my husband… Please help me. I have no one else."

"All right, my child. The other mixture is easy. Take it at night, two thimblefuls. Go to bed and sleep. You will have pain and cramps, but you will lose the babe. But, you must act soon, for every day counts. You should have come to me before."

"Will it… it? Can I…?"

"What, my child?"

"Will I be able to hide it from my husband? If he suspects… or the housekeeper suspects… She is…"

"Have you someone you can depend on?"

"Yes," Mariana told her, picturing Elin. No, Elin was no good for she believed the baby was the product of her union with Griffith. Before she could think of anyone else, Mrs Williams advised:

"Go to them for a day or two. You will find the loss of the babe affects you in both body and soul. Don't do it, Mariana, unless you really have to. You are not unmarried, like some I've known. Speak with your husband. No one else need know or, if you prefer, give him my special medicine. Choose very carefully. Now I will fetch the potion for you."

Mariana watched whilst she waddled away. How could she see anything without a candle? How did the old crone know which potion she was selecting? Afterwards Mariana wondered even more, but soon she had two bottles safely in her pocket, hidden underneath her skirts, lying in place of the shiny coins which Mrs Williams had secreted on her person.

"Use the green one first, my child," implored the witch as Mariana slipped through the door and into the full fury of the wind.

MRS JONES

Mrs Jones salted the shoulder of lamb she had prepared and attached it to the spit using iron 'locks' to prevent it from cooking unevenly with the heavy side falling down, despite the dog turning the wheel!

She sighed. The house was too quiet. Ever since the new squire – her own favourite Master Edward – had left, she had found time dragged. Initially, without thinking, she had continued to make huge meals, but these days she offered meat only on Thursdays and Sundays. The staff no longer benefited from eating the leftovers from their betters' table but Mrs Jones felt obliged to cut down on the cooking. Some money did come from Sir Edward via his steward, Owen Lewis, but winter was approaching and before long she would be unable to supplement the meals with food from orchard or garden.

It was the first time for nearly twenty years that there had been no master or mistress living in the Manor House and the whole place was eerily silent and listless – without a rudder, she would say! After Miss Mariana was married, there had been only that Mrs Struley to feed and she liked the table set with a goodly number of dishes without stinting. Then Sir Edward had turned up, unexpectedly, and Mrs Jones' heart had gladdened. However, the man had come back from visiting Miss Mariana in a terrible rage, ousted his eldest sister (which was no bad thing, Mrs Jones reckoned) and then spent a week lost in his cups, only playing with any food she put before him and returning many of the plates untouched. It took Mrs Jones back to the time when the old Squire – Sir William – had been mourning the departure of his second wife. However, that had lasted for over a year, whereas Sir Edward stayed hardly a week before setting forth, with Wilson and Thomas in tow, to London.

Why had he left again and so soon?

Mrs Jones aimed a slap at the dog who had tried to slip out of the wheel and dash into the yard.

"You lazy animal!" she cried, standing to watch for a moment, checking the creature had settled down. Then she placed newly garnered beetroot, which she had washed previously, into a cauldron, ready to boil and serve with the salad later. She had sent Peggy and Kate to ask the gardener if there was any rocket left. Although autumn was advancing, she hoped one or two more leaves could be found. Presently, apart from the meticulously harvested fruit in the loft, most of the food would be preserved rather than fresh.

The two young maids were good girls but she missed Elin and even Biddy, although the latter had been a great one for disappearing just when her help was needed the most, like the dog. In fact little Peggy seemed to be learning the same trick. It had all started in the summer or maybe that was just when she had first noticed. Almost every day she had had to scold the youngest member of the staff, now a sturdy nine-year-old, she recollected.

"Have you put the mutton bones on to boil, Kate?"

"Yes, Mrs Jones."

"They'll need a good two hours."

"Yes, Mrs Jones."

"Mix that suet in well with the meat and then we can add the gooseberries and spices. I've chopped the thyme and parsley. I've got the saffron here for your oatmeal pudding. We must be careful with it as it's very expensive. Do you remember the recipe?"

Kate nodded her assent. Mrs Jones wasn't sure why she had asked the girl because she knew that Kate remembered *every one* of the recipes which the housekeeper taught her. And Mrs Jones believed she understood the reason for this: it was because Kate had decided to follow in Mrs Jones' footsteps. Shyly Kate had shared her hopes, one humid evening, when Peggy had retired to bed and she and Kate had been alone.

"I don't want to get married, Mrs Jones. And I don't want children. All I want is to be like you, a cook in this house."

Mrs Jones suspected that with Sir William being laid to rest at the end of week, Kate's dream was about to start to come true. Mrs Jones had planned dozens of dishes to be cooked for the vigil and, unhesitatingly, she had turned to Kate for help. At this time of year, even if there had been no vigil, usually the Manor House would organise the mid-summer revels – already the wood had been piled up for the bonfire last week. Yes, the young maid was going to get much experience over the next days which would put her in good stead for the preparation of future feasts!

Mrs Jones neither read nor wrote well. Accordingly, she was teaching her willing pupil to hold all the ingredients – the amounts and the order of assembling them – in her head as she did. Mrs Jones had discovered that Kate had begun going over them to keep them fresh ever since she had attained her tenth birthday. The child had been living in this house since she was five, doing all sorts of tasks and duties but, apparently, it was the cooking that had caught her imagination. Mrs Jones had noticed that, during the last year, Kate had made sure that whenever there were eggs to separate or blackcurrants to be washed or meat to be diced she would volunteer before her sister, Peggy. Not that there was any competition there. Peggy raced through life doing as little as she could, chattering to all and sundry, not resenting her jobs (not to Mrs Jones' knowledge) but working perfunctorily because her thoughts were on to the next task whilst she was doing the first still! The sisters were quite different; Peggy had a rather disorganised mind whereas Kate preferred order and routine. The two youngsters looked quite different too, with Peggy's stout body bursting buttons and ripping seams at least once a week, whereas Kate's slender bones left her clothes hanging from her shoulder – until that is…

Mrs Jones watched Kate squeeze the aromatic ingredients between her slim fingers. The girl had the beginnings of a bosom! She observed a tiny smile form on the damsel's lips and wondered if this change to her body was what was animating her. She had been a sober child, ever since Mrs Jones had known her, taking her responsibilities seriously, but now she was becoming a woman!

A movement out of the corner of her eye caused her to cry:

"Peggy! Be careful!" Remember there mustn't be a single drop of yolk with the whites or they won't whip! Kate, can you help your sister? And then you'd better go into the dairy and turn the cheeses. I need some soft cheese today. You said you had some, didn't you?"

"Yes, Mrs Jones."

Wiping her hands on a cloth, Kate rescued her sister and after checking the bowl of egg whites, expertly she divided six more eggs whilst Peggy edged towards the kitchen door. There it was! The youngest maid must be hoping that no one would observe her departure. Was this the answer? Perhaps it wasn't the different characters of the two sisters but the budding maturity of the one compared with the other! One very much remained a child whereas the other was maturing into a fine young woman!

"I've finished, Mrs Jones," Kate announced. "I'll go to the dairy and then be back to make the oat pudding. We have got those intestines haven't we?" The smile was gone. Kate appeared to be concentrating on the recipe. "And I'll need the saffron then and eggs. Is it all right for me to make it? You did say and I think people like the…"

"Peggy!" The housekeeper broke across her. "Where are you going? You must fetch the fruits the gardener has picked. Take this basket and don't dawdle on the way! Do you hear me, child?"

Carrying a jug of water from the kettle over the fire, Kate had left for the cool of the dairy room and Peggy had skipped out, swinging the basket from her hand and Mrs Jones was alone.

She was alone again right at the moment, but with no feast to prepare for a vigil, just a single meal for the servants, to be served later. How could the house be full to bursting one month and shrivel to emptiness the next? Never had there been no representative of the family dwelling here surely! Or was it just her advancing age that made her prone to loneliness?

Mrs Jones checked the simmering beetroot in the pan, grunted a gruff noise of warning towards the dog, daring it to run away, and then heaved her body into the rocking chair. Most days she contemplated going to see her sister, Keren. She had rejected the plan when she had first hatched it on the day of the funeral because she had decided that the new Squire would need her to take care of the estate, but now… Would it be inappropriate for her to ask Sir Edward for the loan of one of Owen Lewis' sons and the cart (the carriage had been taken by the master himself) and be away for a fortnight? Increasingly she believed that the running of the house – well, really it was just the cooking since the cleaning, dusting and making beds had been cut down to the minimum – could be left in the compact but capable hands of Kate.

And here was the young woman herself. Kate had developed not only a bosom since July but had grown several inches. Although she remained skinny, her added height gave the lie to her tender age.

"Mrs Jones?"

"Oh, I'm all right, dearie. Just my old bones aching. Where's that sister of yours?"

"She's coming with Hugh the Post. He's got a letter for you and he says it's from the Squire. And he has news. There's a sickness come. Half the village and people in outlying cottages have fallen ill."

"What kind of sickness?"

"Fever, Mrs Jones, fever and very loose bowels and much vomiting!" It was the post boy.

"Don't you come a step inside this kitchen!" commanded the housekeeper, getting out of the chair. Puffing across the room, she barred the doorway. "Have you visited any of these people?"

"Of course. The Parson has been kept very busy and…"

"Don't, I say! Don't come any nearer."

"But I have some post for you."

"Give it here then. Peggy, come away from Hugh the Post. Kate, stay back. Go, now! I won't offer you anything today, my man! Be on your way! We've no sickness here and we don't want it!"

"But don't you want me to read what is written?" Hugh protested.

"No, Owen Lewis will read it to me. Go!"

MARIANA

Mariana sat on her bed in the privacy of her room and stared at the two bottles which she held, one in each hand. They were identical in size, small enough to conceal in the palm of her hand, powerful enough to change the whole course of her life. One was made of green glass and one was colourless, although it appeared black because of its contents.

Mariana weighed each vial in her hand, up and down, whilst she tried to decide. How many times had she sat here, willing herself to make the final decision? Today, she had received a third bottle: larger and filled with a foul-smelling liquid which made her heave. Its smell was vaguely familiar, although she could not quite identify it. The answer sat on the very edges of her memory. This new bottle had arrived with a letter from Penelope in which her sister apologised for the delay. It was nearly ten days since her visit to Penelope. The letter explained that Penelope's arm had remained swollen and thus the handwriting was Robert's. Here Robert had included a note from himself that he was spending all his spare time writing letters to his wife's friends, but he was grateful not to have to write out all of her diaries too! Mariana had skipped Robert's comments, which appeared regularly through the missive, and raced on to what her sister was saying to her. Penelope explained that the bottle contained the solution to Mariana's current problem without mentioning it in words. Obviously Penelope had not shared Mariana's troubles with Robert. The medication had been bought from a travelling peddler who had assured Penelope that his 'elixir of life' would produce the desired effect. Then the script had described details of the past few days on the farm and was full of trivialities.

Mariana put down one of Mrs Williams' bottles and picked up the one from Penelope. Nowhere were there any instructions on how much to give or how to administer it. When she had received it, Mariana had decided not to use it; as it had turned out she did not need it now. She was grateful to her sister but Penelope might as well have saved herself any time or effort, since she herself had been to see Mrs Williams.

The last week had been frustrating in the extreme. When Mariana had returned from to the old crone, she had resolved to act quickly. However, Griffith had greeted her with the news that he had to go and help at the funeral of one of his old friends, another clergyman, who had been an incumbent near Betws-y-Coed. Mariana could scarcely protest without giving a reason. Whilst Griffith was away she had considered taking the potion for herself, but her natural horror of disposing of the baby convinced her that she must at least try with her husband one more time.

When Griffith returned, he had shut himself away in his study, explaining to her that he was behind with all his work and had not even started on his sermon. Mariana had chafed at this further hindrance. Once again she thought about her medicine; once again her heart contracted against it. Never had she been so indecisive. Never had she been so alone.

Last evening and the evening before she had stood with the bottle poised over Griffith's food, but on both occasions she had been interrupted: the first evening by the Parson himself and then by the housekeeper. She had understood then that this was not going to be an easy task, but tonight she would go down early to the dining room. She had to succeed or there would be no decision to make; she would have to take the medicine for herself. She picked up the colourless bottle and squeezed it in anguish. If she did not triumph tonight, then, she promised herself, tomorrow she would drink this black mixture and be done with it.

There came a tap on the door. Elin poked her head around the door. Mariana thrust the bottles under the covers of the bed. Slipping the green bottle for Griffith into her pocket, she stood up to greet her maid.

"Why, Elin, whatever is the matter?"

Elin's eyes were misty with unshed tears.

"Oh, Miss Mariana, I was just coming to help you dress when I met your… your husband. He says that he's been to see my… my family, and he says that I'm to go straight away. They've got the sickness and he thinks my father is… is dying."

"Oh, Elin," grunted Mariana, encircling her maid in her arm. "You must not delay. Never mind about tidying up the room or anything. Just go! What about the carriage?"

"No, Miss, no! I don't want any trouble here. If I don't tarry, I'll be there soon enough."

"Of course. Don't waste a moment."

"Will you manage, Miss Mariana... Mrs Owen? Biddy has gone over to the Manor House, and Rosie's little boy is unwell himself so I'm not..." Elin's anxiety was written all over her face.

"Elin, you know me! I'll throw all my clothes in a heap and curl up like a cat and sleep all night through. Don't worry about me. I had no idea the house was so chaotic. Come now."

With their arms linked, the two young women walked down the stairs. Mariana's thoughts remained disordered and hardly was she aware of what others might think of mistress and maid walking close until they met the housekeeper. Elin must have seen the same look of disapproval as Mariana because she tried to withdraw her arm but Mariana tightened her hold.

"Stay as long as you like. Only come back when they're out of danger," Mariana instructed Elin, releasing her maid at the threshold of the servants' quarters.

Mariana turned to speak to the housekeeper, who was striking the gong possibly deliberately. Mariana marched into the dining room. If only *that* grim woman would catch the sickness and die rather than Elin's father. She allowed the door to close behind her and glanced around. It was empty of servants or master! She reached inside her pocket for the potion. Should she put the drops into Griffith's soup? It was served already on the table, sending up clouds of steam to the ceiling. No, for the Parson would drink wine with his meal and she would never persuade him upstairs in an hour.

At that moment, her husband entered. His features were drawn and he had not changed his clothes as was his custom before the evening meal. He looked utterly exhausted. Mariana stepped towards him.

"Griffith!" she burst out with a smile. She must remember to be charming tonight. "Come and sit down and eat. You look worn out."

"Thank you, my dear. I have been out all afternoon and have been to four houses where there is the sickness. '**I was sick and ye visited me.**' I saw your maid's family. What is her name?"

"Elin."

"Has she gone to them?"

"Yes. I sent her post-haste. I appreciate you for allowing her to go. She rarely takes any time off for herself and, although she doesn't often visit her family (because she and her stepmother don't.... don't get on), she loves her father dearly. Is he very sick?"

"Unto death," proclaimed the Parson ominously. "Now let us thank the Lord for His many mercies to us." He began a rambling prayer which covered not only gratitude for the food but also the sick people of the parish. Mariana allowed her nostrils to be filled with the aroma of the soup whilst she planned what she was going to do.

For a few minutes after the prayer was finished, neither of them spoke. Then, when Rosie made an appearance, Mariana enquired:

"Is it the same sickness everywhere?"

"Yes and the death toll is high. Let us hope our Father will be merciful. **'O spare me, that I may recover strength, before I go hence and be no more.'** Mr Lloyd is being kept very busy, but there isn't much that can be done to alleviate it. There seems neither rhyme nor reason to who survives. Often the weak recover and the strong die."

"Should you have gone yourself, Griffith?"

"My dear, as I have already said, Jesus commands us to visit the sick," rebuked the Parson. "'**And the King shall answer and say unto them, Verily I say unto you, Inasmuch as ye have done it unto one of the least of these my brethren, ye have done it unto me.'** We have to imagine that each one of these people is Jesus and treat them as you would treat Him. You went to see old Mrs Williams recently, didn't you? That's commendable."

Mariana flushed. She did not want praise; her motives had not been pure! She explained about the gammer falling whilst she nodded to the maid to take her soup plate away.

Again the room was silent because of the presence of servants and both man and wife were preoccupied with their own reflections. Mariana did not feel any tension and she allowed her mind to dwell on its usual problems. She was beginning to have doubts that this was the evening when she would be able to seduce Griffith. He seemed irritable in his tiredness and yet she was desperate to solve her dilemma!

Without warning, Griffith exclaimed:

"I'm not hungry! I've seen and smelt things today that…" He pushed his plate aside and stood up. "I think I'll go to my study…"

"Wait!" cried Mariana in a panic.

"What is it?" he thundered.

"Nothing. I'm sorry. It's nothing."

With her husband's departure from the table, Mariana lost her own appetite. Her schemes had failed! She was just about to rise when Rosie returned. There followed a short discussion which ended up with the mistress not leaving, but sampling an almond pastry which Rosie herself had made, following Cook's instructions. Not only was the food delicious but it gave Mariana an idea. Maybe all was not lost! In fact, Griffith's early retirement from the table might just serve her purpose. If she held back until later and then took him something to eat, with the potion dropped on it...

"That was excellent, Rosie," she complimented the other woman. "Not too heavy. You'll soon be taking over from Cook."

"Oh, don't say that, Madam. I've caused enough discord here already."

"Discord? Is it because of your son? Is he better? Elin said you were worried about him."

"Oh, he's recovered. He wasn't eating and I thought he might be coming down with the sickness but I found out that he had been nibbling all afternoon when Cook was making your meal. I wasn't watching him because I was concentrating on the pastry."

"What a relief! So, what were you referring to? Have you got into trouble with Mrs Beacon?"

"No, Madam, I shouldn't have said that. I'm very happy here. I want to give you my thanks for what you have done for my Ted and me. That man! He was a..."

"Was he your husband?"

"No, Madam. I... I am a widow. Ted's father was... was killed in the war."

"I'm sorry."

"No need to be, Madam. It wasn't recent..."

"Where did you come from originally? Or was your husband with the fair too?"

"No, Madam. I came from London. That's where I lived with my husband. I was offered a job with the fair after he died. I took it. Soon enough I found out my mistake."

"Don't let anyone else bully you! You've been very discreet tonight and not admitted that there is any strife between you and the housekeeper but don't let her bully you either. It won't be good for you or your son if you leave one bully and end up under another! Incidentally, where is she? Mrs Beacon?"

"She has lost a locket somewhere and is looking for it, Madam. That is why she sent me with the pastry."

"Yes, the pastry was delirious. Could you leave it here? I might have some more later. Would anyone notice?"

"No, Madam. Mrs Beacon would be the only one to notice and she's in a fluster because of this locket."

"I suppose she thinks someone's stolen it."

"Oh, I hope not, Madam! She will point the finger at me."

"No, Rosie, that's not just."

"Well, Madam, I am a newcomer and a foreigner and…"

"If you have any difficulties, you send her to me. Now don't forget. I employed you and you are answerable to me only."

Mariana carried the food up to her room and laid it on her windowsill with care. To her surprise her bed had been straightened out and the covers turned back. Even some of her clothes had been folded. Had Elin returned? What a boon she was, and she was the closest person Mariana had to a friend nowadays. Yet Mariana could never quite bring herself to bare her soul to her. Was it lack of trust? She knew that Elin was a great talker but if she ever specifically requested Elin to keep a secret, the maid did. So, it must be more than that. Was it their different stations? It could not be anything to do with age or sex since they were of a similar age and generation. But then was age important anyway? Her father had been her companion in many ways. There again, often she had kept facts from him because she knew he would have disapproved of them as too frivolous. Henry had been her friend. Would he agree with her plans to get rid of the baby? She did not know. It was not something she had ever thought to face. What about her sister? Was she an ally? She had hesitated even at speaking to Penelope about the true situation. Penelope was almost old enough to be her mother but Mariana had not felt she could confide in her. In the past she had found that Penelope had some very strong views on certain topics! Without warning she would speak vehemently against something one had said. Mariana reckoned that her sister was prim, in spite of her married state, and she had very strict moral codes which must arise from her religious beliefs. She *had* sent the potion.

Strange how it had turned out! That, in her time of need, she had no one to appeal to for help. She stood by the window and stared, unseeing, towards the garden. She felt forsaken. She might be surrounded by others (family, husband, maids) but still she felt isolated. What was to become of her? Her married life seemed particularly lonely and it stretched ahead of her, forever.

Griffith. Her husband. The Parson. He had been very untalkative tonight, probably because he was tired, but then they never really communicated. They would speak of other people and everyday matters, but she suspected that if she told him some of her views of life, he would lecture her. In the first few weeks of her marriage she had been sunk in that awful lethargy and once she felt better from that, she had been trying to please Griffith by her manner and conversation. She did not want to alienate him anymore. Never once had she ventured her opinion, especially if she believed it would go against his own. She knew Penelope and Robert were not just partners in marriage, but they were good friends too. She and Griffith were not that! No indeed! Could it be because Griffith was years older than her? No, for her father and she had related well together. Maybe it was because she did not love him. Surely it was not because of their separate tragic secrets?

Mariana sighed and picked at the pastry on the plate. Why was she feeling so moped tonight? Usually she was irked by Elin's endless chatter and yet, this evening, she would have welcomed company. She placed her hand on her stomach. When she was naked, she could see the swelling: the child.

"Are you there, baby?" she murmured. "Can you hear me? Why did your father have to die? He would have known what to do in this situation. But then if he had still been around I wouldn't ever have married my present husband. I wonder who your father really was? Do you know that I never knew his real name, but I liked him? He was easy to talk to and he wasn't a prig. Well, look at it like this: if he had been, you wouldn't be here now! Ridiculously, he regretted loving me. I didn't! You are a problem to me, but I wouldn't have missed that experience for anything. No, my mistake was marrying the Parson. If only I had known about him. No, if only I could hide where you came from I might be able to find happiness." She stroked the front of her gown. "No, I would still be lonely. Even if my husband and I did… did lie together, he doesn't ever really talk to me. I have to hide my true self. I told your father once that I had to hide myself from my betrothed too. His name was Henry. If I'd married him, you'd never have come along. Nevertheless, Henry and I could not talk about everything. I wonder if your father and I had known each other for longer whether we would have been able to talk about everything. We certainly had some very interesting discussions together, like we are doing now. Why am I talking to you?"

Mariana moved away from the window.

"I can't kill you," she lamented loudly. "I ought to. I have the potion, but I can't do it! No, I must do it. I must kill you. I must kill you."

She flung herself on to her bed and buried her face in the covers.

"Dear God, help me, help me," she prayed.

Where was the bottle? She would do it now and no more indecision. Where had she left the vial? She had kept both receptacles hidden behind a piece of loose panelling in the wall. She arose and hurried to her secret place. She prised open the wood but the space was empty. She felt inside her pocket. One of the bottles was in there. She had taken it to the meal, she recalled, and the other one and Penelope's bottle she had… done what with? She had stuffed them under the covers when Elin had come in. Elin. Elin had made the bed. Had the maid found them?

Mariana walked slowly towards the bed with her heart beating wildly. They had to be there, but she knew they were not for she would have felt them a few minutes ago when she had lain there. Elin had found them! She glanced around the room. Had the servant moved them? On the table beneath the glass was her perfume bottle, amidst the creams and paints, but there were no other bottles. Be calm, she urged herself. Elin would not realise what they were for. Probably the maid would ask her about them when she returned. She could say that one was to help her nausea and the other… the other… She would have to think of something. At least, she had the one she needed for the Parson still! She must stop wasting time and prepare herself for him. After all, this was to be her bridal night. She must not worry, for Elin was loyal to her. Even if the other girl knew the truth, Elin would not tell anyone. Thank God she had the green bottle in her pocket! If Elin had moved that one, all her plans would have gone awry!

Mariana stood in front of the glass. She had taken a long time to prepare herself and, at last, she was satisfied. She had washed in cold water, since she did not want to order hot water from the kitchen. She had applied just a dab of perfume because she was not sure if Griffith would approve. She had braided and unbraided her hair several times. Finally she had decided that her husband had seemed to like her hair loose last time and thus it hung down her back as glossy as a mane. She had removed her cumbersome petticoats and was dressed simply in her shift. She had administered the five drops of liquid carefully to the slice of the pastry and she was ready to go.

The house was quiet except for the ticking of the clock, but she surmised that her husband had remained in his study, for there were candles alight on the stairs. She knocked timorously on the study door, not just because she was nervous as to whether Mrs Williams' magic would work, but because she was aware nobody was allowed to disturb Griffith once he was in his study. She was rewarded with the door being opened.

"Mariana! Is everything all right?"

"Yes. I… I wondered if you were hungry. You ate so little at…"

"That's very thoughtful of you. Come in."

Griffith took the plate and Mariana followed him into the study. This was her first time inside his sanctum and she glanced around but the room was unilluminated, with its corners hiding in shadows, because there was only one candle supporting a flickering flame.

"Oh, I'm sorry about the dark but I was praying. '**But thou, when thou prayest, enter into thy closet and when thou hast shut thy door, pray to thy Father.**' I'll light some more candles."

"No, please don't," contradicted Mariana. "I think it's… er… snug like this. May I sit down?" Griffith nodded. "Aren't you going to eat?"

There was silence whilst the Parson devoured the food and then he began to mumble:

"I was feeling hungry and faint. Maybe what I needed was a sweet pastry." He looked at her. "You're ready for bed. Your lovely hair is unbound." He rubbed his eyes. "Can I help you? You've never been in here before. Is something troubling you? I'm sorry I was irritable earlier. Dizzy. I feel dizzy. God is in control. All life. All death. Barbara died of the sickness. But if she hadn't, then I wouldn't have married you. You are so ravishing, Barbara." He stared at her in confusion. "No! You are Mariana. Beg pardon! My head is spinning."

Mariana moved towards her husband. Initially she had waited for the potion to start to work. When he had mentioned her hair, she had hoped that his pulse might have quickened at the sight of her disrobed. Now fear, not desire, was racing through her blood. Griffith seemed disorientated and almost delirious. Was it the potion which she had given that was making him ill?

"Griffith?"

"Yes, m'dear. I'm sorry but I'm not feeling well. You see, Barbara, it's not my fault. I think I had better retire. I don't think I can finish the sermon tonight. Can you give me a hand?"

The Parson rose unsteadily to his feet.

"It's very dark, my dear. It's all so very dark," he whispered before falling with a moan to the floor.

Mariana froze in horror, scanning her husband's prone figure. Sweet Jesus, what had she done? She had measured the drops very carefully and a month had not passed since she had been to see Mrs Williams. Had she killed him? She knelt beside him. No, he was still alive.

Mariana ran across the chilly hallway as the clock struck eleven. She opened the door to the servants' rooms. There were no candles burning here and it was unfamiliar to her. She halted.

"Mrs Beacon!" she screamed frantically. Her own voice echoed back along the empty corridor. "Mrs Beacon, come quickly! It's the Parson."

Much to her relief, a light appeared at the end of the passageway and here was the housekeeper, candle held aloft, fully dressed and not retired for bed!

"What has happened?" Mrs Beacon's voice was as cold as the floor under the thin soles of Mariana's flat indoor slippers.

"My... my husband has fallen," Mariana stammered. "He... He is ill and I think that we should..."

"Get out of my way!"

Mariana was pushed aside and left to follow in the wake of the servant. She felt like a child who had been dismissed. She stubbed her toe in the dimness and silently cursed the housekeeper for running ahead with the candle.

"Fetch John," Mrs Beacon barked at her over her shoulder as she entered the study. "Send him for Mr Lloyd."

Mariana turned to do her bidding but, without warning, there were the servants in their night attire in the hall, confusion on their faces. They must have been awakened by her eerie call reverberating around the house. Once again the mistress found herself excluded. She realised that her assistance was not only not required but not wanted. Whithersoever, she crept up to her own bedchamber and opened her window. Taking the bottle from her pocket she threw it as hard as she could into the velvet darkness. There was no wind tonight and no sound of breakers on the shore and she leant far out and gulped in mouthfuls of fresh air to try to calm her beating heart. No one must know! No one must know that she had given her husband a potion! She laid her head against the rough wood of the window frame and wept with fear.

ELIN

Along the muddy track and over stiles, slipping on the bedewed grass in the fields, Elin ran and then, when she felt that she might burst if she didn't catch her breath, she walked, but at a fast pace nonetheless. A nearly full moon shone from behind a veil of misty cloud, not exactly lighting her path but preventing her from tripping over rocks or logs as she scurried on. However, she did fall once in the copse at the brow of the hill because of the gloom amongst the trees. Before long she had a pain in her abdomen and she paused to bend over with a groan. Soon she pressed on, remembering Thomas' haste all those years ago when Mrs Jones had cut her head. On that occasion, quick thinking and a stitch or two had saved the life of the older woman, but today she doubted very much whether she would be able to save her father's life with such a concentrated effort.

Almost she called in at the Manor House but the windows were darkened and she reckoned that Mrs Jones and her sisters might be abed. Since she and Biddy had left with Miss Mariana – Mrs Owen – the staff at *Trem-y-Môr* was much depleted. She had heard that the Squire had gone away and, until his return, she supposed, there was no call for extra servants. She halted, overlooking the familiar house and a wave of homesickness swept over her. How she missed everyone here – they had become like family to her over the years! *And* there was Sir Edward too. How many weeks had it been since she had set eyes on him? Now she worked and lived at the Vicarage, any hope of being near him was gone. Deliberately, she had suppressed her feelings until rarely did she think of him, except at moments like this! Where was he? What was he doing? Would he ever come back? He had visited his sister, although Elin, herself, had not seen him, and from the Vicarage had returned to the Manor House, but from there, she knew not where he had gone. Not back to a captaincy, surely. Why did he stay away from North Wales? Was he seeking a wife before he settled down? Or had he no intention of returning?

For a brief moment, she allowed herself the luxury of picturing him in her mind – with peg leg and smart hat – and then she shut it out and allowed memories of her early childhood to take its place. These remained bright and clear but once that dreadful woman – her stepmother – had entered their cottage, Elin's home and life was lost forever. Yet if that witch hadn't come sweeping out their cottage, she wouldn't have been sent off to look for work and she and her siblings wouldn't have met up with Thomas and subsequently entered the Manor House for the first time. That day – that momentous day, although she hadn't realised it then – the family's abode had received a thorough clean; the walls brushed with the broomstick; the rafters dusted with a goose wing and the woollen bed curtains and bed linen flung over a rope line, but the lives of the individuals, who dwelled inside the croft, had been turned topsy-turvy too!

Almost never did Elin reflect on what the weeks and months would have been like if she hadn't come to work here, but remembrances flooded her as she began to half-trot again. She had not spent one night under the same roof as her stepmother, but her siblings had experienced a sharp taste of Widow Davies' rule during the time she, Elin, had made herself indispensable at *Trem-y-Môr*. However, when she heard the tales of Widow Davies' doings, she had managed to rescue at least two of her siblings, Kate and Peggy, from the brutality, after only a sennight.

Widow Davies! Straight as the pole to squeeze the water out of your clothes, with angry eyes and a caustic tongue! Widow Davies! Elin knew full well that the witch was her father's wife and therefore shared her own name, but to Elin she would always be Widow Davies. It wasn't just that the woman dressed in black every day of the year, it was the shadow she cast over the cottage and the rest of her brothers and sisters. Fear and cruelty. Subtle, of course, Elin had had to admit, so that her father didn't seem to be aware of what was going on, but apparently Widow Davies' stick could catch you unaware and from almost any angle and her little sisters had spent the last few days in their birth home avoiding both woman and wood. The young ones had arrived with red weals on the back of their legs and bumps on the side of their heads. From that moment, Elin, who had cared for the rest of the family with love and kindness after their own mother's death, began to loathe Widow Davies.

Seconds had passed, of course, and during the last six years, her elder sister, Anne, had escaped and was now married with children of her own. Elin's two middle brothers, thirteen and fifteen last birthdays, had found work as shipwright and glazier respectively, and both had fled the hearth once they were apprenticed. Only John, who had straddled her hip long ago all the way to the Manor House, and baby Mary, who had known no other mother than Widow Davies, were left in the witch's domain. John, at eight, had grown tall and helped his father in the fields and young Mary, seven next June, would be taken into service soon. Then none of her mother's offspring would be left and, Elin guessed, Widow Davies would rejoice. She suspected that if her father died from the sickness, her widowed stepmother wouldn't take long to marry for the fourth time without a backward glance!

By the time Elin reached the patch of land outside her family home, she was hot from the exertion and the emotions which the reflections had exposed. She paused to compose herself, observing that the vegetable garden had been neglected badly, and then pushed open the door.

Pungent smells assailed her and she recoiled and then re-entered with the end of her shawl across her nose. By the glow of a single rush light she saw the woman who had filled her thoughts just a few moments ago squatting over a pail in the corner of the room, moaning unintelligibly. Elin hastened across the room, past the open peat fire and gazed behind the partition. Lying in the family bed was her father – silent and motionless – and she moved towards him first, fearful that she was too late. Down his nightshirt was fresh vomit and she gagged involuntarily. Putting out her free hand she felt the warmth from his sweat-glistening brow and she exhaled a short breath of relief. Tucked at the edge of the bed were her two youngest siblings, both curled up, possibly against the pain of the illness, both giving small yelps in their delirium.

Having ascertained that all the family were alive, dismissing the thought that the Parson might have seen her relatives lying in such filth and squalor and how embarrassing that was, Elin began to clear up. She searched for a precious candle, not caring at the expense. If she was going to work all night, she reasoned, she would need something stronger than a rush light to light her tasks! Assisting her stepmother back to the stained sheets, she built up the fire ready for heating water for washing.

During the hours of darkness she lost count of the number of times she slithered to the soggy bank of the stream and back. Tenderly she washed and changed all four occupants of the cottage, even the hated Widow Davies, before pressing the cold water that she had collected to their lips and encouraging them to drink. She struggled to place clean linen across the straw of the bed, wishing she could replace the yellow strands with new, since all the patients were weak and querulous. At intervals, buckets and basins were used by the patients and, controlling her own gagging, Elin emptied these receptacles outside, rinsing them before leaving them at arm's length of the bed, ready to be used again. Unaware of her own stoicism, Elin toiled on, sweeping the floor, tending the fire, tidying the place, until the candle burned low and spluttered out in a puddle of wax. Only then did she crouch on the only chair and dozed, half an ear open for any cries for help. Her perseverance was rewarded by everyone falling into an uneasy sleep.

Elin woke with a start. Where was she? Dawn had broken and a murky light was seeping through the unglazed windows. Already she had decided that she would return to the Vicarage and beg bed linen and clothes for the family from Mrs Beacon's chest in the upper hallway. Was it too early to set off? No. She was sure the kitchen in her mistress' house would be bustling with servants preparing the first meal of the day. Checking once more that there were noggins of water nearby and basins for vomiting, she didn't even stop to explain where she was going. None of the people seemed to be awake enough to understand her. She left, gently pulling the door shut behind her. She hoped not to be too long.

Weariness slowed her steps and she didn't run today! She guessed it had been raining by the wetness underfoot but at present there was pale cerulean blue above her head. In the distance, underneath the ceiling of cloud was a line of loose puffs looking like the smoke from a chimney – as if the sky had lit its own fire and was billowing out the waste. The rain seemed to paint the grey masses a darker shade of black around their peripheries as the wind carried them away.

Elin was surprised that there was no one in the Vicarage kitchen and she wandered out into the servants' corridor in search of someone – anyone. It must be earlier than she had imagined. Then she heard a strident voice coming from the housekeeper's room:

"I loved him, you know, Cook. He was only a curate then but I loved him. I had no dowry but I hoped and prayed that he would notice me. I was somewhat of a beauty in those days. You wouldn't know to look at me now but then... But he didn't even see me. Instead he married Barbara. To think that he chose my thin, shy cousin and not me. All because she had a dowry. Do you remember her, Cook? Do you?"

"Of course, my dear. I think you should…"

"Well, I wasn't going to let anyone know that he had broken my heart so I upped and married my Mr Beacon. He was only a shoemaker and didn't care that my parents couldn't raise a dowry. We were married for four years. I had a daughter too. Such a sweet child, but when my husband died from the fever and Barbara asked me to come and be the housekeeper for the Parson, she said I had to leave Winifred behind. It took me ages to understand why I wasn't allowed to bring the babe, but I'm convinced it was because of her barrenness. My cousin couldn't bear to see me with a child when she couldn't have any! What could I do? How could I miss out on the chance to be near the man I had loved for years? And to have money and a roof over my head, for when Mr Beacon died, Winifred and me – we were homeless. I reckoned that the little one would have a better life if I could send her some of my housekeeper wages, so I left her with my mother and joined my cousin and her husband.

"It was all a mistake though. Not with Barbara! She and I became firm friends but Winifred will have nothing to do with me. She's married and has two sons. She lives in the mountains but I am not allowed to visit! She believes I didn't love her and that's why I left her. She won't talk to me at all!"

"I remember Barbara," Cook's voice was soft compared to the harsh tones of Mrs Beacon. "She made the most delicious preserves and her embroidery…"

"Oh, I'll say this for my cousin: she was a very talented woman. She came to accept that God did not want her to have any children and she threw herself into her duties as a vicar's wife. I never mentioned my daughter to her. Maybe she forgot that I had Winifred. The vicarage was always very quiet and I never brought the child here. I always went to her in my parents' home."

There was a pause or perhaps Elin just couldn't hear what was being said. Then Mrs Beacon was speaking again:

"I was devastated when Barbara died. She was such a good friend…"

"But didn't you hope that the Reverend would notice you then?"

"Of course not! No! Well, perhaps just in the very back of my mind."

"You must have still been quite striking. I remember the first time I met you, Mrs Beacon. What a head of hair you had! And you and the Parson had been living together for years. It's not unheard of, you know. To marry your housekeeper."

"It may be but it wasn't what happened. My dear Parson never gave me the slightest reason to believe that he was... that he loved me in return, and I was just happy to show my love for him by running his home smoothly, and I've done that, haven't I?"

Elin shifted from one foot to the other. She knew she shouldn't be eavesdropping and, although the revelations were quite interesting, she had to hurry back to her own family. Should she knock on the door and make her presence known? She lifted her bent fingers.

"And then he married that chit!"

Elin's hand stopped in mid-air.

"She's a slut, you know!"

Elin sucked her breath in! Her dear mistress – Miss Mariana – was no slut!

"She was trouble right from the start. She's as unlike Barbara as is possible. No accomplishments! No manners! And the things you hear around the parish... You would hardly credit it but I saw it with my own eyes. That Lloyd fellow – the surgeon or whatever he is. Here in this very house. I heard them arranging to meet and when I walked in they were kissing. Right here in the Parson's front parlour! But I didn't speak to the Parson. No, not me! I'm not a tittle-tattle."

"Why didn't you tell, Mrs Beacon?"

Elin had stood back from the housekeeper's room door but now she leaned forward to hear the reply. It couldn't be true what she was saying – Miss Mariana despised Mr Lloyd!

"I... I..."

"Did you dream she would run off with him and leave? After all, what can you do with a young woman when her tail is ripe?"

"No, I did not! How dare you! But what I've overheard tonight I shall report to the Parson when he's better!"

"Are you sure you're right? Murder is..."

Murder! Why were they talking about murder? Elin had no intention of leaving at this moment!

"Will you stop interrupting, Cook? Don't you want to hear what has happened?"

"Yes, I do."

"Well, I lost my locket, as you know. It's my only piece of jewellery and I've worn it every day since my grandmother gave it to me, when I was a child. I half wondered if it had fallen into the soup but surely I would have heard it. Then I thought it must have dropped when I turned back the covers on the Parson's bed. I've been doing that for every night for the last twenty years! I searched there and then I went into *her* room. How untidy it was! She never does a thing – leaves it all for the maids to pick up as if she was some kind of a lady! And some afternoons she just sits there and does nothing – not working on any craft or... Anyway, I forget myself. I went into that wastrel's room just perchance the locket had found its way in there. I know I have the right to go into her bedchamber but usually I don't. The door was ajar and I crept in. What chaos! I couldn't stand it! Clothes thrown down and the bedcovers crumpled and I knew no maid would straighten it out. Those two who came with her have both gone home to see their families! In the middle of the week! When it's not their half day off! But the Parson gave his permission.

"Anyway, I stood in the centre of the room and looked around. Before you could count to ten I was making the bed and picking up some of the clothes. I couldn't help myself. I heard it then – the chink of glass when I pulled up the covers and there they were. Two bottles – right in the bed. I opened one and it smelt horrible – like the poison I bought last year when we had that rat infestation. Do you remember? Well, I was a bit surprised. What was the Parson's wife doing with rat poison and in her bed too? But I took both bottles downstairs and put them on that top shelf at the back of the larder. If that was poison then it was dangerous and I didn't want any of the young maids finding it. I resolved to speak to *her* about it. Ask her if she'd seen any rats, and if she had, then why hadn't she asked for my advice, and then I got on with my evening tasks. I even forgot to look any more for the locket."

"Have you found it?"

"Yes, yes." The housekeeper sounded impatient with her fellow-servant. Elin remained motionless, in shock! What had her mistress being doing with rat poison and who had she murdered?

"Was it in Mrs Owen's bed?"

"Of course not! It had fallen down behind the table in here. Look! I've got it on again. I took it off when I brushed my hair yesterday morning and..."

"I don't understand. Why do you think that Mrs...?"

"Be quiet! Stop asking questions! I'm about to tell you. It was after the meal that I was passing *her* door and I heard her. She said: 'I must kill you. I must kill you.'"

"What!"

Cook's exclamation echoed inside Elin's head. Miss Mariana would never have said such a thing!

"Then I understood." It seemed the housekeeper hadn't finished yet. "I had heard the words myself, but who was she going to kill? And into my mind came an image of *her*. It was last week, if I remember aright. She was standing with a bottle, holding it over the plate of steamed fish which was laid out for my Parson. She was going to murder her husband and now he's upstairs and near to death. If he dies, I shall tell everyone that it was her. She killed him! Scheming hussy! She won't get away with it."

Elin listened no more! In a trice, she had run down the corridor and up the back stairs. She must see her mistress and warn her.

MARIANA

Mariana pulled her cloak more tightly around her shoulders and began to walk quickly away from the house and towards the sea.

She wanted to scream in defeat. What was happening? For nearly a fortnight she had not even glimpsed her husband, let alone been near him! As effectively as erecting a stone wall, Mrs Beacon had shut Mariana out of the nursing of Griffith. The housekeeper cared for the Parson all day and half the night, only sleeping when the sick man himself slept and then only in a chair next to his bed.

Mariana had watched for a chance to creep into Griffith's bedchamber. She planned that, when Mrs Beacon went downstairs, she could sidle in, but the other woman never left his side. Mariana noticed that it was Biddy who had to traipse up and down the stairs at the behest of Mrs Beacon. Even in the dead of night Mariana could not tiptoe past the guard, for Mrs Beacon was only dozing.

Mariana understood that the household had been rearranged to cover the crisis. Rosie had to make the meals instead of Cook, who, in turn, was doing Mrs Beacon's tasks. Biddy was expected to work all day, filling in any gaps whenever they appeared – as Mariana herself had observed – and, accordingly, Jennett was reinstated to answering the door and serving at table.

Mariana looked in vain for an opportunity to be at the bedside of her husband but Mrs Beacon refused to allow her over the threshold of his bedchamber. It was Cook who had informed her that the reason for this was because everyone was too worried in case the mistress was struck down with the same illness as the Parson. Meanwhile, Mrs Beacon had spoken no more than a few words to her. Part of Mariana accepted this – she and the housekeeper had never conversed easily, but to be treated to pursed lips and single word replies suggested that there was more to the housekeeper's denying access to Griffith's room than simply concern for the mistress. If the latter was the only reason, then wouldn't Mrs Beacon be civil to her and give her information about her husband's malady, not glare at her every time she saw her?

Mariana recalled hazily that Elizabeth Parry had mentioned something about the devotion of Mrs Beacon to the Parson. Was the older woman consumed with anxiety for her employer? All the same, what about her own fears? Surely a wife – however newly married – should be kept abreast of the plight of her sick husband?

There was a simpler explanation which nagged at Mariana, magnified by her own guilt: the housekeeper suspected that the mistress was responsible for the Parson's condition. But she had thrown the bottle away on that terrible night when her husband had collapsed and, she reasoned, Mrs Beacon could not have found the other bottles because the servant never visited her bedchamber.

A week passed and Mariana had no idea how the Parson fared. She was forced to abide by the housekeeper's reason for her being barred from her husband's bedchamber. She could not voice her conjectures; instead Mariana told everyone of the tireless and sacrificial work of the attentive matron. No one else seemed to have noticed the constraint between mistress and housekeeper.

Why was it that Mariana could not quite rid herself of the doubt that Mrs Beacon *did* suspect something? Was it because she had been unable to speak actually to Elin about the bottles? She had ridden to see the maid, who was continuing to nurse all the members of her family. When she had arrived at the mean cottage, Elin had urged her not to dismount or come any nearer. Contagion was the reason given, just like the housekeeper's excuse! However, whereas Mariana accepted the faithful maid's anxiety and turned Mars around without arguing, she couldn't be at peace about being excluded from Griffith's bedchamber.

Discomfiture, over her inability to speak to Elin, had risen in her throat whilst she rode home. Yet, she chided herself, what else could she have done? It would not have been wise to interrogate Elin about the bottles in a loud voice for all to hear. She was convinced that the vials must be kept a secret, since if it became known that she had potions in the house when Griffith was ailing, someone might start to ask questions.

This conclusion brought her full circle! Had the housekeeper already done so? Had the housekeeper found the other two bottles or had Elin taken them when she tidied up? Admittedly, it would be very uncharacteristic of the maid to remove her mistress' belongings from the room, but Elin had been distraught with worry over her family's plight. It was possible that she had taken them to her room in her haste to be away. Mariana had not searched Elin's quarters nor grilled any of the other servants, again not to arouse suspicions. No, best say nothing.

Nonetheless, if the housekeeper *had* found the vials, would that explain her strange behaviour? Desperately, Mariana wanted to believe that Mrs Beacon's total control of the sickroom simply arose from a possessiveness which came from nearly a lifetime of serving the Parson. Nobody had mentioned to her that the housekeeper was behaving oddly. Did everyone else believe that Mrs Beacon was just doing her duty? Mariana did not know, for the whole household was in upheaval.

Ever since the Parson had been struck down, the doorbell had never stopped ringing. It seemed that all the parishioners were very concerned about their vicar. Since Mariana had to have some information to give the endless stream of visitors, she was forced to resort to asking Mr Lloyd for reports on her husband's progress. She hated having to interact with Lloyd ever; she was very wary of him. What would he try this time? Therefore, she kept their conversations short and usually aimed to talk to him immediately he left Griffith's bedchamber in order that they were not closeted in a room together where he might be tempted to overstep his position again. Such was her desire to see him go, and her mortification over their last encounter, that she never even thought to question him about Jack.

Mariana had found the days dragged. She was no nearer to solving her own problem and, in truth, no longer did she have any potion to take, even if she did decide to rid herself of the child. Her heartache was aggravated by her anger at Mrs Beacon; she found that the days were prolonged into nights of tossing about in the bedclothes.

Over the last few mornings she had risen early to walk. Brisk exercise, whether riding or walking, eased her vexations and prevented her from screaming at the servants or beating down the door to her husband's room.

Her usual route led her towards the coast where Henry's body had been found, but she was saddened to admit to herself that, after the first day, she no longer spent time thinking about Henry; rather she was caught up with her present trials. Genuinely she was concerned about Griffith and full of self-reproach that it was she who had made him ill. Lloyd had informed her that the Parson was suffering from the same plague as his parishioners, but

Mariana could not quite accept this. It would have absolved her somewhat if she could have nursed him, but she could see no opening. Hopefully now that her husband was recovering (for Lloyd had told her that his condition was improving daily) she could insist upon seeing him. She would not be prostrated herself at this stage. No physician understood how these illnesses were passed from person to person, but neither Elin nor Mrs Beacon had succumbed and they had cared for their patients from the start.

Mariana stood and gazed at the horizon where sea and sky were indistinguishable. It was one of those soft, autumnal days which defied the onset of winter. The air would be warm later when the sun ripened but, for the moment, the yellow ball lingered low behind Mariana's back as if unwilling to surmount the hazy sky. Even the waves were undulating unenthusiastically towards the pebbles. However, the rules were made and the sea *had* to caress the land permanently and the sun *had* to travel across its dome and Mariana *had* to fulfil her duties and responsibilities.

Suddenly Marina longed to fling off the restrictions of her life as a married woman and the Parson's wife. If only she were free. Free to go where she liked, do what she liked and say what she liked! There were countless messages left unsaid between people, veiled with polite, clipped sentences which were meaningless. There was Mrs Beacon, who when she said the words, "The Parson is still indisposed," aligned her frowning forehead and eyes to say, "Keep away!" And then there was Mr Lloyd, who when repeating the exact same words as Mrs Beacon, allowed his eyes and mouth to invite her to, "Come near." Same words, different messages. And she was forced to pretend too. All those stilted, boring conversations she had to endure when people came to enquire after their 'dear Parson' whilst, she guessed, behind his back they were complaining about his sermon or the way he ran the parish. Hypocrites! Why did not people just say what they really thought? No, civility laid down the rules as firmly as nature decreed that the sun rise and set each day. Mariana was fed up of being polite and she wanted to do something different and spontaneous. If only she could be free…

Wait! Peradventure, she *could* be free! Crossing the expanse of grass to the beach, noting that parts of the sea remained wrapped in their misty night attire, she realised that if Griffith died she would be free. Not only free to leave the depressing confines of the Vicarage and the malevolent eye of Mrs Beacon, but free from her anguish over the child! Who would know, if

Griffith departed this life, that the marriage was unconsummated? No, she would be a widow and her child would be fatherless, not illegitimate. How could she have missed the truth of this? Why had she prayed for Griffith's recovery when his demise would be the perfect answer?

She almost gave a skip of delight. If Griffith's malady ended in death, she could return to *Trem-y-Môr* where she was among friends and where she was familiar with the routine. Oh, how she had missed it all! In the last weeks, she had gone several times to the Manor House and nothing had changed. If only she could live there again!

Mariana stepped gingerly on to the beach. The reluctant sun had not wiped away the dew from the pebbles and it was slippery. Like her own life! Optimism faded. She was walking on very unstable hopes here. Was there any chance of Griffith dying? Were her dreams improbable? Did such easy solutions ever occur in life?

Immediately she turned for home. She had to know for herself how her husband was faring. Were Mrs Beacon and Lloyd telling her the truth about him? Was he recovering or was he dying? She had to know. She had to know for herself because it affected her future.

When she climbed back up the slope of grass the early sun broke forth and bathed her with indulgent, apricot rays. She squinted against the brightness. The strength of the sun made her feel strong and determined. She would go now and insist upon seeing her husband. It was her right! Perhaps one unwritten rule of marriage which would work in her favour. After all, the guard shielding the Parson was only the housekeeper, whereas she was the mistress! She had been patient long enough. This hour she must find out the truth. Did Griffith even have the sickness which was rampant in their community? She had heard that others experienced vomiting and loose bowels but some were delirious. Was Griffith in a delirium? Was he close to death?

Two brown rabbits, which had come to sniff the morning air, froze nervously with fear as Mariana passed by. Normally she would have stopped to see their twitching whiskers and blackcurrant eyes but she gave them no more than a glance whilst they fled back to their burrows with a flick of their white tails.

Mariana revelled in the heat of the rapidly rising sun. What a mild autumn it had been! How clement the weather and how kind the sea! Today was the sort of day she would have swum in the sea for, although the water would be cool, the sun was hot. She had not been in the sea since that afternoon, months ago, with Jack. No chance these days! The Parson's wife had a groom in attendance and could not bathe naked in the gentle waves!

By the time Mariana reached the Vicarage the maids were scurrying back and forth with plates of food for her meal. Since she had begun to go for a walk each day her appetite had returned and the servants had responded accordingly. She paused. Should she stop to eat? No! She had resolved to deal with the housekeeper right away! Hence she marched straight up the stairs and rapped loudly on the door to Griffith's bedchamber.

Mrs Beacon opened the door a crack.

"Yes?" she frowned.

"I want to see my husband," demanded Mariana. "Now."

"Now?"

"Yes, now. And I think you should be using my correct title, Beacon. I expect you to call me 'Madam' when you address me. Let me by. I want no more prevaricating. I am the Parson's wife and I want to see him for myself to assure myself that he really is recovering." Mariana moved her foot surreptitiously towards the door ready to prevent the other woman from slamming it shut.

Incredibly it was Griffith who answered:

"Tell my wife that I shall see her in her bedchamber in a few moments."

Mariana opened her eyes in surprise as if somehow Mrs Beacon had replied using her husband's voice. He sounded well and vigorous and… and angry. Mariana lifted her head and called:

"I shall await you there, Griffith."

Mariana looked out of the window whilst she tarried for her husband. She could hardly believe that she was going to see him. Had he known that she wanted to see him? Could he have been intending to join her for a meal today? Would that explain the frenzied activity of the servants downstairs? She would be able to ask soon.

Her bedchamber was at the back of the house and overlooked the large, walled garden. Beyond the flower beds she could glimpse Anglesey, although the satin blue edges of the cliffs were hidden in the mists of the early morning. However, the lawn was flooded with sunshine and she could hear a blackbird singing. From the first day of her marriage, she had decided that the secluded enclosure must be a haven of peace with its high walls that protected one from prying eyes and wild winds. Yet she had never sat in it; she would have felt that the members of her own household could have watched her in the same way that she observed the gardener at work.

Mixed feelings swirled inside her whilst she waited. She was dispirited – how easy it had been to arrange a meeting with Griffith. She had not been forced to battle with Mrs Beacon at all! She was glad, on the one hand, that he was well enough to visit her in her room, because it meant that she had not poisoned him too severely; on the other hand, she was sad that the advantages of widowhood that she had worked out earlier had been so short-lived. Underriding these sentiments was curiosity. Why had he asked to see her in her bedchamber and not at the meal table?

Turning from the window she looked up as Griffith entered. He was dressed immaculately, all in black, in the suit that he used for special occasions. Had he risen from his sickbed to make an important visit? Yet the jacket hung uneasily from his shoulders. The illness had robbed him of the last of his protruding stomach and he looked not just shorter but like a different man. Contributing to his altered appearance were his blazing eyes. He seemed consumed with rage and Mariana had never seen him look at her this way. She shivered involuntarily.

"I have something to say to you…" he announced.

"I should hope you have, Griffith, since it is a long time since we have been in each other's company." She hoped that her light reply would lessen his ire, but it appeared to increase it. What had she done wrong?

"There is no need to be frivolous." Griffith moved towards her whilst he spoke and she found herself with her back pressed to the windowsill.

"What I heard yesterday morning has made me stir myself from my bed." He halted. Mariana sucked in her breath. "I was told yesterday that the reason that I have been so very ill – nigh on death – is that I was given a dose of poison by my wife."

Mariana opened her eyes in horror when Griffith produced the bottle which Penelope had sent her.

"Ah, I see you recognise it!" His lip curled. He put the vial back in his pocket. "I knew…"

"No, I…"

"Don't!" he roared, stepping forwards, almost jumping the last few feet between them. "Don't deny it. I have a witness who says that she saw you trying to give it to me on several occasions. The night you finally succeeded was the night on which I fainted."

Griffith grabbed her shoulders with iron fingers. Mariana could not take her eyes off a bubble of spit which had formed on the edge of his mouth and was threatening to fall on his long wig at any moment. Her attention was brought back forcibly to what Griffith was saying when she heard:

"The reason I am so furious is because of your motives for trying to poison me. You are consorting with another man. Lloyd. And don't try to deny that either for I have heard him confess it with his own lips."

He released her but before she could move he slapped her across the face. Mariana's head was flung backwards with the force of the blow and she hit it on the edge of the window alcove. For a moment she was stunned and then Griffith was striking her again and her head wobbled from side to side like a doll's head loosened from its body.

She hardly heard his gasp:

"How could you do it?"

Her senses were spinning, pain shooting through her and she sank to the floor, her palms covering her face. Would he stop now? she cried silently. Yet, far from being halted by his wife's collapse, Griffith seemed more enraged, and he began to tear at her clothes.

Mariana sat leaning against the wall, unresisting, whilst she tried to steady her reeling head. She pressed the back of her hands over her lips as layer after layer of her clothing fell away. All reasonable thought was driven from her. Just one question drummed in time to the throbbing of her bruises: who was this stranger who had taken over her calm, Bible-loving husband?

When he reached her bare skin, he gave a growl of anguish.

"Ah, it's true!" he stormed. Her swelling abdomen was revealed. "You're carrying another man's child!"

For a brief second he moved away and weakly she prayed he had finished with his assault, but then he cursed, "You harlot!" and he was upon her once more.

Unconsciously she curled her knees to protect the child while he aimed blows upon her white, naked flesh. Shock and pain clouded her senses but a basic animal instinct to escape made her turn on her side. A fist in her eye earlier had left her vision blurred and her disarrayed robe hampered her efforts to avoid his punches. She was on her hands and knees when she heard him stripping the last remains of her petticoats away to reveal her legs and buttocks. Like a wild beast he grabbed at her hair and she came up short when a fresh agony shot through her head. She twisted, trying to free herself, but he wrapped the long strands around his hand and she was jerked still.

Mariana spluttered as blood from a cut on her cheek ran into her mouth. What was he doing now? His hold on her black tresses never lessened but he was no longer striking her. She tried to look over her shoulder and, out of the corner of her eye, saw him undoing his breeches with his other hand.

"No, Griffith," she sobbed.

"I'll show you," he spat at her whilst he pulled her hair until she was upright on her knees, half-dressed, half-undressed. With one swoop he had her on the floor and she stared up at him.

"No," she repeated. Strength sped through her veins and she began to fight back, catching at his fingers which still entangled her hair in a painful mesh.

He released her locks and encircling her thrashing wrists with his own hand forced her arms above her head.

"No, Griffith, not like this. Not now! Stop! Please stop!" she groaned. "You don't understand. I…"

Her words did not appear to pacify him.

"I *do* understand what you have done. I am your husband and only I have the right to… I am going to show you what you could have had from me."

Mariana turned her face from him despairingly; then she cried when a new pain assaulted her. Roughly he forced her legs apart with his knee and thrust himself inside her, again and again, passion and anger making him beyond reason.

She lay beneath him, inert and subservient, her strength gone with the same suddenness as it had come, and wept in agony and shame.

SPRING

FRANCES

Edward leant forward carefully against the swaying of the carriage and grasped his wife's hands.

"Well, Frances, we are nearly there," he advised her. "I do hope that you like my home."

"My dearest Edward, of course, I will," she laughed in reply. "I have seen so much of the south of England but both the countryside we've seen today, and now the deep turquoise colour of the sea in these parts, remind me of Portugal. However, apart from all this, if you are happy here, then I shall be. All I want is to be close to you for the rest of my life."

Frances frowned when Edward released her hands and sat back to look out of the window. She knew she should not have said that final sentence but she could not stop herself. She loved Edward Rowlands and the last few weeks had been as near to heaven as she had ever found.

She remembered incredibly clearly the day they had married. An image flashed through her mind of the mysterious, dark interior of an ancient church with just the front pews filled with their wedding guests. Was this when her cup of happiness had flowed over? No! The day she had thought her heart would split with joy was the day he had asked her to be his wife. Was it really four months ago? It might have been yesterday!

Edward had returned from North Wales in a sad mood. Yes, she had noticed it, although he had tried to hide it. He had resided with his aunt in the same house as Frances and had not just set about encouraging her find out what had happened to her father, but also escorted her to many of the famous sites in and around London. Outwardly he had been in a charming, jolly mood, teasing his aunt and, with the passing days, her too. But she had observed the look in his eyes.

What had happened in North Wales to bring him back to London in not much more than a sennight? He had not said. When he had left her he had hinted at marriage, but he had returned single and very soon afterwards proposed to her. He had never mentioned his 'friend' near his home and she had been too frightened to ask him in case he retracted his proposal to her. Yet, why did she fear this when the reverse was true? It had been *she* who had nearly thrown away her chance of paradise!

Her mind was filled with pictures of the sunny parlour in his aunt's house. Frances had grown fond of the elegant town house where Anne and Richard – they had insisted that she did not address them as 'aunt' and 'uncle' – lived. The previous owner had been a silk weaver and all the rooms had high ceilings with cornices. There was much panelling – mellowed with time and polish – and in the parlour carefully chosen pictures adorned the walls, a thick rug reached almost to the edges of the floor, and there was an abundance of chairs so all the family could meet and converse in this room. The house wasn't filled with expensive objects like her father's home in Portugal but the main rooms were redecorated each year, in accordance with the fashion, and Frances felt relaxed and comfortable within a few days of her arrival.

Her bedchamber was at the top of the five storeys and tended to be rather cold; increasingly she chose to sit in the agreeable parlour, usually in the company of Anne. Nevertheless, on that morning, she was alone when Edward entered through the grand door, his wooden leg sinking into the blue-grey carpet.

"Frances?"

"Oh, Edward, how timely! Here is the latest letter from my uncle and I was just about to reply to him. I would appreciate if you would advise me. He wants me to go and stay with him in Ipswich, but I feel I should remain in London until my father reclaims his possessions. What do you think?"

"How is his gout? No better?"

Frances scanned the indistinct script for the passage about her uncle's health. This was the fourth missive she had received, the first coming via the docks the day after Edward had departed for North Wales. As Edward had predicted, the non-arrival of her uncle, on that night when they had disembarked, was due to a very ordinary explanation: he was laid up in bed.

"He's still indisposed. And this is another reason why I don't want to descend on him! Entertaining guests can be quite tiring. But, I am worrying that I am a burden to your aunt and uncle. They have been incredibly kind and welcoming but it is possible to outstay your welcome."

Edward came towards her but did not pin her down on the settee.

"Frances," he began. "There is something I want to say. It's important. Will you put down your letter and listen to me?"

Frances closed her mouth with a snap. She had been about to continue but his solemn tone checked her.

"I'm sorry, Frances, that sounded rude. I am willing to advise you about your future and where you should reside but what I want to say to you may have some bearing on that. Do you mind?"

Frances smiled, immediately forgiving his interruption. She laid down the parchment on an inlaid walnut table by her side.

"Of course, Edward. I shall give you my full attention."

However, the man turned from her and limped across to the window. He appeared deep in thought and when the silence stretched between them, Frances' imagination conjured up several possible events which she did not want to hear him say. He was departing to take up another captaincy. No, worse than that! He was going to fight in the War. No, worse than that! He was returning to North Wales to marry his sweetheart.

No noise could be heard from the servants' quarters; no hawkers selling their wares were out this afternoon; no carriages were passing with snorting horses and no children played in the streets. Frances saw particles of dust floating through the haze of sunshine spreading from the window and across the pattern of the rug, possibly disturbed by the inhabitants of the room. Slowly they fell and nothing stopped them. She felt as if she was swirling down and down too.

"Edward?" Her nerves were in shreds! Had he forgotten her? She stood up and moved towards him.

He swung around and once again she observed such a depth of feeling – was it sorrow or grief or despair or all three? – in his eyes that she felt she was seeing right into his very soul. He shook his shoulders in a quick shiver.

"Frances, I wonder if you will do me the pleasure of becoming my wife."

Whilst he spoke, he crossed the distance between them and by the time he had her hands enclosed in his all trace of that dark emotion was erased. Where had it gone? Had she been mistaken? How had he learnt to cover such agony with lightness because his proposal had been said with warmth and sincerity? Was it all an act and, if so, what was she supposed to believe was behind those words?

Despite her confusion, her heart was shouting out her assent, overriding common sense with abounding joy! She pulled her fingers from his and looked away from him. Now it was her turn to be silent.

"Frances?" He sounded desperate.

But he would have to wait whilst she considered, as she had been kept in suspense a few moments ago. Why had he made this request if he didn't want her? She knew he didn't love her but they had spent many hours together and, apart from the melancholy, she felt she was getting to know him. There had been companionship almost from the first time they had met! Her love – oh, yes, she loved him – had grown without her realising it and she had longed and prayed for today but now… What was wrong with her? Was it the unexpectedness of it all? He had given no clue previously of what he was thinking. Or was it the manner in which he had made the proposal? The lengthy introspection as if he was plucking up the courage to ask her. Yet no one was forcing him to do it! What had been going through his mind just prior to those magical words being uttered? Had he been seeing another woman's face? It couldn't be that he was composing the question – there had been no flowery talk, just a conventional request!

"My answer is 'Yes' but…"

"Oh, Frances, I am thrilled. When you did not speak, I wondered if I was wrong and you had no feelings for me and…"

The door opened and Anne arrived, halting on the threshold of her own parlour.

"Ah, my dears, I beg pardon. I was looking for you, Frances, but I will come back later."

"Don't do that, Aunt!" Edward cried. "You are the first to hear. Frances has agreed to become my wife!"

Edward left her side and encompassed his aunt in a huge hug. Delighted noises, muffled by his jacket, came from Anne and before Frances could deny her acceptance, she was being included in the merriment. From nowhere came Richard and Edward's cousin, Sarah, and within minutes the entire household was aflame with the glad tidings. Frances looked from one enthusiastic face to another, aware of a sense of relief in the air, particularly from Anne, and suddenly her own doubts and concerns vanished. Who was she to bring this kind of rapture to an end? And why would she want to? Her own heart was alive with excitement. She loved Edward and surely love could overcome all things. Didn't the Bible talk of this? She gave herself up to the congratulatory speeches and beamed and beamed.

The wedding had been small and private but she had continued radiant. Even when she heard on the eve of the nuptials that her father was dead and she saw that Anne thought she should be grieving, nothing dimmed her rosy glow. The man who had treated her like a servant was dead! Killed in a shooting accident, she was told. In other words, one of his victims had fought back! She had wanted to shout, "Hurrah!" She did not care that if his will was found she would not be included, because she and Edward knew that she was sitting on a fortune. All her father's treasures were in her chests. Was this why Edward had married her? Her doubtful heart questioned. No, for when he had asked her he had believed, with her, that her father was even then making his way to London. If uncertainties ever raised their ugly heads she struck them down. Nothing would be allowed to mar her felicity; this would be her only husband – she would love him forever – and she was determined to appreciate and enjoy her short betrothal, the marriage service and the first night in his bed.

After his proposal, Edward had agreed to go and search for her relatives and, in particular, for her mother. She had wept secretly at the fear that now her father was dead she would be unable to trace her mother, but there had been no need. When they had tracked down her paternal grandmother, this redoubtable woman had told her willingly where to find her mother. She and Edward had travelled to Bath forthwith to see her.

Frances shook her head at the memory. Her mother was totally disinterested in her. She was living with another man who everyone thought was her husband and, it appeared, the last thing she wanted was for her grown-up daughter to arrive! If it had not been for her marriage to Edward, Frances would have been cast adrift in the world with nowhere to go. The older woman refused to see Frances alone and there had been no chance to find out her reasons for leaving her baby daughter all those years ago.

Frances had wept then that she had *found* her mother. If she had never found her, she could have kept her dreams, but as it was, the reality was too upsetting. Edward had witnessed this bout of weeping and had held her in a sympathetic embrace. Since then he had become her solace. It had been he who had suggested that rather than return straightaway to his estate, they travel around the country in order for Frances to explore some of England. Frances suspected that Edward's motives were not entirely pure. Maybe he did not want to return to North Wales himself, but she did not mind, since, once they settled at the Manor House, she would have to share him with all his responsibilities; whereas whilst they journeyed, she had him all day, every day, with her.

Together they had gone from inn to inn, without haste. Edward was the perfect husband; courteous and pleasant, caring for her needs – whatever she desired. They slept in each other's arms all night and rose late each morning. Once it became known that they were on their honeymoon, most of the innkeepers smiled indulgently at their patent love for one another.

Love.

Frances glanced at Edward, but he had his eyes towards the window. Was he avoiding looking at her? She loved him even more than when they had married, but he did not love her yet. She could not criticise his behaviour for, to all outward appearances, his actions were of a man who loved, but she remembered that never had he said that he loved her and he did not like it if she made any reference to her love for him. Was the latter because he felt guilty that he had married her under false pretences? Frances trusted not, for she had accepted his proposal with the knowledge that he loved another from the beginning. She had been trying to form the words to explain her perception of his feelings when Anne had walked in on them. Once the chance had passed, she had sworn to herself not to mention her concerns but, nevertheless, she hungered for him to share with her the heartache which shadowed his face often. Had she hoped she would not experience this again? No. You can't live with someone and hide every emotion from them, she argued to herself. They were too much in each other's company not to glimpse any inner heart anguish. Despite this, she dreamed continually that if she was patient, in the end he would love her in return. For the present, she must learn to keep her mouth shut. No, that was not fair. Those truthful words she had spoken a few moments ago – "All I want is to be close to you for the rest of my life" – had not been rash but deliberately said. She had wanted to remind him that he was loved by her. He seemed incredibly lonely and far away from her sometimes. He was lost in thought on many occasions. Where was he now, for instance? What was he meditating on? She could not guess but she had observed that the closer they travelled to his home, the more taciturn he became. Unlike in London, when mostly he was able to hide his sorrow behind a jovial countenance, recently he had appeared unable to keep up the pretence.

"Are… are you all right?" she piped up softly.

"All right? Yes, of course I am." He smiled. "I won't be sorry to arrive. It's been a tiring journey and the roads have definitely disintegrated in the last day or two. We must order a new carriage. What do you think?"

"Yes. I think that's a good idea," Frances smiled in return. They had no shortage of money. It was like living in a fantasy world. She had never had possessions or coins before and nowadays, everywhere they went, she and Edward bought things. Too much for everything to be carried in their coach! Many parcels had been sent ahead of them. They had written to tell those at *Trem-y-Môr* they were arriving and Edward had informed them that he was bringing his new wife. Frances was concerned that she would be a disappointment to the servants. She knew from Edward that there had been no mistress in the house since Mariana's mother. Nevertheless, no time to fret, because the horses were turning down a muddy track and here was the house in front of them.

The sky was overcast and the wind was whipping a froth of white lace on the waves, but, when Edward held out his hand to aid Frances, he insisted:

"We must go in the front of the house even if it is cold. It's not far and…"

"I can manage!" protested Frances with a laugh. "I'm not decrepit yet. Thank you, Wilson, your master helped me." She nodded at the man who had clambered down stiffly from the front of the vehicle and was waiting to assist her. "Edward, you didn't tell me how tall the Manor House was!"

"It probably isn't all that much larger than your home in Portugal, but it's not on one level. Would you like my arm?"

They had become accustomed to linking arms when they walked together. She believed that it helped to steady her husband when he wasn't carrying a stick and she never minded being close to her beloved. The strong breeze caught at her hair and hat and she lifted her free hand to prevent the headgear from blowing away. Perhaps they rounded the corner of the house, the full force of the wind hit them and they faltered.

"I'm sorry, Frances. Maybe we should go in the back and…"

"No. We're practically there. Who's that?"

Edward turned away from her to observe a woman marching towards them up the rough paving stones from the beach. The gale was behind her and it looked like it was trying to make her break into a trot. Her black tresses – half loosened from their pins – hid her face from them but Edward must have recognised her for he released her and declared:

"Mariana! I didn't expect to see you here."

He moved towards the other woman and the two met near the front door.

"Ah! Edward, have you just arrived?" Frances heard her call back whilst scraping her hair from her eyes. "I went for a walk and hoped to be back…"

"A walk?" Edward's surprise was evident. He stood barely a foot from her but did not stretch out a hand to touch her. Now it was Frances' turn to be surprised. If this woman was 'Mariana', then she was his sister, but no embrace occurred. Only her black gown blew against him, wrapping itself around his leg.

"Yes, I try to go for a walk each day." Mariana seemed to be busying herself, hastily plaiting her raven locks and then tucking the thick strands around her head before stepping past Edward. Offering a dainty hand to shake, she welcomed Frances.

Suddenly, Frances shivered and not just with cold. Yes, the wind was whistling through her clothes, in spite of her cloak, but she sensed deep undercurrents running between the other two people and she felt left out. Surely it was her husband's place to introduce her! She wondered how much longer they would pause here.

"Let's go in," suggested Mariana. "All the servants will be lined up to meet you." She pushed open the large door. "You had better go first, Frances."

Frances wanted to shrink back. Why was she upset? This young matron and Edward's frigid greeting must have unnerved her. Their exchange of words seemed innocuous, so what was wrong? And why didn't her husband cross the threshold before her? Each of them was hesitating. Yet, before they had arrived, Edward had been purposeful and decisive. He and she had been going to enter through the front door as Squire and mistress.

No opportunity to analyse! It must be some hidden family tension. One mercy, Mariana could not be the woman who had jilted Edward, that is, if he had been jilted. Frances withdrew the foot she had just extended. Whatever had made that notion drop into her head? She had purposed *not* to search among her husband's acquaintances for the probable woman who had broken his heart, but already she was dwelling on it!

"Thank you," she repeated. Thus far these had been her only words to her sister-in-law! "Edward?"

Frances went into the gloomy hall. It was only midday, but the candles should have been lit. Initially her two thoughts were that she was grateful to be out of the tearing gale, and that there were not as many servants as she had expected. A straggle was standing near the stairs and she found herself smiling. They looked even more nervous than she felt!

An elderly woman stepped out from the ranks and Wilson moved towards her also. She felt easy with Wilson, because he had been with them from the start. He must have walked in the rear of the house and round here before them. As usual he was immaculate. Certainly he did not look like he had been outside even!

"Wilson, how did you miss the wind?" she teased to break the silence.

"Ah, Madam, we should have allowed you to enter from the courtyard on a day such as this. May I introduce Mrs Jones to you? She is the housekeeper and cook."

Mrs Jones dropped an awkward curtsy and stuttered:

"Ma... Madam?"

Frances felt Edward come up behind her and grip her elbow and just then, from the back of the line of servants, there was a commotion. One of the maids had fainted. Immediately all decorum was forgotten. Frances watched her sister-in-law sweep past her.

"Rosie?" Mariana burst out whilst the others made way for her.

Frances looked at Edward for guidance. Did this constitute an end to the introductions? Edward's own face was white. Frances had no time to frame her question before Wilson was instructing her:

"I think, Mrs Rowlands, it would be best if you come into the parlour. The fire is lit and some light delicacies are available for you. Sir, your wife could meet the rest of the staff later."

Edward made no reply.

"Edward? I think Wilson is right, don't you?" Frances answered instead. What was wrong with her husband? What was happening? Edward had not spoken to her since he had seen his sister all those minutes ago outside.

"Ye... yes." At last he responded. "You go ahead. I'll just give a hand here."

"No need, Edward. Rosie's all right." It was Mariana. She had bent over the prone figure of the woman. Frances saw that the servant's eyelids were fluttering – she was reviving! "Oh, Frances, what must you think? What a farce! I hope you don't think we're all country bumpkins! Let us go into the parlour. Wilson, are you taking our cloaks?"

Mariana led the way and Frances followed her. She glanced around the room. How incredibly old-fashioned and cheerless! This room was practically bare of furniture. When she remembered of all the expensive tables and cabinets which had housed her father's treasures, this room seemed very crude. She hoped her bedchamber would be more welcoming. Nonetheless, the bright fire was beckoning and she moved towards it, putting her icy fingers up to the crackling flames. Why was she so cold? The wind had chilled her right through. Or was it the change which had come over Edward?

She swung around. It was impolite to stand with her back to the others. But there was only Mariana in the room.

"I must apologise," Mariana spoke in a bright tone. "Rosie has never fainted before. She must be sickening for something. We had a terrible sickness before Christmas which claimed many lives, including my husband's…"

The door opened and Edward came in. The colour had returned to his face. He held out his hands to his wife as he spoke:

"Everything is under control now, dear. What a beginning! Don't think too…"

"Don't mind me," intercepted Frances. "I'm not sure I approve of a servants' parade. I suppose it's so they can see what I'm like, but it must be an ordeal for both parties, especially when there is a language barrier. I remember some of the English wives when they first arrived in Portugal."

"Portugal?" Mariana said. "Have you been to Portugal? Is that where you met?"

Frances frowned at Edward. Had he not told his family about her?

"Yes," acknowledged Edward. "Frances and I met when I was out there…"

"Is that where your secret voyage was to?"

"Yes. Frances' father was anxious that his daughter did not get caught up in the war."

"I'm not surprised. No one wants to be forced to stay in a place when war is threatened! So, will your father be joining you later?"

"No, I have since heard that he was accidentally killed." Frances looked away.

"Oh, I am sorry!" exclaimed Mariana. "I did not mean to…"

"There's no need to apologise to Frances," put in Edward. "She did not have a close relationship with her father like you did with yours... ours. Why don't we sit down? We can catch up on all your news. I didn't expect to find you here. I hope you didn't come all this way just to greet us."

"I... I was unable to tell you..." she began in a fluster. "I hope you don't mind, but I have... I have been living here for... I would have asked you but we had no address to write to you at..."

"I don't understand," frowned Edward. "Why have you been living here? Is your husband away from Holyhead?"

"No... Griffith died just before Christmas and I..."

"Died!" Edward struggled to get up. "Do you mean to say you are a widow?"

Both the women stared at Edward.

"Of course she is, Edward," stated Frances, giving him an indulgent smile. "That's what a woman is when her husband dies. Now it is my turn to offer my condolences to you, Mariana." She faced her sister-in-law; Edward limped away to the window. What in God's name had got into him? He was behaving as if he had lost his reason.

Mariana shook her head.

"Like you, I wasn't heartbroken. Griffith and I had only been married a few months and, although we had become accustomed to each other, I could not say that I was grief-stricken. He lay delirious for a fortnight and then on the very day he left his bed, he had a relapse and the sickness took him. I suppose his constitution was weakened."

"What a shame though for the baby!" concluded Frances. She was curious when she saw Mariana blush. Had the younger woman not grasped that her gown did not disguise the fact that she was with child?

Out of the corner of her eye, Frances saw Edward glance at Mariana. Frances got to her feet purposefully. She was exhausted and wanting to change her travel-stained clothes and she did not understand all the friction between brother and sister. She had anticipated that it would be a strain to meet Edward's family, but it was worse than she could have imagined. Not because of the new people she was meeting. No, indeed, Mariana seemed sensible and kind. It was Edward. It was Edward who was behaving in such a strange way. Frances decided that she would be better able to cope when she had sorted herself out and unpacked a few of her belongings. Also, if she left Edward and Mariana alone they would be able to talk freely and iron out any difficulties which appeared to have arisen.

"Would you excuse me? The jolting of the carriage has given me a headache," she lied. Much to her dismay Mariana arose, exclaiming:

"How selfish of us! Let me escort you to your room. It's not a very big house, but you might get lost on your own."

Frances smiled. She liked Mariana. That was fortunate, because obviously her sister-in-law lived here and there could have been trouble between them. If there was to be disharmony it might be between herself and her husband.

"I'm sure Wilson would show me the way, but if you would like to accompany me, I don't mind. Edward?"

"You go ahead, my dear," Edward responded distractedly. "I'll join you when you've had a little rest."

MARGARET

Margaret leant her body against the massive iron-studded door of the round tower and stepped across the stone threshold. To her left was a staircase and before her an open door to the ground floor chamber which her son and his wife used as a drawing room. She knew winding down from this room was a narrow spiral of steps leading eventually to a dungeon built beneath the rock of the hill, because the parlour was the old guardroom where the custodians took their ease.

Ignoring the warm air wafting towards her from a fire that she could smell but not see, she began to mount the stairs, pausing on every third step. There was no banister but she put her hand on the worn stone walls, thinking briefly of all the soldiers who had run up and down countless times before her! Her bulky frame made her breathless but on the first floor was someone whom she wanted to see desperately and, however long it took her, she would persevere until she arrived. Fortunately she had to climb just the single flight of stairs and then there was a corridor with wooden floorboards to be traversed and she was there.

Soon another heavy door barred her way, but she pushed it open with authority and here was the object of her belaboured exertion and her reason for living: her grandchild. Her daughter, Susanna. Well, of course, Susanna was her granddaughter but Margaret loved her as her own for her son's wife had been abed with a fever since the delivery. The baby was in the arms of the wet nurse but Margaret claimed the child and the servant withdrew without protest. The maid knew who was in charge here.

Carefully cradling the precious bundle to her ample bosom, Margaret headed for the rocking chair set in the window recess. Built over 400 years ago, the castle had been made to withstand fierce attacks from enemy forces and the walls were ten feet thick. By each window was a deep alcove which gave privacy from the rest of the chamber. Not that there was anyone else nearby, but Margaret craved her solitary times with the babe.

Susanna was not robust; her tiny limbs were like sticks and her head was not much bigger than a man's clenched fist. Susanna's fragility had brought out all Margaret's motherly instincts; added to this was the relief that she had not had to suffer any pain to bring this infant into the world! Susanna's mother had laboured hard and long to give birth but that didn't concern Margaret. Here was the child, *her* child, born of her line, belonging to her, and she had no intention of sharing the babe with anyone else.

Crooning softly, rocking the chair back and forwards, Margaret closed her eyes and rested. The climb up the round tower stairs had been tough on her bones but worth it! By God, yes!

Whispering sweet nonsense, she adjusted Susanna's clothes and blankets, tucking everything tight around the thin frame. They were sitting away from the roaring fire in the room but Margaret believed that her own body heat would pass to the child.

Stroking the soft new skin of Susanna's cheek, Margaret allowed her mind to marvel at how far she had come. Was this really the Margaret Struley who had cursed nearly every day of her existence? How had she stumbled upon such contentment and from such an unexpected source? The Margaret Struley who had ignored her only sons when they were young; the Margaret Struley who had decided that motherhood was a hateful state; the Margaret Struley who had never imagined that living with her husband's brother could be increasingly peaceful and satisfying. How had it happened? How had her life turned around so completely?

The days and months flew backwards and with the child fast asleep, Margaret half dozed herself, recalling the past.

* * *

Margaret had driven away from her sister's farm – *Pen-y-Bryn* – in a high dudgeon. She was full of hostility towards every one of her relatives and determined not to forgive them. Recalling her weariness and hunger on arriving at *Trem-y-Môr* for her father's funeral, she decided that she would stay a night just a furlong or two from the castle in order that she could arrive fresh and ready to face her drunken husband and his noisy brother and wife and children. Consequently, she had rested the last night of her journey at the inn in Heathsfield, knowing her destination was almost within walking distance.

The day was surprisingly mild for autumn and shortly she was passing through the grand gates of her husband's ancestral home. First came boggy grassland, cropped short by sheep, and then there was the thick wood which squatted at the base of the final hill on which stood the castle. Margaret knew that in the olden days all the land beyond the moat was kept clear – no enemy army would be allowed to creep up unnoticed – but in recent times, when the occupants inside the walls were not at war with any of their neighbours, domesticity had prevailed and trees were planted to enable the lord and his lady to wander through in spring and observe the early bluebells and snowdrops. When the drive began to ascend, the road twisted round in a series of serpentine corners and once above the treetops she had views of the far distant peaks and dells. With increasing height Margaret saw the hills give way to their grander cousins – blue mountains, hazy in the morning light, growing paler and paler into the distance. A shimmering flash reminded her that there was a lake where fish was freshly caught before being hauled up to the service gate at the back of the castle and into the kitchens where a team of cooks would prepare wonderful dishes to tempt the palates of their superiors. In every direction lay the moors, dressed in greens and browns where her brother-in-law, Ralph, rode his splendid mounts, usually with a party of his boisterous friends.

"Nearly there, Madam." It was Perrin, sitting on the other seat of the carriage, who interrupted her thoughts. "I'm sure you are glad to be coming home."

Margaret didn't deign to reply. She had an entire head of different emotions, but, at least because of her shrewdness she wasn't exhausted by a bumpy journey or famished from hours spent between irregular meals.

Across the moat, the wheels rumbled on the wood, through the portcullis, which had never been closed in her time here, and then they were in the original cobbled courtyard with a gentle rectangular lawn set symmetrically in its centre. When the castle had housed a modest, loyal army there was no grass but again, now the place had become a family residence, a garden – albeit rather plain – suited the owners better.

Margaret descended from the carriage, immediately aware of the silence. Where were her rackety nieces and nephews? Where was Ralph's reined horse, munching on a tasty nosebag? Where even were the servants scurrying to fulfil their duties? It all seemed much quieter than she remembered.

To the left of the gateway they had just come through was a flight of eight wide, shallow steps leading up to the main rooms of the castle where Ralph and his family lived their unconventional lives – all in each other's pockets from dawn to dusk, laughing and playing and interacting with no rebate or hush! Yet today all was eerily silent.

No Tamberlein, the butler, ushered her in, and she stood undecided by the door leading to the Old Hall. This was an ill-lit room with dark oak furniture – chests and cupboards and unadorned settles – whose walls were decorated with spears and swords from a previous age. Its only redeeming feature was an enormous fireplace where great logs burned summer and winter. Guests were entertained in here after riding or when they first arrived and usually stood around drinking hot ale, their booming, hearty laughter clearly audible in every area of the castle. But all was deserted.

Margaret glanced behind her, wishing that Perrin had followed her in instead of going to their own quarters on the opposite side of the lawn. She was completely alone. At that moment she heard footsteps on the wooden staircase straight ahead of her which led to the salon and parlour and dining room on the middle floor before leading up to the bedchambers above. Still she hesitated, bracing herself to be greeted by Ralph or one of his sons. Nevertheless, she could not have been more surprised by whom she saw than if he had been an angel, for through the doors at the end of the corridor came her husband, Walter.

Both she and Walter gasped simultaneously and it would have been difficult to discuss which of them was more shocked.

Margaret glimpsed a picture of her young husband – the man whom she had not encountered for many years. Yes, his skin was wrinkled but his stance was straight and tall and his eyes were clear and responsive.

"Walter!" she cried as he pronounced her name.

"I wasn't expecting you!" They enunciated the same words at the same time.

"My dear Margaret." He spoke again before her. "I am delighted to see you, although I wish the circumstances could have been more congenial."

"What do you mean?" she snapped, foreboding filling her mind. "What has happened?"

"Let's go into the hall. We can talk there. I was just coming to find Tamberlein." Walter rang one of the bells which hung inside the front door.

"What has happened?" she repeated. "Tell me, at once."

"I will, my dear, but I think you should sit down and have a drink first.

Nothing has happened to our boys which needs to worry you and…"

"Who is it, then?"

"Ralph met with an accident some weeks ago and the household is still in upheaval."

"Is he dead?" Margaret couldn't keep the hope out of her voice.

"No, he is not, but he is incapacitated." Whilst they conversed, Walter tried to turn her towards the Old Hall but she refused to be herded in there.

"Where is he? Let us go upstairs and…"

"No, Margaret. He is still weak and should not be disturbed."

"Where is his wife?"

"Therein lies a tale. Please come with me. The fire will be lit and we can exchange news."

Margaret conceded defeat. This was a new Walter – strong and in charge. She could smell no liquor on his breath and his eyes were no longer bloodshot. It must be all of twenty years since he had been sober. She allowed herself to be led back into the frowzy vestibule, offered a tankard from the lately-arrived butler, curbing her impatience until she and her almost unrecognisable husband were alone together. No, that wasn't quite true. Here before her was someone whom she remembered from her youth – Walter in his prime!

During the following hour, she heard the story of how Ralph had set out one summer's day to hunt with a party of other men, all in high spirits. Ralph's horse had tripped on an unseen rabbit hole, which was serious enough but magnified by being less than a yard from a steep cliff. Ralph had been catapulted over the beast's head and down several feet to the bottom of a canyon, landing half in a rushing stream and half on the boulders that lay strewn across the rocky ravine. Carried over several miles in a makeshift stretcher, by the time the physician arrived, Ralph was barely clinging to life. Unconscious and with multiple breaks to his pelvis and legs, Walter had been summoned to pay his last respects. However, Ralph must have had hidden reserves of strength because on the third day he awoke, calling for food in his customary loud voice, and declaring that he would be riding by the end of the month. Unfortunately his confidence had taken a battering too and the prognosis was that he might never be able to walk again, let alone ride.

"The pain has been very debilitating," Walter explained, "and the bones have not set quite right. One of his legs is shorter than the other. He will always be a cripple but I think it is his spirit which has taken the worst knock. You know what a lively man he was – full of fun and active from the second he got up in the morning. Because of this, I'm convinced, the weeks of being chained to his bed, as it were, has disheartened him. I don't think it helps that his wife isn't here but he won't allow us to contact her."

"Where is she?" Margaret asked half-heartedly. Feverishly her thoughts were planning what all this would mean to her. One very obvious outcome was her husband's abandonment of the bottle and she would be grateful forever for this, but wouldn't the running of the estate now fall to him also? To think that she had hoped that Walter could be Edward's steward! The care of the castle and its grounds and tenant farms, not to mention the rest of the lands that the Struleys governed, seemed to have fallen on Walter's shoulders. "And what about his sons? The eldest must be of age by now."

"They've gone to Greece. All nine of them. No one could have foreseen such a tragic accident and the entire family, without Ralph, of course, left not long after you went to your father's funeral. They are due back in the spring. Everyone agreed it was a wonderful idea to meet all their relatives in Greece and there was such rejoicing at the feast on the eve of their departure. I think…"

"And you say that no message has been sent to them. Even when it was thought that your brother wouldn't survive."

"We knew that the party could not get back here in time and we were all concentrating on willing Ralph to come round. I didn't sleep for the three nights he was in a stupor."

"I see. Well, shall we go and visit him? I'd like to express my condolences."

"You will be… be kind to him, Margaret, won't you?"

"Of course, Walter! I'm not in the habit of kicking a man when he is down!" Margaret saw the hurt on her husband's face. Did he believe that she had done this very thing to him? "I'm sorry, Walter." She was surprised to hear herself apologise, but it seemed that God had not forgotten her – perhaps His favour had descended on her at last! Excitement began to fill her veins. "We have much to talk about apart from Ralph being crippled. Let us go and see him and then we can retire to our own rooms. I want to hear all the other news."

"And I would like to hear about your family too."

Margaret was touched by Walter's patience whilst they climbed the two flights of stairs. He did not stride ahead; in fact, within a few moments, he had taken her arm and was supporting her. She rested repeatedly and then he waited whilst her breathing returned to normal on the landing outside her brother-in-law's bedchamber. She didn't admit to Walter that she had never been inside this room or that she was relieved that her sister-in-law and the unruly children were not there to see her distress. The thought did enter her head that now maybe she would be able to eat less since fortune had begun to smile on her; she suspected that her breathlessness when walking up any kind of incline and the pain in her knees might be due to the weight she was carrying.

In spite of the details included in Walter's account of the accident, Margaret was disturbed when she saw Ralph. Here was a second man she would not have recognised! If her husband had thrown off ten years, it looked like his brother had aged by the same amount. He wore no wig and his own hair was snowy white, but she had no way of knowing if this whitening had come since his fall because she had never met him before without his wig. More importantly, it was the fact that he had shrunk from a burly, middle-aged man to a wizened patriarch that made such a difference. He didn't resemble his father, but she glimpsed her first husband, the simple Humphrey, in his strained features. His twisted body screamed out the pain which she had been told he lived with and all shred of animosity towards him drained away when she strode towards him and grasped his thin fingers.

"Margaret." At least his voice hadn't changed, although it had lost some of its heartiness.

"I am so sorry." She found she meant every word.

"I am delighted that you have returned to us. Your Walter has been my right hand man. Without him I don't reckon I would have survived."

"No!" put in the object of his praise. "It was your own perseverance which brought you through."

"I don't agree. If I hadn't known that you were taking care of my affairs and I could trust you to do this, I think I might have gone mad."

"You have had a good physician, I understand. Have you medicines?" Margaret glanced at the vast array of bottles set on a table near his bed. She reddened. "Is there anything I can do?"

"No, my dear. I have a host of servants who rub my sores and anoint my scars and who bully me to move as much as I can. The doctor practically lives here. I think he has had to abandon all his other patients. But I pay him well. In fact, that sounds like him now. Come back later, Margaret. When I am abandoned and needing company."

Margaret found herself planting a kiss on Ralph's pale forehead and then she and Walter took their leave. She did not know how she was going to ascend those steep stairs to visit, but in that moment, she determined to call every day.

Walter and she made their way in silence to the other side of the courtyard where there were a suite of rooms which they called their own. Unexpectedly she felt a real sense of coming home when she stepped into their own parlour. Here were rugs and pictures, chairs and ornaments that she had chosen. Peradventure she might get the walls repainted and send for some new tapestries from London. Notwithstanding, today, she was comforted by the room's rather shabby interior, although there was no excuse for the dust on the side table and writing desk. Soon she would badger the maids but, for now, her thoughts were filled with her brother-in-law's condition.

"What a tragedy!" she whispered to no one and again she was sincere.

"The physician says his vigour will return. Knowing him as I do, he will get on to his legs by sheer willpower but I have found that we have developed a closer relationship than we had even when we were boys together. Humphrey wasn't able to join in and Ralph was my senior by several years but since the calamity we find we..." Walter faltered.

"I can't say that I wish it hadn't happened. You are..."

"I have given up the bottle. I haven't touched a drop since the day he was carried in half dead and bleeding. And I won't touch it again. I am sorry, Margaret, if I have caused you pain over the years."

Margaret faced her husband. What was happening to her? It was as though a boil had been lanced and the yellow pus of bitterness had been squeezed out, leaving an ache but a clean wound with the hope of full healing. Again she was apologising!

"You! I too have not been... I could have been a better wife and mother. Talking of which. Where are our sons?"

"Ah, Margaret. There is something else you should know. Our eldest son is... He married recently."

"Well, that is all right, isn't it? It was arranged."

"No, he did not marry Hannah."

"What! Who did he marry?"

"Not anyone you know. Oh, Margaret, you weren't here and I wasn't sure what to do. He came to me with this stranger who was in a towering rage. It was Ellenor's father. Walt had… had… There was a child and Ellenor's father was demanding that Walt marry his daughter. I didn't know what you would want. I talked to Walt and he said he loved Ellenor and wanted to marry her."

"Who is she? I mean what is her family line? Who is her father? Not a servant, I trust." She felt some of her old self return!

"No, not a servant but one of Ralph's tenants. And she's a sweet-natured girl. The child is not born yet. It will come in the spring. Please say that you will see Walt. He is here – in the other room, waiting for you to summon him."

"I will see him, of course." Margaret's unforeseen joy and humility was overshadowed by disappointment. Not so much with the baby – she guessed her sons did things that she was unaware of – but that the marriage between such disparate families had taken place whilst she was away!

But when she saw her son and both he and his father began to cry, she found it in her heart to forgive them. And then when the child was born…

* * *

Margaret returned to the present. She couldn't say that all her bitterness disappeared on her homecoming but as she began to forgive others, she was able to forgive herself too and even her father. Love seemed to be a difficult plant to grow but sympathy for Ralph had led to a few green shoots of love sprouting in her heart. She had learned to respect his courage and determination and looked forward to their daily sessions together. Most days she read to him because supporting a book gave him discomfort and pain. Then yesterday a letter was delivered to say the family would be back within the week and Margaret's brand new feelings had taken a sharp knock. Hence her visit to Susanna this morning. Here was something – someone – she could love without fear of them not returning the sentiment. Apprehensions shook Margaret's cosy world. Questions haunted her.

What would happen to Walter when Ralph's eldest son returned? He was young still, only twenty-three, but would Ralph hand over the running of the estate to him or would Walter's steady hand on the reins convince his brother that he was capable? Certainly there was no sign of a return to Walter's excessive drinking habits. Would he go back to the bottle if he was usurped?

What would happen to her too? Would Ralph's wife forbid her to help, overlooking all the good she had done in the last few weeks?

Would Ralph's wife insist that her husband accompany her to warmer climes – to her own family doctors?

And Susanna's mother, Ellenor? Would she recover from her childbed fever and wrench her baby back, or would Margaret continue to have a large part in the upbringing of the child she thought of as her own?

Softly she began to sing a lullaby, rocking the chair in time to the tune. She had no answers to these or any of the other hundred queries that flooded her mind. She would have to face each day when it arrived. She must remember how far she had travelled already from the old Margaret who could see no virtues in others.

She had heard of Griffith's death from Penelope and cried a few tears of regret and sadness. Maybe she would return one day to North Wales but, at the moment, her own dear ones claimed her time and energy and she was resolved to get the most out of the coming months and years. She would continue to write to her sister and keep abreast of family news. It transpired that Mariana was well advanced in pregnancy. From reading between the lines of her sister's missives, it appeared that Margaret had been right to encourage Mariana to marry the Parson. The wild child had settled down to her intended role as wife – well, widow and soon-to-be mother.

"Mariana's baby won't be as wonderful as you, my sweet Susanna," she crooned. "Sweet Susanna. Sweet Susanna."

Slowly Margaret's anguish ebbed and she was able to find peace. All would be well. Ralph would not turn against Walter or her once his wife and children arrived. Too durable a friendship had been forged! All would be well.

FRANCES

Frances bent over the chest and pulled out the linen folded inside it. She was angry. Very angry. Her first intuition had been correct. She had been living here at *Trem-y-Môr* for nigh on seven weeks and the only problems she had experienced were with her husband. How could a man be this changed? She could scarcely recall what Edward had been like on their travels. Even in Portugal he had not been so... How could she describe it? Almost surly. Moody, yes. Distant, certainly. Unloving and uncaring. She had not exchanged more than a few sentences in private with him in all the time they had been here. They might as well have been living in different countries for all they interacted!

Frances piled the old sheets and pillibars, or pillowcases, onto the floor. Why was she doing this? Her bruised mind knew the answer: she had to keep busy. She had flung herself wholeheartedly into being a good wife and mistress. Over the weeks, parcels and packages had arrived full of all the purchases which she and Edward had made. Barely could she bring herself to open them. Only her pride kept her going. No one, least of all her husband, was to perceive how miserable she felt.

She had hoped, in the beginning, that if she behaved totally normally, then soon Edward would get over his sullenness, but to no avail. Rather he had immersed himself in his work and hidden in the library with a bottle of drink whenever he was at home. She had discovered that there were many who applauded the way the new Squire was taking his responsibilities, but she felt he was neglecting her in preference to his duties.

Frances halted in her job of emptying the carved chest. Was her husband doing what she was? Keeping busy in order that he had no time to dwell on his problems? She shook her head. Even if it was true, it did not excuse him. She *did* fill the hours of each day with housewifely tasks, but readily she would have laid them down *if* he had ever invited her to accompany him or help him. She had an excellent head for figures; she could have assisted him in his accounting. She would have liked to have been consulted

639

on decisions concerning the estate, but it was not simply that he did not discuss any plans with her, he spoke to her hardly at all.

Savagely, Frances threw the last of the linen on the floor and started to sort it. What increased her ire was that he seemed to be taking out his melancholy on her as if it was her fault! And she knew it was not! She had not behaved any differently since she had arrived here. In fact, she had gone out of her way to be the same as always. She had made no demands on him, but had waited patiently for him to recover. She had not remonstrated with him for keeping silent at the meal table, but instead had kept the conversation flowing between herself and Mariana and any other guests who might have come (although they had been precious few!). She had not nagged him to spend more time with her and certainly had not berated him for coming to bed so many hours after her that it was obvious that he did not desire to be alone with her. She had missed his companionship and, although she didn't want to admit it even to herself, she missed the physical comforts that they had shared each night.

Damn all men! she shouted inside her head. Why would he not talk to her? She might be able to ease his pain. What was wrong with him? Was it just regrets? Did he regret marrying her? Whom did he love? She had not seen him flirting or watching any woman since they had come here. No, that was not true!

Frances stood up and put her hand to her bodice. She had a pain. She had experienced a recurring pain in her chest, almost as if she had eaten a meal too fast, for several days recently. Since… since last Friday when she had overheard a conversation.

She had been leaving the kitchen when voices had reached her from the buttery.

"…. I tell you he does! Like you I didn't believe it, but I've seen it with my own eyes." It was Mariana's voice.

"Who is it then?" This, Frances recognised, was the maid, Elin. She sounded bewildered. Frances had almost turned away but her curiosity was aroused. Who were they talking about?

"I don't know. It was a woman. There was no doubt about that! I watched my brother dismount and enter the house. Two minutes later a woman with a shawl pulled tightly around her head appeared from over the dunes and went inside and…"

"Don't tell me anymore." The maid sounded close to tears. Mariana must have heard it too for she continued:

"Elin? What is the matter?"

Frances had not listened to the reply for her feet had carried her hastily to her room where she had bolted the door.

Now she closed her eyes. Was there an old adage which warned against listening at keyholes? How she wished she could turn back the clock and not have heard those few sentences! Apparently everyone but herself knew that Edward was having an affair and since they had been here a mere two months, it must be an old relationship. It must be. He would not have started anything now he was married and in such a short time, would he? Surely not! her wounded heart cried. No, he must have been caught up with the woman whom he had always loved. Frances had lain awake, night after night, trying to decide what course of action she should take.

Her first response was anger. How dare he cheat on her? She had wanted to hit out against him. Then had come hurt. Terrible, gut-wrenching hurt. He preferred someone else to her. She had longed to hurt him in return. Above all this was the soul-searching question: what was she going to do about it? Nothing, if she wanted to keep him and she did! Dear God, how she loved him! She had concluded that she would do anything to stay with him. Her everyday life was lonely but she did not want to lose him and she guessed that if she accused him of his infidelity he would insist on separate rooms and then when would she ever interact with him?

In the last few days, she herself had become mute when she and Edward were together, whilst she pondered on what she had heard. After the initial reaction when she had wanted to follow him and find him and *her* in each other's arms, she was forced to school herself and her behaviour in order that no one guessed she knew. Fortunately, the inventory of household linen and the list of what needed to be replaced kept her occupied, but she could never quite stop thinking about her husband and what he had done.

Frances went and sat on the windowsill, hoping that the spasm in her bosom would ease. Was it her heart? Was her heart breaking? No, she was made of stronger stuff than that! She had suffered before and survived. She must wait. Wait for him to return to her. At least now she understood why he never sought her out in bed. In truth she was partly relieved, for if he came near her she would be unable to prevent herself thinking of the other woman.

Who was she? Who was she? The question would not be silenced. She had retraced that brief interchange which she had heard so many times that she had wondered if she was going mad. She felt sure that the woman must not be of the same social standing as Edward and that was why he had been unable or unwilling to marry her. A shawl. A shawl. Would *she* wear a shawl? No, a cloak. She and Mariana wore cloaks.

Was it one of their own servants? She had gone through this train of thought a thousand times. Not Elin, since Elin had been one half of the conversation. Rosie, then. No. Everyone knew that Rosie had come to Holyhead only recently and she was Frances' personal maid. Frances decided that she would have known if Rosie was involved with her husband! Yes, Edward had not been enthusiastic when Frances had told him that she had chosen Rosie to be her maid, rather than searching for a new servant, but that could have no bearing on the matter. It could not be Rosie. Repeatedly the woman talked about leaving and she would not do that if she had ensnared the Squire! Anyway, Mariana had told Frances that the groom was interested in Rosie and the boy – Ted – was a link between them. No, it could not be Rosie. There was no one else at the Manor House. Only Mrs Jones and the other servants were children – even Biddy was just a lass. She couldn't be more than thirteen. It must be someone else from another estate.

Yet what if it was a lady who wanted to disguise herself as a maid in order to confuse people? What if she was of their own class really? Maybe even married herself. Frances closed her eyes. There were no answers! She could not stoop to ask Mariana, even supposing her sister-in-law knew the identity of the adulterer, and she would not follow Edward, in spite of her initial impulse. She would behave with dignity... and with love. Yes, it was her love for him that prevented her doing anything. She did not want to destroy her marriage. One day Edward would tire of his lover and return to her. One day. One day. And until then she would hide her desolation and be fulfilled as mistress of her own house.

How much she had done in the last few weeks! She had ordered new, modern furniture, even going so far as to sketch what she wanted, in order for local craftsmen to produce exactly what she was looking for. She had hired a sewing woman who had started making sheets and curtains. Nothing was to be mended. There was no need. There was plenty of money. Of course, she did not throw away any material which had some life left in it still (torn sheets could be made into pillibars or cloths for the kitchen), but much was discarded.

Originally she had hoped that if there were any household articles which she could not get in this area, then she and Edward could go in the summer to Chester or London or even Dublin, but nowadays she no longer planned outings like that! Spring was passing, yet she made no suggestions. Probably her husband would refuse anyway, she reckoned, citing his work as the excuse when really he could not bear to absent himself from his mistress. No chance to recapture those halcyon days when they were first married!

Frances looked up when there came a knock on the door.

"Come in."

It was Mariana.

"Ah, Frances, Mrs Jones said you were in here. How are you doing? Do you need any help?"

Frances moved back towards the heap of linen. Mariana was very heavy with child and was confined to the house for most of the day. However, Frances knew, she trudged whenever she could. Her sister-in-law had admitted that the hours dragged slowly. In the evenings, Frances was teaching her how to sew tiny baby clothes with exquisite embroidery but Mariana concentrated only for a short while. These days Frances welcomed her company for it stopped her disconsolate mind revolving continually around her own vexations.

MARIANA

Mariana faltered. The great chair was in pieces because Frances had embarked on making fresh covers for it. Her fine, neat, gobelin stitching in vivid silks was forming a picture of a castle and its rose garden already and Mariana marvelled at the speed with which the older woman sewed. Frances had instructed the moving of two other chairs to the bedchamber to replace it and now Mariana perched on one of these. Mariana had found herself spending many hours in her sister-in-law's room. Seldom did she think of it Edward's room too, for he was never in it.

"Oh, I'll be pleased when my son has come," she sighed, trying to get comfortable.

"I hope, for your sake, it *is* a boy," laughed Frances.

"It will be."

"Have you decided on a name yet?"

"Yes."

"Griffith, after his father?"

Mariana bit her lip. She wanted to scream at Frances not to mention the name of that man, but she couldn't without explaining the depth of her abhorrence. Ever since she had been attacked she had concentrated on blanking out what had occurred.

Sometimes she could still feel the weight of the man on her, pressing down both on her physical body and her soul. When he had finished he had stood up. Automatically and very slowly she had reached out a shaking hand and tried to cover her nakedness with a shred of petticoat....

No, she would not think of that morning. However her mind raced backwards.

Had he whispered an apology in truth?

"Oh God, forgive me. I shouldn't have raped you."

Then his tone became harsh and she questioned whether she had heard him aright because he went on:

"You will be punished for your sins. The whole world will know of your unfaithfulness. You…"

Griffith stopped. Mariana held her breath. Was he about to start assaulting her again? With her eyes closed tightly she felt rather than saw him swaying. She thought she heard his bowels churning and grumbling beneath the sound of his voice.

"I've been feeling better – quite recovered lately. Now I think I am going to be sick. I must go back to bed before…"

No, she would not think of that morning. Yet her thoughts spiralled down across the weeks.

A long time after Griffith's departure, she decided that she must rise up. She opened her uninjured eye. She was lying not too far from the edge of the bed. If she used it to support her she might be in a position to get off the floor…. Was it viable? Painfully, she dragged herself towards one of the heavy oak legs, trying to make her trembling, abused body work.

Her hand came upon something cold and smooth. It was the bottle. The bottle of so-called poison. It must have dropped from her husband's…

No, she would not think of that morning. But her memories wouldn't be quenched.

Pulling herself onto her knees, she had felt the sticky discharge dribble down her leg and had started to gag. The thought of what had just occurred flooded her with nausea. She leant her cut face against the wool of the bedcovers. Oh God, help me, she moaned.

It was several minutes before the sickness passed but then she was able to grip the post of her bed and heave herself up. Immediately the room shifted before her vision and she fell onto the covers. She longed to get undressed properly and wash herself from head to foot in clean, icy water but she was too dizzy. She would lie down until she recovered. Folding part of the sheet across her body, she brushed against her belly. The child! Stretching her fingers across her extended abdomen, the tears began to fall. Had the baby been damaged by the violence? Wearily she rested her head on the pillow. Presently she would think about the unborn infant, surely the root cause of that man's rage. In a moment she would get up…

"Madam?"

Mariana heard the voice from far away. She tried to move to turn from her side but her limbs were stiff. She opened one eye; the other was too puffy and swollen.

"Oh, sweet Jesus!" exclaimed Rosie. "What has happened to you, Madam?"

"Ssh! I'm all right," insisted Mariana from between dry lips.

"Oh, Madam, what can I do to help you? Who did this to you?"

Mariana watched the maid inspect the entire room, presumably observing the clothes strewn on the floor, before her gaze came to rest on her own half-naked body.

"Mrs Owen?"

"Water. Please, could I have a drink of water?"

Rosie walked to the bedside table where a flagon and a glass stood. She poured some water and held it to Mariana's cracked lips.

"Oh, this is awful," the maid spoke softly. "Madam, who has done this to you? Who could have got in here and done this?"

Mariana felt the cool liquid trickle down her parched throat. She was only half listening but Rosie seemed to be talking to herself anyway. Certainly Mariana did not feel the need to reply; pain thumped around her head. The maid was saying:

"The Parson... The Parson is ill in bed – he's had some kind of a relapse. That surgeon fellow has been called. Was he in the house already and came in here? Oh, Lord, I only knocked on your door because no one had seen you all day since... Jennett told me you came in from your walk and went upstairs and then she hadn't seen you again. Cook said it wasn't our place to question our betters but I decided that I should find out if you... if you wanted anything. You didn't answer but something made me push your door open. Thank God I did! Oh, Madam, who did this? Did someone come to visit you up here? You don't usually entertain people in your bedchamber. Who...?"

"I need to wash and clear up... all this..." Mariana interrupted, trying to erase the recent past.

"Now, don't you fret. I'll tidy up the room after I've tidied you up. I'll go and get some hot water."

"Rosie!" Mariana wasn't sure where she got the energy from to speak, but her gruff, quiet voice had an urgent tone. "No one must know."

"Very good, Madam. I'll take the liberty of locking the door and then no one else can come in."

No, she would not think of that morning. Nonetheless, clear images pressed in on her.

It was after Rosie had bathed her cuts and dressed her in a clean shift and was tidying the room that the second attack had occurred. She had just instructed her torn gown to be burnt when the door was flung open.

"Oh, Madam!"

In Rosie's exclamation Mariana understood all the regret the maid was experiencing in not bolting the lock on her return.

In the doorway, Mariana could make out the figure of Mrs Beacon, but it wasn't until she heard the words that she realised the older woman was consumed with rage.

"You murderer!" she snarled.

Without warning, she sprang towards the bed. On her face was written what she was intending to do and the sight of her mistress' already bruised features did not seem to register in her fevered mind and cause her to halt. Barely did Mariana had time to cower beneath the blankets when, for the second time that day, someone was raining blows on her.

Then all went quiet. Mariana felt the splashes of water; she surmised that Rosie had thrown the bloodied water in the basin over the housekeeper. Almost immediately others ran into the room but Mariana dared not raise her head. She sensed that Rosie had drawn near her, hopefully putting herself between the mistress and the demented servant.

"You murderer! You murderer!" Mrs Beacon hissed repeatedly. "I'll see you hang for this. You poisoned him."

"Mrs Beacon!"

It was Lloyd! Mariana started to shake. Not him! Not now! Oh, the shame! She had not wanted anyone to view her degradation but for him to enter the bedchamber at this time...

"Come now, dearie." That was Cook's voice. She must be here too.

"I know you were in on it," Mrs Beacon ranted. Who was she speaking to? "I'll get you both. You planned it together. You murdered my Parson so you could have each other."

She must be addressing Lloyd. Mrs Beacon must have seen too much when she had chanced upon them in the dining room all those weeks ago! Mariana was faint with fear.

"Be silent, woman! You do not know what you are saying." Something in Lloyd's voice made Mariana believe that he was grasping the housekeeper's arm. She imagined Mrs Beacon trying to shake him off but he would not allow the woman her freedom. Then came the accusation:

"Let me go, you murderer! You may think that no one knew of your plot, but I saw the poison and..." Suddenly she burst into loud sobs.

"Peggy, I think you should lie down." This from Cook. Would she be taking a gentler hold on the distressed housekeeper?

"No!" Mrs Beacon words were indistinct. "He's gone. My beloved Parson is gone and it's because of her and her evil plans. I should have warned him before."

"Come now, dearie," Cook repeated. "Come with me. We'll talk about this later. You've hardly had any sleep for days and everything seems worse just at the moment."

Mariana could not hear if the two old women had left but she sensed Lloyd's approach and she emerged from the covers with a frantic whisper:

"Rosie?"

"I'm right here, Madam."

Mariana would not look at Lloyd but she felt his intent gaze on her when he asked:

"Is there anything I can do for you? I have my bag with me because I was called to the Parson's side."

Mariana reached out to grip the maid's hand in panic.

"Don't leave me! Cutlass. Matthew Cutland is my physician."

"I'll send for him, Madam." The maid's tone was strong both in reassurance to her and implacable towards the man. "Your services are not needed, Sir. You close your eyes, Madam, and rest until Mr Cutland arrives. I shall send Biddy for him. Maybe he can call in on…"

"The Parson is dead." Lloyd remained where he was standing as if he was not going to be ordered around by a lowly maid. For a second Mariana remembered his tenacity when interrogating.

"I was going to say 'Mrs Beacon'," continued Rosie. "She seems very distraught."

"The woman is insane. Such ridiculous accusations! I suspect she will be put away…"

"Sir, I have asked you to leave according to my mistress' wishes. Will you kindly do so?"

Mariana was surprised at Rosie's bold stance; but then the maid was not acquainted with Lloyd or had she learnt to defend herself and her son when she had lived with that Tom who had masqueraded as a husband?

Lloyd left without another word. Mariana heard the door close; at last, her limbs, ready for flight, could relax.

No, she would not think of that morning.

Wait! She could think of that morning because the Parson was dead. Dead and gone! Glimmers of hope had lightened her heart: the man who had abused her was dead! Judgement for him and freedom for her!

Within seconds apprehension had overthrown her hopes; darkness had extinguished the light because of the housekeeper's invectives. Yet, she had wondered, would Lloyd, in defending his own reputation, clear her name? In her youth, she had shuddered with the conviction that Lloyd was her enemy; perhaps he would become an ally after all. Surely he would condemn Mrs Beacon as a lunatic and with his position in the community people would listen to him and not the accusations of a servant, albeit a housekeeper. If the Parson had been alive, he might have lent credence to Mrs Beacon's tales, but he was dead. Dead. No more!

"Mariana? Are you feeling all right? Is it time?"

Frances' question scattered the tormenting echoes.

"I am fine. I just have the occasional twinge. Now, what were we saying? Oh, yes, you had asked me what I was going to call the child? I have decided on 'Charles'."

"Is that a family name?"

"No. I just like it. I did think of calling him after my father, William, but I've chosen 'Charles'."

"And if it's a girl?"

"No!" Mariana was half lost in the past still. Desperately she tried to erase the evil threatening her soul. Mrs Beacon had been taken away. Not to the notorious Bethlem asylum in London – nicknamed Bedlam – as the rumours had asserted, but to her daughter on the mainland. There had been shock on her departure; no one had realised she had any family. Therefore, Mariana reminded herself, her forebodings had no foundations; usually her fearfulness was confined to the night hours. Why was she so agitated? It was sensible to fight to control her dark recollections and not dwell on that fateful day, especially as she was not alone. She must collect her wits or her sister-in-law would suspect that something was wrong! She gave a laugh, which sounded hollow even to her own ears, and announced: "You're as bad as all the others! It will be a boy. I can feel it."

Mariana closed her lips firmly around the words, recalling an idea which came into her head repeatedly: she wanted to call the child "Jack", but did not dare. She watched whilst Frances began to itemise the contents of the chest.

"It could be twins," went on Frances. "You are rather large, aren't you?"

"Yes, he could be and then I would have two sons." Mariana decided to change the subject. She guessed that the size of the child growing within was talked about by many and she had begun to wonder if her secret would remain hidden. Initially, after the Parson's death, Mrs Beacon had tried to ruin her reputation. Amazingly, much to Mariana's relief, folk took not the slightest notice of the housekeeper's continual mutterings. Rantings and ravings they were, everyone said. The ravings of a woman who had worshipped the Parson all of her life. Thank God! Fortunately there did not seem to be a single person (apart from that ancient crone, Mrs Williams) who had any idea of the Parson's problems, but…. but, if the child came too early, talk would spread from household to household again. Nevertheless if she could survive Mrs Beacon incriminating charges, she could definitely conquer any lesser insinuations.

Not long after her husband's death, Mariana had returned to the Manor House and kept herself to herself. Of course, she had been unable to recapture her youth again in her childhood home. The horror of her final encounter with the Parson and the child swelling her abdomen had changed her. Finally, it appeared the wildness had been beaten out of her and she was resigned to conforming. She spent her days learning from Mrs Jones and Elin the kind of skills most girls learnt at their mothers' knees. Occasionally she longed to ride but, now the babe had been saved from an ignominious death, she had no desire to lose him and she resisted the urge to take out Mars.

* * *

Only the news of Edward's marriage had upset her outward calm, for she had fretted about what his wife was like and whether she should seek another place to live. All to no avail, because, from the first, Frances had made it plain that she neither resented Mariana's presence at *Trem-y-Môr*, nor required her widowed relative to move. Thus Mariana had found herself behaving with complete propriety and privately she grimaced ironically at the thought that she had told Jack that she would never have settled as Henry's wife.

"So, is Edward going to buy you a mount?" Mariana queried. This would be a safe topic of conversation, wouldn't it?

"No, not at the moment." Frances shook her head.

Her companion looked up and Mariana scrutinised her face. Consternation was written there. What was wrong? What load of care was her sister-in-law carrying? Was she aware of Edward's meetings with the woman in the derelict cottage? No, it was impossible! And yet, if perchance Frances had found out, surely she would not share it with her, Mariana, for Frances believed she had been a Parson's wife and would know nothing about infidelity!

Why didn't her sister-in-law want a horse? Was it because she had discovered it was when Edward went riding that he met his lover? Should she tell Frances? What should she do? Mariana allowed a frown to crease her brow. Should she recount to Frances all the gossip concerning her brother? No, not gossip. Truth. Mariana had witnessed one of the trysts. No. Frances would not want to hear that her husband was being unfaithful to her. She, Mariana, would not have wished to be told that her husband was consorting with another woman! This would have been funny – the idea of the Parson having a mistress – if Mariana could forget what Griffith had done to her but she could not forget. She pushed away the upsetting images. No, what she must do was tackle Edward. Yes, she would do it. She would dare because of Frances, her friend.

Dear, faithful Frances! Mariana was beginning to believe that Edward was not good enough for his wife. He did not deserve her. Frances was a congenial person, not beautiful in the strictest sense but with an inner beauty. She had an attractive demeanour, if Edward would only come out of his hole and look!

What a disappointment Edward had been as she had come to know him! Mariana mused. He had stayed such a short time when Jack was here and she had been grieving for her father and was full of the assumption that he was her big brother who could save her from anything. But he had not saved her. He had deserted and he had failed her. And now he had failed his wife too. What was wrong with him? She was beginning to find his sullenness unbearable. She accepted that at times in her life she had been subdued, but she had always had a genuine reason to be so, whereas Edward had no reason to be perpetually moped.

He was newly married with an estate well within his capabilities of running. Was he melancholy because he had left the sea? Did he miss being a captain? Mariana could not say because Edward did not confide in her.

Well, enough! she decided. She could see that Frances was very unhappy. Edward's wife did not weep or sit around doing nothing but Mariana had observed how she looked at Edward, willing him to notice her.

Mariana rose to her feet. She would find Edward as soon as possible – maybe even this morrow and inform him of her observations. Yes, she would tell him that he ought to be taking more care of his wife or she would pine away with misery.

EDWARD

Mariana might have been dumbstruck if she could have read her brother's thoughts at that exact moment, for he had come to the same conclusion: he was not worthy of Frances and her love. He had not meant to wound her, as he surmised he was doing, but he had been unable to help himself. Events, outside his control, had overtaken him and it was impossible for him not to be influenced by them!

He had gone to London in turmoil after nearly strangling that... that toad, the Vicar. All during his time in Portugal, his passion for Mariana had bolstered him up and he had planned and rehearsed how he was going to win her hand and then had come that dreadful scene in the Vicarage! It had filled him with deadly acrimony and he had sworn that he would never marry. Yet Frances had charmed him. How had she done it? He did not know. All he knew was that when he saw her again he found her easing some of the pain and he had reneged on his private resolve. He had to accept that Mariana, his love, was gone from him forever. Without a fuss, he returned the letter to his aunt and said no more, keeping his grief to himself. Before long, he had set about pleasing Frances and, in return, she had pleased him.

Those weeks when they had been on the road had been one of the happiest times in his life that he could remember. Nonetheless, the nearer to Holyhead they had come, with its bitter-sweet memories, the more he was sucked back into his moods. All the same, for Frances' sake, he had purposed to hide his feelings as best he could and he would have done this if Mariana had still been the wife of the Parson and residing in Holyhead. But the woman he desired and whom he had tried to erase from his conscious thoughts, was living in his home and was a widow! Free to marry him if only he had kept to his decision to remain a bachelor! He could not deal with his bewildered feelings and he had turned to his old solace: drink. Such a comfort when it blurred the mind but no good when its effects wore off! Why did happiness and contentment elude him? He seemed destined to be miserable.

As if these facts were not enough to turn a man's brain, he had discovered that his circumstances were even more complicated. Not only was Mariana living at *Trem-y-Môr* but the winds of the gods had found Ally and her son – his son – and swept them irrevocably into his life. Of course, she called herself 'Rosie' now, but he had understood why she had fainted, because he had felt dizzy with shock too when he had seen her standing there amidst his servants.

In the beginning she had avoided him, until Frances had taken it into her head to choose Ally to be her maid. He had tried to dissuade Frances but what excuse could he give? To this end, he had to bear with having the woman he had rescued from the streets and had treated like a wife on his shore leave, serving his real wife in his own bedchamber. He kept away from that room for most of the time, only going there when he was confident that Ally was finished for the day. In fact, what with trying to avoid Ally *and* Mariana, there were not many places in the house where he could go! For this reason, he usually retired to the library and when he was jaded with of being indoors, he had his horse saddled and galloped away.

If he had suspected beforehand that one day he would meet with Ally on one of his rides, maybe then he would have avoided that pastime as well!

It had been a blustery day and his mount was nervous with the gusts of wind. He had dismounted near the sea and walked the animal. On the very edge of his land, lying next to the waves, was a dilapidated dwelling place. Edward had passed it on many occasions but suddenly it came to him that this must be the house which Wilson had told him would be suitable for a steward and what with the wind and the first few spots of rain, he had decided to shelter. Remembrances flooded his mind.

* * *

He left the horse in the lee of the wall and pushed open the door. Straightaway he sensed he was not alone and in the dim light he saw her.

"Ally!" he gasped.

"Sir? Is it you? You gave me a fright."

"You startled me too. Are you sheltering from the rain?"

"No, Sir. I often come here."

"Don't call me 'Sir', Ally. Surely we know each other better than that?"

"I don't know you at all, Sir, except that you're my master."

"Oh, Ally, stop pretending! You may call yourself by whatever name you like, but, I recognised you, on the day I arrived, as you did me. How did you end up here?"

"Sir, my name is 'Rosie' and…"

Edward moved forwards to and silenced her denial with a kiss. Not a short peck but a deep, intimate kiss which he found was returned hungrily.

"You can't deny it, Ally, after that!" he breathed against her carrot hair. She made no reply and, with a step backwards, he went on:

"Where did you go? I searched for you everywhere. Why did you disappear?"

"I thought you no longer wanted me." Ally's voice was trembling.

"Whatever gave you that idea?" he demanded.

His words brought tears.

"You never… came," she muttered.

"I was ill with fever." He gathered her back into his arms, forgetting that he was married; he was caught up with bygone years. For a moment neither of them spoke.

"I know that now," Ally confessed eventually. "I… I asked Mrs Jones when you had lost your leg and she told me…."

"Oh, Ally! What am I going to do?" He didn't try to hide his desperation.

"Nothing, Sir." She pulled free from his grasp. "It's all in the past."

Edward saw a variety of emotions flit across the woman's features. Above all seemed to be a determination to be steadfast even though she wanted to tell the whole world who she was! He realised that she could assert that she had the first claim on him and he was the father of her son. He spoke aloud the conclusion of the soundless certainties he had watched on her all familiar face.

"No, everything is not past because of the child. Ted is mine, isn't he?"

Ally looked away from him whilst he continued:

"Ally, don't try to deceive me. I know you too well. You were never any good at lying to me. I *know* he's mine. I asked at 'The Bear' and they told…"

"All right, he's yours," she conceded with defeat in her tone. "But, there is nothing we can do about it. You are married and your wife would not want to acknowledge…"

"You'd be surprised! Frances is a very broad-minded woman! However…"

"No, Sir… Edward. No." Ally moved away and leant against the damp wall. "*I'm* not prepared for everyone to know that… that… It would look as if I came all this way to find you and cling to you, whereas I had no idea that I was working for you."

"How *did* you come to be here?"

He listened whilst she explained about the encounter with his sister at the fair, but she denied adamantly that Mariana or anyone else suspected the sad truth. She ended by saying:

"I must go or Mrs Jones will begin to question where I have got to."

"No!" he cried. "Don't go! We must decide what to do…"

"There is nothing to do. You have a wife…"

"I came…" he started. "I travelled to London to ask you to marry…"

"Please, Edward, Sir, don't. It is all too late."

He went towards her and gripped her shoulders.

"I… I can't never meet you again and never have the opportunity to speak to you except in front of others. I must see you. I need you."

He held her gaze but was unable to read her thoughts as easily this time. He glimpsed indecision before she pulled away from him again.

"I'm sorry, Edward, but it's just not possible. I am your wife's maid and it would be wrong to…"

"Still the same Ally, eh? Fine morals! You always were very moral. That was why you would have made an awful prostitute. You would have been wracked with guilt and…"

"Stop it!" she shouted hurrying towards the door. "You don't know anything about what I have been…"

"Oh, Ally, I'm sorry." Edward stumbled towards her. "I didn't mean any offence. Honestly. It's just that I've got myself into a terrible mess and I remember how good you were at listening and… yes, and advising. You have a wise head on your shoulders."

Ally wrenched the door open and the gale howled in, lifting up the dead leaves and sand which lay on the floor.

"I'm not going to discuss it anymore. I shall go and collect Ted and pack my belongings and leave."

"Ally!" Edward thundered and then he fell, with a loud crack; his wooden leg had caught on the uneven floor.

Ally turned just when he landed heavily on his side. Without hesitation she jumped to his aid and as she bent over him he pulled her into his arms with a groan. If she had any lingering resolves, he reckoned they flew out the smeared window with his. They gave themselves up to each other, oblivious to the cold earth beneath them and the wind whistling under the door.

* * *

Edward stood up restlessly, his heart quickening with the memory of that day. He recalled the ardour and how his troubles were forgotten in the ecstasy.

Afterwards no words were exchanged whilst she helped him to his feet; each of them lost in their own reflections. Without delay she had slipped out of the cottage. He had taken longer to leave, spending a few minutes trying to brush down his coat. He was concocting a story (to explain the muddy cloth to Wilson) and not troubled by his conscience.

How had he come to meet her again? He began to pace up and down but the library seemed too small to contain him. How had he come to meet her again when he had decided on his way home that it would not reoccur? He had absolved his initial guilt with the easy explanation that it had just been a slight aberration – he had been bound up with the jolt of the fall and of encountering her alone, he argued inside his head. He had not planned the tryst – in fact, he had resolved not to – and yet it had happened.

Chance had played its part on that second occasion too. He had seen her in the vicinity of the cottage and directed his horse towards her. He had ridden right by her, without any acknowledgement, and led the way to the ruined building, willing her to follow him. Thus they had met and soon he had begun to arrange a rendezvous. Not regularly, and not at the same time of the day, but definite appointments so that he did not have to fret that he would not see her again. They did not talk much; it was too chilly for conversing. She had gathered some undergrowth and piled it in a corner when he arrived for the third time and on the fourth occasion she had procured a blanket which he vaguely recognised as coming from the Manor House. A wife at heart was Ally. She had never failed to give him a welcome on his arrival home from the sea all those years ago. They had not dared to light a fire in the dirty grate in case someone saw the smoke, but their love kept them warm and when it was over they parted promptly to hasten back to their separate lives.

Nevertheless, Edward knew that it must end. He had always accepted this and yet he had pursued it. He would not have imagined that his indiscretion would disturb him to such a degree. He acknowledged that he was cheating on Frances and increasingly he could not bear the guilt any longer. He had admitted that to himself eventually last night. It had been thanks to Wilson that finally he had come to his senses. He recalled yesterday and the personal conversation he had exchanged with his servant.

Edward had been sitting in this very room – his father's sanctuary and now his: the library. He had been working his way through a bottle of French wine whilst the hands of the clock had ticked slowly towards midnight. At the precise moment he had thrown the contents of his glass at the smouldering fire in a fever of anger, Wilson entered.

"Sir?"

"Oh God! I wish I was dead!" exclaimed Edward.

"Is there anything I can do to help?" asked Wilson quietly. Edward heard no censure in the other man's voice.

"No. I... There's no one who can help me. I got myself into this mess and I must get myself out. Maybe the best way is just to put a pistol to my head."

"You could do, Sir, but there might be a less drastic way out of your problems."

"Oh, Wilson, what am I going to do?"

"It depends, Sir, what you have done and what kind of trouble you're in."

"Have you ever been in love?" remarked Edward abruptly, pushing his chair around in order to face the other man.

"Yes, Sir."

"Come here, Wilson. Don't stand over there near the door as if you were my servant."

"But I am, Sir."

"No, you're not. Not tonight. Do you remember those times we had on the way to London? How long ago it all seems! It's less than a year. Do your recall how we used to sit until the sun came up, discussing all manner of topics? Yes? Well, come. Let's pretend we're in some inn somewhere near.... near Chester and let's talk. Come and sit down. Don't stand on ceremony anymore with me, Wilson. Wilson. That's not your name. What is your name?"

"Richard, Sir."

"No, Richard, no more 'Sirs' tonight. For tonight we will be equal. After all I have contemplated death and after death there will be no masters and servants, will there, Richard?"

"No, Sir."

"Richard!"

"What would you have me call you, Sir?"

"Edward, of course. That's my name, isn't it?"

"I can't, sir. I've had a lifetime of..."

"Well, you can try and that's an order. Sit down. You don't drink, do you? Why don't you drink alcohol?"

"Because I saw what it did to my mother."

"And what did it do to your mother?"

"It brought her nothing but misery, Sir."

"And now you're going to say that it will do the same for me, aren't you?"

"No, I wouldn't advise you..."

"Well, you must, for I need your advice. I love a woman and she... she is not my wife. Not that my wife is not a good woman. She... she does not... It's not her fault. I loved this woman before I met Frances and... and now I can't love Frances because... of her."

Edward looked straight at the other man.

"What would you do, Wil... Richard?"

"It depends on what you want, Sir."

"What do you mean?"

"Do you want to be happy?"

"Well, yes, of course I want to be happy."

"Then, Sir, you must decide..."

"Ah, choose between the women. I knew you would say that."

"No, Sir, that is not what I was going to say. You must decide what you are going to do about it."

"There's nothing I can do about it. Even if I.... I could get rid of Frances, which I don't want to do. Even if I did find myself without a wife, I could not marry the woman I love."

"Then the choice is easy, Sir."

"What choice? I have no choice."

"You do, Sir. You have the choice, and the power, to mould your own future. If you want to be miserable for the rest of your life, you can be, but you can be happy too."

"How?"

The beginning of a smile lifted the corner of the servant's mouth.

"You can face the truth and act on it. You have told me that there is no chance of you ever having this woman you love. So, therein lies a decision. You can't erase your love but you can consciously resolve not to let it affect your other relationships. For example, with your wife. At the moment you can't see your wife and her... excuse my frankness, Sir, her excellent character. You are allowing your love to ruin your life. Admit to yourself that it is a lost cause. Don't try to fight it for it will simply rear its head again and again. No, accept it and relax. Have it as part of you, but don't let it be your master. Don't let it come between you and your wife..."

"But it does. I can't help myself."

"Very well, then, let it ruin your life. You can be miserable for the rest of your life. You will have a failed marriage and you will never claim your love." Wilson stood up. "So, Sir, is there anything I can get you before I retire?"

"No, wait! Don't go! I don't want to be miserable for the rest of my days."

"Then face it, Sir. Face the truth. Your love will be unrequited. There is no chance for it, but it is not too late for your marriage. That is, unless you're deceiving me. Is there any chance of you having a relationship – an open, honest relationship, I mean – with the woman you love?"

"No." Edward bent his head.

"Then face the truth, once and for all. You are tough enough to take it. I know that, Sir. You have a robust character, like your sisters too. You are able to take a few bumps in life. You already have, Sir. So make up your mind to start afresh. Let your love be your slave; command it to go as you do me. Not all the time, for it is part of you. But, when it threatens to come between you and your happiness. An act of will. Your will is much more powerful than your sentiments."

"I'm not sure, Wilson, if I can..."

"You can try, Sir. Try and see. You might be surprised."

"What about Frances?"

"Your wife? She will help you. She also is not made of jelly. Your marriage is young. Since you arrived you have been caught up with the estate and… and your own thoughts. Now the Manor can run without you being in every place at every second. Spend more time with…"

"But you don't know who it is I love, and…"

"Who she is bears no relevance to your problem, since she is not your wife. Remember, an act of will – an attitude of mind – can overcome the ups and downs of your feelings. It won't be easy. When is life ever easy but, if you want to be happy, you must persevere, and each time you fail, pick yourself up again. And, remember, Sir, I will be here if you ever need me."

Edward returned to his seat behind his desk as the past merged with the present. He had not told Wilson the whole truth: he was entangled with two women. That aside, he tried to use the same principles, which unknowingly Wilson had laid down about Mariana, to his relationship with Ally. There was no future in that either. Therefore he must tell her that, not only could he no longer meet her, but it would be best if he found her another place to live. He could afford to give her enough money for her not to have to work, but she, and his son, must go away to somewhere where she was far, far from him.

MARIANA

Mariana glanced back over her shoulder as the wind tore at her cloak and skirt. Suddenly she wished she had not come, but she had seen Edward ride out and was determined to catch him and his mistress together. She felt the occasional pain in her belly but she ignored it. She was nearly at the house where she knew the two met and once she had said her piece she would go home and straight to bed.

If there had been any sun it would have been low, near the horizon but the dingy, grey clouds had been draped across the heavens all day and the darkness was already claiming its victory. The wind was very fierce; it must be carrying the clouds away but new, identical ones replaced the old and there was never any break in the overcast sky. As yet it had not rained, but Mariana reckoned that probably there would be a downpour in the night.

Mariana acknowledged that it had been foolish for her to set out for her walk this late, but her task was an important one. She believed that if she did not find Edward actually with the woman in his arms she would be unable to challenge him. Therefore she battled on, against her better judgement and the intermittent stabs of pain which made her halt often.

She had been in the stables when Edward had come for his mount. She and Thomas and young Ted had been watching whilst Mars was eating the warm mash which they had prepared for him. The horse had been running a fever for several days now, but today, it looked as if he was beginning to recover.

Instantly Edward had quit of the yard, Mariana had excused herself, and set forth. She realised that Edward would arrive at the dwelling place sooner than her but that would be opportune, for it would give his partner time to arrive as well. Mariana could not have said how she was so certain that Edward was making for his tryst, but she was sure that she would find him there. If it had not been for the wind, she would not have found the walk too arduous, but she was feeling exhausted already and longing to turn back.

She was not frightened of what Edward would say, or expecting to be embarrassed. Her only thought was a kind of righteous indignation on behalf of her sister-in-law. She considered that Edward was treating Frances contemptibly and since no one else would be brave enough to tackle the Squire, then she, his younger sister, would! Someone had to tell him that he must stop. What madness to have an affair on his own doorstep, with all his tenants and acquaintances watching! He should have been more discreet. Although she had to admit that she hadn't discovered the identity of Edward's mistress.

As she reached the brow of the dunes, Mariana gave a sigh of relief when she saw Edward's horse tied up beneath a rickety piece of wood which acted as a roof to a shed. At least her belaboured journey had not been in vain.

Pushing the door open Mariana heard her brother call:

"Ally? I thought you were never coming!"

"No, I'm not 'Ally'."

"Good God! Mariana! What are you doing here? I would have thought it was too windy for you to be traipsing around the beach."

"I came to see you, for…" Mariana stopped as another pain caught her.

"Come to see me? Why come here? It would be better to see me at home at the meal table at…."

"Don't be ridiculous!" snapped Mariana. She paused whilst the discomfort receded. "What I want to say to you could not be said in front of Frances. She does not know what you are doing, but I do!"

"Well, shall we go towards home as we converse? It will soon be dark and…"

"No, I want to meet Ally and, anyway, she will wonder where you are if you have gone."

"What are you talking about? Who's Ally?"

"Sweet Jesus, Edward! Don't start playing games with me! Everyone knows about what you are doing!" The recurring pains and the effort of the journey made her short-tempered.

"What am I doing?"

Mariana gazed at her brother through the gathering gloom. What a depressing place to meet one's lover! Really she had hoped that the woman could be here already, but as it was she would just have to keep Edward talking.

"I suppose you want me to spell it out in words of one syllable! You are having an affair with some… some…" Mariana caught her breath. The pain was here again. What was it? Surely it was not time for her travail! Even by *her* calculations the baby was not due yet! It must be something she had eaten, but she could do without the distraction at the moment with an onerous difficult conversation ahead of her. In truth she needed to sit down. She looked around the derelict cottage for somewhere to sit. In the corner was a bed of hay. A bed! She knew what that was for! She must not lose sight of why she had come here, birth pangs or not!

"Don't deny you meet a woman called 'Ally'," she accused when she felt better, "for I myself can testify to your first words and…"

"What makes you so sure that I am having an affair?"

"Oh, Edward." She frowned at him with frustration. Obviously he was not going to admit anything to her and it dawned on her that she could not keep him here. The gripe was too compelling. Even thinking straight was becoming increasingly difficult. "Look, Edward, I must go for I am not… I am sick, but what I want to say to you is: please end it for… for Frances' sake. She loves…"

"I really don't know what you are talking about. I simply arranged to meet a woman here who is selling me some cloth which I am having…"

"Edward! Don't lie to me! I've seen you before but I've only had the courage to speak to you now for I have heard others comment on your clandestine meetings. Oh, why are you doing it? You are breaking your wife's heart."

"My *wife's* heart?" emphasised Edward. "Then why are you here and not my wife?"

Mariana stared at her brother. Why *had* she come? She might have guessed he would not listen to reason. Why had she interfered?

"It's none of my business really," she conceded quietly. She had been a fool to meddle, after all. "I just hate to see Frances sorrowing because you do not return her love."

"I have never returned Frances' love and she accepts it. She married me although she was aware I loved another. Not everyone marries for love, as you should well know!"

"Who do you love?" started Mariana. Then what Edward had said registered in her mind. "What are you saying? That I did not love the Parson? You have no idea why I married the Parson."

"No, I don't. So I'm asking you now: why did you marry that man?"

"It's none of your business why…."

"My point exactly, my dearest Mariana. And what goes on between me and my wife is *my* business and not yours, but I can assure you that Frances is not suffering as much as you would think."

"What do you know of what she is suffering? You never seem to go near her nowadays! You hardly speak to her…. or me, for that matter. You aren't civil to anyone but spend all your time in the company of a bottle!"

"How dare you set yourself up as judge!" retorted Edward. "*You* have no idea of all the agony that… that I've been through!"

"What agony? You have no reason to be distant from us as if you are above us. You are newly married and…"

"Mariana, I think we should go before we say things which we regret." Edward's voice was gruff; it was as if he sensed danger here.

"No. What reasons do you *imagine* you have for your behaviour? Tell me."

"No. You would not want to hear them."

"Try me."

"No, Mariana. We had best forget this conversation ever took place. You have no need to concern yourself about…."

"I want to know what your problem is. When I first met you I thought it was wonderful to have a brother, but since you've returned, I've often wished that you had never come back."

"My God!" burst out Edward. "I had thought you grown up at last but you still behave like a child sometimes. *Trem-y-Môr* is mine by right and I am the Squire. *You* are the guest now. I don't have to allow you to stay but…."

"I shan't be staying, don't you worry! I had already determined to leave when…"

Edward went towards her with the reassurance:

"Oh, Mariana, don't listen to what I'm saying! I didn't mean it. You made me angry. Of course, the Manor House is your home too and you are…"

"No! I don't want to stay anymore." Mariana turned on her heel. She must get home to bed. This whole interchange had not worked out as she had hoped and she felt ill.

"Mariana, don't go! Hear me out!" Edward caught at her cloak but she wrenched it from his grasp. Immediately he shifted and even with his false leg he reached the door before her, for the pains were preventing her from moving quickly. He barred her way. Softly he pronounced the words:

"Don't go, Mariana. I like to have you near me. I'll tell you my reasons for drinking. It's to prevent me from thinking so much because I love someone who does not love me. Can you guess who it is? No, of course you can't. Don't even try to guess. It doesn't matter anyway."

Mariana looked up at her brother's face. What she saw there made her shiver.

"How... How can you love...?" She shuddered. For a moment there was silence between them and then she concluded, "You can't love me. I'm your sister."

"Oh, Mariana," he sighed. He cupped her face in his long, cold fingers and she started to tremble. What was he going to do? If only she could get past him and out the door but he was a big man and his body covered the exit.

"You are not my sister."

She closed her eyes. The bold statement was barely audible, but she could not prevent herself from hearing them.

"I swore I wouldn't tell you," he groaned, "but it's worse that you think that I might love my.... my sister than to hear the truth. We are not related by blood, my sweet Mariana. Oh, the torment I have gone through!"

He released her gently as Mariana felt the stabbing pain start again, but apparently, he had not finished speaking and now his words alone held her in his grasp. She would not meet his eyes.

"I have loved you from the moment I saw you. I had to go away that first time when I went to London because I thought you were my sister. But, when I discovered that... that Father was not your... that you were not related to me, I returned to... I was going to..."

Mariana backed away from him and put her hands over her ears. His voice came from far away, whispers which made her head spin. She could not believe it. Father! Father was not her father. Edward desired her. It was she whom he loved and all the time she had been looking for someone else. No, it was obscene, horrible, disgusting, sinful to love one's sister. And her father and mother. Who was her father? How could her mother have... have lain with another man? No more! No more! She could not stand to hear anymore. The agony which had begun in her abdomen was engulfing her heart.

"Don't, Edward," she pleaded but he took no heed. It was as though now he had begun to speak he had to finish. Fortuitously, it came to her that he was so engrossed in his monologue that he was not really aware of her! First she was beside him and then she was pushing past him, her wretchedness giving her added strength.

Her escape made him stop his declaration of love!

"Mariana!" he shouted, following her. "Wait!"

The wind snatched his call but Mariana didn't halt. Glancing back, she saw him floundering because his leg had sunk into the sand. She calculated that by the time he had righted himself and fetched his stick and untied his horse she would be gone.

* * *

Mariana fell through the front door of the Manor House, shaky and breathless. Concentrating on straightening herself she did not notice Frances emerging from the shadows at the bottom of the stairs and jumped.

"Mariana, are you all right? You are very pale."

The younger woman stared silently at her sister-in-law. She had not realised there was anyone there. She had hoped, against hope, that she would reach her bedchamber without being seen in order to lie on the bed and still her beating heart and calm her raw nerves. She felt sick with the shock of what she had been told and the hazardous journey home.

"I'm… I'm just… The wind is fierce."

"What in heaven's name made you go out in this weather?"

Mariana gritted her teeth against the aching discomfort. Frances glided towards her and grasped her arm.

"You ought to be more careful," she admonished. "Here, let me take you up to your room."

"I'm… Aah!" cried Mariana.

"Mariana! Are you in pain? Is the baby coming?"

"No!" Finally Mariana had her breathing under control. "I slipped on the sand and I'm feeling uncomfortable." No one must know. The child must not arrive yet! It was too soon! Not even an idiot would believe the child was the Parson's if it came today!

"Let me help you. Please, lean on me. I'll call Elin…"

"No, I'm all right. It was just… I landed badly…"

"Where did you go?"

Whilst Frances questioned Mariana, she led her up the stairs.

"I… Not far…"

"Well, I think you should either stop your daily walking or take someone with you. I'll willingly accompany you. It's too dangerous. What if you fell and there was no help for you."

Mariana allowed Frances to do the talking. The ache was easier already. Please God, it would lessen now that she had returned. If she could just lie down possibly it would go altogether, although she surmised that the agony in her heart would not be so easily assuaged.

Luckily, it seemed that Frances required no replies and it was not until she was lying under here covers that Frances enquired:

"You didn't see Edward whilst you were out, did you?"

Involuntarily Mariana clenched her fingers. She was aware that Frances had noticed. Would her sister-in-law think it was another spasm?

"No."

"Are you…? Has Edward upset you?" persisted Frances.

"No," she strived to keep her voice normal. If only Frances would go! "I think maybe I'll have a little sleep. Thank you for your concern."

Frances smiled.

"I'm glad that you got back safely. I will leave you and check that Edward is not in the library."

Mariana closed her eyes as she heard the door being pulled shut. *At last* she could cry. All the way home she had battled against nature, pushing her thoughts down. She had told herself that she must reach the house before she collapsed. No weakness until then, but finally she was alone and she could cry… cry for the terrible loss which lay deep in her very bones. Desperately she tried to forget what Edward had said but instead she was hit with the full force of not just this latest horror but past nightmares; everything seemed magnified by memories of the rape which had burst out from behind the wall she had erected to contain them.

Immediately the tears flowed.

"Oh, by the way," Frances remarked, coming back in, "Mrs Jones asked me to… Oh! What is it?"

Mariana covered her eyes with the crook of her arm. Sweet Jesus, was she never to be left alone? She felt a gentle touch on the bedclothes.

"My dear sister," she whispered. "What has happened?"

Mariana knew there was no chance of hiding her distress but she could not reply even if she had been able to form a logical sentence. Her voice was choked and her mind was in chaos. She had gone to the cottage to try to save Frances' heart from breaking and had ended up with her own life in tatters. She had told no one of the ordeal she had been through, never discussing it even with Rosie, and had tried to hide the desolation and shame behind the normal routine of each day. Yet she had been living a pretence and, without warning, like a dam cracking, her held-in emotions were rushing out.

Eventually she became aware of Frances' cool hand placed near her, but still she could not begin to share her confusion and suffering. However, the other woman did not insist on any explanation.

"I'm sorry," Mariana mumbled after she knew not how long. "I had not meant you to see…"

"You should not be alone when you're this upset. I remember when…. when my husband, my first husband was… died, I needed someone to talk to and there was no one."

"How did he die?" enquired Mariana, grateful to focus the attention away from herself.

"My… My father killed him."

"Your father?"

"Well, I thought he was my father, but he wasn't. He told me himself that I was not his child."

Mariana removed her arm from covering her face and gaped at her sister-in-law.

"You… You… Your father was not your father. I… Did you… you think that he was before this time?"

"Yes, and I was extremely unsettled when I first heard. It was as though the very foundations of my world had shifted."

"If… If what you say is true, then I think I can tell you what I'm… I'm crying about," confided Mariana in a hoarse whisper.

THOMAS

Thomas walked along by the stalls, talking to the horses, stroking their muzzles, patting their necks and whispering encouragement. He assured them that they had plenty of hay in their mangers and that they should be asleep since it was well past midnight. Returning along the same brushed walkway, with the animals on his right, he reached the sleeping boy. Ted was stretched over two bales of hay and Thomas stopped to pull the edge of the frayed horse blanket around the child's loose limbs and touch his golden locks.

He had become increasingly fond of Ted and a warmth stirred in his breast as he watched the small face, vulnerable in his oblivion. Again he was struck by the boy's resemblance to the Squire and he wondered afresh at the relationship between them.

Thomas had enjoyed what he called "his adventure" in London. Never could he have imagined the all-consuming noise and the bustling lives of the masses who dwelt in the capital city. Nothing seemed to rest, even in the moonless hours of night, and he had found himself unable to wind down and sleep each evening. Time after time he had seen something new to investigate and observe and, initially, he had revelled in it. But, with the passing weeks, he had begun to long for a sight of a wide open expanse of sky with its fast-moving clouds racing across it; he had yearned to feel the wind blow past him with the tang of seaweed and the freshness of ocean depths carried on its wings; he had wanted to sit astride the broad back of one of his charges and canter along the sand and glimpse far distant mountains etched on the horizon; he had wished to be able to stride freely along a track instead of stepping gingerly around mounds of stinking rubbish or even the prone body of a beggar; he had craved to hear his mother tongue in his ears but most of all he had desired to meet with his familiar family and share some of his experiences with them, and they tell him of the happenings of their lives.

Nevertheless, on his return he had found many changes. His father seemed to have grown in stature and now rode around the estate as grand as the Squire himself, collecting rents, settling disputes and keeping the tenants in order. Gone was the stooped groom who had crept around the yard looking haggard and ill-used.

His eldest sister, Biddy, had left to work in the Vicarage, maturing with her recent promotion, and either it was the real distance of her new place of work or her sagacity which meant he felt he no longer knew her. Of course she was sixteen now and being courted by a man from Bodedern too, a thatcher whom Thomas had met but once. Was this new relationship coming between their childhood closeness?

His other sister, Martha, had stepped into his mother's shoes, after her death, and was growing more and more like his *Mam*, in both mannerisms and voice (and sometimes even in facial expressions), although Thomas reckoned that the household and his younger siblings were better behaved and cleaner in the care of their new 'mother'!

Then there was his all-consuming first love, Mariana, who had been married and widowed all in the space of a few months. She was near the time of her delivery and Thomas did not believe that Mariana was one of those women whom pregnancy or widowhood suited. Her lustrous hair sat demurely beneath a cap and her exquisite figure was hidden by the girth from the child, but it was her mischievous grin and irrepressible high spirits which he missed the most. Etched on her pale face were unseen-so-far lines of worry or sadness, he could not decide which, and her new lifestyle meant she rode no more and he only saw her when she came to offer titbits to her beloved Mars, stabled again here when his mistress returned home.

Of course, Mrs Jones looked more elderly and Elin had brought her two youngest siblings, Mary and John, with her to be employed after the demise of their stepmother and father. Elin's sister, Kate, had grown into a pretty girl from being a child, shooting up almost like the spring growth of a tree. He accepted that Peggy was the same as ever – cheery, stolid and with a gift of being able to avoid work if at all possible!

Elin was different – thinner in her grief – and more silent perhaps. She and his brother, Morgan, three years his junior, were often found together and hesitantly Morgan had confided in him one day that he was hoping to marry her in the not too distant future. These confidences had got Thomas thinking of his own future. For the two children who had arrived with Elin were not the only additions to the Manor House staff. Ted and his mother, Rosie, were here too.

He stroked the soft curls of the sleeping boy once more and then made his way back to his own bed, not much more substantial than the boy's bales of hay, but longer and wider.

Rosie.

Was it the romance of Biddy and her thatcher, or Morgan wanting to woo Elin, or even the quiet acceptance of Mariana's bereavement which had made him consider his own lonely bed? He had intended to court his friend, Joanna, last summer. But, again, whilst he had been "traipsing around the country" – Mrs Jones' words, not his – Joanna had married a farmer from the other side of Anglesey – a serious man with prospects who had fallen in love with Thomas' comely friend and had not hesitated to snatch up his new wife and bear her off to live under the same roof as his aged parents until such time as he inherited the farmhouse and lands. Thomas had not even set eyes on Joanna, let alone conversed with her, but he had been informed, albeit by her smug family, that she was settled and very happy with her ambitious husband. Thomas was glad but it left him alone and rather jealous when he saw his younger brothers and sisters and their partners hand in hand or even kissing on their afternoons off. He was the eldest and he was lagging behind! That is, until he met Rosie.

Maybe it was her pronounced London accent (which reminded him of the fun he had in that city) that had attracted him or her curly auburn hair and bright blue eyes; perhaps he came to know her caring side when she collected Ted from the stables each evening (before the child had begged to be allowed to sleep near his favourite horses); certainly her shy smile and the abundance of freckles had not escaped his notice. He would not have been able to explain what exactly had drawn him to her but she was very different from any the local girls, who lived around him and he had known from childhood. He found himself looking forward to Rosie's visits to the yard and that his gaze would often stray to her round face or slim-boned hands when the servants convened around the kitchen table for meals.

The first time he had acknowledged that the boy, Ted, had Sir Edward's chin and nose and even his eyes was when his master was hoisting the lad up onto the back of the mare and their faces were close together. Then Thomas had wondered how this could be and decided that he was mistaken. Never did he observe Rosie looking at the Squire, as if she was acquainted with him from her earlier life; in fact, she seemed to recoil from the man, tiptoeing back to the house if Sir Edward was ever collecting his mount when she arrived. It was only last week that Thomas had discovered that Rosie's apparent avoidance actually covered a secret because Thomas had seen master and maidservant meet in the broken-down house on the seashore. He had been exercising one of the Manor House's horses and was returning from his ride. Over the fields, he had just emerged from the shelter of some sturdy trees when his keen eyesight had picked out Sir Edward's mount, riderless and grazing by the ruined boundary of the cottage. Thomas reined in but before he could go and investigate whether the Squire needed help, a woman had appeared along the path from *Trem-y-Môr*. The wind that day had been gusty and had caught the shawl from around her head; even from that distance, Thomas recognised the glowing red of Rosie's locks. He had ridden away swiftly. All the jumbled thoughts and the questioning of Ted's resemblance to Edward and, of course, the child's name, a derivative of Edward he had realised, came into focus sharply. Thomas knew…

The door of the stables opened and swung back against the stone with a clang. Thomas leapt out of his bed, surprised that the weather had loosened the bolt and there stood the very woman he had been thinking about.

"Rosie?"

"I'm sorry to… it's so late but I've come for Ted."

"Come for Ted? Why? Do you want him sleeping in the house again? He's quite safe here and no trouble." When Thomas reached the woman's side he saw her bag.

"You're not leaving?" he lamented.

"Yes."

"Why?"

"Because I want to get a good start towards the mainland and…"

"No, I don't mean why are you leaving tonight. I mean why are you leaving at all? Are you not happy here?"

"Yes, I'm happy. It's just that I'm very homesick for…"

"No, Rosie." His recent musings and his acknowledgement to himself that he was increasingly attracted to this woman made him bold. His command of English had improved enormously whilst he had been away – with both the Squire and Wilson tutoring him – but he spoke slowly for he did not want to make a mistake and allow Rosie to depart before he had declared himself! "You're not homesick. Everyone knows how much you like it here and you yourself…"

"Please, please don't ask me any questions. I have my reasons for wanting to go."

"What are your reasons for wanting to go?" he echoed. When the woman did not reply he continued, "Well, if you won't tell me what they are, then you won't mind if I try to stop you going."

"Stop me? Thomas, why should you want to stop me going?"

"Come and sit down the other end so we don't have to whisper. Not much wakes Ted but… but what I want to say to you is not… I don't want him to hear."

Rosie's shadowed features showed confusion but meekly she followed him to his quarters and he placed the lantern high up on a hook where it threw eerie shadows onto the whitewashed walls.

He gestured towards a kitchen chair (which had been discarded by the new mistress recently and he had grabbed for himself to try to make his 'bedchamber' more homely) and then he perched on the edge of his bed. Silence drew out between them whilst, once again, he translated what he wanted to say into the foreign tongue. Afterwards, he wasn't sure if he had said something wrong or if he had been too abrupt but her shriek of denial reverberated around the bare surroundings when he asked her to marry him. Testing all his brain power, aware that the hour was late but guessing this might be his only chance, he tried to explain that his proposal was serious. Listing some of her attributes and adding that he had become very attached to her son, blushing himself when she blushed, he stumbled on. However, Rosie continued to shake her head and soon arose.

"I thought when you said you wanted to speak to me it was to ask if I would leave Ted here and go away on my own. But I could never do that! I am flattered by your proposal but, not only do I not know you, but, as I have said, I have my own private reasons for leaving and it must be tonight."

In desperation Thomas spoke out without preamble:

"I know you have been meeting the Squire but I am willing to move away towards Holyhead. If you no longer lived in the Manor House, you would not have to see him every day."

Rosie sat down abruptly as though he had struck her.

"You know! Oh, this is terrible! How many others know too? I thought if I went today… I had decided that I would meet him no more… I should never have agreed... You mustn't believe that I am a loose... I can't think straight..."

Thomas squatted down next to the woman and took her shaking hands between his own.

"Hush! Don't fret! I'm sure that not many, if any, people know about your meetings in the cottage..."

"No! Mrs Owen went there today! I saw her go inside and turned back myself. Edward was inside already. I rushed back to the house and I've been waiting to be summoned by Mrs Owen. When Mrs Rowlands came and asked to speak to Mrs Jones I was convinced that I was to be dismissed but then I found out that Mrs Owen had fallen. All Mrs Rowlands wanted was a tray to be set so Mrs Owen could eat upstairs. But the minutes of fear made me resolve to leave tonight. Oh, but Thomas, you must not think that I have ensnared the Squire and taken him from his wife. I must tell you all."

She withdrew her hands and awkwardly Thomas stood up and returned to his perch on the bed. He listened to her tale incredulously, only interrupting when he heard that his master had abandoned his common law wife. Throughout, she denied that Sir Edward had behaved badly. For the entire story, including the confirmation of Ted's parentage, her love for the Squire shone out and when she confided that she had lain with no other man except for the hateful Tom who had forced himself on her, Thomas blushed for a second time. Increasingly he realised that she could not stay since it would be torture to live close to the man she loved and not have that love acknowledged. She seemed to respect the Squire's wife genuinely, even after such a short time and had some kind of bond with Mariana too. He understood that she had served Mariana when Elin had been away caring for her own family and had seen her then mistress through the loss of her husband, the Parson.

His own tentative feelings – not real love yet, he would say – seemed immaterial. Before tonight he had reasoned that she might accept his offer because she must guess that the Squire was using her for a while, whereas he could offer her the security of marriage, but when the facts were told, he understood that nothing was that simple. He had hoped that eventually she might come to return the attraction he felt for her but her ardour for Sir Edward seemed all-consuming. Thomas accepted that he could not put anyone through what he had lived with for years – he could still remember his infatuation with Mariana too well. Nonetheless, he managed to dissuade her from setting out on her journey tonight. He knew that all the servants arose much earlier than the master and mistress and assured her that she would be away hours before Mrs Rowlands had read the letter which Rosie had left for her. He offered to take her part of the way on the back of a horse, smiling then and saying that this might stop the boy from protesting too much at being forced to leave!

"I suppose you don't want to go back to the house now."

"I dare not. I have already risked waking Kate and Peggy. It was hard enough to pack my belongings into my bag without any of the little girls seeing. I might even disturb Elin. Can I stay here? Lie next to Ted?"

"There's not enough room where he is. You can take my bed and I will find somewhere else to lay my head. I only need one blanket."

"Absolutely not!" she exclaimed. "I couldn't possibly take your bed."

"Don't argue with me, Rosie. You look worn out." He pulled her to her feet and gave her a light push towards the bed. She turned back to him and unexpectedly stood on tiptoe and kissed his cheek saying:

"I am really touched by your offer."

He left her and the lantern and prowled around the stable, trying to decide where he could rest. The cobbles by the stalls were cold and damp and he found himself returning to his snug hideaway. Rosie was fast asleep, fully clothed, her breath showing misty in the night air. Flinging the blanket around him like a cloak he hunched up on the wooden chair but sleep eluded him. Finally he sat on the floor at the end of the bed; his head began to loll against the bedclothes swathed around Rosie's feet and he dozed off when exhaustion overtook him.

MARIANA

Mariana awoke with fear running through her veins. Something was wrong with Mars. She could sense it. Quickly she threw back the covers of her bed and heaved her cumbersome frame out of the bed. The child was very large now. She could feel his little foot underneath her skin, on occasions kicking and other times still and, for some reason this made her understand that he was a real person with moods – living out his own life inside her. How she longed to be free of the burden of carrying him; she wished her body belonged to her again!

Forgetting the babe she recalled her reason for waking – Mars! Hastily she lit the candle on the mantelshelf over the smouldering coals, since she did not want to fall, and her eyes saw her cloak hanging on the back of the door. She reached for it as she left the room.

Her heart was racing. What could be wrong with Mars? Was his fever raging once more? This morning Thomas and she had decided that he was well on his way to recovery. She must hurry to find out what ailed him. She moved as fast as she could but her wide girth slowed her and the tiny flame of the candle kept blowing towards its death. She dare not let it go out because everywhere was pitch black. She had no idea of what o'clock it was but she concluded that everyone must have retired long ago and be asleep.

When she pushed open the door to the servant parts of the house she perceived a faint orange glow in the corridor. The kitchen fire must be burning brightly, or could someone have lit the bread oven? She was puzzled. It was Mrs Jones' custom to damp down the fire before she retired, removing both kettle and pans. Creeping along the tiled floor, intending to enter the kitchen, she discovered that the glimmer was coming from outside. Nonetheless, her anxious mind did not register the explanation of the mysterious illumination until she stepped out of the house and smelt the night air.

Fire! The stables were on fire!

Momentarily she stopped, stunned, horror paralysing her, for already the flames were at the windows and the smoke was billowing across the yard. Then she revived.

Screaming an alarm at the top of her voice, she sped across over the cobbles with only one thought in her mind: she must save Mars. At least she knew now why she had awakened.

Moving towards the burning building, she saw that the worst of the violent flames were at the other end of the stable where the vehicles were kept. Were the wheels and body of the carriages fuelling the monster's appetite? The heat was less intense at the end where the stalls were, where the animals were kept; maybe she would be able to free the horses after all; hope rose in her breast.

When she reached the stable door, she paused. Caution filled her. Would the fire lick out towards her when she opened it? she asked herself. The persistent wind of earlier was high and presumably was fanning the flames. Yet she could not be defeated by forebodings. Courage must override frightening possibilities. She leant her shoulder against the wood, pleased not to feel any searing temperatures and stepped inside the stable. The whole of the far end of the building was ablaze and against the brightness she could see the outline of the horses, agitatedly prancing. Above the roar of the fire, she heard them whinnying.

With no more hesitating, she headed towards the nearest horse, catching at its mane, pulling its head downwards. She spoke to it, soothing it with nonsense words, as she strived to move it out of the stall and towards the door, but the beast, maddened by the loud sounds and thickening smoke, would not budge.

Mariana tried to squeeze behind it, intending to shoo it from its rear with a well-aimed slap, but the unborn babe prevented her. In that moment she perceived the danger of being trampled underfoot. In a trice she made up her mind. She would leave this crazed animal and save her favourite. Once Mars was out she could return to this horse.

Mars' stall was nearest the furnace and he should have been kicking against the partition, but Mariana realised that the hot, spark filled air, must be overcoming his breathing and confusing him. When he heard his mistress' voice he neighed – was it with relief? He seemed only too glad to follow her lead, trusting in her whilst she guided him away from those terrifying flames.

Mariana was delighted with how easy Mars was to handle. She could not believe that he was walking sedately towards escape and freedom. When she reached the entrance to the stables, she heard a crash and saw, beyond the broad back of her horse, that his stall had collapsed. She had only just been in time. When she turned her head to focus again on getting out, something else caught her attention: the child! Ted was lying, as if dead, near the horses' stalls. She flung open the door.

To her surprise the yard was full of people, none of whom she recognised at first. Who were all these strangers? Where had they all come from? Who had summoned them? Why were her own family and servants not here? Then she observed Frances, in her nightclothes, feverishly scanning the crowds.

"Frances," she called and then instructed: "Take the horse. I must go back for Ted."

"No!" shrieked her sister-in-law, but Mariana took no notice. She reckoned that Mars would find his own way away from the obnoxious odour of the all-consuming dragon and the crackle of its furious heat. She smacked his rump and returned to the stable. It would only take a moment to find the child.

However, she was mistaken. In the few seconds she had been outside, the building had been overcome with smoke and she could see nothing. Panic incapacitated her. She began to gag and then jumped when she felt something touch her.

"Mariana," chided Frances, "go out. You must look after yourself and the baby. I'll find the boy. Where is he?"

"He's over there somewhere. Let's go together. I know where he is and you don't. You can carry him, if you like."

Whilst they talked there came an eerie bray of fear. The other horses! Mariana grasped Frances' hand and together they walked, blinded and trembling, through the choking atmosphere, towards the sound of the animals. Both of them were coughing but the image of the child kept Mariana going. Where was he? Their senses were disorientated and they bumped into a wooden partition, not the stable wall as Mariana had expected. Behind it loomed the body of a horse. Surely this was the first one which she had tried to coax out. At last Mariana had her bearings.

"He's over there," she informed her sister-in-law, releasing her hold on Frances' fingers and pointing to her left. "You take him. I'll try to get this horse out."

"No, come with me," begged Frances, clinging to her. "We mustn't be separated."

"I must try to save this horse. You take the child. Follow the wood along like this. Honestly, he's just over there."

Mariana was surprised at her own calmness but she was aware that valuable minutes were being taken up in fruitless argument. She thrust Frances away from her and she was alone. The smoke had completely swallowed up the other woman.

Without warning, terror flooded her and she wished she had listened to her sister-in-law and remained by her side. Trepidation beat in her breast. She could not breathe. She could not breathe. She was going to die. She stared with smarting eyes at the floor. The smoke looked thinner down there. She crouched down awkwardly, struggling to get her head lower than the bulge of her stomach and took a large gasp. The air was by no means sweet but it cleared her thoughts and she devised a plan to save the horse. Speedily she pulled her cloak from her back and gripped it, ready to throw over the animal's head. Then, with another gulp, she stood up, holding her breath, and turned around the corner of the stall.

Unpredicted, the horse reared, pawing to be released and catching her shoulder in its agitation. With a howl of anguish she fell, twisting around, at the last juncture, to try to save herself from the thrashing hooves of the terrified animal.

"Mariana!"

She heard her name being called and then she heard nothing more.

FRANCES

Frances wept with fear. She could not find the child and she could not see her sister-in-law.

"Mariana," she panted desperately, but the sound of the horse crashing down the wood, finally out of control, prevented her from discerning any reply. That is, at first. Then she heard another cry, close by. It was a whimpering sound, not an animal this time, but a child.

"Mammy," the boy was saying and there, miraculously, a bare three feet away from her, was Ted.

Frances grabbed the sobbing child and fell to her knees; she could see the air was less fetid near the floor and she began to crawl towards the door. All of a sudden she heard the thunder of hooves and she crouched over the child as the horse leapt from the confines of its stall. She felt a searing pain in her elbow when the animal knocked her with his hoof and then the beast was gone. She could hear it running around the confined space of the stables. She must move before it came back.

Frances lay over the child. Her arm was hanging at a strange angle and she was in agony. Could she reach the door? The pain was excruciating. She cradled the child with her undamaged arm.

"Ted," she ordered. "You must crawl with me. You must crawl with me."

She lifted herself from the child's body and watched as Ted raised his head.

"Mammy," he repeated.

Frances dared not look at her arm. Was it broken? Out of the corner of her eye she could see it was dangling there horribly. She turned to her goal instead: the door, but whilst she gazed across the building, a burning rafter fell from the roof across her path. The flames leapt high, illuminating the way. Frances heaved herself upright and lifted the child with her uninjured arm.

Then, calling on God for strength, she ran towards the door, jumping the flames to burst through the entrance. When she hit the wood, a fresh pain shot along her arm and she felt it click, but her only thought was that she was out! Thank God she was out! The air refreshed her smoke-filled chest, but she could not keep on her feet any longer. She sank to the hard cobbles, the child slipping from her grasp to the wet yard.

All around her was the bustle and noise of the fight to contain the fire. Water splashed over her as people threw the life-saving fluid to try to douse the flames. From out of the confusion a man strode towards her. Not Edward, she registered, since he had no peg leg. She did not recognise him, but he lifted her up tenderly, encompassing the boy too, and carried her towards the house, away from danger.

"No," she entreated. "Leave me! You must go back for Mariana. Mariana is in there."

Without hesitation the stranger ran the last few steps to the back door. There he placed her carefully on the step and she leant against the wood, Ted in her lap, her throbbing arm resting between the child and herself.

The man had gone before she could say anything else and she watched him race towards the burning building. He paused only to throw his shirt into a bucket which was standing on the cobbles. Scattering droplets everywhere, he wrapped his head in the wet material and darted into the stable.

Frances closed her eyes. He would never survive, whoever he was, for the roof was alight and the windows shone copper and brass. He would be burned with Mariana. Gone. Dead.

The boy shifted himself and pains shot through her. He struggled to leave her lap, with a moan of distress. She let him stand, but caught at his shirt tails, in case he wandered too near the heat or was trampled by the throng. He appeared dazed, crying for his mother, but Frances could not see Rosie anywhere.

She knew she ought to go indoors and bandage her arm, possibly even lie down because her head was spinning. Her chest hurt from the smoke but she could not exert herself to rise up and walk the pace or two into the house. Mariana was dead. All for the sake of a horse. Mariana was dead. She could find no tears; her injury seemed to be numbing her, but she wished she had dragged her sister-in-law out with her a few moments ago.

From behind her, nearly knocking Frances over, came a woman. The child turned with a cry:

"Mammy!"

However, it was the maid, Elin.

"Madam!" she enunciated almost stumbling over the threshold. "Are you all right, Madam?"

"Yes, but you must take the boy. I'm afraid he will run back towards the stables in his search for his mother. Have you seen Rosie?"

"No, Madam. Come, Ted, *cariad bach*. Come to Elin. We will go and look inside for your mother."

When she swung around to go, there came a bellow from the stables and then, with the remainder of the roof collapsing, the stranger appeared with a bundle in his arms. Frances stood up with joy. He had done it! He had brought Mariana. Her senses reeled and she sat down again whilst figures ran forward to relieve the man of his burden. Frances was not elevated enough to see, but when Elin enquired: "Who is it?" She instructed:

"It's Mariana. Go for me, Elin, and see if she is alive."

They transferred the boy's grubby hand between their own.

Frances watched a crowd of people surrounding the two who had come out of the furnace, but she saw the maid push her way through. The gap left by the others moving aside afforded Frances a view of her sister-in-law who was being laid on the cobbles, her white shift black with soot and ashes, the unborn baby's shape rounded and stark. The hero was removing his shirt from around her face and head but Elin knelt down, checking her mistress. Frances found herself holding her breath but she exhaled it as the cry went up:

"She's alive!"

Elin stared up at the man who had risked his life in the rescue and exclaimed:

"Mr Jack! Mr Jack, what are you doing here?"

Frances thought she heard him reply:

"Repaying Mariana for the time she saved my life!"

Even from that distance she caught his wide grin. He heaved Mariana back into his arms whilst he reassured everyone:

"Don't worry. She's alive. It's just the smoke."

"You must take her to her bed, Sir," advised Elin.

Frances closed her eyes in relief. Perhaps only she and this Mr Jack were aware of what a miracle had occurred – how close to death her sister-in-law had come. When the man with his precious load reached her, with Elin in tow, Frances stood up to make way for them. She noticed how tightly he was holding Mariana and it was as if he could not stop smiling. His skin was dotted with burns, but his hair appeared to be only scorched.

Once more Frances' legs buckled beneath her but she released the boy's hand and Elin grasped it and led him inside after the rescuer. She sat a few moments longer, allowing the truth of Mariana's remarkable escape to sink in, oblivious to the crowd. No more water was being thrown on the blaze but the people remained to stand and watch. No one should have come out of that building alive. Was the stranger an angel? How had he survived the terrible heat? From where had he found air to breathe? Yet, he could not be a heavenly being because Elin had recognised him. Who was he? A neighbour? Briefly Frances resolved to get out more and visit those who lived in nearby houses. She was sure that folk from quite a distance away might have seen the flames leaping into the night sky and had come to offer their assistance. Mr Jack must live in the area but Edward had not invited him to dine yet. But, when had Mariana saved his life? Frances shook her head; she could not think straight with the pain and the crackle of the flames and the roar of the wind.

Before her eyes, people wandered almost as if sleep walking. Initially, when she had come out of the house she had found that the crowd was organised, lines of willing hands transferring buckets and basins, any receptacle which could be used – she had even seen a hat or two – to form a chain to bring water from well or sea to the yard. She guessed that by unspoken agreement the aim was to keep the fire from reaching the Manor House but now, she noticed, everyone had given up working. All faces were turned towards the still brilliant flashing blaze, dancing and prancing in the darkness. Hope of putting out the furnace was over and Frances saw what others must have seen that the wind was blowing any stray sparks away from the other buildings and the quietly milling people. The threat of spreading appeared to have receded.

Once again Frances scanned the masses. With their backs towards her, it was hard to distinguish who was who, but she was looking for only one person and in an instant she accepted that her husband was not there. His unusual leg and her love for him would have made him stand out before her quaking vision! Frances found some she recognised – the lads who worked in the stables and the Manor House's steward, Owen Lewis and Wilson too, but no Edward.

Slowly Frances raised herself, placing her good hand on the bricks of the house to steady her trembling limbs. She had not seen Mrs Jones in the fray but surely the elderly matron would not have been able to help in a crisis such as this. Probably the housekeeper was inside tending to Mariana. The younger maids had not left the house – had they been prevented from coming out by Rosie or Elin or had they slept right through the commotion? Where was her maid? She could do with some support but, presumably Elin had found Rosie and the woman was comforting her son after his narrow escape.

Where was Edward? Why was he not here to aid her? Yes, he had not returned this afternoon for his meal or to their bed – which was not unheard of nowadays – but would he not have witnessed the smoke and flames and hurried home in the company of his neighbours? In fact, she had been lying awake pondering as to her husband's whereabouts when she had heard the cry of "Fire!"

Hobbling inside she felt anger against Edward fill her heart. She would manage to get upstairs to her bed, but if it hadn't been for the man Mr Jack, then Edward would be arriving home to the news that tragically his sister had perished. She decided that she must wrap something around her own arm and then go and check on her sister-in-law.

However, by the time she reached the deserted kitchen, she was near collapse again. It was as though she had exhausted all her supplies of strength back there in the stable. She calculated she would be unable to mount the stairway and, gratefully, she fell into the rocking chair, closing her eyes, praying that the pain would decrease.

After a short while she inspected her arm. In the light of the candles she could see that it was swelling and already purplish bruises were visible through the thin cloth of her shift. She hoped that no bones were broken. Where was everyone? Was there no one to help her upstairs?

The door opened and Biddy came in. This girl had returned recently from the Vicarage when a new vicar had been appointed; the Parson's wife had brought a whole bevy of servants with her and Biddy was surplus to requirement. Frances had been told that Biddy had been brought up here – most of her family worked at the Manor House – and Frances suspected that Edward would not refuse to re-employ her. Money was abundant. Nevertheless, all was not as it had been, since the maid slept on the top floor with the other children and not in her old home. Frances knew not why but there was plenty of room up there for one more.

Frances observed that Biddy's eyes were red-rimmed from crying and Frances soon discovered that the lass's eldest brother, Thomas, did not sleep in the family home either but in the stables and was presumed dead. Biddy was stuttering that some were saying it may have been Thomas who had started the fire, accidentally knocking over a lantern. On hearing the girl's grief, Frances considered embracing the maid but Biddy stood stiffly by the table, twisting her long unbound hair between her fingers whilst she explained to her mistress that Mrs Jones had wrenched her ankle in her hurry to get out of bed when the alarm was raised and that Elin was comforting Ted because there was no sign of Rosie.

"And the children, Biddy? Where are…?"

Footsteps interrupted her question and the stranger entered.

"Mr Jack!" Biddy's surprise echoed Elin's earlier exclamation. "I didn't know you had come back!"

"No, no one knew I was coming," he admitted. "I wonder if there is a shirt I could borrow. Mine is rather past its best." He looked from one woman to the other.

"Of course," answered Frances. "Run, Biddy, and find the gentleman a shirt in the laundry room. Mind you, one that is ironed."

When they were alone, she asked:

"How is Mariana?"

"She is still insensible. I suspect it's the effects of the smoke. I've put her on her bed and covered her with a blanket. I met Elin and she has promised to look in on her once she has settled the children. I thought I had better go outside and see if…"

"There's no need for that. The blaze is beyond control now. The others are just letting it take its course. They are only putting out any burning pieces which fly near the house. Why don't you let me find you some ointment for those burns of yours?"

"No, they're nothing."

Frances rose to her feet.

"Butter. That's what's needed. I should…" Her words petered out as the room swirled around her.

"Here, let me help *you*," offered Jack. "I think bed is the place where you need to be. You've hurt your arm. Let's have a look and then I'll carry you upstairs."

"Oh, no! You can't do that," protested Frances whilst Jack guided her back to her seat.

"Why ever not? Do you think that your arm is broken? Can you move it?"

Frances shook her head.

"It hurts too much to move. When the horse kicked it, it hung oddly, but now it's more like normal. But, it's torture to move. Are you a physician?"

"No," he laughed, "but I've had wounds to dress in the past."

"Here's a shirt for you, Mr Jack." Biddy proffered the garment. "Is there anything I can do?"

"Yes," smiled Jack. "You can get me some bandages for this friend of yours."

Biddy turned puzzled eyes on the man, but before Frances could explain that she was mistress of the house the girl had sped away for the second time.

"I…" started Frances.

"Could you bear me to tear away your sleeve?" Jack interrupted, pulling off his own torn shirt and replacing it whilst he talked. "What is your name?"

"Frances."

"Well, Frances, can you stand the pain?"

She nodded. Producing a sharp knife from his belt, he eased the material away from the injuries. Frances closed her eyes.

Oh, where are you, Edward? she cried silently. She wanted to scream out against the agony and she longed to have her husband here to comfort her. Not that this man wasn't being careful and sympathetic, but she wanted a familiar face – her own dear Edward!

It was when the last of the material came away that Frances remembered that she was dressed only in her shift and it was clinging to her tired body. She was embarrassed.

"I… I think…" she began.

"*I* think that cold water might ease the swelling."

"I think I had better go… My husband will…"

Biddy pushed open the door and quickly, while she was distracted by the maid, Frances found her arm being bandaged. It was as if the man had picked up from her half-finished sentences that she was about to refuse any treatment. She could speak no more but sat with her eyes shut, biting her lips. If she had thought the pain was bad before, despite the gentleness of this man's tending, now it was beyond belief. All modesty was driven from her mind. With Biddy supporting her arm away from her body, he wrapped her elbow and fashioned a rough sling for it.

"There, all finished," he advised her.

Frances felt the tears squeeze beneath her closed eyelids.

"You've been very brave and…" he started.

"Where is she?" Edward's roar jerked her away from her suffering.

Edward came to a standstill when he saw the occupants of the room. Frances could imagine what the scene looked like to him. She in her insubstantial, grimy nightclothes, her arm caught across her breast, her cheeks white as her bandages, with strained eyes; a tall stranger leaning close over Edward's half-naked wife; and one of the maids – hardly adding any propriety to the situation.

Frances tried to stand up and then the blackness, which had been threatening her ever since she had flung herself from the stable, overtook her. She was aware that it was not her husband who caught her before she reached the floor. Fluttering in and out of consciousness she heard what the men were saying.

"Good God!" swore Edward. "Jack! Where did you spring from?"

"It's a long story. If you'll excuse me, I'll just carry my patient to her bed. Which garret does she sleep in?"

"She doesn't sleep in a garret, Jack. She's my wife."

"Your wife! Oh, I am sorry. I had no idea."

"I'll take her."

"Don't be ridiculous, man. You wouldn't manage her with your leg."

Frances stirred against Jack's chest. She must *do* something.

"Is she badly injured?" Edward asked when Jack began to move.

"No, not when you think that she was in that burning building. She saved a small child who…"

"A small child? Ted! Is he safe?"

"Yes. Follow me, Edward."

"Is Mariana safe too?" enquired Edward somewhere along the way. "They told me outside that someone rescued her. Was it you, Jack?"

"Yes. I went to lift your wife from where she had collapsed near the building and she told me that Mariana was inside. I… I went in to find her."

"Thank you, my friend. How will I ever repay you?"

"Edward?" grunted Frances.

"He's right behind me," soothed the man who was carrying her.

"I'm here, my dear. We are nearly there."

She felt a firm hand touch her foot which dangled across Jack's arm. Oh, if only she was in her husband's arms! Barely a breath away and her wish came true. When she was laid on the bed, the stranger stood back and it was Edward who gathered her upper body against his jacket. She became aware that he was crying but all she could say was:

"Please, don't. It hurts when you press me."

"Oh, Frances, can you ever forgive me?" he whispered.

"Will you manage now?" It was her saviour, Mr Jack; she had forgotten his presence.

Edward nodded and then they were alone.

*J*ACK

Jack closed the bedchamber door quietly behind him. He had guessed that the couple had forgotten him already and abruptly he knew where he should go. Some instinct made him hurry to check on Mariana. He had stood for many minutes over her unconscious body before going down to the kitchen, willing her to open her eyes. Reluctantly he had left her, after checking her breathing for the third time, telling himself that he should return to the fire since there was nothing more that he could do for this woman. Then he had become entangled in dressing Edward's wife's wounds and half an hour must have passed since he had left Mariana. Had she come to by now? If he knocked, Elin would tell him how her mistress fared.

It only took him a moment to walk along the corridor before he was standing before an identical entrance to Edward's bedchamber. He rapped his fingers on the hard wood but no answer came. Was Mariana still insensible and if so, why was Elin not with her? He heard a noise and tentatively entered. What he saw made him hurry to the side of the bed.

Mariana was half-sitting up, gasping and panting. Her legs were bent beneath the covers and when he reached her, she crouched over them, her face red with straining.

My God, the baby was coming! he thought.

"Jack," she hissed through gritted teeth, leaning back on the rumpled pillows. Her skin was moist with sweat, but before he had time to speak another pain was upon her and she caught his hand and gripped it fiercely. He waited until the spasm had passed before he suggested:

"I'll get help for…"

"No!" she thundered. "Don't leave me! Don't leave me!"

Out of his depth Jack watched as the agony took its toll on her lovely face and then she ranted:

"I… I was alone. No one was… was here. Is it you, Jack? Is it really you?"

"But I don't know what to do," he stated, scanning the room. There was a pint jug in which he might find some water, but it would not be hot water. Hazy thoughts of childbirth and needing hot water raced through his mind.

"Just… just stay with me. I… I need you. He's… he's coming," she wailed, sitting forward to push.

Jack caught at the sheet across her legs. There was nothing for it but to assist her. She was right. The child was about to be born; its head was gleaming darkly between her thighs.

How long before the babe arrived? He did not know! What he had told Mariana was true – he only had the sketchiest idea of how a child was delivered! All he realised was that there was hardly a pause between her contractions and he could not leave her at this time to go and call for help. Where, in God's name, was Elin? She had promised that she would come as soon as the boy was settled, but Mariana must have awoken with the pains upon her and found herself abandoned.

"Come on, Mariana," he urged, kneeling on the edge of her bed and encouraging the straining woman. All thoughts of fetching a midwife flew from him; he entered wholeheartedly into receiving the babe from the womb. He hated to see Mariana so tortured and he willed the child to leave her body. He found that with each push the tiny round crown came out further and it seemed like only a few fleeting seconds before the whole child slithered from its mother in a gush of fluid.

Jack had no need to encourage the infant to breathe for it opened its mouth and yelled even as he gathered its slippery body from the bed into his hands. He had not even rolled up his sleeves on his borrowed shirt but he did not care!

"It's a boy," he announced, but his triumph passed when he observed the amount of bloody matter which had followed the child out and the coil of umbilical cord. Dear God! he swore silently. Was this usual? How could anyone survive losing all that blood?

Mariana was lying back on the bed, looking exhausted, but she managed to ask:

"Is he all right?"

"He's… he's fine," Jack felt panic rise inside him but he quelled it, determining to keep it to himself. Nevertheless, he must go and find help and he had better go right now! "Two legs and two arms, two eyes and a nose and very healthy lungs! Is there something I can wrap him in?"

Mariana gestured towards the cot in the corner of the room and Jack stood paralysed in indecision. Then he left the child on the soiled bedclothes and raced to fetch a sheet into which he bundled the child and the frightening mess and cord together. Again he hesitated.

"I must go and fetch hel… hot water," he stuttered. "Shall I put him in the cot?"

"No, give him to me. I want to see he's all right. Give him to me. Our son."

"Don't unwrap him 'til I get back," he advised, not taking in her last words, speeding through the door and descending the staircase two, and sometimes three, steps at a time. He couldn't bear to think that, having rescued Mariana from the fire, he might lose her again!

He was not sure what had made him run down and not up the stairs in search of aid, although at the back of his mind he registered that Elin would be up in the attic with the boy. Like streaked lightning he made his way down to the kitchen, intending to go outside and shout for assistance if that room was empty. However, he was met by a crowd in the kitchen and servants' hallway. Barely could he get through the door and he did not see a single face he knew immediately. Who were all these people and what were they doing here? They must be those who had come to extinguish the blaze in the stables. He halted, pondering his best course of action. Should he call out for a midwife? There were plenty of women mixed in with the men and even the odd child or two, passing around what looked like slices of bread and tankards. Then he saw someone he recognised.

"Biddy, can you help me? Is there any hot water? Mariana's baby has come and…"

"What!" A fat, old woman stepped up to him, blocking his path towards the kettle. "Did you say the baby has been delivered? Who did it?"

Jack stopped in the middle of the host of faces.

"Are you a midwife?" he breathed out, relief flooding his whole body. "Mariana needs help. There's a lot of blood. I didn't know what to do."

The whole room hushed and all eyes turned on him. He reddened.

"You?" accused the belligerent old crone. "You were with her to deliver the child?"

"Please, if you are a midwife, can you go upstairs? I think Mariana needs…"

"A man!" stormed the fat woman. "A man being present at childbed! It's unheard of! Out of my way, whoever you are. I must check that all is well.

Mary, come with me."

Jack found himself shouldered aside as the two aggressors snatched the jug which Biddy had brought to him and left the room.

"Don't worry about Mrs Parry," advised a jolly fellow who was standing nearby. "You come and have a drink. You look as though you need it. Mrs Parry believes that nobody, not even another woman, has the right to bring babies into this world. She'll sort everything out. Fancy Mrs Owen having a son! I wonder if he looks like his father."

Suddenly Jack's legs gave way. After all the excitement, he felt light-headed. Would Mariana really be all right? What if she had bled even more heavily since he had left her? What if the baby died? What if Mariana died? What if it was all his fault? What if his very inexperience had led to the tragedy?

"Hey, make room. This man needs a seat." The kindly stranger shooed a slight woman from Mrs Jones' rocking chair and Jack half collapsed.

"Sorry," he apologised.

"Ale!" ordered the man who had befriended him. "Oye, you, is there any more ale?"

"Wilson?" gasped Jack, appalled that the old retainer was being spoken to in such a manner.

"Shall I get you another shirt, Sir?" It was Biddy.

Jack gave a rueful nod.

"Mrs Owen is in the best hands," went on the young maid. "Mrs Parry knows what she's doing. She's got a sharp tongue but she knows what she's doing. She often helped my *mam*."

EDWARD

Edward stood up from his seat on the bed and watched his wife's sleeping face. At last she looked at peace, but she had been restless during the night – he suspected with the pain from her arm. He was amazed to find himself attracted to her. He remembered all the good times they had shared together before they had returned to *Trem-y-Môr*. If it had not been for the dark shadows under her eyes and her bandaged arm he would have woken her this very minute, and held her close. But he understood she needed to sleep. So he would leave her and go and find some food. He had been feeling the gnawing pangs of hunger for ages.

He moved to the windowsill and watched as the horizon lightened. The wind had scattered the clouds and behind them was a backcloth of clear, blue sky. Rapidly the moon and stars, pinned to their black curtain, were being pulled aside to reveal the day-time heavens. The dawning of a new day was like the sentiment in his breast. He had been given a new, fresh start too.

What an incredible woman his wife was! To have forgiven him was so generous of her. How could he ever have cheated on her? He allowed himself to recall what had passed between them, after Jack had left. Remembrances of last night forced themselves into his mind.

***

When Jack had laid her solicitously on their bed Edward's heart had contracted with remorse. He *had* to hold Frances and he put his arms around her. He should have been here tonight, he cursed in his head, not drinking himself under the table at the inn in Holyhead. Owen Lewis had told him how Mariana had nearly died, but obviously Frances had been courageous too. To think she had saved his son! If he owed Jack for his part tonight, he owed Frances as well for Ted's life. Ironic that she should save his son. The son of the woman he had been seeing. No more! He would not meet Rosie again. Whatever else happened, he would try to love his wife from now onwards.

"Please, don't," protested Frances. "It hurts when you press me."

"Oh, Frances, can you ever forgive me?" he whispered.

"Will you manage now?" enquired Jack.

Edward nodded. He could not speak; his voice was choked with tears. How close he had come to losing both his wife and his son! He would learn his lesson and keep his drinking for social occasions only.

He heard the door close on Jack's departure and he took Frances' uninjured hand.

"My poor lamb," he crooned. "How are you feeling?"

"I'm better for… for seeing you, Edward. I kept wishing… and wishing you could be here."

"Oh, my dearest Frances, how can I forgive myself for not being here? What would I have done if I had lost you?"

His wife frowned.

"I really mean it," he declared, lifting her fingers to his lips.

"How selfish I have been," he murmured. "Ever since we arrived here, I have ignored you. Can you forgive me?"

"Of course, my love." Frances pulled her hand away from him and placed her palm on his cheek. "Will you… you kiss me?"

He bent to her mouth and smelt the fire on her. All of a sudden, he realised how awful it would have been if she had died before he could repair the damage he had foolishly done. Barely did he brush her lips with his before he stood up and limped away. Then he swivelled around to face her.

"Oh, Frances, thank God you're all right! This… this terrible event has cleared my mind. It's made me see… see what you mean to me."

Frances shifted in the bed whilst he continued:

"I… I want to start again with… with our relationship, but first I must confess something to you." He came and sat down again. "Please don't," she repeated softly.

"Oh, but I must. It wouldn't be fair if I didn't confess that… that I haven't… haven't been faithful to you and…"

"Ssh!" she silenced him. "You don't need to tell me. Suffice that you are here now and…"

"No," he insisted, "I must tell you. My heart is burdened with guilt."

His wife covered her eyes with her uninjured hand but he could not stop. He had to tell her everything.

"Oh, Frances, it was not your fault. Don't ever think that you haven't been an excellent wife to me. No one could ask for a better wife. What happened... I didn't mean it to happen... It was... The woman... I knew her... from before we were married. She and I had... had been intimate before."

Frances turned her head away and hunched her shoulders.

"Dearest? Are you in pain?"

"Yes," she admitted.

"Then all I want to say is that it's finished. Over. It will never happen again."

He watched her face, hoping for some response, but she would not meet his gaze.

"Will you forgive me?" he whispered, reaching out for her hand again. "Frances?"

"Of course I do, Edward." At last she looked at him, and gave a crooked smile.

"Are you sure? Is there anything I can do for you? We could go away together like we did before and..."

"It's all right, Edward," she soothed. "You don't have to make it up to me. Let's forget it."

Edward embraced her, keeping his body away from her because of the injury, and kissed her, sighing with contentment.

* * *

Edward rose and hastened across the room. His heart felt light this morning. He would not be tempted again. He would make it up to her. He would. He was completely resolved that he would tell Rosie at the earliest opportunity that he could never see her again. If Mariana had not cornered him yesterday, he would have spoken to Rosie already. He had been shocked when Mariana had turned up in the cottage. Initially, he had determined to deny whatever she accused him of, but silently he cursed that she should have chanced upon him on the very occasion when he had decided to end the affair. No, he realised that Mariana's arrival was not by chance. She had come with a purpose. But what exactly had she found out? And if she had observed him, then who else had seen him and Rosie? He might have reckoned that nothing would be kept secret in a small community!

However, recalling the conversation that had occurred between himself and Mariana reminded him of his finishing words and the stupid declaration of the truth: that he was not her brother. How could he have claimed that he loved Mariana and then treated her so cruelly? He should never have told her; it was too great a burden to bear, as he himself had discovered. How could he have broken his promise to himself not to ever mention it? He had suffered deeply with the secret knowledge and now he had passed it on.

"Yes," he whispered out loud. He might have made his peace with his wife but there was someone else he needed to speak to: Mariana. He would go right away whilst Frances slept and summon Rosie to the library. It would not be suspicious – he could say that he needed to talk to the maid about his wife's condition. And, then, afterwards, he would seek out Mariana and ask for her forgiveness too.

Descending the stairs he was surprised that there was no noise of servants working. Was it that early? Hope sprang up; perhaps he would find Rosie alone and he could speak to her without any witnesses. His stomach rumbled loudly and he recalled his original plan. He would scour the larder himself for something cold to eat before embarking on any of these conversations.

WILSON

Wilson stood in what was called 'The Butler's Pantry' but was in fact his bedchamber and sitting room. Near to the cellars, since the butler was the servant in charge of the wines, and boasting only a slit window high up – which was at ground level outside – it was dark and depressing.

All those years ago, when Sir William, had decided to settle at the Manor House, Wilson had chosen to sleep (and live) in a narrow room next to the Squire's bedchamber on the first floor of the house. Then, when Sir Edward had returned with his pretty wife, Wilson had suggested that he retreat downstairs to give the newly-married couple some privacy. With Elin's help he had tried to lighten the place.

Nothing could be done about the dense, nearly black oak cupboard in the corner, which contained the family silver, including several valuable tea caddies. Originally a footman might have slept here to guard these treasures but these days, with such a depleted team of servants, there was no danger of staff running away with the contents of the homemade safe and with stout locks (from the local locksmith) on both cupboard and room door, no thieves could have gained entry anyway. Elin had found a cheerful Welsh wool blanket to lie on his bed – reds and cream with a recurring purple pattern and with the addition of a wash stand, a high backed armchair, hooks for his clothes and an antiquated chest-of-drawers, for his undergarments, he and Elin had made the space comfortable at least, if not inviting.

Wilson swayed with exhaustion and took an indecisive step towards the basin. He had been up all night fighting the blaze and the smell and the feel of the soot had sent him back down the years to when he was a chimney sweep. He'd forgotten how sticky the whole aftermath of fire was! He was sure that some of the younger maids could have told him with their daily cleaning out of the grates in all the rooms!

Once the immediate danger had died back, Wilson had offered hospitality to all the people who had come to help, although the kettle and some of the pots borrowed from the kitchen had to be retrieved first. Subsequently Wilson had tried to make sure that everything which had been appropriated from *Trem-y-Môr* was returned. Owen Lewis helped him collect buckets, pots and pans, the odd milk pail – and even a milk churn. They had smiled grimly to find a few bedpans thrown down, but who owned the abandoned hip-bath they had not found out! People's ingenuity during a crisis seemed limitless!

After dawn broke, most of the fire fighters walked away to snatch a nap before getting up to go to their daytime jobs and Wilson had left Owen and two of his children gloomily guarding the embers. It was obvious that Owen's eldest son, Thomas, had perished in the furnace and someone raking through the ash had found a metal buckle which another said belonged to Rosie's bag. Since no one had seen Rosie, it was being passed around that she had died too.

Wilson had thrown off his own grief with hard work but now it squeezed back into the edge of his mind; he had become fond of Thomas during their trips to London.

Wilson had been excited to return to his birthplace after eighteen years away. Of course, London had lost its very core in the Great Fire in the month of September in the year of our Lord 1666. The ancient city was completely destroyed. Wilson and his master had been away from their town house at the time but afterwards it was calculated that 400 streets, 600 churches and 14,000 houses were consumed in the tragedy. Now nothing familiar was left of where he spent his childhood for him to see, but something did trigger his memories and that was the smells. Almost from the moment they neared the capital, the stench stripped off the years and Wilson was a seven-year-old again, fearful and hungry, alone and vulnerable.

Like today. The fumes from the burnt out stables had shaken him. Why were smells so evocative of the past? Distance caused the fading of the sharpest memories but the whiff of perfume or the sniff of a pungent odour could conjure up bygone days instantly. How did the sense of smell drown the present and take you backwards through time?

He had understood that after the Great Fire, Londoners were devastated. Where do you start when your very heart has gone? Thank God that the Manor House had been preserved! Horses had been lost and one, maybe two, servants but much heroism had saved both Mrs Owen's and a young boy's life.

Wilson sighed with relief. His heart had not died this night! Travelling away from North Wales had made him accept that this symmetrical mansion, on a windy corner of Holy Island, was his home. Of course the death of his master last year had rocked his world. At first he had pondered the idea of retiring. Sir William had been more than Master – he had been a dear friend and Wilson was bereft. However the arrival of Sir Edward had changed all this. Very soon Wilson had become involved with the new Squire. He remembered the lively lad who was sent away to school and was dismayed to see how troubled the mature man had become.

Wilson knew all about the agony of spirits which descended on Sir Edward. He had observed the Squire's love for his sister, Mariana, flare into life on that very first eve and he had a shrewd idea who was the mother of the stable boy, Ted. His advice, given the night before last, came out of a deep desire to see his master throw off the past and start afresh. The mistress, Lady Frances, was a fine woman with many talents and gifts, but most of all she was brimful of love for her husband and Wilson was old-fashioned enough to believe that love could conquer all!

How alike father and son were, not least in their taking solace in the bottle! Yet their circumstances were continents apart; Sir William had lost his second wife on the birth of the baby but Sir Edward's wife was alive and willing to help and support and care for her husband. Wilson had become fond of both his employers and now could not leave them even if he had wanted to and had a place to go!

Yes, on this latest return, Wilson had relaxed in the safe, regular routines of rural life, mostly not even resenting the hole underground which was his domain. At least he did not spend his time off there. Indeed, the week after Sir Edward and Lady Frances had arrived, Wilson had proposed that he train up a man to serve the Squire in case anything happened to him – that is, if he died. This had led to him finding himself with time on his hands, not only because he had insisted that the younger servant be given (and take) some regular hours off but two pairs of hands got through the work at twice the speed. One of Thomas' brothers was offered the post: Adam. The youngster reminded Wilson of himself when he had been rescued by Sir William from poverty and surviving on his wits. The boy had a look of Biddy about him but the mannerisms of Thomas. Wilson had enjoyed learning Welsh from Thomas during their sojourn in London and teaching him his own tongue, but Adam was quicker and brighter than his eldest sibling and spoke precise English already, with hardly an accent at all. The child was shaping up well and Wilson had found his own enthusiasm and strength double when he took on the role of teacher. Adam remained living at his father's hearth each evening and Wilson had encouraged him to go there this morning, telling him only to come back after he had rested.

In fact he also ought to lie down and try to snooze before Adam returned – the lad was not ready yet to assist Sir Edward without supervision. All the same, Wilson wondered if sleep would elude him. He guessed that memories, former and latter, would keep him awake.

Nevertheless, he did come to one decision. He drew fresh water from a jug and began to scrub the grime and soot from his hands and face and neck, leaving a frothy scum on the rim of the basin. Slowly he started to disrobe. Surely he would feel better once he had changed and had clean clothes on!

His mind recalled the past few months. On his return, before Adam was employed, loneliness surrounded Wilson. If Sir William had been his friend then the older man had been his only friend. There were male outdoor staff working on the estate, but no one his age and increasingly he found himself dwelling on the years which were gone and which the next generation knew nothing about. Unable to settle in the Butler's Pantry, when his tasks were done, he had started to venture forth to walk the seashore and nearby paths, finding, as he exercised, his body became fitter and he could go further and further. He would never run like Adam and his brothers but there was a quiet satisfaction in being out in the air, with the sights and smells of the sea and country around him.

And on one of these outings he had found a friend. On a sunny afternoon in March, he had bumped into Matthew Cutland and the two had struck up an easy conversation which had led to an invitation to Matthew's house on his next afternoon off. He and Matthew were of a similar age and found much in common to talk about. It wasn't long before he met the shy woman, Pearl, and heard about Matthew's worries over her future. Realising that they were man and wife, Wilson had suggested that his new friend make these congenial arrangements official and legal. It transpired that Matthew had many concerns about Wilson's idea but two stood out: the age gap and whether Pearl would be accepted into the community. Wilson had advised the retired surgeon that often it was difficult to guess the age of people from other cultures, adding that he would never have known how young Pearl was if he hadn't been told. On the latter disquietude, Wilson had hatched a plan.

"I suspect that if Pearl wore western clothes, it might help her to fit in more. Also, if you present her as your wife, whom you have just married, rather than someone who has been your servant for years, it might smooth her acceptance. Why don't you say that you are travelling to Liverpool to meet Pearl, marry her away from this area, and then return with her after the deed is signed and sealed?"

Matthew must have thought over what Wilson had said because he purchased a carriage in which he smuggled out his Chinese servant, dressed in her tunic and trousers, and went away for several weeks before arriving home with an attractive wife attired in bodice and skirt, her black plaits hidden beneath a very fashionable bonnet. Nowadays, Mr and Mrs Cutland were seen everywhere together.

It was fortunate, mused Wilson to himself, that the Cutlands were away at the moment, since usually their horses were stabled here and would not have survived last night. Of course, Matthew's expert knowledge would have been useful to anoint and bind the various minor burns which inevitably had been sustained by the helpers. Wilson had found himself, aided by Biddy and Elin (once the child had fallen into a restless sleep) acting as surgeon and doctor during the hours of darkness. Fortunately, in his opinion, the news of the fire had not reached the ears of that obnoxious man, Lloyd, although he remembered Lloyd had not been seen in this area since the scandal of his supposed affair with Mrs Owen which the Vicarage housekeeper had announced from every street corner.

Stiffly, Wilson removed his stained breeches, jacket and shirt. He hesitated once more and then washed all over in the cold water, shivering, goose pimples appearing on his naked flesh, before dressing quickly.

Ah, that certainly did decrease his tiredness and heartache! The loss of Thomas would hit him later but, finally, he felt able to go back upstairs and visit the housekeeper. He had been informed about Mrs Jones' fall, but there had been no time to offer her comfort. He suspected that she would have been both relieved at not having to play a part in extinguishing the fire and frustrated at not being able to mix with everyone, in charge of refreshments and queen of her own kingdom.

Wilson gathered up the discarded clothes, ready to leave them in the laundry and balanced the basin full of dirty water on his arm. He liked order in both his quarters and in his master's rooms. Revived by the wash and change and some solitary moments of reflection in his room, he left, pulling the iron-studded door shut behind him.

As usual he felt like he was leaving a prison but today his spirits lifted. Something had happened last week to bring wings to his feet: Matthew had offered him bed and board in *Tŷ Craig* – Matthew's solid house perched above the waves – if ever Wilson did decide to retire. Wilson was delighted. *Tŷ Craig* was near enough for him to visit those he counted as family but not a house on the Squire's estate that would make Wilson feel that he owed Sir Edward for his kindness. One fly in the ointment was that Matthew had confided in him at the same time as the invitation was extended, that Pearl and he were to have a child. This might complicate the situation but right now Wilson was glad that he had found friendship in his dotage which included such a generous offer, allaying his own fears about the future.

Up the wide, worn stone steps Wilson trod, aware, unexpectedly, of hunger. Perhaps he would eat before taking up his tasks. Arriving in the kitchen, after depositing his burdens in the laundry room, he was met with the sight of Biddy in the embrace of a young man.

"Oh, Sir! I'm sorry. This is Edmond."

"I have met Edmond before. Good day to you both."

"Edmond heard about the fire and came across straight away to check I was not hurt. He was so worried that he has asked me to marry him and I have agreed. We will go and see the new Parson this week and arrange to have the banns read."

"Congratulations to you both, but don't you think you should speak with your father or the Squire first?"

"Oh, I haven't told the Squire yet."

"What haven't you told me yet, my girl?" It was Sir Edward, dressed and looking as though he had slept all night, which Wilson guessed he had not! There was a teasing tone in his question.

Biddy reddened before repeating her news. Edward suggested that the young couple went and spoke to Biddy's father and valet and master were left alone together.

"Wilson, is the blaze out?"

"Yes, Sir. Everyone has gone home and most of the house is asleep and…"

"And you? Have you had any rest?"

"No, Sir, but I don't need much sleep nowadays. How is your wife, Sir?"

"She eventually fell asleep a short while ago. It's what she needs most. Tell me, is Jack about?"

"No, Sir, he returned to his ship, but he told me he would come back in the morning."

"Ship! What ship?"

"Supposedly he came by ship, Sir, and some of his men helped dampen the fire. You can see the vessel from your library window, Sir."

Edward led the way into the library. Both men observed a brigantine sitting at anchor off-shore.

"It's a fine vessel. Is it his ship?" enquired Edward.

"I don't know, Sir."

Sir Edward left the window and looked around the room.

"There isn't much light in this room, Wilson, is there?"

He did not say anything more but Wilson surmised that his master felt that this room was full of unhappy memories. Sir Edward was continuing:

"What say you that we make some changes here? Maybe we can sort out some of these books and get rid of some of them or place shelves all around the house so that this room isn't so cluttered. Or maybe we can extend the house. Yes, if we built an extension, we could fit another bedchamber upstairs. We are going to have to rebuild the stables, and I'm wondering if we could redesign the house too. What do you think Wilson?"

"I think improvements could be made, Sir."

"Were any horses saved last night?"

"Yes, Sir. By some miracle Mrs Owen managed to lead her own stallion from the fire. She will be pleased, for, now she's been delivered of the baby, she will want to ride again and then there was…"

"Has the child come?"

"Yes, Sir. Last night. The women were chattering in the kitchen that the shock of the fire had brought on the birth pangs, but, although the child was early, he is fit and healthy, even if a little under sized."

"A boy, then," breathed the Squire. "And how is… my sister?"

"I haven't seen her myself, Sir, but have been told that mother and child are very well."

"Strange how I didn't hear any cries. Our room is only next door. I suppose it's the thick walls. Still, never mind." He straightened his shoulders.

"What do you say, Wilson, to a morsel to eat? I'm famished. Like you I haven't slept, but my appetite is not affected. Rather it is increased by all the activity in the night."

"Very good, Sir. I can boil a kettle and bake eggs and…"

"That sounds most acceptable, Wilson."

Barely had they begun to search for the necessary cooking utensils and food, when they were joined by Elin. Her face was worried and she held a folded piece of paper in her hand.

"Sir," she said. "I… I have just found this in the room where Rosie sleeps. I did go in there last night but in the dark I missed it. It's addressed to your wife, Sir."

EDWARD

Edward felt the colour drain from his face.

"I'm sure Mrs Rowlands won't mind if I open it," he observed, snatching the paper from the maid. He could not wait to find out what it contained. What had Ally written to his wife? He prayed that she had not confessed her part to Frances. He scanned the neat writing. "Well, I'll be damned! It says she has gone to London because she is homesick and…"

"Gone to London!" Elin interrupted, evidently forgetting who she was talking to. "But she left the child."

"Yes, indeed. That's surprising. What do you make of that, Wilson?"

Before Wilson could reply, Elin commented:

"I can't understand it at all. I have spent all night trying to calm her little son. He cried himself to sleep finally, over the fact that his mother wasn't to be found."

"You don't think she was in the fire, Sir?" suggested Wilson in a quiet tone.

"I… I…" stammered Edward. His Ally dead! Could it be true? And Frances saving her child and his. If she had known the identity of his lover, would she still have risked her life saving young Ted? Ally dead! Please God, no! Although it would solve one of his problems, he would not want that!

"Oh, no, Wilson," argued Elin. "The letter explains where she has gone."

"Did anyone see her go?" questioned Edward whilst he sought out a seat for himself. Exhaustion overtook him.

Wilson and Elin shook their heads.

"There is a possibility that her bag was…" began Wilson.

"Maybe we'll never know," Edward went on. He must not show any feelings otherwise these servants might suspect something and that would be a pity since he was reconciled with his wife now. His head swam; he needed food urgently. "Wilson, is there anything I can eat?"

"I'll cook you a meal, Sir," put in Elin and immediately started to bustle about.

It was as Edward broke his fast that Jack knocked on the door. He was well dressed this morning, with no signs that he had nearly lost his life in a terrible blaze last night. He smiled at the occupants of the kitchen.

"May I come in?" he asked.

"Jack!" exclaimed Edward. "Come and join me. I'm just having a meal. You owe me… well, all of us, an explanation."

"I won't eat, but I'll sit with you. I have already eaten on board ship and…"

"Yes, you sly fox!" interposed Edward. "You never told me you were a sailor."

Jack laughed.

"The last time I saw you, I did not even know my name!"

"Well, who are you?"

"My name is Philippe Salisbury and I come from… from France originally, but from all around the world recently."

"And how did your memory return?" remarked Edward.

"Ah, that's a long story. I'm afraid it didn't come back all in a flash, like lightning, but gradually over the months. The best result… I mean when I made the greatest step forward, was when I saw something familiar – my ship. Of course I could recall all of the time I spent with you and the fact that I was dragged from here, against my will, one night and…"

"That's not what we were told!" gasped Elin. "We were told you were found by a friend, who whisked you back to your home in Scotland."

Jack cast puzzled eyes at Elin.

"Who told you that?"

"Miss Mariana," confessed the maid.

"Mariana. Well, I've yet to speak with her. We were too busy for polite conversation last night!"

"What do you mean?" demanded Edward.

"Mr Jack delivered the child, all by himself, Sir, much to the anger of Mrs Parry," declared Elin.

"How is Mariana this morning?" Jack broke in before Edward could exclaim on this unusual event.

Edward and Wilson both looked at Elin for an answer.

"When I last put my head around the door, she was asleep with her son tucked in beside her. I had a peek at him and he is very sweet. He doesn't look like Miss Mariana or his father. At least, I don't think so!"

"Who was his father?" queried Jack in an undertone.

"The Parson," grunted Edward with a grim expression on his face. "God alone knows why she agreed to marry him! Like you I was not here when she married him."

"I think, Sir, she thought that there would be no one else." Elin seemed quick to defend her mistress.

"And has the Parson seen his son?"

Jack's question was met with silence.

"The Parson is dead." It was Edward who replied eventually.

Jack made no comment, but simply crossed his legs and leant back in his chair.

"So, you haven't told us what you did when you recovered your memory," scolded Edward. He found that he did not want to talk about Mariana.

"There wasn't much I could do. Initially I was trussed up like a chicken on its way to market in the hold of an unknown ship." His usually amicable face was serious.

"Who were your captors, Sir?" Wilson spoke for the first time.

"That I didn't discover for several days. Hazy memories danced in my mind just out of reach and, later, when I remembered everything it turned out that this was the second time I had been tied up. The night I was shipwrecked on your shore, I was also a prisoner."

He paused.

"Go on," urged Edward.

"As I've already said: it's a long story."

"We've plenty of time, haven't we?" persisted Edward.

"I must go back a bit then and I shall tell the tale as if I never lost my memory for the ease of the telling. I have been a proud owner of my own ship since I was twenty-one. My father ran a fleet of ships which brought merchandise from all over the world to France – before the war, of course. On my twenty-first birthday he gave me my own ship. Needless to say, she, the 'Antoinette', and I became fast friends. She took me all across the seas, through hurricane and calm. So, when pirates attacked and stole her, I was not pleased. They came in two boats, when we had just left the Americas fully laden, and my loyal crew and I fought like mad men! Some of my sailors were killed in the battle with a dozen of the pirates, but those of us who were still alive were divided between the two vessels and taken prisoner on the pirate ships. But '*Antoinette*' sailed away, captained by a sly pirate whose name I knew as 'Red Knife'.

"Before many days had passed my men were pressed into service but I was left in a cramped hole below decks, often chained but with my thoughts ranging far and wide. I had no idea where we were, since I couldn't see the night sky, but we must have been crossing the Atlantic. When the storm hit us, it was the pirate ship which sank off your coast here. As you know there were no other survivors – all my men, who were captured with me, were drowned – and, when I got my memory back, I remembered what had happened. I can't believe no one else managed to get ashore. I know the hull of the ship cracked wide open when we hit rocks and I was catapulted into the waves. Amidst the grief of losing my crew was the realisation that if I hadn't been transferred from '*Antoinette*' to the pirate ship, it would have been my ship at the bottom of the sea not far from the Manor House. Whereas…"

"Did the pirates recapture you then?" piped up Elin. "The second time, I mean."

"No, they don't bother with that, my dear. I'm afraid at that time, I had no idea not only why I was lying in a ship's hold but that it hadn't been many weeks earlier that I had been imprisoned before. It was days, or so it seemed to me, before we reached our destination, and I was in no fit state to care who had taken me or where I was. It later transpired that we had anchored off a private beach on the west coast of Ireland. I was manhandled before the man who had ordered my capture: Mr Lawrence Murphy.

"One look at me, even in my dishevelled state, and he began to curse his men. I was apparently not the right man. He had sent his men to search for someone who had seduced his wife and then escaped to North Wales by boat. All he could give his men was a sketchy description, although he had caught… caught the man and his wife in rather compromising circumstances and knew he would recognise him again instantly. But I wasn't the man.

"His crew had come to Holyhead and heard about a stranger who had lost his memory. However, there was a rumour that I was faking! They decided that I was their quarry and I was trying to hide my identity with a tale of lost memory. They had observed me on several occasions and I fitted the description they had been…"

"What kind of fools were these people?" intercepted Edward. "They could have killed you and you, an innocent man. I hope this Lawrence Murphy recompensed you well."

"He did," laughed Jack. "In the end very well indeed. I can't say I was glad about my treatment. I developed a bad cough in my chest and my head would not heal for weeks, but I was alive."

"Is the ship we can see in the bay yours then?" Edward wanted to know.

"Yes, and she is the reason why I have taken this long to return here. Whilst I was recuperating I decided that I wanted to come back here and... and see you all and thank you for everything you did for me. My intention was to make Mr Murphy bring me back and then I would go to my family in..."

"What have your family being doing during this time? Have you a wife?" Edward was caught up in the story and had almost forgotten his own problems.

"I did. She died seven years ago. My relatives are well used to not hearing from me for months and months, but I sent them a message from Ireland. I intended to send one here but I thought I would reach you before it did.

"At dusk one evening I saw my ship. She had a new name but there was no mistaking her! I rushed – well, hobbled, might be a better word – to my captor-turned-host and asked him to lend me some of his stalwart men. He was most happy to aid me; in fact, he wanted to come too. We were going to creep down in the dead of night and board my '*Antoinette*', but someone warned the pirates and we had to pursue them. Hence the delay. Mr Murphy once again came to the rescue and furnished me with a ship and a full crew.

"I must say that my recovery was much quicker once I was a captain again! Visions of my dead and dying men spurred me on. I'd seen broken bodies before – no one survives falling from the top of the mast – but when the men who served me so faithfully were cut down by a horde of marauding devils intent on capturing my vessel, that was not to be tolerated! On we sped, although Mr Murphy's vessel wasn't as fast as my '*Antoinette*'. Needless to say we lost her almost immediately, but some instinct made me set a straight course to where the original attack had occurred. Sure enough, we found her moored not half a mile down the coast from the scene of the bloody battle. It appeared that we had strayed too close to the pirates' base camp on that fateful day and this was why two ships were sent to sink us. There were not meant to be any survivors. But then, I believe, Captain Red Knife took a fancy to my '*Antoinette*'. The cargo in my hold was valuable to me. I intended to make a profit but there was no gold or treasures to interest such men as these, except one prize. My brigantine is well built and fast, very fast! I'm not sure why any of our lives were spared. Did the pirate captain of our vessel disobey his orders? Or were we simply being used to man the boat until we reached our destination, where we would have been disposed of and then the storm sank us? I couldn't say and I didn't bother to find out when we came face to face with the pirates.

"Amongst Mr Murphy's sailors were a battalion of hardened soldiers – some of whom now work for me – and the actual victory was not very spectacular. We hid in the next bay and then rowed around under the cover of darkness. With only a skeleton crew on watch, it was surprisingly easy to climb on board and overtake them. Then we sat down and waited for Mr Red Knife to return. I personally had the pleasure of running a sword through his heart.

"Now '*Antoinette*' was mine again. Again I resolved to return to Mari... to you all and thank you for your hospitality. But the winter storms had arrived. Subsequently, once the weather was fair, we had to sail with only half the number of men I needed, back to Ireland, alongside the other half of Mr Murphy's men, and then recruit a new crew. It was more difficult than I had expected. Hence the protracted delay in arriving."

"Nonetheless, a very timely arrival, if I might say so, Sir."

"Wilson is right, Jack," agreed Edward. "Your arrival could not have been more timely. My wife has told me how you bravely saved Mariana's life."

"Foolish girl to go into such a blaze! But I suppose you couldn't expect her to think sensibly when Mars was in danger. Apparently she went in to rescue him." Jack half smiled at Edward when the door opened to reveal Peggy.

"Please, Elin, can you come?" she entreated. "The baby is crying and Miss Mariana needs you."

"Will you excuse me, Sir?"

Edward nodded and whilst Elin dashed away, Wilson began to clear the table.

"Shall we go into my study, Jack?" offered Edward.

Jack rose from the table and the two men walked slowly out of the room.

"Your wife is a very courageous woman, Edward. Where did you meet her? Incidentally, how is she today?"

"She is sleeping. She was in a lot of pain. I'm going to call Cutlass to see her today. By the time I had thought of it last night, she was asleep. You bandaged her arm, she told me."

"Yes. I don't think it is broken, but Cutlass will know. How is he?"

"He hasn't been here for a week or two. I... I have been very busy with the estate."

"Are you here to stay now?"

"Yes. Frances' home was in Portugal, but her only relative there died recently, so she is contented to settle here. And, of course, there is the threat of war... I miss the sea, I'll admit to you, although this damned leg of mine is a great hindrance aboard ship. I'd like to see your vessel, if I might."

"Of course. Any time."

Edward waved a hand towards a seat for Jack to take and then he pondered:

"What are your plans? Are you bound for faraway lands?"

"It all depends on... on your sister. I want to ask for her hand in marriage. Would you agree to such a proposal?"

Edward sat down in shock. So, this was why Jack had returned; he wanted Mariana too. Edward felt jealousy spring up inside him, but he cast it aside. Mariana was not for him. He had resolved to be faithful to his wife and Wilson had urged him not to ruin his life by dwelling on a relationship that could never be realised. Was this a solution to his personal problems at last? If Mariana moved to France with Jack...

"Where is your home?" he rejoined.

"I don't have a home, as such. It is a long time since I lived with my parents, but I..."

"But when you were married. Where did you and your wife live?"

"She... she lived with my parents. They have a large house and she was only seventeen on our wedding day. We were married three days after my twenty-first birthday and a week later I left on my newest possession, *Antoinette*. Much later my wife accused me of being in love with my ship and I suppose I was, in a way."

"Where did you learn such good English?"

"My father is English, my mother French. My father set up his business in France because it suited him. He argued with my grandfather and was happy to live a reasonable distance from his relatives. His family come from the north of England. I haven't seen any of them for years."

"And your wife? What was her name?"

"Magdalena. She and I did not spend more than four months in total together, even though we were married five years. She... I came home one time and found that she had... had taken up residence with my younger brother. I was furious and was all for killing the pair of them. My mother told me that it was my own fault; that I ought to spend more time on shore. She told my brother of my intentions and he and Magdalena fled. By the time I returned from the next voyage, both my brother and my wife were dead from fever." He paused. "I did not think to marry again. My marriage is with the sea, but, like you, I have been thinking of settling down. Your sister is too... too..."

"Delectable?"

Jack laughed.

"Possibly. I was thinking more along the lines of 'unpredictable'! She would not cope well if she were left alone for lengthy periods of time alone. However, I suppose with a child, she will have matured. I have enough money to retire but..."

"What do you feel about caring for another man's child?" mused Edward.

"I hadn't thought. I... When I arrived last night I was caught up with the fire. Of course, I saw immediately that she was with child and I assumed I was too late... That she already had a husband. If I was too late, then I would have only myself to blame for chasing after my ship before coming and wooing Mariana. It seems I have learnt nothing in the six years since my wife died. Now, I have discovered from you, a few moments ago, that she is a widow. I've hardly had time to take it all in. And, of course, there is Mariana herself. She may not want me. We... we did not talk of... of anything like this when I was last here. Henry filled her mind and she was grieving over the death of Sir William and I had no idea whether I was married or not. So..."

"She would be a fool not to take you!" retorted Edward.

"Ah, but I was hoping that my wife, this time, would return my love."

"I suggest you go up and find out, Jack. Send Elin away with the child and talk to Mariana."

JACK

When Jack knocked at the door of Mariana's room, he was ushered into a quiet place.

"Where's the baby?" he enquired.

"He's asleep in his cradle," explained Mariana. "Come and see him, Jack."

Whilst he leant over the cot, which had been moved to the side of the bed, mistress and maid exchanged a muted conversation before Elin left.

"What do you think, Jack? Isn't he gorgeous?"

Jack put one finger to stroke the child's forehead. He was lying on his side, tucked under the blankets, and all Jack could see of him was a tiny snub nose and a thatch of black hair. Already he looked different from last night.

Jack glanced around. Everything was in order; no sign of any panic. Evidently, the delivery had been normal and he blushed to remember his own fears. He brought his eyes back to Mariana. She too was looking better than when he had last seen her. Her resplendent hair was brushed and neatly plaited, hanging in a thick rope over her shoulder. Her young face was full of delight and pride. He smiled.

"Congratulations! I think he is a grand baby."

He walked across the room and sat on the window seat, gazing out to sea.

"Jack?" she muttered. "I suppose I shouldn't call you that. Elin says your name is 'Philippe' but…"

"But my middle name is 'Jacques', therefore I don't mind. What else has she told you?"

"Not much. Charles was crying. We had our hands full."

Silence fell. Jack wondered why it was so difficult to talk to this woman. He recalled the dozens of conversations that had flown between them nearly a year ago – easy, not stilted, and relaxed and with no drawn-out pauses. And what about the intimacy they had shared on his last day here? This was Mariana, his friend, his love, for God's sake!

"Mariana…" began Jack as she started simultaneously:

"I hope that…"

Jack laughed and shifted to face the woman in the bed in order to see her clearly.

"You first," he offered.

"No, you. What were you going to say?"

"I have much to recount… We have a great amount of news to catch up on. Many things have happened. It's been… How many months?"

"An eternity," he thought she whispered, but when he enquired she did not repeat what she had said.

"I thought you were dead," she shuddered.

"So did I, when I first awoke."

"Matthew Cutland saw you being taken away. At least, he did not realise it was you, until I told him you had disappeared, without trace."

"I'm sorry. It wasn't intentional."

"I couldn't believe you had gone. I… I did as you suggested. That very morning I apologised to Margaret for attacking her and then…"

"Margaret! What ever happened to her?"

"She and Edward argued… argued over my marriage to Griffith. He thought…"

"Edward is still very bitter about you marrying the Parson. Why did you marry him? You…"

"Edward is wrong to be bitter about it. He… he was not here when I needed his… his advice, and…"

"And neither was I." Jack discontinued before saying, "We all left you, Mariana. Was it very perplexing?"

"Yes," she sighed. "But, looking back, I can't help wondering if it wasn't good for me, in a way. It showed me that I could manage on my own and nowadays I don't need anyone."

"Are you thinking of getting married again?" He trusted he gave no clue of how important her reply was to him.

"No. I've experienced a loveless marriage and I don't want to repeat it. In fact, I know I've said this to you before, but I really mean it this time: I'm never going to get married."

Jack kept his voice level.

"And the babe? What about him? Will he grow up all right without a father?"

"I had no mother," came the rapid reply.

Jack heard something in her tone which made him stand up and walk to the end of the bed, where he had stood to deliver the child. Pushing remembrances of that both terrifying and amazing moment, he asked:

"And what if you loved someone? Would you change your mind then?"

For a second or two she did not answer, but plucked at the bedclothes. Then she sniffed:

"It's very difficult to say. It's just conjecture. It would depend on… on many factors."

Jack retraced his steps to the window, away from her direct gaze in case she observed his dejection. Obviously she did not feel anything for him! Conjecture, she had said. She did not love him in return. Oh, God, what was he going to do? He had believed and prayed that she would want him too!

"And you?" Mariana spoke in a subdued voice. "The last time I saw you, you did not remember if you had a wife. Do you?"

Jack put his hand to the cold windowpane, trying to collect his anguished thoughts. He had never imagined that his suit would be unsuccessful, if Mariana was free to marry him, in spite of what he had said to Edward downstairs. He had come here full of excitement to find that he had nearly lost his beloved to the Grim Reaper. Then, he had seen the unborn child and concluded that Mariana was already married and he was too late. Earlier this morning his heart had leapt with joyful anticipation when Edward had told him that Mariana was a widow. All to end with this: the woman herself had no love for him.

What should he tell her about his wife? he asked himself. He could say that he was still married. He could not bring himself to make a formal proposal after what she had just said. She would only refuse and he would look foolish. Yet, he found he could not deceive her about his wife. No, he must just finish the conversation as soon as it was polite to do so and be on his way. He might have guessed that life would not be that uncluttered! Maybe he had based his hopes of her loving him because of her willingness to lie with him all those months ago, but he should have known that Mariana was too untamed to fit in with normal expectations.

"I did… I was married once, but… but she ran away with my brother." He kept his face from her, watching his ship, out in the bay, rocking on the waves. '*Antoinette*' had been his life before; she would have to be again.

"Oh, don't think that I blame her," he went on quickly. "It was my fault. I neglected my wife. I am a captain of a ship and I spend months away at sea. My wife could… could not wait for me to… reappear."

Jack's words petered out and all that could be heard was the peaceful snuffling of the sleeping infant. Nevertheless there was no peace between this comely woman and himself – discordant tension appeared to crackle across the gap. What more was there to say? Mariana remained silent. He felt compelled to fill the pause with conventional courtesies:

"I came to express my gratitude to…"

"You did more than that," interrupted Mariana. "You repaid me by saving my life. And, there's an end to it."

"Yes," agreed Jack in a whisper. "An end."

He swung around and gave the ghost of a smile.

"I'm glad to see you looking very much… much like your old self this morning. No ill effects from the fire?"

"Incredibly, no! I'm only in bed because Elin has insisted. But, later today, I'm going to get up. I don't even feel particularly tired. It's marvellous to be free of the baby and he's such a darling. I love him already."

"Yes, I'm pleased you've got him." Jack stepped towards the door. "Mariana, would you mind excusing me? I have much to do. My men ought to be able to replenish our supplies without me, but I must check on them. Also, I did promise Edward that I would take him…"

"You will come and say… farewell?"

"Naturally. I won't be sailing today. The wind is in the wrong direction."

Jack descended the stairs, grinding his fist into the palm of his hand. What was he going to do? What was he going to do? Mariana! Mariana! his heart cried. How he loved her! All this time he had carried around a picture of her in his mind and now, when he closed his eyes momentarily, he saw her, etched on his very eyelids it seemed, as she had been only a few minutes ago: fragile, young, winsome beautiful and very, very desirable. He had described her to others, this woman he loved, but today he realised that she was more enchanting than before. She had been radiant over the birth of her son and this had enhanced her usual magnificent looks. Blatantly the troubles she had been through had refined her features, which he remembered extremely well. Yet there was something new about her also. She appeared fragile today and defenceless. He desired her so much that it cut him like the blade of a knife to think of her lying in the arms of the lustful Parson. He had not forgotten the agony she had suffered in the night, nor his awful fears concerning the delivery, and all for the sake of a son who should have been his! He had deflowered her – wrongly – outside marriage, but nonetheless she belonged to him and he wanted to lift her up and carry her away from all her disagreeable memories, stroke away the worries which creased her brow and have her to himself for the rest of his life.

But she did not love him! The words rang in his head like a death knell. And she did not want another loveless marriage. Who could blame her? Could he plant love in her soul, he who had begun to teach her of fleshly love? He wished he could, but he would not force her to marry him, and she would have spoken up if she had wanted to. After all, she had invited him, an unknown stranger, into her bed, when he had been too ill to oblige her last year. She had been outspoken since first he had met her, not holding back on what she thought. And he had given her plenty of opportunity to say that she was interested in him. Yet she had said nothing. He had best leave her to her son, who appeared to fulfil her needs, and hope that, with time, the fever that burned inside him would pass.

He decided to take Edward aboard his ship sooner rather than later and then he would be free to leave whenever the wind obliged. He knocked on the library door. Even while he waited for a reply, he heard voices from the dining room and he went to find the Squire in there.

FRANCES

Frances looked up when her champion from last night entered the room and with his arrival recollections of the events of yesterday flooded her senses.

How could he have hurt her so, this husband of hers? Bad enough to have had an affair without prolonging the mortification by insisting on confessing it! Somehow Edward's insistent apology had made it real. Before he began to talk, it was just fears, gossip, hearsay, whispers in her mind, as delicate as wisps of mist on the gorse bushes, but with his words, the deed was set in stone. She'd tried to stop him, but he had carried on regardless of her exhausted desolation. The ache of her physical injury was swallowed up in the sorrow of her bleeding heart.

Initially she had questioned his sincerity, wondering if his protestations were to cover up his intention of continuing to meet the unknown woman. Then he had refused to kiss her, after she had almost begged for him to prove his love for her. In that moment, she had concluded, in her anguished thoughts, that he was wishing himself in the arms of his lover and not in their bedchamber. She had felt tears prick her eyelids, but she would not blink; at least he would not have the satisfaction of knowing how discomposed she was!

Then had come that desolate statement:

"I must tell you. My heart is burdened with guilt."

She had wanted to shout at him then. Scream that she could take no more tonight, after all she had been through. Make him understand that she did not want to hear what he had to say and urge him to forget it. She knew he had a mistress but she did not need to hear all the sordid details, and especially not to discover the identity of the woman who had lain in his arms in *her* place! Yet, instead of berating him, she had closed her eyes and unconsciously turned her head away in an attempt to protect herself from the thousands of tiny stab wounds his loud declarations were inflicting on her!

He must have noticed her flinching because he had enquired about her pain. Pain! No, she was not in pain, she was being torn in two by an evil torturer! She had managed to squeeze out a single word of assent in the hope that now he would refrain but still he ploughed on!

"It will not happen again," he had promised, but how could she trust him? How could she ever believe anything he said ever again? Evidently guilt was flooding through him this evening, perhaps enhanced by his worried conscience that both his sister and his wife had played a huge part in the tragedy in the stables. But what about in the morning? Or when he met this woman again? What if the witch cast her spell over him again?

When he had asked for her forgiveness, Frances had bit her lip. What could she say? He was penitent and he absolutely intended not to stray again, but… Nevertheless who was she to question his ability to keep his promise? Could she forgive him? She would have to if she wanted to regain him as a husband! And, in her innermost being, she did want him back, but not right away. Privately she wanted him to suffer too. She longed to withhold her forgiveness and make him understand that nothing would ever be the same again. Probably, even with the passing days, it would not be possible to recapture the closeness which they had experienced at the start of their married life.

"Of course, I do, Edward." Where had she found the grace to make such a statement and to smile too?

Now he was suggesting that they forget it, after he had insisted on unburdening himself! Oh, selfish man! I will never forget it, her treacherous heart had cried, but she released no sound. When he had embraced and kissed her, ever so gingerly, she had submitted but found that she had to pretend. Pretend that she wanted him that close. It will take time, common sense asserted, when Edward laid his head on her shoulder. Be glad that he has returned to you, she had urged herself, allowing a single tear to fall on his wig.

Edward had sighed with apparent contentment but she had found no rest then or all through the hours of darkness. Finally she had succumbed to sleep, through sheer exhaustion, but she had awoken too many times to count and despair had enshrouded her! She had tried to chide herself, pull herself together and overcome her maudlin thoughts, but it wasn't until the sun had risen and she had woken from a frightful nightmare (where she saw a woman in a shawl and raced to unmask her, only to find that the adulterer had only a black hole instead of a face), that she had shaken herself inwardly and forced herself to be positive.

Three statements she repeated out loud (for the room was empty by morning).

You are alive.

You are no longer a slave but mistress of an extensive estate.

Your husband has returned to you.

Then, calling on all the strength of character she had cultivated over the years of imprisonment by her father, she had climbed out of bed.

Her arm ached abominably and her head swam dangerously. Where was her maid? Surely by now the child, Ted, could be left and the woman could return to her duties? How was she going to get dressed with no help?

Fortunately Edward had appeared just in time to aid her and he had brought with him news of most of the household, including the birth of Mariana's baby. Frances was able to smile and planned to hasten to her sister-in-law's side first, but what her husband announced next drove all desire to visit Mariana from her. He mentioned, offhandedly, the sad news of Rosie's death. Something in his tone made her look up at him and in that moment it dawned on her that Rosie was the mysterious woman. No logic explained how this could be – the maid did not hail from this area and his affair was supposed to be of long-standing – but the revelation would not go away however hard she tried to expunge it from her thoughts!

Yet outwardly, to a casual observer, the next half an hour had been like the first days of her marriage – her husband lovingly playing maid to her. The difficulty she encountered in donning her clothes covered any embarrassment there was between them over her state of undress, and they had even laughed at her inability to get attired appropriately, although she felt her laugh was forced. Finally they were obliged to cut one of her bodices and now a light shawl covered her bandaged arm and any gaps which made her apparel immodest. She had ignored Edward's suggestion that she stay in her room and had walked to the dining room without stumbling.

She greeted the man who had been so kind to her last evening with the glimmer of a smile.

"Ah, Mr… Salisbury, is it? You are just in time to partake of some food. Wilson, bring another plate."

Jack shook his head and then replied:

"Thank you, Mrs Rowlands, I…"

He seemed... What was it? Indecisive? Frustrated? Did he not want to stay? Was he fretting to get back to his ship? She could not discern but interrupted him with a request.

"Please call me 'Frances', as you did last night."

"I owe you an apology," flashed back Jack.

Frances could not help her eyes twinkling with amusement, despite her heavy heart and cast down spirits.

"You did not realise I was the Squire's wife, but I think you can be forgiven your mistake. In all the chaos... I suppose there's not much difference between master and servant when we are stripped of our roles."

Edward frowned.

"That's dangerous talk," he warned his wife.

"Not at all. I lived like a servant for many years, although I was the daughter of the house."

Edward did not answer her but anxiously asked:

"What was Mariana's reply, Jack?"

"She is not interested in marriage where there is not love," announced Jack softly.

"But you told her you loved her!" stormed Edward. Frances started at her husband's vehemence.

"That was not necessary." Jack took his place at the table. "She made it abundantly clear that she was not interested in me. I suppose I allowed my own love to overrule my common sense. We... We became good friends after your departure to London, Edward, but I mistook friendship... Well, I simply hoped that..."

"But she loves no one else," persisted Edward.

"How do you know?" argued Frances mildly.

Edward turned to her, almost angrily, but then evidently bit back what he had been about to say, for he agreed:

"Yes, my dear, I suppose you are right. It is none of my business."

Frances looked from one man to the other. She could not understand why Edward was so determined to see his sister married and, at the same time, she could not believe that Mariana would turn down a proposal of marriage from such an interesting and handsome man as Mr Salisbury. Yes, she admitted to herself, from the instant that Jack had picked her and Ted up from the sooty cobbles, she had been drawn to him. She found him undeniably attractive, and without realising it, her betrayed heart wanted to wound her husband in return. Before she had discovered that Edward had a lover, she would not have looked at another man, but Jack had turned up, acting out the part of a hero in the fire, and she was surprised to find her eyes resting on him often whilst the meal progressed.

Nonetheless, the man showed no interest in her. His countenance was drawn, his eyes dull. His discourse with Edward was disjointed, as if his mind was elsewhere, and she sympathised with him because she was finding it hard to concentrate too. Her arm throbbed and the weight of it in the sling was giving her a headache. She found she was not tempted by the dishes set before her by Wilson and instead, whilst the men spoke at some length on seafaring matters, she quizzed their head servant about the wellbeing of Mrs Jones, Elin, Biddy and even the young boy, Ted, despite acknowledging that this child was the son of her husband's lover. After all, she reasoned, his mother's behaviour was scarcely his fault!

"I think I'll return to bed," she announced when there was an interlude in the conversation. Immediately both men rose to their feet.

"I'll help you," they said together.

"I don't need any help," she rejoined, but neither man took any notice of her refusal. Both hovered near her but she did not trip or feel dizzy at all on the journey up the stairs. It was just the pain and a debilitating tiredness which kept sweeping over her in waves, she explained as they walked.

"I will be fine from here," she assured them when they reached her bedchamber door. "Please go and finish your meal."

"I must tarry no longer." Evidently Jack's initial haste had returned!

"I shall go and see Mariana."

"Please don't berate her, Edward." Jack's voice was firm. "She mustn't be coerced into another mismatched marriage."

"As if I would!" retorted her husband. "I was just going to congratulate her on the birth of the baby."

"Should I come with you?" enquired Frances, although her whole body was begging to be allowed to lie down and sleep, and she was not sure that she would be able to keep up her mask of the Squire's wife for much longer.

"Of course not, my dear. You have a rest. I am sure Mariana has been told about your injury and is not expecting you 'til later."

"Edward?" Jack appeared to need reassurance.

"Don't worry, my friend. I shan't upset Mariana. I shall keep my mouth closed, but I would advise you to plead your cause at least one more time. Women at the time of childbed are notoriously contrary. I reckon the strain on their bodies affects their thinking, don't you, Frances?"

"I wouldn't know. Jack… Mr Salisbury, I trust I shall see you again before you leave. It has been more than a pleasure to meet you – your courage yester eve has put us in your debt forever."

Jack demurred with a mock salute and then Frances was through the door and in the privacy of her own room. She exhaled a huge sigh of relief whilst she leant against the comforting wood and then headed straight for the bed where she lay down fully clothed on the covers, curled up in a ball, and gave herself up to her tormented forebodings.

ELIN

Elin gathered her youngest sister, Mary and the orphan boy, Ted, into her arms. Both children were crying and she suspected that secretly each one was competing with the other to see who could sob the loudest! Admittedly, Ted had a real reason for weeping since his mother had disappeared and it was assumed around the Parish that she had perished in the Manor House fire. However, Mary's grief on the death of her parents should not lead her to dissolve into tears practically every day; her solemn visage was rarely lifted by a smile.

Recently, Elin had asked her what was wrong and she had bleated that she missed her *mam*! This answer had shocked Elin because it the child was grieving for their stepmother – the hateful Widow Davies – not her natural mother. How could Mary be missing her? How could she love someone who had regularly beaten her? The ways of the heart were a mystery to Elin and not just her sister's heart but her own as well!

Here she was, only returned to *Trem-y-Môr* a few weeks, and she had abandoned her love of the Squire. Yet, was this true? Did she really no longer love Sir Edward, or was her heart frozen, with its inner core no longer warm, by the gamut of feelings she had experienced recently? When had it all begun?

Was it the night her father had died? Or was it seeing her beloved mistress, Miss Mariana, haggard and sad at the Parson's funeral? Or was it the morning Thomas' father, Owen Lewis, had ridden by and told her that now her father and stepmother were deceased other tenants would be moving in and she had one day in which to vacate the property? Or was it on hearing that the man she thought she loved was not just married but carrying on with a lover, right before their very eyes?

Elin could not say. All she knew was that, unlike the little ones sitting on her lap and wrapped in her arms, she could not afford the luxury of tears, and she believed that her heart had turned to stone. She stroked their heads and their cries lessened.

Without wanting to, Elin's mind returned to the day she had pulled the door shut on her childhood home.

* * *

Elin pressed her hands into the aching small of her back. She decided she must be getting old because the spring cleaning she had just finished had taken a far greater toll on her than she would have thought possible. Ever since the steward's horse had disappeared along the wooded path, she had been cleaning and tidying. In fact, she considered that from the moment she had arrived in the cottage to tend to her sick relatives barely had she paused for breath. Each day her brother and sister's condition had improved whilst, at the same time, her father's state and that of Widow Davies had deteriorated. No matter how assiduously Elin tried to nurse them, their symptoms worsened. She had taken no time off except to attend the Parson's funeral, where, from the edge of the crowd, she had glimpsed her beloved mistress.

That day the icicles began to grow around her heart. When she arrived back at the side of her patients, her father had tried to talk to her but he was so debilitated that his usually strong voice was but a mere whisper and she took no comfort from his words for he explained to her that he was near the end. Two days later and he was gone. She was left only with one person in her care. It was at this point that she had wondered if she should send Mary and John to her elder sister, Anne, but Anne had two infants under the age of three and there was still the worry that the bad humours might spread to them. And it wasn't as if the children were any trouble – both remained listless and weak, although, at last they were eating proper meals and the awful loose bowels had disappeared. Although, Mary did tend to follow Elin around, sometimes literally holding on to her older sister's skirts, but John was a slight help, collecting sticks for the fire from the surrounding woods and fetching half buckets of water from the stream.

The Widow Davies lingered on, day after day, delirious and fretful, calling for people Elin had never met and shouting at her attendant on most occasions. Elin did not know where she got the strength or patience to continue to nurse but, although she admitted it to no one, she was glad when the querulous woman passed away.

Then had come the visit from the steward, a mere twenty-four hours ago, and here Elin stood on the threshold of the family home with a meagre collection of belongings which represented the entire lives of three people: her father, her mother and Widow Davies.

The Widow had left the largest item – that chest with its initials AG, which she had brought to her third marriage so proudly six years earlier. Elin had heaved it outside this morning as she was working her way from the farthest corner of the cottage towards the front door, sweeping and dusting, tidying and clearing. She had been told that the new tenants were a young couple with a baby and it wasn't just the fear of infection which had made Elin use her last ounce of stamina but her natural pride – she didn't want any aspersions cast on her housewifely talents! Well past midnight she had worked, like the first night when she had arrived, breathless and anxious, from the Vicarage, and it wasn't until now that she had a chance to open the chest and investigate what was inside.

Elin reckoned the chest might have belonged to a seaman originally for next to the initials was the carving of a sail-boat. She opened the stiff lid and was horrified to see that it was stuffed full to the top! No, this was not the time to peruse its contents! Faded papers, yellowed lace, a brass candlestick, spotted and tarnished, she saw before she pulled down the lid and fastened the clasp.

Turning her attention to a much smaller box – more the size of a loaf of bread – she picked it up and held it to her breast. This was all that was left of her own mother and she knew intimately what it contained: locks of hair from her brothers and sisters (and presumably herself) when they were babes; a posy of dried flowers which her mother had carried on her wedding day; a wedding band (this had been added later) – not valuable but kept by her father for sentimental reasons after her mother's death; three brightly coloured ribbons dulled to muted copies of their original hues; a tin which seemed to contain tiny teeth – another memento of the children's infanthood; a favourite sewing needle and spool of thread; some silver coins; a 1662 prayer book – not that her mother could read but it had been given to her by her only cousin and… and not much more, if Elin remembered aright. All that remained of a dearly loved mother's life! Was this all that showed that her mother had lived?

There was a third box, but not near her side or pressed against her breast; it was in her memory – the coffin in which her father had been laid. The roughest coffin – no carving like on Widow Davies' chest or polished wood similar to her mother's treasure box – just the cheapest box had been bought to contain all that was left of her father once his final breath was expelled. No further evidence of him existed except his body – wasted and shrunken in life by the sickness, peaceful in death – even any tools he had used in his work had not belonged to him!

When she considered the span of her father and mother's lives, from cradle to grave, there didn't seem much to show for a lifetime of toil and trouble, unless... She paused in her reverie. Unless you counted children. Maybe that was the only mark someone left on the world! But was that...?

"Can I go back inside?" It was John.

"No!" Elin shouted, more fiercely than she had intended. "I've just finished cleaning it. If only I could have whitewashed the walls but there was no time. Anyway, what do you want to go back inside for?"

"Just to see."

Elin put down the box and gave him a quick hug.

"Sorry, *cariad*. Yes, let us all stand in the doorway one last time."

Holding hands, brother and sisters peered into the gloomy interior. The mud floor was swept and the partition scrubbed. Elin had procured fresh straw to put on the family bed, whose aroma masked any lingering odours of sickness. There were no furnishings in the room because her sister, Anne, had collected several pots and pans and a few blankets on the eve before, after receiving a message from Elin to come. Anne had suggested that Elin might keep these household items for her own cottage one day but Elin was convinced that she would never marry and would end her days living in the Manor House like Mrs Jones, the housekeeper. The bare starkness which they observed, combined with the absence of a glowing fire in the hearth – surely the very centre of a home – and the echoing silence with no sounds of a family going about its business, meant the place was as dead as its latest occupants.

"Come," Elin said decisively. "Let's get on our way to the Manor. Stand still, Mary, whilst I tie this bundle to your back. Can you manage yours, John?"

Elin placed her mother's box in the centre of a shawl; she wrapped a few clothes around it to protect it before knotting the corners of the shawl and throwing it on to her shoulder and securing it under her arm, leaving her hands free. Then she strapped an identical but lighter pack on to her sister's childish frame. Her own scant belongings had been sent ahead to the Manor House from the Vicarage, packed up by Biddy – she herself had not returned to the Parson's abode after the night when she had overheard the housekeeper's terrible accusations – and she knew that everything was waiting for her arrival there this afternoon.

"Now, the chest. John, can you and Mary take one end – there's a handle, see? Can you take that end and I'll take the other?"

They had gone not more than ten steps before the children put down their end of the chest and Mary began to snivel. Elin groaned inside. Should she leave the chest by the side of the path and send someone to collect it? But would the cart get up this narrow stretch of the road? And what if a passer-by chanced upon it and rifled through it and stole from it? Did she care? Widow Davies' past didn't concern her. But, her canny nature overturned these possibilities and she tried to grasp both ends of the chest and lift it on her own.

"Good day!"

Elin turned to see who was greeting her and smiled when she saw one of Thomas' brothers.

"Oh, Morgan, can you help us?"

"I was coming to do just that! They told me at the House that you were moving out today and I decided to come and lend a hand. What, little one, is all that noise? Here, if you stop crying, I'll carry you and the trunk."

Suiting action to words, Morgan flung the Widow's chest on to one shoulder, balancing it with his hand on its curved lid, and bent down to scoop Mary up in his other arm.

How easy it looked! Elin knew that Morgan was a year or two her junior but he had filled out in the last months, maturing into a man you would look at twice. He towered over his eldest brother and father and did not resemble any of the rest of the family. Mrs Jones said he was the image of his maternal grandfather who had measured six foot six in his bare feet. With curly chestnut locks and merry brown eyes Morgan was popular with the girls, but Elin admired him this morning for his bulging muscular forearms and gentle teasing of Mary out of her weeping.

* * *

Elin came back to the situation of the woebegone children in her lap, to find Ted had fallen asleep and Mary was watching her with doleful eyes whilst she sucked vigorously on her thumb. Nevertheless, the picture of Morgan striding before her would not go away and she recalled how she and he had met again and again. Was he seeking her out deliberately, or was it chance? She wasn't sure. Mary had got into the habit of running away almost daily. She never got far and usually was found fast asleep beneath a bush by the side of the path. It was Morgan who had suggested that she might be trying to return to the cottage where she had been born. Elin was surprised at his insight and interest; often it was he who returned the child to the Manor House kitchen and her own anxious arms.

"I shouldn't fret," he had advised. "I suspect she's not sure of the way, nor could she find the place or even walk the mile to it. Let her grieve in her own time. Hopefully, she'll soon forget."

Now Elin allowed Ted to slip to her side on to the bed. She was relieved she had chosen to sit there and not in the only chair in the servants' quarters up under the eaves. The two children were no longer infants and were heavy. With one burden released, she was able to stand up and she intended to lay Mary next to Ted, but the girl clung tightly to the front of her bodice.

"Mary, you must let go. I have to get on with my work and Mrs Jones asked you to fetch some potatoes from the gardener, didn't she? That was ages ago."

Elin noticed Widow Davies' chest in the corner of the room. Would its contents one day be as precious to Mary as their own mother's box of treasures was to her? Suddenly she was glad she had not abandoned it by the side of the path or offered it to Morgan on the day he had told her that he was thinking of signing up on a vessel bound for the Americas. Elin had discovered that Morgan had dreams, and the daily jobs on the estate did not satisfy him. He was considering his future even at the moment, and with Elin noticing the sailing boat carved on the chest she had wondered if she should give it to him. Unconsciously had she thought to 'pay' him for his help on their moving day? But it was good that she hadn't, because if Mary was missing her stepmother this much then the chest could go to her little sister and might comfort her in the coming years.

Elin sighed. She was reluctant to admit to herself that she was disappointed not to be able to give the trunk to Morgan, for the more she saw of him, the more she enjoyed his company and the idea of giving him something to take on board which would remind him of herself had pleased her. Was her icy heart melting?

Certainly she felt nothing but coldness towards Sir Edward. He, who had once filled her waking hours, was now never in her mind, and at least her duties meant she rarely encountered him. If she dared to review her feelings for him, she reckoned that the love she harboured for him had begun to erode when he had abandoned his sister to marry that terrible Parson, but the final collapse had occurred when she heard about his affair. Tears had sprung to her throat when Miss Mariana had told her, but they were not for herself but for the new mistress, Lady Frances. How could she, Elin, love a man who betrayed his marriage vows in such a fashion?

A whisper fluttered into her mind – a question that would not go away: had she never really loved him? She hadn't known him very well, but had put him on a pedestal like Miss Mariana. Had his handsome face and dashing peg leg seduced her heart? Could it be that with the passing weeks and months, she had seen the truth about his character and her feelings had changed? If this was so then she could never have loved him – real love wasn't that fickle, was it?

Elin tried to put her sister down on the floor but the child bent her legs and clung to Elin's upper arms.

"Mary, that's enough! Stop playing about! Stand up, please. I have to go. You may accompany me. We'll leave Ted to doze. I'll come and check on him later. Mary, are you listening to me? If you are good I'll see if Morgan will come and we can walk along the seashore."

The child placed her feet on the floor and took her own weight at the mention of Morgan's name, and Elin had to admit that she relished the idea of seeking out that tall, broad-shouldered young man with his white, even teeth and friendly grin too!

MARIANA

Mariana stood in front of the glass with her legs shaking. Guessing that Elin would not approve of her arising, she had dressed herself. She had chosen a becoming emerald green gown which hid any curves left from the babe and at last she was ready, but her thoughts were still in the past.

She had left her bed not long after Jack had departed and sat on her window seat, pondering on what to do. Within a short time she had seen Jack striding across the beach. He had climbed into the waiting rowing boat and been carried out to his ship. Her heart had bled as she watched him growing smaller and smaller.

When he had walked through the door in the middle of her birth pangs she had believed he was some kind of vision, although the severity of the pain had negated the possibility that she was dreaming! Once the baby – Charles – had arrived she had wanted to ask her friend a host of questions: what he was doing here, how he had turned up right on cue, where had he been, had his memory returned? But he had rushed away, mumbling about hot water. Why? Had he more important tasks to attend to – like putting out the fire in the stable? Had the blood and mess repelled him? She would not have thought that the Jack she knew was squeamish. And he had not returned but sent that interfering Mrs Parry to attend to her! Her baby was wrenched from her grasp and the umbilical cord tied and cut. Despite her loud protests Charles was washed and swaddled and laid in the cot. She herself was subjected to no less a thorough wash and was asked where clean linen was kept. Mariana had bit back the caustic retort she would have liked to say, and given instructions to Mrs Parry's companion so that the woman could fetch fresh linen and blankets.

In truth, she had found that she did feel more comfortable when the room was set in order. Several moments were taken up putting the babe to her breast to suck, but he was very sleepy and was returned to his cot on the other side of the room. Suddenly she missed having him at her side; that previous quarter of an hour of holding him in her arms straight after the birth seemed an age ago! She suggested that the cradle be brought nearer, but neither attendant was listening to her. She suspected that the midwife was trying to find fault with Jack's timely help, but both she and the babe were fine! She had enquired of the fate of others in the household but no news was forthcoming – she knew better than to expect information about her horse, as the women were not interested in anything but the delivery of the baby. Mariana had repressed a smile when they had left finally – they were repeatedly exclaiming over the horror of a man seeing a woman's travail.

Once she was alone again, Mariana threw off the covers of her newly-made bed and sat up. Whatever it cost she would get Charles and bring him back to bed with her. She would unwrap him too. She did not hold with swaddling and she wanted to observe his frail, thin limbs free and unrestricted. It did take the last of her strength to fetch her son and, although she had supposed that she would lie awake fretting over the wellbeing of the other members of her family, she had found that she fell asleep instantly with her newborn son resting in the crook of her arm.

It had taken until this morning for anyone to check on her, and it was Peggy who had stuck her head around the door. By then, Charles was yelling at the top of his voice and Mariana had sent the servant girl to fetch Elin. Whilst Elin instructed the inexperienced mother on how to feed the babe, the maid had told Mariana much detail of the night's happenings. All the queries her mistress fired at Elin about the reappearance of Jack were not answered. Elin had proposed that Mariana wait until she was receiving male visitors and then direct her enquiries to the man himself.

Yet, when Jack had entered her room, truly not dead after all, but in the flesh, healthy and hale, her curiosity had dried up and silent restraint had grown between them. Fear that what Elin had reported – that Jack was here simply to see the entire household – had made her heart lurch with anxiety and she was tongue-tied. She had castigated herself inside, recalling the number of times over the last year she had longed to talk to him and pour out her introspections and forebodings to him and receive wise advice and solace back. Why could she not phrase the words?

In the end, the conversation had taken a different direction from the one she had yearned for! His inability to meet her eyes had unnerved her. What was wrong? Why could they not pick up their friendship where they had left it? Isn't that what really good friends did? Why did he stand at the window again and again, his face turned from her? Obviously he did not love her, but he did not seem to want to be even in the same room as her. Was he longing to be back on board his ship – what had Elin called it? The '*Antoinette*'. He appeared far away from her, lost in a world she knew nothing about and had never shared.

Then her dreams had come crashing down like an avalanche of stones falling into the sea when he had admitted that he was married. For a second she had pitied him, since he had suffered what Frances was suffering – betrayed by his own wife – but then her own sorrow had overwhelmed her, almost causing her to stop breathing. She had not been garrulous before but now she was unable to say the shortest of sentences whilst despair enfolded her.

It wasn't very many minutes later that he had gone! It was evident that he had been unable to sense that her hopes and imaginations and plans had been swallowed up by the whirlpool of truth. He had used to be so sensitive to her, interested in what she had to say, perceptive to her innermost desires, happy to counsel, ready to aid her and now... Now, it was as if he could not escape from her presence fast enough! Couldn't his first mate have supervised the restocking of the ship's supplies? He had not been wielding the oars but she had observed how the boat had sped across the waves at a terrifying pace. Had he instructed his men to hasten? What ailed him? What had frightened him here in the Manor House?

A tiny hiccough from the baby gave her a clue. Of course, it was Charles! She had wondered that he had not commented when she had told him last night that Charles was his son, and suddenly a dazzling light shone on her speculations. It was the babe who frightened him. It must be the responsibility of fatherhood. He was concerned that she would try to tie him down and insist that he stay to bring up the child with her! How could she have been so dim-witted? How could she have mistaken a man that much? Never would she have described Jack as a shirker, a weakling, a deserter.

And she had dressed to go out on to the boat to offer herself to him. Standing before the looking glass, she wondered if this latest realisation changed what she had resolved to do earlier?

Gazing at her own image she saw how her conclusions enslaved her very features. Downcast eyes and a lined mouth reflected the dark state of her very soul. She might as well have been dressed in sackcloth. It wasn't surprising that she was desolate since her memories refused to stop churning over and over.

Aware that soon Jack would not just be leaving the four walls of *Trem-y-Môr* but sailing away across the horizon, whilst she was getting up, she had tried to test to see how she would feel when he did actually go. Immediately she had acknowledged to herself that after all she had been through, she would shrivel up and die if she lost Jack a second time. She could not bear to continue her life without him.

What was she going to do if she allowed him to go? She had told Edward that she was thinking of setting up her own home, but she dreaded being all alone. There was Charles, of course, but he was only a baby. She wanted the company of adults and in particular a man. No, more than that, she needed the company of one man: Jack. Whilst she had sat and stared out the window, finally she had accepted with her intellect what her heart had been telling her for months: she loved Jack. This was the moment she had resolved to hurry to him and, if need be, beg him to take her with him. He had told her that he had a wife, therefore he could not marry her, but he appeared estranged from his wife. Thus, she would ask if she could simply accompany him on his voyages and be his mistress. After all, the situation was not unlike Edward and Frances, for presumably Jack's wife did not love him.

Edward. There was her brother to consider too. That final meeting when he had informed her that he loved her... It was unbearable that she should stay here. At last she understood all those covert looks he had given her – right from the first! But she was his sister, at least in name if not in truth, and it would be impossible for her to live under the same roof as him knowing that he... he desired her. Also what about his wife? What if Frances found out that Edward loved her? Surely Frances would begin to hate her sister-in-law. No, it would not do. Mariana shook her head, imagining the consequences. She would have to leave the Manor House.

Fleetingly she wondered if she should just ask Jack to take her as a passenger to wherever he was going, but at once she perceived that she would be unable to hide what she felt for him. No, she would explain her feelings and if he was not interested in her, then she would have to find herself somewhere else to live.

What if Jack did not want her? a tiny voice inside her head had mocked her. She sighed, for she could not conceive what she would do if he rejected her; she could hardly bear to think about the anguish and hurt. All she understood was that she had to speak to him. The false conversation this morning had not been sufficient. She knew Jack better than that, did she not? If only he would accept her proposal to be his mistress, then she could cling to him, because she felt thrown into a sea of confusion since Edward had told her about her father.

Who was she? Who were her parents? Where did they come from? In the few hours she had had, yesterday evening, after Frances had talked to her, before going to sleep, she had concluded that she would have to search to find out her true identity. She had decided that she would quiz Edward (maybe with Frances in the room for protection!) about what he remembered about her mother and father. From there she could try to discover more. Anything to take away this feeling of being lost and soulless.

Then had come the fire, the child and the reappearance of Jack.

Today, she had to unravel where her priorities lay. Did it matter that she did not know who her real father was? Without warning the words sprang up: not if she had Jack. She was forced to admit this to herself. No, Jack's return had changed everything. She must seek an answer from him first and only if he turned her away would she begin to trace her genuine family. For the present she still thought of Sir William as her father. He had been her father in all but blood and she loved him and missed him. (Dare she admit, even privately, that she missed him?) What would he advise her to do, were he still alive? She knew the answer without hesitation: he would urge her to go after that which she craved, for he had wanted the best for her on every occasion! Yes, she must speak to Jack before all else.

That was when she had started to get dressed. And now…

Had all the musings of the past hour been in vain? She crossed to the cradle and touched her child. He was fast asleep, small and helpless. What was to become of him? His father had rejected him already. Was he to grow up never knowing his father?

Abruptly she settled on her actions. She *would* go to Jack. She would explain to him that she did not require anything from him for the child – only for herself. She could tell him that Charles was the Parson's son – that what she had said before had been incorrect – spoken because of the pain and disorientation of giving birth.

Mariana sat down on the bed. No! No more lies! Her relationship with Jack had not been founded on untruths and it would not be good to start on this day! She would have to go to Jack and ask him outright where his affections lay. Not mention the baby. She needed to know what Jack felt about her – that there was no coercion for him to take her because of the child!

Disquietude assailed her. She could not do it! Take courage, she urged herself. Dread threatened to bring her plans to a standstill but a glimmer of hope pierced the darkness. Maybe she was wrong – perhaps there was another explanation to Jack's uncharacteristic behaviour. If the worst happened, she would face it at that point. But, if she did not venture forth, then for the rest of her life she would wonder what would have happened if she had spoken to Jack.

Back to the glass she went, determining to look her most alluring. But her indecisiveness lingered still. What should she do about Charles? Should she drag him out to the ship? Should she just wait here until Jack visited again? No, for what if he did not come for days or when he arrived she had no opportunity to speak to him alone?

Yes, she must take the child. The entire household was in chaos and she could not trust anyone but Elin with the babe, and if she told that sensible woman of her crazy intentions, she could almost hear what Elin would say! She dare not leave the infant unattended and, anyway, he was part of her and he would come too, if Jack would have her. She was not sure what kind of a life it would be for a boy to be the son of a woman who was someone's mistress, but how would he grow up if she tried to quell her attachment to Jack and permit him to sail away without telling him? No, she would become bitter and resentful or even go into a decline and waste away! She would take Charles with her!

She wrapped the baby in several blankets and tiptoed along the passage. It was like the old days, creeping out of the house, although she was dressed as a woman, not a lad! She must be stealthy for no one would approve of her being out of bed, quite apart from throwing herself at a man! It was not dignified, they would chide, or not done or foolish or childish or… She did not care! For the last time she was going to allow herself to do something wild and non-conforming – her happiness depended on it. Then if she was rejected, she would apply herself to widowhood and never venture anything like this again.

Much to her relief there was no sign of anyone, not family nor servant. During her mental perambulations, she had given some thought to the problem of how she was going to reach Jack's ship. There was an ancient rowing boat which belonged to the Manor House, but it had not been used since last season. She dare not risk using it with a newborn child. No, she would go to her friend, Matthew. He would help her. He had promised that if she needed anything she was to call on him. If, by chance he was not there, she would borrow one of his small crafts, for she knew they would be seaworthy. It was quite a walk to his house for someone who had just given birth, but she felt resolute. She was not allowing herself to contemplate a refusal from Jack. As with Henry, on the night of the storm, when she had feared for his life, she must think positive thoughts – think that she was going to succeed. Whatever his answer, she must discover it and act accordingly. Not to express her heartache would lead to regrets.

When she left the house, she pulled her cloak to cover the child, and hurried across the beach. She was surprised at how cold it was, but she was pleased to have left her home without being challenged.

It was whilst she was descending the steps to the sand, that a movement, out at sea, caught her eye. As luck would have it, here was the yawl from Jack's ship. At first she wondered if the captain himself would be aboard, but when it drew closer she saw it had only two sailors in it. Temporarily she stood undecided again. If the men could be persuaded to take her it would be much easier to travel with them, for the sea was choppy and she would find rowing difficult with Charles with her, but would they agree to take her?

JACK

Jack looked up from the papers on his desk. He had reached a decision. He would not disembark again. Accordingly, he had sent a note to those at the Manor House to say that he was setting sail with the tide. He had thanked them all, including Mariana, for saving his life and promised that he would come to see them whenever he was in the vicinity. Privately, he had decided not to come here for a long, long time!

He stretched his legs out before him and glanced out the window. He observed that his men were coming back. They had been very quick in delivering his missive! He squinted. Who was that in the boat with them? He stood up and moved in order to get a better view. It looked like a woman. It must be a woman; the figure was too small for a man. He frowned. His unrequited love must be deceiving him – the third person could almost be Mariana. However, she was still in bed after her ordeal of the night. He waited whilst the party approached. It *was* a woman! It *was* Mariana! What was she doing here?

Jack hurried on to the deck and arrived as the yawl was being steered against the tall side of his ship. Many of his sailors were leaning over the edge to stare at the woman with luxurious hair, who seemed to be coming aboard; her beauty lit up the grey waves and barnacled wood. When they saw the Captain approaching they scattered immediately.

"Mariana!" Jack called. "What, in God's name, are you doing here?"

She raised her face towards him with a saucy grin. Momentarily, he was back to last summer, but then the boat was carried by the waves and hit the side of the larger vessel and she grimaced. When the yawl tipped drunkenly, Jack noticed that she had the child in her lap under her cloak. He shouted to Wright, his First Mate, to help with the baby and he himself went to aid the woman he loved.

"Give the babe to Wright, Mariana." Jack instructed.

"I… I… Is it safe?"

"You'll need both hands for the ladder. Wright won't drop him."

Jack's anxiety appeared to be reflected on the young woman's face when she clambered aboard eventually. There had been an alarming moment when her skirt had become entangled and the ladder, with its precious climber, swayed dangerously.

"Please be careful of my son," Mariana pleaded, glancing over her shoulder towards his First Mate.

"Don't worry," reassured Jack. "Wright has four children of his own."

Nonetheless, he himself was relieved when the fragile bundle was again in Mariana's arms. He watched her check the infant as soon as she held him, but he could see that the babe remained asleep and appeared oblivious to his surroundings.

Jack longed to question Mariana about her unexpected journey but there were too many listening ears. Therefore he led her to his cabin, telling his personal servant to serve them drinks.

It was only when some colour had reappeared in the woman's cheeks and the baby was settled in a drawer from one of his chests that he observed:

"Why did you bring your son?"

"I... I couldn't leave him. He looked so tiny and... and defenceless and..."

"But why have you come at all?"

Mariana was focussing on the sleeping child.

"How incredible that you should be so unruffled, sweetheart!" she crooned before continuing, "I wanted to have a look at your ship."

"Did you not get my note?"

Mariana's gaze flew to meet his and then back to the infant.

"No. What did it say?"

"It said I was due to sail with the tide and..."

"You mean you were going to leave without..." she accused him.

"I said all I wanted to in the note. What happened to it? I must see Pierce about it immediately."

"No, there's no need to deal with your men right this minute because you can't sail with me aboard and you mustn't..."

"I ought to, just to teach you a lesson!"

She stared at him. He was finding it hard to keep a straight face and a terse tone despite the severity of his words; he thought she looked relieved. However, she moved away from him and the makeshift cot, gliding towards one of the large windows at the stern of the ship.

"Why were you leaving?" she mumbled.

Jack gave no answer but sat down behind his desk, leaning back with his fingers interlocked behind his head. What had been her real motive in coming? he asked himself. Not the ship, for she seemed in no hurry to be given a guided tour, and it did not explain her bringing the infant. He scrutinised his companion. She was incredibly attractive to him – her figure gave no indication of the trauma of the last twenty-four hours, her curves remained sensuous and he could feel desire beginning to flow through his blood; yet silence reigned.

After several minutes he countered with another question:

"Why did you come, really?"

"I wanted to see... To talk to you." Her voice was low with an unidentified tension making it tremble.

"What about?"

He could hear a heart thumping loudly and it took him a second to realise it was his own, and not hers! Still she did not turn and then she swung around, stuttering about how much she had missed him when he had disappeared.

"I know we had only known each other for a few weeks but I considered you my friend. Are you my friend, Jack?"

He smiled at her broadly whilst he confirmed his friendship. He watched her pace the floor in some agitation, ending up beside the child. Bending over the infant and tucking a corner of the blanket down from his cheek, she seemed to be collecting her thoughts.

"Are you still alive, little one?" she whispered to her son. "Your breathing is so shallow." She looked up. "Oh, it's too difficult to explain it,' she cursed softly.

"You can try," he encouraged her. "After all, we have time. As you yourself have said, I can't sail now, can I?"

"Sweet Jesus!" she murmured. "I longed for you, Jack, when you had gone!"

Jack relaxed, feeling his heart's frenzied pace slow. Everything would work out, but he must test the depth of her affections. She was speaking again.

"Not only were you my friend, but you were my ally against my sister, Margaret and..."

"The Parson?" he interjected.

"Yes, and the Parson. I did not want to marry him but… but I had to." She paused. "I was… was with child."

Jack rose and came around the edge of the desk. He did not touch her but, like her, surveyed the infant.

"Are you saying that the Parson was not his father?"

Mariana stepped away. He wondered if she needed to be further from him to enable her to think clearly. In truth, her presence was disturbing him. Could it be the same for her?

"I could think of no other way to save… save myself and the child from disgrace. I had no one to advise me. I simply took the only way out I knew."

"And the Parson was the only available…?"

"It had to be someone who would marry me quickly. I had no time for courtship." She sounded defensive.

Jack retreated to his seat when Mariana walked towards the door. She was very restless and did not appear to want him close to her. He would have to be patient and allow her to articulate whatever it was she wanted to say. All the same, he could afford to abide passively because he had heard her whispered confession and blatantly she had not loved the Parson. His whole being was aglow with happiness because there was hope for his suit! He would not interrupt her; he was in no hurry. Everything was going to work out, in the end. He would not allow her to leave without declaring his love!

Almost he spoke out because he could observe her misery as she grappled to explain what was going on in her soul. Hardly could he bear to watch her suffer so, but yet he tarried. Whilst the cogs inside her brain turned, it was as if her limbs had to be free to twirl too. She ignored the settle and went again to the window, pressing her fingers against the panes of glass and scanned the sea. Jack had stood there himself very recently and could imagine what she could see. The waves were stirred into a white froth – were her thoughts tumbling and whirling as well?

"It was… It was…" she stuttered again. "It was a difficult decision, but all my… my friends had gone. I did not find the Parson attractive, but he could shield my child and me from…"

Without warning she broke off, her face paled. What was the matter with her? Did she have memories that were upsetting her? He hesitated for the twinkling of an eye before standing and crossing the space between them. Tentatively he put his hands on her shoulders.

"You don't have to tell me all this," he informed her quietly. "In fact, why are you telling me all this?"

She turned and pulled away from him. Without warning her voice was angry.

"I'm trying to explain how it was that I came to realise that I..." she screeched. She took a deep breath and panted, "Oh, there's no point in my trying."

In rage or agitation, he knew not which, she began again to walk up and down across the polished floor.

"No point? What do you mean?" Jack leant against the wall of the cabin and folded his arms. This was like the various discussions they had shared on his previous visit to this remote island.

"You are a married man, Jack. I always said that you talked as if you were married, for..."

"Stop!" It was practically a shout. He leapt to attention. "I was married, but my wife is dead."

Mariana halted her frantic pacing, a look of real shock on her confused features.

"Dead?" she repeated and he saw a shiver run through her body. "How?"

"I told you that she ran away with my brother. Months later she and he both died of fever."

MARIANA

Mariana gaped at Jack in amazement. All her fears had been in vain! He was free to marry her. Yet even with this knowledge she could not fling herself at him. Where was the easy companionship that they had experienced before? Had they really not known each other better than this? She reasoned that she had changed but then Jack had too. He was a stranger to her. This was not Jack but a man called 'Philippe'. He had a past now. He even looked different. He was back to his full health, his frame tall and straight, his head held high, his craggy cheeks sunburnt, his blue eyes drawing her towards him and… and passion began to burn inside her. If only he would come and hold her again like he had begun to do earlier. Surely that would smooth over their difficulties, but he was keeping his distance. However she could not blame him, for it had been she who had torn herself away from him. Had he ever held her? It hardly seemed possible for it had all happened long ago, yet the living proof was lying over there in the drawer.

Without warning she felt the room spin and hastily she sat down on the settle. Almost immediately she regained her composure and enunciated calmly:

"So…o, have you anyone else?"

"Yes," he answered. "Yes, I have, but, I have been unable to ascertain her feelings for me. As you said to me this morning, I have no desire to marry someone who does not love me."

"Love? What is love? Such a short word. It's very hard to define. It's easier to say when you don't love someone, isn't it? I assume you did not love your wife, Jack?"

"I might have, but I did not give love a chance. I did not understand that love had to be nurtured. We were both young. If circumstances had been different… Who knows? It's too difficult to say in the light of what happened."

"Did you hate your brother?" she asked.

That made him laugh and she wanted to cry out to him to come to her side and embrace her and kiss her, but he had retreated behind his desk. She had believed that she would never hear that laugh again and yet there was the man she doted on, sitting only a few feet away from her, but still she did not dare to declare how her heartstrings were singing in case he turned her away. She could not tolerate being rejected after what her husband had done to her and what Edward had told her. She needed to be accepted and appreciated and… and loved. As well as this, she had a desperate need to be held by him, physically held close to him. No man had touched her since… since that soul-destroying day. Yet she wanted to be reassured and comforted by… by a man. No, by Jack. Come to me, Jack. She willed him to hear her silent plea.

"I certainly did." His answer cut across her concentration and she wondered what he was replying to, so disorientated was she! "I wanted to kill both him and my wife, but all these years later, I can see that it was my fault and not theirs. I should not have left her alone. The temptation was too great…"

"Nevertheless, she should not have… have done it. She had promised to be faithful to you. She knew you were a captain when she married you and she should…"

"Probably. But, if I'm truthful I can't censure her. My mother told me that she and my brother loved one another. Love again, Mariana. It's very strong… and compelling. It demands things of you. I can't say I blame her. If *I* had found love whilst I was married to her, I would have wanted to follow its call."

"I suppose you're right. Love makes you do all sorts of things which you wouldn't otherwise do."

"You sound as if you speak from experience. Do you? Are you referring to your love for Henry? You said you did not love the Parson."

"Well, I told you once before that I behaved differently because of my love for Henry, so, in one way, I speak from experience. But, I was thinking of baby Charles. Even though I did not know him when he was growing inside me, my love for him made me behave in certain ways. I would never have married the Parson if it had not been for the baby."

"Ah, Mariana, how you've changed! You never liked babies before! At least that's what you told me."

"Somehow it is different when it's your own child, but Charles is very special to me. Remember, he's all I have left of his father."

Jack leant forward and put his elbows on the desk top.

"Mariana, you... you said something... something last night. Did you mean it?"

"What was that, Jack? I don't remember much of what I said last night. I... I really want to thank you for rescuing me."

"As I explained to Elin: you had saved my life, therefore I owed you your life."

Mariana watched the man. Why was he being so malapert? He would often keep his comments light but this sounded too roistering even for him.

"What brought you here, Jack, at that precise moment?"

"I was in the area and I saw the flames. I came to help. I had no idea you were inside the stable, until Edward's wife told me."

"Yes, dear Frances. How is she? Do you know? Have you seen her this morning? I... I came straight to you... your ship."

"Yes, I have seen her. She was up in spite of being in pain. She seems a very personable woman."

Mariana heard something in his tone which made her sit up. Surely he was not attracted to Frances! That would be worse than a tangle of embroidery silks! What with Edward having an affair already! Her spirits sank. No, her heart shrieked. Not with Jack! She could not bear if someone else had him! Who was it he loved? Should she just tell him that she adored him? She had bearded Edward in his den and spoken to him about his liaison and yet she could not speak openly to Jack. What was wrong with her?

"Yes, kind Frances. She has been a great encouragement to me," she confided. It was easier to speak about others. Mariana recalled last night – before the fire. Talking to Frances had eased some of the pain caused by Edward's revelation about her father but it had been the arrival of the baby which surprisingly had been the most comforting. He had given her an unexpected identity. She was no longer just someone's daughter; now she was someone's mother. "I shall miss her."

"Miss her? What do you mean? Are you leaving? Is that what you came to tell me? Where are you going to?"

Mariana kept her eyes lowered but she could sense that he was watching her. She longed for him to come and sit next to her on the settle.

"In a way, yes." She was addressing him but not looking at him. "I came to discuss my plans with you. I'm... I'm not quite sure yet, where I'm going to, but, I don't believe it's right to stay at the Manor House. Edward and Frances need time on their own and I am…"

"What do you mean?"

"Oh, nothing. Just that they are still only newly married and they need time to…"

"But, isn't *Trem-y-Môr* your home? Where could you go to? To one of your other sisters?"

"No."

Mariana folded her hands together. Why could she not just utter the truth and announce her love? Why was she spending all this time talking about her brother and sister-in-law? "It's just that Edward… Edward needs a fresh start… Without having memories of…"

"Mariana." His voice was gentle. "What are you trying to say?"

"Nothing. Nothing." She shook her head in desperation.

"Well, you're not making any sense. You don't want to be moving with a young child. Why can't you stay? Has Edward asked you to go?"

"No!" At last she raised her eyes. "It's not him. I… It's me who's decided it's time to leave."

All of a sudden Jack got up and came and sat down next to her.

"You sound upset." He paused. "Can't you tell me what's troubling you? You always used to."

"No." Steadfastly she fixed her gaze on the piles of papers on his desk. "I've become accustomed to… to liv… to managing without… without anyone to share my burdens with."

"You said earlier that we were friends. Are you no longer my friend? Is it my fault? Something I've said? Because I went away for so long? Was it really terrible? Could I have helped you?"

Mariana turned away. Why had he come to perch next to her? She wished he would go further away; she did not want him reading her expressions. She was not ready for him to sit this close, even though her body was nearly fainting with desire to reach out and touch him.

"I…" she stated in as steady a voice as she could muster. "I still think of you as my friend. I can't blame you for leaving. Initially I was confused and hurt, but when Matthew told me what he had seen, I knew it was not your fault. It's just that…"

"But you covered up my disappearance," he reasoned. "Why?"

"Because I didn't want to be made a fool of!" she gasped, involuntarily staring at him. She saw his compelling cobalt eyes very near and caught her breath. "I didn't want people…" she finished. She could not recall what she had been trying to say.

Peeping at him from beneath her eyelashes, she sat in silence and then he whispered:

"You're more attractive than even in my dreams, Mariana."

Their gaze locked and she could not look away. She was paralysed, unable to speak, with her heart beating wildly.

"When I woke up on that ship, all I could think about was you." His voice seemed to be coming from far, far away. "Were you all right? What had happened to you? Had your sister attacked you again? I should have come back from Ireland for you at once, but I was weak with illness. For two months I coughed and coughed and no amount of herbal potions could cure me. My head ached whenever I sat up and I could not get out of bed, but I thought of you each day. I should have left my ship and come to fetch you sooner. If I had, you would not have been put through all you have."

"Whenever you had come," she remarked languidly, unable to relinquish the hold he had on her vision, "it would have been too late. I have explained to you that I had to marry Griffith in a hurry."

"Who is the father of Charles? I hope…"

"You are." The merest murmur.

Slowly he stretched out his hand to enclose her fingers in his. She did not pull them back but purred:

"He looks like you. He has your eyes. I just hope others won't see it."

"It won't matter if we're married, my love," Jack prophesied. Mariana opened her mouth in surprise as he pondered, "Why have we talked around and around? Why did I not tell you this morning what I have been wanting to shout from the rooftops? I love you, Mariana."

She turned her hand and squeezed his whilst she leant towards him. How easy to say the words, after all!

"I love you, Jack."

"I didn't know until I lost you."

"I fought against the idea that you were dead." She was close enough to feel his breath. "Matthew told me you were lifeless when he saw you. I… I prayed each night that you would be alive. I was so alone and trapped and con…"

"Was the Parson kind to you?"

She jerked backwards, breaking the contact with him and folded her arms across her bosom. He had shattered the spell.

"Mariana, what have I said?" He sounded distraught and he stretched out his hand hesitantly towards her but she made no answer and he did not actually touch her.

"Mariana, my dearest, I'm sorry. I didn't mean to upset you."

She closed her eyes, battling with herself. Could she tell him? She had told no one else but he was her friend – maybe her very best friend... and she loved him. Could she cope with recounting what had passed between herself and her hated husband? She swallowed a lump in her throat. No. She had carried it around on the very edges of her existence all these months. She could feel the pain in her chest, day and night, heavy like a chain encircling her.

"Mariana?"

Afterwards she never knew why she started to speak, but she heard her own voice telling the strange tale of her plot to cover the illegitimacy of the baby, her husband's inability to consummate the marriage; the acquisition of the medicine bottles and Griffith's subsequent accusation of her trying to poison him. Halfway through, Jack caught her fingers for the second time. She resisted for a split second but soon he was stroking her delicate fingers tenderly, until, at last, he put his lips to them. He reversed her hand and caressed the very centre of her palm.

"I love you," he declared, during a long pause, possibly wondering if she had finished, but manfully she struggled on.

When she shared how she had nearly killed the unborn child, tears pricked her eyelids but she determined not to cry. She managed to relate how the Parson beat her but when she tried to describe what had occurred on that haunting morning, the words choked on her lips and her account faded away.

Abruptly Jack pulled her into his arms, fiercely hugging her to him.

"Ssh!" he soothed. "You don't have to tell me anymore. I don't think I can bear to hear it anyway."

She laid her head on his shoulder, but surprisingly the tears never fell. She could feel a pulse beating in his neck and she listened to its regular beat until her trembling stopped. One day she might be able to describe it all. For now, she was content. She had found someone stronger to lean on.

"I thought I was angry when I discovered my brother's treachery." His comments sounded like an aside. "I imagined that I would never again feel that angry, but now there is a terrible… terrible rage pumping in my blood. Thank God the Parson is dead or I could not be held responsible for…"

Slowly Mariana sensed his wrath being replaced with a different sort of passion. He kissed the top of her silken hair.

"My sweet, sweet Mariana. My own dear Mari. How I've longed for this moment! Let us think no more of the past. Will you become my wife? Say that you will and then my joy will be complete."

"Oh, Jack, are you sure?" she cried, pulling away from his comforting embrace. Would he still want her? Maybe she should not have told him about her violent husband. She had made so many mistakes.

"Sure? Of course I'm sure."

He put two fingers beneath her chin. Without further words he placed his lips on hers and she put her arms around his neck and returned the kiss. Unconsciously she leaned against him, pressing her womanly curves against his masculine body. Sighing silently with pleasure, she lost herself in the delight of having him enfold her. He was rock solid and trustworthy. Finally she had come home to port. She had been through some savage storms – those storms of life – and nearly been sunk on several occasions, but now she had arrived where she ought to be and she was safe, safe within the harbour, and she was never going to venture away again.

PENELOPE AND ROBERT

Carrying a jug of water from the kettle over the kitchen fire, Penelope entered the shade of the dairy room. At this time of year, thanks to the rich grass, the milk from the cows was excellent for making cheese and Penelope was proficient at the art of cheese-making! She had this staple food in various stages of preparation. Above her head hung muslin cloths with dripping juices – the first stage after the rennet had separated the curds and whey. She knew the nursery rhyme and glanced around but there were no spiders in her dairy! Everywhere was spotless. She would take one of these 'bags' to Miss Swann before she left. Mayhap a few herbs would be added and the soft mixture eaten today.

Penelope did her tasks in the same order each day. She would add the hot water from the kettle to the fresh milk and cream to bring it to the right temperature for the ingredients to separate before stirring in the rennet. Then she would turn her attention to the contents of the wooden press. The muslin from yesterday would need changing before putting the unmatured white wheel of cheese back – but only if it needed more squeezing. If not she would wrap it in its cloth cover and put it next to the other drying cheeses. Every day the big rounds (which would make a hard cheese) had to be wiped with salty water, helping the rind to form. She didn't worry about the mouldy bloom – it was all part of the rind – but religiously she would turn the lump over – in order for it to dry evenly – before putting them back on the shelf. Over the years, she had learnt how very important it was that one side of the round was not left underneath becoming pappy – the whey had to drain from each side over two to three months – because these would have to be their supply the whole year through, when the grass was sparse. Eventually she would return to the original rennet-added mixture, sieving the contents of yesterday's bowl, lifting the curds from the whey either with two small wooden paddles or her bare fingers, before tying it up in its own cloth and hanging it up with its neighbours.

Whilst she worked, Penelope's mood lifted slightly. What a winter it had been! First the failed harvest and then the darkening nights of autumn and the harsh weather of January – she had longed for the spring and despaired of it ever arriving.

No, she shook her head. It had not been the rain or sleet or shortened days but the loss of the unborn baby which had upset her and taken away her usual peace and happiness. Even the presence of her dear friend, Miss Swann, had not dispelled the lump of sadness in her breast. She had tried to hide it but both Miss Swann and her husband had noticed her grief, although she hoped the children were unaware of her melancholy.

How could it have happened? Why had God allowed it to happen? She had never lost a baby before but the bleeding had started one morning and the tiny babe had come out, half-formed but definitely human, and Penelope had insisted on burying the misshapen creature in the front garden. No priest or vicar was called but she had held a short service which was attended by her two closest friends.

Then she had imagined that she could get on with her life, but nothing was the same. She could not rid herself of the image of the ill-fated child and found Sarah's merry chuckling laugh grated and her sons' lively banter irritating. She had withdrawn into herself and kept her own counsel. She knew her conversation tended to be monosyllabic and her warmth in the marital bed had cooled, but how could she tell those she loved so dearly that she was lost? Lost in a fog of anger and self-pity and her God had hidden His face from her. Yes, the longer she went without being able to pray the worse it became and in the end she did not recognise herself and therefore did not blame others for their changed attitude to her.

No, that wasn't quite fair. Were people behaving differently towards her or was it her perception? She understood that any awkwardness came from her, not from others, but where would it all end? Would she ever come out of the gloom and depression and be able to take up her cheerful outlook again? How could the death of one so small and insignificant have caused such…?

"Penelope."

It was her husband.

"Penelope, are you in here? We're ready to go."

Robert entered the ordered confines of the cheese room and regarded his wife. She was dressed in her usual working clothes, her hair untidy and straying around her pale face, her hands wet with curds and whey.

Simultaneously impatience and pity rose inside him. Why was she in here, performing her tasks, when she should be changed into her Sunday best and climbing into the cart ready to attend her sister's marriage? Yet, beneath this unspoken question was a deeper one which daily attended him: where was his sunny-tempered Penny, the wife he worshipped?

He grabbed a cloth and passed it to her.

"Come, my dearest," he said mildly. "You need to make haste. Wipe your hands. Leave this for Mary to do. The boys are lined up in the cart. Sarah and Miss Swann are waiting to wave us farewell."

Robert watched whilst Penelope rubbed her fingers slowly. He had learnt that he could not hurry her. It was truly as if she lived in another world to him and the rest of the family. Resisting the urge to scold her, he tarried in the middle of the room. He dare not leave her or she would never appear, but he did go to aid her when she began to gather up a bag of muslin.

"Miss Swann may want to eat this today with Sarah and…" she started.

"She might well, but you have already left a mountain of food on the table."

Come back to me, he wanted to shout. Where have you retreated to? How his patience and love had been tried over the past few months. Initially he had allowed her to behave in whatever manner she liked, believing that the grief would lessen, even agreeing to that unsanctified burial of the scrap of a corpse, hoping that if she was given full rein to do as she wished, she would recover more quickly. In truth he was surprised to find his love increase, but with the passing weeks, when there was no sign of improvement, he had found his forbearance wearing thin.

Admittedly, she did keep up the daily toil of being a farmer's wife – she seemed to take comfort from the order of routines – but he felt she neglected the children and, in particular Sarah, who had received no praise or encouragement to walk or talk like the boys had been given in their first year. Penelope was distant even with their visitor and he had apologised to the elderly woman but had been told:

"Don't you worry about me, Robert. Penelope has been in this lonely place before. When she was younger, she would often retreat into isolation. Give her time and she'll come back to you."

Give her time! That assurance had been pronounced on the eve of the old year and now spring was nearly turning into summer! He himself wanted to burst the bubble of self-interest that his wife lived in. He had grieved for the lost baby and had thought that the best way to recover was to plan another child but Penelope shunned all advances that he made and sometimes he wondered if her fear of getting pregnant again would stop the intimate side of their marriage for the rest of their days.

Penelope allowed herself to be led from her tasks, taken to her bedchamber and assisted into her favourite blue skirt. It wasn't many minutes later that she was sitting next to her husband and they were on their way. Vaguely she wondered whether she ought to leave instructions for Miss Swann about the care of Sarah, but she decided that the little girl would be fine under the supervision of her experienced companion.

It had been comforting to have Miss Swann with them over the winter, but Penelope had found that there was no renewal of their close relationship of years ago. Of course it was twelve years since she had married and both of them had grown older. She did not perceive any radical changes in her friend and half concluded it must be she herself who had altered or was it just that she had matured? No confidential chats or helpful advice was exchanged – she was a farmer's wife with endless jobs to do from sunrise to sunset – she had no time for idleness or unfruitful chatter. Notwithstanding, it wasn't long before Miss Swann took up the task of tutoring her elder sons – Penelope guessed that the other woman felt at ease in her customary role of teacher. She had not minded to see her companion thus engaged until last week that is, when it was suggested that Llewelin was not only clever enough to be sent to school and university but it would be a terrible waste if he was denied the opportunity. That comment had pierced the armour Penelope had donned, and she had spoken out vehemently against such a scheme.

"Llew is destined to take over the farm from his father," she explained haughtily. "He needs to remain here to learn all the necessary skills! What would be a real waste would be for him to learn subjects which have no bearing on running a farm!"

Robert broke into her agitated remembrances.

"What a beautiful day, my love!" he commented. "Don't you think so? Mariana couldn't have wished for better weather. The sea will be calm and there will be no trouble getting out to the ship for the ceremony."

Penelope nodded her assent. Mariana. She had not seen her sister for an age. The news of the fire had reached them within hours – probably whilst the flames continued to burn. Then they were informed of the return of

Jack and following, two days later, was the invitation to the wedding today. Penelope had known she must go but her enthusiasm, never high at the moment, was dampened even further by the knowledge that her eccentric younger sister had arranged for a friend of Jack's, a sea captain, to marry the young couple aboard a ship! Penelope had not been away from the farm for many weeks, finding the strain of meeting others too debilitating, but she had never been much of a sailor and just the thought of a brief trip in a rowing boat filled her with trepidation.

"I'm not sure if…"

"You will be fine. I'll come with you in the boat if you are frightened. You wouldn't want to miss your sister's special day, would you?" Robert put his work-worn hand over hers, which were clasped anxiously in her lap.

Penelope shook her head. She felt strange. She ought to be revelling in the journey, lifting up her eyes to take in the vista of rolling fields and dry stone walls, breathing in the aroma of sea and farmland, but she could not shift the heaviness – had her heart turned to stone? Oh, God, where are You? she cried mutely from the very centre of her suffering crippled soul.

The nearer they got to *Trem-y-Môr* the more she fretted. She knew she shouldn't but she found herself snapping at the boys in the back of the cart. They were fooling around, full of high spirits, excited and joyful. She wished she could join in the adventure of the day but all she could do was harangue them. They took no notice of her until their father spoke to them sternly and then they sat in the back demurely and played a word game, their best clothes only slightly dusty, their hair needing only a quick pat to repair their tidy good looks on their arrival

They were greeted by Wilson and led in by the front door.

"Robert?" Penelope felt panic rising.

"It's all right, sweetheart. Here's Peggy to take you upstairs. Mariana is apparently waiting for you. I am going into the library to find Edward."

Penelope was disorientated. Wasn't it her habit to come in through the kitchen?

"This way, Mrs Roberts."

Penelope gazed at the young maid before timorously following her up the stairs. She wanted to turn around and go home. What if the room was full of women all attending to the bride, giggling and talking? But Mariana was on her own, apart from Elin.

"Penelope! Oh, how glad I am that you have come! Look, I have received ever such an odd letter from Margaret, full of assurances of her best wishes, telling me that she is a grandmother now and how much she loves the baby. Aunt Elizabeth has written too and sent love from all the family and in particular Esther who has a baby of her own. Talking of which, you must come and meet Charles. I've been longing to introduce him to you."

Mariana grasped her arm and dragged her across to the cradle. Penelope averted her eyes. This was the last thing she wanted to see. A baby. How could she have forgotten that Mariana had been safely delivered in childbed, whereas she…?

"Penelope? Do you want to hold him? Is Sarah downstairs with Robert? Where are your boys? I thought they would be…"

"Miss Mariana," interrupted Elin. "You must sit down and allow me to finish your hair."

Penelope stood with her back to the others, thankful that they could not see her tightly closed eyes. She was aware of her sister chattering and then into the silence of a pause she heard a gurgle – the sound of a very young infant. A baby. Charles, Mariana had called him.

Penelope opened one eye and found herself staring into the solemn blue gaze of the child. Another gurgle. Penelope stepped closer and the smell of milk and damp cloths and… and newborn babies broke through her defences. Here was a baby.

Without conscious thought, Penelope reached out to touch the velvet cheek of the child and then, whilst his mother prattled on gaily, Penelope picked up the babe.

Like the smash of a rock hitting glass, the wall she had erected around her cracked and collapsed. Expertly she wrapped the blankets around the fragile frame, supporting his wobbly head, unaware of the tears splashing down.

"Therefore, Penelope, we are expecting her and her husband any time. They are staying in the inn in Holyhead. They arrived yesterday but have not visited us yet. I can't believe it. To meet my sister, Katherine, after all these years. When did you last meet her, Penelope? Did you know she was widowed within a month of marrying her second husband and married to her third husband almost immediately? They have just got back from Venice. Venice. She also sent me a letter and she writes of the marvels of ices – yes, desserts made using ice from ice houses. She wishes me well in my marriage too and says that she had no idea that marriage could be so satisfying until she married her new husband. He's called Daniel and is many years younger than her. Did you know about him? Have you ever met him? I can't believe it. Everyone is being very kind, wishing me all sorts of felicitations. Penelope?"

Penelope swallowed hard. She knew she ought to give some reply and turn around. One more minute, she pleaded silently. Just to compose herself. She felt dizzy and light-headed! If she'd had to describe her feelings, what would she say? That she had come out of a tunnel? No, that would be an understatement – she felt as if she had been living in an underground cave for weeks and weeks. What was happening was more than emerging from hazy, unsubstantial shadows! The scales of self-delusion had fallen from her eyes and sunshine had flooded into her heart. Indeed a Damascus road experience, and she was sure she had heard a voice inside her head which had said: "I will never leave thee nor forsake thee."

Remorse for her unnatural and selfish behaviour – in particular towards her own daughter and sons – struck her like the stab of a long knife. And how could she have ignored her familiar friend and companion, Miss Swann and… and then there was her husband? What must he have gone through? To have rejected his care and love, repeatedly? She could not cope with the depth of her guilt and remorse!

"Penelope?" repeated Mariana.

"I am sorry." Her voice sounded hoarse but she struggled to make polite conversation. "I am sorry that I haven't come to see you sooner. What a charming baby! I heard about the fire and…"

She felt a touch to her elbow.

"Penelope, what is it?"

Then she was being embraced and the tears flowed faster. Between the sobs, she gulped out a sketchy explanation of her distress until the baby bawled his displeasure at being squeezed between his mother and his aunt. This brought laughter – a bit too near hysterics for comfort – but nonetheless, real. Soon Elin issued handkerchiefs to both women and with a calmer atmosphere, the bride seated herself, allowing the maid to minister to her again, and Penelope perched on the window seat, Charles clutched to her, weak from the crying but able to exchange more trivial news.

Into this convivial atmosphere came a stranger – their sister, Katherine, willowy and prepossessing and expensively attired – with a train of children all stroking and calling to a delicate dog who followed her mistress through the door. For several moments chaos seemed to fill every corner of the room and then Elin shooed out both Penelope's younger two sons and the Manor House maids. It was Peggy who entreated from the doorway:

"Can we take her, Miss? Can we take her for a walk along the beach? She'll be quite safe with us."

"Peggy, John, Mary." Elin spoke firmly. "I will hold you responsible for this dear creature. You must not take it around the back to meet that rascal who turns the spit or, in fact, anywhere near the kitchen. Mrs Jones and Kate have enough to do preparing the feast and Mrs Jones is still in pain with her ankle. I don't want to hear that…"

"I don't think Phoebe wants to leave me," protested Katherine, but the animal was looking up at the children adoringly, licking their outstretched fingers and fawning around them.

"She looks happy to me," interjected Mariana. "Let them take her. If they go on the beach and not into the stable-yard there won't be any danger from carriage wheels. Go, you noisy rabble! Look, you've upset Charles!"

The baby's face was crumpled up and it did appear as if he was about to protest. Penelope rocked him back and forth and he relaxed when the room was emptied of youngsters.

Penelope was aware that she should have taken control of the situation, not least since her sons had made up some of the gang of children, and she supposed that really she should stand up and welcome their long-lost sister but exhaustion from her recent experience kept her in the background.

Mariana was dancing around in her wedding apparel, seemingly forgetting that she was a widow with a new babe, excitement and jubilation spreading round the room.

"Oh, Mariana!" Katherine exclaimed. "You are identical to your mother. I can't see our father in you at all! No, I tell a lie. You are more beautiful than your mother ever was. You must come downstairs and meet my husband, Daniel. I'm sure he'll be desperate to paint you. What amazing eyelashes you have! And such silken skin. Your incredible hair – it nearly reaches the floor and what a figure! Is it true that you have just given birth? They were saying downstairs that you have a son. Where is he?"

Possessively Penelope held on to Charles but Katherine did not approach her. She was continuing:

"You and I are very alike. Both of us lost our husbands and remarried. I understand your Jack has quite a saga to tell. Oh, I do hope you will find the same happiness as I have. I can hardly believe that marriage to two different men can be so different. My Daniel has taught me much in such a short time."

Penelope ceased to listen. She found this loquacious woman was not how she had imagined Katherine would be from reading her letters. She would have described her elder sister as nervous and pedantic, not someone who was joining hands with Mariana and prancing around the room with as much vigour as one of her sons, Llew or Robbie. Surely Katherine detested noise and disorder and only took pleasure in the strokes of a master painter or the music of a virtuoso violinist? How could such a transformation have occurred? It must be thanks to this latest husband, the young Daniel! Could a person shed twenty years of age by marrying a mere boy?

It took several minutes of conversation, with Mariana, Katherine and Elin all talking at the same time, to ascertain that indeed the bride was ready to descend the stairs, climb aboard her flower-bedecked boat to be carried by softly caressing winds to her love. Evidently Elin was very flustered, her countenance red and her voice raucous, but Penelope couldn't blame her – the two other women continued to shriek with as much gusto as any common maid and it was up to Elin to calm them both before they joined the men folk.

Charles' needs for the next hour had to be planned for too. Penelope was surprised to hear that the baby was to accompany his mother to the marriage ceremony, but she volunteered to care for him, arguing persuasively that it would not be seemly or practical for a bride, especially one this buoyant, to carry her own child up the makeshift aisle on the deck of a ship.

Thus it was that Penelope descended the stairs with the infant, awake and watchful, in her arms.

Robert uncrossed his legs when his host announced:

"That sounds like the women. What a cackle they make! Robert, Daniel, shall we go? There is a veritable fleet of boats to transport us across the bay, but I think it might take some time for the ladies to climb aboard in their skirts, so we must hasten there."

Out of the library the men went, to stand at the bottom of the stairs. First came Mariana, radiant as all brides are, her dress shimmering and sparkling, but Robert only glanced at her because he was looking for his wife. How was she faring? The party tripping down to meet them seemed lively and full of banter. Would Penelope be overwhelmed in the company of such high spirits?

Behind Mariana came Katherine, whom Robert had met when the clock had struck the last hour and now the small hand stood only at half past. There was no doubt that she was a sensational sight with her golden locks, with not a strand of grey, and her smooth skin belying her age. Robert might have mistaken her for Edward's daughter, not his sister, if he had not known better! Was it her fine good looks or her youthful husband that deceived the perceptions? He glanced at Daniel but the man had eyes only for Katherine and Robert remembered his own spouse.

Robert looked up, half-expecting Edward's wife, Frances, to be next, but the maid followed Katherine, an assortment of garments hung over her forearm, and here was Penelope finally. Robert gasped.

Whatever had happened in the upper rooms? Gone was the bent over, timid woman whom he had escorted from the cart to front door. If he'd anticipated that female company would break through the barrier which surrounded her, he would have insisted she came months ago! Suddenly here again was the woman he loved – his own familiar Penny – and then he noticed the baby. This must be Mariana's child. Edward had been regaling them with an account of the fire and Jack playing midwife. Could this paltry bundle be responsible for Penelope's metamorphosis? He knew her incredibly intimately – every line on her scarred face, the deep pools of her eyes, the turn of her head, the lift of her shoulders, and he could observe, even at this distance, that her posture and countenance was bright. She seemed to be searching for someone. Was it him?

Robert did not want to hang back anymore but the lower hall was not spacious and it was crowded with people. Before he could reach her side, the children returned through the front door with shouts of glee, the mincing dog barking with apparent delight. Robert's teaching experience welled up inside him and, unthinkingly, he found himself speaking with authority. Without intending to, he was left in charge of the gaggle of youngsters whilst the adults exited the Manor House. Robert was swept away from his wife and unable to talk to her.

"Will you be quiet?" he shouted above the uproar, manhandling aside his own sons until he reached the excited animal. Gathering it up in his arms away from the grasping hands of the little ones, he managed to bring order and peace into the situation.

Skilfully he instructed his own offspring to go down to the beach and within minutes he was left with an elfin girl and the trembling dog.

"What's your name?" he asked but no answer was forthcoming, except that the child sucked her thumb intensely.

"Her name is Mary." Here, at last, was Edward's wife. Robert half-bowed towards his hostess but he was shocked to see how drawn she looked, with dark shadows under her eyes. By her side walked a diminutive child, dressed in a miniature green suit, complete with tricorn hat!

"And this is our son, Ted," the woman continued. "Say 'Good day' to your uncle, Ted."

The boy hid behind his mother's skirts.

"I'm sorry. He's still upset by the loss of his real mother in the fire. However, Edward and I have decided to adopt him and he now sleeps in the back bedchamber and soon we will get a tutor for him. For now, Elin cares for him but she is going away with Mariana. Don't you think that he has a look of Edward about him?"

Robert surveyed the shy child.

"I can't say that he does but he is very lucky to have been adopted by such kind people." Something in her tone made him add, "Are you all right?"

In the silence which followed he cursed himself. He did not want confidences from this woman! He did not know Frances very well, having only met her three times, but some inner instinct had picked up her distress; perchance his own wife's anguish made him more sensitive to others' troubles. What was the matter? He recalled her words. Why had Frances mentioned that the child looked like her husband? Surely she wasn't hinting that this was Edward's offspring in truth? Had her observation been a cry for help? He held his breath, marvelling anew at the private pain people endured. What was he supposed to do?

"I hurt my arm in the fire. Mostly I put it in a sling but today…" Her voice trailed away and Robert thought he saw tears in her eyes.

Robert tried to exhale quietly. Thank God she had chosen not to bare her soul – possibly because of the presence of the children – and had taken his question to be referring to physical injuries!

"Your arm does look swollen. Has a physician seen it? I'm surprised Edward hasn't waited for you. Shall we hurry and catch him up?"

Mary burst into noisy sobs and Ted sat down on the hallway floor.

"Oh, dear," pronounced Frances, in a more normal tone. "It looks like we have a mutiny among the ranks. Come, Ted, your new father is expecting you and he won't be pleased if we are late."

"Shall I take this young miss to Mrs Jones? I was wondering, Frances, if I could ask a favour of you. Could you travel in the same boat as my wife? She's not very confident on water but I suspect that all the women are going together and I won't be welcome. What if Ted comes with me and we'll follow you once Mary is settled in the kitchen? It might be that we would be allowed to sample some of the cooking – just to keep us from fainting – before we travel across the bay. What do you think, Ted?"

The lad scrambled to his feet and placed his hand in Robert's curled fingers. Holding out his other hand towards Mary, the children appeared to communicate with gestures, not words; the girl stopped crying and allowed herself to be led to the servants' quarters. Robert gave Frances a nod of grateful thanks over his shoulder.

Robert was correct in his hopes because immediately they entered, Mrs Jones gathered Ted into her ample arms before sinking on to a wooden chair next to the table. The young master accepted both titbits from the table and the housekeeper clucking over his wellbeing. The child, Mary, ran to an older maid, who was busily whisking eggs, and clung to her skirts.

Robert was stunned at the amount of food being prepared. If he had thought his own kitchen table was laden down with dishes to tempt Miss Swann then it was as nothing compared to the delicacies arranged over every available space in the Manor House kitchen. Through the door behind him came a maid he recognised, Biddy.

"Mary, leave your sister alone," she commanded. "Sir, can I help you?"

Before Robert could answer he felt a bunch of small fingers pushed into his hand and looked down to see his youngest son by his side. Where had he appeared from?

"*Tad*? I don't want to go on the boat without you," he whispered.

"Well, it's a good thing you've returned," replied Robert, "because Ted was just deciding whether he wanted to come too. Mrs Jones, Mrs Rowlands was particular in wanting her son to attend the wedding. Are you taking time off from your cooking to…"

"Me?" laughed the round woman. "I can hardly get along the corridor to my room let alone climb a rope ladder! Sir Edward has promised me a rest once today is over and I'm off to see my relatives. I was all set to go a sennight ago before events outside my control took over. Once I get to my family, I shall sit with my feet up and allow others to serve me, but for today I must stay and supervise Kate and Biddy and the three maids who are coming from the village. So, if you would take the young master away and this little imp, Mary, then I can get on with my tasks."

Penelope sat on a coil of thick rope, one arm cradling the baby and the other around the waist of her son, Robbie, who had found his way through the crowds, with Llewelin, to stand by her side. The marriage ceremony was nearly over and Penelope was ashamed to admit that she had not heard a word of it. Her sister-in-law, Frances, had been a great solace on the crossing in the rocking rowing boat. Penelope had pressed her for details of the fire and the injuries sustained and it had eased her anxieties to concentrate on someone else. The actual changeover from small craft to ship, even though she wasn't hampered by the baby, was rather frightening and the solid refuge of the brigantine seemed altogether more stable and she relaxed, refusing to contemplate the journey back to shore. She was presented with the sleeping child as soon as she had rearranged her skirts and placed her feet firmly on the wooden decks, and it wasn't many minutes later that she was proffered her makeshift seat. She was grateful for the kindness of the stout, rough sailor because her arm ached with the weight of the infant.

Everywhere was very crowded and there was no sign of her husband, and this was the main reason why she had not concentrated on the proceedings. She was desperate to converse with Robert and apologise to him. Eventually, at the back of the mass she saw him standing, next to Frances, who had been joined by her husband. There seemed to be a cluster of children surrounding them and it was at this point that she was approached by her two elder sons. Guilt made her reach out to them with her free arm but her eldest stepped away, reddening apparently at his mother's open embrace, but Robbie leant against her and laid his head on her with a whisper that she did not catch.

Much singing – some slightly bawdy songs – ended the ceremony and then Jack gathered his new bride into his arms and Penelope observed that others followed suit. There was Edward kissing his wife fully on the mouth and squeezing her tight; nearby was Elin (soon to be married herself) almost disappearing inside the hug of a huge bear of a man. This must be the much-talked of Morgan. Mariana had informed both her sisters, during their conversation in the privacy of the bedchamber, that Morgan had signed up as a member of Jack's crew and since Elin was to accompany her mistress on Jack's travels, it was only proper that maid and man were joined together in holy matrimony before they set sail. Penelope observed Katherine cuddling her handsome spouse and had to admit to herself that they made a striking couple. Which only left her! Where was Robert? He ought to be at her side, not across the other side of a host of faces. She sought a glimpse of him and sighed with frustration.

At that moment, she sensed him approach and turned to see her husband, their youngest son sitting on his shoulders. He dropped David to the floor to stand by Robbie.

"Penny, my dear," he said, encircling her and their boys. "Is there room for me in this small family?"

"Oh, Robert, you have come. I want to go home. Can we go home?" Suddenly it was as if he and she were the only people on board. All the noise of the wedding guests faded when their eyes met across the heads of the children.

"I love you," she stated boldly.

Without another word, Robert leaned across to kiss her, but the lads wriggled free and pushed into the crowd away from their parents. Now only the babe was between them.

"I love you too," he replied.

"Can we go home?" she repeated.

"My dearest Penny, Mrs Jones has prepared a feast. We are expected to stay. I believe Jack and Mariana sail tonight for we know not where. They may not be back for months. Would you deny them our presence for a few hours more?"

"Well, you must not leave my side then. You promised to come in the boat with me!"

She was sure that he heard her deliberate teasing for he smiled.

"We are already home, my love. You have come home to me."